1-17-18

Thank you for your
contributions to the
Touro family in helping
to repair the world.

Mike

First Do No Harm

Michael B. Clearfield

VANTAGE PRESS
New York

This is a work of fiction. Any similarity between the characters appearing herein and any real persons, living or dead, is purely coincidental.

FIRST EDITION

Published by Vantage Press, Inc.
516 West 34th Street, New York, New York 10001

Manufactured in the United States of America
ISBN: 0-533-13701-2

Library of Congress Catalog Card No.: 01-126751

0 9 8 7 6 5 4 3 2 1

With my love for Susan, who gave me
Daniel, Libby, Jason, and Jake

First Do No Harm

Prologue

"I'm sorry, A.T., there's nothing more I can do." Jacob Brown shook his head in disgust and frustration. His brow furrowed, eyes glazed and misty—he was spent, both physically and mentally. Over the past three days he had exhausted every therapy, every conceivable combination, every dosage . . . all to no avail. Two patients dead and a third comatose, hanging on by the thinnest thread of hope. How he hated spinal meningitis.

"I know, I know." A.T. put a comforting hand on the shoulder of his friend and colleague. A.T. knew all too well the ravages of meningitis but this was different; this was his family, his children. Tears welled in his eyes as he assessed how this disease had, in a matter of days, decimated his family, his life.

The weather had changed recently from the frigid cold of winter to a balmy spring. But now the dark shroud of winter was making an unexpected return. A.T. knew these abrupt changes in weather frequently heralded disease, but he never envisioned the pain this spring would bring.

A.T. walked to the window, opening it a crack, allowing a chilling Kansas breeze to enter, hoping to clear some of the must of disease that permeated the room.

Dr. Brown silently returned to his seat at the side of the bed, continuing his vigil. He once again opened the *Materia Medica*, the ultimate reference text on the practice of medicine, its pages tattered from repeated use. Jacob Brown searched the same pages over again hoping to find the cure, yet knowing it was pointless. A page accidentally tore off in Jacob's hand and he clumsily attempted to reinsert it back into the text.

A.T. pulled up a chair on the opposite side of the bed and held the limp hand of his daughter in his own. He studied the body, trying to separate his emotions from his professional perspective. The ulcerated lips, cheeks and tongue, the excessive

1

salivation, all a likely result of the calomel, the supposed curative medicine, rather than the disease itself. As he gently wiped the bloodstained saliva from her lips, a tooth loosened by the inflammation of her gums fell into his hand. Tears streaming down his cheeks soaked his beard.

Why? A.T. silently screamed. *Why this? Why now? Why me?* It was only five years ago when A.T. had lost his first wife, Mary M. Mary was beautiful, kind, and abounded with love, yet she had been taken prematurely from him. Now two of their children had gone to join their mother. *How could this be?*

A.T. trudged toward the back room where his second wife fitfully slept. Mary E. filled a void A.T. had thought impossible to fill. Mary E. had remained steadfast by her dying children. The fact these children had been born to a different mother made no difference—she loved them with all her being. For seventy-two sleepless hours Mary cared, loved, and wept for her children, fighting off sleep. Once they were gone A.T. sedated Mary so she could finally get some needed rest.

A.T. often mused that he had been blessed to have found not one but two Mary's. Mary E. didn't replace his first Mary, but complemented her. Mary E. allowed A.T. the space to regain his spirit and his life. She counseled, advised, encouraged, and supported him in his time of need. She was his lover and his best friend. But now he heard her cries of anguish and knew it was her time of need. He was a doctor—yet their children, their beloved children—were dying. How could he let this happen?

A.T. sat on the edge of the bed where Mary slept. His bloodshot eyes stared into space. A vacant, morose stare. A.T.'s mind wandered but kept returning to the complexity of this disease, this disaster. A.T. surmised it was as much the cure as the disease that had placed his little girl at death's door. He had frequently prescribed calomel, a potent cathartic, so he was aware of its potentially devastating side effects. It was the knowledge of his own inadequacies and those of his profession that was now tormenting him.

A.T. returned to his daughter's bedside. Jacob looked at his friend but said nothing.

"The war," A.T. mumbled, shaking his head.

"What?" Jacob asked.

"The war," A.T. repeated. A hint of smile attempted to break through his beard. "My family made it through the war, only to be struck down with this." It was not a smile, but a smirk, reflecting the irony. Yet even the smirk was again to be replaced by the anguish and the torment of the moment.

The two physicians silently sat at the bedside until the last breath was expended from A.T.'s little girl. Just as A.T. had kept watch over two of his sons, he now saw his daughter die. Her frail, gaunt, emaciated body, covered with ulcers, was finally and mercifully at peace. A.T. could imagine no greater pain, no deeper sorrow than he felt at that moment. His entire being precariously balanced on the edge of the abyss, yet with an inner strength he turned his pain into a promise to honor his children.

A.T. accompanied Jacob to his carriage. The north wind increased off the Kansas fields, bringing with it a noticeable chill and a light rain. A.T. looked into the sunset. "You know, there has to be a better way."

Jacob, already feeling guilty, didn't know how to respond. "I did all I could."

"I know you did all you could." A.T. agreed. "What I mean is, these diseases of organic decomposition, I think we're approaching them the wrong way."

"Wrong way? What do you mean?" Jacob backed off his defensive posture.

"It seems the harder we try to rid our patients of their symptoms, the more harm we do." A.T. paused as a gust of wind seemed to lower the temperature several degrees. "There has to be a better way. And I'm going to try to find one."

"A.T., my friend, I'm sorry for your loss. I know things seem impossible now, but somehow I hope this will all make some sense." Jacob embraced A.T. It was an embrace of friendship, collegiality, empathy, and fear. It could have easily been Jacob's family, not A.T.'s, visiting the Grim Reaper.

As Jacob climbed aboard his carriage the rain turned to snow. "Looks like winter's back."

A.T. turned to look back at his home. He had to tell Mary of their most recent devastation. A dark, empty feeling over-

3

whelmed him. Little did he realize at that pivotal moment in his life he would change the course of medicine. For on that cold spring day in Kansas in 1864, A.T.—Andrew Taylor Still— made a pledge to find a better way. And he would spend the remainder of his life on that quest. A quest that would lead him to believe that the remedies necessary for health already exist in the human body and that these remedies are integrally related to the structure and function of the human mechanism. The result of his efforts would result in the birth of a new field of medicine: osteopathic medicine.

Well past a century later, Walter Ambercrombie, chief advisor and political strategist to the president of the United States, entered the lobby of a brownstone on O Street in the historic Georgetown area of the city. Ambercrombie had used this apartment for years for his various liaisons. He was very discreet and always a stickler for details, in order to minimize, if not totally eradicate, any evidence of his indiscretions.

The weather had turned considerably colder. Ambercrombie had forgotten his overcoat and shivered as he fumbled for his keys at the door. Racing up the stairs to the second floor, he entered the apartment and turned on the radio while he prepared for his guest. Veronica loved Walter's martinis.

The knock at the door interrupted Walter's preparation of his infamous martini. He checked his watch; Veronica was forty minutes early. Walter peered through the peephole of the door and to his surprise it was not Veronica waiting on the other side.

"Veronica sent me." The voice barely penetrated the door, but the Southern accent was very apparent.

Walter did not want to risk a public scene, so he opened the door a crack, leaving the chain in a locked position.

"Hello darlin', Veronica sent me." The tone was barely louder than a whisper.

"Where's Veronica?" Walter mumbled back.

"Well, she was detained. So she asked me. I hope you don't mind." The voice, a discreet whisper, dripped with Southern charm.

Walter sighed while he reviewed his options. Why had

Veronica put him in this situation? Walter opened the door, the option he decided to be the least onerous.

The woman who entered the room was older than Veronica but just as attractive. She wore a low-cut evening gown, adorned with a pearl necklace and complementary earrings. She completed her outfit with elbow-length gloves, all very tasteful and elegant. A subtle waft of her perfume went straight to his head, further arousing his already heightened senses.

The woman extended her hand, palm down, very daintily. "Hi darlin'. My name is Beth." Walter noticed a slight overbite when Beth talked.

"Why are you here?" Walter was intrigued, yet irritated,

Beth appeared confused and bewildered. "Ah, I'm sorry, sir. I was under the impression Veronica had called."

"No, she didn't," Walter responded abruptly.

"I'm so sorry. I'll be on my way. Can I please use your phone to call a cab?" Her face flushed slightly with a hint of embarrassment.

Walter suddenly felt ashamed. His displeasure was not with Beth but with Veronica, who had sent her. "Yeah, um, of course, you can use the phone." He pointed to the phone in the living room.

"Thanks." Beth bent over to pick up the receiver, exposing her ample cleavage.

Walter had always been attracted to a woman's breasts, and these breasts were magnificent. The combination of Beth's breasts, perfume, and long legs excited him, but it was her cute little overbite and the Southern accent that drove him over the edge. "Do you have to leave so soon?" He blurted out.

A sensual smile appeared as Beth replaced the receiver. "Of course not, darlin'. I have all evening if you wish."

Walter walked over to where Beth was standing. His arousal was already evident. "Would you like something to drink?"

"Maybe later," Beth said coyly, as she leaned toward him, again exposing her cleavage.

Walter, without saying another word, grabbed Beth and plunged his face into her bosom. His tongue licked her soft, creamy breasts, while her hands stroked his hair. She tasted as good as she looked. She felt so soft and smooth.

Beth moaned as Walter exposed her left breast and his tongue circled her erect nipple. "Oh, yes."

Focused on her luscious body, Walter did not notice the eight-inch needle Beth extracted from the slit in her evening gown. With the precision of a surgeon, Beth inserted the needle into the nape of Walter's neck. With a flick of her wrist the needle destroyed Walter's central nervous system. His body contorted as he breathed his last breath. Then Beth skillfully removed the needle, letting Walter's body fall to the floor.

Beth wasted no time. She entered the bathroom where she had earlier hidden a bag containing her makeup, a housedress, a pair of shoes, a wig and other accessories for disguise. Within five minutes Beth had transformed herself from a high priced call girl into an elderly matron.

She checked her watch; she was on schedule. Veronica should be there in ten minutes. Beth surveyed the scene, carefully wiping away the small amount of blood that emerged from the puncture wound in Walter's neck.

A hobbling, old woman carrying her weathered bag exited the brownstone, a marked contrast to the young, exquisitely dressed woman who had entered thirty minutes earlier.

While Veronica circled the block searching for a parking spot, she didn't notice the figure emerge from the shadows. Screeching to a stop, she barely missed the old lady, who, unfazed, continued to cross the street. The car stalled. Veronica sighed deeply while she collected her composure. The old lady, oblivious, disappeared into the night.

Jackson Placard pulled into 1600 Pennsylvania Avenue, passing the guard station as he had done a thousand times before. He glanced at the illuminated dial on his watch; two A.M. Although he wasn't told what this meeting would be about, all indications suggested this would be another of the countless nights without any sleep. Jackson was met at the door by Mark Smith, the other key player on the president's strategic planning committee that Walter Ambercrombie chaired.

"Cold as shit out there," Jackson lamented.

"Well, that shit just hit the fan here." Mark shook his head. "Follow me, we can't talk here."

Jackson's demeanor changed the instant Mark asked him to follow. What could be so important that they couldn't discuss it in a secured hallway in the White House? This was more serious than he expected.

Mark led Jackson into a secured room in the west end of the building. The man waiting in the room was immaculately dressed in a three-piece suit. Jackson had met Horace Jamison, the Secretary of Health, twice before and each time he had been left with same impression—this is one intense individual. However, something was different. Jamison's gait was slow and deliberate, far different from his usual bounce. His head and hands were trembling almost imperceptibly as he approached.

"Thank you for your quick response." Jamison extended his hand toward Jackson, the lilt in his voice gone. Jamison's riveting blue eyes underscored his intensity and his depression. "Please be seated."

Jackson Placard's eyes darted from Jamison to Mark, then back to Jamison. The usual calm that Jackson had relied on was gone from Mark's face. They both sat nervously on the edges of their chairs.

"Gentlemen, we have a serious problem." Jamison paused to emphasize the importance of what was to follow. "Walter Ambercrombie is dead."

"What! How?" Jackson blurted out. He had just seen Walter earlier that evening.

" What I am about to tell you cannot leave this room. Is that clear?" Jamison's remark was more of a command than a request.

Both men answered in the affirmative.

"It appears Walter was murdered." Jamison's stone cold stare was laced with anger. "He was pithed."

"What?" Mark asked.

"Pithed!" Jamison replied. "It's a ritualistic type of death used by the Colombians. They insert a needle into the neck and kill the command center of the brain. It's quick, clean, and very effective."

Both Mark and Jackson looked away in disbelief.

"I've talked to the chief of staff and the president. We need to change our strategy for the campaign. We all feel that the war on drugs is not in our best interest as the lead message. Not now." Jamison shook his head.

"Because of this?" Jackson asked.

"Yes, because of this. You see, Walter was found by a prostitute. A woman he had been seeing for some time. If this gets out it could be politically devastating to the president's reelection."

"Yeah, I guess you're right." Jackson couldn't think clearly. He kept imagining the image of his recently deceased friend and colleague.

"But all the work we did on this . . . what about that?" Mark's grief was sprinkled with anger and frustration.

"We'll use it, but at a different time. We need to quietly investigate this nightmare and find out if this was the Colombians. But that will take some time, and we don't have any of that to spare." Jamison looked out the window at the White House lawn. The rain had turned to snow, covering the grounds like a soft white blanket.

Mark and Jackson both silently stared at Jamison's hunched shoulders as he gazed into the cold night. Jamison slowly turned. "I need you both to help spearhead the president's new initiative on health-care reform. This is the issue that will now take center stage."

"You're kidding, right?" Jackson said. "We tried this before and got crucified."

"No, I'm not kidding." Jamison's blue eyes gave no doubt of his sincerity. "The last time we made some bad moves. This time we can't afford the luxury of mistakes."

"We'll need the support of the doctors, then," Mark said.

"Screw the doctors," Jackson responded.

"I'd like to, but we need them to pull this off. We can always screw them later." Mark's face hinted at a smile.

"Do what you need to do. But do it quickly and do it right," Jamison said, pounding his fist decisively on the Eisenhower coffee table.

"We'll do our best." Jackson looked to Mark for some encouragement, but his face was blank.

"Look, I know this is asking a lot, but none of us has a choice. Health care is a universal issue that isn't working. You have to help us find a better way." Jamison stood and left the room, leaving them both stunned.

1

"These are the good old days"—the reprise of a lyric he had listened to many times, but had heard for the first time this evening, was drowned out by the roar of the police siren, while the flashing light intensified his already pounding headache. As the officer approached, Steven Callison thought *what an appropriate way to end a horrendous week*.

"What's the problem, officer?" He realized he had been speeding, but this time he felt he had a legitimate excuse.

"May I see your license and registration, please?" The officer's badge signified his last name was Halliday.

"Officer Halliday, I can explain. You see I'm a physician and I'm on an emergency call to the hospital."

Officer Halliday wasn't impressed. "License and registration, please," Halliday reiterated.

Callison decided to try again. "Officer, I really am on an emergency call and we're wasting precious time."

Halliday was now becoming irritated. "Listen sir, you were going seventy-two miles an hour in a fifty-five zone. Can I please have your license and registration?" Halliday's tone and manner were now much more emphatic.

Callison handed the license and registration to the officer, who returned to his car. Several thoughts entered Dr. Callison's mind, none of which were of any real significance, yet their cumulative effect was a magnification of his splitting headache.

"If you're really going to an emergency and can prove this emergency, the judge may let you off with a warning." Officer Halliday said, returning Callison's license. "Personally, I wouldn't. If you get into an accident neither you or your patient would be helped. So Doc, drive carefully and obey the speed limit," Officer Halliday said, as he handed the doctor a ticket.

Callison was in no mood for a lecture and sped off defiantly down the interstate toward the hospital. As he left the blinking lights of the police car in the distance, Callison started to think of the events of the last several days. Although he had driven the route to the hospital thousands of times, the speeding ticket had added frustration to the tedium of the road. Callison muttered to himself, "What did I do to deserve this?" Then the voice in the back of his head answered immediately, "This is your life— accept it."

As reality started to rear its ugly head, a feeling of apprehension and concern began to grow. This was a familiar feeling, almost like an old friend who had been a traveling companion during hundreds of cases over the years. Twelve years of practice preceded by four years of residency—and this feeling, this sensation, had not really changed. As he approached the hospital the images of the various hospitals fused with a myriad of faces. Faces of patients and their families, of nurses, of technicians, of students, of colleagues and of clergymen were all connected in time by this feeling—this old companion—this "friend."

Another component of this feeling wasn't nearly as friendly. It was composed of memories of holidays and other meaningful life cycle events missed: movies and plays that were interrupted, parties that were never meant to be, numerous nights and weekends without sleep and that gut-wrenching feeling of losing a patient in spite of all his efforts and prayers.

He walked quickly from the garage to the emergency room. The concerns of the day, the week, the past and even the headache were all gone as he focused on the issue at hand, Mrs. Kodack. Over the years Callison had established a special relationship with the Kodack family.

Mrs. Kodack had been one of his first patients twelve years ago. He had inherited her case because at the time she was essentially considered hopeless: too complicated, too ill and too much effort. The intensive therapy and long hours of care eventually paid off for both Mrs. Kodack and Dr. Callison. For her, a new lease on life, and for him, a reputation as an excellent, caring doctor.

The details of Mrs. Kodack's case were still ingrained in his mind, which was quite unusual; he frequently forgot the details of a specific case within several days, but not Mrs. Kodack's. He mentally reviewed the pertinent facts: coronary heart disease, congestive heart failure, diabetes, renal insufficiency, hypertension and hyperlipidemia, all of which were probably contributing to her current status.

He entered the emergency room. The bright light from the first treatment room outlined the silhouette of an approaching figure.

"Dr. Callison, she's in . . ." Before the nurse could finish her sentence Callison entered the first treatment room, the eye of the storm. Crowded around the stretcher were: Dr. Greg Jones, the emergency room physician; Dr. Peter Lopes, the medical resident on call; another person in a white coat, whom Callison assumed was a medical student; and two nurses.

"How long?" Callison asked the nurse whose name tag said Perkins. She was obviously new and somewhat unnerved.

"Let's see." Nurse Perkins fidgeted with the paper and looked at the clock twice. "Let's see, it's now one-twelve, the code has been going on for about eighteen minutes." Callison knew that a code lasting this long generally had a poor prognosis. He quickly surveyed the situation: the student doctor was adequately compressing the chest; Dr. Jones was ventilating Mrs. Kodack via an endotracheal tube according to protocol, one ventilation for each five chest compressions; Dr. Lopes was monitoring the electrocardiogram while asking Nurse Vasquez to prepare another vial of epinephrine for intravenous injection. Nurse Perkins was documenting everything on the appropriate form.

Lopes looked up as Callison approached, his expression conveying both concern for the patient and relief that Callison was finally here.

"What's the story?" Callison said.

Lopes looked toward Jones, apparently hoping he would respond, but Dr. Jones was preoccupied with the CPR.

Lopes took a deep breath before answering. "She came in with signs and symptoms of decompensated failure and a questionable history of unstable angina. While the nurse was rechecking the vitals she seized and coded. So far she's gotten two amps of epi."

Nurse Perkins interrupted, "Actually three amps of epi."

Lopes continued, "Okay, three amps of epi, and um, one atropine."

Lopes paused for a reaction. Getting none, he continued, "We actually got a rhythm of V tach and started Lidocaine, but the rhythm deteriorated into V fib."

"How many cardioversions?" asked Callison.

"Three or four."

"Actually five," Nurse Perkins interjected.

Lopes didn't acknowledge the correction, as Nurse Vasquez announced that the epinephrine had been injected.

Callison looked at the EKG, still V fib. "Okay, let's get ready to defibrillate."

Lopes placed the paddles on Mrs. Kodack's chest. "Clear the table, ready to defibrillate 300 joules!"

Everyone moved away from the table as Lopes released an electrical charge to the chest of Mrs. Kodack that momentarily lifted her body off the stretcher.

Callison motioned with his hand to temporarily stop CPR until he could review the rhythm strip of the electrocardiogram. To his surprise there appeared to be a perfusable rhythm. "I believe we have sinus tachycardia. Check for a pulse."

Dr. Jones placed his index and middle finger on Mrs. Kodack"s neck over the right carotid artery. A wry smile appeared on his wary face.

"You SOB, I have a pulse!" Jones exclaimed.

Nurse Vasquez immediately inflated the blood pressure cuff, placed the stethoscope in her ears, and carefully listened for a blood pressure. "BP 100 over 60," Vasquez said softly, with cautious optimism.

Mrs. Kodack was still unresponsive. This was expected following a seizure. In fact, she would probably remain in this unresponsive state, this postictal state, for quite some time.

Dr. Lopes inserted a needle with a glass syringe into Mrs. Kodack's right arm, puncturing the radial artery. The syringe started to fill slowly. The red color of the blood suggested adequate oxygenation, another positive sign. The tension in the room was reduced. Orders were reviewed, and Mrs. Kodack's condition appeared to stabilize. Dr. Lopes was now able to review the details of the case with Dr. Callison.

The medical student hung onto each word of the discussion, attempting to assimilate what he had just experienced.

Callison left Dr. Lopes to write the admitting orders as he went to find Mr. Kodack.

Enos Kodack was a working man's man with a large, broad muscular frame, pot belly, and distinctive creases where facial lines used to exist. These creases were a testament to his forty odd years of ranching in the hot Texas sun. The expression on Mr. Kodack's face immediately told Callison he had prepared himself for the worst. Callison escorted Mr. Kodack to a corner alcove in the waiting room where they could have some privacy. Knowing how to handle a delicate situation, Callison initially assured Mr. Kodack his wife was alive, but still in very critical condition. On realizing that his wife was not dead, Mr. Kodack began to cry, tears of gratitude. He had been positive he had lost his Annie.

Once he regained his composure, Mr. Kodack thanked Dr. Callison for all his efforts. Before Callison left to return to his patient, he again cautioned Mr. Kodack that his wife was still very unstable. Mr. Kodack firmly grabbed Dr. Callison's arm before he was able to walk away. "Is she gonna live?"

Callison responded as honestly as he could. "I don't know. She's had a cardiac arrest and seizure, which is definitely not good. Her diabetes is out of control and she hasn't regained consciousness." It was a habit of Callison's to initially give the negative facts in such cases, so as not to build unrealistic expectations.

Callison could see much of Mr. Kodack's hope drain from his body as he completed his remarks. He knew he had to rekindle some optimism, so he continued, "However, the possible good news is, I don't think your wife has had a heart attack, the diabetes should be fairly easy to control, and it usually takes a person a while to wake up from a seizure. Hopefully Mrs. Kodack will continue to improve."

15

Callison placed his hand over Mr. Kodack's. Mr. Kodack released the formidable grip he had on Callison's arm. The additional words and the physical contact had eased some of Mr. Kodack's fears. He again had some hope for his Annie's recovery.

"We'll transfer Mrs. Kodack to the coronary care unit and I'll see you up there." Callison slipped through the door, leaving Mr. Kodack with his thoughts, fears, and hopes.

The CCU was generally quiet this time of night except for the occasional sound of a monitor alarm and the low frequency hiss of the ventilators as they delivered their oxygen. The lights were dimmed and most of the patients in the twelve-bed unit were asleep. A respiratory technician was giving a treatment to a patient who was experiencing an asthmatic attack; otherwise everything seemed under control.

Irma Wiggins, the head nurse on the night shift in the CCU, was one of the few nurses who predated Callison's arrival twelve years ago. "Fancy seeing you here again. This is getting to be a nightly occurrence," Wiggins said empathetically.

"We have to stop meeting like this." Callison said.

Wiggins chuckled at Callison's response, then inquired on the status of Mrs. Kodack. Once informed on the details of the case, Wiggins asked Callison if Mrs. Kodack was on her way from the emergency room. Before Callison could answer, the doors to the CCU opened to Mrs. Kodack's stretcher, accompanied by Dr. Lopes, Nurse Vasquez, and an orderly. As the nursing crew were busy transferring Mrs. Kodack to her CCU bed, Lopes and Callison reviewed the case. Callison was satisfied that, at least for now, Mrs. Kodack was stable. He went to the waiting room of the CCU to see if Mr. Kodack was there. Except for a corner lamp, the room was dark. A couple huddled in a corner briefly looked up and asked if anything had changed in the status of patient Edison. Callison shook his head, and they again attempted to find a comfortable position to try to sleep. As he left the waiting room, he noticed Mr. Kodack walking down the hall accompanied by a woman and a child. As Callison approached the trio, Mr. Kodack spoke. "Dr. Callison, I'd like you to meet my daughter, Margaret, and my granddaughter, Sally."

16

Margaret shook Dr. Callison's hand, "It's a pleasure to finally meet you. I want to tell you how much we appreciate the wonderful care you've given my mother over the years."

Mr. Kodack nodded his head. Callison never really expected any acknowledgment, but like most of his colleagues he appreciated when his efforts were noticed.

"It's nice to meet you." Callison returned Margaret's handshake. "And you." Callison extended his hand toward the child, Sally.

Sally retreated behind her mother. Margaret attempted to coax Sally from her sheltered position, but to no avail. Mr. Kodack patted Sally gently on her head and then began to caress the back of her neck.

"She doesn't speak," Mr. Kodack said, sadly shaking his head.

"Oh," Callison nodded, as if he had been aware of the child's affliction, but had forgotten. He redirected his attention to Mr. Kodack, informing him that his wife was stable in the CCU and if he wished to see her he could do so now.

Mr. Kodack followed Dr. Callison into the coronary care unit. Like most people the CCU intimidated Mr. Kodack with all the machines, computer screens and technology. However, what was most unnerving was the realization that each room housed a person who was in a condition similar to his wife's. Even worse was the smell, a distinctive odor, which he had detected before when his brother was in such a place. For him, it was the smell of death.

When they reached Mrs. Kodack's room, Callison led Mr. Kodack to her bedside, then quietly left. Mr. Kodack gently caressed her hand and kissed her forehead, whispering so only his Annie could hear. There was no response. Nurse Wiggins interrupted to check the status of the intravenous line, and Mr. Kodack decided to return to the waiting room to be with his daughter and granddaughter.

Before leaving, Callison reviewed his therapeutic plan for Mrs. Kodack with both Lopes and Wiggins. On his way out of the hospital, he decided to stop in the emergency room to thank Dr. Jones for his help. Jones was completing his paperwork when Callison approached.

"Do you believe a patient came into the ER at two-thirty in the morning with a complaint of hiccups? No wonder the cost of medical care is going through the roof!"

Callison nodded his head. "Well, what else is there to do at two-thirty anyway?"

Jones completed his paperwork, looked up at Callison, and asked how Mrs. Kodack was doing. Callison said she appeared stable and thanked him for his assistance. He started to leave but Jones spoke again.

"I'm curious, what took you so long to get here?" Jones seemed to be noticeably upset. "I'm busting my butt coding your lady, and you meander in and after one dose of epi she converts to a sinus rhythm." Callison was stunned. He didn't know if Jones was serious or not. He was about to respond when he noticed a huge grin on Jones' face. "I'm just busting your chops," Jones said jokingly.

Callison attempted to smile, but couldn't. "With the week I've had, it wouldn't have surprised me if you were totally serious."

"Bad week, huh?" Jones asked. "That's why you look like shit." Jones laughed, trying to lighten the conversation, but Callison did not see humor in the remark. He was exhausted both physically and mentally. Callison was all too aware of his changing physical characteristics—the bags under his eyes, the graying of his hair, the love handles around his waist.

"Do you believe I got a damn speeding ticket coming here tonight?"

Jones was agitated, "You're kidding; didn't you explain you were going to an emergency?"

"I tried to explain but the cop wouldn't listen. Anyway, it was totally consistent with the way my week has been going," Callison said as he slumped into a chair opposite Jones.

"You must have had some week!" Jones leaned forward as he positioned himself in his chair to hear more details.

Callison decided to oblige, but only with the most benign particulars. "I've been here nearly every night this week and Tuesday I missed a surprise party that I'd been looking forward

18

to for months. I've also been stressed out at work. Our division's last quarter income was way down. Now Mrs. Kodack, maybe my longest established patient, is knocking at death's door." Callison felt a lump rise in his throat as he spoke about Mrs. Kodack.

Jones nodded in agreement. Callison felt the compulsion to go on. "And that's not the half of it! For a good part of the last three years I've been attempting to get a Primary Care Preventative Medicine Grant from the NIH. My first application was two years ago, and although the grant was approved, it wasn't funded. The priority score was decent and I was encouraged, hell, I was basically told to reapply and I would get funded. After resubmission, the new priority score was excellent. I was told off the record every grant receiving a similar score had been funded. So, I made some changes administratively to accommodate the grant, anticipating that the funding was in the bag. This week I received the Dear John "approved but not funded" letter. I try to call my so-called representative on the grant selection committee who won't return my damn call. Finally after numerous attempts, the last few bordering on threats, I get my representative who also can't believe the grant wasn't funded. She states the reason she didn't return my earlier calls was to verify that a mistake hadn't been made. Then she apologized profusely for misleading me regarding the potential funding."

Jones did not seem surprised. "Do you think the decision was political?"

"Political?" Callison repeated. He knew what Jones meant. Although the thought had actually crossed his mind, it had been immediately discarded.

"Yeah, osteopathic versus allopathic—it wouldn't be the first time," Jones said.

Callison thought about his profession and whether his being an osteopathic physician was the reason his grant wasn't funded. Callison was aware of the difficulties of being in a minority profession, even though it was 100 years old. He was still asked on occasion what an osteopath was and how it differed from the MD's—the allopathic profession.

Everyone knew what an MD was, but many had never even heard of a DO or of the osteopathic profession. Callison would explain that they took the same courses and frequently the same licensing exam, but there was a difference in philosophy. Osteopaths also used manual or manipulative medicine. It had taken the better part of the twentieth century for the osteopathic profession to attain the same practice rights in all the states as did their MD counterparts.

Despite the growth and acceptance of the profession, it still was an enigma to much of the nation. Some of the patients under the care of an osteopathic physician were unaware that their doctor had a DO, rather than an MD degree; they were only concerned as to whether or not he or she was a good doctor. But there were others, patients and doctors alike, who did care, who thought the DO degree was inferior. It was very possible some of these physicians sat on the grant review committee and decided not to award Callison the grant strictly on the basis of his degree and not on the merit of the grant itself.

Before the conversation could go any further, Nurse Vasquez appeared to inform Dr. Jones of an unstable patient who had just arrived. Jones excused himself, and Callison proceeded to the parking garage.

Jones' remark haunted Callison on his drive home. He couldn't decide if a political decision would be more tolerable than a decision based on merit. He finally decided that the result was the same, so worrying about the deciding factor was of no significance.

Callison's mind wandered and he recalled some of the negative events of the week which he had not related to Jones. The fiscal problems were not new, but they were approaching a critical juncture where decisions reflecting salaries would have to be made. These problems were the worst part of his job as the head of the Division of General Internal Medicine. Not only were the members of Callison's division colleagues, they were all friends. To cut their salaries would be a difficult and painful decision.

Callison was able to rationalize the fiscal problems, and to a significant degree he could rationalize the loss of the grant. But there was yet another problem that he could not come to terms with. The week had started with a letter from the Texas Medical Foundation (TMF) regarding a potential issue dealing with the premature discharge of a patient from the hospital which had resulted in the patient being readmitted to the hospital. The allegation stated Callison had not provided the necessary quality care for the patient, which resulted in the patient being discharged while still at significant medical risk.

If Callison felt he stood for anything, it was quality of patient care. This letter was a direct affront to his ego and reputation. If this was upheld, the TMF would disclose this information to state and federal licensing and accreditation bodies, thus tarnishing Callison's spotless medical record—a record he was most proud of. The mere fact that this accusation had been made gnawed at his stomach, leaving a repugnant aftertaste like a bad burrito.

Callison decided to turn on the car radio to take his mind off his problems. He couldn't believe he was hearing the song again, with the refrain "these are the good old days." He didn't know whether to laugh or cry. Since he never cried, he did neither.

2

"Can you tell me what room Senator Hargrove is in?" The man was handsomely dressed in an Armani suit appointed with a Nicole Miller tie and a solid gold Rolex watch. His manner and style not only suggested wealth, but also authority.

The frail white-haired lady at the information desk frantically rechecked the hospital's in-patient list to confirm what she already knew. Mrs. Polk had volunteered every Tuesday and Thursday at the hospital for the last twelve years. She would definitely remember if a senator was a patient in the hospital.

"Are you sure you have the correct hospital?"

"Of course I'm sure. This is the Osteopathic Hospital of Detroit, isn't it?" The tone of his response was louder; the cadence of the speech was slow, enunciating each word.

Without acknowledging her nod, he continued. "I am Lance Darby. I work for Senator Hargrove, and I know he is a patient in this hospital. Now, if you will please let me know what room the senator is in, I'll stop bothering you. Here's my identification to verify that I'm an executive assistant in the senator's Washington office." Darby handed Mrs. Polk a laminated identification card which Mrs. Polk immediately returned.

"I have no reason to doubt you are who you say you are. But the fact remains there is no Senator Hargrove on our daily census. I have looked under Hargrove, Senator Hargrove, Douglas Hargrove, and Hargrove Douglas. Also, for the record, as you political types like to put it, although I am seventy-eight years old, that does not mean that I am either deaf or stupid."

Darby's expression showed his surprise at her response as he stammered, "I apologize for any inference I might have made. I never intended to be insulting. As I'm sure you're aware, that is the bane of a politician."

"Apology accepted. Now, I might suggest contacting my

supervisor to see if the senator might be listed under another name." Mrs. Polk forced a smile as she walked off to find her supervisor.

She returned within several minutes, escorted by a woman in her late forties who was introduced as Ms. Taylor, the supervisor. After checking his credentials, Ms. Taylor informed him that the senator was in a private VIP suite on the tenth floor.

The tenth floor was decorated differently than the rest of the hospital. The wall coverings and carpets were all color-coordinated in teal, mauve, and violet. The paintings accented the décor, as did the furnishings. Even the nursing stations were color-coordinated and stylishly integrated. The rooms were all suites, with a sitting room and an adjoining additional bedroom. The senator's room, 1002, was directly across from the nursing station. Although the door was ajar Darby decided to knock anyway. As the door opened, Darby was greeted by Delores Hargrove, the senator's wife.

"Hello, Lance. What brings you all the way from D.C.?" Delores extended her hand.

"The trip from D.C. was a snap compared to finding what room the senator was in. It nearly took an act of Congress . . ."

Before Lance could complete his thought, a response bellowed from the corner of the room. "You know Congress would never act this quickly! Come on in."

The sound of the senator's voice was upbeat. He was sitting on the side of the bed. An intravenous was connected to his neck, and another tube was draining what appeared to be blood from under his hospital gown. Blood usually didn't bother Darby, but the sight of the senator and his bodily fluids left him a little lightheaded. Delores, noticing Darby's unsteadiness, quickly offered him a seat. Once seated, Darby rapidly returned to his normal composed state.

"Don't let the blood bother you, Lance. It's normal after prostate surgery. Actually, it's clearing up. Even a little blood when mixed with urine appears much worse than it really is." Although the senator's response seemed plausible, Darby wasn't convinced. He decided to change the subject.

"I hope you're feeling better, Senator." Darby skillfully

23

avoided any eye contact with the bloody bag draining from the senator.

"Actually, I do feel much better. You see this tube going into my neck?" The senator pointed to a tube that was feeding intravenous fluids. Fortunately for Darby, the point of entry was covered by an adhesive dressing.

"This intravenous is called a subclavian line. I have this fear of needles so I asked if there was an alternative to multiple needle sticks—after the first day I felt as if I was a pin cushion. After some lengthy discussions and some arm twisting, I convinced them to put this in me. They explained that there were risks associated with this line, but it would last longer and hopefully prevent additional needle sticks. Anyway, to make a short answer long, since this has been in me I've felt much better. I dreaded the needle more than the surgery because I knew I would be out during the surgery."

"I had no idea you had such a fear of needles." Darby studied the intravenous line in the Senator's neck; it looked uncomfortable.

"So, Lance, what brings you here?"

"Senator, there's been a leak. A reporter from the *Post* called me regarding your condition."

"What did you say?" The senator cocked his head and shot Darby a concerned look.

"I pleaded ignorance. Unfortunately, he didn't buy my answer and asked for a meeting. At the meeting he handed me this." Darby held up a photocopy of a detailed description of the senator and his disease. The story further suggested the senator was covering up this disease for political reasons.

Although the story was accurate, it wasn't true. The senator was well aware of the political ramifications of his illness. He knew, as did all politicians, that any of the three A's could be career ending: drug addiction, Alzheimer's Disease, and AIDS. He also knew the big C came in a close second. And he knew, unfortunately, that his prostate cancer needed to be dealt with personally, as well as politically.

It disturbed the senator that this information had leaked out. When he had gone in for his yearly health exam and was

24

told of a possible growth on his prostate, he had immediately flown to Detroit to confer with his personal physician. Not only was Harris Terbanion an excellent physician, he was also a very close friend. If it was feasible to keep this quiet, Harris could do it.

The leak had to have come out of Washington, although Darby and Garrison Hammer were the only people on his staff who knew of his condition. Garrison was his oldest and closest friend and chief advisor. There was no way he would leak this. That left Dr. Laskans, who had done the initial exam, but that suggested a major breach of confidentiality. He couldn't imagine the doctor as the source of the leak. The only other person with knowledge of his disease was Darby himself. Could Darby be that stupid?

The call startled Dr. Terbanion from a deep sleep. Awkwardly grasping for the phone he knocked the receiver to the floor. Picking up the instrument Terbanion asked, "What time is it?" His eyes couldn't focus on the clock.

"It's three A.M., Dr. Terbanion, and I have some awful news. Senator Hargrove has died."

Terbanion bolted upright in the bed, not believing the words he had just heard. "What did you say?"

"I'm sorry, sir, but the senator is dead."

"What . . . how?" Terbanion shouted, waking his wife.

"I'm not sure. The nurse found him cold in bed about twenty minutes ago. We initially tried to revive him but he was already cold. I think it must have been a big P.E. . . . ."

"Pulmonary embolus? He looked great when I left the hospital at eleven! I can't believe this ! Did you notify his wife?" Terbanion's head collapsed in his free hand.

"She was asleep in the adjoining room. She's obviously quite upset."

"I'm on my way. Leave everything just like it is." Terbanion slowly replaced the phone.

Judith Terbanion was crying inconsolably in bed, having pieced together the one-way conversation. Harris hugged his wife and joined her in tears. They had both lost a dear friend.

Upon his arrival at the hospital Dr. Terbanion was met by Dr. Alton Randolph, the chief of staff.

"We'd better use the service elevator to avoid the crowds and commotion." Dr. Randolph escorted Dr. Terbanion to the elevator where he was greeted by two men in dark suits and darker demeanors.

The tenth floor was abuzz with idle chatter, moanful sobs, and serious conversation. Although Terbanion arrived within twenty minutes of the phone call, he was almost the last to arrive. All the physicians associated with the senator's case were already present, as were most of the hospital's administrative staff, the senator's local staff and family, several nurses, hospital security, and the men in the dark suits.

After a cursory review of the few details available, Dr. Terbanion proceeded to console Delores Hargrove, who had already been given a sedative. Following several minutes of nonsensical conversation, Judith Terbanion intervened and convinced those present to allow Mrs. Hargrove some privacy.

The men in dark suits introduced themselves as secret service agents and asked Dr. Terbanion several questions relative to the medical care rendered to the senator. During the interrogation, Dr. Terbanion noticed Lance Darby nervously conversing with one of the senator's top aides. Dr. Terbanion excused himself momentarily from the agents, to inquire what had Darby so upset. The substance of his concern dealt with informing Garrison Hammer of the senator's death. Terbanion assured Darby he would personally inform Garrison, much to his relief.

The ring of the phone startled several of the staff who had already begun the mourning process by quietly reflecting on their individual relationships with the late senator. Robert Mulse, head of security, answered the phone. He muttered something, swore softly, then forcefully, yet quietly returned the phone to its base. "The media is in the lobby."

There was a collective moan. Someone verbalized the questions they all were pondering: *How did they find out so soon? And from whom?* There was no response.

The senator's staff, along with the hospital's administrative staff, prepared themselves for a very long day.

26

Thousands of miles away, the staff on the surgical floor at Laguna Beach Community were frantically scurrying about attempting to stabilize Mrs. Peters, whose hypotensive state was now becoming unresponsive to usual therapy. Her physician, Dr. Arnold Freewald, was generally very calm, collected, and rational. But not tonight.

Her blood pressure continued to drop, in spite of their careful monitoring of her fluid balance. Mrs. Peters was rapidly approaching a comatose state. Her fever was remittent in spite of broad spectrum antibiotics.

Freewald thought to himself what a mistake it had been to agree to do the surgery locally. It was part of his unwritten law that, whatever could go wrong, would, if you were taking care of a physician or a physician's family. The second part of this unwritten law was that the degree of complications were directly proportional to the stature of the recipient. In the case of Mrs. Janet Peters, the stature was indirect, yet monumental. Mrs. Peters' brother was none other than Dr. C. Arnold Prentiss, arguably the most renowned physician in the country—a Nobel laureate, the inventor of the Prentiss valve (which revolutionized heart surgery); and the recipient of virtually every prestigious award given by the medical profession. Dr. Prentiss was a legend. When Mrs. Peters insisted on having her surgery performed locally, Freewald had asked the best orthopedic surgeon on staff, Marvin Pearle, to perform the operation.

There had to be something else they could do, some missing piece of data that would explain this downhill course Mrs. Peters was taking.

"Her pressure's not responding to the vasopressors," Dr. Pearle stated, as if expecting Dr. Freewald to miraculously reply with a solution.

"Let's review the data again," Freewald said.

Opening the chart they started another review of the case. 'She was stable at the time of the surgery. All her vital signs and laboratory data were normal. She had been a smoker but quit ten years ago. There was a history of borderline hypertension, never treated with medication, and a hysterectomy for fibroids over twenty years ago. She broke her leg in an accident fifteen years ago, which resulted in a gait abnormality aggravating her degenerative joint disease, causing her knee to become unstable and refractory to conservative therapy." Freewald shook his head as he asked and answered his own question regarding the necessity o the surgery in the first place. *Was it really indicated?* His answer to himself had not changed. The surgery was clearly indicated.

Dr. Pearle continued to thumb through the chart. "The surgery was straightforward and without any complications. On the second post-op day she spiked a fever, complained of some mild shortness of breath and some abdominal pain. We cultured her up, started a broad spectrum antibiotic, and monitored her status, which has progressively deteriorated."

Freewald interrupted. "Her lung scan's negative, her EKG's normal, and X-rays of her chest and abdomen essentially normal. When we put in the central lines yesterday, her initial pressures suggested some fluid depletion. Her pressure initially responded to the fluids, but over the last twelve hours again started to drop, even though her wedge pressures were more than adequate. Vasopressors have had little-to-no effect and her cultures have remained negative." Freewald twirled his pen aimlessly in his fingers as he mulled the case over.

Pearle chimed in, "And now she's slipping into a coma." Pearle shook his head. "Why?"

"I don't know." The words barely were audible.

Pearle started to talk, then hesitated before asking, "Arnold, would you consider asking Jasper to consult on the case?"

Freewald had never been a fan of Dr. Jasper and hadn't asked for his opinion on a case in years. "I wouldn't feel comfortable calling Jasper myself, but if you think he would be of any assistance, by all means, call him." Freewald was beyond allowing his personal feeling to interfere.

"I'll call him now," Pearle said.

Ethan Jasper was an older internist trained in the days before much of the current technology was available. Dr. Jasper and his colleagues at that time were required to refine their bedside diagnostic skills to a level that generally surpassed those of physicians who had become more dependent on the new technology. Over the past several years, Jasper had limited his practice, accepting no new patients and rarely taking care of any who were hospitalized. If a patient needed hospitalization, Jasper would call on several of the staff internists to tend to them, only offering advice if it was requested.

Before Jasper had phased out of his hospital practice, Pearle had frequently consulted him. Over those years Pearle had been consistently impressed with Jasper's medical knowledge and diagnostic skills.

Jasper was at the hospital within twenty minutes. Once Dr. Jasper had completed his examination of Mrs. Peters, he returned to the small conference room where the exhausted and frustrated Freewald and Pearle were leaning over their coffee.

"I have some suggestions. First I would repeat the CBC with the bleeding parameters, electrolytes, and also pick up a cortisol level followed by a short cortico-tropin stimulation test. Then I would give a steroid bolus." Jasper spoke softly, but confidently and with authority.

"So, you think she has acute adrenal insufficiency?" Freewald asked, as he pondered Jasper's comments.

"It's a possibility. I think we need to consider acute adrenal hemorrhage as a cause for her resistant hypotension."

They followed Dr. Jasper's recommendations. Within hours Mrs. Peters' condition began to stabilize and her blood pressure returned to normal.

Freewald had been keeping the immediate family informed from the start but had intentionally avoided the call to Dr. Prentiss. When Mr. Peters informed Dr. Freewald that Dr. Prentiss was on the phone and would like to discuss his sister's status, Freewald had no choice but to oblige.

Although cordial, Freewald could sense Prentiss' critical evaluation of his every word. To Freewald's relief, Prentiss asked to confer with Dr. Jasper.

"Jasper here."

"Dr. Jasper, this is Arnold Prentiss. I would personally like to thank you for your care of my sister. Doctor, could you please review your perspective of her care and how you concluded she had acute adrenal insufficiency?"

"Thank you for your kind words, but the diagnosis really wasn't that difficult," Jasper said.

"It's apparent to me that you are an excellent physician with laudable diagnostic skills. My sister is fortunate you were there."

"Dr. Prentiss, I'm humbled by your remarks."

"No, Dr. Jasper, it is I who am in your debt. Please take my personal phone number, and do not hesitate to call me if I can be of any assistance to you in the future. Again, thank you very much."

"Thank you, Dr. Prentiss." Jasper replaced the phone. A feeling of pride and worth overwhelmed him. He hadn't experienced that type of satisfaction in years. Hearing the words of Dr. Prentiss caused Jasper to recall his mentor, Dr. Jonas Cisko, who had a profound influence on his medical career. Although he hadn't talked to Jonas for over a year, he felt the need to talk to him, as he did in the old days when he wanted to discuss an interesting case.

Jasper's beeper interrupted his thoughts. It was his office calling. He looked at his watch and only then realized that the night had given way to the dawn. His office hours were about to commence. He was fully energized and ready for a full day of practice. Prior to leaving the hospital, Jasper checked the status of Mrs. Peters, who had now regained consciousness and was well on her way to making a remarkable recovery.

Dr. Freewald was overflowing in his praise of Dr. Jasper, who accepted his remarks graciously before leaving for his office.

The remainder of Dr. Jasper's day was a blur. As soon as he returned home, he felt compelled to share this feeling with someone. The person he knew who could appreciate how he was feeling was his friend, Jonas Cisko. As he dialed Jonas in Chicago, he thought about how wonderful medicine could be.

3

Dr. Jonas Cisko put down the phone and sat back in his old, battered recliner. It was the only piece of furniture he had kept after his divorce was finalized four years ago. He decided there were too many memories, both good and bad, associated with the old furniture, as well as with the home in Northbrook. His wife—rather, his *ex*-wife—wanted virtually nothing tangible from their thirty-six years of marriage save their art collection and various mementos and photographs of their only son, Jordan. Dr. Cisko donated all his furnishings to charity with the lone exception of his recliner of twenty-some years, which he referred to as his "fortress of solitude" in that sea of hostility he had called home for all those years. His new home was a modern condominium on the Magnificent Mile offering a beautiful view of Lake Michigan.

The knock at the door surprised Dr. Cisko. He wasn't expecting visitors and the security guard at the front desk hadn't notified him. Peering through the peephole in his new mahogany door Jonas Cisko recognized a face that he hadn't seen for over thirty-five years. Cisko opened the door to greet Harvey Kahn, who still possessed an ingratiating smile, full of large pearly white teeth.

"How the heck are you, you old geezer?" Harvey enveloped Jonas in a bear-like hug. Jonas had forgotten how large a man Harvey was.

At a loss for any meaningful remark Jonas decided on the banal. "You look great. How many years has it been?" Harvey did look great. His tanned face, deep blue eyes, and white hair accentuated his pearly whites, all complementing a robust physique.

Harvey returned the compliment, but Jonas knew this was merely a courtesy, since the years, especially the last four, had not been as kind to him.

As Jonas motioned Harvey to enter his home, he noticed

another man standing in the shadow of Harvey's large frame. Harvey, aware of Jonas's reaction, realized he hadn't introduced his companion. Harvey's friend was dressed completely in black: black shoes, black pants, black shirt, black tie, black jacket and even black sunglasses. Harvey introduced him as Van Gregory, but Jonas did not hear the introduction. He was distracted by his attire and wondered why this man was wearing sunglasses at night.

After a reintroduction, Jonas and the man in black followed Harvey into the living room, where he had already made himself at home. Harvey was lounging in Jonas's prized recliner. His body barely fit and the force of his weight appeared to bend the frame.

Suddenly memories of Harvey flashed across Jonas' mind and he realized he never liked him. In fact, he recalled he had actually disliked Harvey. Jonas wondered if Harvey had changed or if his aversion would span the decades. Jonas remembered Harvey as a pompous, egotistical braggart but with style enough to enable him to manipulate many people and most circumstances. He also recalled that people with intelligence and insight universally saw through Harvey's panache to the opportunist who could not be trusted.

When Jonas saw the figure sprawled on his sentimentally retained recliner, he had to refrain from saying something he would later regret. "So Harvey, long time, no see." Jonas had to bite his lower lip to limit his remarks.

"Yeah, over thirty years since the old California days." Harvey said. "I've kept up with your career over the years, and it appears you've come a long way from our days at L.A. General."

Jonas nodded, his curiosity was getting the better of him. "So what brings you here?"

Obviously anticipating the question, Harvey sat upright in the recliner and leaned forward. The expression on his face changed to reflect a much more serious tone. "I'm here as a friend and a colleague."

Jonas's face remained expressionless. He had no idea where this was about to lead.

Harvey continued, "This committee you're on, the primary-care liaison committee, has been charged with a very serious assignment. The ramifications of this assignment will have tremendous significance, not only for yourself, but for our entire profession."

Jonas was nonplused. "What are you talking about?"

Van Gregory, seated on a couch adjacent to the recliner, now abruptly stood and faced Jonas. "Maybe I can clear this up. I represent some of our colleagues who are very concerned about what recommendations may come from your committee. These colleagues, who I might add are very influential, would like to know your position on any proposed merger."

Van Gregory was now face to face with Jonas, which made Jonas uncomfortable. Jonas maneuvered himself a safe distance from Van Gregory and then approached Harvey, who was now standing. "You said this would have significant ramifications for our profession. What does that mean?" The tone in Jonas's voice intensified as he continued. "Also, what colleagues, influential no less, are you referring to?"

Before Harvey could respond, Van Gregory interjected, "For now, who these colleagues are isn't important. As far as the significance of the committee on the profession, you can imagine what an impact the profession can make on primary care in this country. This committee may be the ticket to achieve such an impact."

It quickly became apparent to Jonas that the only reason Harvey was there was to allow this stranger access to Jonas. Although angered by this approach, Jonas didn't want to lose control of the situation. "What the hell did you just say? Harvey, can you translate for me?"

Even through Gregory's dark glasses, Jonas could see he was irritated, a reaction that pleased Jonas very much. Harvey, unaware of the silent conversation between the two, started to laugh, but the laughter ceased as Gregory spoke again.

"Let me simplify this for you, Dr. Cisko." He virtually hissed the "s" in Cisko's name. "First, we need to know, tonight, your opinion on any merger between the professions. Second, we'll discuss your response with our colleagues, who will remain nameless at this time. Third, when and if we're ready, we'll reveal who our colleagues are. At that time you'll realize why it was important to keep their identities unknown." The tone of Van Gregory's voice was both demeaning and condescending. Jonas was infuriated.

"Who the hell do you think you are to talk to me in that manner! Also, who the hell are you? What do you have to do with our profession? Are you a doctor? A DO? And what do you mean the names of these so-called 'colleagues' are irrelevant, you pompous asshole!"

Jonas was on the verge of totally losing control when Harvey intervened, attempting to restore some propriety. "Whoa, Hoss, simmer down—I'm sure Van didn't intend to insult or offend you." Harvey glanced at Van, who nodded in agreement.

Harvey continued as they all sat down. "Van only meant that because of the delicate nature of these negotiations, some of our colleagues would prefer to remain anonymous at this time. You see, Van works as an advisor for both the AMA and the AOA, and therefore is sensitive to both sides of the issue. What we really would like to know is your perspective on the potential merger issue."

Harvey's response was controlled and rational. Both Jonas and Van appeared calmer, yet each was internally harboring a strong disdain for the other. Jonas had never trusted Harvey after his wife pointed out Harvey's many character flaws those many years ago. One of his ex-wife's best attributes was her ability to accurately assess someone's character, and she had Harvey figured out within seconds. Jonas did not need the help of his ex to size up Van Gregory.

"As I'm sure you're both aware, the information and the discussions from the committee are supposed to be confidential. Obviously this confidentiality has been compromised, but not by me. I'm afraid I cannot reveal my opinions nor any other information regarding any merger referable to the committee."

Jonas's comments were followed by several seconds of silence, finally broken by Van Gregory. "I was afraid this would be your answer. I don't know if you realize that your performance on this committee will be carefully watched by many concerned parties. A good number of these parties can either directly or indirectly influence your career."

"I hope you're not trying to threaten me." Jonas's fists were clenched so hard his fingers started to blanch.

Van Gregory's smirk belied his answer. "This isn't any threat, just a statement of fact. You must know that we can help you in your career and that's why we're here."

Harvey walked over to Van and whispered in his ear. Van then excused himself to the restroom. Harvey, mustering a sincere look, approached Jonas. Jonas had seen this look before. It was the look Harvey had used when he wanted to delude someone.

"What Van just referred to is real. What I mean is, you could essentially write your own ticket career-wise, if you cooperate on the committee. I hope for your own sake, you seriously consider our conversation. I've always admired your integrity, as well as your common sense, and I'm confident that you'll do what's best for the profession, as well as yourself. We're not really asking you to break any confidences, rather to just discuss options with some friends who are also deeply committed to the profession. Why don't you sleep on it tonight and I'll contact you tomorrow?"

Harvey extended his hand and Jonas reciprocated. Van Gregory was already standing at the door.

The one thing that really bothered him was Van Gregory, who had offered little to the conversation except for the implied threat. Why was he there? Although not intimidated, Jonas was uncomfortable with the entire situation; and after considering the circumstances, decided that his best option was to discuss the matter with one of his favorite patients and confidants, Marcus Merker.

4

Dr. Cisko arrived early at his office to complete his medical charts and to review several additional medical records where the insurance companies had denied payment.

His receptionist was the first to arrive at a quarter to eight. Dr. Cisko interrupted her preparatory work to inform her that Mr. Merker would be coming in this morning, and that he should be shown into the office as soon as he arrived. The morning schedule was routine, with several patient revisits and one emergency that required hospitalization for pneumonia. At ten-forty Marcus Merker entered the waiting room and was promptly escorted to Dr. Cisko's private office.

Dr. Cisko entered the room and slowly sat in his chair. After an awkward silence, Cisko sighed and focused his attention on Merker. "Marcus, thanks for coming on such short notice."

"No problem at all. What's up?" Merker asked.

"I need your advice and possibly your help," Dr. Cisko said as he tapped his pen worriedly.

"I'm all ears."

Dr. Cisko reviewed the conversation of the previous evening and asked if he should be concerned.

Merker reflected for about a minute before responding. "Before I give you my opinion, I'd like to clear up some points." Cisko nodded as Merker continued, "This committee you're on, is it that powerful?"

"I don't think so. It's really a subcommittee that has been charged with developing policy on one issue. Also, I don't think we're the only committee discussing that issue."

"What's the issue?" Marcus Merker had jotted down some notes from Dr. Cisko's introductory remarks and now held his pen poised.

Cisko hesitated. "The issue deals with the potential merger

of the two medical professions, the allopathic and osteopathic professions."

"Say what?" Merker asked.

Cisko smiled. "Allopathic doctors are the MDs, and the osteopathic doctors are the DOs."

"Oh." Merker said. "But what's the difference?"

"Your question is a good one, and until recently, a question I had ignored. But this committee has forced me to formulate my own answer." Cisko folded his hands in front of him and leaned forward.

"So what's the answer?"

"Before I answer the question I first need to give you a little background on the profession."

"Fine." Merker said agreeably.

"The osteopathic profession is over a hundred years old, and for the majority of the time we've struggled to overcome many obstacles to become accepted by the government, the military, and the MDs. Over the last half century the profession was transformed from a profession characterized by manipulative therapy to a full-service health-care profession."

"What does that mean?"

Cisko straightened himself in his chair. "It means, we started as a splinter group from the MDs, and in fact, A.T. Still, the founder of osteopathic medicine, was an MD. He founded the profession in an attempt to find a better way to deliver health-care which included the use of manipulative techniques."

"Do you mean, you know, um, what is it . . . chiropractic?"

"Sort of but not exactly." Cisko smiled and rubbed his chin, as he thought of a response. "I believe the chiropractors use manipulation or adjustments, as some call it, to restore normal function to the nerves that are malfunctioning." Cisko winced. It had been awhile since he tried to explain this. "We also use manipulation, but incorporate the basic principles of medicine with it, to create a more comprehensive approach."

"Let me see if I understand this. It seems to me you're describing a marriage between the MDs and the chiropractors. Is that it?" Merker asked, to the relief of Cisko.

"Not exactly, but close enough." Cisko paused to regroup his thoughts. "Besides our emphasis on manipulation, our profession has also emphasized primary care and specifically general practice."

"Isn't that sort of what everybody's talking about today?"

"Exactly" Cisko smiled at Merker.

Merker continued, "So let's cut to the chase, how much money is involved with this merger?"

"Money?"

"Listen Doc, if you were really threatened, then there must be money involved. As my daddy used to say, 'All of life's conflicts can be boiled down into two issues, money and sex, and most of the sex issues were really about money.' So I ask you, where's the money? Who's gonna profit from this merger? Once we answer these questions, then I can tell you whether you have something to be worried about." Merker folded his arms across his chest and sat back in his chair.

"Well, a merger would probably mean the reallocation of funds to various institutions. It could possibly affect the practices of thousands of physicians."

"Not a bad start; what else?" Merker clasped his hands in front of him as he listened.

"Let me think. Because of the health-care reform being bantered about, there is legislation being formulated around primary care."

"Primary care, you mentioned that before. What the heck is that exactly?" Merker asked.

"Good question. I won't bore you with my opinion but the working definition for primary care includes those physicians who have initial and primary contact with the patient. That usually includes general and family practitioners, general internists, and general pediatricians, although some also include obstetrician gynecologists."

"Isn't that what you said your profession is about?" Merker asked.

"In a manner of speaking, yes." Cisko answered, gently nodding his head.

"So that could be the money," Merker said enthusiastically.

"What?"

"If the laws are changing and more money is thrown at primary care, then anyone in primary care should do okay."

"Theoretically. But to date this hasn't happened. Although some money is there, most of the money in medicine is still in specialized care."

"So what are you saying? There isn't much money involved in this merger?"

"No, I wouldn't say that."

Merker smiled. He was about to continue the conversation when Dr. Cisko abruptly stood and walked over to his white coat removing an envelope from the outer pocket.

Before he could inquire, Dr. Cisko explained. "This conversation reminded me that I received a letter yesterday from the committee. I was busy at the time and put it in my coat. So let's see what the letter says."

Dr. Cisko opened the letter. He had to readjust his arm position to be able to read what it said.

"Why don't you just put on your glasses?" Merker asked.

Dr. Cisko chuckled, "Since my divorce I've been feeling quite sorry for myself. So recently I decided to do something for me. I started to play golf again and my glasses became an annoyance so I decided to have Lasik."

"Huh?" Merker had no idea what Dr. Cisko had just said.

"You know, laser surgery to correct nearsightedness. Since the surgery, my vision's corrected for distances, but now my near vision's gone. My old glasses are useless." Cisko removed his glasses from his desk drawer and tossed them on the table. "So, I have an appointment next week to get fitted for a new pair of reading glasses."

Merker, sorry that he asked the question, continued, "So what does the letter say?"

Dr. Cisko read the letter. It was a reminder of the meeting scheduled for next week. An updated agenda was also enclosed with the merger as a major item to be discussed.

"Marcus, do you think I have anything to be concerned about?"

"I'm not sure. Why don't I check out the two guys who visited you yesterday and see what I can find out. What're their names again? And do you have any idea where I can find them?"

"Dr. Harvey Kahn is the internist who I believe still lives in California. I think the Redondo Beach area. The other guy's name was Van Gregory. He's probably local, from Chicago. Harvey mentioned that he had ties with both the AOA and the AMA, so maybe that would be a good place to start." Dr. Cisko continued to describe the physical characteristics of both Kahn and Gregory as Merker jotted down the pertinent details.

That evening Dr. Cisko got a call from Harvey Kahn asking if he would agree to meet with him. Reluctantly, Cisko agreed, as his curiosity got the better of him.

There was a distinct air of tension when Harvey entered the living room, again accompanied by Van Gregory. Jonas had placed several medical journals on his recliner to prevent either Harvey Kahn or Van Gregory from sitting in his seat.

Van broke the silence. "I'd like to apologize for last night. I've been working real hard, and my edges are a little raw."

"Apology accepted." Cisko felt the tension in the room start to dissipate.

"Have you thought about our discussion of last evening?" Harvey said.

"Obviously I have, but I'm still not sure what you want." Cisko focused on Harvey Kahn but kept Van Gregory in his peripheral vision.

"Not to offend you, but can I make a suggestion?" Van Gregory offered.

Dr. Cisko shrugged his approval.

"You're going to be part of a meeting dealing with this issue of a merger. Several people in this meeting will come out strongly for this merger."

Kahn noticed the shock on Cisko's face and interrupted. "Jonas."

Cisko changed his attention from Gregory to Kahn. Gregory sat back on the couch. Using his softest, soothing tone, Kahn continued. "Let me try to explain. Some members of your committee will recommend that the osteopathic medical schools be incorporated into the allopathic system. Each osteopathic school will be formally or informally associated with a larger allopathic school, hospital, or both to form a larger consortia. This consortium will allow the allopathic school a base for a generalist curriculum, while preserving the osteopathic tradition for primary care."

"So our schools will become the illegitimate children of the MD schools?" Cisko said curtly.

"No, not at all. In fact, hopefully this type of agreement will give our schools the support necessary to be the leaders in this new health-care reform. As you are well aware, there is an alarming recent trend even in our profession to specialize. Over the past several years, the percentage of our graduates entering allopathic residencies has grown significantly. Hopefully this will allow this trend to reverse."

"I'm having difficulty seeing how this type of change would be beneficial to either profession." Cisko said.

"Please don't take what I am about to say the wrong way. As we are all aware, there are major problems with the medical system in its current format. Sweeping reforms are being proposed and we must be prepared. As the financing for medicine changes, so will the competition. When push comes to shove, the osteopaths will not be able to compete with the AMA, whose lobby is still very powerful and will not allow another profession to significantly impact on its turf. Thus this merger will hopefully allow both professions to come out winners."

"Explain again how the osteopathic profession will come out a winner?" Cisko rubbed his forehead forcefully.

Harvey placed his hand on Cisko's shoulder. "I understand your concern. Believe me, I have similar concerns myself. But if you really think about it, what are we as a profession doing differently? How can we justify not merging?" Harvey threw his hands up in the air.

Cisko didn't like what Harvey had said. Although he believed some of what he said was true, the gist of Harvey's comments infuriated him. "Do you honestly believe what you just said?"

Harvey's voice cracked. "Yes, I really do. I feel this type of merger will at least preserve the essence of the profession, and allow our colleagues to continue their professional careers."

41

"Just as the essence of homeopathy was preserved," Cisko replied sarcastically.

"I can't believe you'd use that comparison," Harvey exclaimed in astonishment. Now he also was becoming irritated. "Homeopathy? Wasn't the premise of homeopathy based on a concept of using a substance that has potential toxicity to treat that same illness, like using poison ivy to treat a rash."

"That may have been part of it, I really don't know." Cisko answered. "But what I meant was . . ."

"I know what you meant." Harvey interrupted. "But this example actually may emphasize my point. I believe, homeopathy also suggested using remedies in very small doses, a concept that has merit, but hasn't been scientifically proven. Just like manipulative treatment, which also has merit but hasn't been scientifically proven either."

"I think you've totally missed my point," Cisko said. "I'm aware that substantive research is still needed to prove the true effectiveness of manipulation, but that's coming. What I meant was, when a smaller profession is absorbed by a much larger profession, it's only a matter of time until the smaller profession is nothing more than a historical footnote, like homeopathy." Cisko's cold stare focused on Harvey.

Harvey Kahn began a retort, but Cisko's mind started to wander midway through his diatribe. Something in Harvey's response reminded him of Merker's remark, "Where does the money fit in?"

Without considering the ramifications of the question, Jonas interrupted Harvey, "Let's cut to the chase, what about the money?"

"What money?" Harvey asked.

"The funding, you know, government contracts, grants, research dollars, reimbursements—all that stuff." Jonas wanted to put them on the defensive.

Van Gregory took a clue from Harvey and offered a response, "That all needs to be worked out and probably will not be even considered until after the merger is completed."

"You're not serious. Funding will have to be a major portion of any negotiations regarding the merger." Jonas now understood why Merker had brought up the issue of money.

"What I mean is, the details of any funding probably couldn't take place until the merger was complete. Then it would be worked out on the local level. But you don't have to worry." Van Gregory gave Cisko a self-assured grin.

"Worry? Why would I worry?"

"You wouldn't, we'll take care of you," Harvey replied.

"What are you talking about?" Cisko was struggling to maintain his composure.

"If you agree with the proposed plans for the merger, you can basically pick whatever position you'd like within the framework of the merger," Harvey said. He looked at Gregory, who nodded his head in concurrence.

"Are you asking me to sell out the profession?" Jonas felt his heart palpitate.

"I don't see it that way at all," Van Gregory said sharply. "What we're asking is for you to cooperate in a merger that will save your profession."

"I'm sorry I don't see it that way." Jonas said, clenching his teeth.

"I'm sorry you don't," Van Gregory said, reacting to the change in Jonas's mood.

"I think it's time for you to go." Jonas motioned with his arm for them both to leave.

"By the way, have you spoken to your son recently?" Van Gregory replied without moving.

"What does my son have to do with any of this?" Jonas's thoughts focused on his son, a prominent judge in Philadelphia. *Could he be part of this?*

"Nothing, nothing at all. I just heard that your son was in line for a very important appointment, to the Federal Court of Appeals." Van Gregory's words dripped with acrimony.

Dr. Cisko sat back down as he prepared himself for the hammer to fall.

"You know how they check and double check all potential candidates these days," Van Gregory said. "Wouldn't it be a shame if they found out about a college drug bust years ago?" A smirk appeared on Gregory's face as he removed his sunglasses.

"You son of a bitch, how dare you drag my son into this?" Jonas's face was flushed and his neck veins were distended.

"I'm not dragging him, you are," Gregory said smugly as he folded his arms across his chest.

Jonas could feel the rage building inside.

"Listen, all you need to do is what is right for you, your profession, and your son," Gregory said.

"And if I don't?" Jonas barked.

"Well, who knows what could happen to both you and your son's careers if . . ."

Jonas could not control his temper any longer. He jumped from his chair and charged the man in black, flailing wildly. Harvey positioned himself between the charging Jonas and Van Gregory. Suddenly Jonas fell limp into Harvey's arms. Harvey lowered Jonas's body to the floor, simultaneously feeling for a pulse. Jonas's eyes were half opened and his pupils dilated. He lay motionless.

"He's arrested!" Harvey started to position himself to institute CPR when he felt Van's hand on his shoulder.

"Leave him. The dumb asshole deserves to die," Gregory said emphatically.

"What?" Harvey Kahn looked up with astonishment and disbelief in his eyes.

"Leave him. We can't be found here."

"But he'll die."

"He's probably already dead." The words which rolled off Gregory's lips were as cold as his stare.

They both looked down at the limp body, the face already losing color, the jaw ajar, and the blank, lifeless stare.

"I can't leave him like this." Harvey's eyes were welled with tears and he was physically nauseated.

"Sure you can," Gregory said without emotion.

"But this is really wrong . . ."

"Listen to me. If we do anything to him we'll have to call for help. Then we'll have to explain what we were doing here, and our associates wouldn't like that at all. In addition, he was being difficult and would have probably caused a great deal of trouble. Not to mention putting our positions in fuckin' jeopardy."

"I guess you're right." Harvey couldn't think clearly as he wiped away a few tears and the nausea started to subside.

Van Gregory nodded.

"Van. Can we at least place him in his chair instead of leaving him on the floor?"

Van lifted the journals Jonas had put on his recliner and placed them on the end table adjacent to the chair. Together they placed Jonas's body into his recliner, his fortress of solitude, now for eternity. Jonas's body slumped over the side of the recliner, knocking over the end table, jarring his glasses and a magazine, *The New England Journal of Medicine* onto the floor.

They stood back to evaluate their handiwork. Harvey replaced the glasses on Jonas and the magazine on his lap. There was no question Jonas was dead. Meanwhile Van Gregory systematically retraced their steps, wiping away all their fingerprints.

Van Gregory placed a hand on each of Harvey's shoulders and stood face to face to ensure he had his total attention. "I think it's time to leave. When we leave, I want you to walk at a normal pace. Don't do anything that would bring attention to us."

Van went to the closet and removed a camel hair jacket and adjusted it over his own black sportcoat. Then he removed his sunglasses.

"Do you wear glasses?" Van asked Harvey.

"No."

Van went into Jonas's bedroom and found another pair of glasses by his bed, then returned to the living room.

"Put these on," Gregory ordered.

Dr. Kahn placed the glasses on his face and looked in the mirror. What he saw there was terrible.

"Again, when we leave walk normally. Don't look at anyone directly, but don't intentionally avoid them either. When we leave the building, we will turn right, circle the block, and approach the car from the opposite direction."

Dr. Kahn was still in a state of shock as he looked over to his lifeless colleague hunched over the recliner, motionless.

45

"Did you hear what I said?" Van Gregory asked in a petulant tone.

"Yeah, I heard." Harvey's response was barely audible.

Van Gregory gave one last perusal around the room before opening the door to the hallway, which was empty. So was the elevator. When they vacated the elevator, they passed a couple engrossed in conversation, seemingly oblivious to their presence. The night doorman wished them a good evening, and Van Gregory responded in kind. They faded into the darkness of the evening, indirectly heading for the car. They reached the car, but it was apparent Harvey Kahn was almost to the point of panic. Van removed the camel hair jacket and tossed it into the back seat of the car. He opened the door and assertively escorted Harvey Kahn into the passenger seat.

"Get a fucking grip, there was nothing you could do," Gregory said.

"How do you know that?" Kahn asked, guilt tearing him apart.

"Listen, it's a moot point now anyway."

Harvey just shook his head in disbelief.

"When you get home, destroy the clothes you wore tonight." Gregory inserted the key, started the ignition, then turned toward Harvey Kahn extending his hand. "And give me the glasses."

Without speaking, Harvey handed him Dr. Cisko's glasses. Harvey Kahn realized something Van Gregory already knew. He was in way over his head.

5

Merker had called the AOA office claiming he was a friend of Dr. Kahn's who had heard that Dr. Kahn was in Chicago and would like to surprise him. Initially there was some reticence to assist Merker in his request. However, after several minutes of small talk and hollow compliments, Merker was able to convince the staff to assist him. They informed him that Dr. Kahn was staying at the Drake Hotel.

It had been years since Merker had visited the Drake. As he entered, he thought to himself how he preferred the older, grander hotels in the city, especially the Drake, where he once had spent a memorable evening with his wife when they were first married.

Merker had forgotten the lobby of the Drake was raised above the street, and could be exited on either Walton Street or Lake Shore Drive. Since he couldn't cover both exits, he needed to improvise. The valet parking was on the Walton Street side of the building. To Merker's amazement, he found a legal spot a half block from the hotel on Walton.

Merker's detective skills were not as fine-tuned as they had once been, but his mind was still sharp and his forte was improvisation. Merker had an adequate description of Harvey Kahn from Dr. Cisko and he felt comfortable that he would be able to recognize him. Once he identified Harvey Kahn, he would reevaluate his options.

Merker reacquainted himself with the hotel. He studied the lobby, exits, elevators, stairwell, and the hallways before returning to the lobby. Merker located the house phones. The lobby was empty this time in the morning. It was now six-thirty.

"Dr. Kahn's room please, Dr. Harvey Kahn."

"Sir, we generally do not forward the phone this early in the morning," replied the telephone operator.

47

"I'm calling to confirm a limousine reservation for seven-thirty this morning."

"I'll connect you sir, one moment."

The voice on the line was raspy and partially incoherent, it was obvious he had been awakened from a deep sleep. "Hello."

"Dr. Kahn."

"Yes"

"This is Lake Shore Limousine Service confirming your limousine reservation for seven-thirty this morning."

"What are you talking about?" Harvey's enunciation was now clearer and he was much more coherent.

"I'm sorry, I am calling for a Dr. Kahn at the Drake Hotel."

"This is Dr. Kahn, but I didn't reserve a limousine."

"This is strange. A Dr. Kahn called for a limousine. Our records indicate that Dr. Jeremy C-o-n-n in room 412 at the Drake Hotel made this reservation yesterday."

"This is Dr. Harvey K-a-h-n in room 502. You must have the wrong Dr. Kahn."

"I am so sorry, doctor. Please forgive me, I hope I didn't awaken you."

Harvey was too tired to be overly irritated. "That's all right, good-bye." Harvey hung up the phone before Merker could respond.

Merker wasn't surprised with the ease in which he was able to acquire Harvey Kahn's room number. He proceeded to the elevators. On the fifth floor, Kahn's room was close to a sitting area strategically placed at the center of the hall, opposite the elevators. Merker decided to wait in the sitting room for Harvey Kahn. Once identified, he would follow him.

Merker realized it could be hours until Dr. Kahn would leave his room, but waiting didn't bother him. Actually, Merker relished the possibility of a protracted wait. It would give him time to read the newspaper. Merker loved to read the paper, but was very selective as to what he actually read.

Merker was a sports fanatic, devouring every detail of virtually every sport printed in the paper. The other section of the paper he read religiously was the obituaries, a habit he had acquired after the death of his wife. When Merker looked for her obituary notice he had recognized two other names: one a childhood acquaintance, the other a retired ex-officer from the police force. Since that day, he read the obituaries regularly. As for the remainder of the paper, he really could care less. The news was generally bad, and he wasn't interested in current events if he wasn't directly involved.

Merker positioned himself in a chair that would afford him a perfect view of anyone entering or leaving the elevator. He was set. He had completed every column twice and was halfway through his third reading when a man fitting the description of Harvey Kahn summoned the elevator. Dr. Kahn appeared to be somewhat preoccupied, so Merker decided to join him when the elevator arrived.

Merker noticed that Dr. Kahn was holding what appeared to be a suit of clothing crumpled in his arms. Kahn was conspicuously avoiding any eye contact. Although this behavior appeared strange, it worked well for Merker. In the lobby Kahn was met by a man dressed in black, just as Dr. Cisko had described. Their conversation was brief as they walked out the lobby exiting onto Walton Street. While Harvey Kahn and Van Gregory waited for their car from the valet, Merker had ample time to retrieve his own car.

Merker double-parked his car, positioning himself across the street. He had his camera even longer than his car, but it still consistently took a good photograph. He was able to snap off several candids of both Harvey Kahn and Van Gregory before the valet arrived. As they pulled away, Merker got a clear view of the license plate and snapped a final shot before he entered the traffic.

Their first stop was at the offices of the American Medical Association. Merker parked his car and was able to track the duo to the offices of Graduate Medical Education, where they were meeting in the office of Dr. Victor Rasta, an AMA representative from the Government Affairs Office. The meeting lasted several hours. Merker was not sure why he was surprised when they returned to the Drake, since he had no reason to expect them to go elsewhere. Nevertheless he was disappointed. Parking his car illegally, he placed his police identification placard on the visor to avoid being ticketed or towed. As Merker crossed the street, he glanced back at his car. It was in a perfect position.

In the lobby, Merker noticed both Harvey Kahn and Van Gregory sitting in the restaurant adjacent to the lobby of the hotel. They were engaged in an intense conversation. Merker sat diagonally across from their table, positioning himself so he could not be seen, yet close enough to overhear. Unfortunately a harpist began to play. Although the music was pleasant and added to the ambiance, it virtually drowned out the conversation between Kahn and Gregory.

A waitress handed Merker a menu for afternoon tea. In his fifty-five years, Merker had never experienced afternoon tea, but today would be different. Merker opted for the traditional tea service, which included an assortment of finger sandwiches, a currant bun and a scone, whipped cream, and strawberry preserves with a choice of pastry.

As Merker looked over the menu, he noted the conversation between Kahn and Gregory had escalated into a mild shouting match. The exact content of their discussion was still obscured by the music, but it was evident they were not happy.

The waitress soon delivered the complete tea service to Merker's table. Before Merker could complete his tea time, Kahn abruptly exited the restaurant with Van Gregory in pursuit. Merker placed a twenty-dollar bill on the table and followed them to the lobby. They were both more controlled in the lobby and concluded their conversation in a civil manner. Dr. Kahn then left in the direction of the elevator, while Van Gregory left via the Walton Street exit. Merker debated whether it was of any additional benefit to follow Gregory. Instead, he decided to visit his old police station, the Twentieth District.

The police station at Foster and Damen had been his home for his last ten years on the force. Although he was retired, Merker still felt the adrenaline rush when he entered the building. There were so many new faces he almost felt out of place, but then he recognized an old familiar face, his old friend Sergeant Marvin Powell.

"Merker, you old SOB, how the hell are you?" Powell exclaimed.

"Good, real good. You look the same," Merker answered in a sarcastic tone. Powell had gained at least fifty pounds.

If they hadn't been friends, Powell would have taken offense at Merker's remark. Instead, his response was equally sarcastic. "Yeah, sure I do. I hear your detective agency is really cleaning up." Merker's business sense was about as effective as his ability to refrain from ice cream.

"Anyway, enough of the formalities. I need your help." Merker's voice carried a much more somber tone.

"How can I help?" Powell asked.

"I need you to run some plates." Powell hesitated. Before he could respond Merker continued, "A concerned friend of mine, a good friend, may need my help. I need to know if the owner of these plates is clean."

Powell didn't hesitate with his answer this time. "Give me the numbers and let's see what we can find out."

Merker handed Powell the sheet of paper on which he had written the plate numbers. Several minutes later Powell returned with his information. "The car is registered to a Van Gregory who resides on North Sheridan Road. There are no outstanding warrants or anything like that. There was a notation of an old aggravated assault charge that was dropped years ago before records were computerized, so I don't have any further info on it."

"Thanks a lot, Marv. How's the wife?" Merker asked as he transcribed the information into his notepad and put it in his pocket.

"Fine, how are you doing, really?" Powell's deep voice took on a deeper more serious resonance.

"I'm doing better, thanks for asking." At the time of his wife's death, Marvin and his wife had been one of the few couples who visited Merker, a fact he would never forget. They gave each other a firm handshake that conveyed more than just a greeting—more like let's keep in touch.

Upon arriving home, Merker called Dr. Cisko to update him. There was no answer. Merker reflected momentarily about Dr. Cisko's situation. He couldn't decide whether this was a legitimate situation requiring his help or not. He finally decided he didn't want to think about the case any further that evening. He set a portable television on top of his console, allowing him to simultaneously watch the basketball playoff game and the baseball game. Merker was content, at least for the moment.

Dr. Alexander Jourge had been hand-picked to chair the primary-care liaison committee. He was respected in the medical community, having held several prominent positions including a recent directorship at the National Institutes of Health. The committee was formed at the request of the head of the president's task force on health-care reform in conjunction with the secretary of health and the surgeon general's office, so it appeared more than a coincidence that Dr. Jourge was a personal friend of both the president and the first lady. Dr. Jourge was chosen for his abilities, not his political connections, although many thought his selection was entirely political.

Now, more than ever, Dr. Jourge's insight into health-care were considered relevant even if they were disparate. Jourge realized how important this committee could be in the process of health-care reform, and how critical it was to ensure each member of the committee was truly representative of their constituency.

When Jourge was notified of the untimely death of Jonas Cisko, he knew he had to convene several key members of the committee immediately to choose another candidate. Jourge chose two committee members to consult about the replacement for Dr. Cisko: Victor Rasta and Chester Timmons.

Victor Rasta was an old friend whose pioneering work in the field of cancer research and immunology placed him at center stage in the burgeoning field of AIDS research. Chester Timmons was a strong advocate for the osteopathic profession. Dr. Timmons began his career as a cardiologist, but over the years he aspired to political positions primarily dealing with postgraduate education, hospital administration, and community relations. During his career as a cardiologist Dr. Timmons was unique, because he incorporated osteopathic manipulative therapy in his routine care of his patients.

That evening the three met at the Embassy Suites Hotel at O'Hare airport. Jourge frequently chose the airport for short meetings. Since both he and Rasta were already in the city, it was a logical choice. Fortunately most of the preliminary work, such as selecting an alternative list of potential committee members, had already been completed when the initial committee was appointed. The list of alternate candidates was short—only four candidates had to be reviewed.

"I can't tell you how much I appreciate your willingness to meet on such short notice," Jourge said sincerely after they arrived.

The three ordered room service so they could begin. They decided to start by individually reviewing each potential candidate's credentials. Both Rasta and Timmons were given folders containing all the pertinent material regarding the candidates. Jourge had already reviewed the material in detail and patiently flipped back and forth through the packet. By the time Rasta and Timmons had completed their review of the potential candidates dinner arrived.

"I would prefer to discuss each candidate separately before we make any recommendations." Jourge said. "Upon the completion of our discussions I would like to reach a decision on a single candidate tonight."

Rasta's mouth was partially full of his salad "Let's not rush the process and bully us into a single choice."

"It is not my intent to bully anyone. However, we need to make a choice tonight so I can contact the rest of the committee tomorrow."

They reviewed each candidate in depth. After a lengthy discussion, they agreed on eliminating two of the candidates, but Rasta and Timmons were split on the two remaining. They both were equally adamant in support of their respective candidates.

Jourge agreed the two candidates left were the best, but had difficulty choosing one over the other. Both Rasta and Timmons agreed that the other's candidate was acceptable, yet neither was willing to concede his choice. After hours of discussion Rasta's arguments wore Timmons into submission. Jourge agreed, making the decision unanimous. Their choice for Dr. Cisko's replacement on the committee was Dr. Steven Callison.

6

Steven Callison's week had gone considerably smoother. This was his last week on the teaching ward service and all was under control, at least concerning the hospital practice.

The group followed Dr. Callison as they entered Mrs. Kodack's room. Dr. Callison was in the lead, closely followed by the resident, Dr. Wickerman. Then the students, with the student assigned to the patient in the lead. For this case, the student on the hot seat was Sean Gilbert, a bright student who had excelled on the rotation. The rest of the students quietly filed into the room, fading into the background.

Student Doctor Gilbert was updating the group on the status of Mrs. Kodack when her husband, daughter, and granddaughter entered the room. Mrs. Kodack's room had become the favorite spot of their daily patient rounds for several reasons. Mrs. Kodack's daughter Margaret was an excellent cook and frequently would have an array of tantalizing delicacies for them to enjoy. Mr. Kodack was also a tower of strength, not only for his wife but also for the staff and students. Lastly, there was little Sally, usually hiding in the corner of the room, her big, blue eyes taking it all in, yet saying nothing. During the week several students had attempted to bring Sally out of her shell, but to no avail. Any encroachment into her space caused Sally to retreat to the arms of her mother.

They had been able to ascertain the cause of Sally's silence. Two years ago while driving home with her father, Sally had been involved in an auto accident that killed her father. Dr. Wickerman learned the graphic details in a conversation with Mr. Kodack. A drunk driver had run a red light, broadsiding their car, instantly killing Sally's father, who was not wearing his seat belt. The impact caused her father's body to ricochet off the passenger side with his head landing in Sally's lap. Sally was wearing her seat belt which had jammed, trapping Sally in her seat unable to move while looking at her dead father's fixed stare. She hadn't spoken since.

However, what permeated the air whenever they entered the room was a sense of pure love that the Kodacks had for each another and this love was captured in those large blue eyes of little Sally. The entire group greeted Sally and her mother as they entered the room. Mr. Kodack was standing by the bed, and Mrs. Kodack was holding his hand as they were listening to Student Doctor Gilbert update the group on her status.

"Do you have any questions, Mrs. Kodack?" Student Doctor Gilbert said, as he placed his stethoscope on her chest.

"No Sean." Mrs. Kodack blushed slightly. "I mean Dr. Gilbert."

The alarm on Dr. Callison's beeper sounded. This was quite atypical, as it was generally known that he was not to be disturbed while making teaching rounds. Dr. Callison excused himself and left the discussion in the hands of Dr. Sharon Wickerman, the third year medicine resident who had performed exceptionally on this rotation.

The message on the beeper was for Callison to call his academic office immediately. As he dialed the number, he wondered what new disaster was about to descend upon him. "Helen, what's so important that I have to break from rounds?"

Helen Hunter had been Callison's secretary for the past two years and she was by far the best secretary he had ever worked with, always appropriate and supportive. Callison knew if she interrupted him, it must be an urgent call. "I'm sorry to disturb your rounds but I think this is a call you may want to respond to immediately."

"Okay, let me have it." Callison bit his lower lip, expecting the worst.

"The dean's office called and asked me to contact you immediately."

"The dean's office? Did they tell you what this is in reference to?"

"No, they just said they need you immediately."

"Need me, you mean in person?"

"Yes, in person."

Callison was at once relieved and aggravated. This was probably about some bureaucratic issue, which almost never amounted to anything significant. What irritated Callison was the fact that he had to interrupt rounds to deal with whatever this was. "Helen, please call them back and tell them I'm on the way."

Callison hung up and returned to Mrs. Kodack's room. He explained to Dr. Wickerman that he would return as soon as possible, and if she needed him, she shouldn't hesitate to beep him.

The walk from the hospital to the Administration Building of the Medical School was less than a block, but Callison was in no hurry. If they could disturb his rounds, he could take his time getting there. When Callison finally strolled into the administrative suites he was greeted by the dean's secretary, who was even more harried than usual and obviously glad to see him.

"Thank God you're here. I was just about to call you again! The dean really needs to speak with you, so go right in." The secretary opened the door to Dean Hoffnagle's office, curling her lip, sneering as she peered over her bifocals, motioning with her hand that Callison should enter.

Dean Hoffnagle greeted Callison at the door. "Please have a seat."

Callison sat in one of the dean's oversized dark leather chairs. He recalled how deceptive the chair was. It appeared comfortable but in reality was probably the most backbreaking chair he had ever sat in. Callison couldn't remember the last time a meeting in this office had been pleasant—and try as he might, he couldn't blame that solely on the chair. Usually Callison could read the dean's face, but this time the expression was unfathomable.

Before the dean could take his seat, he was interrupted by a phone call. "Excuse me for a moment." Hoffnagle's face changed as he started his conversation. Callison recognized this expression. It was a mirror image of his countenance the last time Callison was summoned to his office. Hoffnagle had asked Callison to review a draft of a proposed grant for the effectiveness of supervised therapy for tuberculosis in the local homeless shelter.

Callison had spent the better part of a week reviewing, critiquing and rewriting the proposal, only to have Hoffnagle decide not to provide institutional support for the grant. It was never submitted. Callison actually felt sorry for the person on the line.

As soon as the phone conversation ended, the undefined expression reappeared.

"I apologize for the interruption, but that was a call I had to take. I unfortunately had to give a department chairman some bad news." Hoffnagle said, and then smiled. "But now for the good news. Congratulations!"

Callison was beyond confused. "Excuse me, what exactly are you congratulating me for?"

"Oh, in my excitement I forgot to tell you."

This entire scenario was quite unusual. The dean was always in control and composed. Hoffnagle's expression was one of unadulterated enthusiasm. When had Callison ever seen the dean this excited? No wonder he didn't recognize his expression.

Dean Hoffnagle continued with his train of thought. "Do you remember several months ago, I asked your permission to place your name in nomination for a committee that was being formed by the secretary of health dealing with our profession and the issue of primary care? Well, I just got a call from a Dr. Alexander Jourge, the head of that committee. He asked if you would still be interested in serving on the committee."

"Why would he ask you if I'd be interested?"

"Because this committee might take some significant time commitments, and he needed to know if institutionally you would be supported. He felt it inappropriate to place you in a position where you would need to ask for institutional leave. He stated he would rather first obtain the institutional support, before he would ask you. Of course, I readily agreed to support this effort. I also asked him if I could notify you myself. I can't tell you how great an opportunity this position is for our institution, as well as for yourself." Dean Hoffnagle's face returned to the previously undefinable expression.

Callison was sitting in a state of disbelief; not because of the fact he was invited to sit on this committee, but because of the dean's response. "I thought they had selected another physician for the committee. I'm sure I was notified of that several months ago."

"Your memory's correct. They selected a Dr. Jonas Cisko from Chicago. Did you know him?" Hoffnagle's expression changed.

"I knew the name, not the man. Did something happen to him?"

"M.I., a couple days ago, and you were the first alternate."

"I guess I should be flattered." Callison didn't know what to say.

"I would say so." Hoffnagle's expression again was enthusiastic.

Still not knowing how to respond, Callison decided to skirt the issue. "When do I have to let them know?"

"Are you even questioning whether you would do this or not?"

"Frankly, yes I am."

"Don't you realize this is the opportunity of a lifetime? This type of opportunity will never occur again." Hoffnagle's eyes were wide and his mouth agape.

"Nevertheless, I need to know how much time this will take. I need to know some more details. And I need to discuss this with my wife." Callison had learned from previous meetings to hold his ground and not let the dean force the situation.

Hoffnagle rubbed his forehead. "I think those are all excellent points. Let me reiterate that I will guarantee whatever support you need from our institution. Also, you can expect a call from Dr. Jourge either later this evening or tomorrow. I do . . ."

Almost as if planned, Callison's beeper sounded. "Sorry to cut short the conversation, Dean, but I have to go. One of my patients is coding. I'll think about this and talk to you tomorrow." As he completed his sentence Callison promptly exited the room. His mind quickly switched to the hospital. The beeper suggested the call originated in the dialysis unit and the suffix signified a cardiac arrest. That meant another of his favorite patients, Robert Lincoln, was dying.

Robert Lincoln had been Callison's patient for over five

years. The major reason Callison was so fond of Robert was his vivacious personality. No matter what obstacle was placed in his path, Robert would always confront it head on, with a positive attitude. He sucked the marrow out of life, getting every drop of pleasure he could.

As a bon vivant, playboy, man about town, he had led a colorful, flamboyant fifty-five years. Robert had been married five times, divorced five times, and had at least five affairs to show for each of his marriages. What was unique about his relationships with his ex-wives was that he was able to remain close with each of them. He had no formal education, but he knew people and was a keen observer of the human experience.

Over the years he had amassed several small fortunes, only to eventually lose them. His expertise was as a salesman, where some of his exploits were legendary. He had sold real estate, automobiles, securities, insurance, and succeeded in every area. But his real prowess was as a master of the flesh. Robert loved women: women of all types, colors, and shapes, and they loved him right back.

On one occasion, Callison had asked Robert how he was able to maintain such a relationship with his ex-wives since he had cheated so many times on each of them. His answer was that he was, and always would be, the best lover they would ever have. Once he had a woman, she would always be his. Callison had asked him if he had a secret to sexual prowess but this was the one question Robert wouldn't answer. He would only respond with a grin from ear to ear.

This fact was actually confirmed when Callison had the occasion to meet two of his ex-wives at a party. Both admitted they still needed a "Robert injection", as they called it, every once in a while. Callison hadn't the nerve to ask them what was so special about Robert. He regretted this. Callison had examined Robert and couldn't help but notice that his penis was on the large side, but in his opinion wasn't so large as to warrant such acclaim.

Over the years, Robert would disclose his latest sexual escapades, and Callison would again attempt to find out the secret of his success. But to no avail. Callison enjoyed hearing

Robert's stories and often suggested he write his memoirs, as he was sure they would make a best-seller. Robert never seriously considered Callison's suggestion, although Callison was quite serious.

Robert also loved his own version of sex, drugs and rock and roll, which was rhythm and blues, fine wine, Chivas Regal, and rich foods. It was the excesses that brought Mr. Lincoln to the doctor and eventually to kidney failure, and for the last eight years, dialysis. Over the years Robert's exploits often culminated in various hospitalizations, usually to control his diabetes or his kidney disease. But possibly the most devastating result of his disregard for his health was the recent onset of impotence. Generally an extremely secure person, the impotence had wreaked havoc with his self-confidence. This hospitalization was intended to correct his impotence with a curative procedure.

Callison entered the dialysis unit. He was greeted by a medical student who seemed to be laughing, which Callison thought inappropriate. In the dialysis unit, he noted a group of doctors, nurses, and students crowded around Robert Lincoln. Some were smiling, there were a few quiet giggles, and two student-nurses were standing off to the side appearing embarrassed.

The dialysis unit was set up in a semi-circle with the sixteen dialysis chairs facing the central nursing station. Before Callison could make his way through the crowd surrounding Mr. Lincoln, he was intercepted by Dr. Wickerman.

Dr. Wickerman started to explain the circumstances heralding the cardiac arrest of Mr. Lincoln. He had been on the dialysis treatment for approximately twenty minutes, when a woman entered the dialysis unit with a message for him. This woman was an entertainer hired by one of his ex-wives to give him a surprise strip-o-gram for his birthday. As was his custom, Mr. Lincoln would occupy the center stage chair so he could adequately survey the entire unit. It was also his custom to wear a loose fitting hospital gown while he was having his dialysis treatment. He did this so he wouldn't soil his clothing, but it was common knowledge that his real reason was to allow him to occasionally expose himself to the staff.

Dr. Wickerman continued to explain in some detail that the

woman who delivered the strip-o-gram not only was extremely well-endowed, but was a very accomplished erotic dancer. Her performance had captivated not only all the patients, but the staff as well. As her routine was reaching its climax, so was Mr. Lincoln. He evidently had gotten so aroused that he was able to achieve an erection for the first time in months. He had removed his penis from his pants, exposing his erection.

At this juncture in the conversation Dr. Wickerman began to giggle and suggested Dr. Callison go see for himself. The crowd parted as if Moses were crossing the Red Sea. There in front of Dr. Callison was seated Robert Lincoln, motionless and obviously dead. What was just as obvious as the fact that he was dead, was the secret of his sexual prowess. Although his penis in a non-erect state was only moderately enlarged, when it was fully erect it was enormous, but that wasn't the key to his success. When erect, the tip of his penis bent at an angle of about sixty degrees. The base of his penis had several large bumps of what appeared to be calloused skin. It was now obvious where his sexual power over women had come from.

Callison realized his mouth was ajar. He couldn't help but stare at the deceased, yet still stiff penis of Robert Lincoln. It was at this point Dr. Wickerman continued her story.

Mr. Lincoln had gotten so excited and his erection had gotten so large, that they theorized he shunted a significant portion of his blood supply to his penis. Realizing that dialysis itself can compromise some of the blood supply, the combination of the two, plus the excitement of having an erection, was more than his heart could stand.

Callison was now fighting off his own inclination to laugh, when he looked at Robert's face, and saw a grin from ear to ear. Wickerman reminded Callison that Mr. Lincoln had signed a "Do Not Resuscitate" order to which they had eventually complied. Callison asked Wickerman to clarify her last statement, but he could see she was doing all she could to restrain herself. He then noticed several of the other nurses and students, also on the verge of hysteria. He grabbed Wickerman by the arm and escorted her into a small conference room.

The conference room off the dialysis unit was slightly larger than a closet. A small round table with four chairs and a cabinet that held a coffee pot were crammed into the room. Wickerman remained on the verge of hysteria, and Callison couldn't determine whether this was secondary to fear, laughter, or anguish.

"I'm very sorry, Dr. Callison, but you need to know the rest of the story." A tear slowly trickled down her cheek.

"Please go on." Callison said.

"We had just finished rounds when I was paged to the dialysis unit. John James, the nephrology resident, called me to tell me about the surprise birthday present for Mr. Lincoln. The dancer had started her routine by the time the students and I arrived. The music was pretty loud, and I guess it masked the sound of the alarm on the dialysis machine. By the time the nurse noticed Mr. Lincoln, he was already unconscious and unresponsive. Yet his erection was, um, I don't know, it was enormous! Things then got a little crazy."

"What do you mean then?" Callison asked.

"Several people started shouting orders. Someone was ordering to give fluids through the dialysis machine; another was asking for a crash cart, another was asking for his chart, and so on. All the while, this dancer was gawking at Mr. Lincoln. She had plenty of company. It was quite an unusual sight."

"To say the least."

Wickerman continued. "The music was still playing, so it made communication that much more difficult. We had started basic CPR, when somebody yelled 'get on him'... or something like that. Anyway, this dancer reacted and grabbed his penis and started to, you know, suck. I guess she thought that's what they meant by get on him."

"You're kidding, right?" Callison's eyes were wide open.

"No way. Everybody stopped whatever they were doing, as we were all stunned. At this point I believe Mr. Lincoln regained consciousness momentarily to smile and ejaculate, ejaculate all over the place I might add, before he went out again. The dancer had his fluid all over her face and hair because she had pulled away when he, sort of, responded. Several people were laughing, but most were in a state of shock. The dancer then realized what had happened and ran out of the unit in a state of frenzy. We again started to perform CPR on Mr. Lincoln. But, someone looked at his chart and realized he had a signed Do Not Resuscitate directive. That's when we called the code."

Callison could not believe the story. He wanted to ask Wickerman once more if she was kidding, but he could see in her face she was serious. Callison didn't know what to say.

Wickerman continued, "I hope you're not too upset with us, but we decided to leave him essentially as he was, so to speak. We, or I, felt you'd want to see him."

As visions of this episode were playing through Callison's mind, he was having trouble restraining his laughter. "What happened to the dancer?"

"Security caught her in the stairwell and escorted her to their office. I was told she was quite upset."

"I would think so." Callison was trying to get a grip on his laughter.

"By the way, I heard security was holding her for the police."

"For the police, why?"

"Somebody told them she blew him away."

Callison fell on the floor nearly convulsing with laughter.

Once everyone had regained their composure, they all returned to their routine. Callison reflected on his memories of Robert Lincoln and smiled. Knowing Robert for the last five years, Callison felt that if Robert had chosen a way to leave this life, he couldn't have scripted a better scenario himself.

Later Callison remembered that he had a dinner engagement with his wife, Natalie. He looked at his watch—he was already an hour late.

Callison called home. "Hello, Nat, is it too late to go?"

"I don't know, how do you feel?" She sounded somewhat irritated.

"I'm still game if you are. Can you see if you can change the reservations, and I'll be home in twenty minutes."

Her voice sounded surprised but pleased. "You still want to go to Dallas?"

"Sure. Anyway, we can talk in the car. Be home soon." Callison hung up the phone.

Natalie Callison was used to waiting. Over the years she had grown accustomed to late dinners, eating alone and postponed plans. As a third grade teacher, Natalie had found her niche. She had rejected a position as an assistant principal the year before because she truly loved her job. She was as committed a teacher as Steven was a physician.

Natalie had occasionally sacrificed her career for his—a fact that didn't escape either of them. Although Natalie was at the age when her biological clock was ticking a little louder, the subject of children was no longer an issue. Earlier in their marriage they had decided against children for several reasons: they both had careers; they both loved their independence and ability to travel at will; and they both were concerned about raising a child in a world whose future was so tenuous. Yet about three years ago they changed their minds. After a year of futility, they went through an infertility evaluation. They were told that they were essentially infertile and the likelihood of them conceiving was extremely remote, if not impossible. So they decided to forgo any type of contraception, and go on with their lives. Once the decision was taken away from them, they accepted the fact they would be childless. This allowed them to focus on each other, as well as their careers.

As Callison pulled into their driveway, Natalie greeted him. "Let's go—I'm starved."

On the drive to Dallas, he described what was being shared around the hospital as the "Lincoln assassination." As they pulled up to their favorite restaurant he realized he hadn't even mentioned the appointment to the Primary Care Committee. After they were seated and had ordered, Callison decided to broach the subject.

"Do you remember several months ago, the dean recommended me for a national committee dealing with primary care?"

"Vaguely."

"Well, apparently they want me to be a member of this committee."

"That's great, isn't it?" Natalie's smile vanished as quickly as it came.

65

"I'm not sure. I haven't talked to anyone on the committee, so I'm not sure how extensive a commitment this may be."

"Then who notified you about this?"

"Hoffnagle. He was really enthusiastic about this position and thought it could be a great career move." Callison raised an eyebrow.

Natalie knew intuitively that he was asking for her support. "I think you need to decide if this is something you really want to do. If you feel this is a good opportunity for you, then you know you have my support." She leaned over and kissed him, just as the waiter arrived with their meal.

Callison already knew that he would have Natalie's support no matter what he had decided, but he still felt better hearing the words. He needed more information before he could make any final decision. Before he could say any more, they were interrupted by the high-pitched staccato of his beeper.

"I'm starved. I'll call the service after I eat." Callison said as he looked at the number on his beeper.

"Good idea." Natalie said as she gave a exaggerated nod.

The answering service said Dr. Jourge had called from Chicago. Natalie suggested that she drive home, while he returned the call on the car phone.

"Hello, Dr. Jourge this is Steven Callison."

"How nice of you to return my call so promptly. I assume you know why I'm calling?"

"Yes. I had an earlier conversation with David Hoffnagle. He told me to expect your call."

"I hope you understand your dean was adamant about notifying you himself. I would have preferred notifying you myself but . . ."

"I understand."

"Thank you. Have you been able to make a decision?"

"Not really. I need more information before I can commit."

"What type of information?" Jourge inquired.

"To start, what exactly is the mission of the committee, what are the goals and objectives, and what is the timeline." Callison looked at Natalie as he talked. She momentarily glanced in his direction and smiled, then returned her attention to the road.

"Some of the goals and objectives are confidential, but the mission of the committee is to evaluate primary care under the rubric of both the allopathic and osteopathic professions. The timeline requires a consensus statement complete with recommendations from the committee within the next eight weeks."

"How much time will this committee take up?"

"Initially I would envision a significant time commitment on your part to bring you up to speed. If you agree to participate, I would suggest you come to Chicago next Monday. That will afford me a day or two to spend with you, to help elucidate the charge to the committee—what we have accomplished to date, and our future direction."

"Can you tell me who's on the committee?" Callison asked.

"There are twelve members—six DO's and six MD's. I would be glad to name them for you now if you wish."

"Yes I'd like to know who they are."

"The MD's on the committee are Robert Thornhill, Andrew Percy, Victor Rasta, Angela Mendoza, Woodrow McMillan and myself. The DO's are Chester Timmons, Susanna Michelson, Peter Probst, Jacob Danzinger, Harold Teitelman, and possibly you."

Callison recognized the names of Percy and Thornhill. They were both very well-known physicians of international repute. Callison had actually met Andrew Percy years before while he was interviewing for his medicine residency. Callison could recall that interview as if it had been yesterday. During the interview Dr. Percy told Callison it was a mistake he was even asked to interview. Dr. Percy had stated he would never take an osteopath into his program. Percy explained that he had numerous applicants from prestigious Ivy League schools, and no matter what Callison knew or how good a doctor he was, these were far better candidates.

Callison couldn't believe the irony of his being selected to sit on a committee with Dr. Percy, discussing the potential merging of the professions. Of the DO's, he knew Teitelman personally and had heard of the others. He recognized that this was a quality group and from that perspective, it was an honor to be asked to participate.

"Dr. Jourge, the committee is quite impressive. But I need to discuss this with my wife. Can I let you know my decision tomorrow?" He again looked at Natalie, who smiled when he mentioned his wife.

"That would be fine. By the way, if you decide to participate I will send off a packet for you to read prior to our meeting next week. I sincerely hope you decide to join the committee. I am sure you will find this to be one of the most worthwhile ventures of your medical career."

Callison hung up the phone. Natalie glanced quickly in his direction. "Are you going to do it?"

"I think so, but I want to sleep on it."

7

Merker awoke refreshed and looking forward to reading the paper. Not only had the Bulls won, but so had the White Sox and the Cubs. It was a glorious day. Merker decided to make himself a cup of tea, instead of coffee, in celebration of his newfound interest in tea. As was his routine, he opened the paper initially to the obituary page, before getting immersed in the world of sports. Merker rubbed his eyes not once, but twice, hoping to remove a film that wasn't there, a film that distorted the words that he wished weren't true. It was a modest column, in no way representative of the man it depicted. Nevertheless, it was there in print.

CHICAGO— Dr. Jonas L. Cisko, a renowned physician and surgeon, died Tuesday at his home. He was 65. Dr. Cisko's career as a distinguished physician included many awards and honors. Funeral will be today at 12:30 at Oak Lawn Funeral Home. Burial will be at Emerald Hills Memorial Park in Chicago. Survivors: son, Honorable Jordan M. Cisko of Philadelphia, PA; sister, Amanda Childress of Tampa, FL; two grandchildren.

Merker read and reread the words, desperately wanting them to change. How could this be? He had just met with Dr. Cisko and he was just fine, looking healthy and fit. Obviously, the column lacked detail, which suggested to Merker that it had been written in haste. Merker sat and aimlessly stared out the window for over an hour. Images of Dr. Cisko, his wife, Alice, and numerous friends and relatives who had passed on, appeared in his mind. In an attempt to rationalize his grief, Merker realized that with the death of Dr. Cisko, he also lost another part of Alice, as her illness had originally brought them all together. A tear fell from Merker's cheek onto the paper. The sports section had lost its relevance. Merker went to his closet to try on his black suit. He hadn't worn it in years. He wanted to make sure it would still fit.

The chapel in the funeral home was at capacity, nearly two hundred people. Merker noticed Dr. Cisko's ex-wife sitting in the first row next to their son, Jordan, his wife, and their two children. A woman who resembled Dr. Cisko sat on the aisle of the first row, obviously his sister. She was sobbing inconsolably in the arms of a man Merker assumed must be her husband. Over the past several years since his divorce, Dr. Cisko had become something of a recluse, but as he had mentioned in their last conversation, he was starting to emerge from his shell. Yet Merker had the definite impression he was still out of the mainstream. So where did all these people come from?

Dr. Cisko had an excellent reputation as a physician, but, as Merker scanned the room he felt most of those in attendance were not physicians. Merker overheard a conversation between two elderly couples comparing notes on their years under the care of Dr. Cisko. It was so obvious. The vast majority of those attending the funeral were his patients. What an appropriate testimonial to Jonas Cisko. A satisfied smile appeared on Merker's face as he realized how his friend had made a difference in so many lives.

Merker continued to scan the audience. Many were deeply affected by the loss of Dr. Cisko. While surveying the crowd, a shadow of a man caught his attention, standing in the back of the room, silhouetted against the wall. At first Merker couldn't place him, then he realized it was the man in black, Van Gregory. Gregory wasn't wearing glasses and almost everyone was dressed in dark clothing, so his black suit blended into the crowd, but it was him. Merker was positive. *What was he doing here?*

From their conversation, Merker remembered how Dr. Cisko was concerned about Van Gregory and his friend Dr. Harvey Kahn. *Why would Van Gregory show up at Dr. Cisko's funeral? And where was Dr. Kahn?* Merker thought if Van Gregory was there, he would surely be accompanied by Dr. Kahn. Merker started to canvass the audience. No sign of Dr. Kahn. Merker glanced again to the back of the room where Van Gregory had been standing alone. He was gone. The crowd was dissipating. The service was over and Van Gregory was nowhere to be seen...

Most of the patients didn't attend the brief gravesite ceremony. Also absent were Van Gregory and Dr. Kahn. Merker had to know why Van Gregory had attended the memorial service; he felt he owed it to Dr. Cisko to find out.

Merker went home immediately after the funeral. He disliked wearing a suit of any kind and this particular suit itched and was uncomfortable.

Merker couldn't get Van Gregory out of his mind. His sixth sense told him something wasn't right.

Merker called Marvin Powell to see if anything out of the ordinary had been reported pertaining to the death of Dr. Cisko. There was no formal police report, since the death was considered to be routine. Still, Merker felt uneasy about the situation, especially about Van Gregory.

Merker decided to call the medical examiner's office. Again he was told the death was considered typical: sudden death secondary to acute myocardial infarction. In other words, he had died of a heart attack, the most common cause of death in this country. For the remainder of the day, Merker kept wondering why Van Gregory attended the funeral. It still made no sense.

The following morning Merker was feeling slightly better,— a good night's sleep had helped. He opened the paper to the obituary section, hoping to find at least a small column about Dr. Cisko. There was a column, not about Dr. Cisko, but about a man who died late Wednesday evening in a car accident on Sheridan road. The name of the victim was Dr. Harvey Kahn of Redondo Beach, California. Merker was familiar with Sheridan Road and knew there were many twists and turns. An accident, even a fatal accident, would not necessarily engender any suspicion. But Merker was suspicious. He now had his explanation as to why Harvey Kahn didn't accompany Van Gregory to the funeral. Merker's sixth sense was right; something was amiss apropos to Van Gregory.

Merker's first stop was the police station to visit Sergeant Powell and to review the accident report. According to the report, it was estimated Harvey's car was going fifty miles an hour around a treacherous turn where the speed limit posted was twenty miles an hour. The car, out of control, crashed into a large tree and burst into flames, killing the lone passenger, Harvey Kahn, instantly. The results of the autopsy were pending, but the police didn't suspect any foul play. There were no witnesses. A standard report was filed, and the only information they had on Dr. Kahn was that he was divorced, with no children, had a brother and a sister, and was in practice at a hospital in Redondo Beach where he had been chief of staff.

"So, did you find anything helpful?" Powell asked Merker.

"Not really. But my sixth sense tells me otherwise." Merker winked at Powell.

"Oh, not that damned sixth sense again. That gets you into more trouble." Powell said while shaking his head.

Years before, when Powell and Merker were partners, Merker's sixth sense told him that a highly decorated lieutenant was on the take. Merker's allegations suggested a connection to a local drug dealer. Unfortunately, Merker's key witness mysteriously disappeared and without additional proof Merker was ostracized in the department. Marvin Powell stood by his partner. Months after Merker raised the issue, Internal Affairs confirmed the allegations and the lieutenant and several other officers were accused of conspiring in narcotics trafficking. The damage in the department was irrevocable, resulting in both Merker and Powell being transferred to separate precincts. Powell was assigned a desk job and Merker eventually retired.

"Yeah, I know. Anyway, I need to ask another favor. Can you get me Dr. Cisko's phone records for the past week?" Merker patted Powell on the shoulder. "If not for my sixth sense, then for old times."

"Okay, for old times."

The scenery on Sheridan Road was beautiful. The sun sprayed light through the tree branches. Merker meandered down the scenic and peaceful road. A scorched tree loomed ahead—the lone remains of Kahn's fatal journey. The curve in the road was acute, and anyone going fifty miles an hour would have extreme difficulty controlling their vehicle. What Merker did find unusual was the absence of skid marks on the road. Did Kahn drive directly into the tree on purpose? Or was there another explanation?

Merker mulled over how he would approach the medical examiner in an attempt to get the information about Cisko's death. After imagining several scenarios Merker decided on the truth. The medical examiner who performed the autopsy on Dr. Cisko was Dr. Rami Ramariz. Dr. Ramariz was a small man with a slender build, nearly bald, with a thick black mustache.

"What can I do for you?" His accent was difficult for Merker to understand.

"My name is Marcus Merker and I was hired by Dr. Jonas Cisko prior to his death to investigate a situation which he felt was potentially dangerous. I was wondering if there was anything you found at the autopsy that was at all suspicious?"

Ramariz seemed to have as much trouble understanding Merker, as Merker had in understanding him. "I'm sure you're aware that the autopsy information is confidential."

"I understand." Merker almost laughed at himself. He could barely understand anything Ramariz had said, but he needed to find out as much as he could. "Dr. Cisko was a close friend of mine and I have a feeling that his death wasn't an accident. I know the police aren't considering foul play, but I have a feeling they're overlooking something."

"Look, I really can't tell you anything specifically, but I can tell you that our report indicated that your friend died of natural causes."

"There were no unexplained bruises or evidence of drugs or anything?"

Ramariz shook his head. "Again, sir, I cannot give you the details, but I believe you are on a wild moose chase."

For a second, Merker thought to challenge Ramariz. Moose or goose, who really cared. However, Ramariz' accent was growing somewhat easier to understand. "Can you tell me what he was wearing?" Merker asked.

After considering the request for several seconds, Ramariz agreed to Merker's request on the condition he would not continue to probe for any other details. Ramariz returned in several minutes with the file on Jonas Cisko.

"Dr. Cisko had been dead for several hours when we arrived; rigor mortis had probably been present for some time. He was wearing a sports shirt and pants along with shoes, socks, underwear, his hearing aid, and glasses."

Merker questioned his talent as a detective. He hadn't ever noticed that Dr. Cisko wore a hearing aid. Just then Merker realized what Ramariz had said. "He was wearing his glasses and hearing aid?"

"Yes, is that surprising? He was found in his reading chair—apparently he was reading something when he died."

Merker controlled his excitement. He had confirmed his suspicions, his sixth sense was dead on. "Thank you very much, Doctor. If you think of anything else, can you please call me at this number?" Merker handed the doctor a scrap of paper with his phone number and promptly left the building.

Jonas Cisko's voice echoed in his head. During their last conversation Dr. Cisko told Merker that he recently had undergone eye surgery and his glasses didn't work anymore. Whoever was responsible obviously didn't know that. Merker now knew that the death of Jonas Cisko was staged and was no accident. His prime suspect was Van Gregory. Merker's mind quickly flashed to Sheridan Road and the fatal car crash of Harvey Kahn. Another victim of Van Gregory? If Van Gregory was guilty, Merker would find out. Merker had lost a friend and he was determined that the death would be avenged.

8

Merker's quest led him to Cynthia Cisko, the ex-wife of Jonas Cisko.

Merker had called Cynthia Cisko, who requested they meet at her home in the northern suburbs. Merker parked in the street in front of her two-level townhome. The air carried the smell of freshly cut grass. He loved that smell, it reminded him of his childhood. Merker inhaled deeply before he knocked on the door.

"Mrs. Cisko? I'm Marcus Merker."

Mrs. Cisko briefly shook his extended hand. "Please come in," Cynthia Cisko said. She had dabs of paint sprinkled over her face, hair and clothing. "Please excuse the mess, I was just painting. I hope I didn't get any paint on you."

"No, I'm clean." Merker said, examining his hand.

The foyer was jammed with canvasses at various stages of completion. Merker followed Mrs. Cisko's lead through the maze of paintings into her living room. Every inch of wall space was filled with abstract paintings of all types, shapes and colors.

"I like your work." Merker said. He really didn't, but wanted to be polite.

"Thank you." Mrs. Cisko smiled. "Please sit."

Merker sat opposite Mrs. Cisko on her black leather sofa, which was covered with hundreds of mini paint spots.

"Now, what can I do for you?" Mrs. Cisko asked, folding her hands and placing them on one knee.

"I was a friend of your late husband."

"Ex-husband." Mrs. Cisko corrected curtly.

"Yes, ex-husband. Anyway, I was wondering if you could answer some questions about Dr. Cisko?" Merker jotted down 'ex' on his pad.

"Why?" Mrs. Cisko asked, the lines in her face deepened

as her expression intensified.

"Before his death, your ex was concerned about his safety and asked me to check into some things."

"You don't think. I mean, you don't . . . " She couldn't say the words.

"No. I don't think he was murdered, but I feel the need to finish the job he hired me for." Merker did not want to scare Mrs. Cisko.

"Okay, shoot," she said as her facial lines diminished.

"When was the last time you spoke to your ex?" Merker asked.

"Over a month ago. We've kept in touch off and on since the divorce. You know, I still cared for him, but I just couldn't live with him." Mrs. Cisko could feel a lump in her throat.

"I understand." Merker said. "Could you tell how he was doing?"

"He seemed troubled. But I couldn't get him to admit it."

"Did he mention anything about the committee he was working on?"

"No. What committee was that?"

"A committee dealing with health-care reform." Merker said.

"No. He never mentioned that committee."

"I see." Merker couldn't help but feel discouraged. "Did he ever mention a man named Van Gregory?"

"No."

"How about Harvey Kahn?"

"Now, that's a name I haven't heard in a long time."

Merker beamed. "So I take it you know him?"

"Oh, yeah." Cynthia shook her head, squinting her eyes, and gnashing her teeth. "A real slime."

"Really? That's interesting."

"No. Not really." Cynthia said frowning, the deep facial lines returned. "It was the summer of '61 and we were living in L.A. It's funny, I can remember that time like it was yesterday." She paused to take a deep breath and sighed. "It was the beginning of the end of our marriage." Tears welled in her eyes.

"If you don't want to talk about this—" Merker offered sympathetically.

"No, it's all right." Cynthia wiped her eyes. "There was this big meeting in which hundreds, maybe thousands of DO's got their MD degrees."

"What?" Merker exclaimed.

"You know, they changed degrees."

"How did that happen?" Merker said, his eyes fixed intently on Mrs. Cisko.

"I don't know. It just happened and then they merged."

"Merged?" Merker fell back into the couch.

"Yeah. They merged the DO's and MD's in California, sometime the following year."

"A merger?" Merker said, as he stared blankly at the ceiling.

A scowl replaced Cynthia's tears. "That damn merger forced us to leave L.A., our home. It was right after that, Jonas went to Chicago for a job interview. His friend, the slime, came over our house and, you know, tried to seduce me."

"Kahn?" Merker returned Mrs. Cisko's scowl with one of his own.

"The one and only. What a slime."

"Can you remember anything else?" Merker asked.

"About Kahn? Or the merger?"

"Either." Merker's scowl was replaced with an anticipatory grin.

"Well, I don't remember much about the merger except Jonas, Harvey and some others were pretty involved politically at that time."

"Wait a minute." Merker said, holding his hand in the air. "Harvey Kahn was involved in the merger?"

"Oh yes. He and Jonas were both very involved."

'Hum, that's interesting." Merker said. Thinking, he gently chewed on his lower lip. "Can you think of any others involved with the merger?"

Mrs. Cisko rubbed her forehead smearing a red drop of paint. "A friend of Jonas's, Amos Wilcox, was also heavily involved. In fact, it was he and his partner . . . oh, what was his name . . ." She again rubbed her forehead, further spreading the paint. "Something Trulof. I'm sorry I can't remember his first name."

"That's okay." Merker said. "Please continue."

"Anyway, they were sort of the ringleaders of the group."

"The group?" Merker asked.

"The group against the merger."

"Oh, I see." Merker said. "Do you know where I could find Amos Wilcox?" He underlined both Wilcox' and Trulof's names on his pad.

"Sorry. I haven't had any contact with Amos since California."

"No problem. I'm sure I can find him." Merker paused to look at his notes. Then asked, "Can you think of anything else?"

"Only that that damn merger just about ruined all their careers. And changed Jonas. He was never the same and neither was our marriage." Cynthia shrugged, as her voice faded.

"I'm sorry." Merker said, not expecting an answer. "I won't be taking up any more of your time. I imagine you want to get back to your painting." As Merker stood, he handed Mrs. Cisko his number. "If you think of anything else please call."

Leaving Mrs. Cisko's home, Merker finally had some possible leads. And what about that merger . . . was there a connection between a merger in California in the sixties and Dr. Cisko's committee?

On his drive back to the city Merker reviewed the status of his investigation. The coroner's report added nothing new. He had interviewed Cisko's neighbors and the staff of his building, again coming up empty. And his preliminary investigation into the backgrounds of Harvey Kahn and Van Gregory was not very informative.

Kahn, who stopped practicing medicine in the eighties, recently held several administrative positions at a hospital in Redondo Beach, California. But now he was dead. Was his death an accident?

The information on Van Gregory was also minimal. Merker learned that Gregory currently resided in the Chicago area but was unable to find out much more. Even checking Gregory through the police computers was of little help. Gregory, a veteran of the Korean War, had worked as a freelance agent following the war. The details were sketchy, but Merker was able to piece together enough information suggesting Gregory had worked in counterintelligence during the war and later as a consultant to the private sector specializing in surveillance. However, what his relationship was with the AMA, AOA or Harvey Kahn was still a mystery.

At a stop light, Merker referred to his pad. He had one friend, J.T., who worked for the FBI. Merker jotted down J.T.'s name next to Van Gregory's. Hopefully, J.T. could help in the investigation of Gregory.

"Hello, Mr. Merker. This is Judge Cisko calling. You called about my father."

"Yes, thanks for returning my call Your Honor." Merker said. "Would you mind if I ask you some questions about your father?"

"Who are you?" barked the judge.

"I'm a private investigator; your father hired me just before he died."

"Why would my father hire an investigator?" The words sounded harsh.

"I can't reveal why I was hired. But I can tell you he was concerned about his safety," Merker said.

"The hell you can't. My father's dead and I need to know what you know."

Merker was not surprised by the judge's response. After all, Dr. Cisko was his father and he was a lawyer. "Okay, I'll tell you. Your father was on a powerful committee about health-care reform. This powerful committee deals with some powerful issues and your father was a key member."

"Tell me something I don't know," the judge said sternly.

"Well—did you know your father was concerned for his safety?" Merker asked.

"You mentioned that before. What does his safety have to do with this committee?"

"That's what I'm investigating." Merker knew he was talking in circles.

Frustrated the judge asked, "Who's paying you?"

"Your father paid me."

"Why are you calling me?"

"To see if you knew anything about the committee or if your father confided in you."

"All I can tell you is this committee was important to him and he was determined to give it his best effort. He never mentioned anything about his own safety," the judge said, his tone subdued.

Merker could sense this conversation was going nowhere. "That's all I needed."

"Let me ask a question of you. Why are still investigating my father's death—wasn't it of natural causes?"

"Yes. His death was of a natural cause, but I still feel an obligation to see this investigation through. Out of respect for your father." Merker's response was only half true. The other half was personal. Since his wife's death, Merker had lost his passion for work, or, for that matter—life. He was merely existing. For some reason Jonas Cisko's faith in him, rekindled his spirit and vitality. He needed to see this through as much for himself, as for Dr. Cisko.

"If you find anything out, you will let me know." The judge's statement was as much an order, as a request.

"Sure. Thank you, Your Honor."

"Good bye."

Merker stared at the phone. The conversation had given him a headache.

9

Having contacted all Dr. Cisko's relatives, Merker now focused his attention on the phone calls originated and received from Dr. Cisko's phone. Most of the calls related to medical topics. One call was different. It was an incoming long distance call the night before Cisko's death. The call originated where a merger had taken place several decades before and where Harvey Kahn had lived. Yes, this call was suspicious. The call was from a Doctor Ethan Jasper.

Merker called Dr. Jasper, who wasn't aware of Dr. Cisko's death. From his reaction, it was evident to Merker that Jasper was so upset by the news of Dr. Cisko's death that he was not able to continue the conversation. Jasper did indicate before he hung up that he would like to talk to Merker at another time.

Merker felt Dr. Jasper would be more receptive in person. Since he was already contemplating a trip to California, he arranged to meet him later that week at Jasper's office.

Merker surmised his best bet was to investigate the committee that had originally concerned Dr. Cisko. Specifically the person who had taken his place on the committee, Dr. Steven Callison. Obvious questions begged to be answered: *Is Callison involved in the death of Dr. Cisko? Is he a pawn, being manipulated by others? Or is investigating Callison barking up the wrong tree?* Merker knew he could only answer these questions by actually talking with Callison.

Natalie Callison quietly sat while her husband dressed for his trip to Chicago. The last few days had been hectic for both of them. Callison had immersed himself in the volumes of paperwork Dr. Jourge had sent him, and Natalie was in the middle of a potential teacher walkout. Neither had been home for any quality time since their dinner, and they both felt overwhelmed by their current circumstances. Sex had been totally abandoned, and Natalie realized Steven would now be gone for several more days. This would be their last opportunity. If this were a decade ago, she wouldn't have hesitated seducing her husband. But now, their relationship was more staid and less spontaneous. She was afraid she would be rejected, so she decided not to pursue her inclination. Steven finished packing for his trip to Chicago while Natalie made a fresh pot of flavored coffee, her latest passion.

"Steven, do you want some coffee?"

"Sure, could you also put a bagel in the toaster for me?"

"Are you prepared for your meeting?"

"I read all the material Jourge sent. Most of it was total bullshit, but some of it was very provocative. I think this meeting could actually be meaningful." Callison chuckled as he mumbled to himself, "What a contradiction in terms—a meaningful meeting."

"Did you say something, hon?"

"No, I was just talking to myself."

"What time do you take off?"

"In about an hour and a half. I guess I'll leave for the airport in twenty minutes or so." Callison hated to wait at airports. He had honed his plane-boarding technique to a fine edge. He consistently arrived at the gate just as they were announcing the last call for passengers to board. He prided himself on never missing a flight.

The flight to Chicago was uneventful. Callison had some time free of distractions to review the information Jourge had sent. He reflected on his opinions of the many issues raised. The cab ride downtown was tedious, as usual, because of continued highway repair and the residual of rush hour traffic. The meeting was to be held downtown. A room had already been reserved for Callison at the hotel. Upon arrival, the receptionist gave Callison a message to contact Dr. Jourge.

Jourge was waiting for Callison's call and suggested they meet in his room because he had an adjoining sitting room. Jourge was dressed casually in a pair of khaki pants and a work shirt. Callison felt a bit self conscious, still wearing his suit and tie.

"Please come in! I am delighted you assented to join the committee. It is my pleasure to finally meet you."

"Likewise, it's nice to meet you, Dr. Jourge."

"Please call me Alex, or Al, that's what my friends call me. Feel free to remove your jacket and tie. We have a great deal to accomplish."

"Thank you, Alex, and please call me Steve." Callison removed his suit jacket and tie while he followed Jourge into the sitting area where he had been working, as evidenced by the papers and manuscripts strewn about. They both sat at the table. A file with his name caught Callison's attention. Jourge observed Callison staring at the file. "I have compiled files on all the committee members. Please feel free to review it." Jourge smiled as he handed the folder to Callison.

Callison perused the documents containing his full curriculum vitae, letters of recommendations he had solicited over the years, and some letters that he had never solicited. There was also a brief personal description of his interests and hobbies, as well as his wife's biographical data. In addition was a form yet to be completed dealing with other personal matters.

"I hope you can appreciate, we desired as much pertinent information as possible before we effected our decision. Each member has corresponding documents on file which are available for review. I will distribute your file to the other committee members only after you have scrutinized the file and have sanctioned me to do so. The other document is a disclosure statement, requiring your completion. We must ensure total autonomy. There must not be any conflicts of interest with our personal holdings, stocks, etcetera, since we will be dealing with fiduciary issues which cannot be construed in any way as self-serving."

Callison quietly reviewed the documents as Jourge talked.

"I'm not sure whether I feel comfortable with how and why this information was compiled and who will have access to this information." Callison said.

"I can assure you that you are not alone in your incertitude. The information is strictly confidential and only accessible to members of the committee. At each meeting all the confidential

83

documents are collected and stored at the office of the AMA in a secured safe."

"Why do you need all the personal information on me?"

"The committee decided at our first meeting to compile such a file on each member. Some of the recommendations could have considerable impact on a myriad of interest groups, powerful groups, who could be most inconsonant. We deemed it imperative to provide this documentation to allow us to function without fear of compromise." Jourge gently rubbed his right eye.

"Do you mind if I think about this before I give you permission to distribute my file?"

"As you are aware, we have a full committee meeting tomorrow. Without your approved file, you would not be permitted to attend the meeting." Jourge continued to gently rub his right eye.

Callison thought before he responded. "I don't mean to offend you, but why didn't you tell me this on the phone? It might have saved both of us time and aggravation."

"I understand your concern. I do apologize for placing you in such a position. However, it was my decision to discuss this in person, because I felt this sensitive information cannot be adequately conveyed over the phone. I know you feel your privacy has been invaded, but because of time constraints I felt this was unfortunately unavoidable. I understand fully if you feel you cannot participate, and I'm sure the rest of the committee will likewise understand."

By bringing Callison to Chicago and confronting him directly, Jourge had left him little choice. If Callison declined, he might be perceived as concealing something. He felt compromised by Jourge's understated ultimatum. "I realize the committee is under some pressure, time-wise. But I need an hour or so to think about this."

"You can have as much time as you need. If you need me I'll be in the next room." Jourge left the sitting area and retreated into the bedroom, leaving Callison alone with his files and his thoughts.

Callison took the better part of an hour reviewing the files. They were accurate and thorough. The disclosure document also appeared to be appropriate, considering the potential contentiousness of some of the issues involved. Callison decided to comply and filled out the disclosure document. When he completed the paperwork he notified Jourge of his decision. Jourge seemed pleased.

"Now that we have the preliminaries out of the way, we need to delve into the business at hand." Jourge's expression turned serious; lines of concern appeared on his furrowed brow and his voice deepened. "As you know the president stridently campaigned for health-care reform, only to have his initial efforts thwarted. Alas, he is a stubborn man." Jourge said, shaking his head. "He has again embraced the challenge. However, this time he is actively inviting the full participation of the medical community. Our committee is routed through the secretary of health, but also has a reporting line through the surgeon general directly to the White House. Our recommendations will be personally reviewed by the highest authorities and therefore should have a significant impact on the final recommendations emanating from the president himself."

"After reading all the documents you sent, I'm still not totally clear on the mission of the committee." Callison said.

"To better explain the mission, I first need to review what the committee has discussed to date and what our meeting tomorrow will encompass." Jourge again rubbed his right eye as he spoke.

Callison sat intently listening to every word.

"Pardon any repetition, for the documents I had sent to you had pertinent details intentionally omitted." Jourge coughed and readjusted his collar before he continued. "As you are aware there are many elements to the health-care reform agenda such as universal coverage for all Americans: a cap on national expenditures for health-care; a mandated core health benefits package from all insurers; centralized price control; the use of the political process for setting prices possibly by instituting state committees; and an emphasis on primary-care providers as the gatekeepers for the entire system. It is the last issue our committee has been charged to address."

Callison nodded. He had surmised what Jourge had said,

but was pleased to hear his assumptions were correct. Jourge coughed before continuing. "Although we have not heard much from the administration relative to the details, what seems unequivocal is that this new system cannot end competition, nor fee-for-service, nor consumer choice, but will have to change the way we approach all these issues."

"What about other issues such as malpractice reform?" Callison asked.

"Malpractice reform is not under the purview of our committee; however, issues such as medical education reform, graduate education, and the funding for these educational efforts are under our jurisdiction. Not a small task, huh?"

Callison was speechless. He had realized this committee had the potential to be powerful, but for the first time he realized how powerful.

Jourge continued his remarks, "Dr. Jonas Cisko, your predecessor on the committee served a critical role on a subcommittee evaluating the potential implications of a merger between the allopathic and osteopathic professions."

"Implications?" Callison asked.

"By implications I mean, is this feasible? If so, how could it be accomplished? I would like you to consider filling Dr. Cisko's position on this committee and if you agree, to chair the committee."

"Why would you want me to chair a committee when I'm the least informed member on the committee?" Callison was confused.

"Just because you are new to the committee does not make you uninformed. In fact, as you are now well aware we investigated your background in some detail, and I believe you have the most desirable perspective pertaining to the global picture of any of our current members. I have reviewed in great depth the articles you have written on your profession, and yours is the type of critical thinking and insight needed to direct this subcommittee."

Callison was surprised at Jourge's confidence. "I guess I'm flattered by your confidence in me, but I still doubt that I should chair this subcommittee."

"Before you respond, I would like to discuss some of the

issues you have raised." Jourge took out his notes.

Callison nodded.

"We have started to address, albeit insufficiently, the dearth of primary care physicians in this country." Jourge paused to cough before continuing. "Others have mentioned the racial and ethnic composition of the nation's physicians is not reflective of the population as a whole, and how this can contribute to the decreased access of health-care to underrepresented groups. Most of this is not new, but you then take these concepts one step farther. By highlighting the osteopathic approach to this issue you suggest a different perspective. Could you elucidate?"

Callison replied. "The osteopathic profession should not only emphasize primary care but should redefine it. There has never been a time in history when our philosophy coincided more with the political climate of the country. By aligning manual medicine with traditional medical therapy, while orienting more toward disease prevention and health promotion, I think we can better meet the needs of the new millennium."

"I see." Jourge said. "What intrigues me is the concept of using what has already been developed in osteopathic medicine and evaluating why a significantly greater number of osteopathic graduates follow a career path in primary care in contrast to their allopathic brethren. Then to expound on those concepts to create a new generalist physician for the future." Jourge stopped once more to cough and adjust his collar. "I may have taken some liberties in elaborating some of your opinions but I don't believe I have misrepresented your position on these issues."

"No. I must say that on the whole I agree with what you have said but my philosophy goes beyond even what you have attributed to me," Callison said in a quiet, understated tone.

"See, you have justified my original opinion of your expertise in this area. You would be perfect to chair the subcommittee." Jourge gave Callison a knowing smile.

Callison chuckled. "All right, I may reconsider your suggestion, but first I need to know who else is on this subcommittee. What are the objectives of the committee? What's the timeline to achieve these objectives? What resources will be made available to the committee to achieve these objectives?"

Callison had paused for a breath when Jourge intervened, "Is that all?"

They both grinned.

"Well, that will do for a start. Once I have those questions answered I might be able to give you an answer."

"The subcommittee consists of two other physicians selected by Dr. Cisko, Andrew Percy and Susanna Michelson. You are probably aware Dr. Percy is a past president of the American Medical Association, and Dr. Michelson is the current representative from your profession to the National Select Committee on Women's Issues in Health Care, as well as a dean of one of your medical schools. I don't know how well you knew Dr. Cisko but his death was a loss not only to your profession but to all of medicine. He was a good man."

"I only knew of him, but what I had heard was uniformly positive. I have also heard positive comments about Dr. Michelson, and Dr. Percy's reputation speaks for itself."

"So you'll head the committee?" Jourge coughed once more as he asked the question.

"No, I didn't say that."

"Oh, that's right, you had other concerns. As I have previously stated, the charge to this subcommittee was to explore the possibility of merging the two professions. There are many ramifications of such a merger that you and your committee need to explore and adduce to the committee as a whole in six weeks."

"Six weeks? That's hardly any time."

"I concur. But we have a window of approximately two months to finalize our report for review, before a global policy can be presented by the president."

"What type of resources are available?"

"Essentially whatever you and your committee members request—within reason."

"Before I can accept any subcommittee assignment, I'd like to know what the others on the committee are evaluating?"

"Excellent point. There are other subcommittees. I was hopeful I could convince you to chair the merger committee, but if you would rather participate on another committee, I reluctantly could accommodate you. The other committees encompass other substantial areas affiliated with primary care, including research efforts focusing on primary care, postgraduate programs in primary care, undergraduate reform for primary care curriculum, and the reorganization of other health-care services."

Hesitant to give his answer too soon, Callison requested additional time before he could commit to the merger committee. Jourge agreed to not press Callison for an answer until they met tomorrow. With that settled, Jourge told Callison of the progress of each subcommittee and the agenda for the meeting. By the time Jourge had completed the specifics it was time for dinner.

As they adjourned for their meal they were both mentally exhausted not only from the massive amount of data they had reviewed but also from the anticipation of the even greater amount of work that lay ahead of them.

10

The committee meeting was scheduled to begin promptly at 9:00 A.M. When Callison arrived at eight, several committee members were conversing in front of a panel of massive picture windows. Standing in front of massive pictures, Robert Thornhill, Woodrow McMillan, Jacob Danzinger, and Peter Probst were intently discussing the ominous skies. It was strange how eerie the streets appeared as the last glimmer of sunlight vanished and the streetlights reappeared.

The group's attention shifted from the impending storm to Callison.

McMillan was the first to greet Callison. "So nice to meet you. I hope you're prepared for a long day."

"Don't scare him off before we start." Probst said half-jokingly. "It really isn't bad at all. Actually I find the entire process to be extremely educational." Probst's remarks appeared to contain equal parts of humor and sincerity.

"Educational? What a unique way to describe these meetings," Danzinger said as he shook Callison's hand. "Frankly, the amount of data reviewed at these meetings is usually voluminous, but I don't know if I would call it educational. It's more like informational. Anyway it's nice to meet you."

All eyes then centered on Thornhill, who was older than the others. Thornhill had that sort of stern, hardened, weathered face that made you feel you were being judged. His voice, deep and raspy, reverberated as he spoke. "Why don't you sit down so we can get acquainted?"

As Thornhill finished his remarks McMillan, Probst and Danzinger simultaneously responded, as if it were a command, each bringing over a chair to the table. When they realized they reacted in kind, they looked at each other and laughed, since the table was now overrun with chairs. Callison chose to seat himself between McMillan and Probst only because that was the closest seat to where he had been standing.

Upon taking his seat Callison noticed two other committee members entering the room: a Hispanic woman who appeared to be in her late fifties and a man he recognized as Andrew Percy. Percy was now considerably older than the last time Callison had met him, but he could sense that the man was as arrogant as ever. Even at a distance Callison felt Percy's cold, slate-gray eyes critiquing him, his profession, medicine in general—everything. Then Callison realized he was probably being overly sensitive and paranoid. It had been over sixteen years since he last saw Percy, and the past was history. He needed to concentrate on the present.

Within minutes the remainder of the committee arrived. Callison was introduced to each of them. As a group they appeared to be cordial, yet there was something about the group that didn't feel quite right.

The storm was rapidly approaching. A flash of lightning was followed by a dull rumble of thunder several seconds later. Callison hoped this storm wasn't the harbinger of things to come.

The meeting started promptly at nine. A large mahogany table shined under the fluorescent lights. The table was arranged in a circle, each position affixed with a name card and a microphone. Several packets were placed at each seat, containing the biographical data on each of the committee members, the minutes of all the previous meetings, the agenda for the current meeting, and the reports from each subcommittee. Other than the committee itself, the only other person in the room was a woman seated behind Jourge, who appeared to be taking notes. Prior to the meeting this woman placed a cassette into the recorder, which she started when the meeting began.

Jourge formally introduced Callison, and he was again warmly greeted by the committee members. Following his introduction Jourge suggested a moment of silence in memory of Dr. Cisko. He followed with a brief summary of Callison's background and suggested the group review his file at their leisure. After reviewing and approving the prior meeting's minutes, Jourge referred the group to the agenda for the day.

The first report was an update by Jourge on the general status of the health-care reform movement and how it specifically pertained to their committee. Many of the statistics Jourge mentioned were familiar to Callison but some were new and quite revealing.

It appeared as if night had fallen when Dr. Thornhill started to present his subcommittee report on undergraduate reform. Thornhill was the most prestigious member on the committee, with the possible exception of Jourge. Dr. Thornhill was a tall man with a full head of white hair, a white handlebar mustache and a formidable presence. Dr. Thornhill's raspy voice was monotone and understated, yet his words were carefully thought out and insightful. The problem, he surmised, in shifting the undergraduate education toward primary care was primarily due to fiscal constraints.

Dr. Thornhill continued at length discussing how the proposed health-care reform would only exacerbate this problem by decreasing income to the schools via their medical practice plans. He concluded his remarks by describing this pernicious cycle, and how his committee was frustrated in their lack of ability to solve this dilemma.

Almost on cue, as Thornhill completed his remarks, the room exploded with a thunderous burst of light and sound. The lightning bolt rattled the windows and shook the building.

Jourge, undaunted by the storm, continued the meeting. The next report to be given was by Jacob Danzinger on postgraduate programs in primary care.

Danzinger briefly reviewed the data that had been previously presented, including the impact of the governmental freeze on postgraduate positions. As with the undergraduate curriculum, there were many problems associated with the current postgraduate system. However, Danzinger noted the marketplace had already started to shift, and he discussed a plan that would further increase the incentives for medical school graduates to pursue a career in primary care. The result would help meet the societal and educational needs currently lacking in the system. Funding shifts would be necessary to facilitate this new paradigm where the majority of the graduates would now enter primary care.

After the first two presentations Callison needed a break, not only to digest the information discussed but to investigate the impact of the storm. Callison wasn't alone in his curiosity. Several other members of the committee joined him in monitoring the progress of the storm. Sheets of rain pummeled the windows. A brave pedestrian attempted to cross the street in front of their hotel. The wind was so intense it inverted his umbrella. He struggled to right it but to no avail. Soaked and frustrated, he tossed the useless umbrella in a trash can and stomped off, cursing and shaking his head. Callison turned to make a comment on the unfortunate pedestrian, only to find he was standing alone.

Jourge reconvened the group for one additional presentation before they would break for lunch. The last presentation of the morning would be given by Angela Mendoza, who was the chief advisor to the assistant secretary of health and human services, a detail that had somehow escaped Callison. Fortunately Callison had kept his ignorance to himself.

Dr. Mendoza had a no-nonsense demeanor which Callison thought probably served her well in this male-dominated profession. Her black-rimmed glasses complemented her coiffure, highlighted by a streak of white that shot through the left side of her thick black hair. Her tightly bound bun reminded Callison of his third grade teacher.

However, when Dr. Mendoza started to talk, her voice was captivating, almost melodious. The thunder had subsided, but the steady patter of the rain against the windows continued. The background rain meshed with Mendoza's voice, making her presentation all the more captivating. She described how the National Institutes of Health (NIH) only spent about 20 percent of its budget on research related to disease prevention and health promotion.

Dr. Mendoza explained that the greatest strides in the general health of the public over the last century has been in the field of prevention, rather than intervention. Dr. Mendoza recommended strongly that the government increase its support of research on prevention at the expense of the traditional science-based research.

Dr. Mendoza's recommendations elicited more discussion and heated debate than the previous two presentations combined. In an attempt to justify her position Dr. Mendoza noted that seven out of the top ten leading causes of death in this country are due to unhealthy behavior. She further stressed how poorly we, as a nation, are addressing these issues.

Most of the members on the committee were either previously or currently funded by the NIH or another similar national funding source. Since their research dealt primarily with basic scientific concepts, they as a group were less than supportive of Dr. Mendoza's ideas. It was a difficult task for the committee members, including Callison, to separate their own self-interest from Dr. Mendoza's remarks and suggestions.

The discussion dealing with the research appropriations continued over lunch. Jourge asked Callison to stay behind so they could talk privately.

"What was your opinion of the morning session?" Jourge said appearing genuinely interested.

"Very informative and interesting," Callison said cautiously.

"I'm not looking for the politically correct answer. I would much prefer to know your honest opinion."

"Too many details and not enough time to really discuss each issue to the depth it needs to be discussed."

"Is that all?" Jourge studied Callison.

"No, not really. Several people seem to dominate the discussions and others who possibly may be better informed seemed less free with their opinions. I think you need to encourage and even actively solicit their participation. Also, I feel the subcommittee reports need to follow a more rigid format, so the group as a whole can make some decisions and recommendations relative to each presentation."

Jourge smiled. "I appreciate your candid comments. As the newcomer to the committee, your opinions are fresh and aren't as biased by personalities or preconceived notions. If you have any further comments or suggestions, please feel free to discuss them with me."

By the time the afternoon session started, the rain had subsided to a dank drizzle. Victor Rasta's presentation on the reorganization of health-care services initiated the afternoon session. When Rasta started, Callison was aware Jourge was watching him, which made Callison uneasy. Rasta's remarks reiterated much of what had already been stated, but not as eloquently. Where Rasta differed from the previous presenters primarily dealt with his remarks about non-physician practitioners who currently constitute about 20 percent of all primary care providers.

When Rasta discussed his diatribe on the perils of relegating care to nurse practitioners, physician assistants, and nurse midwives, Andrew Percy quickly chimed in with his own concerns. Up to this point, Callison was trying to give Percy the benefit of the doubt, but his remarks about the non-physician providers mirrored his remarks about osteopathic physicians two decades before. Callison could feel his face flush and his blood pressure rise. This was the same asshole who wouldn't interview him because of his degree. He hadn't changed.

The last presentation of the day was to be given by Andrew Percy, in place of Dr. Cisko. Percy reviewed the fact that annually there are about 16,000 graduates from allopathic medical schools receiving the MD degree, and about 2000 graduates from osteopathic medical schools receiving the DO degree. He also mentioned that of the 750,000 physicians in the country, only about 45,000 were osteopathic physicians. Since DO's were fully licensed in all 50 states, able to serve in the military physician pool, accepted in post graduate programs in allopathic medical training programs, he felt eventual merger of the two professions was inevitable. Percy continued to show the trend of osteopathic graduates seeking allopathic training programs, especially in primary care area. He concluded that in essence the merger was unofficially already taking place.

Susanna Michelson was the other member of the subcommittee. Dr. Michelson was an attractive, trim woman with ivory skin and electric blue eyes. Callison did a double take when he noticed her age to be 59. She could have easily passed for forty. Dr. Michelson had a stack of documents—which she had previously reviewed, placed on the table in front of each seat. These documents included reams of data that had been accumulated from a variety of sources detailing the history of the osteopathic profession and the primary care efforts of the allopathic profession.

During Susanna's presentation, Callison took the opportunity to review her file. There was an interesting bit of historical information, especially in lieu of her presentation. According to her file, both her parents, her maternal grandfather, and her son were all DO's. Her grandfather must have been one of the pioneering DO's, since the profession was just over 100 years old.

Andrew Percy responded to Dr. Michelson's presentation, concentrating on the consequences of such a merger from the perspective of the allopathic profession.

Percy noted the increase in the non-primary physicians did not increase the access of care for the underserved or enhance the health of the public, another task the committee had been charged to address. Percy suggested the current physician-to-population ratio was adequate and the problem was not the number of physicians, but how they were distributed. How would the merger impact these statistics? Percy suggested that since less than half the osteopathic medical schools were state supported, the majority were private institutions dependent on private funds and thus he was concerned for their financial stability.

Without the merger, Percy was concerned that many of the osteopathic schools and programs would not survive, thus depleting further an already scarce commodity, the primary care provider. With the merger, the osteopathic schools in fiscal jeopardy could be supported or incorporated into the allopathic system, thus maintaining their primary care roots. This would allow the teachings of Dr. Still and Dr. Osler to be integrated into a new brand of medicine for the future.

Dr. Michelson did not refute or challenge any of Dr. Percy's remarks. What was also perplexing was that none of the other DO's on the committee made any comments either. Thinking there must be a logical explanation, Callison refrained from offering his point of view. He decided to wait until the meeting was over to canvass his colleagues. After Michelson concluded,

Jourge suggested they take a short break.

Before Callison could confront any of his colleagues, he was approached by Chester Timmons who asked Callison to attend a meeting of the osteopathic physicians on the committee later that evening. Timmons intimated this was not the time or place to have any further discussion about the meeting. Callison decided not to pursue the issue any further at this time, but was prepared to get an answer later.

When the meeting reconvened, Jourge handed out a manuscript that summarized the morning session. This document was to be reviewed by all the members for approval when they met in the morning. Jourge also explained that before the meeting would conclude tomorrow, each committee would need to form objectives utilizing the data presented. These objectives would be used to formulate strategies and outcome measures. Once determined, they would prioritize the objectives and from the prioritized list would codify their consensus statement.

By the time the meeting disbanded the rain had stopped, positioning massive puddles, fallen tree limbs, and several downed power lines as a reminder of its intensity. Callison left feeling even less comfortable than before.

The evening meeting was scheduled to convene in a private dining room at the Ambassador East Hotel at eight P.M. The rain had cleansed the city, dropping the humidity and leaving the air fresh and delightfully cool.

Chester Timmons and Peter Probst were already seated in the hotel bar when Callison arrived. Both Timmons and Probst appeared to be in good spirits and fully enjoying each other's company. While Probst motioned to Callison to join them, he inadvertently spilled his drink on Timmons' lap. Timmons instinctively reacted by jumping out of his seat, unintentionally knocking his knee on the edge of the table. In pain, Timmons hopped on his left leg losing his balance momentarily, falling into another table. Using his hand for balance, Timmons accidentally upended a bowl of popcorn, catapulting the popcorn into the air, covering a couple seated at the table. From Callison's vantage point, the entire incident appeared like an old slapstick comedy. Fortunately for Timmons, the couple at the table also saw the humor in the incident.

"Come on over, but watch your step." Probst slurred his words slightly, suggesting he'd already had plenty to drink.

Timmons apologized to the pelted couple while Callison took a seat. When Timmons returned to the table, he appeared to be sober. "So glad you could make it. I apologize for the show." Timmons said feigning embarrassment.

"No need to apologize to me. Aren't you the one who had a drink spilled on him?" Callison said.

"You know, you're right." Timmons gave a side glance at Probst. "Anyway, how did you like the meeting today?"

Callison wasn't sure how to answer the question. Before he could respond, Susanna Michelson and Jacob Danzinger arrived. Danzinger was a statuesque man with a deep tan, dark gray, neatly trimmed hair, and a dark mustache. Susanna was the female equivalent of Danzinger; tall, lean, with her whitish-blond, shoulder-length hair also neatly trimmed. They both appeared much younger than their years. One could never tell they barely knew each other. They gave the appearance of a couple that had been together for decades.

Just as the three gentlemen stood and offered Dr. Michelson a seat, the waiter informed them that their table was ready in the private dining room.

"Should we wait for Teitelman?" Michelson asked.

"No. He's always late and I'm hungry." Timmons said. "He'll be able to find us." The group followed the waiter into a private dining area.

They were assured they could conduct their meeting in complete confidentiality. They were all seated around a large table and had started to order when Teitelman arrived.

"I'm sorry I'm late," Teitelman said as he sat at the empty seat between Callison and Probst.

Timmons started the discussion formally, then explained, "I feel it's imperative we meet as a group to help our colleague Steven with his subcommittee."

Callison was stunned: he had no idea that his committee

would be the topic for this meeting. He glanced at the faces around the table. He wasn't sure whether this attention was intended as a compliment or an insult.

Timmons continued, "I am pleased, as I'm sure the rest of you are, at our restraint today during the meeting. I think Susanna will back me on this. I believe Jonas wouldn't have wanted us to make an issue of the merger at this time."

Susanna nodded in agreement. A waiter entered the room offering a selection of wine. After the wine was poured and tasted, Timmons continued.

"Steven, we are all here to assist you on your committee. As soon as the word is official, you will be bombarded by DO's offering you their opinion on the merger issue. I, as the other members of the committee, implore you not to be swayed by their politics. Everybody has a different agenda."

Susanna interrupted, "What Chester is saying is true. People I barely knew came out of the woodwork offering me their opinions, both for and against a merger." Susanna's manner was completely controlled. She didn't seem to over analyze or fret. Perhaps that was the key to her ageless mien.

Timmons continued, agitated by the interruption. "As I was saying, we need to depend on each other. If we're going to use outside consultation, I feel we need to discuss this first, so we can agree on who and what type of consultation we need to solicit."

"I wholeheartedly agree," Probst said. "If we don't control our outside resources, this entire process will get totally out of hand. The result would be chaotic."

"Is this review of a subcommittee typical? Or is this unique to my committee?" Callison still couldn't decide if he should be upset or thankful for the input.

"The answer to your question is, yes. What I mean is, your committee is unique, and we also have to share our opinions and insights on the other committees as well." While Timmons answered Callison's question, he looked to the other members of the group for consensus.

"Ah yes, unique." Callison shook his head, but was not impressed with Timmons' answer.

As Timmons concluded his remarks, the waiters arrived with their entrees.

Teitelman, who had been conspicuously quiet turned to Callison. "It's good to see you again." He smiled tentatively.

"Likewise; what have you been up to?" Callison said.

"Well, I recently applied for the dean of academic affairs. If I get the position I'll have to give up the chairmanship of pediatrics. To be quite honest, I'm not really sure I want this position, primarily because I feel there is still a lot more to do at the department level."

Callison hadn't expected this random response. However, he couldn't help inquiring further. "If you enjoy your present position and aren't sure about the dean position, why are you applying?"

"Good question. To be frank, so many people are encouraging me to apply I can't distinguish whether this is something I want or something they want."

"I don't mean to pry, and tell me if I'm out of line, but can you really let others make this type of career decision for you?"

"They're not. Not really—it's just the unknown. You see, I know what my current job requires but this new position will be much more demanding." Teitelman's face contorted as he spoke and Callison could sense his confusion.

"I'm sure it will be." Callison was surprised at Teitelman's lack of insight into this position. Teitelman had been two years ahead of Callison in medical school, and had been the chief pediatric resident when Callison started his medicine residency. He had been intelligent, organized, and appeared to be a natural leader. Although Callison had not kept up with Teitelman's career, it was evident he continued to excel. In addition, Teitelman had a reputation as a leader in the primary care arena. Callison assumed it was Teitelman's leadership in this area which led to his selection on this committee.

At the completion of the meal, Timmons resurrected the topic of the evening. "Before we leave, we need to agree on several basic principles. First, we need to agree to assist each other on our committee assignments. Second, we need to agree as a group, before we request any outside consultants. Lastly, Steven,

100

we will all help you get up to speed on your committee. Your committee has the potential to affect all of us in a very profound way."

"Before I can agree to this, I need some answers," Callison said decidedly. "First, do we not trust the MD's on the committee? Second, if we do trust them, why are we meeting secretly? Third, if the subcommittee is so critical, should I decline to chair the committee in lieu of someone with more experience? Lastly, I understand the rationale to maintain confidentiality at this point, but somewhere down the line, don't we need to involve the profession? This could potentially change the lives of thousands of colleagues."

Probst responded, "Of course, we trust the MD's on the committee, but only to a point. We must first represent our profession, and on occasion this requires a meeting such as this evening. There are issues that many of us feel uncomfortable discussing with the whole gathering before we get a consensus of our own group. I know for a fact that the MD's have on occasion done the same thing."

Danzinger and Michelson both confirmed Probst's comments.

Timmons resumed the conversation, "I can only speak for myself but I, like Jourge, have total confidence in your abilities. He believes you're the best candidate, and most qualified to chair the committee." Timmons' eyes focused on Callison with a steady, unrelenting gaze.

There was no further discussion on Timmon's last comments. Callison appeared to be the only one uncomfortable with Timmons' statement. He always had a problem accepting a compliment.

Timmons noting no further discussion continued. "The last point about letting the profession in on our discussions has merit on the surface, but in reality would be a catastrophe. Did you ever ask a DO to define osteopathy? Even in this room, we would get many different variations on a theme. If we canvassed the profession at large, it would be utter chaos."

Danzinger interrupted, "May I tell a joke?"

The group was stunned by his question. Since nobody

rejected his request, Danzinger continued "An Indian, a Frenchman, and an osteopath were at the zoo. They were all standing in front of the elephant cage studying the elephant. An Englishman passed the trio and asked what they thought of the elephant. The Indian said, 'When I see the elephant, I see a mammoth creature—mighty, regal and proud.' The Frenchman said, 'When I see the elephant I see a sensuous animal that is as graceful as it is sexual.' The osteopath said, 'Before we discuss the elephant, let me tell you about osteopathy."

The group, including Callison, started to laugh.

"Okay, I get the point," Callison softly chuckled. Timmons continued. "Once we work out the details, whatever they might be, we will meet with appropriate officials of the profession to discuss in depth the committee's conclusions. Hopefully we will at least get the majority of the profession agreeing with our decision."

This answer made Callison feel better, yet he was still a little uncomfortable. The hour was late and everyone was exhausted. He decided to not pursue any other issues at this time. They adjourned the meeting. Callison started to leave when Timmons grabbed him by the elbow and asked him to remain behind.

Timmons escorted Callison to the bar of the hotel, where they both ordered coffee. "I couldn't tell you this in front of the others, but I have some information from a very good source that may aid you on your committee."

Callison had no idea where Timmons was heading, but listened politely. "Are you aware of the Omnibus Budget Reconciliation Act? This act requires all physicians rendering care to Medicaid beneficiaries who are pregnant, or are under 21 years of age, to have board certification in family practice, pediatrics or obstetrics, by the American Board of Medical Specialties."

"I don't know what you're talking about." Callison had never heard of this and didn't know how it applied to him, since he had little contact with this segment of the population.

"Let me clarify. If this is enacted, not having AMA board certification essentially excludes all our physicians who are certified through the AOA. As you may or may not be aware, many of our colleagues' practices are dependent on Medicaid patients. Even though we represent about 5 percent of the physician population, we care for about 25 percent of the Medicaid patients. This action will not only have a devastating effect on our profession, but will also place a quarter of the nation's Medicaid patients in a lurch for quality health care."

Callison was still confused as to how this applied to him. "This must be a mistake. Isn't it?"

Timmons shook his head. "I wish it was just a mistake. We have been told that this act, when initially passed, inadvertently overlooked AOA board certification, but I think otherwise. I've been told that if we are moving toward an agreement, a merger of the two professions, this act will become a moot point and can literally salvage the practices of thousands of our colleagues. Otherwise the act is scheduled to take effect the first of the year. I'm sure it goes without saying how sensitive this issue is. Our conversation must be kept strictly confidential."

"So what you're saying is that if we agree on the merger the MD's will help us continue with our Medicaid practices? And if we decline on the merger, will they support this discriminatory action?"

"I'm not sure on the latter point. But we need to consider this in conjunction with the other issues pertaining to the merger."

"Who told you this?" Callison said angrily.

"I can't reveal my source but it's reliable. Plus it makes sense. If we're in the same profession, then there's no issue."

"I don't like ultimatums or threats, real or implied, and I certainly don't like this." A scowl appeared on Callison's face.

Timmons was now attempting to calm Callison. "Maybe I overstated the issue. Let's sleep on this and we can discuss this in the morning."

"Okay, but I have one more point that begs for an answer. If they're successful in excluding us from taking care of the Medicaid patients, who do they have in mind to pick up the slack? And that doesn't address the over 37 million uninsured that will almost certainly enter the system if a universal health-care policy is approved."

"I don't have an answer for you. But I again implore you to keep this to yourself until we can get some more information."

Callison agreed to keep this information confidential, but he could feel his stomach churning.

They hailed a cab to return to the hotel. In his room, Callison noticed the red flashing light indicating he had a message. He called the front desk. The message said: "Please call Dr. Teitelman when you get in."

Callison called Teitelman's room. He answered the phone after the first ring. "Hello, Callison?"

"Yes."

"Thanks for returning my call. Would you mind meeting with me tonight, just for a few minutes?"

Callison's first inclination was to decline, but he grudgingly agreed. Teitelman was at Callison's door within two minutes. Callison could tell Teitelman was anxious, and this anxiety made Callison even more uncomfortable than he already was.

Teitelman entered the room and fidgeted, rolling a small crop of his hair between his right index finger and thumb. "I needed to clarify something I said tonight." Teitelman avoided eye contact while he spoke.

"What's that?"

"I feel I left you with the impression that I am being forced into applying for the deanship. Um, in reality this is a position I have wanted for years. Now that I have an excellent chance of getting the position, I'm not sure I can do the job." Teitelman still avoided any eye contact as he talked, which only increased Callison's anxiety.

Callison wasn't sure why Teitelman had chosen him for his catharsis but he was sure he didn't have the patience for a prolonged dialogue. "If this job is really something you want, then go for it. What do you really have to lose?"

"That's just it. Um, I feel I have a lot to lose. Once I give up the chairmanship of the department, it's gone. I've worked for years to get to this point and I'm afraid to possibly lose it all." Teitelman finally looked at Callison.

"But you won't. No matter what may happen if you take the

new position, you will still have your administrative skills and experience, along with the knowledge that you gave it your best shot."

Teitelman sat quietly for a moment contemplating Callison's words. "You know, I haven't discussed this with anyone until tonight. I don't even know why I chose to dump on you, but thanks for listening."

Callison actually felt some relief for Teitelman, although he still didn't think Teitelman had made any definitive decision. "You're welcome."

"Not to change the subject, but I'm really glad you're on the committee."

Callison felt flattered by the remark.

Teitelman continued, "I was really getting a little paranoid. It seemed I was the only one under the age of sixty. I couldn't figure out why I was selected when they had the choice of other more seasoned and experienced docs. Then when they chose you, it made me feel more comfortable."

"Comfortable." The word resounded in Callison's head. Was that the reason he felt *un*comfortable? Was it that he was of a different generation than the other members of the committee? "Why do you think you initially felt uncomfortable on the committee?"

"I'm not sure. But I had this feeling that I was selected because they felt I could be manipulated. I know that sounds ridiculous, but something just didn't set right." Teitelman again avoided direct eye contact with Callison as he spoke.

"I doubt that."

"Yeah, I guess you're right. It's late and I've already taken up too much of your time. Thanks again for listening and for your advice. See you in the morning." Teitelman shook Callison's hand and promptly left for his room.

Callison sat on the edge of his bed, thinking. *Why would they want to manipulate him? To what end?* As much as he didn't want to believe that Teitelman's concerns had any validity, he couldn't shake the feeling there was a ring of truth to his paranoia. Was Timmons' speech an attempt to sway or manipulate Callison? He was too tired to think. His mind wandered to Natalie. He would be home tomorrow and she would help him clarify what was real. As he fell into a sound sleep, he thought of his wife and whispered softly, "Good night, I love you."

11

The second day of meetings started without incident. After reviewing the minutes of the previous day's proceedings, assignments were issued. Other than some minor disagreement with the new charge for the research committee, this portion of the meeting was uneventful.

Callison could sense, as could the others, the meeting was about to end. He was ready to go home. "Before we adjourn, I would like to take a moment to reflect on the progress of the group." Jourge's brow furrowed and his voice deepened, slowly enunciating each word. "To succeed, to achieve the formidable task assigned, we must function as a unit." Jourge coughed. "When we dissent, we do it in this room. With this group. Together." Jourge started to slowly move his head in a circular motion, coughing at the completion of the circle.

Silence. Jourge's words reverberated in Callison's head. His head down, he blankly stared at the table.

Timmons broke the silence. "I agree."

The other committee members nodded.

"Very well. We all have our assignments." Callison raised his eyes from the table, focusing on Jourge as he spoke. "Are there any further comments?"

"I know we've had our differences. Which is fine," Rasta said. "Whatever's in the past is over. Let's move on."

"Thank you, Victor." Jourge said, followed by another cough. "And thank all of you for your attention."

Jourge stood. He approached Timmons and shook his hand. "Have a safe journey home. I'll be in touch."

Timmons smiled, "I'll look forward to hearing from you."

Rasta slapped Probst on the back. "Nice move." He laughed.

"Well, what can I say?" Probst shrugged his shoulders.

The mood changed. The embarrassment of the moment subsided and the group was again one.

Jourge shook Callison's hand. "I told you this was an interesting meeting."

"You weren't kidding," Callison replied.

"Anyway. If you need any assistance, call me." Jourge smiled and patted Callison on the shoulder.

"Thanks. I will."

Waiting to check out of the hotel, Callison's mind wandered to the previous night's meeting.

"I guess we were pretty naive thinking they wouldn't find out." Teitelman said, startling Callison.

"I guess." Callison answered, still embarrassed.

Callison did not notice the man studying him. The photocopy of the photograph Merker had received from the medical school yearbook was more than adequate to identify Callison. Merker wasn't sure how, but he was certain Callison was an integral part of the puzzle surrounding the death of Jonas Cisko and probably Harvey Kahn.

Over the past several days, Merker had immersed himself in the detailed work he had so despised while he was a policeman. As a police officer, he often felt this work went for naught because the system would frequently screw up even the best evidence, wasting his efforts. But as a private detective, the knowledge he acquired on the force allowed him to attain proof, which utilized the same system to assist, rather than hinder his cases. Understanding the system from both ends gave Merker a distinct advantage, which gave him the latitude he didn't have as a cop.

Merker had searched for the whereabouts of Dr. Amos Wilcox, finally discovering he had died in 1966.

The other name Cynthia Cisko could recall had been a Dr. Trulof, who had been Wilcox's partner during the controversy. Merker was able to confirm Trulof's full name—Richard Tyler Trulof—but could not locate Dr. Trulof through the California Medical Association, the AOA, the AMA, or any of the usual sources. It was as if Dr. Trulof had vanished.

Merker started to cross the lobby toward Callison. An image

appeared out of the corner of his eye. It was the figure of a man dressed in black, lurking in the shadows of a large marble column. The man was Van Gregory. Merker, never changing his gait, walked past Callison, not glancing in the direction of Callison or Gregory.

Exiting the building Merker hastened to his car, which was parked two blocks away. Pulling the car adjacent to the hotel, he noticed Callison enter a cab. Gregory was not in sight. Merker followed Callison's cab to O'Hare airport. When Callison exited the cab, Merker scanned the area looking to see if Gregory was in pursuit. There was no sign of the man in black. Merker double-parked his car in front of the terminal, to the chagrin of the attendant who was attempting to control the flow of traffic

In the terminal, Merker noticed Callison standing in a long line awaiting his turn to be checked in for his flight. Merker returned to his car just as the attendant summoned a policeman. By the time Merker returned to the terminal, Callison was gone. Merker checked the flight board and noticed the next flight scheduled to depart for DFW was in forty minutes. He still had time to talk to Callison.

At the gate Merker noticed Callison seated in the waiting area, quietly reading the newspaper. Before approaching Callison, Merker surveyed the waiting area for Gregory or anyone else who might appear suspect. The waiting area was very crowded, not an empty seat. Several small children were playing tag as their parents attempted to control them; a couple was huddled saying their good-byes; the usual businessmen were scattered about; a nervous couple kept trying to convince each other that flying was actually safer than driving.

Merker noticed Gregory cleverly hidden, almost totally camouflaged into the dark background. He didn't need to see Gregory's eyes through his darkened glasses to know he was watching Callison. Merker moved to another waiting area adjacent to the Dallas flight. Here he could observe both Gregory and Callison from a distance.

If Callison was working with Gregory, why were they still non-communicative? Merker had a frightening thought: what if they were on to him and he was being watched? Without showing any sign of alarm, Merker slowly rose and walked toward the restroom. His senses heightened. He couldn't detect anyone following him. There was no reaction at all, by either Callison or Gregory. Relieved and embarrassed, Merker returned to his previous seat and studied them both to see if there was any hint of nonverbal communication. There was none. Now more than ever he needed to talk to Callison.

Merker realized he still had an advantage on Gregory. Gregory had no clue that Merker was also following Callison. Merker could not approach Callison with Van Gregory watching, so he decided to abandon his current pursuit. He already had a plane reservation for L.A., where he was hopeful that Dr. Ethan Jasper could shed some insight into this case—if this really *was* a case. If not Jasper, then maybe he could discover some more information about Dr. Kahn or possibly locate Dr. Trulof. Callison would wait until after California. Maybe by then he would have a better handle on what to ask and whether he should confront Van Gregory.

As Merker left the airport he thought about Van Gregory. He turned on the radio. The Cubs were at home against the Pirates. He relished the distraction. His mind wandered back to Callison and Gregory and all the possibilities. Merker felt a slight tinge of anticipation; he hadn't experienced this feeling in some time. It was exciting. He was alive again—and it felt good.

Callison debated whether he should stop off at his office before going home. The main thing he hated about returning to work after several days off was the amount of accumulated paperwork that typically piled up. This time his decision wasn't difficult. He knew his wife would be awaiting his return; he would definitely bypass the office. Natalie had prepared his favorite dinner, which he could smell even before he entered the house. He was affectionately greeted by Natalie, and they exchanged a long passionate kiss.

"Smells great." Callison was famished.

"It's your favorite, lasagna."

Callison loved Natalie's lasagna. It was the first meal she prepared for him when they started dating and it was fantastic.

"So, how did the meeting go?"

"I was assigned the chair of a subcommittee responsible for evaluating a possible merger between the osteopathic and allopathic professions."

"What? Why would you do that?" Natalie quizzically stared at her husband.

"I know at first it seems outlandish, but when you start to think about it, the possibility has some merit."

"I can't believe you would even consider this as an option."

"My committee is investigating the possibility of such a merger. We'll study both the good and bad points of the merger and then present our conclusions to the committee as a whole. It's very possible our conclusions will be that such a merger would be detrimental, and therefore, we would be against it."

"You don't have to meet to decide that . . . do you?" Natalie had already formulated her opinion on this subject.

"Actually there are some valid points in favor of the merger."

"You're serious?"

"Yes, very serious." Callison raised his eyebrows, surprised at Natalie's rigid stance.

"Okay. Educate me." Natalie defiantly folded her arms across her chest.

"First, the difference between the two professions appears to be minimal, at best. The major difference is probably not the manipulative component. Many practicing DO's don't routinely use manipulation." Callison hesitated for effect. "It's more philosophical."

"So what about that, then?" Natalie still held her arms across her chest and now began to rhythmically tap her right foot.

"Let's say our philosophy is committed to the sanctity and proliferation of the primary care physician."

Natalie rolled her eyes back.

Callison, frustrated, decided to try a different tack. "After a dinner meeting in which we discussed the importance of this committee and especially my subcommittee, I was cornered by Chester Timmons."

"Who are you referring to? Who's the 'we'?" Natalie's toe-tapping intensified.

"We met, just the DO's on the committee. We thought if we could meet confidentially to discuss matters sensitive to the profession, we could come to some sort of consensus."

Natalie shook her head. She stopped tapping her foot but her arms remained tightly folded across her chest.

"Well, Jourge found out about the meeting and he was pissed. He sanctioned the entire committee against meeting privately. It was embarrassing. Anyway, after our meeting Timmons pulled me aside. He told me of some new legislative act passed by Congress that will disallow DO's who were trained in accredited osteopathic programs from taking care of Medicaid patients under the age of 21 or if they're pregnant."

"Are you kidding me? How can that be?" Natalie's mouth was agape and her arms fell to her side.

"I'd heard of this act but only in vague terms. Since then, I've substantiated this as accurate information."

"So what can you do about this?" Natalie scowled.

"This is where it gets interesting. Timmons inferred that if our committee supported the merger and if we all became MD's, then the discriminatory component of this act would become a moot point, because those programs would then be considered allopathic."

"In other words, if you support the merger, your profession will be allowed to continue to care for their Medicaid patients, and if you don't . . ."

"And if we don't, although he didn't say this in so many words, many of our family practitioners, pediatricians, obstetricians and gynecologists will literally be out of work."

"Wow, what are you going to do?" Natalie lowered her voice.

"Well, I got a couple of options. I could go to the AOA and ask them if they know about this." Callison paused. "No, I don't want to do that." Callison belched loudly. "Excuse me." *Was it the lasagna or the committee that had upset his stomach?* Callison continued, "Or I could confront Timmons. You know, he may be bluffing. Or I could bring this up to the committee and see where that goes." Callison's burp was silent this time. "Or I could quit the committee. What do you think?"

Natalie sat quietly reviewing the dilemma. Suddenly a

spark appeared in her hazel eyes. "They're bluffing."

"You think?"

"They're bluffing! They could never enforce such a discrimi-natory rule. This Timmons wants to bully you into this merger. Probably setting you up as the fall guy, because when the profes-sion hears about this, they're going to want somebody's ass." Natalie's mind was racing. The more she thought about it, the more she was convinced she was right.

"Why are you so sure?"

"Because it makes sense. If they tried to go through with this, there would be such an outcry by the Medicaid patients! Public opinion would crucify whoever was responsible."

"How can you be so sure? What if they have a plan to rectify the problem and offer other care? What if they sell this to the public as an improvement in the health-care system?"

"What if you're right? Could they have such a plan?"

"I don't know. It doesn't seem likely. Timmons told me a sta-tistic that surprised me. Although the DO's constitute only around 5 percent of the physician population, they take care of about 25 percent of the Medicaid population. Even with Medic-aid going more to managed care, that's still a lot of patients." Callison's stomach growled, as he suppressed another belch. "So to answer your question, it appears to me that the MD's would need the DO primary care providers to take care of all these patients. And this doesn't even begin to address the issue of how we'll take care of all those who are currently uninsured if they suddenly become insured via some sort of universal insurance program."

"This is complicated. You need to be very cautious in your recommendations."

"Hon, I really don't know what to do." Steven looked up at his wife, a look of self-doubt in his eyes.

"Listen, you must be exhausted. I know I'm tired. Let's go to bed and discuss this in the morning."

Without saying another word Natalie took Steven's hand and led him into their bedroom.

The extensive paperwork Callison had feared more than

fulfilled his expectations. After several hours of separating the essential from the superfluous, he needed a break. He walked over to the hospital to pay a visit to Mrs. Kodack, who was participating in the cardiac rehabilitation program. The smile on Mrs. Kodack's face lifted his spirits. This was what medicine should be about, not the bureaucratic red tape, the endless paperwork, or the politics and meaningless committee meetings.

"Look how well my Annie is doing, Doctor." Mr. Kodack was beaming with pride. "She's getting stronger every minute and is gonna come home in a day or so!"

Callison placed his hand on Mr. Kodack's shoulder, "She sure does look good. I couldn't be more pleased."

"Doctor, once my Annie's home, do you think she'll stay healthy?"

"Mrs. Kodack's a very strong woman who has fought the odds and has already accomplished more than I would have thought possible. And hopefully with time her heart will continue to get stronger." Callison knew he really didn't answer the question, but his response was what Mr. Kodack wanted to hear.

Callison excused himself to return to his paperwork, but his short interlude with Mrs. Kodack reenergized him.

Sorting his mail, a letter from the Texas Medical Foundation caught his attention. The issue of the premature discharge from the hospital had been hanging over Callison's head since he became aware of this as a potential medical mismanagement case. Callison had responded explaining his point of view on the issue, and he assumed this letter would be their decision. He took a deep breath before opening the letter, then quickly perused its contents. It was nothing more than a form letter acknowledging they had received Callison's reply and stated their response would be forthcoming.

The remainder of the mail was routine with the exception of a letter addressed to Callison stamped, "confidential." Callison noted the envelope had no return address, which made him suspicious. Callison opened the letter not expecting much. He frequently received letters that had been similarly stamped as confidential but were usually either offering to loan him money or suggesting a less than optimal practice opportunity. This letter, however was different.

Dear Dr. Callison,

I have learned that you have been appointed to the committee that will be reviewing the possibility of a potential merger between the DO's and the MD's. I will be contacting you in the near future to see how I may be of help.

Fraternally yours,
A Concerned Colleague

As Callison reread the letter, he reflected on Jourge's concerns and the need for security and collegiality. He had just returned and had already he received an anonymous letter— so much for security and collegiality. Although there was no return address, the letter was postmarked in Chicago. Could it be from a co-committee member? Were they testing him? The wording was too ambiguous to get overly concerned about, but it nevertheless bothered him.

Callison decided to keep the letter to himself at this point. He would reevaluate whether he should inform Jourge or Timmons at a later date.

Callison's secretary, Helen Hunter, called to remind him he had a meeting with the chairman in five minutes. Harold Zamba, or Dr. Z as he was frequently referred to, had been the chair of the Medicine Department for about twenty years. He had recruited Callison over a decade ago and was the one who had selected him to develop the Division of General Internal Medicine. Callison found Dr. Z to be fair, honest, always direct and to the point. No elaboration or small talk.

Dr. Z's office was down the hall from Callison's. He was escorted into Z's inner sanctum by the secretary, Hilda. Before Callison could sit, Z initiated the conversation. "The first quarter's income from your division was down from last year. Also the expenses are up. This trend is not good."

Callison was well aware of this and had been dreading this conversation for some time.

"Now for the good news." Dr. Z actually smiled, which might have been a first.

Callison was not prepared for any good news, so this statement came as a pleasant surprise.

"The dean has informed me that he will personally underwrite any losses in your division for the year. He feels that the work you're doing on your new committee is important enough to warrant such a guarantee. The only addendum I would add is that even if he bails you out this year, if you carry too large a deficit we will need to look at changes in salary when we project our budget for next year."

"That sounds reasonable." Callison knew that Z wouldn't hesitate to cut salaries if he felt it was necessary. Three years ago they had gone through a lean year and had to cut salaries, although they euphemistically called it an "adjustment." Callison had promised himself he would never let the division get in that type of financial difficulty again. It was too painful to make those cuts, or adjustments.

"By the way, the dean mentioned he'd like to see you when you're finished here. Since we're finished, I suggest you pay a visit to the dean and thank him for his generosity. I believe the offer he made in your behalf is unprecedented in the institution." Dr. Z rose from his chair and accompanied Callison to the door.

Callison left without saying another word.

Dean Hoffnagle's office was overflowing with a least a dozen medical students meandering about, complaining to each other. Callison sensed that something major was amiss when he noticed a second contingent of students huddled outside the office, presumably planning their strategy. Callison was promptly escorted into the dean's office, to the total dismay of the students, who had been waiting to have their audience with the dean.

"What's all the commotion outside about?" Callison said as he walked in.

"Nothing special, just a typical day in the land of entitlement." The dean winced as he shook his head.

"What?"

"The land of rights and entitlement. Just being here gives

116

them their rights and entitles them to every little thing their heart desire. Now they're complaining they haven't been given ample time off between their classes and the final exams. I'm trying to be understanding. But the last time we gave them time off to study, half the class took off for the coast for sun and relaxation. Anyway, that's life today."

Callison could sympathize with Hoffnagle's plight as he had been there many times. On the other hand, he had just heard only the dean's version.

"How's the committee going? I take it Harold told you of my little proposition." The dean leaned back in his chair, cupping the back of his head in his hands.

"Proposition? Harold said that you would underwrite any divisional losses for the year. What proposition?"

"What I'd like from you is to keep me apprised of the recommendations coming forth from your committee. My proposition to you would guarantee that any financial losses you or your division might incur over this fiscal year will be totally covered by my discretionary funds. It's simple." The dean beamed with pride. It was the rare occasion he could make such an offer, and he wanted to milk it for all he could.

"I'm not sure I fully understand what you're talking about."

"Let me give you an example. Let's say your committee is about to take a stand, a strong stand, on how the government will change its priorities on the funding of research with a new emphasis on behavioral medicine. If we knew about this, then we could have a better chance as an institution to get funding in that area, which as you know, is getting tighter and more competitive every day."

"Is that ethical?"

"Ethical?" The dean barked. "Of course it's ethical. It's the game we all have to play to survive in this world. We're not doing anything different than they're doing at every other institution where a member of your committee is on faculty."

"Yeah, I guess you're right."

"This is a game. You should know this as well as anyone. It's not only how good a job you do, or how well your grant is written. It's who you know. It's are you a player, a member of the club?

Well, welcome to the club. You've just arrived."

"You know I care for this school and will do what I can to help it prosper." Callison swallowed hard. "But I can't break any confidences."

"What confidences?" The beam was gone from the dean's face.

"I promised the other committee members that I would keep the information confidential. If we discuss the issues and utilize them for our own gain, they'll know I broke my word."

"I see." The dean's face reddened. "I don't want you to feel you have compromised yourself or your word. What I'm asking is if there's information that can be shared with me that doesn't compromise your position on the committee, I'd appreciate your cooperation. I still feel there will be many issues discussed that won't violate any breach of security and may afford our institution a slight advantage. The funding support isn't totally contingent on your cooperation in this matter, but I must say in all candor, I will take it into account."

"I know you can appreciate my concerns. I'll see what I can do." Callison had no choice, and the dean knew this. He had to cooperate or else he would be forced to cut salaries.

"That's all I can ask." The dean smiled, but more superficially.

"Is there anything else?" Callison wanted to leave.

"Only if you have any suggestions dealing with the land of entitlement."

"No. I'll leave that to you."

As Callison left the office, the band of students was mobilizing for their assault.

Callison started to think. Was it possible to use his position on the committee to get his grant funded, yet maintain his integrity? Was it possible to assist the dean, yet maintain his word? And lastly, was it possible to maintain the profession without sacrificing its members and their practices. He had no answers for any of these questions.

12

Merker arrived at LAX and headed directly for the rental car he had reserved. It had been many years since he had last visited Los Angeles. His wife had just been diagnosed with cancer and requested that they vacation in a place that would be as far from their reality as possible—the world of make-believe and of Disneyland—Los Angeles. It was their first and only visit to Los Angeles, and the memories were still vivid in Merker's mind. These were some of his best memories of his marriage. Although there had been an underlying sensation of dread and fear, they were able to suppress those emotions and substituted excitement and discovery. Maybe it was the warm weather, or the vast Pacific, or the wonder of Hollywood, or the child in them that Disneyland unveils. It was probably a little of each that had freed both Alice and Marcus Merker temporarily from the deadly cloud that had hovered over them. The cloud of disease and despair recurred as soon as they returned to Chicago. Alice would never be able to leave the city again.

The weather was hot even by California standards and the air conditioning felt refreshing. The community hospital at Redondo Beach was a modern facility, reflecting a new style of suburban hospital which focused greatly on amenities, resembling a fashionable hotel as much a medical center. Merker walked past the waterfall that dominated the lobby to the information desk. A woman with purple hair and matching purple eyes directed Merker to the administrative offices, the entry to which was flanked by extravagant but attractive exotic plants. Merker searched for the desk of Ms. Decker. He had learned Ms. Decker had been Kahn's secretary at the hospital for the last year. Ms. Amanda Decker was seated at her desk concentrating on her computer screen, deeply involved in her work.

"Excuse me, Ms. Decker." Merker's voice was subdued. It was so subdued she didn't even respond. "Ms. Decker!" Merker's voice was now definitely audible.

Decker, startled, looked up. "Yes, can I help you?" Her tone was agitated.

"Yes, my name is Merker. I called you two days ago . . ."

"About Dr. Kahn." The tenor of her voice changed dramatically to a very somber almost tearful tone.

"Yes, do you have a little time to discuss Dr. Kahn?"

Ms. Decker abruptly stood up, she was much shorter than she appeared while seated. She probably wasn't even five feet tall. She told the other secretary that she would return later.

Amanda Decker led Merker to the cafeteria, where they both poured cups of coffee and then seated themselves in a remote alcove.

"Thank you for allowing me to talk with you," Merker said, intentionally assuming a passive manner to allow Ms. Decker the space to trust him.

"Ever since your call I have been intrigued as to what type of information you wanted and why."

"To answer the why question, a very good friend of mine, an acquaintance of Dr. Kahn's, recently died too. I know they had met during Dr. Kahn's trip to Chicago and I was wondering if their deaths were somehow connected."

"Are you serious? Are you trying to say that Dr. Kahn's death wasn't an accident?" A look of disbelief overcame Amanda Decker.

"No, not really." Merker didn't want to alienate Ms. Decker. He quickly decided to change the focus of the conversation. "Can you tell me what kind of man Dr. Kahn was?"

It was the correct move. A quiet calm soothed her. "Dr. Kahn was a gentle and kind man—always considerate—never harsh. He was the best boss I ever worked for, and I genuinely miss him." Tears formed in the creases of Ms. Decker's eyes. They slowly started to drift down her cheeks, running her mascara.

"I'm sorry if I upset . . ."

Ms. Decker motioned with her hands. She was momentarily indisposed.

Merker waited several seconds before continuing. "Do you know why he went to Chicago?"

"He had a meeting."

"Do you know what the meeting was about?"

"Not really, only that he was staying at the Drake Hotel and he was representing the AMA." Amanda Decker grabbed a napkin from the table and discreetly blew her nose.

"Do you have any idea what was the purpose of the meeting?"

"Only what I told you already. But I'm curious. Why are you asking these questions?"

"I'm just trying to find out if there's any connection between the death of my friend, your boss and this meeting in Chicago."

"Well, I honestly don't know the purpose of the meeting." She seemed to grow a little more distant, and her voice sounded slightly sarcastic.

Merker realized Ms. Decker was becoming less than enamored with him. He resolved not to press the subject. "Do you recall anyone who might have wished any harm to Dr. Kahn?"

"No!"

"Is there anyone else who might have some additional information about Dr. Kahn?"

"I can't think of anyone at this time. But if you leave your name and number, I'll call you if I think of someone."

The remainder of the morning was frustrating. Merker was not successful in contacting the chief hospital administrator, Mr. Brandeis, who had been Dr. Kahn's immediate superior. However, he was able to arrange a meeting with him for early the following morning.

The one piece of information that did appear to have some promise was the former address of the late Dr. Kahn.

Dr. Kahn's townhome complex was very upscale, with a private security gate, complete with guard. Merker had no trouble convincing the guard to allow him access to the complex, which was situated overlooking the Pacific Ocean. Merker had located the landlord who was on the premises. He thought Merker had been sent over by Kahn's lawyer. As Mr.

Tacasura, the landlord, explained, Dr. Kahn's personal posses-
sions had been removed by his lawyer and his other posses-
sions had been donated to charity. Mr. Tacasura's log book not
only corroborated his story, but also listed both the specific
charity for each item donated, and the name and address of
Kahn's lawyer.

Merker copied the name of the charity, the AIDS House of
Greater LA, and the lawyer's name, Robert Simon of Simon,
Simon, and Harbister, while he endured Tacasura's harangue on
the value and benefits of his townhome complex. Mr. Tacasura
showed Merker Dr. Kahn's now emptied home, which was in the
process of being prepared for new occupants.

That evening Merker returned to his hotel room. He found it
unusual that he couldn't uncover any gossip about Dr. Kahn at
the hospital and hoped he would gain some insight when he
interviewed the hospital administrator, Mr. Brandeis and Robert
Simon, Kahn's lawyer.

The morning sun had broken through the haze. Its bright-
ness nudged Merker from his sleep. He had a full day, starting
with Mr. Brandeis and ending with a night game at Dodger Stadium—the Braves versus the Dodgers.

The meeting with Mr. Brandeis was short and to the point.
Brandeis had only been at the hospital for six months, so he
hadn't much information on Kahn. He did, however, have some
insight pertaining to the meeting in Chicago. The AMA had
asked for several local administrators and representatives to
assist in a panel to discuss some of the new health-care reform
proposals. The group was to meet in Chicago, and Dr. Kahn had
been asked to participate because of his experience in a capitated
health-care program he had helped create.

The next stop on Merker's agenda was the law offices of
Simon, Simon, and Harbister. The lobby was ostentatious,
highlighted by large abstract paintings interspersed with
Ansel Adams photographs. In stark contrast to the vibrant
paintings was the furniture, all mahogany with leather padded
seats. Merker had no interest in interior design or decor and
realized his opinion had no relevance, but he was aware there
was something wrong. They were trying too hard to impress,

and the result was just the opposite. At best, Merker was uncomfortable.

When he explained he wanted to discuss Dr. Kahn, Merker was surprised how quickly the secretary escorted him into Mr. Simon's office.

Robert Simon appeared to be about fifty years old, graying at the temples and thinning on top. He had a robust tan and was wearing braces on his teeth. His clothing was expensive but garish and even that was overshadowed by the gold jewelry adorning his fingers and wrists. Mr. Simon's attire was consistent with the decor of the office—overstated and pretentious.

"Won't you please have a seat?"

Merker was confused by Simon's informality. His previous contacts with lawyers, even if he knew them, was not nearly as favorable as this. Merker sat in one of the large leather chairs in front of Simon's oversized mahogany desk.

"So you knew Harvey Kahn?"

"No, not really. But a friend of mine knew him."

The expression on Simon's face abruptly changed, as if he had been duped.

"A friend...I see...So what can I do for you?" Simon leaned forward, resting his elbows on his desk.

"My friend, like Dr. Kahn, recently died. Dr. Kahn had just visited him and when they were together, several photographs were taken. These pictures were the last photographs of my friend, Jonas Cisko. Jonas's family asked me to see if I could get a copy of these pictures because of their sentimental value."

"I don't recall any pictures that would fit your description."

"If it wouldn't be an inconvenience, I'd appreciate it if I could look for myself. I promised the family."

"It wouldn't be an inconvenience at all. However, I don't have his personal items any longer. As stipulated in his will, they were destroyed." Simon sat back in his chair, distancing himself.

"Shit. Um, how unfortunate." Merker decided to try one other ploy. "How were they destroyed?"

"Excuse me?" Simon again leaned forward, his eyes scrutinizing Merker.

"How did you destroy his personal items? It seems a strange request, doesn't it?"

"Not really. As lawyers we get many unusual requests, much more bizarre than this. I followed his wishes and had his personal objects incinerated and mixed with his ashes."

Merker found the answer so strange he actually believed it. "Can you think of anyone who might have any copies of the negatives?"

"I really wouldn't know. I was just his lawyer."

"Do you know anyone else who was close to Dr. Kahn who could help me?"

"I'm sorry." Simon looked at his watch.

"Thank you for your time."

"Sorry that I couldn't have been more help. But if you leave your business card, I'll contact you if anything comes up."

Merker couldn't decide whether to give Simon the mock or legitimate business card. He decided to give him the actual card.

Simon glanced at the card. He remained controlled. Merker could sense a feeling of uneasiness.

"So, you're a private detective?" The calm in Simon's voice was replaced by uncertainty.

"Yes, I thought I had mentioned that." Merker was fully aware that he hadn't.

"If I think of anything I'll call you, Mr. Merker."

Merker thanked him once again and shook his hand, which was now clammy and trembling slightly. Merker was trained to notice even minor changes in posture, speech, or gestures. Merker appreciated Simon's cool outward demeanor, but he knew the lawyer was rattled on the inside.

As soon as Merker left the building, Simon picked up the phone to make a long distance call to Chicago. Merker had a little more insight into Dr. Kahn now than he had before he arrived in L.A., but not enough to make any sense out of Simon's reaction. Discouraged, Merker decided to concentrate his efforts on Jonas Cisko.

Tomorrow Merker was scheduled to meet with Ethan Jasper, the last person that Cisko had talked to. Now he would return to his room, remove his uncomfortable suit, and change into his baseball clothes. He had a game to catch.

The game went into extra innings. Merker savored every moment. It had been almost a month since he had experienced a live baseball game, which was much too long. Merker anticipated he would be exhausted, but he awoke feeling unexpectedly refreshed. He needed his baseball fix.

The drive to Ethan Jasper's office was quicker than he had expected. The traffic was surprisingly sparse. Dr. Jasper's office was quite a contrast from the lavish law offices of Robert Simon. A plain, one-story building without any pomp, it reminded Merker of his childhood and the office of his old family doctor. He tried, but he couldn't remember his old doctor's name.

Several amateurish paintings adorned the walls of the simple, but clean waiting area. Merker felt much more comfortable in this office but something was missing. It came to him. There were no patients. A lone person was seated at a desk mulling over some papers.

"You must be Mr. Merker. The doctor is expecting you." The elderly lady shuffled from her chair to escort Merker to the back of the building where Jasper had his office.

"My name is Mary." Her hand trembled as she grabbed Merker's arm.

"Nice to meet you, Mary; my name is Marcus."

Mary led Merker into Jasper's office. *This is an office*, Merker thought to himself. Books and magazines were strewn everywhere, yet Merker could sense a strange type of orderliness to this jumble.

Jasper removed several large textbooks from a chair to make space for Merker to sit. "Please take a seat and excuse the mess."

Merker had to shuffle his feet slightly to clear an area that was free of manuscripts. Jasper reminded Merker of his grandfather—both men had eyebrows that connected in the middle, large ears, and large bulbous noses. Jasper either looked like his grandfather or a troll. Actually Jasper was probably just a few years older than Merker, but Merker thought of himself as much younger. "I appreciate your making time for me."

"My pleasure. When you told me that my friend and colleague Jonas Cisko had died I nearly collapsed." Jasper's eyes welled with tears.

"I'm sorry, I thought you already knew," Merker said apologetically.

"No real harm done, just a bit of a shock. Now what can I answer about Jonas?" Jasper sighed as he thought of his friend and mentor.

"As far as I can tell, you were one of, if not the last person to speak with Dr. Cisko. I wonder if you can remember any of that conversation."

"You came all this way to ask me that?"

"First, I had to come to California for some other business. I also wanted to discuss Dr. Cisko with you in some detail and I felt I could do this best face to face."

"Fair enough. I called Jonas about a medical case. Over the years when either of us had a particularly difficult or interesting case, we'd call each other to discuss the details. After we discussed my case in some detail, I could sense from Jonas's tone that he was either preoccupied or depressed. He told me some confidential information that I'm really not a liberty to discuss."

"Information about the committee?"

"You know about the committee? Maybe it wasn't as confidential as I thought." Jasper gave Merker a thoughtful look.

"Can you tell me about it?"

"Before I can trust you with what I know, why don't you first convince me of what you know."

Merker understood. "I was a good friend of Dr. Cisko's. He called me the day after you spoke to him. He was worried about a committee he was on. He was also worried about his safety."

"His safety?"

"Yes. At first I was surprised at his concern, but after I started to investigate I think his concerns were justified."

"I don't mean to sound condescending, but why would he confide in you?" Jasper asked.

"Like I said, we were friends. Good friends. Plus, I'm a private detective."

"So what did you find in your investigation that concerned you?"

"Do you know a Dr. Harvey Kahn or a Van Gregory?" Merker inquired.

"I know Harvey, but not the other person. What does Harvey have to do with this?" Jasper's interest was piqued.

"They both visited Jonas the night he called you. Did he mention anything about their meeting?"

"No, nothing at all."

"I was hoping you would have some insight into that meeting. From what Jonas told me they sort of threatened him, and that was probably a large part of his concern."

"What was their threat?"

"I really can't remember. You see, I'd taken Dr. Cisko rather lightly and agreed to follow these guys around for a day or two to see if I could turn anything up. Unfortunately, I never got back in touch with Dr. Cisko before his death. I feel guilty for this. I really owed him."

"So do I. Jonas Cisko is and was very special to me. When I was in my residency he was my trainer and my role model. As you can see, I'm a year or two older than Jonas; maybe he took me under his wing, because he felt sorry for me.

"In my former life, before becoming a physician I was a pharmacist. I didn't find that as rewarding as I initially thought it would be, so I decided to apply to medical school. In those days it was fairly competitive and I was initially rejected. My grades and board scores were adequate but not great. My medical school advisor suggested I apply to an osteopathic school, since they were generally easier to get into and were much more receptive to people who were a little older and had a previous career. So I became a DO.

"After I completed my undergraduate work I was accepted to a residency program in Internal Medicine. Jonas Cisko was one of my first trainers. He was remarkable. Very intelligent and caring and an excellent teacher. He definitely went out of his way for me and I still feel indebted to him for that."

"I thought you were an MD?" Merker recalled the MD designation outside Dr. Jasper's office.

"I am. I was just getting to that. While I was in my residency there was a amalgamation of the DO's and MD's in the state of California."

"The merger," Merker said.

"Yes, the merger. You've heard of the merger?"

Merker nodded.

"Anyway, I felt torn between the profession that gave me the opportunity to become a physician and the possibility of joining what I perceived as mainline medicine. Although Jonas fought the merger initially, when he realized it was an inevitability he dropped the fight. He knew he couldn't conciliate, so he looked for other options for himself. Yet, he counseled me to become a MD. He convinced me that at my stage it was a smart career move."

"So you became a MD because of his recommendation?"

"Not exactly, but Jonas's recommendation was probably the deciding factor." Jasper squinted. When he did that he definitely looked like a troll.

"If he recommended you to become an MD, why didn't he?"

"It was a little different for Jonas. Because he had already completed his training, he would either have had to get additional training to maintain his specialty or be designated as a general practitioner."

"Interesting. And you kept in touch over the years?"

"Not as much as I would have liked. But we called each other, as I said before, on interesting cases and sometimes just to say hello."

"Is there anything else you can remember from your last conversation?"

Jasper hesitated. "There is something else. I felt he was distracted by something. Jonas mentioned something to me, something I hadn't thought about or heard for thirty years. He mentioned he thought they resurrected Caldo." Jasper again exhibited his troll expression.

"What's that?" Merker leaned closer.

"Well, it's a theory or speculation or something in that vein. Back when the merger was taking place there were hundreds of rumors, maybe thousands. One rumor that kept recurring was

Caldo. Caldo was a list of DO's, influential DO's, who were marked by the MD's. As the story goes, there were a group of MD's who over the years collected information, incriminating information, initially on other MD's and then on some DO's. These MD's would then use that information as an inducement to make the other docs do things."

"You mean blackmail."

"Yeah, I guess basically it was blackmail. The trouble was no one could ever prove any of this. When the merger was finalized all this discussion essentially ended. Although he never said anything to me, I think Jonas was on the list."

"What makes you say that?"

"Just a hunch. It was the way he acted when the subject was brought up in conversation. I don't know, just a hunch."

"He brought up this Caldo when you last talked?"

"Yes, but indirectly. I can't remember how he exactly put it but it was something like 'this committee reminds me of the old Caldo days,' something like that."

"I see, that's a bit strange." Merker thought for a second before he continued. "Do you believe Caldo exists?"

"I did back then, but doubt it would have remained in hibernation all these years," Jasper replied.

"What makes you think it was in hibernation?"

"Good point. I guess it could still be active doing other deeds."

"Why Caldo? What does it mean?"

"Oh, it stands for California DO. Cal-DO, get it?"

Merker gave a half-hearted grin. "You mentioned bringing back Caldo, do you know who *they* are?"

"No, I have no idea."

Merker stopped and looked at the ceiling, then looked back at Dr. Jasper. "Can I ask you a totally off-the-wall question?"

"Sure"

"Do the names Wilcox and Trulof mean anything to you?"

Jasper again resembled a troll. "You have to be kidding!"

"No, why?"

"Wilcox and Trulof were both DO's and very politically active at the time of the California merger. Although I was in my residency and basically tried to stay out of the controversy, I knew who they were. They were very outspoken. I could be wrong on this, but I'm pretty sure that they were the ones who started the rumors on Caldo."

"You're kidding me?"

"No, but remember this was a long time ago, and I really wasn't as involved as many others, but I believe they were the ones who started it all. You know who would probably remember them better than me? Harvey Kahn. Harvey was involved in all of that stuff. I believe he was pretty friendly with either Wilcox or Trulof. He'll be able to help you."

"Harvey's dead." Merker clasped his hands and rested them on his lap.

"No, when?"

"Couple of days ago, car accident."

"Do you think any of this is related?"

Merker shrugged his shoulders. "Do you know how to get in touch with Trulof?"

"No idea, or for that matter Wilcox either."

"Wilcox died in '65," Merker said dejectedly.

Jasper shook his head. "I think I knew that. You can see how out of touch I really am. But I'll tell you what I'll do. Let me ask around. Maybe I can find out what happened to Trulof."

"That would be great. I can use all the help I can get."

"I'll see what I can do. It's the least I can do for Jonas. Although I hadn't seen him in a couple of years, I'm really going to miss him."

"Me too. He was a special person."

They were both silent for a moment.

"By the way, do you know a Dr. Callison, Steven Callison?" Merker asked.

"No, that name doesn't sound familiar at all."

"He's the doc that took Dr. Cisko's place on the committee."

"Nope, never heard of him." Jasper shook his head.

"Anyway, I have to get going. I have a plane to catch, going to big D."

"I'll keep in touch."

Merker gave Dr. Jasper his card and wrote his home number

on the back. "Call me any time on this number. It's a machine, but I check the messages daily."

Merker left for the hotel and then to the airport. Hopefully he now had something to go on.

13

Merker arrived at the Dallas-Fort Worth International Airport during one of the infamous summer thunderstorms he had heard about. The storm had definitely lived up to its reputation. The turbulence on the airplane was quite impressive, creating an experience any roller coaster aficionado would envy. Merker felt fortunate he did not have to use his little bag. Many of his co-passengers left the plane accompanied by a greenish complexion and a little bag full of memories.

By the time Merker had rented the car, the storm had passed and the sun was attempting to peek through the clouds. Merker drove to Callison's office in Fort Worth, which was located in the Medical School complex and afforded one of the best views of the skyline of the city. When the storm abated, a rainbow outlined the city just as rays of sunlight started to break through the clouds.

Once in the complex, Merker was directed down a long corridor to the reception area for the Division of General Internal Medicine. The receptionist then referred Merker to Callison's secretary, Helen Hunter.

"May I help you?" Helen Hunter inquired, peering over her glasses.

"Yes, I was wondering if I could see Dr. Callison?"

"Do you have an appointment?" Helen glanced down at her appointment schedule for Dr. Callison.

"No, not exactly. But I only need a couple of minutes."

"Can you tell me why you need to meet with Dr. Callison?"

"It's a private matter."

"I'm sorry, but Dr. Callison isn't scheduling any meetings at this time. If you care to give me your name and number, I'll be glad to leave him a message."

Merker realized this was going to be more difficult than he

had anticipated. "My name is Hack Wilson." Merker gave her the name of his all-time favorite Cub, a name he routinely used as an alias.

"I'll give him the message." The tone in Helen's voice suggested it was highly unlikely Merker would get a meeting with Dr. Callison any time in the near future.

Merker was tired and still a little shaken from his flight. He decided to check into the local hotel and take a nap. He could deal with this much better once he had rested.

The following morning Helen gave Callison the message about Hack Wilson's request for an appointment. As usual she added her editorial comment, "he was either selling something or had a complaint." Callison disposed of the message in the trash. He couldn't be bothered. He had more important things to do. Mrs. Kodack was being discharged from the hospital and they had overbooked his outpatients.

The Kodack family was eagerly awaiting Callison's arrival, anticipating his discharge instructions. The mood in the room was even more upbeat than usual. Mrs. Kodack wouldn't allow anyone to feel sorry for her during her illness; she demanded they all keep a positive attitude.

Over the past weeks Callison had spent many hours with the Kodack family unintentionally allowing his emotions to enter into his professional relationship. The Kodacks had reciprocated Callison's feelings with their own. They exchanged some pleasantries before Callison reviewed the detailed instructions for Mrs. Kodack's care at home. After he completed the instructions, Mrs. Kodack gave Callison an all-encompassing hug, conveying her gratitude and appreciation for all he had done. This was one of those moments that reminded Callison of why he went into medicine.

Outside Mrs. Kodack's room Callison stopped to review his patient list. He didn't notice the man in the seersucker suit who was following him. When Callison pressed the down button on the elevator, he was tapped on the shoulder by the stranger in a seersucker suit, Marcus Merker.

"Dr. Callison?"

"Yes, do I know you?"

"No, but you might have known a friend of mine, Dr. Jonas Cisko. My name is Merker, Marcus Merker."

"Jonas Cisko?" Callison knew that name but couldn't place it.

"Yes, Jonas Cisko—the man you replaced on the . . ."

"On the committee. He was a friend of yours?"

"Yeah, a good friend and a good man."

"That's what I heard. What can I do for you?"

"If it wouldn't be to much of a bother, I was wondering if you would have a couple of minutes to talk."

"Actually, now is a little inconvenient, but if you leave me your number I'll call you when I finish rounds."

"If you don't mind I'll just wait for you."

"I might be several hours."

"No problem. I have no plans and would really like to talk to you."

This conversation seemed strange to Callison, but there was something about Merker that interested him. "All right, why don't you wait for me in the cafeteria on the second floor. I'll be there as soon as I can."

"Thanks Doc, I really do appreciate this."

Callison and Merker left in opposite directions, Callison to the top floor of the building and Merker down to the second floor cafeteria. Callison continued his rounds, but couldn't fully concentrate. Merker's remarks had been distracting and his curiosity was getting the better of him.

It was actually a little less than an hour when Callison joined Merker in the cafeteria. Merker had completed the paper and was people-watching when he noticed Callison and waved.

"Can I get you another cup of coffee?" Callison asked before he sat.

"No thanks, Doc. I've already had my quota for the day."

"How about a soft drink?"

"No, nothing. Thanks anyway."

Callison grabbed a diet soda and joined Merker at his

table. "So, why are you here?"

Merker didn't want to give Callison too much information, especially if he was part of some larger plot. "I was asked by Dr. Cisko's family to see if you were given any of Dr. Cisko's papers."

Callison looked puzzled. "Did you come from Chicago to ask me that?"

Merker realized his question was a little too shallow. "Actually, that was only part of the reason. The other part was to find out what you knew of Dr. Cisko."

"I never knew Dr. Cisko, nor have I received any of his papers from the committee. Even if I had, they probably would have been confidential and I wouldn't have been able to give them to you anyway."

"No, you don't understand. I don't have an interest in any of the stuff from the committee. The family is convinced Dr. Cisko was in the process of rewriting his will. They thought his will might be mixed up with the papers from the committee, since he was probably working on both sets of papers at the time of his death."

"Let me make this perfectly clear—I have never received any papers from Dr. Cisko, no papers pertaining to the committee nor to his will. Do you understand?"

"Crystal clear." Merker knew this line of questioning would get him nowhere, so he decided to try a entirely different topic. "Does the name Caldo mean anything to you?"

"Caldo? Never heard of him."

Callison was either a very good liar or he had no idea about Caldo. "Doesn't really matter," Merker mumbled. He realized his technique was stale and too roundabout, undermining his effectiveness as an investigator.

Callison was getting irritated at the trivial nature of Merker's questions. "I don't want to be rude but if you don't have any further questions, I really do have to get going."

Merker pulled out a photograph he had taken of Van Gregory and Harvey Kahn. He handed the photo to Callison. "Do you know either of these two men?"

Callison studied the picture for a few seconds. "No, don't know either of them. Why? Is one of them Caldo?"

"No, neither of them is Caldo." Merker thought, *This guy is good.*

"So who are they?"

"The one in the glasses is named Van Gregory, he works for the AMA. The other one is Dr. Harvey Kahn. You won't be running into him, since he just died recently."

"Why would you ask if I knew either of them?"

Merker decided to go with the flow of the conversation. "They were the last people known to have been with Dr. Cisko."

"So?"

"So, I think they might have had something to do with his death."

"You think they killed Dr. Cisko?"

"No, not necessarily killed him." Merker paused as he pondered whether to delve any further. "Can I be totally frank with you?"

Merker now had Callison's complete attention. "Sure."

"Dr. Cisko was concerned about the committee."

"My committee?"

"Yeah, your committee. He asked me to check out these two guys." Merker pointed to the pictures of Gregory and Kahn. "Anyway, while I was in the process of checking them out, he died. Something about Dr. Cisko's death made me suspicious that his death wasn't exactly on the up and up. Which brings me to you."

"Why me?" Callison raised his voice, which caused two women at the opposite end of the cafeteria to stop their conversation and look.

Merker and Callison looked at the women, who returned to their own conversation. Merker continued. "If Dr. Cisko's concerns were real, then maybe somebody wanted you on this committee instead of him."

"Who would want me? That doesn't make any sense at all." Callison's voice cracked.

"You're probably right. But I still feel Dr. Cisko's death wasn't totally innocent."

"What makes you say that?"

"I'd rather not go into any more details at this time but trust

136

me, his death wasn't natural."

"Why should I trust you? I don't even know you." Callison was getting irritated.

"I know that, but before this committee is over you'll need to trust someone, and that should be me."

"Listen, I don't know why you're telling me all this and I don't appreciate it. The committee is fine, I'm fine and you sound totally paranoid. I'm sorry that Dr. Cisko died. He obviously was a close friend of yours, but I think you've blown his death totally out of proportion and you need to get on with your life. If you're trying to scare or frighten me, you're not succeeding."

"No doctor, please don't take this the wrong way. I have no intention at all of upsetting you." Merker thought carefully. "I just have a feeling that some people, possibly some very powerful people, want to have some influence over your committee."

"And they would kill to gain this control? I find this highly unlikely." Callison's sardonic tone was not lost on Merker.

Merker wanted to retaliate but controlled his response. "Maybe so, and maybe I'm being a bit paranoid but if you notice anything out of the ordinary, or if you happen to run into the individual in the photo, please be careful, just in case."

Callison said nothing.

Merker realized the conversation was over. He had revealed much more than he intended, but there was nothing he could do about that now. He felt confident that Callison had nothing to do with Cisko's death, so he had accomplished his main objective, and that would have to suffice. "I'm sorry to take so much of your time. If anything comes up, I'd appreciate if you could call me collect. I wrote my number and name on the back of this picture, which I'd like you to keep."

"Okay, I'll do that." Callison said passively. He placed the picture in his pocket as he stood up from the table. Merker followed his lead, they shook hands and Callison left.

Merker sat back down at the table and reviewed the conversation in his mind. He had revealed more than he had found out. It had been some time since he needed his investigative skills—he had to do better. He looked at his watch. He could eat dinner in the hospital's cafeteria and still make it back to the hotel in time to catch the Cubs game on cable. He also needed to call to make his reservation for his return flight to Chicago. It was time to go home.

Callison returned to his office still troubled by his conversation with Merker. He was seated at his desk going through his mail when Helen entered. "I see Mr. Wilson caught up with you."

"Who?"

"Mr. Wilson, you know the man you were talking to in the cafeteria."

"Wilson? He said his name was Merker. In fact, he wrote it down on this picture." Callison pulled out the photograph that Merker had given him and read the name printed on the back, Marcus Merker. "Are you telling me that was the man who was here earlier and called himself Wilson?"

"Yes, that was the Hack Wilson who was in this office yesterday."

"Why would he lie about his name?" Callison was perplexed.

"Got me." Helen shrugged her shoulders.

"Me too. He's probably nuts." Callison tossed the photo into the top drawer of his desk and returned to his mail. Helen took his hint and left to resume her work.

14

The cab turned onto 44th street in front of the Algonquin Hotel. As usual, there were several cabs congregated in front so one more wouldn't matter. Rasta loved this hotel because he felt it exemplified the quintessential New York experience of a bygone era. Rasta had preceded the others in "the group," who would be arriving tomorrow, so he could ensure that all the accommodations were in order. He had reserved a special dining area he had used previously, which combined the appropriate atmosphere with the needed privacy.

The following evening the four members of "the group" convened in the lobby of the hotel. They sauntered past the Rose Room where Dorothy Parker had held court with the various wits and literati of her time. Rasta hoped, somehow, their wisdom had lingered and would inculcate their conversation this evening.

The members of the "group" included Rasta, Chester Timmons, Marvin Barnes, and Lazlo Wilovsky. Lazlo Wilovsky, the eldest of the group by about ten years, was rehashing the consequences of his recent, second bypass surgery, which was complicated by a post-operative pneumonia, leaving him in his current weakened and debilitated state. Lazlo's white hair had thinned considerably and he had lost forty or fifty pounds.

Marvin Barnes on the other hand had gained the weight that Lazlo had lost. Marvin could never have been described as thin but he was now morbidly obese. In spite of his intellect, which was impressive, Marvin still lacked common sense. He had never learned the art of tact or restraint. He also still had the annoying habit of smoking large, expensive Cuban cigars, and still took offense when others were less than tolerant of his unhealthy habit.

The four members of "the group" were seated in a quiet

alcove off the dining area in the Rose Room, cocktails in hand, ready for a serious discussion.

Rasta began. "I want to thank you all for coming on such short notice. I know your schedules are very hectic."

They all acknowledged each other.

Marvin Barnes was not a fan of such pleasantries and started the discussion in earnest. "Why the secrecy and immediacy of this meeting?"

"There are several serious matters that we all need to be apprised of and then we need to make some tough decisions," Rasta said. "Because of the delicacy of the topics to be discussed I felt it necessary to meet in person. I'm sure when you hear what they are, you'll agree."

They silently looked at each other.

Rasta continued, "Let me start with a brief review of what's new with the organization." The organization was the group to which they all belonged, both as members and administrators. It had started decades before, actually during the Second World War. It was started by an MD by the name of Wayne Tatum. Dr. Tatum had been serving in the Medical Corps of the Army during the Battle of the Bulge, when he came into contact with a medic by the name of Miles Gance. Gance had been totally committed to the healing arts, working endlessly helping his compatriots in their hour of medical need.

Stationed near the front lines, they were setting up a triage unit when a sniper infiltrated their camp and shot Dr. Tatum in the chest. Without any hesitation, Gance administered the appropriate first aid and literally saved Dr. Tatum's life. From that moment, Dr. Tatum felt a profound obligation to Miles Gance. Since Dr. Tatum came from a large and very prestigious family, based in both New York City and Boston, his sphere of influence was extensive. When Tatum learned Gance had been turned down for acceptance to medical school because his medical board scores were inadequate, he made it his personal quest to assist Miles Gance in his lifelong dream of becoming a physician. Tatum achieved his quest, and Miles did get accepted to medical school after he was discharged from the Army. Unfortunately, Miles never actually attended medical school. He was

140

killed in a hunting accident two days before he was scheduled to start school.

After his grieving, Tatum realized there was something he could do to honor Miles. Tatum decided to create a system to assist students who for some reason were unable to gain acceptance to medical school but like Miles had his passion for medicine. These were people who needed help from an organization with significant political and medical clout that could circumvent the normal system. It was called the Gance system and was to function as a legacy to Miles Gance.

In the early fifties Tatum was able to assist several deserving students who had been rejected from medical school for sundry reasons. Their successful careers would be a living testament to Miles Gance.

By the mid-fifties the Gance system had mushroomed into a large scale effort, forcing Dr. Tatum to recruit one of his first proselytes, Dr. George Alexander, to help him administrate. With the assistance of Dr. Alexander, a new system was formalized and the organization was instituted, out of which "the list" was introduced. "The list" contained all the pertinent data relative to all those assisted by the organization. "The list" was initially referred to as either the Gance or the Tatum list, which was shortened to just "the list" by the time Dr. Alexander took control of the organization.

In 1957 Dr. Tatum was diagnosed with colon cancer, resulting in a rapid deterioration of his health, eventually forcing him to bestow full control of the organization to Alexander. Dr. Tatum died on New Year's Day 1958 after assisting nearly sixty individuals in fulfilling their dreams to become a doctor.

Under the leadership of Dr. Alexander the organization flourished while taking on a somewhat different viewpoint. Alexander did not have the political connections of Dr. Tatum, nor his style or panache, but what Alexander did have was the insight to see the potential power intrinsic to such an organization. Alexander realized that many of the initial benefactors of Dr. Tatum's generosity had now completed their medical training and had already been placed in prominent positions. Using the information he had, Alexander was able to ask certain favors of these individuals, initially to help promote the careers of other graduates of the Gance list, thus forming a powerful infrastructure within the medical community.

Alexander significantly increased the numbers of those helped and "the list" doubled in the first few years under his direction. Alexander also accepted candidates who did not meet the same rigorous standards, nor the same quality and commitment, that Tatum had demanded. By the end of the decade, it was not unusual to require an endowment to the organization to enable someone access into medical school. This new policy, with its resultant cash flow, greatly expanded "the list," increasing the sphere of influence of the organization, while creating a lucrative side business for Alexander.

Alexander also utilized a similar system to assist people in achieving admission to law school. Over the years Alexander had amassed quite a stable of physicians and lawyers. By the early sixties he was poised to see how powerful the organization had become. He needed a pilot program to test the political influence and work out the kinks, if any existed. His pilot program was called the Caldo project. His objective was to merge the osteopathic profession into the allopathic profession in California and then the rest of the country. There were several DO's who had been products of the Gance system; however, their numbers were small, and Alexander had virtually exhausted all his osteopathic resources to fulfill his California initiative.

A similar program had been attempted in Pennsylvania, but had failed miserably without their political connections in the osteopathic profession. It was the failure of the Pennsylvania project that initiated Dr. Alexander's downward spiral. Much of the infrastructure had been lost in the Pennsylvania debacle, and by 1969 Dr. Alexander had lost control of the organization to Dr. Alan Smithee, who wanted to return to the precepts originated by Dr. Tatum. Shortly after Smithee gained control, George Alexander committed suicide.

In 1970 Smithee decided to recruit four members to help administrate the new organization. He called these four the administrative group, and they were charged with restoring the mission of the organization back to its roots. Those four members were Doctors Rasta, Timmons, Barnes, and Wilovsky, later referred to as simply "the group."

Each had been recruited because of their various skills and talents as well as their respective positions in the medical community. They were also bonded by their ties to the organization, which had assisted them when they had strayed prior to their medical careers.

Over the years they had met to discuss various controversial issues. The issues they needed to address today were as contentious and dangerous as any with which they had ever dealt.

"We recently had to hire Van Gregory again," Rasta said. "Mr. Gregory was brought in to investigate a member of the organization, Jonas Cisko, who had been given a key position on a committee on which both Chester and I sit."

"Why weren't we informed Gregory was brought in?" Barnes seemed to be irritated he had not been included in this decision.

"I believe it was felt to be a fairly routine investigation. As you should recall, we decided many years ago to let the local administration in Chicago handle these routine investigations and only include the group if there was a complication. Well there was a complication, and that's why we're meeting now."

"I don't know if I have the stamina to go through another lengthy process like some in the past." Wilovsky's concerns were legitimate; he appeared to be exhausted before they even started their discussion.

"Lazlo, I believe I speak for all of us. We will support you in whatever decision you make, but your input is really invaluable." As Rasta concluded his remarks, the others shook their heads in agreement.

"I appreciate your support, all your support." Wilovsky acknowledged each of them with a nod and a grin. "As you know I've had some serious medical problems recently, but as long as I can physically handle the stress, I'll try to do my share."

Rasta continued. "Mr. Gregory did confirm Dr. Cisko was wavering on his position apropos to the merger situation, which we had discussed in detail in the past. Gregory attempted to use an argument that had previously been effective in persuading Dr. Cisko. Unfortunately, this line of reasoning had lost its effec-

143

tiveness. So Gregory resorted to his alternate plan, which involved using Cisko's son, who is currently in line for an appointment to the Federal Court of Appeals." Rasta gave a wry smile before he continued. "It appears Gregory had uncovered some indiscretion in the past that could tarnish Cisko's son's career. Anyway, when Gregory broached this subject with Cisko, he became so upset it appears to have precipitated his infarction."

"Was Gregory present when he arrested?" Barnes asked.

"Yes, so was Dr. Harvey Kahn. They decided, after their initial assessment, to leave and not notify the authorities."

"Are you serious? They left him lying there?" Timmons was appalled.

"Think about it. He was dead. If they called in the authorities it would have complicated matters greatly. It might have led them to us."

"I doubt that. And even if it did, so what?" Timmons was still horrified by the fact that they left a man to die.

"Gregory felt, and I agree, it wasn't worth the risk." Rasta realized he was on shaky ground. He wasn't convinced Gregory's decision was correct, but knew he needed to support him.

"I agree with Timmons," Barnes said emotionally. "I can't envision a physician could passively watch as a colleague was dying. The more I think of it, the more it infuriates me that nothing was done. In addition, once you were notified, you compounded the offense by remaining silent." Barnes' emotion increased in intensity with each word. "I find this entire scenario to be unconscionable, and I refuse to be any part of this."

Barnes' voice started to escalate, and some of the patrons of the restaurant turned to see what the commotion was about. Barnes was now standing, his face flushed and the veins in his neck distended.

Wilovsky slowly stood and stretched his arm over the shoulder of his friend—a gesture that had an immediate calming effect. "Marvin, calm down. You're among friends and we can discuss this in a quiet and rational manner. I'm also upset, but we don't need to bring any additional attention to our meeting." Wilovsky's words seemed to calm Barnes, and their audience returned to their own meals and conversations. Wilovsky and Barnes quietly sat in their respective seats.

"You're right, Lazlo, I just get so incensed sometimes." This was as close to an apology as Barnes could muster.

Wilovsky and Barnes were again seated when Wilovsky focused his attention on Rasta. "Marvin's right. That type of action is reprehensible. After all, we are physicians dedicated to the preservation of life, not this. We must do something to rectify this situation and notify the authorities." He stared directly at Rasta. Although Wilovsky had lost some of his physical strength he was still a strong man, and his gaze was intense.

"I don't think that would be such a good idea." Rasta returned Wilovsky's stare with one of his own.

"I think you're outvoted." Barnes' voice once again started to intensify.

"Before we get carried away, I think you need to hear the rest of the story . . . so we can make an informed decision." Rasta turned to face Barnes and then back to Wilovsky.

"Fair enough." Wilovsky sat back in his chair and folded his arms across his chest.

Rasta waited for any other remark. Hearing none he continued. "After the death of Dr. Cisko, Dr. Kahn started to become unnerved. Mr. Gregory informed the organization of Dr. Kahn's condition and . . ."

"Are you telling us that Kahn was killed?" Barnes interrupted.

Rasta hesitated. His facial expression along with the perceptible pause in the conversation, confirmed his query. "Let's say that his death might not have been an accident."

"I can't believe what I'm hearing! Are you nuts? You're implicating all of us in murder." Barnes was on the verge of losing it again.

"I didn't say he was killed. I believe his death was probably accidental, but I have my suspicions. I really don't know—nor do I want to know." Rasta looked past Barnes to see if anyone had overheard their conversation. There was no indication anyone was even aware of them since Barnes' outburst.

"What you are saying does seem to involve us in the deaths

of both Cisko and Kahn. And I personally don't appreciate it," Wilovsky said slowly, his eyes meeting Rasta's again.

"I realize this information is unsettling. Now you can appreciate why we had to meet in person."

"So what are we going to do about this?" Timmons, overwhelmed by the circumstances, could barely voice his concerns.

"That's why we are meeting—to discuss options. However, there is more." Rasta almost appeared to be enjoying this.

"You got to be kidding." Timmons was nearly in tears and Barnes was starting to fume.

"Before we proceed, I feel we need to decide whether we can handle any more of this type of news at this time." Wilovsky said.

Rasta appreciated Wilovsky's concern but was compelled to press on. "We need to discuss this sometime and now seems as good a time as any. Anyway the rest of the story isn't nearly as disagreeable."

"Let's get on with it," Barnes said matter-of-factly.

"After the deaths of Cisko and Kahn, Mr. Gregory was given an assignment that appeared on the surface to be benign. He was to follow the new member on the committee, Cisko's replacement, Dr. Steven Callison. This was fairly routine. We had made similar inquiries on all the other members on this committee."

"I remember discussing this in the past," Wilovsky said.

"Me too," Timmons assented.

"Anyway, Mr. Gregory followed Callison back to Texas strictly for observation purposes and was essentially finding nothing of any importance to report. Then I get a phone call from Robert Simon, who happens to be Dr. Kahn's lawyer in California. He was the one responsible for settling Kahn's estate."

"Why would he call you?" Timmons asked.

"I'm getting to that. It seems a Marcus Merker, a private detective from Chicago, visited the offices of Robert Simon inquiring about Harvey Kahn. Simon told me he felt Merker was probing for something, although he wasn't clear what that something was."

"How did he have your number?" Timmons said.

"Harvey Kahn had left instructions in his will to call me if anyone inquired about his professional career after his death. I wasn't aware that Harvey had done this, so the call came as a surprise to me."

"Knowing Harvey and how concerned he was about maintaining his image, it really isn't that surprising that he would extend his concern to his life after death." Timmons gave a trace of a smile.

Rasta forced a smile in return and continued. "I had someone check out Marcus Merker. He was a personal friend of Jonas Cisko."

"Holy shit!" Barnes blurted out.

"My sentiments exactly." Rasta continued, "Merker told Simon that he was working for the family of Dr. Cisko, looking for the last photograph taken of Dr. Cisko. Simon thought this to be a feeble excuse. After Simon's call we made some further inquiries; however, we're not sure whether his intentions were as he stated or not. But there is some data to suggest Merker is investigating the death of Jonas Cisko. What we don't know is why."

"This is very disconcerting." Wilovsky's face began to flush.

"Indeed it is. But there's more. When I was given this information about Merker, one of the individuals I discussed this with was Van Gregory. Mr. Gregory did not know Mr. Merker, but asked if I could fax him a copy of the file we had on him. I saw no reason not to comply, so I sent the fax. Two days ago I got a call from Gregory that Merker had just met with Callison in Texas." Rasta sat back and watched the others. He felt drained, yet at the same time a tremendous weight had lifted.

"This is quite a predicament." Timmons was scratching the back of his head furiously.

"That's an understatement. What are we going to do?" Barnes for lack of anything better to do, lit one of his imported cigars, only to be asked to extinguish it seconds later.

"As difficult as it was to tell you this, it was much more difficult to keep this information to myself until now. How this got so out-of-hand I can't explain, but I'm concerned it won't go away unless we do something about it." Beads of sweat appeared on Rasta's forehead and one drop slowly moved down the side of his face, tracking next to his eye like a tear.

"Let me review the information we have," Wilovsky said. "First, Dr. Cisko's death was, as far as we know, natural. Correct?"

"Correct." Rasta answered.

"Second, to our knowledge, Kahn's death was accidental. Correct?"

"Correct," Rasta and Barnes both answered.

"Third, we have no real knowledge that this Merker person is investigating the death of Dr. Cisko. He may in reality be working for Cisko's estate as he said. Correct?"

"Correct," All three chimed in unison.

"Do we know if Callison knew Merker prior to any of this?"

"No," Rasta replied.

"Then we need to get more information before we can make any informed recommendations. The last thing we need is another Chalitz incident." Wilovsky's point was well taken since they were aware of the gravity of the situation, and its potential consequences.

The consequences from the Jennifer Chalitz misfortune had bonded the four members of the group since the incident occurred in 1972. The group had been recruited only two years before and by 1972 had effectively streamlined the organization, so that only major issues would need their attention. An administrative secretary by the name of Jennifer Chalitz had made a formal complaint about Dr. Dudley Pector, a physician rapidly gaining national and international prominence and a loyal member of the organization.

While Dr. Pector was in undergraduate school, he was accused of raping a coed. The charges were reduced to assault. Nevertheless, it kept him from being accepted to medical school. Pector's record prior to the incident was flawless. With the assistance of the organization he was able to have the charges dropped. After his residency, Pector's career was on the fast track. He was being groomed for a directorship at the NIH. It was powerful people like Pector that the organization needed to assist them.

When a complaint was filed by Jennifer Chalitz, claiming she was physically attacked and assaulted by Dr. Pector, it was temporarily misplaced so the organization could first investigate. The group met with Ms. Chalitz and found her story compelling, but without any other witnesses, not convincing enough to make any formal recommendations at that time. The group decided to hire a man recently retired from covert operations. The man they hired was Van Gregory.

Mr. Gregory learned Ms. Chalitz had had an affair with a married man, her boss, the previous year. At the time of the affair her boss had been separated from his wife, but they had since reconciled. Mr. Gregory discovered an encounter in which they had one last liaison after her boss' reconciliation. Gregory informed Ms. Chalitz her affair would have to be revealed if she pursued her complaint.

Dr. Pector countered with his defense, stating he was the one seduced. He stated he could prove Ms. Chalitz had a history of similar types of sordid affairs in the past.

Gregory approached Ms. Chalitz, and suggested if she were to drop her charges before they were formally filed, none of this information needed to be divulged. The group agreed with the recommendations from Mr. Gregory and decided to ignore the previous report in the file, suggesting this might have been a repeat offense by Dr. Pector. The charges were never officially filed and three weeks later, Jennifer Chalitz was brutally raped and murdered by Dr. Pector. There was a routine investigation of her death, but Van Gregory was able to bury any evidence that could have implicated the group.

Pector killed himself shortly after Chalitz' death, thus severing the last link to the group. From that time and forevermore, the group was inexorably linked with each other, as well as with Van Gregory. Since that time in 1972, the name Jennifer Chalitz was never mentioned again . . . not until this evening.

15

Callison had been in a sound sleep when he was startled awake by the ringing of the phone. The hospital had called to inform him of a patient in the emergency room with a stroke. The resident assured Callison the patient was stable and wouldn't require his attention that evening.

Callison had just fallen back asleep when he was snapped awake. It was the phone again, only this time it was Mrs. Kodack who was in the emergency room. A veil of depression overcame Callison as he expected the worst. Natalie, who virtually never awakened from the phone calls in the middle of the night bolted upright in bed sensing this call was different. While Callison dressed, he thought of Mrs. Kodack and her courage and fortitude. Somehow thinking of the Kodack family and all they had endured placed his problems in a different perspective.

When he reached the hospital and entered the room where they were working on Mrs. Kodack, Callison knew immediately she was gone. CPR was still being conducted and all eyes immediately turned in his direction. The remainder of the code was surrealistic—Callison could recall the events, yet at the same time felt distanced from the entire episode. When it was officially over, there was an inexplicable calm.

In all the years and codes and deaths he attended, this one was different. It was almost mystical. He could sense Mrs. Kodack was truly and finally at peace. Callison chose to inform the family. Although the chaplain of the hospital offered to accompany him this was something he needed to do alone.

The small room where the family had been sequestered was quiet. Mr. Kodack, his daughter, and granddaughter were all seated on a couch, huddled together clinging to their last ray of hope. When Callison entered they knew without a word being said. They all sat and cried. Callison wanted to join them in their

150

tears, but he had lost the capacity to cry years ago. He spent the better part of an hour with the Kodack family. Though he had consoled many families through the years over the death of a loved one, this was as different as the death itself. The family grieved, yet celebrated her life and the love they had for her. For Callison this was a special moment.

Callison, like many of his colleagues, had spent years perfecting the art of distancing himself emotionally from his patients. This was a defense mechanism most doctors used to survive, so they could muster up the strength to face this situation time and again. Callison was impressed with the strength the Kodack family displayed, especially Mr. Kodack.

Margaret, the daughter, was outwardly more upset and unable to hold back the stream of tears, but with each tear came an acceptance of her mother's death and a new strength. Her daughter Sally held tight to her grandfather's chest as she silently sat on his lap.

Callison wanted to allow the family some time for themselves. He also realized he needed time for himself, so he excused himself and walked to the cafeteria to get a cup of coffee and collect his thoughts.

The cafeteria was officially closed, the lights dimmed, but a pot of coffee was kept warm on a heater and couple of picked over donuts remained scattered on an oversized plastic plate. Callison cautiously felt the coffee pot to ensure it was still hot. He had been fooled in the past and there was nothing worse than swallowing a large gulp of stale, cold coffee. He poured some out and carefully tasted it: lukewarm and bitter, but better than nothing.

Out of the silence came a voice, muffled yet familiar. Callison surveyed the room. It was empty, not a soul in sight, yet the voice was real. Carrying his coffee cup, he followed the trail of the voice toward a small meeting room off the cafeteria. The door to the room was ajar, and the light from inside filtered into the cafeteria, streaking across the empty tables.

As he neared the crack in the doorway, Callison could see the backs of two people sitting at the conference table. The voice was clearer now, but he still couldn't place it or hear what was actually being said. As he neared the door he held his breath, so he could hear better. Still the voices were soft, restrained but not yet discernible. He was now eavesdropping in the doorway. There was a momentary silence. Callison still hadn't breathed, when the door suddenly opened. Callison gasped, spilled his coffee on the floor, and backed up several steps.

"Steven, what are you doing?" The voice that he couldn't place was that of Sydney Snyder, the head of neurosurgery.

"I heard a voice and followed it to this room. Sorry if I'm interrupting anything." Embarrassed, Callison awkwardly wiped the coffee off his hand where it had spilled.

"No, not at all. Come on in, we're just talking."

Callison followed Snyder into the room. There was a large pot of freshly made coffee, which filled the room with its fresh aroma, and Callison discovered where the rest of the donuts had gone. They were piled on a small plate in the middle of the table. Snyder took his seat at the table where two others were already seated, Stanley Kolomy and Paul Jaffe.

Callison hardly knew Kolomy, who was relatively new on the staff, but he knew Jaffe and was aware of some of his unusual habits, such as making hospital rounds in the middle of the night.

"Good evening, gentlemen." Callison smiled as he sat in an empty seat next to Kolomy.

"Gentlemen, where? Did I miss something?" Jaffe said kiddingly, hoping to get a response. There was none.

"Scared you, didn't I?" Snyder asked Callison.

"Maybe a little." Callison refilled his coffee cup.

"A little, what's that puddle around your feet?" Jaffe guffawed. "That's what you get when you spy on us,"

"I really wasn't spying; I was just curious." Callison chuckled slightly at himself.

"Sure you were," Jaffe said sarcastically. "Anyway, what are you doing here?"

Callison had momentarily forgotten about Mrs. Kodack. When he remembered he took on a more solemn demeanor. "I lost a patient tonight, a special patient—if you know what I mean."

The three simultaneously looked down at the table, humbled by Callison's sincerity. "Sorry," mumbled Jaffe.

"Isn't it a little late to be having a meeting?" Callison said, intentionally changing the subject.

"No, not for the midnight club." Jaffe answered.

"What's the midnight club?"

"This is the midnight club," Snyder replied.

Jaffe continued, "Actually, I have always stopped off at the cafeteria whenever I'm in the hospital around midnight. It's a bit of a superstition of mine. It just so happens that Snyder's often here awaiting surgery and recently Kolomy's been here admitting someone from the ER. You see, Kolomy here has sucked up to the ER docs and has been establishing a nice little practice through the emergency room."

"That's not true." Kolomy appeared embarrassed by Jaffe's remark.

"Yeah, whatever you say. Anyway, whenever any of us are here around midnight, we make it a point to get a cup of coffee and meet in this room just to talk a little. Alderman and Belding also are members of the club but they're not here tonight."

"So what do you talk about?"

"Everything and nothing."

"Tonight we've been hearing part 98 of Jaffe's theory on how we're all getting screwed in medicine," Kolomy said in jest.

"Yeah, that's right, I'm pissed at the entire system. With the changes that are being proposed it's only going to get worse, and it's already intolerable." Jaffe's diction had a faint lisp which was accentuated and accompanied by a moist spray when he got excited.

"Intolerable? Don't you think that's a slight exaggeration?" Callison said, attempting to add some balance to the discussion.

"No, I don't think I'm exaggerating at all. More doctors than ever are leaving the profession. Malpractice claims are running rampant, third-party carriers and their managed care cohorts are constantly adding more paperwork. When added to the other busy work there's little time to actually practice medicine. Then when you do get a chance to practice, some managed care outfit is telling you that your care is too costly, you order too many tests, use too many expensive medicines, and they don't want you to take care of their patients any longer. So you try to adapt by containing costs, decrease the diagnostic testing, use generic medicines, and then you get slapped with a malpractice suit because you didn't do what you were originally doing. Now a bunch of lawyers, no less, are meeting to make up new rules which will screw up the system even more. No, I don't think I'm exaggerating." Jaffe was lisping all over the place. By the time he finished his speech, the table in front of him was soaking wet.

Kolomy poured himself a cup of coffee. "The other day a patient in my office demanded we discount their office visit. They stated that doctors make too much money and they were ripping off their patients. My office manager tried to explain our costs were in line with the other physicians in the area and we'd work with them in designing an appropriate payment plan. Before my business manager could finish, the patient became belligerent. It got real scary when several other patients also chimed in on how expensive medical care was. Just about when things were about to get totally out of hand, an elderly patient shuffled over to the crowd that had started to form. The man, who was in his eighties, interrupted the hostile group of complaining patients and asked if they would allow him to give his opinion."

Kolomy's beeper vibrated indicating he had a call. He glanced at the number on the beeper and then continued with his story. "Where was I? Oh, yes. About this time my nurse summoned me from my examining room. I arrived in the waiting room just as this old man started to talk and watched him blow them away. It was beautiful."

Kolomy gave a huge grin and sighed, then he continued. "He asked the patient who started complaining if he knew how much training it took to become a doctor. The guy tried to finagle his way out of the discussion, but the old guy wouldn't let him. When he asked the man who was complaining how he spent his decade from the age of 21 to 31, he gave some glib answer. Then this old guy responded, how would you like to have given up those years of partying to schooling, studying and working over 80 to 100 hours a week. He went on about the time, the costs, and how long it takes before school is done. I tell you, you could have heard a pin drop. The man took out his checkbook and wrote a check for the full amount and left. Some of the patients applauded, a few silently took their seats. I went back to work."

As Kolomy finished his story he sipped on the coffee he had just poured.

"That supports just what I was saying." Jaffe said. "The patients still think we're a bunch of money hungry profiteers who are to blame for all their problems relative to the medical system."

"I think this could be interpreted differently." Snyder said. "Most people do appreciate the care they're given and are satisfied with their physicians. They realize the system's out of control but don't blame the doctors solely for this. We as a profession have not done a good job at controlling those of us who do abuse the system. We have for years looked the other way, and now we're paying for it. Unfortunately, it only takes a few to taint the whole profession. Those few have put us all behind the eight ball." Snyder watched for a response.

Jaffe stammered as he started to reply. "Unfortunately, nothing is that black and white. What are we to do when they stop paying for our time, our knowledge, our expertise, and our efforts? Medicare's reimbursing less than forty cents on the dollar. Frequently it's more costly under these circumstances to see a patient than not, since the reimbursement frequently won't even cover the overhead. So what do we do to make up these deficiencies? We maximize those procedures that do get reimbursed at a decent rate. I don't consider this profiteering, but prefer to look at it as using the system they established."

"You realize your system of maximizing any procedure is now passé," Callison interjected.

"Yeah, I know that managed care now rewards less procedures. I was only reminiscing for the good old days," Jaffe lamented.

"It seems almost ironic." Kolomy said cautiously. "In the past, a good day was when your office was filled with patients. Today, in a capitated world, a good day is one when nobody shows at all. We get paid the same, whether we do something or not."

Jaffe shook his head in disgust. "Yeah, what a system."

Kolomy broke the silence. "Sydney, weren't you about to say something before all this?"

Snyder reflected for a second before responding. "Yes, I remember. In fact, this story is really quite apropos to our conversation. Last weekend, I get a call from this oncologist. I'll not mention names to protect the innocent." They all nodded. Snyder continued.

"Anyway, he had this case he wanted me to see. It was a forty-year-old woman he had taken care of two years ago for some type of cancer for which they never found a primary source. Anyway, it's early Sunday morning. Her husband calls this oncologist telling him his wife is severely constipated and is having difficulty walking. He tells the husband to meet him in the emergency room, since he's going to be making rounds at the hospital.

"Several hours pass, rounds are done and still no patient. The oncologist calls the husband back. The husband tells the oncologist he was able to reach her doctor. Actually, it was someone on call for her primary care doctor who never had even seen this patient. Anyway, the on-call doc tells the husband to give the patient an enema and if she's still constipated come in Tuesday to the office. The husband relates this to the oncologist. On further questioning, the husband now tells the oncologist that he had to carry his wife to the toilet. The oncologist tells the husband to bring his wife immediately to the hospital. The husband balks at this idea, saying the primary care doctor won't approve the emergency visit and he can't afford to pay. The oncologist assures the husband of an approval and convinces him to bring his wife to the emergency room. While waiting for the patient, the oncologist calls the doctor who recommended the enema. Initially this guy continued to refuse to approve the emergency visit, stating that specialists are frequently alarmists, and in his experience an enema should suffice."

Snyder hesitated a moment for effect. "They had some heated words, and the oncologist eventually hung up on him. When the patient arrived in the ER, she had a classic cord compression. Sensory level and all. Her bladder was grossly dis-tended and her anal sphincter tone was gone. So, he calls her pri-mary care schmuck back to let him know what's going on with his patient. Not only does he refuse to come in and see his patient, but he argues to the value of a MRI of the spine. He would prefer a plain X-ray."

"You're kidding, right?" Kolomy asked.

"No. He thought the added cost of the MRI was excessive. What can I say? Anyway, the oncologist convinces him to approve the visit—as well as the MRI—as well as my consultation." Sny-der paused, a look of disgust on his face.

"So, how did she do?" Kolomy asked.

"She did okay. I was able to relieve the obstruction, but unfortunately she has diffuse metastatic disease. However, she did get her legs back, and her bladder and bowels are almost back to normal." Even though she was temporarily improved, they all knew she was terminal. But if it weren't for this inter-vention she would have suffered and languished considerably more. I was able to give her some quality time, for which she and her husband were eternally grateful.

"Managed care." Jaffe scowled.

"No, this wasn't managed care's fault. This was bad medical care. Period!"

"I don't buy that. If this patient wasn't with the HMO then the referring doc wouldn't have been as concerned with the cost of the ER visit or the MRI." Jaffe was again lisping and spraying.

"I'm not so sure. A bad doctor is a bad doctor, no matter what system he's in," Snyder countered.

"Really?" Jaffe raised his eyebrow.

"I wasn't referring to you when I said that. Don't be so inse-cure."

When Snyder concluded his remarks Jaffe looked at his watch and excused himself. It was time to start his rounds. Kolomy followed Jaffe, but was diverted to the emergency room. Snyder called surgery to see if his patient was prepped and ready to have his head cracked open.

Callison decided to use this opportunity to ask Snyder's opinion on some of the issues he had been dealing with pertaining to the committee. Over the years Callison had only modest contact with Snyder, but had always respected him and his views. Callison had never confided in Snyder on any substantive matter, but maybe it was time.

"Do you have a couple of minutes?" Callison said hopefully.

"Sure, they just got the patient on the table and anesthesia is still tied up with another case. They said it will be another 20 minutes or so."

"What I'm about to tell you needs to be kept confidential," Callison said with all sincerity.

"No problem." Snyder took Callison's request in stride.

"I don't know if you're aware I have been assigned to serve on a committee that's exploring several options regarding some of the issues dealing with primary care. One of these issues specifically deals with how osteopathic medicine will integrate into the new health-care system."

"Sounds interesting."

"It is interesting, but it's also very complicated. Can I ask you a question?"

"Of course."

"I know you've had offers to go to larger hospitals and more prestigious medical centers. Why did you stay here?"

Years ago Snyder had been courted by a rival medical center to join their staff. Callison had been privy to the discussions and eventual strategy used to keep Snyder on staff at their institution.

"I guess you're referring to the time I was being recruited by the medical center in Dallas. Actually I never seriously considered leaving. The money might have been better and the institution was larger but I was very satisfied where I was. However, they continued to pursue me, and I started to have second thoughts. Then came the incident which made my decision. The chief of staff of the center told me I was too good to be a DO, I would be more comfortable being around MD's. His statement really ticked me off and I told him that I would never consider practicing in an institution that judged me not on my abilities but on my degree. I detest the stereotype that many MD's have about us, that we're not as well trained or as

158

competent as physicians. I'm proud to be a DO, to practice in a DO hospital and I'm comfortable here, knowing my place and standing. I don't need to prove myself to anyone. My record speaks for itself. So why should I go elsewhere?"

"Why do you feel so strongly about the profession? Especially since you did your residency in a MD hospital?"

"This is the profession that gave me my opportunity to be a doctor. I like the feel of our profession. To me the profession is a closer fit to who I am. Yes, I trained in large MD institutions, but I feel more comfortable in our smaller hospital. I like that we have more contact with our students and residents on a one-to-one basis. I also like that we touch our patients, which I feel brings an entirely different perspective to patient-doctor relationship. This goes beyond manipulative therapy, although that's a large part of it. I also like that many of us had previous careers and have chosen this profession because of a true longing and not strictly as a continuum of our premedical education."

As the words flowed from Snyder, Callison envied Snyder's sincerity and dedication. Callison had felt some of what Snyder had stated, but not nearly as deeply or passionately.

The hour was late, and Snyder needed to proceed to his surgery. Callison decided not to pursue this any further.

"I'll let you go. Thanks for your candid answer."

"Glad to do it . . . and good luck on your committee."

"By the way, are you here every night?"

"No, not at all. I'll stop in the cafeteria if I'm here but that isn't very often, thankfully. I do get a kick out of Jaffe, though. He's always complaining and moaning about how he's getting screwed by the system, all the time he's taking all this money to the bank. I think he's a scream."

"Yeah, he's pretty funny," Callison added.

"He's so predictable and it's so easy to push his buttons. He's here almost every night." Snyder's beeper sounded. "Anyway, I got to go, surgery is calling."

Callison walked Snyder to the surgery suites and then went to revisit the Kodack family before he left the hospital.

When Callison returned to the waiting room, he noticed the

hospital chaplain and the head nurse were both in attendance. Little Sally was asleep on her grandfather's lap and Margaret was silently sobbing in the corner, her body heaving intermittently in an attempt to restrain her emotions. She caught the silhouette of Callison in the doorway and quietly rose to approach him without disturbing either her father or daughter.

"I'm glad you returned." Her sobbing was more controlled. She grabbed Callison's arm, squeezing it ever so slightly. "I need to ask a favor of you."

"What can I do for you?"

"I'm concerned about my father. You see he and my mother had, how can I put it, a very special relationship." Margaret's bloodshot eyes stared at the ceiling in an attempt to hold back her tears. "They had a bond that was so special, so complete, it was magical. Their love for each other was so fulfilling that I don't know if my father can survive without my mother. I know this sounds corny but I really believe this to be true. My parents had few friends because they had each other as best friends and therefore they really never needed others to confide in. They were not well educated, neither graduated from high school, yet they both insisted I be educated, so they scrimped and saved to send me through college and graduate school. Yet, the knowledge and wisdom they imparted to me was far greater than anything I ever learned in all those years of formal education."

Callison was impressed with how composed and focused Margaret was, considering the situation. "I know what you mean." Callison placed his hand on Margaret's shoulder.

"I married an attorney, but my marriage failed. I feel a major reason for the failure of my marriage was because I wanted from my relationship what my parents had. It isn't that I didn't love my husband. I did, but the intensity of the love and total commitment wasn't the same. They would do, and give to each other without ever expecting anything in return. They would never hesitate, when it came to each other's needs, no matter what it was or how it might negatively impact on their own needs. They were totally absorbed in each other.

"As much as they loved me, their only child, and my daughter, their only grandchild, it paled in comparison to their love for

160

each other. Growing up I never realized how remarkable their relationship was. I only really started to grasp it after my own marriage failed and I started to critically look at the relationships of my friends and acquaintances. So I guess what I'm trying to say is, can you help me look after my father?"

Margaret couldn't continue. Her eyes welled with tears, and her sobbing robbed her of her voice. After a few seconds, she managed through the sobs, "He's all Sally and I have left and is very important to the both of us. I'm concerned he'll start to neglect himself and wither away now mom is gone."

Callison had listened intently. Her words struck a chord deep inside him that reverberated throughout his body. Did he have such a commitment to Natalie? Did Natalie have such a commitment toward him?

Callison knew one of the greatest risk factors for a sudden death was the loss of a significant other. He would do what he could as a physician, but he realized that this was far beyond anything medicine could offer. "I'll do what I can to help. Why don't you make an appointment for your father to see me in the next week or two, and I'll give him a complete evaluation."

"Thank you, doctor. Thank you for everything."

"No, I need to thank you and your family. You're all very special people. I'm just so sorry about your mother."

"It was her time. Now she's at peace." Margaret embraced Callison genuinely. "Now it's time for you to go home to your family. We'll be all right."

Margaret returned to the waiting room where her family was seated. Callison started to follow, but she motioned for him to leave. It was time for him to go home.

Callison had difficulty sleeping that evening. He was haunted by the memory of Mrs. Kodack, but even worse by his conversation with the midnight club. Jaffe's remarks were nothing new, but Snyder had evoked a sense of guilt in Callison, as if he had compromised his professional life. Images of Marcus Merker kept appearing, and Callison couldn't get them out of his mind. Then there was the anonymous letter about the committee.

The following morning Natalie noted how tired he looked. They needed a night out. They agreed to meet for dinner that evening.

Natalie had already started her meal because Callison was thirty minutes late. She wanted to make sure they had a place at the sushi bar, even if he was late as usual.

"Sorry I'm late. Do you remember the case that dealt with the quality issue from the TMF?" Natalie nodded. "Well, the initial letter I sent back explaining why the patient was discharged was not enough. They wanted a more detailed explanation so I complied. Now they want to schedule a formal hearing or they'll nail me with a level three medical mismanagement charge."

"What's that mean?" Natalie put down her tea so she could concentrate on his response.

"A level-three severity is the worst. It means they consider this a medical mismanagement having significant adverse consequences to the patient, possibly leading to a serious condition such as unconsciousness or even death." Steven shook his head, he couldn't believe this was happening to him.

"I thought you said this was no big deal."

"That's what I thought; this really threw me when I received the letter today. They're claiming that I discharged the patient prematurely, putting the patient at an increased risk. The irony to this whole situation is that everybody and their brother is asking, hell, *forcing* us, to discharge our patients earlier and earlier, or not to even admit them at all. I try to do as much as possible as an outpatient, so that's what I did, and this happens. I swear the system is really starting to suck." Callison heard the words coming out of his mouth and a cloak of panic overtook him. He was sounding like Jaffe.

"So what happens next?" Natalie placed her hands gently over her husband's.

"I guess I have to prepare my case to present to this review board, which is scheduled in three weeks."

"What if you lose?"

"If the class-three sanction is upheld, then that automatically mandates a triggered intervention, which means the details of this case will be sent to the Licensing and Accreditation Boards, as well as the National Data Bank. What happens after that, God only knows."

The sushi chef handed them their meal over the counter. They both used this as an opportunity to concentrate on their appetite and not their problems. They devoured the sushi in silence.

"Let's order some more," Callison said when he finished. For some strange reason Steven had an appetite. Maybe it was because he hadn't eaten all day after he received the letter from the TMA.

"Okay."

After they ordered their second round of sushi, Natalie restarted the conversation. "I think we're being watched."

"What do you mean?"

"I think we're being watched." Natalie barely moved her lips as she talked.

Steven looked at Natalie, thinking she was joking. "Yeah, sure."

"No, I'm serious." Natalie was now a bit perturbed. "The man sitting in the far corner by himself wearing the dark glasses. I'm sure he's been staring at us all evening."

"Why would anyone stare at us? You're just being paranoid."

"I have a feeling about this; he's been watching us. Why, I don't know."

"Where is he again?"

"Behind you, facing me in the far corner. Don't be too obvious." Natalie continued to talk without moving her lips.

"Thanks for your confidence." Steven dropped his napkin onto the floor. While he slowly leaned over to pick the napkin up he furtively glanced in the direction Natalie suggested. There was a man half in the shadows, dressed in black. He immediately turned in the opposite direction as Steven momentarily glanced his way. There was something about him that seemed vaguely familiar, but Steven could not place him. As he sat upright in his seat, Steven asked, "What's he doing now?"

"Nothing, just eating his meal."

The second course of sushi was being served, but they were

now preoccupied with this strange man. "You know, I think you're right. I think he's watching us. There's something about him that's familiar. Do you recognize him?"

Natalie was growing increasingly concerned. "No, I don't recognize him at all." Just then her eyes opened widely and her voice started to crack. "He's getting up and moving in this direction."

Steven sat still in his chair trying to read Natalie's face, to tell him what was going on. Her startled look receded into a quiet resolve. "He's paying his bill." Her voice was now calm and collected.

"Did he look in our direction?" Steven purposefully looked only at his wife.

"Didn't even glance. Now he's leaving the restaurant. I guess we're both overtired and our imaginations have gotten a little out of hand."

"You're probably right. Let's finish our meal."

During the remainder of the meal the man's image bothered Steven. He suspected he had seen him before, but he couldn't establish where.

That night Steven couldn't sleep. The image of the man in the restaurant was haunting him. Then, as if struck by a bolt of lightning, he realized where he had seen him. He was the man in the photograph Merker had given him. It took all his willpower to refrain from going to his office to confirm his suspicion. Once Steven reconciled who the mystery man was, he was finally able to fall asleep.

Steven woke early. He told Natalie he had a breakfast meeting as an excuse to leave home earlier so that he could go directly to his office. Not that he really needed an excuse but it made him feel better.

In his desk he found the photo Merker had given him. As he studied the picture, there was no question he was the man they had seen in the restaurant. Now Callison had to decide whether or not to call Merker. He didn't want to tell Natalie anything until he had some more information. There was no reason to needlessly alarm her. He decided instead he would talk to Jourge about this, when he visited Chicago for his subcommittee meet-

164

ing in two days. Pending Jourge's response, he would then decide whether he would discuss this with Merker. Callison looked at the photo again, almost in disbelief. He thought, *What the hell is going on?*

16

Of the messages awaiting him on his answering machine, only one had any real significance to Merker. J.T. had left a cryptic message stating they needed to meet. Merker had known J.T. from his police days and had never known him to be an alarmist, so he figured J.T. must have discovered something significant. The message contained no details, but that was not surprising. Merker's curiosity was piqued.

Merker called J.T. at work. He was out of the office and his secretary told Merker that J.T. would be at Buckingham Fountain in Grant Park at 4:00 P.M. She asked if he could meet him there.

The drive down Lake Shore Drive was unusually beautiful that day. The sun was bright, people were walking, biking, playing, and jogging. Lake Michigan was at its bluest hue, matching the color of the sky. Merker arrived shortly after three. He sat on a bench soaking in the sunlight when he felt a tap on his shoulder. It was J.T.

J.T. had on a beige suit but had removed his tie, his way of being casual. He was wearing sunglasses and had grown a mustache, which made him look older but not more distinguished. Merker hadn't seen J.T. in several years, but he really hadn't changed. His stocky six-foot frame with his thick neck never had looked comfortable in a suit. That was no less the case today.

"Let's walk to a more private spot." J.T. had a no-nonsense attitude that surprised Merker because he was usually more casual and relaxed. They found a bench several hundred yards away from the fountain. It was surrounded by trees and about as secluded a spot as they could find.

"This should do. Please sit." J.T.'s formality made Merker somewhat uncomfortable.

"What's all the secrecy about?" Merker said half kidding,

hoping J.T. would loosen up.

"What do you know about this guy, Van Gregory?" J.T.'s face was stone-cold serious.

"Not much. He was following a friend of mine who died, Dr. Jonas Cisko, and I was wondering if there was any dirt on him."

"Is that all?"

"No, I know he has worked for the AMA, the American Medical Association." Merker hesitated for a second to see if J.T.'s expression changed. Seeing nothing, he continued. "He has also been following another doctor, a Steven Callison, who lives in Texas. Lastly, he was seen in the company of a Dr. Harvey Kahn, who was killed in a car accident just last week. That's about it." Merker again studied J.T.'s face.

"Well, you really opened up a hornet's nest." Merker didn't think it possible, but J.T.'s expression became even more intense. "I started out with the usual standard procedure inquiring about his background and all hell broke loose." J.T. stopped and looked around before he continued. "If anyone found out what I am about to tell you, my ass would be cooked." J.T. picked at some gravel by his feet and threw it into the grass.

"No problem. You know I can be trusted."

"The file on this Gregory guy is classified, because he worked for the Bureau in the past."

"You're kidding?" Merker was stunned.

"No shit, he worked on some special assignment in the fifties that came out of his military experience in counterintelligence. The bureau fired his freelance ass after he screwed up his assignment, which, by the way, had to do with surveillance." J.T. accentuated the word *surveillance*. "Anyway, since that time we've kept an eye on him. Over the years he worked for several organizations, including the AMA, but also the AOA, the American Osteopathic Organization. He mostly did surveillance work and helped them when they had labor problems. His specialty is strong-arm tactics. The guy seemed pretty penny-ante, so you could imagine my surprise when his name created such a commotion."

"Why? What you've told me doesn't sound that important."

"I agree. This is where I need you to swear to me that you

167

won't ever repeat what you're about to hear to anyone." J.T. removed his sunglasses to allow his eyes to emphasize the serious nature of his request.

"Okay, I swear." Merker had never seen J.T. this intense.

"Both the Bureau and the CIA have been tracking Gregory. We think he's part of a group responsible for bribing federal officers, as well as high-ranking political figures, possibly including members of the president's Cabinet. I can't divulge the details, but this is some heavy shit."

"Wow! Why are you telling me this?" Merker realized why J.T. appeared so intense.

"It appears your little investigation can potentially screw up our big investigation. Get my drift?"

"So you want me to back off."

"*Want* is such a polite term for what we want, but in essence, yes."

"What if I refuse?"

"Don't."

"What if?"

"Don't be stupid. If he's guilty we'll get him. But if your little investigation tips him off that something might be going down and he backs off, well, then we're all in for a world of hurt."

Merker's mind drifted momentarily to something his father had told him: never trust a man with an initial instead of a name, and that goes double if they have two initials. Merker had trusted J.T. in the past, but that was easy; now he was stepping into a personal agenda.

"So what do you want me to do, nothing at all?" Merker felt powerless.

"Actually, you may be able to assist us in our investigation."

"How can I do that?"

"This Dr. Callison that you met with, tell me about him."

"Not much to tell. I don't think he had anything to do with any of this. You know, an innocent bystander."

"We're not so sure. We'd like you to pursue your relationship with him to see if you can come up with something which might tie Gregory in with Callison." J.T. replaced his sunglasses.

"There's nothing there."

"We have sources to suggest otherwise. Since you have a relationship with Callison, we feel you can be our entree."

"I wouldn't call what we have a relationship."

"Whatever, just do it, please. We'll be very grateful." J.T. gave Merker a patronizing smile.

Merker wasn't pleased but surmised he had no choice, at least at this time. "Okay, I'll do it. Tell me what you have on Callison that makes you feel he's part of this whole mess."

"Fair enough. I don't have his file with me but I'll get it to you within 48 hours. Then we'll talk again."

"Can you tell me anything more about these bribes? Who's involved?" Merker doubted J.T. would reveal such information, but there was no harm in asking.

"Believe me, the less you know, the better off you are. Marcus, I like you. Just trust me on this one." J.T. again removed his glasses.

There was that word *trust* again. Two letters instead of names. Merker hoped J.T. was the exception to his father's rule. "So I'll wait to hear from you."

"I'll be in touch within the next couple of days." J.T. walked away, leaving Marcus alone on the bench with his thoughts. Marcus' initial instincts were correct; Gregory was up to something and his concerns about the death of Dr. Cisko probably did have some merit. Why else would the Feds be involved?

Something still bothered him about J.T. Why did they want him to pursue Callison? Surely they had agents who could do what they were asking of him. What ulterior motive could they have in hoping to divert his attentions away from Gregory and toward Callison? Maybe they had none. He would wait for the file on Callison before making any final conclusions. If he wasn't convinced, he would do what he needed to do.

Callison had called Jourge and arranged to meet with him the day before his subcommittee meeting. Jourge's office was in the AMA building on the third floor. Callison noted as he passed the office for Primary Care Initiatives that Victor Rasta was listed as its office head. Jourge's office, although on the same floor, was part of a different complex of offices at the end of the hall called National Affairs. There were five secretaries for the offices of National Affairs. Jourge's secretary, Alberta Reynolds, escorted Callison into the corner office, where Jourge was waiting.

"Steven, how good to see you."

"Likewise, how's everything been going?"

"Fine, you said you had something important to ask me which couldn't be discussed over the phone?"

"Yes. Do you know this man?" Callison showed Jourge the picture of Kahn and Gregory.

"Yes, this one on the right is Harvey Kahn."

"How about the other man?" Callison pointed to Van Gregory's picture.

"I think he's been following me."

"Why would he be following you and why would you think I would know him?" Jourge said, looking perplexed.

"I was visited by a man in Texas who told me that this man was hired by the AMA and might have had something to do with the death of Dr. Cisko."

"Who said this?"

"His name is Merker and he's from Chicago."

"I don't know him or know of him. But I can assure you this entire scenario is totally preposterous. I obviously don't know all the employees at the AMA, but I promise if he is our employee, I'll get to the bottom of this. Dr. Cisko died of a myocardial infarct at home. What possible association could there be?"

"He was reticent to confide in me, but he said he thought Dr. Cisko's death wasn't totally innocent. I blew him off until I recognized Gregory following me. Am I being paranoid?"

"I don't know. I can't envision why anyone from our office would be following you. This is the first time I've heard Jonas Cisko's death was anything but of natural causes. But I'm not prepared to ignore this. Because of the potential implications, we need to be very discreet. In view of my high profile, I would prefer to remain uninvolved. May I impose on you to assist me with the initial investigation? I could assign you my best assistant, an executive secretary who is superb. Her name is Maxine Wells, and she is the most thorough, conscientious, reliable, and veracious person I know."

170

Soon Callison found himself being introduced to a woman dressed in a navy pants suit, her dirty blond hair neatly compacted into a bun. Maxine Wells extended her hand to meet his. Callison found himself alone in Jourge's office with Maxine.

"How can I be assistance to you?"

Callison handed the picture to Maxine. "Do you recognize either of these men?"

Shaking her head, she said, "No, I don't believe I've ever seen either one of them before."

"The one in the dark glasses is named Van Gregory, does that name ring a bell?"

"No, never heard the name. Why?"

"I was told he was an employee of the AMA."

"There are hundreds of employees here. Do you know what department he's assigned to?" Maxine asked.

"That's where I need your help," Callison answered.

"That sounds simple enough. We can go over to my computer and I can look him up in the personnel files. I have the security code allowing me access to all employees." Maxine gave Callison a little smile; it was becoming. "Follow me."

Callison followed Maxine to her computer, which was situated off the main corridor in a small, isolated office. The office had a desk, a lamp, a small file cabinet, and a computer. A name plate on the desk was partially obscured by a photograph in a frame. The photo had a portrait of a child about ten or so and a man. "Is this your family?" Callison returned the smile that Maxine had given him.

"Yes, that's my husband and my son, James."

"Nice family."

"Thanks. Anyway how do you like my spacious office?"

"Real plush." They laughed.

Maxine sat at the computer. "Now, you said his name was . . . ?"

"Van Gregory."

"Van Gregory." She repeated the name as she typed it into the computer. The screen went blank. Maxine repeated the procedure several times with the same result each time. "The computer doesn't have any information on a Van Gregory. Are you

171

sure he's still employed here?"

"No. I was told by someone he was employed here, but I don't know this for a fact. Are there any employees that aren't included in this list?"

"Not that I'm aware of."

"I'm confused. Why would he lie to me?" Callison said thoughtfully.

"Who? Who are talking about?"

Callison looked quizzically. "His name is either Merker or Wilson."

"What do you mean, either?"

Her question hit Callison like a tidal wave. *Of course, if he lied to me about his name, why would he tell the truth about anything else?* "He told my secretary his name was Wilson and he told me it was Merker."

"Sounds real honest to me." Maxine gave Callison a knowing look.

"Yeah." Callison felt foolish.

"Other than checking on whether there's another list of employees, is there anywhere else I can be of assistance?"

Callison reflected for a moment. Why was Van Gregory following him and who was he? Who wrote the letter? Who is Merker–Wilson and what does he really want? Why was Jourge so eager to shunt this onto him?

"I have a committee meeting all day tomorrow and I'll be leaving the next day," he said finally. "Maybe you could check out this Merker–Wilson person; he left his phone number on the back of the photo. Why don't you keep the photo and check him out tomorrow? Also, any information you could find on Van Gregory would help. But I have no idea how to find him."

"I'll see what I can do." Maxine said, as she smiled.

"I appreciate your help." Callison said, returning her smile.

"No problem." Maxine said matter-of-factly.

"I'll call you, or better yet, you call me tomorrow evening. I'll be at the Drake Hotel. Depending on what you find, we can decide tomorrow on whether we need to meet again before I leave town."

"I'll call you tomorrow night at around 9:00 P.M." Maxine jotted down the time in a small notebook.

"Well, I guess that's enough for now. Thanks again for your help."

Maxine reiterated. "I'll call you tomorrow."

"Okay, until tomorrow night, then." Callison had a good feeling about Maxine, and he hoped she would find out some information. He couldn't decide if he felt comfortable enough with her to tell her about the letter. He would wait until tomorrow and reevaluate.

17

Since arriving home Merker hadn't made the time to do his domestic chores. He decided today would be reserved to accomplishing those basic necessities he had been ignoring. He started the day by cleaning the debris from his refrigerator. Once he completed the cleansing and fumigation of the refrigerator, it was time to restock the essentials.

Before he would attempt the cleaning and vacuuming of his home, he needed a break from his chores. The Cubs were in town and the rain had ceased—it was a beautiful day for a ball game. Before he would leave for the game, Merker attempted again to phone J.T., but as before he was only able to leave a message.

The game was rained out in the middle of the second inning, and Merker reluctantly returned home to complete his household chores. He was greeted by a flashing light on his answering machine. J.T. must have returned his call. There were two messages, the first was from Marvin Powell and the other was from Ethan Jasper. Merker's initial response was disappointment. He still hadn't heard from J.T., but on reevaluation he was intrigued by the call from Ethan Jasper. As he dialed Jasper's number, Merker started to mentally review his previous conversation with Dr. Jasper.

"Hello, Dr. Jasper, this is Marcus Merker returning your call."

"Yes, Mr. Merker. How nice of you to return my call so promptly." Jasper's voice sounded enthusiastic.

"So, Doctor Jasper, why did you call?"

"I think I've got some information you'll find very interesting." Merker's pulse increased. "At first I was very frustrated in my attempts to find out what happened to Dr. Trulof. Every lead came to a dead end and it appeared he had literally vanished. I was about to give up when I was contacted by a colleague from the past, who had heard via the rumor mill that I had been inquiring about Tyler Trulof. He asked me to keep his identity anonymous and the reason for this will become apparent in a few minutes. Anyway, he gave me the address and number of a Dr. Tyler Truelove in Phoenix, Arizona. I called Dr. Truelove and he verified he was the former Dr. Trulof."

"Why did he change his name?" Merker asked.

"This is where the story gets interesting. In the early sixties Trulof and a Dr. Amos Wilcox had a very successful practice in internal medicine. When the possibility of the merger was made public, both Wilcox and Trulof became very vocal in their opposition to the merger."

"Merger?" Merker wasn't sure what Jasper was referring to.

"The California merger between the DO's and MD's . . . "

Merker interrupted. "Yeah, yeah. The California merger."

"Anyway, their efforts earned them the reputation of troublemakers, but also of staunch supporters of maintaining the presence of the osteopathic profession in California. Once the merger was finalized they had tremendous difficulty maintaining their practice. They lost most of their hospital privileges, which made them both very bitter. Wilcox became obsessed with attempting to reverse the merger. He started to investigate a theory about a list of DO's who were under the control of the medical establishment, who wanted this merger to take place."

"The Caldo list," Merker said hesitantly.

"Exactly. When Wilcox started to accumulate some information that could be incriminating, both he and Trulof started to receive some threats. Wilcox was able to withstand the threats, but Trulof succumbed. What caused Trulof to back off was the fact he was a closet homosexual. In the sixties most gays were in the closet, especially if they were physicians. If he was exposed as a homosexual Trulof's practice would be totally decimated. He decided to change his name and vocation."

"He changed his vocation?"

"Once he officially changed his name, he moved to Ohio and pursued a residency in radiology."

"Radiology?" Merker asked as he jotted the information in his notebook.

175

"Yes, radiology. After he completed his residency he moved to Michigan where he changed his name again, this time to Truelove. A year later he moved to Arizona, where he has been ever since. Over the years Dr. Truelove became a very respected radiologist. Anyway, he came out of the closet several years ago and states he now has nothing to hide."

"Help me here, Doc. Where are you going with this?"

"Patience, I'm getting to the good part. Truelove told me that he feels Wilcox's death was not an accident as reported. He thinks Wilcox was killed because of the information he had about the Caldo list."

"Why would he think that?"

"Because of several factors that occurred at the time of death. First, Wilcox called Truelove several days before his death. Truelove hadn't heard from Wilcox for several years prior to that call. Wilcox informed Truelove he was about to get possession of the Caldo list which implicated several prominent doctors who were key figures in the California merger. Second, he told Truelove during that conversation he was concerned for both his safety and Trulof's. Third, Wilcox was an excellent driver and never drank. After Wilcox's death, Truelove inquired how his ex-partner had died. When they said he was killed in a single vehicle accident while intoxicated, Truelove was convinced his friend and colleague had been killed."

"So what did he do?"

"Nothing. Truelove was scared. Since he had no real proof, he decided to remain silent. Over the years this has eaten away at him. He'd now like to make amends and is willing to help you anyway he can."

"Would he mind if I contacted him?"

"No, not at all. In fact he's expecting your call. Let me give you his number."

Merker jotted down the number on a note pad. "What about the person who told you about Truelove, could I contact him?"

"Remember I said he would like to remain anonymous. All I can tell you is that he was a close personal friend of Trulof's in his California days."

Merker understood and didn't press the issue. "I don't know

how to thank you, Doctor. You've really been helpful."

"My pleasure. Jonas Cisko was a dear friend. If there has been any foul play I'll do whatever I can to assist you."

"Again, thanks a lot."

"One last favor," Jasper requested.

"Anything."

"Please keep me informed on anything you feel is pertinent. I'd truly appreciate that."

"Be glad to."

Merker hung up the phone feeling energized. He had another source confirming the Caldo list and two people who were willing to help. Before he would call Arizona, he decided first to call Marvin Powell.

"Hello, Marvin, this is Merker."

"Marcus, hold the line for a moment while I change phones." There was some shuffling in the background. "Okay, hon, you can hang up the phone now," Powell yelled to his wife.

"So, Marvin, what's the problem?" Merker asked.

"We need to talk." Powell's voice sounded serious.

"Okay. Let's talk."

"Do you remember the Garza case?"

When either of them referred to the Garza case, it was a code that indicated they were under surveillance, possibly being watched or listened to. "Yeah, wasn't Garza the guy who lived on Lawrence?" Merker grabbed his note pad and wrote down Lawrence Avenue.

"No, he was the guy who lived for seven years on Lincoln."

Merker and Powell understood the code. They would meet at Lawrence and Lincoln at seven P.M.. The remainder of their conversation consisted of idle chatter.

Merker lost any interest in calling Truelove, at least for the time being. He would hold off until he had resolved whatever the issue was with Marvin Powell. The phone rang, which startled Merker. Was it Powell calling back? The voice on the phone was obviously not Powell's—it was a female.

"Mr. Merker, please."

"This is Merker." Merker was irritated, he was in no mood for a solicitation call.

"Mr. Merker. My name is Maxine Wells and I work with Dr. Steven Callison."

"What can I do for you?" Merker remembered Callison, but who was this woman?

"I have been asked by Dr. Callison to see if you could give me some information on a Mr. Van Gregory."

"Why would I do that?"

"You told Dr. Callison that Mr. Gregory worked for the AMA. I wonder if you could confirm your statement?"

"Listen Ms. Wells, I don't know you from Adam. Why would I tell you anything about Gregory or anybody else?" Merker suspected she was a plant by the FBI, maybe even working with J.T.

"Would you be willing to discuss this with Dr. Callison himself?"

Merker knew he needed to meet with Callison eventually. First he needed to review the file from J.T. "Why? Can you make an appointment with me and Dr. Callison?"

"Yes, I can do that. Do you have a time and a place you'd like to meet?"

"What do you mean? Here in Chicago or in Texas?"

"Here."

"Callison's in town?" Merker was agitated that Callison hadn't personally contacted him.

"Yes, and I can be available to meet, say tomorrow night?"

"Okay, tomorrow night, nine P.M. at Gino's East. Do you know Gino's?" Merker's mouth watered at the thought of Gino's pizza bread.

"Yes, I know that restaurant, so I guess we'll see you then."

Merker's agenda was suddenly full. First he had to meet with Marvin Powell, then he needed to meet with J.T. before he could meet with Callison. Finally he needed to call Truelove and confirm Jasper's story. But first things first, he needed to meet with Marvin Powell.

There was a light mist in the air, a residue from the rain and humidity, when Merker pulled his car up to the corner of Lincoln and Lawrence. He noticed Powell in his car sitting patiently.

Merker parked his car and walked over to where Powell was waiting. Powell opened the door and Merker joined him.

"Why all the secrecy?" The concern was apparent on Merker's face.

"This guy, Kahn, you asked me to check out? Well I do this routine check and the next thing I know the FBI is on my ass." Powell grimaced as he spoke.

"The Feds?" Merker grimaced in return.

"Yeah, the FBI. They had been checking this guy out for something and they wanted to know my interest."

"What did you tell them?"

"I told them I was checking out some of the fatalities on Sheridan Drive. I said, I nearly had an accident there and wanted to see if any accidents had been recently reported at that spot."

"Did they buy that?"

"I really don't know. But I can tell you they were serious. What the hell's going on?" Powell said, snorting his contempt for this predicament.

"I'm not sure."

"Listen, you don't have to tell me anything if you don't want to. But I need my job, and if they find out I'm helping you, well, you know . . . "

"Damn!" Merker mumbled. "I'm sorry for getting you involved here. I really had no idea."

"I know, I just hope this is worth all this."

"Me too!" Merker knew he had placed his friend in an awkward position.

"Anyway, I was limited in what information I could get. But the scuttlebutt is that drugs may be involved."

"I don't think so, but maybe I'm missing something." After Marvin's comments about the FBI, Merker found himself repeatedly looking into his rear view mirror.

"I don't know." Marvin grinned as he noticed what Merker was doing.

"Why didn't you want to discuss this on the phone? Do you think the line's tapped?"

"Like I said, the Feds were acting really strange about this.

179

It wouldn't surprise me if they did tap the phone. I decided to play it safe."

"I appreciate your concern."

"I did this as much for me as for you. Probably more. I can't afford any hassle, not this close to retirement."

"I'll try to keep you out of this but if anything else comes up . . ."

"Don't worry, you'll be the first to know." Powell placed his hand on Merker's shoulder and squeezed.

"You're a true friend," Merker said seriously.

Without saying another word they exchanged a handshake and Merker returned to his car.

Callison had arranged for a small meeting room at the Marriott where the subcommittee was to meet. Callison, Michelson, and Percy were accompanied by a secretary supplied by the AMA and Maxine Wells, who was now assigned to coordinate their research needs.

The subcommittee discussed in detail the mounds of information they had amassed. Culling out the pertinent material lasted the entire morning, leaving them the remainder of the day to formulate their recommendations. They adjourned for lunch, believing their greatest task had been completed.

Maxine Wells cornered Callison before they convened. She told him of about her conversation with Merker and of the meeting for later that evening. Callison thanked her and returned for the afternoon session.

The discussion in the afternoon alternated between recommending and not recommending the merger. After ten arduous hours they were unable to come to a consensus. They decided to table any final decision until they each investigated their individual concerns in greater detail.

18

Merker had finally been able to contact J.T., arranging to meet him later that morning. Before the meeting, Merker decided to call Dr. Truelove.

The phone was answered without a ring. "Hello, Dr. Truelove?"

Truelove was perplexed, since he had just lifted the receiver to make a call himself. "Yes, this is Truelove. Who is this?"

"My name is Marcus Merker. I believe Dr. Ethan Jasper told you I'd be calling."

"Of course, you're the private detective investigating Caldo, right?"

"Well, sort of. Actually I'm investigating the death of Jonas Cisko."

"Jonas was a good man and an excellent doctor. How can I help?"

"Dr. Jasper gave me quite a few details..." Merker then reviewed his discussion with Jasper. He had kept notes of his conversation with Jasper and he attempted to be as thorough as possible in his recounting. When Merker completed his remarks, he waited for a response from Truelove. There was none. Merker had to break the silence.

"Dr. Truelove—are you still there?"

"Sorry, I was just stunned at your detailed description of the events of my life. It was as if you were listening to my conversation with Ethan Jasper."

Merker was concerned he had broke a confidence. "I hope I didn't speak out of school."

"No, I told Ethan to tell you everything. I wanted to know if this interested you and if it did, to what extent."

"I found this to be very interesting. That's why I'm calling."

"Before I tell you anything else, I need to ask you some questions."

"Shoot."

"Ethan told me you were a private detective and a personal friend of Jonas Cisko. Is that correct?"

"Yes."

"Fine. Why are you doing this?"

"Before Dr. Cisko died he asked me to investigate two people, Dr. Harvey Kahn and Van Gregory. He was really worried and thought these guys were a threat to his safety."

"How?"

"To be honest, I'm not sure. He thought that they would or could do something to him which would mess up his standing on the committee. But there might have been more than that, I just can't remember."

"So why are you still actively investigating this case?"

"There are several reasons. I owe it to Dr. Cisko."

"What are the other reasons?"

"I know how much this committee meant to Dr. Cisko. Just in talking to him about this I saw a spark in his eyes that I hadn't seen since his divorce. I had to find out for myself what this committee was about."

"Is that all?"

"No. There's one more reason, but it's more personal."

"Listen, if I'm going to confide in you, I need to feel that this is a two-way street. Otherwise our conversation is over."

"Okay. Since the death of my wife I haven't been worth two nickels. I've filled my time doing basic stuff, like domestic investigations. You know, checking on people whose spouse thinks they're cheating on them. Stuff like that. Boring and definitely not challenging. Then Dr. Cisko gives me this assignment. I thought this was more of the same, but after checking these two guys out, I got the feeling this was something different, bigger. Anyway, after Dr. Cisko died I did a little snooping around. I feel, no, I know, that Dr. Cisko's death wasn't totally an accident."

"How do you know that?"

Merker hesitated. After a few seconds he realized Truelove definitely should be trusted. He was the one who had changed his name and gone into hiding. "It was the glasses. You see, Dr. Cisko just had some eye surgery done and his glasses were useless. But when he was brought to the coroner he was wearing his glasses. Why would he be wearing glasses if they were of no use? Somebody had placed his glasses on him after he died, someone who didn't know that he recently had surgery and his glasses were unusable." Merker pulled out his notebook, anticipating Truelove's cooperation.

Truelove reflected on Merker's comments before continuing. "Why couldn't he have placed his glasses on out of habit at the time he had his heart attack?"

"He was supposedly reading when this heart attack occurred, but I know for a fact he couldn't read up close and he had an appointment scheduled to have his eyes checked, but the appointment was scheduled for sometime after his actual death. So he wouldn't be reading or wearing his glasses."

"I believe you. Now you're going to have to believe me."

"Okay, fine, I believe you. But there's one more thing you should know. This case is important to me. It is the first time, in a very long time, that I feel I'm doing something worthwhile. Besides, these guys have really ticked me off. I want them to know they made a big mistake when they mucked around with one of my cases and more importantly one of my friends."

"I see." Truelove hesitated momentarily. "I didn't tell Jasper the whole story."

"Oh." Merker was surprised by Truelove's remark and sincerity.

"Do you recall my concerns about the death of Amos Wilcox?"

"Yes."

"You're convinced Jonas Cisko's death was no accident; I feel just as strongly about Amos. Amos was an irascible, arrogant man who would never back down from a fight if he thought he was in the right. Anyway, a couple of days before his death, I got a call from him. I hadn't talked to him in years before that call. We were pretty close when we practiced together. I trusted Amos and he trusted me. When I decided to leave, we agreed that we would not keep in close touch. We were both concerned about the possible consequences from being as outspoken as we were. Amos was especially concerned for me because he was aware of how fragile I'd become by the constant threats."

"Constant threats?" Merker questioned.

"Yes, there were dozens of threats. I couldn't handle them as well as Amos. Anyway, Amos told me he continued to investigate the Caldo list and was about to get some real evidence that was verifiable. He died before he got the evidence, but before his death he sent me a letter, which I received after his death, that summarized his entire investigation." Truelove cleared his throat before he continued. "Over the years I wanted to pursue this but was afraid. Back then I didn't have the courage to follow up what Amos had started and probably lost his life for. But I'm not afraid any more."

Merker knew Truelove was telling the truth. He was as sure as he could be. But he needed to know more. "Can you tell me what's in the letter?" A sudden thought entered Merker's mind— *What if the phone is tapped?*

Before Truelove could respond, Merker interrupted. "Listen—come to think of it maybe you shouldn't read the letter."

"I couldn't do that anyway because I don't have it."

Merker was simultaneously relieved and aggravated. He would find out what happened to the letter when he called Truelove back on a phone he knew wouldn't be tapped. "Listen, Dr. Truelove, someone's at my front door. Do you mind if I call back later?"

"No, by all means, do what you have to do."

Merker hung up the phone and immediately went to his neighbor's apartment. His neighbor Rudolph was always home; he had mastered the art of indolence. Rudolph let him in and was glad to lend Merker his phone, since Merker was willing to reimburse him double for the cost of the call.

Truelove picked up the phone on the first ring.

"Dr. Truelove, Merker here."

"That was quick."

"Actually, there really wasn't anyone at the door. But I got worried someone might have tapped my phone and I needed to stop our conversation. I'm in my neighbor's apartment and I know this phone is safe. Now can you tell me what happened to the letter?"

"The letter is in a safe deposit box." Merker sighed with relief. "I placed it there years ago. You see, Amos sent a cover letter with the Caldo letter. In his cover letter he told me he was concerned his life might be in danger and this letter contained all the information he knew on Caldo. He also said that I would know when the time would be right to use the information, but until that time keep the letter in a safe place. I can't tell you how many times I wanted to destroy that letter! How many times I wanted to pursue the information contained in the letter, to find and then reveal the list. How many times I wanted to totally forget the letter existed. Now I know this is the time to do what's right, for Amos, for Jonas Cisko . . . for myself."

"Can you get the letter?"

"Of course."

"Does anyone else know about this letter?"

"To my knowledge, no. Amos stated in his cover letter, this was the only letter he sent and cautioned me that there were many people who probably would kill to avoid the list becoming public." There was a protracted silence on the other end of the line. "Merker—are you still there?"

"Yeah, I'm still here. Listen, you need to keep the letter where it is. Don't get it. Do you understand?" Merker spoke forcefully. "It's just that if the phone was tapped, then others know about the letter. As long as it's in a safe place you're probably safe but . . . "

"But if they get it . . . I'm dead." Truelove's voice trailed.

"Listen, I'm not even sure the line was tapped. It probably wasn't."

"Fine then. I won't get the letter if you think it's not advisable."

"Yes, that's my advice."

"I do remember several facts from the letter. Would you like to hear what I remember?"

Merker wondered if he should hear what Truelove had to say. He was sure this phone line was secure, and if something should happen to Truelove he at least had something else to go on. "Okay, tell me what you can remember," Merker said with note pad in hand.

"The letter detailed the history of the Caldo list which started sometime after the Second World War. A doctor by the name of Tatum started the whole thing as a way to help people get into medical school. His intentions were honorable and many people were helped. I can't remember the details, but somewhere in the fifties Tatum died and the list was taken over by a Dr. Alexander, who used the list to gain power. It was under this Dr. Alexander that the Caldo list was formed. Using a group of hand picked DO's, he was able to achieve the merger in California. Then he formed another group in Pennsylvania. Maybe they were called Pado, I don't know. But they couldn't pull it off. From what I can remember, the period after the failed merger in Pennsylvania was real chaotic. Alexander wound up losing his power to a Dr. Smith and his right-hand man, a Dr. Rasta."

Merker recognized the name of Rasta as one of the members on the committee. "Did you say Rasta? Victor Rasta?"

"Yes, do you know him?"

"Are you sitting down?" Merker asked.

"Yes."

"Good, Victor Rasta is a key member on the committee."

"The committee. Cisko's committee?"

"One and the same." Merker circled Rasta's name on his note pad.

"Well! I'll be damned."

"What else can you remember from the letter?"

"Are you sitting?"

Merker chuckled softly. He could tell from the tone of his voice this was going to be good. "What?"

"Rasta had the list."

"What do you mean had?"

"I mean at the time of his death in 1969, Amos had traced the list to Victor Rasta. He had the list back then, whether he still has it is anybody's guess."

"You said the other guy's name is Smith. Do you remember

186

anything else about him?"

"No, I can't remember anything else about him other than he spelled his name differently."

"Like S-M-Y-T-H or something like that?"

"To be honest, I really can't recall. But I could get the letter and call you back."

"No, I don't think that would be a good idea. It might be dangerous. Just stay pat. I have some things I have to get done today, but I'll be on a flight tomorrow and we'll get the letter together. Promise me you won't get the letter without me."

"I won't," Truelove said.

"Is there anything else you can think of?"

"No. I guess I'll see you tomorrow. How will I recognize you?"

"I'll be wearing a Cubs cap and a White Sox T-shirt, and I'll come to your house. Dr. Jasper already gave me your address."

"Well I guess I'll see you tomorrow then."

"See you tomorrow."

As he put the receiver down, Merker noted the time. He was late for his rendezvous with J.T.

Merker rushed to the lobby of the Sears Tower where J.T. should have been waiting in front of the Alexander Calder sculpture. The lobby was moderately crowded with a mixture of businessmen and tourists, but no J.T. Was he too late? Merker caught J.T.'s image out of the corner of his eye, summoning him over to a remote section of the lobby.

"I was about to leave. You're thirty minutes late." J.T. was definitely not pleased.

"Sorry, got tied up." Merker wasn't one for excuses, but he was also a bit miffed at J.T.

"Here's the file on Callison. This is classified material so I can't let you take it with you."

"What? Why not?"

"I told you, it's classified. I shouldn't even remove this from our file room, let alone show it to you."

Merker knew this was an argument he could never win, so he decided to follow J.T.'s lead. "So what now?"

"Follow me." J.T. led Merker down a corridor into a men's

room that had a sign on the door designating the room was closed for renovation. J.T. entered, followed by Merker. J.T. placed his index finger to his lips while he surveyed the bathroom for any patrons. Once he was sure they were alone, he spoke.

"Here's the file. You have a half hour to review it before I need it back. Also I'd appreciate it if you didn't take any notes. Try to memorize whatever information you need."

"Are you kidding?" Merker had his trusty note pad in his pocket.

"Do I look like I'm kidding?"

The expression on J.T.'s face didn't need a verbal response from Merker. Merker retired to the closest stall, put down the lid, and started to read. J.T. watched at a small crack in the door so he could monitor any activity in the hallway.

The file had the usual biographical information. Merker skipped to the data pertaining to his college days, as J.T. had told him earlier the material he needed was probably contained there. Callison had been a member and later an officer in his college's local chapter of the Students for a Democratic Society (SDS). During his SDS days, Callison had been arrested in Washington D.C. while participating in a demonstration protesting the war in Vietnam. That was when the FBI initiated their file on Callison. This was followed by a routine investigation of his political ideology, since much of the SDS's philosophy was based on the writings of Karl Marx.

During his junior year in college, Callison was part of a group that organized a sit-in and eventual takeover of both the administration building and library of the university. Callison was an integral member of the steering committee responsible for the takeover.

Merker shook his head and continued to read. During the height of the protest, a professor of organic chemistry decided to penalize those protesting by giving daily pop tests. Because the protesting students were absent from class, they would receive a zero. The professor could then fail those students without appearing to be overtly arbitrary.

Callison was part of the group who attempted to explain

the rationale of the protest to the chemistry professor, but to no avail. The conversation deteriorated into a shouting match and ended with the professor being accidentally shoved. The professor lost his balance. As a result of the fall, he suffered a mild concussion and lacerated his forehead, requiring twelve stitches. The professor filed formal charges against all those involved in the confrontation, Callison included. Because of Callison's involvement in SDS, the steering committee responsible for the sit-in, and his reputation as a good student, albeit a dissident, the administration decided to make an example of him.

Callison's parents were notified he was in danger of being expelled from the university. Steven was their only child, and as soon as they were notified of his predicament, they decided to immediately drive to the university. They were both killed in an automobile accident before they ever reached the university or were able to talk to their son. The school decided not to pursue the charges against Callison in deference to his loss, if he apologized to the professor, along with his discontinuation of all involvement with the SDS or any other activist group. Callison complied and never participated in any further protest activity.

The file had little more to offer after the college protest incident and the death of his parents. There was a notation about the chemistry professor continuing his vendetta against Callison, among others, to have them all expelled, but his efforts were to no avail. Merker noticed a hand-written notation scribbled in the corner of the last file paper. It read: "Gance?" Otherwise Callison's career after college was uneventful and there was no data suggesting any further activity that could be considered suspect.

Merker felt he had the information he needed and returned the file to J.T.

"I have a meeting scheduled with Callison tonight. Is there anything specifically you'd like me to ask him?" Merker asked.

"What we'd like to know is, if Callison is involved in any way with Gregory."

"I'll see what I can do." Merker placed his hands in his

189

pockets, feeling for his note pad.

"Remember, stay away from Gregory," J.T. warned Merker.

They both went their separate ways. Merker stopped after he was certain J.T. was gone and scribbled on his note pad all he could recall from Callison's file.

19

Maxine picked up Callison at the hotel and drove directly to the restaurant. Gino's was crowded, but there were still tables available. While Callison was asking if there were any tables available in a quiet section, Maxine noticed a man waving in their direction. Callison recognized Merker, seated at a booth in the corner. Merker looked different than Callison had remembered: he was disheveled and had dark bags under his eyes, noticeable even in the subdued lighting of the restaurant. Merker remained standing while Callison introduced him to Maxine Wells.

"Please take a seat." Merker signaled them to sit on the bench facing the patrons, while he sat opposite facing the wall. "I already ordered some garlic bread and a pitcher of beer. I hope you don't mind?" Merker pointed to the bread and the beer already on the table.

"Could I have a Diet Coke, please?" Maxine said.

"Sure." Merker responded with a little chuckle. He caught the attention of their waiter and ordered Maxine her drink.

"So Miss Wells, is it?"

"Mrs. Wells, Mr. Merker."

"Sorry, Mrs. Wells, how long have you known Dr. Callison?"

Merker was perplexed. Why did Callison ask Mrs. Wells to accompany him to their meeting? Her presence made him edgy.

Maxine seemed nervous, and Merker's question unnerved her even more. Sensing Maxine's uneasiness, Callison decided to answer for her. "Actually we just recently met, but I've already found Mrs. Wells' assistance to be invaluable." Callison gave Maxine a nod.

"How nice. So what can I do for you, Doctor? After Texas, I doubted I'd ever see you again."

"Before we start I need to get something off my chest," Callison said suddenly.

Merker could not imagine what Callison meant. "Fine, what's on your chest?"

"When we first met, you lied to me."

"You told me your name was Marcus Merker, yet you told my secretary your name was Hank Wilson."

"Hack, Hack Wilson." Merker was trying to suppress his laughter.

"I'm sorry, I don't see the humor."

"Sorry, Doc. No disrespect intended. I use the name Hack Wilson as my, uh, alternate name. I didn't want to use my real name with your secretary because I had a feeling she wouldn't let me see you. By using the other name, I could call you with my real name and hopefully get an appointment."

Merker's explanation was so absurd that Callison believed him. "The name Hack Wilson sounds vaguely familiar."

Merker laughed, this time not suppressing it. "Hack Wilson was one of my favorite ballplayers. He was a Cub and set the record for most RBI's in a season."

"190." Callison boasted.

Merker opened his eyes widely, protruded his lower lip and nodded. "190, right. I'm impressed."

"Once you mentioned who he was, I remembered the record. I'm a fan myself."

Merker had a new respect for Callison. "Hey, I'm truly sorry I..." Merker struggled for the right word, but couldn't find one... "lied to your secretary, I hope you understand. But like my father used to say. 'If you must lie, be brief.'"

Maxine sat quietly. "I hate to break up this trivia session, but can we order? I'm starved."

Merker motioned for the waiter, who had been hovering, waiting for a break in their conversation. Merker did the ordering for the table.

As they ordered, Callison continued the conversation. "You mentioned a man, Van Gregory, whom you said worked for the AMA. I was wondering how you found this out?"

"Dr. Cisko told me. Also, I followed both Gregory and a Dr. Kahn. Saw them both enter the AMA building where they stayed for several hours."

"That doesn't constitute employment."

"Never said it did. Why all the interest in where Gregory's employed?"

"We checked the files at the AMA and there's no record of Gregory being employed there."

"I personally did the checking and I'm convinced Mr. Gregory is not presently on the payroll," Maxine said confidently.

"I see." Merker again protruded his lower lip and shook his head. "Isn't it possible someone who works for the AMA may be paying Gregory from some other fund, or even out of his own pocket?"

"Yes, but then he wouldn't be an employee of our organization," Maxine said.

"Same difference."

The expression on Maxine's face immediately changed. Callison noticed it. "I beg to differ," he said quickly. "I think there's a major difference in where the paycheck originates. Maxine did a very thorough job in determining the source is not the AMA."

There was a slight but perceptible change in Maxine's eyes, conveying a silent thank you to Callison for his support.

The conversation hit a lull just as the pizza was served.

With a strand of pizza sticking to his chin, Merker again began to talk. "So Doc, why all these questions about Gregory? Did he contact you or something?" As Merker concluded his question a small piece of pizza fell from his mouth onto the table. "Oops."

Maxine put down her fork and looked away, biting her lower lip to refrain from either laughing or vomiting.

"To answer your question, I think I saw Gregory following me in Texas," Callison said.

"I knew it," Merker said as he placed the pizza remnant in his napkin.

"Knew what?" Callison asked while he stared at the crumpled napkin Merker placed on the table.

"I knew that he was up to no good." Merker could see Callison staring at the napkin and removed it to his lap.

"I didn't say that. All I said is that I thought he was following me."

193

"I heard what you said. What I'm telling you is, this guy's trouble with a capital T."

"What makes you so sure?"

"I just know?" Merker said wryly.

"Oh you just know." Callison's response was sarcastic.

"Yeah, I just know. I sometimes get this sixth sense and when I get it I'm always right." Merker's eyes peered directly at Callison.

"Always?"

"Yep, always." Merker gave an ear to ear grin that was highlighted by the strand of pizza which was still precariously dangling from his chin.

"You're kidding right?" Maxine said.

"No, actually this might interest you, Doc. I inherited this sixth sense from my old man."

"You did what?"

"I inherited it. Let me explain. When I was growing up my father told me that all the men in our family had this ability to sense right from wrong. I don't mean RIGHT in the terms of the Bible or the law, but RIGHT in terms of the gray zone. If you get my drift."

Callison nodded, although he had no idea what Merker meant. Merker continued. "I didn't believe him probably anymore than you believe me. Over the years there were times when he would say things like, 'this friend of yours is no good', or, 'don't trust this person.' Stuff like that. Anyway, I wanted him to be wrong, but he never was. Even with all that, I still didn't believe him. I thought he had the same type of insight that all parents have and it wasn't anything special." Merker stopped to eat another piece of pizza.

Callison looked at Maxine who returned his look, both smiling uncertainly.

Merker spoke as he ate. "You see, my father was a plain man, nothing fancy. As a kid he worked in the gold mines in the southwest. He later moved to Chicago, where he met my mom and settled down. He became a cop, and the one thing he always stood for was honesty. He was basically a good man, but a tough father. He was pretty hard on me, always putting me down and

194

insulting me, which eventually resulted in a big fight between us. We didn't speak or even see each other for years.

"Then one day I get a call from my mom telling me my dad is dying from cancer and would I come to see him. I decided to let bygones be bygones and told my mom that I'd come and make up. I was married, and my wife suggested that I bring him a gift, something special, that would break the ice. I couldn't think of what type of gift would be that special. My wife suggested I go shopping with him and let him pick it out. Seemed reasonable to me, so that's what I did. To my surprise he didn't argue. He said he sensed this was the right thing to do. He was pretty sick by this time and had to be pushed in a wheelchair. We went all over the city looking for the right gift. I remember we went to this flea market on the south side and at one end of the market was a bunch of artists selling their stuff. There were sculptures, paintings, all sorts of artwork. While walking through there, I noticed a painting that gave me a strange feeling."

Merker stopped for another bite of the pizza. "That feeling was this sixth sense. I walked over to this abstract type painting as if it called to me. The painting just looked different from the other paintings, and somehow the colors in it reminded me of my old man. I didn't know why. I never really liked that type of art but I knew this was the right gift. I didn't even look at the price tag, I was so excited.

"I rushed back to find my parents, who were at another part of the flea market. I zoomed my father in his wheelchair over to the painting that I found. I told him I found the gift. Just as I started to show him the painting, I noticed the price, it was $450. I'm sure my face changed when I saw the price, but I was still ready to buy this for him. I thought I noticed a smile on his face when he first saw the painting, it was the first smile I'd seen on his face in years. So I asked him what he thought of the painting and he said it was a waste. We got into this big argument, neither of us listening to the other." Merker shook his head and momentarily looked away.

In a softer voice, Merker continued, "I never did buy the painting or any other gift for my father. Several months later, on his death bed, he called for me. We talked and he reminded me of our family's sixth sense, that we might not always be one hundred percent right, but we're never wrong. When it came to the sixth sense, he said it was a special gift and I shouldn't waste it. When he said that, it reminded me of the painting. I still thought that painting was special, but I never mentioned it to him again.

"Several years after his death, I was walking down Michigan Avenue and saw the same painting in the window of one of those fancy art galleries. I still had the same feeling that I had the first time I saw it in the flea market. I asked how much the painting cost and was told it was $20,000! I told my wife about the painting. For the first time in my life, I was right and my father was wrong. I told this to my mother, who told me that my father never disliked the painting, in fact he liked it a lot. He just thought it was a waste. My father had a life insurance policy and my mother used some of the money to buy me the painting. You know, to remind me of my father. Common sense told me to return the painting and give the money back to my mother, but this sixth sense told me to keep it. The look on my mother's face when she gave me the painting will remain with me the rest of my life."

Merker had a lump in his throat. He cleared his throat and continued. "One day several months later I was dusting the frame of the painting when a small card fell to the floor from behind the painting. I picked the card up and read it."

Merker took out his wallet from his pants opened the billfold and handed a small, weathered, discolored card to Callison. Callison read the card and then handed it Maxine. The card simply stated: Artist—Gustav Anschauung, Title—"The Waist."

After they both read the card, Merker continued. "After I read the card I looked up the artist and part of the description of the artist included a translation of his name. His last name means intuition or insight."

"Spooky." Maxine said, clearly moved by Merker's story.

Callison was more skeptical. "So I guess this means this sixth sense is real to you. But I don't think so."

"You're entitled to your opinion. But I can tell you ever since then, when I get that feeling, what I call my sixth sense, I follow it. And to tell you the truth, I haven't been wrong yet."

"What does your sixth sense tell you about me?"

Merker thought for a second before responding. "I think you're an innocent bystander in this mess and you can be trusted."

"Why do you say that?" Callison asked.

Merker knew Callison's background from the FBI's file. He concluded that if Callison was part of any conspiracy he would have been initially selected to the committee. By removing Cisko they—whoever *they* might be—exposed themselves needlessly. What was more likely, he was a secondary choice and the information the FBI had, "they" also had. "Because you're here. And you're getting involved."

Callison mulled over Merker's response before asking, "So what does your sixth sense tell you about Gregory?"

"He's trouble and definitely up to no good . . . and I believe he's somehow involved in the death of Dr. Cisko and probably Dr. Kahn as well."

"Do you have any proof of this other than your sixth sense?"

Merker recounted his story about Dr. Cisko's glasses. When he finished Callison wasn't totally convinced, but he did agree that the circumstances surrounding Cisko's death were suspect.

At this point Merker excused himself and went to the men's room.

"So what do you think?" Callison asked Maxine.

"I believe him," Maxine said confidently.

"I'm not so sure. Why would he be doing all of this? What's in it for him?" Callison still couldn't piece together a logical reason.

"I'm not sure, but it may be as simple as he's doing what he believes is the right thing for his departed friend."

"You don't really believe that, do you?"

"I'm not sure."

Merker returned to the table with a concerned look.

"Is something wrong?" Callison said.

"I think we're being watched."

Callison scanned the patrons of the restaurant. "Where?"

Merker grabbed Callison by the wrist to gain his attention. Maxine had not flinched but kept her eyes focused on Merker.

"Be calm, like Mrs. Wells here." Merker was intently peering

197

into Callison's eyes. "There are two men sitting at a table in the corner. They came in a couple of minutes after we were seated. I noticed them staring in our direction several times tonight."

"How could you notice that? They're not in your line of sight."

"Through their reflection off that picture above your head. I can see them clearly in the glass." Merker bobbed his head in the direction of a poster framed in glass which hung on the wall above Callison's head.

"I think you're being overly paranoid." Callison said.

"Would you humor me then?" Merker asked.

"How?" Callison looked at Maxine as he replied.

"Let's pay the bill and get into my car just for a little ride and see if they follow. If they do, then we know something's up. If they don't, I'll bring you back here." Merker clasped his hands on the table, carefully looking at them both as he spoke.

"What do you think, Maxine?" Callison said.

"My mother told me never to accept a ride with a strange man." Maxine smiled.

"But I'm not strange." Merker returned a gentle smile.

"You're definitely strange but what the hell, I never really listened to my mother anyway. Let's go for a ride." Maxine slapped her palms on the table and stood.

Callison paid the bill as Merker left to get his car. Callison noticed the two men were asking for their check.

Merker pulled up the "Merker Mobile." The car was old and weathered, but was customized. When Merker started his detective business, he had installed his own custom-made security system complete with a refined motion detector, which would trigger an alarm in his hand-held remote. When he pulled up in front of the restaurant he stretched across the front seat to open the passenger door. Despite the exterior, the interior was immaculate, with plush oversized leather bucket seats in both the front and the rear.

"Nice car," Callison said.

Merker wasn't sure whether Callison was kidding or serious, so he ignored the remark. Anyway, he had more important things to do, such as monitor the progress of the two men leaving the restaurant. As Merker slowly pulled away, he noticed the two men in his rearview mirror summon a dark Chevy Caprice.

"We're being followed." Merker didn't have to say I told you so.

Both Callison and Maxine looked out the back window of to see the car in pursuit. Maxine did not seem the least nervous or anxious. "What are all these lights and knobs doing in this old car?" she queried.

"I modified the car for my work. Some are for my security system, some for my communication system, and some for my surveillance system. I also modified the engine so this baby can really rock and roll."

"Not to interrupt this most interesting conversation, but do you have any idea who those people are who are following us?" Callison was definitely more anxious than either Maxine or Merker.

"I don't know for sure, but I'll bet you they're connected to Gregory," Merker said smugly.

"So what do we do now?" There was a nervous crack in Callison's voice.

"I'll lose them in a few minutes, but before I do I want to see how good they are."

"Not too confident, are you?" Callison said less than impressed.

"Doc, when you see a patient and tell them you know what to do to make them better, do you consider that being too confident?" Merker flipped a switch on the dashboard.

"No, that's my job."

"Well, this is my job, and I do it well." Merker flipped two additional switches on the dashboard, which was followed by a low frequency rumble and a subtle downward movement of the chassis.

Merker's remarks silenced Callison, and Maxine said nothing.

Merker kept the Chevy Caprice in his sights, but also noticed another car, a car he had seen before, a black Seville. It was Gregory's car. Merker smiled to himself. The chase would now begin. Merker led both cars onto Lake Shore Drive off

Wacker Drive heading south toward the Field Museum.

"I think it would be a good idea for both of you to use the reinforced seat belts."

"What's a reinforced seat belt?" Callison was becoming progressively more anxious every time Merker made an additional comment.

Merker pulled a harness from the ceiling of his car which fastened into two metal buckles on either side of him. The harness had a double-crossed strap that would protect without inhibiting normal movement. Both Callison and Maxine followed Merker's lead, harnessing themselves into their respective seats. Once they were all secure, Merker again viewed the cars in pursuit. His foot slowly pressed on the accelerator as he moved the car into the passing lane. Merker's car was turbocharged. When combined with his converted overdrive system, modified fuel-injected dual carburetors, and a special catalytic converter allowing him to use a higher octane fuel, it created a very responsive, powerful machine. Merker warned his passengers to brace themselves.

When his foot hit the accelerator, the car immediately responded, jettisoning both Callison and Maxine back in their seats as it swerved through the traffic on Lake Shore Drive at breakneck speed.

"Driving a tad fast aren't you?" Callison commented apprehensively.

Merker again smiled. "Ain't seen nothin' yet, Doc." His foot pressed down further on the accelerator and they sped even faster down Lake Shore Drive, the speedometer reaching three digits. The two vehicles in pursuit were losing ground to Merker. He slowed down slightly, allowing them to close the distance between their vehicles. Speeding in and out of traffic in the ninety-mile-an-hour range, Merker was in total control of his vehicle yet Callison and Maxine were clinging onto whatever they could, praying they wouldn't be projected through the windshield.

The two cars were now closing in on each other. Merker, timing his move to the inner lane, slammed his brakes while rapidly turning his wheel, causing the car to skid into the oncoming traffic going north on Lake Shore Drive. It wasn't clear whose scream was louder, Callison's or Maxine's—the screeching of the tires only partially muffled their frantic shrieks. Merker enjoyed every second of this, as he masterfully maneuvered his car into the northbound traffic, leaving his pursuers aimlessly skidding about the southbound lanes.

Callison had to check his pants, concerned he had lost control of his bladder. He hadn't.

Maxine was energized. "That was great! How did you do that without crashing?" The words poured out of Maxine. Her adrenaline was pumping and her senses heightened.

"I used to teach evasive driving . . . that was just one of the maneuvers I taught. Usually pretty effective. See?" At the completion of his sentence he performed the same maneuver. Before Callison or Maxine could muster another scream they were again in the southbound lanes, leaving the faint odor of burning rubber as the only souvenir. "Now let's see if we can find them."

Merker increased the speed of the car in an attempt to find the former pursuers. The traffic was backed up as the result of his first evasive action, which in his wake had produced a multi-car collision involving both pursuers. Several squad cars were already at the scene of the accident. While they slowly drove by, both the men from the restaurant and Gregory and his companion were attempting to explain their side of the story to the police.

"That was Gregory in one of those cars," Callison exclaimed in amazement.

"Really, I hadn't noticed." Merker responded in a caustic tone.

"You knew all along he was in a car following us, didn't you?" Callison said, somewhat perturbed.

"I had a feeling it was him. Served him right. Listen—I'll take you guys back to your car now if you like." Merker said.

"Fine!" they said in unison.

The remainder of the car ride was in silence. Returning to the restaurant, Merker turned to Callison. "I hope the car ride didn't scare you. But I needed to let you know how serious this really is. I don't even know for sure if the men in the other car were with Gregory or hired by someone else. But I'll find out. I have to go out of town for a few days, but I think it would be a good idea if we keep in close contact."

Callison was having trouble deciding whether he needed to stay in close contact or have no contact with Merker. "You have my home number. I'm leaving tomorrow for home, you can give me a call." Callison opened the door.

"I'll do that. Nice to meet you, Mrs. Wells." Merker gave an imaginary tip of a hat followed by an informal salute.

"Likewise, Mr. Merker." Maxine followed Callison's lead.

"After all we've been through, you can call me Marcus or just plain Merker."

"And you can call me Maxine." She closed the door, and Merker carefully drove down the street into the darkness of the night.

Merker returned home after picking up an extra-large order of guacamole dip, chips and a case of beer. He expected company that evening, but wasn't sure when his company would arrive. The Sox were on television against the Yankees, and Merker desperately needed a distraction. The knock on his door came during the eighth inning, but the game was a rout anyway, so Merker really didn't mind.

Merker looked through the peephole in his door and noticed there were two men waiting, the same two men who had been in the restaurant. Merker opened the door and the two men suddenly rushed through the doorway, one grabbing him in a bear hug, the other maneuvering behind.

"You son of a bitch!" yelled the taller of the two, the one who had the bear hug around Merker.

"I'm sorry, Peter. I didn't know the other car would be there." Merker had worked with Peter Moiner and Paul Abnus on several cases in the past. They were consummate professionals, conscientious and discreet, two qualities Merker sought in anyone he chose to be associated with.

"You know we could've been killed." The smaller of the two, Paul Abnus, was sitting at the table eating chips and dip. He was joined by Merker and the taller man.

"Listen guys, I'm really sorry. Of course, I'll pay for any damages."

"No problem, Merk," said the taller man, Peter Moiner. He was four inches taller than Merker, ten years younger, and his glasses had apparently been chipped during the accident. "No one was hurt and the car had only a couple of dings. To be quite honest, it would be very difficult to tell which dents were already there and which were new."

"So did it at least work?" The smaller of the two was about Merker's size, but not his weight. Paul Abnus was much thinner than Merker, by at least twenty to thirty pounds, and his dark brown hair was tied in a ponytail.

"I think it worked. Callison was definitely rattled, but the woman unbelievably remained cool as a cucumber. I don't know who she is, but we need to check her out."

Merker had hired Peter and Paul to follow both him and Callison hoping that would convince Callison the threat from Gregory was legitimate and help facilitate Callison's cooperation in obtaining the inside information he needed.

Merker had used a similar tactic earlier by sending Callison an anonymous letter with a Chicago postmark, intended to cast a doubt in Callison's mind. Merker hoped this would raise a reasonable doubt from Callison's perspective, which would allow Merker the opportunity to gain his confidence.

Merker wasn't sure how effective the letter had been, but he had accomplished what he wanted in his initial meeting with Callison. Hopefully this little foray would help insure Callison's cooperation.

"No problem; does she have a name?" Peter Moiner asked.

"Maxine Wells. She's married and works at the AMA," Merker said.

"Got it," said Paul Abnus, who was writing down the name on his note pad.

"These chips are pretty good." Peter said, stuffing his face with chips as if they were the last ones on earth.

"Here, have another beer. You've earned it." Merker threw a beer each to Peter and Paul.

The three watched the end of the game, finished the chips

and the beer, before Peter and Paul called it a night.

Several minutes after they left there was a knock at the door. Merker opened the door, expecting to see Peter and Paul, assuming they must have forgotten something. To his surprise, he saw Van Gregory and a friend standing at the door. Merker realized he was out-manned, but he still had his secret weapon, and it was totally loaded in the event he needed it.

Gregory and his companion bolted into Merker's home, pushing Merker into a corner, where Gregory held him by his collar. "Listen, you asshole, I don't know who you think you're dealing with, but you just bought yourself a world of hurt." Gregory's face was flushed, neck veins distended. He sprayed saliva with each word.

"I'd advise you to take your hands off of me." Merker's eyes were piercing as he stared unflinchingly at Gregory.

"You got a lot of balls, you hot fucking dog." Gregory was frenzied.

"Let go, or else." Merker thought about using his secret weapon, but would wait until he knew there was no other option.

The other man was standing in the doorway putting on padded gloves. It was the time to utilize his secret weapon. What was once an embarrassment was now a weapon that Merker learned to control.

During his youth Merker had difficulty controlling some of his bodily functions. It started out primarily as passing of gas from both below and above, but as he got older he had trouble holding back the food he had just eaten, especially when he got upset or nervous. This regurgitation of the partially digested contents in his stomach accounted for many embarrassing moments. But while in the service, Merker had been counseled by a fellow soldier, who was also a hypnotist.

With his help Merker was able to harness his propensity to regurgitate his food. He learned to control the urge and under a self-hypnotic suggestion, was able to induce the emesis when it was to his benefit. The effectiveness of this self-induced vomiting was limited by what he had eaten recently, and thus he had used this technique only a few times. The forcefulness of the technique directly correlated with the quality and quantity of the contents in his stomach. Merker knew the admixture of the beer and the guacamole dip could potentially be the motherlode of his career.

Merker was able to foster his gastric juices along with the guacamole and beer into a torrent of green vomitus directed squarely into Van Gregory's face. The projectile vomitus exploded into Gregory's face just as he was about to say something, and a good portion of the putrid spew found its way into Gregory's mouth, which immediately induced a like response from Gregory. Merker adroitly avoided Gregory's disgusting, yellow bilious discharge and used this opportunity to deliver a forceful kick to his groin, dropping him into the pool of the combined yellow-green, malodorous vomitus.

Merker then turned to Gregory's companion, whose complexion had turned to a color mimicking the mess on the floor, and who had already started his exit. "You want some of this too?"

"No, man, I just came along for the ride. This was his show." The man squinted. He could barely look at Gregory rolling around like a fish out of water, clutching his aching groin, moaning, while floundering in the pool of vomitus.

"Then get your friend, or whoever he is, the hell out of here and tell him not to come back." Merker spit a couple extra chunks of the green discharge left on his lips onto Gregory while Gregory's companion dragged him out of Merker's home.

The incident with Gregory reinforced the need for Merker to use the home security system he had installed, as well as always check before opening his door. He also needed to start carrying his gun again, just in case.

After cleaning up the mess, Merker retired for the night. In spite of the evening's excitement, Merker still needed his rest. Tomorrow would be a long day, which would start with an early flight to Phoenix.

20

Since Merker couldn't sleep, he had no difficulty arriving early at O'Hare for his flight to Phoenix. Merker couldn't resist the temptation of humming the melody of Glen Campbell's record, "By the time I Get to Phoenix," which at first was a pleasant distraction, but then the tune kept recurring in his mind until it was far more than a distraction, but a horrendous irritation.

The flight was without incident but the tune kept returning. Merker deplaned with a headache and a song stuck in his mind.

Merker was scheduled to meet Dr. Truelove at his home in Scottsdale, then they would both go to the bank to secure the letter. Even with the headache, Merker was attentive to his surroundings, especially heedful of anyone who looked even remotely suspicious. There was no evidence of Gregory, J.T., or anyone else Merker would consider as a potential problem. The directions he had been given were perfect, and Merker had no trouble finding Truelove's home, which featured textured stucco walls, squat round towers, and an unusual entry—complete with a cypress door and an arched iron gate, which reminded Merker of the inside of a seashell.

Before Merker could ring the doorbell, the door opened and a slender man with a well-trimmed mustache and graying temples greeted Merker.

"Mr. Merker, I presume? I'm Tyler Truelove. So nice to finally meet you."

"Same here. I really do appreciate your help."

Truelove's arm was outstretched, indicating Merker should go in first. The inside of the house was immaculate. The pattern and matched veining of the granite floors flowed from the entry to the main living area. The use of subtle area rugs and the precise alignment of furnishings with ceilings, cathedral or dropped, defined the spaces.

"Nice house." The decor was not Merker's taste but he could appreciate the effort Truelove had put into it.

"Thank you, would you like a drink of iced tea or lemonade?" Truelove had a youthful, bouncing gait and appeared younger than his actual age.

"A glass of tea would be great." Merker followed Truelove into the kitchen. It was possibly the largest kitchen he had ever seen. There were pots and pans hanging around an immense central island with six separate ceramic burners. There were also four ovens and a microwave. "Nice kitchen, I take it you like to cook."

"It's one of my passions." Truelove handed Merker a glass of iced tea.

"I can tell. So why after all these years did you finally decide to do this?" Merker took a sip of the refreshing mint-flavored tea.

"I've asked myself that same question about a hundred times, and the only answer I can come up with is, it feels right to do this now. Not a very good reason, but an honest one."

Merker finished his drink. "Did you notice anything out of the ordinary since I've talked to you last?"

"Nothing, nothing at all." Truelove's expression changed with Merker's comment, revealing some deep creases in his face around his eyes and forehead.

"Good. I'm sorry if I worried you. I really didn't think the phone was tapped, but I felt it was better to be safe than . . . "

"Sorry." Truelove's face relaxed when he realized Merker was only inquiring.

"Yeah, sorry. I was concerned I might have been followed, but I flew through Denver just in case. Anyway, I didn't notice anything suspicious. I just didn't want to put you in the middle of this whole mess."

"Unfortunately, I was invited to this mess years ago and now I'm finally going to the party. I turned down the first invitation, but I'm going to keep this one. I think it's time for me to get in the middle of all this. Let's get that letter!" Truelove grabbed his car keys and briskly walked out of the house. "I'll drive, if it's all right with you."

"Fine with me."

The drive to the bank usually took about twenty minutes, but Truelove decided on an alternate route that added about five minutes, just in case they were being followed.

Merker assured Truelove there was nobody in pursuit, and that he had probably blown this entire process way out of proportion.

The day was typically hot, and the bank was moderately crowded for the early afternoon. The safe-deposit box was located behind a guarded door. Truelove entered and returned within a couple of minutes. He wore a smirk that signified not only success, but also revenge.

"Do you want to read it now?" Truelove seemed as anxious for Merker to read the letter as Merker was himself.

"Before we go let's make some copies," Merker said. "You can leave one in the safe-deposit box; we'll decide later where to keep the original."

They asked a teller where they could make a copy of the letter, and she volunteered to make the copies herself. Truelove insisted he accompany her to the copier. They were back within minutes carrying five copies of the documents. Truelove then returned to the safe-deposit room to put a copy of the letter in the box while Merker started to read the original letter.

March 20, 1969

Dear Tyler,

I hope this letter finds you in good health and prosperity. I feel sad we have lost touch over the years but it is probably for the best. Anyway, I need to apprise you of a delicate situation that has arisen. I hope you recall the trouble we had several years ago after the merger went through. You know me, I couldn't let a sleeping dog lie. I kept trying to find out if the Caldo list was real or just some fabrication. Frequently I would be on the verge of an apparent breakthrough when the lead would vanish into thin air. But at a New Year's Eve party I ran into an old acquaintance, Douglas Kern. I don't think you ever met him. Doug was dying of leukemia and he told me he needed to get something off his chest before he died. He said he was one of the first members on the list (he called it the Tatum list), but he said it went by other names too. (Gance and Caldo and maybe others.) He said when the list was first

208

made in the fifties, it was used as an aid to help good prospects fulfill their dreams to become doctors. That was when Wayne Tatum was alive and running the show. Tatum was succeeded by a Dr. Alexander, who was the brains behind the Caldo list and the force behind the merger. This is the guy responsible for the destruction of our practice. Kern said that he had heard that over the last few years Alexander had fallen on bad times and had brought in some fresh young talent to help him. Two names he mentioned were an Alan Smithee and a Victor Rasta. Kern told me that they were probably the keepers of the list. Kern said that he felt real bad about what had happened and had heard I was still inquiring about the merger and the list.

After my conversation with Kern, I did some investigating and located Victor Rasta in New York City. The other person, Dr. Alexander, was impossible to find without his full name. I tried to contact Kern to see if he knew Alexander's full name, but unfortunately Kern had died in February. As far Dr. Smithee is concerned, I drew another blank. There was no listing of a Smithee in either the AMA or AOA directories. Then it occurred to me that maybe Smithee wasn't a physician, maybe he had a doctorate in another field. Since Kern was dead I had lost my best source for information and was getting very frustrated. I decided to concentrate on Rasta.

I attempted to approach Rasta in New York, but he denied knowing anything at all about any of this. His protest was so rigorous it convinced me he was definitely involved. That was a couple of months ago, and since then several strange incidents occurred. At first I thought I was becoming paranoid, but now I am sure I am being followed by a mysterious man dressed in black.

Merker put the paper down and looked up at Truelove, who had returned and was reading over Merker's shoulder. "I know who he's talking about. His name is Van Gregory. Believe it or not, he's still part of this whole thing."

"How do you know this?" Truelove was amazed.

"Because he was the man Dr. Cisko asked me to follow, the man who strangely showed up at Cisko's funeral, and the man who followed Callison to Texas."

"Who's Callison?" Truelove asked.

"He's the guy who replaced Dr. Cisko on the committee."

Merker was overcome by a sensation they were being watched. He began to glance carefully around the lobby. His concern was transmitted to Truelove, who also started to scan.

"What, what did you see?" Truelove said with a hint of panic in his voice.

"I'm not sure. I just have this feeling we're being watched."

"Did you see someone?" Truelove nervously continued to scan the lobby of the bank, but had no idea who he was looking for.

"Out of the corner of my eye, I think . . . I don't know. Let's get out of here." Merker wasn't sure what he might have seen, but he wasn't comfortable any longer sitting in the bank's lobby.

"Good idea."

They left, their senses heightened, but neither noticed anyone following them nor anything out of the ordinary.

On the return drive to Truelove's home, Merker reopened the letter. Before he began to read, he told Truelove to keep an eye out for anyone who might be following them. Truelove was so on edge that he didn't even hear Merker. His attention was fixed on the road, the traffic, and possibility somebody might be following them.

Merker opened the letter scanning quickly to where he had stopped.

. . . being followed by a mysterious man dressed in black. I actually confronted him one afternoon. What he said to me still puts chills in my spine. He told me that I was playing a dangerous game, a game that could result in very serious consequences for me and my family. My family! I nearly lost it, but I kept my cool and got my family to a safe place. It was the look in his eyes when he said that, which gave me the chills—his stare was ice cold and without any emotion. It was a dead stare. At that point there was no doubt in my mind this man could and would kill if he had to. That was when I decided to write this letter to you. I'm not sure what this letter will allow you to do, but it summarizes what I have found out over the last few years.

One more point you need to know. Once I had my family safely situated I decided to go after Rasta. This man is more arrogant than me, if you can believe that. Recently I found out about a former associate of Rasta's, who had a major ax to grind with him. His name is Dr. Walter Bartolli, and when I mentioned Rasta's name he was more than willing to assist me. Bartolli said he thinks he knows where Rasta keeps the list and would help, pending one condition—if we revealed the list, we needed to delete one name on it—Walter Bartolli. I told him I would remove his name if I got the list.

This is where I am asking you to help. If I get the files or the list, I will send you a copy. If something happens to me, I would like you to find a way to have Bartolli's name removed from the list. I know you can do that. I'm not sure what you could do with this information but I'm confident you will know what to do and when to do it. Hopefully you won't have to be brought into this mess again. I know I'm really close. In a few days I should have the list and I'll give you a call and we can celebrate like in the old days. I'm sorry for even bringing you into this, but I don't know where else to turn. I trust you more than anyone else I know.

Sincerely,
Amos

Merker looked up from the paper and noticed Truelove was still shaken. "How are you doing?"

"Did you say something?"

"I said, how are you doing?"

"Fine, I've taken several alternate routes and I haven't noticed anything to suggest we're being followed."

Merker knew that if they were being followed by professionals, Truelove would never know, but *he* would. Even when he was reading the letter, Merker was aware of the traffic, and the possibility of Gregory, or J.T., or both.

"Good. By the way, the letter mentions a Dr. Bartolli. Do you know anything about him?"

"After Amos' death I received this letter. I was angry and scared but I felt I needed to do something. So I decided to find Dr. Bartolli. It took me months to finally locate him." Truelove stopped at a red light and looked at Merker eyeball to eyeball. "I found out Bartolli died in a car crash the day before Amos. From that day my fear superseded my anger. That was when I put the letter in the safe-deposit box and tried to forget about the whole thing."

The car behind Truelove started to honk as the light had

turned green. The sound from the car startled both Truelove and Merker. They simultaneously looked toward the sound: a mother with her three children in a minivan.

The remainder of the ride was in silence. When Truelove pulled into his driveway, they both turned to make sure they weren't followed. There was no other car on the street, and they quickly went into the house. Inside, Truelove went to the kitchen to get Merker a glass of water. Merker sat on the couch and started to reread the letter. Truelove entered the living room where Merker was seated and handed him the water, which Merker took and started to drink without looking up.

"So, where do we go from here?" Truelove's voice cracked a little from being dry.

Merker's mind had been sifting the possibilities. He hadn't come to any conclusions but decided to verbalize his thoughts to Truelove. Maybe between the two of them they could decide on a plan. "From the letter, it seems Rasta is the key for us to get the list, and at least he's still alive and kicking." Merker looked up at Truelove. "Now what about the others?" Merker took the letter over to the kitchen table; Truelove followed. "Let's go about this in a logical manner. Do you have a pad and pencil?"

"Sure." Truelove produced a note pad with several pencils and pens from a drawer in his kitchen.

Merker's voice was slightly more upbeat. "Now let's go through the letter person by person. First is Douglas Kern, who is dead. Next is Wayne Tatum, who is also dead. But the letter also mentions a Gance list along with Caldo. Do you know what this Gance is all about?" Truelove shook his head. "Next we have a Dr. Alexander, but no first name, so this one will be next to impossible to check out. Then comes Rasta and this guy, Alan Smithee. Does that name ring any bells?"

"I can't place a face with the name, but it does sound familiar." Truelove was troubled by the inability to place the name, but he was sure he had heard that name before somewhere.

"So Smithee might be still around. Then he refers to that asshole, Van Gregory." A broad smile came to Merker when he thought of the last time he had seen Van Gregory and the state he had left him in. "And last, but not least, is the late Dr. Bartolli." Merker looked at the list he had just compiled. "We'll call this the anti-Caldo list."

Truelove smiled. "So we have a list, mostly of dead people. Where do we go from here?"

"We need to find out if the Caldo list still exists, and if it does, who has it. All we have is this letter, which contains no proof of anything. We can't even prove that it was written by Amos Wilcox."

"I have other letters written by Amos. I can have those analyzed by a handwriting expert I know. He could confirm that Amos wrote the letter. If you feel that's important?"

"I'm not sure. But we may need proof this letter was written by Dr. Wilcox." Merker said.

"No problem. So what else?"

"What else? We have the names of several people who are dead, but they might have spouses who are still alive and might have some information that might be helpful. Lastly we have the unknowns. Dr. Alexander, the man with no first name. Dr. Alan Smithee, the man with no history. And the word or name Gance. And my friend Gregory."

Merker looked back at the list, thinking that something had been missed. Not finding any deficiencies, he sat back and folded his hands across his chest as the plan started to unfold.

"How can I help?" Truelove asked.

"If you wouldn't mind, we could split up some of the busy work. For example, you could try to hunt down the dead spouses, while I try to check out the unknowns. Plus I have a plan on how to find out if Rasta still has the list."

"Really? What's the plan?"

"I'd like to keep it to myself, at least for now. Let me just say that we have a contact within Rasta's organization who may be willing to help." Merker was thinking of Maxine Wells, but before he had Callison contact her on this sensitive subject, he needed to know what Peter and Paul had found out about her.

Merker heard someone at the door fiddling with the lock. He immediately stationed himself against the wall next to the door. The man who entered was of a slight frame, but about six feet tall, wearing a flowered Hawaiian-type shirt and khaki shorts.

He smelled of suntan lotion. He had barely entered when Merker grabbed him from behind.

Truelove screamed. "Stop, Stop! This is my roommate, Earl. Please leave him alone."

Merker was embarrassed by his actions. "Sorry, Earl. Name is Marcus Merker. Pleased to meet you."

"You're an aggressive one, aren't you?" Earl was smiling as Truelove put his arm around his shoulder and gave him a little squeeze.

"Earl, Marcus is the private detective I told you about. He's here to help me with . . ."

"With your obsession with Amos Wilcox." Truelove nodded. "Well, maybe you can help him get over his Wilcox thing, and if you can do that I will be eternally grateful to you." Earl smiled at Merker.

"It's the least I could do since I attacked you in your own home." Merker returned Earl's smile.

"Good, I'm glad you see this the same as me. Listen, if I'm interrupting anything I apologize. I know I wasn't supposed to be here until later. I'll be leaving in a minute or so, as soon as I can grab a change of clothing." Earl retreated to the bedroom, leaving Merker and Truelove standing in the living room.

"I'm sorry about jumping Earl but I thought . . ."

"No harm done."

Merker asked if he could use the telephone to call the airport. Merker called to change his itinerary—instead of returning to Chicago he would first stop off in Texas and meet with Callison. He was able to get the next flight out which meant he had to leave immediately. Merker said his good-byes and left. Merker and Truelove exchanged their work numbers; they already had each other's home phone numbers and agreed to keep in close contact over the next few days.

Merker arrived at the airport and even had ample time to drop off the rental car. He knew there was a tight time line, but that was the way he liked it. He was dismayed when he got to the gate only to find the flight had been delayed an hour due to some mechanical difficulty.

Merker used this newfound time to call Peter and Paul and find out if they had any information on Maxine.

"Hello, Peter. This is Merker."

"No, this is Paul." Merker always confused Peter and Paul on the phone. "So where are you?"

"I'm in the Phoenix airport. I decided to make a side trip to Texas before I come home. What did you find out about Maxine Wells?"

"Very little. She hasn't been working very long at the AMA and has little contact with most of the personnel there. We can't even find out anything about her husband and where his job is. She's a loner at work, but nobody could say anything negative about her. We went to the department to try and check her out from their files but drew another blank. We are attempting to find a way to access her résumé; maybe that will give us some information to go by."

"So you have nothing? Nothing at all."

"Yep, nada, zilch, zero."

"That's great. Just great." Merker needed to know if he could trust Maxine as his inside person, the person to find out where Rasta kept the list, if he still had it. And the person to help him get to the list. "Listen, Paul, I really need you find something out on this lady. I'll call you when I get to Dallas. I expect some information by then. I need to know whether I can trust her and I need to know before I meet with Callison."

"We'll do the best we can."

"My flight will get in about seven. I'll call you at eight sharp."

"Okay, we've got some work to do. Bye."

Merker picked up the local paper and sat down to read the sports page. He was pleased to see the Sox had just moved into first place.

21

Callison immersed himself in his work, in part because he had no choice. Because of his recent exploits in Chicago his paperwork had accumulated. He also wanted to be distracted from Merker and the committee. The paperwork actually was less formidable than Callison had thought, and he was able to catch up in a single day. His clinical obligations were fairly routine, and he had almost completed his preparation for his hearing for the TMF. As long as he could avoid dealing with the issues of the committee, his life appeared to have become almost tranquil.

The resident clinic he was supervising had the usual array of patients exhibiting a plethora of medical maladies.

Jerry McIlhaney, a third-year medicine resident, came to Callison nearly in tears. "I have a problem."

Callison accompanied the resident to an office where they could converse in privacy and without interruption. "What's the problem?" Callison had known Jerry since he started the residency and had never known him to be this emotional.

Jerry sat still with his head lowered and his eyes watery. "Mr. Davis refuses to see me."

"What?" Callison was confused. Mr. Davis was a patient referred for evaluation of his high calcium, and Dr. McIlhaney was assigned his case.

"He doesn't want to see a DO." Jerry had difficulty even saying the words.

"What do you mean he doesn't want to see a DO?" Callison was confused. The clinic and medical school was entirely composed of DO's. By coming to this clinic he was destined to see a DO. Callison thought that maybe Mr. Davis meant he wanted to see an attending physician and not a resident, since that was not uncommon.

"Let me speak to him. I'll reassure him that an attending physician will also participate fully in his care."

Jerry shook his head. "No, he doesn't want to see you either. He doesn't want to see anyone here."

Callison was irritated. "Where is he?" Callison started for the door; he wanted to have a little talk with this patient.

"He left," Jerry said, still shaking his head. "I tried to explain but he kept saying he wanted to be seen by a real doctor. A real doctor! What are we?"

Callison could see the effect this remark had. "Don't take this personally. Some people are still totally ignorant of our profession."

"I know that. But I still take offense to his remark. This was an intelligent man. He appeared educated but he wouldn't even listen to my explanation. I've put in my time. I graduated with honors from a certified medical school and have worked my ass off. Excuse my language." Jerry blushed slightly with his last remark. "I busted my hump the last few years and..."

"I know it hurts, but sometimes that's the price we pay for being a minority profession. We've all experienced similar situations. I know that might not help you now, but at least you know you aren't alone." Callison gave Jerry a supportive nod.

"Thanks for listening. I'm better now. It's just upsetting. What irks me is he was referred here from an MD. Mr. Davis was a member of a HMO and he thought a medical school referral could only be to a MD. I explained to him we were a DO medical school and met all the requirements for full credentials to practice medicine."

"I know." Callison didn't know what else to say. He had experienced this type of ignorance before, but it was still upsetting.

"A real doctor." Jerry shook his head and mumbled. "What an asshole."

A knock at the door interrupted their conversation. Callison opened the door and was greeted by Nurse Johnson.

The nurse informed Callison of a patient who was scheduled to see him specifically, and not the resident. He had been waiting for him and was now becoming impatient. Since the rule in the resident clinic was that all patients were to be seen initially by the resident, Callison was reticent to break the rule. When he began to give his nurse some attitude about why the rules needed to be followed, she informed him that the patient was specifically told Callison would see him. His name was Enos Kodack.

Callison apologized and asked her to please put Mr. Kodack into an examining room. He would be there momentarily. Jerry assured him that he was now more upset with himself allowing this ignorant man get to him. They both left the room, Jerry to attend to his patients, and Callison to his patient.

Upon entering the room Callison quickly perused Enos' medical chart. Mr. Kodack was typical of many of his male patients, in that his compliance with his medical regime was less than satisfactory. The only occasions he would actually seek medical attention were those when he had an acute symptomatic illness, such as pneumonia or a laceration which required stitches, or at his wife's bequest. The appointment today was at his daughter's request.

Taking a deep breath, Callison entered the room. Mr. Kodack was seated in a chair and to Callison's surprise was alone, no Margaret, no Sally. He looked terrible. His face was ashen and gaunt, he had obviously lost weight as his clothes appeared several sizes too large, dwarfing his once powerful frame. His eyes were sunken into their sockets and surrounded by large darkened circles, and a distinctive odor permeated the room suggesting it had been quite a while since he bathed.

The conversation was minimal and Callison had difficulty even maintaining eye contact with Enos Kodack, who looked away at every opportunity. Any reference to Mrs. Kodack was met with a cold, empty stare and any attempt to lighten the conversation was met with silence. It was not a pleasant experience. At the completion of the examination, Callison could find nothing grossly abnormal, except his profound depression and his state of malnutrition. But that was enough. After numerous attempts at breaking Mr. Kodack's silence, Callison conceded. Maybe a psychiatrist who wasn't emotionally involved could do a better job.

In the waiting room Callison was greeted by Margaret, who

also looked as if she had aged a year for each of the eight days since he had seen her last. Only Sally, silent little Sally, looked the same: happy, content, quietly playing with her doll.

The exchange between Callison and Margaret had been scripted thousands of times, in virtually every hospital in the country. Margaret's role was that of the loving daughter, who just lost her mother and was now losing her father. Callison's role was the caring physician who would do everything in his capacity to save this dying man who had lost his will to live. But it was Enos' role of the grieving husband, who had lost his Annie that reached a level of intensity unparalleled in Callison's experience. His was so convincing, even the staff who was aware of his situation and generally hardened were in tears. Even those who had never met either of the Kodacks, could sense his pain, his loneliness, his grief, and his loss of self.

Callison assured Margaret he would do what he could. He had ordered some basic laboratory tests and would refer them to an excellent psychiatrist whose expertise was in treating the depression associated with death and dying. But Callison was concerned, as was Margaret, that Enos' life ended the same day as Annie's and there nothing any of them could do to stop the inevitable.

Callison studied Sally as she quietly played with her doll, knowing that in a very short time she would be without either of her grandparents, and Margaret would be without her parents; they would only have each other. Callison escorted the Kodack family to their car in the parking lot. The sun was particularly bright that afternoon, causing Callison to squint and shield his eyes with his hand.

The man who approached Callison had the sun to his back, so all Callison could discern was his silhouette, but he was walking directly toward him. "Dr. Callison, do you have a minute?"

Callison still couldn't see the face of the man as he approached, but his voice was familiar. He excused himself from the Kodacks so he could approach this man. Before Callison could answer, the face became recognizable and the voice was recalled. "Merker, what are you doing here?"

"We need to talk."

"Excuse me a moment. I need to see these people off." Callison returned to the Kodacks' car and said his good-byes.

Returning to Merker, he said, "Listen, I'm in the middle of clinic hours. How about if I meet you at the bar at Michael's Restaurant at five. It's just down the street and is a quiet place to talk."

"Okay, I'll see you there at five." Without saying another word, Merker disappeared into the sun.

The bar at Michael's was just as Callison had described—off the flow of the restaurant's main stream, quiet, subdued, and cool, close to cold, which was a pleasant distinction from the hundred-degree heat of the Texas summer. Merker ordered a light beer and pulled out the sports page of the newspaper, biding his time.

Several minutes after five Callison arrived. However, Merker was still engrossed in the paper and didn't notice him until he sat. "So what brings you to my neck of the woods?" Callison had ordered a diet soda, and the waitress brought his drink along with a bowl of tortilla chips and salsa.

"We have some problems."

"We? Why am I included in this?" Callison snickered.

"Because you care. Because you're involved whether you like it or not."

"Listen, I've thought a lot about our little escapade in Chicago since I've returned. The conclusion I keep coming up with is, you're nuts."

Merker laughed, a deep belly laugh. "Tell me something I don't know. Anyway, I really do need your help."

"I don't know; something tells me that I don't want to hear what you're about to tell me."

"That may or may not be true. I guess we'll find out afterward." Merker took a sip of his beer.

Callison was still depressed over Mr. Kodack, so this actually helped shift his attention to another subject. "So, what can I help you with?"

"I have a letter here I want you to read." Merker handed Callison the Wilcox letter.

Callison slowly read, trying to concentrate on the details. He reread the parts specifically pertaining to Gregory and Rasta. When he finally looked up, he noticed the salsa staining Merker's chin and the residual dribble on his shirt. Refraining from laughing, Callison asked. "Where did you get this?"

"From a friend." Merker wiped his chin with the back of his hand.

"Listen, if you don't confide in me then I can't confide in you either," Callison said, annoyed at Merker's evasiveness.

"Fine. The friend's name is Dr. Tyler Truelove. He was a friend of Cisko's from his California days. Truelove was actually a partner of another doctor, Amos Wilcox. They both had their practices ruined by the California merger."

Merker grabbed another chip and dipped it into the salsa, this time performing the maneuver flawlessly. "Wilcox believed and probably died trying to prove there was a conspiracy behind the merger, and that conspiracy was based on the Caldo list. You can see from the letter, this list started years before the California merger even took place. We're concerned the list is still active and is the reason for the death of Dr. Cisko and possibly Dr. Kahn, as well."

"Who is 'we'?" Callison asked.

"Truelove and myself. I just arrived from Phoenix where I met with Tyler Truelove and he gave me the letter." Merker looked at the letter for a moment before he continued. "I also hope you can see the reference to Gregory in the letter. Realize this was written in 1969."

"So what you're saying is, Gregory has been around since 1969 and you feel his following me can be connected to this letter? I find this very hard to believe." Callison accidentally dripped some salsa on his lap and wiped at it quickly with his napkin.

"I'm not sure, if there's a connection between this letter and you. But this does appear to be more than a coincidence." Merker studied Callison carefully during the conversation, but either Callison was not aware of Caldo or he was excellent at the art of deception.

Merker needed to convince Callison it was also in his best interest to track down the Caldo list, if it still existed. "Look, I know this seems a bit far-fetched, but if we can find the list, and if Rasta has it, then maybe we can make some sense out of this. Do you think you could help me find out if Rasta has the list? It won't be easy. We can't ask him. But there's always a way to get the information by some other means."

Callison reread the letter, concentrating on the parts pertaining to Caldo. "If you want me to ask Maxine about helping you find the list, well, I have some problems with that." Callison ate another chip, this time without salsa.

"So do I." Merker leaned in toward Callison and lowered his voice. "I did a little investigating on her background. Nothing fancy, just some routine stuff. Well . . ." Merker hesitated before he continued. "She has no history or background at all. I can't document her background education, the fact that she's married or has a kid, there's nothing. This has me concerned. I'm wondering if she can be trusted with any of this stuff."

Callison rubbed his temples vigorously. "How about if I try to find out the information you need on Maxine?"

Merker thought Callison might offer that solution in regard to Maxine Wells. Since Peter and Paul couldn't discover anything about her past, Callison might be his best bet. "Do you think you can find out the information without screwing up your relationship with her?"

"Our relationship is very superficial anyway, and now you've made me curious." Callison asked the waitress for another soda and another beer for Merker. "Not to change the subject, but tell me what you know about this Caldo thing."

Merker reviewed the information in the letter, elaborating on some of the details where he could. He told Callison how both Walter Bartolli and Amos Wilcox had died in car accidents on consecutive days, reminding Callison that was also how Harvey Kahn died. Merker could see this had an impact on Callison. He decided not to discuss the information J.T. had disclosed to him about Callison.

"So do you think Rasta is really involved?" Callison asked.

"Hey, this is no coincidence. Rasta has a major role on your committee and he's mentioned in a letter . . . what . . . twenty, thirty years before. Yeah, I believe he's involved. Up to his neck."

Merker grabbed a handful of chips and dipped them all into the salsa, gorging them in his mouth all at once.

"But what if you're wrong?" Callison avoided watching Merker down his mass of chips. "What if this letter is a fabrication? What if all this is nothing more than a theory that can't be proven and isn't based on anything real?"

"I understand your point, but there was and is a conspiracy. I'm going to get to the bottom of it, with or without your help. Hopefully it'll be with your help."

"How can you be so sure about this? Is this your sixth sense or something?" Callison said sarcastically.

Merker felt it pointless to respond, so he changed the subject. "Listen, Doc, I've brought this little gadget of mine that I'd like to put in your car. Do you remember the security system in my car?"

"Of course, I've never seen anything like it."

"Probably because there isn't anything like it. It's my own invention, and I've brought a modified model to put in your car."

"Why?"

"Let's assume for a second my theory is true. Then we can also assume they have a way of messing up a car to cause it to get into an accident, a fatal accident! My security system will let you know before you get into your car whether it's been messed with. It can't hurt to be on the safe side, and I promise I won't charge you."

Callison laughed, "Okay, my car is parked in the lot outside of the restaurant."

"Is there a place we can go where I can work on the car?"

"Why don't you follow me back to my house and you can work on it there."

They both drove their respective vehicles back to Callison's house, which was empty. Natalie was at a meeting and wouldn't be home for several hours.

"Would you like something to eat?" Callison asked Merker since he was hungry himself.

"Nothing now, maybe I'll get a bite to eat after I put in the security system." Merker pulled a tool chest out of the trunk of the rental car. He had come prepared.

"Listen, Doc, this might take a while, so if you need to do something...I'll give you the instructions on how to use this thing when I'm done." Merker wasted no time. He already had the hood opened, investigating the contents.

Callison used this opportunity to go into the house and heat up some frozen lasagna. Once he finished his dinner and read mail, he checked on Merker's progress. Merker said he was about halfway through with the installation and suggested Callison use this time to call Maxine Wells. Callison decided to follow Merker's recommendation.

Callison reached Maxine's answering machine and left a message asking her to call him at her convenience. Before Callison could return to check on Merker's progress, the phone rang.

"Hello, Dr. Callison, this is Maxine returning your call."

Callison was surprised at the response since he had just hung up the phone. "Hello, Maxine, and please call me Steven."

"I had the answering machine on to monitor calls. Before you tell me what you called about, I have some exciting news for you."

"I'm always ready to hear some exciting news."

"I continued to dig around and found out Van Gregory had been employed not directly by the AMA but indirectly by an employee of the AMA. What's interesting is this employee is a member of the committee, Victor Rasta."

"You're kidding me. Rasta?" Callison slumped in his chair.

"Yes, Dr. Rasta has employed Van Gregory on and off for several years, using another corporation or foundation to pay the bills. Gregory was most recently retained several months ago. As far as I can tell, he may still be on the payroll."

"This is interesting. How did you find this out?"

"I was with a group of secretaries in the cafeteria and we started talking about some of the physicians who were employed here. One thing led to another, and the conversation turned to physicians who, how can I put this, weren't very sensitive to women's issues. One of the first names to come up was Victor, the chauvinist pig, Rasta. I thought my relationship with Dr. Rasta was bad, but what I found out was my contact was actually much better than the majority of the other secretaries. Dr. Rasta just criticized me, but he humiliated others with condescending and sexists remarks. That's when Rasta's secretary, Margo, mentioned a man who made Rasta look like a woman's libber. She said he always wore sunglasses so you could never see his entire face, but you could feel he was constantly carping you with his eyes."

"Carping?"

"Oh yes, that's one of Dr. Jourge's favorite terms. It means he's constantly finding fault with you. You know, how you look, how you act, basically everything. Anyway he's always carping all the women in the office, and Margo said he must be evil because he's always dressed in black. So I asked her if she remembered his name. She said she could never forget it. His name is Van Gregory. I asked her what else she knew about him, and that's when she told me about his being paid on the side by Rasta."

"What a break, huh? Did you find out anything else?" Callison was amazed at Maxine's discovery.

"Of course, she said this jerk had been hired on and off by Rasta and he used this other account, a secret account, to pay him. Then I asked her if she would divulge any information about this account and she asked me why. I didn't know what to say. I didn't feel comfortable telling her about Gregory and our car chase, so I made up a story about someone I knew. I told her a friend of mine had been hired by Rasta as a secretary several years ago and she was accumulating a lot of overtime hours working on a special project for him. After working for weeks on the project, literally doing all the work, Rasta turned in the project and received a hefty raise, yet gave no credit to my friend. Rasta denied her any credit for the overtime and said she had no overtime at all. When she questioned this, he said there was no overtime documented and she couldn't prove she actually worked the hours she claimed because she had no written substantiation. Well, Margo bought the story hook, line, and sinker. She said she had reasons of her own for hating Rasta and would gladly cooperate with anyone who wanted to put him in his place."

"So did Margo tell you anything else?"

"Oh yeah, she said Rasta had made up this corporation and used funds from another source to support the corporation. It was called the Smith corporation."

"Are you sure it is called Smith, S-M-I-T-H?"

"Pretty sure but not positive. I can check it out if you like."

"Please do. Anything else?"

"Yes. This same corporation had paid for Harvey Kahn's trip to Chicago, and as far as I can tell Dr. Rasta has sole control of the funds."

"Did Margo know the source of these funds?"

"No, but I did ask her and she volunteered to try to find out. She said if we could nail Rasta, that would be great."

"This is excellent work. Do you know Margo well?"

"Pretty well. She's very intelligent and resourceful. I'm sure she'll figure a way to find out where these funds originated."

"My concern is her cluing Rasta into our possible investigation."

"I can assure you Margo is more than capable of finding this out without Rasta having a clue. She really wants to nail him and his buddy in black too."

"You're sure of that?"

"Very sure. We discussed the delicate nature of all this and she assured me nobody would know. Now, you said you had something else to ask me?"

Callison almost felt embarrassed having to ask Maxine about her mysterious personal life, but he needed to know, not only for Merker but also for himself. "I don't know how to put this, so I'll be direct." The silence on the other end of the line was unmistakable. "Because of some of the sensitive topics we'll be investigating we did a routine check on your background and . . ." Callison could hear a muffled laugh on the other end of the line.

"I know what you're about to say—you can't find anything out about me or my family, correct?"

"Bingo."

"Let me explain. I was happily married to a man named Albert Napier and had a wonderful son by the name of Sean. They were both killed in an automobile accident ten years ago, and I had a nervous breakdown. I couldn't even stand to see their names or say my own name, that's how bad I was. Anyway, my psychiatrist suggested I change my name completely in order to free myself enough so I could go on with my life. The name change helped. Over the years I was able to accept my loss, to the extent that I was able to keep some mementos of my family and not fall apart. I still have difficulty talking about this, but I can do it. If you need to check out my file, ask Dr. Jourge. He's the only one who knows about my past and he could give you the information you require."

Callison now was embarrassed that he had doubted Maxine's sincerity. "I don't know what to say."

"It's all right. You don't have to say anything."

Callison thought for a second before asking the next question. "I have one other favor to ask of you."

"Sure."

"Did you ever hear of a list that Rasta keeps? It may be called the Caldo list or the . . ." Callison had forgotten the other references listed in the letter pertaining to the list. "Hold the line a second, I got to check something." He quickly ran over to the letter then Callison picked up the receiver. "Hello, Maxine?"

"Still here."

"The other possible names for the list are Tatum, T-A-T-U-M, or Gance, G-A-N-C-E. Any of these names ring a bell to you?"

"No."

"What I'd like you to find out is if Rasta has a file or list under any of these names? And if he does, will you be able to access them without his knowledge?"

"That's asking a lot, Doctor. Do you mind if I inquire why?"

"Let me say for now that if this list does exist, there's a possibility that the information on it could really nail Rasta, as your friend Margo would say."

"Can you repeat the names so I can copy them down."

Callison repeated the potential names from the letter. However, if the letter was written in 1969, a new list could be filed under any name. He knew this was a long shot.

"I bet Margo would know if this list existed. Can I ask her?"

Callison was hesitant, but if Margo had access to Rasta's

files he would probably have to risk this. "I guess it's all right to ask for Margo's help, but this needs to be held strictly confidential. I mean nobody can know about this."

"I get your drift. I know I can vouch for Margo; she's extremely dependable but also very vindictive. She wants to nail her boss badly and will do whatever she needs to accomplish this."

"Okay, but be careful. I doubt you'll find anything, but you never know."

"If it's there, we'll find it," Maxine said with a quiet confidence.

"Maxine, thank you again for all your help." Callison hung up the phone and went outside to see the progress Merker had made.

To his surprise, Callison found Natalie in conversation with Merker. "Hi, hon. Marcus was explaining to me why he was installing a security system in our car."

By Callison's expression, Merker knew he had made a major mistake by telling Natalie what he was doing. So much for Merker's keen insight.

"Nat, when did you get home?"

"A couple of minutes ago. Marcus has been telling me of your exploits in Chicago." Natalie stared at her husband. It was a look he knew and dreaded.

"I was meaning to tell you about all this, but you know how busy we've been."

"Yeah, sure," Natalie said too quickly.

Merker could feel the tension in the air. "Listen, I'm sorry if I said something I shouldn't."

"No, you didn't say anything wrong," Natalie said as she stared at her husband.

"Anyway, your car is ready. Let me give you both the instructions on how the security system works."

Merker proudly explained the intricacies of his system to both of them. By the time he finished, even Natalie was glad he had installed it.

After the instructions, they all retired to the Callison kitchen, where Natalie and Merker ate a pot-luck dinner while

Steven nibbled. The talk around the dinner table was essentially small talk, avoiding the committee, the reason for the security system, and anything that might be controversial. When Merker was about to leave, Callison told him about his conversation with Maxine.

Merker offered to put a security system in Natalie's car the next time he was in town, and she appeared appreciative of his offer. Merker had a return flight to Chicago in the morning and told Callison he would be in touch.

22

Callison had seen Natalie this angry only a few times before, and he had hoped he would never have to experience her wrath again. Natalie's face was flushed and her eyes were shooting darts at him.

"When were you going to tell me about any of this?" She asked venomously, tapping her foot on the floor.

"I'm sorry. The reason I didn't mention any of this was because I wasn't sure any of it was real. And to be honest I'm still not totally convinced."

"Why don't you tell me what the hell's going on?" Natalie's foot was still furiously tapping.

"Why don't you tell me what Merker told you, so I at least know where you're coming from." Callison said defensively.

"No, why don't you tell me first and then I'll tell you what Merker said."

"That's fine. I thought my suggestion might make things a little simpler."

"I want to hear it all." Natalie sat briefly at the kitchen table but was too annoyed. She stood and again started tapping her foot.

Callison sat at the kitchen table after getting a large glass of water. He also brought over a glass of water for Natalie which she ignored. He then took a deep breath and began to talk. "Where to start?"

"Try the beginning!" Her tone had not softened.

"I'm trying to figure out where the beginning is. Do you remember the night at the sushi bar?"

"You mean the night I thought we were being watched? Were we?" Natalie stopped tapping her foot, awaiting Steven's response.

"I believe we were. Merker had visited me at work and had

mentioned he was concerned that the committee I was on could incite a major controversy. By controversy, I mean there are people who want the committee to do certain things, make certain recommendations, and if these people don't get their way, they might play a little rough."

"What people? Be specific." Natalie folded her arms across her chest.

"I can't, because I really don't know. But the man who was watching us may be a hired gun for some of these people. His name's Van Gregory, and he may have been involved in the deaths of several people."

"Are you serious? He's some sort of hit man?" Natalie supported herself on the kitchen table before taking a seat next to Steven.

"Are you all right?" Steven asked.

"I'm fine." Natalie was annoyed at herself for weakening her position. "This person is a hit man?"

"I don't know. That's why I was hesitant to tell you anything. I didn't want to scare you or make you worry needlessly." Steven placed his hand on Natalie's, hoping this would appease her.

Natalie's face changed subtly; the anger was still present but the wrath was fading. "Go on."

"Anyway, Merker told me to watch out for Van Gregory and he gave me this photo." He pulled the photo, crumpled but still intact, from his wallet and showed it to Natalie.

Natalie's wrath was rekindled. "Why haven't I seen this before now?" she demanded.

"Because, I thought Merker was some kind of nut case when he gave it to me. I initially threw the picture in my desk. Then after we recognized Gregory at the restaurant, I wanted to talk to Merker before I told you anything."

"Why?" Her eyes refused to turn away from his.

"Because I had no idea who he was or what he was about. When I met with Merker in Chicago, we discussed several things, and one of them was Gregory."

"And..." Natalie was not accepting Steven's vague answers.

"And, Merker thought Gregory was involved in some sort of

231

conspiracy involving the committee."

"What sort of proof does he have to make such a statement?" Natalie's anxiety was building and she stood again.

"Most of the proof is speculative but compelling. For example, Gregory was seen here, following us, and was also seen following me and Merker in Chicago. Merker states that Dr. Cisko—remember he's the doctor who died and I replaced on the committee?" Natalie nodded. "Anyway, Merker says he was asked by Cisko to check out Gregory because Cisko was concerned about him. Also Merker has a letter written by some other doctor over twenty years ago. The letter also implicated a man filling Gregory's description who was following him back then."

"Wait a minute. Are you trying to tell me a man has been following doctors for over twenty years? Why?" Natalie started to tap her foot again.

"That's the million-dollar question. Now you know why I was hesitant about telling you any of this?"

Callison had gotten through to Natalie, as she again took her seat next to him at the kitchen table. He could see in her facial expression and her mannerisms that she was getting calmer.

Callison, feeling a bit more confident continued, "Apparently a friend of Cisko's from the old days contacted Merker with this old letter. This letter possibly implicates a key member of my committee as a conspirator."

"You're kidding? A conspirator in what?"

"I really don't know, but my best guess would be a conspirator in some sort of plot to influence my committee to come up with a recommendation that would benefit a selected group of physicians, possibly to the detriment of others. The conspiracy may have started years ago when a merger occurred in California between the DO's and MD's. Since my subcommittee is charged with determining whether a merger between the two professions would be beneficial, I think this letter might be more than a coincidence. What concerns me is all this is totally speculative and nothing is substantiated. Before I could even consider saying anything about a Doc whose credentials are impeccable, I would need a lot more hard data than I currently have."

"I can understand that. But you still haven't answered the question, why would they, whoever 'they' might be, want to do this?"

"Remember when I told you about the legislative act prohibiting DO's from taking care of Medicaid patients? You said at the time they were bluffing. Well, I originally thought you were correct. But now with all this stuff Merker has brought up, I started to think maybe there is a larger picture where really big money is concerned, and this committee is a key ingredient in where that money will be allocated in the future. You know, the politics of health-care. I don't know." Callison threw his hands in the air.

"What don't you know?" Natalie was perplexed.

"I don't know if a conspiracy exists or not. If it does, are members of my committee part of it? And if they are, where do they fit in? Where do I fit in this, if at all? And who the hell is this Gregory? And why does Merker feel he is such a threat?"

"There's a lot of questions there."

"You can say that again. I don't need this type of aggravation now, especially with my case before the review board coming up next week."

"Aren't you prepared for that?" Natalie said, trying to be supportive.

"I hope so, but you never really know for sure."

Natalie started to drink the water he had left on the table. Callison reclined in his chair hoping Natalie was appeased. He was wrong.

"So, Steven." Natalie called him "Steven" only when she was upset or needed his complete attention. "What was Mr. Merker referring to about your exploits in Chicago?"

"What exactly did Merker tell you?" Steven nervously started to drink from his glass of water, only to realize it was empty.

"Sorry, why don't you go first," Natalie said.

Callison knew he had no option. "When I went to Chicago I asked Dr. Jourge if he knew of Van Gregory, and specifically whether he was hired by the AMA, as Merker had suggested. Jourge was little help, but he referred me to one of his executive secretaries who assisted in the investigation of Gregory." Steven was now sitting erect in his chair, his body stiff.

"So what did you find?"

"Maxine Wells, the secretary assigned to help me, discovered that Victor Rasta, a member of the committee, actually did hire Van Gregory through another fund, a private fund over which he has fiduciary control." Steven paused. He was concerned Natalie would get upset, but he needed to forge ahead. She would not let him finish without getting an answer. "Remember I told you about a member of the committee who was mentioned in the letter as a potential conspirator?"

"Don't tell me it's the same person, Rasta." Natalie was chewing at her bottom lip, a nervous habit.

"Bingo!"

"So, you're telling me, this Dr. Rasta was named in a letter over twenty years ago, and this same person might be implicated in some sort of continuing conspiracy today, and has hired some type of hit man. A twenty-year conspiracy? Next you'll be telling me he killed JFK." Neither Natalie or Steven smiled.

"Who knows, maybe he did. All I know is Rasta is a well-respected physician and researcher. Why would he be involved in something this sordid? It doesn't really make any sense. Rasta's career is set, he doesn't need the help of this committee."

"Are you sure about that?"

"Well, I don't know for sure but I can't imagine . . ."

"What? That Rasta may have used this Gregory person in the past to help him with his career and now needs him again. That there might be more to this than is readily apparent?"

"I guess you could be right, but I still don't know." Callison's voice grew softer.

Natalie seemed to be getting frustrated at Steven's uncertainty. "What else? What about this car chase in Chicago?"

"So Merker did tell you about the chase. When I met with Merker in Chicago to ask him about Gregory, Merker noticed we were being watched."

"Gregory again?" Natalie nodded her head, waiting for Steven to agree.

"No, they were other men, not Gregory. Merker suggested we go to his car to see if we were actually being followed. Maxine Wells and I cautiously agreed, and Merker's concerns were confirmed when these men followed us. A car chase ensued, primarily instigated by Merker. I think in part, he was showing off. Anyway, we were actually followed by two cars, and guess who was in the other car?"

Natalie did not hesitate, "Gregory."

"Bingo! Merker is still checking into who the other men were and whether or not they're associated with Gregory. That in a nutshell is the escapade in Chicago."

Natalie rose to fill another glass of water. Steven knew Natalie's moods and expressions. He could see she was in deep thought, still gnawing at her lower lip. Natalie turned to Steven, intense and worried. "What are you going to do?"

"I'm not sure." Steven joined Natalie at the sink, looking out their kitchen window into the darkness of the night.

Natalie grabbed Steven's arm and pulled him around until they were face to face. "You're not going to pass on this are you? If any of this is even remotely true then you have to do something!"

Callison could feel the pressure building around him. "I'm doing something, thank you."

"What are you doing?" Natalie snapped back.

They stood in silence for a while. He could see Natalie's mood hanging over her like a cloud. Callison didn't want to answer, but he knew it was not worth the grief it would cause. "I have Maxine, the secretary, trying to find out if Rasta really does have the list, and if he does where he keeps it."

"What list are you talking about?"

"I forgot to mention a little detail. During the merger in California there was a rumor of a list—an inventory of names of DO's and probably MD's who could be counted on to be cooperative or persuaded to help in the merger."

"What exactly are you trying to say?"

"Again, I honestly am not sure, but I think if this list exists

235

it may contain an inventory of individuals who could be influenced."

"Are you saying bribed, or blackmailed?"

"Probably both, but again I don't know."

"Stop being so noncommittal." Natalie's voice carried disappointment. "I know we've discussed this before, but you can't always run away and hide from problems, especially problems with political implications. College was a long time ago. You need to get over it, once and for all."

Steven shook his head. "I don't know, we'll see." Steven knew she was right, but none of that mattered. He still felt responsible for the death of his parents.

It was time to call it a night. They retired to their bedroom, both wanting to have a romantic interlude, but neither willing to make the first move. Instead, they both had a restless night's sleep.

As soon as Merker returned home, he went over to Rudolph's apartment to see if there were any messages, and to tell Rudolph he was elected as Merker's new answering service, a service for which he would be amply reimbursed. Rudolph was home as usual, eating as usual, and as difficult as usual. Fortunately for Merker, Rudolph was also greedy—as usual—and finally agreed.

Merker decided to call Callison to discover what damage he might have caused. He felt comfortable calling Callison at his office, since he was confident his work number was safe. To Merker's surprise, Callison was not only in his office, but was also available.

"I was about to call you myself. After you dropped the bomb and left, I didn't have the opportunity to tell you about my conversation with Maxine." Callison said anxiously.

"Hey, Doc, I'm sorry if I got you in any trouble. Your wife really looked upset when I left," Merker said apologetically.

"No problem. We needed to have a discussion about all this and I'd been reluctant to bring the subject up. Anyway, she's fairly well informed now and we're still on speaking terms."

"Glad to hear that. I was worried I really messed it up." Merker was seated in an old pseudo-leather recliner of Rudolph's that smelled like moth balls, not to mention it was also extremely uncomfortable. He shifted cautiously.

"I have something to tell you. I talked to Maxine last evening and she explained to me the mystery of her inexplicable identity." Callison then recounted the details.

"That's an interesting story," Merker said sardonically,

"What, don't you believe her?" Callison was almost taking Merker's response personally because he was convinced of Maxine's sincerity.

"No, I believe you," Merker said sensing Callison's reticence to discuss Maxine. He decided to pass on this issue.

"Good, because Maxine discovered a source at the office who could help us find the Caldo list, if it still exists."

Callison's remark brought Merker to his feet. "What exactly do you mean by a source at the office?"

"Maxine found a secretary who will assist us in finding the Caldo list."

"Are you kidding? Do you realize what could happen if Rasta found out what we're doing?" Merker was furious. How could Callison trust Maxine, let alone some other secretary at the office? "If Rasta becomes aware of our actions, he'll destroy the evidence, if in fact it truly exists."

"Listen, we have to agree to disagree on Maxine. I trust her and feel confident she won't confide in anyone who might compromise our position. Also, in case you've forgotten, we really don't have much of an option. Maxine and her friend are the ones with access to Rasta. If we intervened, Rasta would surely know. I don't see any option."

Merker grew somewhat calmer. He realized he had no option but to agree with Callison. The die had already been cast. "Okay, so who's this other person?"

"Her name is Margo. She's Rasta's personal secretary, who also has it in for him."

"Why?"

"Apparently Rasta is a male chauvinist pig at its worst and most—if not all—the women would love to turn the tables on him."

"I hope you're right because this entire case is riding on

Maxine and her friend."

"I have a good feeling about this. I'll keep you informed."

Callison hung up the phone and then dialed Maxine's work number.

The phone was answered by someone else, who told Callison Maxine was on another line. Callison asked her if she would tell Maxine he was waiting. Within seconds Maxine was on the line.

"Dr. Callison could you hold for a few seconds longer so I can get to a more private line..." "Are you still there?" Maxine's voice was a little raspy and slightly out of breath.

"Yes, I'm here." Callison answered.

"Do I have news for you. Margo may have found the list. She recalls a list on an old floppy disk, but she couldn't locate the disk at the office. But she is suspicious the list is probably in his home computer files. She also thinks the information can also be found in a paper file he keeps in a locked file cabinet in his study."

"So you don't have the list?"

"No, but if the list is kept at his home, she feels confident we'll be able to access the file." Maxine said excitely.

"Is she sure the list is on a computer disk?"

"Not one hundred percent. She was able to access a master file and found a reference to the Caldo files; however, she could find no evidence of these files in his office at work. She worked at Rasta's home on occasion and knew he kept separate files at his home. That was where she came across the Smithee foundation, not the Smith corporation, which I believe I told you before."

"This is incredible. Are you sure Rasta has no idea about any of this?"

"Positive. What's even better is I have gotten us an invitation to his home this Saturday night. Rasta is having a party and I mentioned to Dr. Jourge you'd be coming in town for some committee business. He told Rasta, who invited us both to the party at his home."

"Whoa, are you suggesting we break into Rasta's home?"

"No, we're invited. Margo told me exactly where to look in his study for the files. I figure one of us could keep an eye out for any intruders and the other could find the files or the disk or both."

"Why are you doing this? If we get caught your job is finished and so is my position on the committee."

"Men like Rasta have always gotten their way, mostly at the expense of others. I have all too frequently acquiesced even when I knew they were wrong. I'm not going to do that any longer. I believe you're trying to do the right thing, and for once I'd like to be on the side of the good guys. You are the good guys, aren't you?"

"I hope so."

"Anyway, this is really pretty interesting stuff, and my life has been so boring and routine, I can really use a little excitement. By the way, I made reservations for you through our travel agency to come in Friday evening and leave Sunday. If you need to change the times of the flights, I believe you have the number of the agency."

Callison's mind was spinning. *Am I getting in too far? Does this make any sense?* Should he go to Chicago to break into Rasta's study and steal the list? The old college Callison would have jumped at such an opportunity, but the post-sit-in Callison didn't feel as comfortable.

"I'll be there." Callison said, rolling his eyes.

"Great. Oh, one other thing. Dr. Jourge asked me if you could find some time Saturday before the party to meet with him and update him on the status of the committee."

"Sure, why not? Could you arrange that?" Callison asked.

"No problem. If you like, I can pick you up at the airport Friday evening." The enthusiasm was back in Maxine's voice.

"That would be nice. See you then."

Callison silently sat and stared at the walls of his office wondering what kind of mess had he gotten himself into.

23

Rudolph frantically knocked at Merker's door. Nobody was home. He nearly fainted when he felt a hand grab his shoulder. He turned in the direction of the contact and there was Merker standing in front of him. Without saying another word, Rudolph grabbed Merker by the hand and pulled him into his apartment before he released his grasp. Rudolph picked up the phone left dangling off the table where he had dropped the receiver.

"Hello, are you still there? Great, here's Merker." Rudolph motioned for Merker to take the phone.

Merker grabbed the phone and sat in the uncomfortable, recliner. "Hello, this is Merker."

"Hello Merker, this is Tyler Truelove, how's everything going?" Truelove's voice was chipper and had a musical flow to it.

"Fine, Tyler, what can I do for you?" Merker was confused by Truelove's flippant tone.

"I've been busy following up on the people from the letter and have some interesting news for you."

"What'd you find?"

"I tracked down the widow of Douglas Kern. This turned out to be quite an experience since she had remarried twice. When I finally reached the former Mrs. Kern, alias Harriet Barker–Kern–Swialki–Gerber, she was of little use. She could not recall any of the names from the letter nor anything even remotely related to that time period.

"Next I was able to hunt down the widow of Wayne Tatum, who's living in a retirement community in Clearwater, Florida. She must be close to ninety and has a marked speech impairment from an old stroke, but was totally lucid and did recall her husband had some kind of a list. She said all his records were discarded years ago long before her move to Florida and her recollection of those times was vague at best. She couldn't really remember any specifics dealing with the list. She was helpful, however, in clarifying one of our unknowns, Gance. She told me a story of how Miles Gance saved the life of Wayne Tatum during the Second World War. The list was originally composed of individuals Tatum assisted in getting into medical school. He dedicated the list to the memory of Miles Gance."

Truelove paused for a second. "Last but not least was the widow Bartolli, who not only remembers Rasta, but still feels he was responsible for her husband's death. Her name is now Helen Sanford and she was most cooperative."

Merker adjusted his position to the edge of the recliner, anticipating Truelove's next words.

"Helen Sanford said she also remembered a man fitting Gregory's description. Although she couldn't remember many details about him, she did remember he was despicable. She also remembered her husband had contacted the widow of Wayne Tatum shortly before he died. She wasn't positive, but she believed Mrs. Tatum could be the one who supplied him with the list."

"Are you saying she has the list?" Merker could hardly say the words as he leaned on the edge of recliner.

"No, she doesn't have the list. And as far as I can tell she still isn't sure the list exists."

Merker fell back into the recliner, exhaling heavily. "But she knows how to find the list if it does exist?" Merker asked with cautious optimism.

"Probably not. What she told me was that Walter, her husband, was being blackmailed by Rasta. Bartolli and Rasta were working on a similar research project and Bartolli discovered some critical component to a compound which could destroy cancer cells. Rasta wanted to market the compound himself, and he used the information he had obtained from Bartolli's college days to blackmail him."

"Do you know what he had on Bartolli?"

"His wife says he was caught with reefer and beer in the dormitory while he was in college. Seems pretty tame today, but back in the late fifties it could mean serious jail time. Anyway, somehow Bartolli got out of his mess, but Rasta was aware of his past record and used it to blackmail Bartolli."

"So he gave in to Rasta?"

"He did, but he regretted it. Rasta patented his compound and sold it to a pharmaceutical company for thousands of dollars and didn't give Bartolli a dime."

"Nice guy."

"Yeah, real salt of the earth. That was when Bartolli swore to seek revenge against Rasta. For over a year Bartolli toiled in his struggle to find the perfect revenge. His wife said it became his obsession. She can't recall how he found out about Tatum and his widow, but she recalls vividly how excited Bartolli became when he visited Mrs. Tatum and proclaimed he finally had found the ammunition for his revenge. It was about that time, she remembers her husband discovered another person who also wanted some information on Rasta."

"Amos Wilcox," Merker said confidently.

"Exactly. She feels both her husband and Amos Wilcox were killed because of the information they uncovered about Rasta. She went to the police with her suspicion, but because of no evidence or motive nothing was done."

"What happened to the information? Was it the list?"

"She doesn't know. She thinks her husband had the papers the night he died, but that's pure speculation. After his death she carefully went through his belongings but didn't find anything that could be the least bit incriminating. She even hired a private detective to investigate her theory, but he was of little use. So she gave up the hunt and went on with her life."

"Did she get back in touch with Mrs. Tatum?"

"She says the private detective initially did, but Mrs. Tatum denied ever giving Bartolli any list in the first place. She told the detective she did allow Bartolli to review her husband's files and take the papers he needed. She discarded the remaining documents."

"That's strange. Why would she discard the files?"

"That's what I wondered too," Truelove agreed. "Helen Sanford said she personally contacted Mrs. Tatum several months after the death of Dr. Bartolli and asked her what she had given to her husband. Mrs. Tatum told Helen her husband found some

242

old files of Dr. Tatum's and asked her if he could keep them and she agreed."

"The list was in his files." Merker closed his eyes and crossed his fingers, hoping he was right.

"Very likely. Anyway, Mrs. Tatum told Helen she had discarded all her husband's files shortly after Dr. Bartolli's visit."

"So did he get the list?" Merker was frustrated.

"Helen isn't sure he ever did. She also suspects others might have been involved in her husband's quest and they might have provided the list, assuming the list did exist."

Merker stood up. His anxiety was increasing. "So what about this private detective she hired, do we have his name?"

"She said he died years ago and was of virtually no help at all in the case. Pretty typical, huh?" Truelove chuckled.

"Very funny." Merker was not amused. "Did you personally talk to both Helen Bartolli Sanford and Mrs. Tatum and confirm that they *don't* have the list, or don't know how to get the list?"

"I'm sure Helen has no access to the list and never did. I strongly doubt Mrs. Tatum has any knowledge of the list, but I never actually confirmed any of this with her directly."

Merker pondered his options. If he could obtain the list without having to utilize Callison, Maxine, and her friend Margo, his case would be much tighter. Was it worth the effort to meet with Helen Sanford and Mrs. Wayne Tatum? Merker decided he had a better chance using Callison and his crew. "Maybe if we just called Mrs. Tatum to confirm she doesn't have the list . . . "

"I could do that if you like."

"That would really help. Thanks."

"Glad to do it. By the way I also talked to Ethan Jasper and updated him. I hope that was all right?"

Merker wasn't overly enthused about another potential leak. "That's fine; next time you talk to him give him my regards."

"Well, that's about all I have. Do you have anything else you'd like me to do?"

"Not right now, other than confirming with . . . "

"Mrs. Tatum, right. I'll contact you after I talk to her." Truelove hung up the phone.

As Callison deplaned he noticed Maxine among the small crowd. She was dressed in blue jeans, short sleeved shirt, sneakers, and glasses. Her hair was in a ponytail. Callison couldn't recall whether he had ever seen Maxine in glasses, or was it her casual dress that made her look different. After exchanging greetings, they left the airport. Maxine updated him on their plans for Saturday, starting with a morning meeting with Jourge, followed by lunch with Margo, and ending with the party at Rasta's house. By the time Maxine and Callison reached his hotel, they had set the itinerary for Saturday.

Callison checked into the Park Hyatt and thought about calling Merker to let him know he was in town. He decided against this, as he was determined to show Merker he could get the list without his help.

Alexander Jourge met Callison in the lobby of the Park Hyatt at precisely 10 A.M., wearing a hand-tailored silk suit. His thinning gray hair was expertly coiffed, and his mildly tinted, steel-gray glasses suggested to Callison a much more formal discussion than the informal talk he was expecting. Callison greeted Jourge feeling woefully underdressed. He was wearing denim jeans, a tennis shirt, and loafers. The morning traffic of tourists and businessmen had abated, and the lounge off the lobby was relatively quiet, sprinkled with sporadic conversations. A waitress asked if they needed any assistance. They both declined, since they found a suitable meeting site in the far corner of the lounge overlooking the famous Chicago Water Tower.

"So, Steven, Maxine informed me you are in town conducting some committee work."

Maxine and Callison had contrived a story to justify why he needed to make an additional trip to Chicago. Their story was not far from the truth. The deadline for the committee report was approaching and much work still needed to be done. Maxine had told Jourge of some new information she had collated that needed his input, and she didn't feel comfortable sending this sensitive material to Callison via fax, e-mail or the mail.

Callison repeated most of Maxine's explanation. Once Callison finished, Jourge furrowed his brow and sighed. "I'm glad you're here because I would have had to call you anyway. I received a call from both the secretary of health's and the surgeon general's offices enjoining us to formally present our committee's recommendations within two weeks. I have been accosted by representatives from the White House soliciting updates on our progress. The burgeoning pressure in Washington and specifically the White House necessitates an immediate plan to help defray the stress.

"Our committee meetings will be scheduled for the week after next. They will allocate up to four hours for our presentation to a select committee appointed by the President himself. There will be representatives from the White House, the Department of Health, the surgeon general's office, and Congress."

"Well, I hope to have our subcommittee report ready within the next two weeks." Callison realized, if he were to achieve this goal, he would have to essentially drop everything else on his agenda.

"Can you facilitate the process so we can have the committee meet before we have to present to the president's select committee?"

"I think so."

"That's a relief. You are the first subcommittee chair I've contacted. I truly appreciate your cooperation." Jourge sat calmly with his hands clasped in front of him.

Callison politely nodded. "So how are the other subcommittees coming along?"

"I believe all the work is on target, but we nevertheless have the major task of condensing our reports into a cohesive plan to be presented within the allotted four hours.

"I'll have my secretary contact your office to coordinate possible dates. By the way, what have you found in your investigation of Mr. Gregory?" Jourge's unruffled expression changed slightly as he asked the question.

Callison realized he had not discussed this issue with Maxine and had no idea what she might have told Jourge. He decided to be enthusiastic and direct "Glad you asked. We actually found some information suggesting Gregory had been employed previ-

245

ously by the AMA, but we're trying to confirm whether he's currently employed."

"Interesting. Do you recall when he was employed?"

"It was several years ago, but I can't recall the exact dates." Callison knew he had to appear confident and composed. He struggled to maintain eye contact.

"Why couldn't we detect the fact he was employed previously when we initially evaluated our records?"

This was the issue Callison had hoped to avoid. Should he reveal the alternate funding source to Jourge? What if Jourge was testing him and already knew the answer? What if Jourge had no knowledge of the other funding source? Would this knowledge then implicate Rasta and undermine his and Maxine's efforts? "We found several sources of funding that are not recorded in the routine manner. Gregory was hired by one of these alternate funding sources. We're currently checking out the origin of the funds to see if this may give us a better understanding of Gregory's role in the AMA."

"Keep me informed on this matter. We cannot afford to have our committee's credibility challenged by any outside agency, and I am still consternated by your allegation about Mr. Gregory."

Callison was relieved Jourge had not pressed the issue. He was equally concerned about Jourge discovering the link to Rasta which would create quite a controversy, especially without any substantiating hard data, other than a letter written decades ago. Maybe tonight Callison would have the hard data he needed.

24

Maxine was accompanied by an attractive middle-aged woman, Callison assumed she was Margo. Margo was dressed in a white pant suit and a black tank top that complimented her tan, her sparkling white teeth, and her firm, compact physique. Margo's silken hair wafted as she walked and her eyes slightly slanted, bestowing upon her an exotic flair. Maxine was dressed in a tan pant suit, her dirty blond hair was tied in a tight ponytail, and she wore sunglasses. Both women walked, stride by stride, with an athletic verve. From a distance it was difficult to tell them apart.

Maxine suggested they walk down Michigan Avenue to a restaurant that had an outside patio so they could take advantage of the beautiful summer day. The humidity was significantly lower than it had been, and the sun was bright, yet not too hot. It was a perfect day for outdoor dining. The small bistro off Michigan seemed an ideal setting for a casual lunch.

While walking to the restaurant, Callison couldn't help but notice how other pedestrians would stare at him being accompanied by a pair of attractive females, one on either arm. Maxine and Margo were both older than Callison, but you would never know that by looking at them.

At the restaurant Callison ordered a chicken salad, Maxine a shrimp salad, and Margo a piece of apple pie. Maxine and Margo dominated the conversation, avoiding the topic Callison needed to discuss. After hearing all he could about office gossip and the plight of the office worker, Callison changed the subject.

"How long have you worked for Dr. Rasta?"

Margo smiled. "How long? Well, I've been his secretary at the office for two years, two fairly long years."

"Maxine mentioned to me that you weren't very fond of Dr. Rasta." Callison said.

"Actually, that's an understatement. Victor Rasta is a brilliant man but not a nice human being. How he picked the medical profession as his career is a mystery to me; he's much better suited to be a lawyer."

Callison smiled at Margo's remark, as did Maxine.

"How did you find out about the Caldo file?" Callison knew he needed to be comfortable with Margo, and this seemed to be the best way to begin.

"When Maxine mentioned she needed some information about Van Gregory, I knew my opportunity had come to pay back Rasta for all the ingratitude and nastiness I had to endure, especially over the past year. As bad as Rasta is, Gregory is worse, much worse."

"How so?" Maxine interrupted.

"Well, you know how abusive Rasta can be at times. Gregory is that way or worse all the time. He is hypercritical and very condescending, which is fairly ironic because I think the guy has the IQ of a kumquat." Margo's voice had increased in intensity.

Maxine laughed.

Margo smiled and continued. "Rasta has been very protective of Gregory when complaints of inappropriate behavior or harassment would occur. This seemed strange to me, as if Gregory had something on Rasta." Margo raised her right eyebrow. "Anyway, Maxine, you don't even know this. A little over a year ago I was aware of an opening in the department, a supervisory position that I really wanted. I knew Rasta was going to be the one to make the final decision, so I approached him about the job. He asked me to go dinner with him because he didn't feel comfortable discussing this at the office. I agreed to meet him for dinner. Big mistake."

"You didn't . . . ?" Maxine's eyes were wide open and her mouth agape.

Margo slowly nodded. "I did. It was so stupid."

"You slept with him?" Callison asked astonished.

"Yes, and of my own free will."

"That's outright sexual harassment. You probably can sue him on legal grounds," Maxine stated.

"For what? Although it was his idea, I didn't argue. Plus he's married." Tears were rolling down Margo's cheeks running her mascara and exposing some of the years which were hidden behind skillfully applied makeup.

"I take it you didn't get the job," Callison wondered out loud.

"Not only didn't I get the job, but Rasta threatened to fire me for seducing him to get a job." Margo wiped away the tears with her hand and then took a napkin from the table to blow her nose. "Anyway I was confused and scared. I needed this job and couldn't afford to be fired especially for trying to seduce a piece of stale salami such as Rasta."

"So what did you do?" Maxine grabbed Margo's hands.

"Before I had a chance to do anything, I was confronted by that lowlife Gregory. He had a tape of a conversation I had had with one of the other secretaries in the office, the one who eventually got the job." Margo raised her eyebrow. "On the tape, I said how badly I wanted the job and would do almost anything to get the job. He also had another tape of a phone conversation I had with Rasta, where I apologized for sleeping with him." Margo looked away and shook her head in disgust.

"Doesn't sound good." Callison shook his head.

"Really, so I just dropped it all and started to look for another job." Margo's expression changed to a sneer. "I found something that seemed good and I was just about to accept it when I decided to take another tack. Before I quit this job, I decided I wanted to get Rasta. I didn't know how, but I knew the opportunity would avail itself. I turned into the perfect secretary, subservient and passive, waiting for the right time." A huge smile formed on Margo's mascara-streaked face.

Maxine acknowledged Margo's smile with one of her own. "And now is the time."

Callison still hadn't had his original question answered. "How did you find out about the Caldo list?"

"I had total access to all of Rasta's files at work, but couldn't locate any reference to any of the names Maxine had given me. That was when I remembered about Rasta's home computer and files. I had worked on several projects with Dr. Rasta in the past which required me to work at his home.

"I know where he keeps his computer disks including his

secret stash, as well as where he keeps his paper files. I think that's where this list is. I also recall a reference to a list in the past. I think it was called Caldo."

"But you're not positive of that?" Callison said.

Margo looked at Maxine for a second before she continued. "The only way to be positive would be to check his home computer and paper files. I know I can tell you exactly where and how to look. If the files are there, you will surely find them. Then you'll have your answer."

Callison waited for his date for the evening in the lobby of the Park Hyatt. He sat strategically for people-watching, as well as for a view of the carport to monitor Maxine's arrival.

Callison noticed a black Ford Taurus pull into the carport. The car was driven by a woman, but Callison could not get a clear view of her face. Callison exited the hotel and peered through the window of the car. The woman in the car waved in Callison's direction, but he didn't recognize the driver. He turned to see if she was waving to someone behind him, but there was no one else. Callison pointed to himself and the woman motioned for him to enter the car. It was Maxine but she looked totally different. Callison sat and buckled up his seat belt all the while not able to take his eyes off Maxine. She had a new hair style, a permanent, and her makeup was exquisite. Callison assumed she had to be wearing contact lenses, since she was sans glasses. The perfume she was wearing was as intoxicating as her appearance. Maxine pulled away from the hotel, but could not help noticing Callison staring at her.

"What are you looking at?"

"I'm looking at you. You look mah-val-ous," Callison said.

"Thank you, you look pretty good yourself." Maxine eyed Callison, who was wearing his navy suit from Paris, a birthday gift from Natalie.

The drive to Rasta's house followed Lake Shore Drive to Sheridan Road, along the shores of Lake Michigan. During the drive they reviewed their plan. They would mingle for several minutes to acquaint themselves with their surroundings, and then slip off to Rasta's study, located on the second floor, first door on the right. They agreed Maxine would initially check the computer to see if she could locate the disk, while Callison would watch for any intruders. If Maxine was unsuccessful, they would change positions and Callison would search Rasta's files while Maxine would assume the role of lookout.

It was a beautiful night for a drive. The sun had just set, still leaving a reddish tint to the evening sky. The air was clear and fresh, and Callison felt confident. Rasta's home was an enormous Tudor with plush landscaping and a large circular driveway. As they drove into the driveway, they were greeted by a valet.

"Quite a spread," Maxine said. Callison nodded, thinking the same thing.

Callison was studying the outside of the house trying to envision where the study was situated when the valet pulled the car away, and Callison got his first full-length glimpse of Maxine in her black sequined evening gown, which tightly clung to her supple body. Callison had seen Maxine at least a half-dozen times before, but he now realized he had never really seen her at all. The first thing Callison noticed was her legs. The gown was split almost to the top of her thigh, and she was wearing black stockings which outlined her very well-proportioned legs. Callison was always a leg man; it was actually Natalie's legs that had caught his eye when they first met. Natalie still had a great pair of legs, but Maxine's were something special.

"Is everything all right?"

He realized the words were coming from Maxine. Maxine started to walk toward him, but it seemed she was floating rather than walking.

"I'm sorry, I was just thinking which room might be the study." It was lame but the best he could do.

"We'll find out which room is the study when we get inside." Maxine motioned for him to follow her.

"Why don't we go in then?" Callison grabbed Maxine by the elbow and escorted her into Victor Rasta's home.

Once inside they were met by Victor and his wife Helena, who were dressed for a formal affair. Callison scanned the crowd to see if all the men were wearing tuxedos, but there was a balance between tuxedos and suits.

Both Victor and Helena were very gracious and friendly toward both Maxine and Callison. Victor even made a special effort to thank Callison for attending their party and couldn't understand why Callison smiled when he thanked him; all the while Callison couldn't help but think of Rasta's response if he knew Callison's ulterior motive for attending.

Maxine and Callison survived the introductions and migrated toward the living area, where a harpist was playing. Callison noted Helena examining Maxine when they left the foyer and started to chuckle softly to himself.

"What now?" Maxine said.

"Nothing, I just noticed Rasta's wife giving you the eye." Callison couldn't take his eyes off of Maxine.

"Why would she do that? I don't even know her."

"Don't be naive. The way you look tonight every man's wife who works at the office will probably be thinking the same thing."

"What a sexist thing to say." Maxine looked around uncomfortably.

"Please—no offense intended. It's just that you look real good in that dress."

"I'll take that as a compliment and drop the rest."

"Thank you. Would you like a drink?" Callison intentionally changed the subject.

"A ginger ale, please; we have to keep our wits about us tonight."

Callison smiled and left to get two ginger ales.

Maxine was admiring the furnishings, which were primarily early American antiques all in superb condition. Paintings circa early twentieth century from both America and abroad adorned the walls.

"Maxine, is that you?" Startled, Maxine turned to see Dr. Jourge.

"Hello, Dr. Jourge, how nice to see you." Maxine smiled at her boss.

Jourge's face was slightly flushed, possibly from the wine he was drinking.

"Maxine, you look ravishing."

Maxine acknowledged Jourge's compliment with a bashful turn of her head. "Did Steven, I mean Dr. Callison, accompany you?"

"Yes, he's getting us a drink."

"I'm pleased you convinced him to come to the party tonight. I really like him and think his contribution to the committee will be invaluable."

"I agree, Dr. Jourge. He seems to be very conscientious and is also very professional and easy to work with."

"Good, I'm pleased." Jourge looked past Maxine, acknowledging Callison with a nod as he returned with their drinks.

"Good evening Dr. Jourge."

"Steven, how are you this evening?" Jourge extended his hand.

"Well, very well. Did you happen to see the spread they have in the other room?" Callison didn't know what else to say.

"Yes, quite the spread indeed," Jourge said politely.

"I'll say. Maxine, you should see the food. They have Beluga caviar, oysters Rockefeller, prime rib, even some sushi, the works." Callison motioned with his head for Maxine to help extricate him from Jourge's conversation but Maxine didn't seem to notice.

"Victor always has a first rate party. A bit pretentious for my taste, but always first rate." Jourge studied Callison carefully to see if his criticism made any impact.

Maxine intervened, "Dr. Jourge, maybe you can help me." Jourge's attention was immediately diverted from Callison to Maxine. "The paintings, are they originals?"

"I believe most if not all are originals. Many are probably worth quite a sum of money, as is the furniture," Jourge said as he surveyed the room.

"I would say," Callison said.

Jourge leaned in between both Maxine and Callison and whispered, "Victor's wife—that's Helena—comes from a very wealthy family." He nodded his head as he whispered the words.

"Oh, I see," Callison whispered back.

Jourge continued surveying the room. "Seems I've misplaced my wife. I would very much like to introduce you to her.

I'll return momentarily."

Callison used the free moment to talk to Maxine. "Listen, we need to keep focused on our plan. I think we need to stay away from Jourge. We don't need him looking for us later, if you get my drift." Before Callison could continue, he saw Jourge approaching them, accompanied by a woman. Callison immediately changed the subject, "Do you believe this place? It's magnificent."

Jourge was walking directly toward them when he was diverted by another couple, only several feet away.

He was still within earshot, so Callison continued his small talk. "They obviously have some bucks. Did you notice that the design on the wall is not wallpaper but it is hand painted." Callison referred to the intricate flowered pattern painted on the dining room walls.

"No, I didn't notice that." Maxine really didn't seem to care how the Rastas decorated their home. "So when do we make our move?" Maxine whispered. She hadn't noticed Jourge was standing directly behind her.

Callison watched Jourge for any reaction; fortunately there was none. Callison knew the time was near, if they were to carry out their plan. He grabbed Maxine by the arm and led her away from Jourge, then whispered that Jourge had been standing behind her.

Maxine, embarrassed, apologized as they continued to walk toward the dining room. Callison stopped and looked at Maxine. "After Jourge introduces us to his wife—we'll go then." Callison looked deeply into her blue eyes.

Callison and Maxine entered the dining area. A huge chandelier hung over the main dining table, which seated twelve. The room was crowded. This would be the opportune time to discreetly slip away, as they surely would never be missed.

Maxine noticed Dr. Jourge escorting an extremely attractive woman, who appeared to be many years his junior. The woman was wearing an exquisite evening dress, accented by a magnificent yet tasteful diamond necklace with matching earrings.

"Maxine Wells, Dr. Steven Callison, I would like to introduce you to my wife, Donna," Jourge said proudly, as if he was presenting royalty.

Callison noticed the jewelry, but what impressed him more was her cleavage. She was a very well-endowed woman, at least twenty years younger than Jourge, and that estimate was generous. After the customary pleasantries Jourge excused himself and his wife. Maxine and Callison watched as Jourge introduced his wife to another couple at the party.

Maxine could not resist saying. "I didn't realize Dr. Jourge was a dirty old man."

"Why do you say that? I'll be bet you she's very nice."

"Yeah, right. Well, is it time to do our deed?" Maxine said, wanting to change the subject.

"I guess so. Let's do it."

They proceeded to the main entrance of the foyer, where the spiral stairway led to the upstairs. Waiting until they were alone, they briskly climbed the stairs.

At the top of the stairs immediately to their right was a beautiful Tiffany desk lamp sitting on an antique end table, just as Margo had described. The door next to the table was the door to Rasta's study. Upon reaching the top of the stairs they both quickly looked up and down the hall. Seeing nobody Maxine swiftly crossed the hall opened the door to the study, and entered, followed by Callison.

The study was just as Margo had described. The focal point to the room was a large antique Chippendale desk, flanked by two walls of bookcases. Maxine turned on the small desk lamp and immediately sat at the desk in front of the computer.

Margo had given her the passwords which should access the system. The computer was an older PC just as Margo had said, and therefore probably didn't have the memory to store much information on the hard drive. Maxine accessed the hard drive to see if there was any reference to Caldo, Tatum, Gance, Smith or Smithee. There was no file under any of these names.

Meanwhile, Callison had the door cracked open so he could peer into the hall. All he could hear was his own heart beating, as beads of perspiration formed on his brow. Callison momentarily gazed over where Maxine was working. "Did you find anything yet?" Callison whispered.

"There's nothing on the hard drive I can find," Maxine said, frustrated. "I found a drawer of disks, but none appear to refer to the list."

After a few more minutes, Callison asked, "Is it time to switch?" His heart was pounding louder than ever and beads of sweat were now freely falling from his forehead. He was still intently studying for any movement in the hall.

"I think we need to try plan two, I couldn't find anything in the computer," Maxine whispered from behind him.

They switched positions.

The cabinet was locked, but as Margo had instructed, there was a key in a plastic holder attached to the bottom of the first drawer on the left side of the desk. So far Margo's directions had been perfect. Callison checked his pocket to make sure he still had his camera.

The key worked and the cabinet opened, giving off a minimal squeak. Callison stopped and looked toward Maxine, who turned suddenly to give Callison a glare. Callison shrugged his shoulders and returned to the file cabinet. Rasta had his files neatly organized in alphabetical order. Callison found nothing under Caldo, Tatum, Gance, Smithee or Smith, or under the L's for list. His heart was pounding louder than and he was also soaking wet from sweat. Just when he thought things couldn't get any worse, Maxine whispered somebody was coming.

Callison was about to jump out of his skin, when suddenly Maxine grabbed him by the arms and without saying a word gave him a kiss. Callison's initial reaction was to back away, but her grip was too strong. He felt her tongue enter his mouth and he opened his mouth slightly to reciprocate. She smelled so good and her kiss was so soft, seductive. Maxine then grabbed his hand and placed it inside her dress. She wasn't wearing a bra and her nipple was erect. Her breast felt soft, full, and warm. He could feel himself becoming hard.

Maxine moved her kiss to his ear and softly whispered, "I think we're being watched. We have to appear to be making love rather than spying."

Maxine straddled his leg, her body squirming as she started to grind her groin into his thigh. They both started to breathe more rapidly. Steven could feel her undo his zipper as she exposed his erection. Steven groaned. The voices in the hall were now a distant echo, but his lust for Maxine had overcome his fear of being caught and the pretense of this just being a charade.

Maxine reciprocated Steven's every passion as he became harder, she became more erect and wet, having him inside her now became her primary desire. Steven had moved from her mouth to her earlobe. Maxine shuddered and gasped. He then worked his way down her neck and finally to her exposed breast. Maxine used her free hand to run her fingers through his hair, then she guided Steven's hand between her legs, so he could feel her wetness through her panties. Their breathing was now louder and the voices from the hall appeared to be getting closer again. Neither Maxine nor Steven could be bothered by the voices in the hall as their desire was culminating.

Callison's pants were now down to his knees and the top of Maxine's gown hung around her waist as he voraciously sucked her breasts and her hardened nipples. Callison used his free hand to tear away her panties, which were now soaked, and used his middle finger to find her slit. Maxine groaned as his finger entered her, shifting her pelvis against his hand to ensure he would find the right spot, while she started to feverishly rub his erect penis. Maxine opened her legs, arching her back and called to him to enter her.

All other thoughts of Natalie, AIDS, Rasta, the list, and the people in the hall disappeared. He was totally consumed with passion as their sweaty bodies fell onto the Oriental rug. Steven entered Maxine and their groans could no longer be contained as they climaxed simultaneously. They were both panting, sweating, and shaking as their orgasms continued. Finally, both spent, they lay on the Oriental rug at the base of the antique Chippendale desk.

They didn't find the list but settled for the lust.

Maxine was the first to speak. "Isn't the door open more than when we began?"

Steven was lying on his back facing away from the doorway. He craned his neck to see the door, which was now opened much wider than he remembered. "I guess we had visitors."

"I'm sorry. It's just that I felt they were about to come into the study and I couldn't think of anything else to do. You looked so scared." Maxine's eyes were still half closed as she spoke.

Callison put his arm around Maxine and warmly hugged her. "You were tremendous. It was a brilliant maneuver. Plus I must admit a lot of fun."

"I enjoyed it too." Maxine leaned over and gave him a gentle closed mouthed peck on the lips.

"We better put ourselves together and get out of here before we have to do that again," Callison said as he stood, pulling up his pants.

"Why? Was it so bad?" Maxine playfully pouted.

"No, but I don't know if I can perform again this soon." They both laughed. "Plus I don't believe there's any list or file in this study, anyway."

They both stood and regrouped. Maxine placed her torn panties in her purse.

Before leaving they looked out the study door. The hall was clear and they hurriedly walked down the stairs and immediately left the house without saying any good-byes. Maxine handed the valet the receipt for her car and they smiled at each other.

"Did you actually see anybody?" Callison asked. He had been so caught up in the moment that the Mormon Tabernacle Choir could have paraded through the study without his knowledge.

"I really can't say for sure, but I do believe somebody did peek their head into the room. I have no idea who that somebody could have been."

"Before this whole thing started, you said you saw people coming down the hall?"

"Yes, one person was Rasta, but I don't know the others."

"Others, how many?" Callison looked about. He had a sense that everybody knew what he had just been doing.

"I'm not sure, it happened so fast but I believe about two or three others."

The valet pulled Maxine's car into the driveway and they got in and drove off.

"I hope you don't think badly of me," Maxine said in a coquettish tone.

"No, not at all. And I hope you don't think badly of me either." Callison brought his hand to his face to rub his chin. He could still smell her on his fingers.

"Of course not. I'm sorry we couldn't find the list. Where do we go from here?"

"Oh, yes—the list. To be honest, I'm not sure, but tonight might have been the final stop. I guess we'll wait and see what the ramifications are from tonight. Then we'll regroup." Callison looked at his hand and placed it on his lap.

The remainder of the ride Maxine and Steven spent in deep thought about the evening. Still fevered from their tryst, both repressed their animal instincts—attempting to put this entire evening behind them.

Maxine dropped Steven off at his hotel and he gave her a peck on the cheek. "I'll call you tomorrow."

25

Callison tossed and turned all night. His inability to find the list bothered him, but not nearly as much as his indiscretion with Maxine. Callison watched each hour pass on the digital clock next to his bed, finally getting out of bed at 5:00 A.M. He completed the paperwork he had brought to take his mind off his problems, but it didn't work.

He could not appreciate the sunrise because the buildings blocked the dawn, but when Callison sensed the sun had arisen he called for breakfast. Since his flight was leaving later that morning Callison decided to call Maxine. The call was transferred to her answering machine but Callison had remembered she frequently used the answering machine to screen her calls.

As he suspected Maxine picked up the phone when he started to leave his message. "Dr. Callison, I presume."

"Good morning, Maxine. Did you sleep well?"

"Like a baby. How about you?"

Callison was embarrassed to tell her he hadn't slept at all, primarily because of her. "I slept okay. What I'm calling about is a game plan, specifically where do we go from here? Do you have any suggestions?" Callison wasn't expecting an answer, but he hoped to determine Maxine's state of mind.

"If you like, I can call Margo and see if she has any ideas."

Callison was still shaken from Margo's last suggestion. He did not want to venture into those waters again, at least not at this time. "Let's keep Margo out of this for the time being. I think we should both return to our respective jobs and give this matter some time before we decide to do anything else."

"Whatever you say, you're the boss," Maxine said calmly.

Callison thought to himself how wrong she was.

"I'll keep my eyes and ears open in case something comes up relative to the list," Maxine said.

Callison couldn't determine if there was some duplicity in the statement, so he opted for another topic. "I do have an assignment for you."

"Great, what can I do?"

Maxine's enthusiasm seemed to be unaffected by the events of the prior evening, but Callison wasn't sure whether that was good or bad. "I'd like you to contact the members of the subcommittee and see if you could coordinate a time when we could meet prior to the meeting that Dr. Jourge is planning."

"That should be a piece of cake."

"Thanks for your help, again," Callison said.

"My pleasure and about last night . . ."

Callison held his breath; this was a subject he wanted desperately to discuss yet felt uncomfortable even thinking about.

"As far as I'm concerned nothing happened," she said, "if that's what you would like." Maxine's voice was without any innuendo.

Callison, feeling slightly ashamed and embarrassed, still didn't know exactly what to say. "I think that might be best for now, and I appreciate your understanding."

"Don't you have a flight to catch pretty soon?" Maxine said, changing the subject.

Her remark caught Callison off guard, but then he realized she had made his reservations. Of course she would know when his flight was leaving. "Yes I have a cab picking me up."

"Have a nice trip. I'll call you with some possible dates for the subcommittee meeting."

As Callison put down the receiver he felt much better about the previous evening, although the worst was yet to come. He still had to confront Natalie. Callison thought about calling Merker, but the effort seemed too much for him at this time, so he left for the airport.

Merker hesitated over his list of things to do. First on the list were the phone calls he needed to make: Callison, Truelove, Peter, and Paul. Merker was thinking which call would be the most informative when the phone rang. To his surprise, it was none of the above. It was Ethan Jasper. Merker felt guilty about not calling Ethan Jasper, but he knew Truelove had contacted him so he was at least partially informed.

"I'm sorry to disturb you, Mr. Merker, but after my conversation with Tyler I felt I needed to talk to you."

Merker considered asking Jasper if he could call him back using Rudolph's phone, but decided to see where the conversation was headed first. "What can I do for you, Doctor?"

"Tyler told me about the letter and . . ."

Merker realized he had made a mistake. He needed to interrupt before Jasper revealed too much information. "I'm sorry, Doctor, but someone's at my door. Can I call you back?"

"Do you have my number?"

"Yes, I'll call you right back." Merker hung up the phone and crossed the hall to Rudolph's apartment. As usual Rudolph was home. He quickly called Jasper back.

"Hello, Dr. Jasper, I'm sorry for the interruption, what can I do for you?" Merker deliberately avoided informing Jasper about the possibility of the phone being tapped. He didn't need another innocent person involved.

"It's more like what can I do for you? Like I said, I had talked to Tyler and he told me about the letter from Amos Wilcox and the possible leads to the Caldo list. How can I be of help?"

Merker didn't want to insult Jasper, but he really didn't want his help. He was grateful to Jasper for having found Truelove and thus the letter, but that was then. Now he had enlisted Callison, who was using Maxine and Margo to find the list, so Jasper wasn't needed. As these thoughts raced through Merker's mind he made a mental notation to call Callison as soon as he was finished with Jasper.

"I think I have most of the investigation under control but maybe you can help with some of the stuff left over from the letter." Merker didn't want to dismiss Jasper, so he would defer him instead.

"I'd be glad to help."

"If you could call Truelove and between the two of you could figure out whether any of the relatives of the people mentioned on the list could be of any assistance. That would be a big help."

"I also have some fairly influential contacts in the profession who might be of some help," Jasper said.

"I think it would be best if we kept this to ourselves, at least for now. Maybe sometime later I'll call you for your contacts, but it's way too early now." Merker doubted any of Jasper's contacts would be of any benefit, but he jotted a note to himself just in case.

"I just want to be involved. Jonas Cisko was a dear friend, and if his death was secondary to someone protecting a list, well, I need to know I've done what I could to make sure the guilty parties are brought to justice."

"I can tell you, you're doing all you can and your help has been invaluable."

"Thanks. I'll be calling back if I find something out after I talk to Tyler."

Merker sat back in the recliner. After a minute he remembered he wanted to call Callison. He returned to his apartment to find the number and then traipsed back to Rudolph's to make the call.

Merker's call was answered by Callison's wife, Natalie, who was remarkably friendly considering the circumstances in which they had last met. "I'm so pleased you called. Ever since that evening I've felt terrible about being so rude and inhospitable. But the story you told me about Steven's trip to Chicago caught me so off guard."

"I'm sorry if I caused any problems between the two of you, but I thought you knew about the trip."

"The trip, yes. The details, no. Steven didn't want to unnecessarily worry me, so he skipped the details. But he spent the better part of that evening telling me all the details he had previously spared."

"I hope it didn't cause any problems?" Merker was concerned. He still needed Callison's cooperation in the case.

"No, just some conversation which was long overdue. I guess I should thank you for opening the door, so to speak. Actually, let me thank you by inviting you to dinner at our home the next time you're in town."

"Thanks, that's very nice. By the way, is your husband at home?"

There was a long silence. Natalie finally answered, "I thought he was in Chicago with you."

Merker thought, *I did it again.* Why would Callison say he was coming to Chicago to visit me? "He told you he was going to Chicago to see me?"

"No, not exactly. He said he was going to Chicago on committee business. I just assumed that meant meeting with you."

"So he's in Chicago now?" Merker silently mouthed the word "damn" to himself.

"Yes, he called yesterday from the Park Hyatt downtown. I hope I didn't just make a similar faux pas."

"I'm not sure. If he's in town, I'd really like to meet with him. If you don't mind I'll try to contact him now."

"I think you have to hurry. I believe his flight gets in later this afternoon, which means he should be leaving there fairly soon." Natalie was searching for the piece of paper that had Steven's flight itinerary.

"In case I do miss him at the hotel, do you happen to know what airline he'd be flying?"

"I'm sure it would be American." Natalie found the itinerary and confirmed the information with Merker.

Merker scrambled for his yellow pages and found the number of the Park Hyatt. He called the hotel, only to learn Callison had checked out moments earlier.

Merker grabbed his keys and sprinted toward his garage. Merker pressed the hand held unit for his car's security alarm system. To his amazement, the red light was flashing, which indicated someone or something had tampered with his car. He didn't have time for this, yet he had no choice. If Callison was in town and decided not to contact him, then so be it. What was now more imperative was the activation of his security system. This was the first time since he had installed the system the security light was triggered.

Merker could not detect any evidence of forcible entry to the car either by the doors, trunk, or hood. He looked underneath for some evidence the car had been tampered with, but found nothing. Merker's forte had never been automobiles, but he was afraid to use the car since the security alarm had been activated.

Suddenly it struck him, he needed to contact Barney Minton, the car bomb expert.

Barney Minton hadn't changed over the years since Merker had last seen him. Still morbidly obese, with his beer belly hanging over his belt and the crack of his ass exposed for all the world to gaze at, day-old stubble over his face, which had considerably more hair than his head. He was still quite the spectacle. Minton had been dismissed from the force because of his inability to pass the yearly physical, primarily due to his excessive weight. Merker estimated Barney to be in the 400-pound range.

Barney always had moved slowly, but was now moving in slow motion even for him. In a way Merker felt sorry for his large friend, but he would never give the slightest hint of this to him. Barney was the type of person who would never allow anyone to feel sorry for him. He made his bed, as he liked to put it, and he was very comfortable sleeping in it. Barney was the first to acknowledge he was his own worst enemy, but on the other hand he was also his own best friend, and he could live with both.

Merker hadn't known Barney well when they were working together, but knew of Barney's reputation as the best mechanic and electrical engineer on the force. He was so good at his job, the former chief of his precinct had fudged his medical reports for years. But when a new chief was appointed, it spelled the end for Barney's police career. Barney held no resentment toward his new chief or the force. He accepted the blame for allowing himself to get so out of shape. They had no choice but to dismiss him.

After leaving the force, Barney opened his own auto repair shop, specializing in rebuilding and modifying engines. However, the skill for which Barney was best known on the police force was bomb squad expert.

Barney drove a customized van which he had gutted and modified for his own needs and specifications. Barney's vehicle could hold all his tools and equipment as well as Barney himself, which was no small task.

The van pulled into the garage where Merker's car was parked and Merker was anxiously waiting.

"Thanks for coming so soon, Barney."

Barney's massive leg slowly found its footing on the floor of the garage, followed by the other as he exited his vehicle. "Long time, Merker. How ya been?" Barney was chewing something but Merker couldn't tell what it was, only that the entire left cheek was hiding a wad of something.

"I've been fair, how 'bout yourself?"

"Never better." A typical Barney response.

"Let me tell you what we have here. I made my own security system for my car and it says the car has been messed with, but I can't figure out where or how. I'm worried the car's been rigged with a bomb."

Barney started to laugh, so much so he almost choked on his gum. He started to cough, hacking up a wad of gum into his hand. "Damn gum, nearly choked on it." Barney looked at the gum and then replaced it in his mouth. "Started chewing gum when I gave up cigarettes, now it's the gum that'll probably kill me." Barney laughed again, although this time much more controlled. "So you think your car's wired with a bomb?"

Merker was feeling foolish but still concerned. "That's why I called you. I hoped you wouldn't laugh."

"Oops, sorry. Let's see what we have." Barney opened the back of his van and pulled out a large metal case which he carefully placed on the ground and then unlatched, revealing a machine that looked part musical instrument, part machine gun. Barney flipped a switch on the side of the machine and a red light went on. He walked over to Merker's car scanning every aspect of the exterior with his device.

Barney then removed a special mirror from his van. The mirror looked like a enlarged version of a dentist's mirror. Barney slowly scanned under the car, first with the mirror and then with both the mirror and his device. He moved slowly and swept them back and forth. After fifteen minutes of this, Merker couldn't maintain his silence.

"So, is there a bomb or what?"

"There's no bomb, but you're right—someone did get into your car. Let me see this security device you used that told you something was wrong."

Merker gave Barney his hand held security unit. Merker

then explained with great pride about his invention and told Barney this was the first time the device had been activated. Barney intently listened to Merker, as an interested student would listen to an instructor.

"Did you patent this?" Barney asked.

"Never got around to it. I guess I really should do that." Merker looked at the ground.

"We'll talk about that later. Let me show you where they broke into your car. See on the hood, these small scratches and the slight discoloration of the paint."

Merker leaned into the car looking carefully at the area Barney referred to. He could barely see the marks. Barney pulled out a magnifying glass from his pocket and gave it to Merker, so he could have a closer look.

"Yeah, I see the marks."

"They pried open your hood and then touched up any scratches with some paint, so it's nearly impossible to see. Now let's open the hood and see what they did."

Merker stood patiently waiting for Barney to do something. Barney looked back at Merker and said, "Don't you have the keys?" Merker nodded. "Then open up the car door and release the hood. The car won't explode, I promise you."

Merker cautiously placed his key into the slot in the door and slowly turned. A loud alarm sounded and Merker dove for the ground placing his hands over his head, anticipating an explosion. Barney never moved his feet, but his protuberant abdomen bounced rhythmically as he laughed. "Forget to neutralize your alarm?"

Merker was looking for a hole to crawl into, he was so embarrassed. Merker crawled over to the car and opened the door, turning off the alarm and releasing the hood-lock. Barney wallowed over to the hood and peered in, rubbing his chin with his right hand. Merker could hear Barney mumbling something to himself as he studiously examined in the engine. Finally Barney said something understandable.

"I don't know what kind of trouble you're in, but whoever did this knew what they're doing. This is very sophisticated stuff. Come over here and take a look."

Merker had already been standing next to Barney, but Barney's left side virtually blocked Merker from Barney's peripheral vision. "I'm right here, Barney, next to you."

Barney turned to his left and then pointed to a small piece of "plastique" attached to a small wire that was barely visible. "Is that a transmitter?" Merker asked.

"I think it's a receiver connected to your brake fluid and brake booster. When this is activated, probably by some type of remote control device or timer, it would make your brakes useless."

Merker blurted Gregory's name in disgust.

"Excuse me." Barney looked up at Merker.

"I think I know who did this and why. There's been some people who've died in car accidents when their cars accidentally collided with different things," Merker mumbled, deep in thought.

"What?" Barney had no idea what Merker was saying.

"You know, they hit things—trees, telephone poles, stuff like that."

"Why didn't you say that in the first place? But something still doesn't make sense."

"What doesn't make sense?" Merker was still angered by Gregory's tactics.

"This would explain someone losing control of their brakes, but why would they all crash into something?" Barney started to scratch his unshaven chin as he pondered his own question.

"Good point," Merker agreed.

Barney lumbered over to the driver's door and angled his way into the driver's seat so he could get a good look at the steering wheel and column "Ah ha, there it is."

"What, there's what?" Merker scurried around Barney's mass attempting to gain a better view of the steering mechanism, then ran over to the passenger side and was able to finally get a decent view.

"These guys are good, real good. See this." Barney pointed to another small piece of plastique, with another wire similar to the piece on the brakes.

"I think by detonating this small device they can lock the

steering wheel, making it nearly impossible to turn the automobile."

"No skid marks," Merker mumbled.

"What? You're mumbling again."

"The most recent car accident was on Sheridan Road, where the car hit a tree but left no skid marks, as if the brakes couldn't slow the car down and the steering wheel couldn't be turned."

"Yep, this could do that. And what's so interesting about this is, only a handful of people have the expertise to be able to tell the car had been tampered with," Barney said matter-of-factly.

"So it would listed as a car accident." Merker nodded.

"Exactly. This is done by someone who knows what he's doing. Do you want me to defuse this now?"

"Sure." Merker couldn't decide what to do with this information. If he notified the police, then his entire investigation could be blown and Merker would never get to whoever was behind all this. Another option would be to discuss this with J.T., but he still didn't trust him, so that was less than optimal. The third option would be to not tell anyone and figure out a way to utilize this information to his advantage. Merker decided on the last option, as Barney let him know the car was now safe to drive.

"Listen, Barney, can I ask a favor of you?"

"What?" Barney was slowly maneuvering his massive body out of the car, grunting and straining with every move.

"I'd rather keep this between us for now until I can figure out what to do."

"No problem. But on one condition." Barney now stood next to Merker.

"What condition?"

"When this matter is all done, I want to work with you in marketing your security system. I've seen a lot of systems but I think yours may be the best I've seen."

"You have a deal." They shook hands. "I added a little extra bonus. I switched their triggering mechanism for the steering wheel with the indicator light for your emergency brake. So, if you're driving and the emergency brake light suddenly appears,

you'll know someone used the remote unit to screw up your car."
Barney winked.

"Thanks, Barney, this may really be useful." This information could come in handy, since the person controlling the device should be in the immediate vicinity of his car.

26

The Rose Room at the Algonquin Hotel was filled to capacity, while the group hovered in the sitting area awaiting Rasta's arrival. They filled the time with idle chatter and a tour of the Hirschfeld caricatures that adorned the walls. It wasn't until Rasta arrived that they were made aware of their accommodations on the second floor for the meeting. Rasta told them he would meet them in the library room momentarily.

The urgency of the meeting was unprecedented and a tidal wave of anxiety overwhelmed the atmosphere of the stately meeting room. The three gentlemen were nervously talking about the crisis when Rasta entered.

"Sorry for the delay, but I just got off the phone with Smithee." Rasta appeared frazzled.

A look of doubt appeared on the faces of Timmons, Barnes, and Wilovsky. They had discussed the issue of Smithee previously among themselves. To a man they had concluded that Smithee and Rasta were one in the same. Why would he continue the charade of the mysterious Smithee and to what purpose? Only Rasta had privy to Smithee, and according to Rasta, this was the way it was to be.

If something should happen to Rasta, then Smithee would choose another to act as the intermediary. The explanation for these unusual conditions was to limit their potential liability and thus protect all the parties, meaning Smithee and the administrative committee, from implicating each other if an issue arose. Rasta had also explained on several occasions that he had never actually met Smithee, and how all their communications were either through a third party or over a secured telephone line, while their voices were electronically altered.

All four participants of the group had just arrived in town, and none knew precisely why they were summoned but each had their own theory. It was after nine and Rasta appeared weary and tired. For that matter, they all looked weary and tired; it had already been a long day and it was about to become considerably longer.

Wilovsky looked as if he had aged significantly in the few weeks since they last visited. His clothes hung limp off his body and his coloring was unmistakable—he had the bluish hue of cyanosis suggesting his heart was failing.

Barnes was nervously chewing on his unlit cigar and pacing the floor. Timmons kept cleaning off the lenses of his glasses in an attempt to remove a seemingly invisible spot, interrupting only to rub the back of his neck. It only took Rasta a second to see he had a nervous group on his hands.

"Please let's all sit down since this might take a while. If you need something to drink, the hotel has set up a private bar with some mints and candies over there in the corner." Rasta pointed to the corner bar which the others had not even noticed until he brought it to their attention.

Barnes, not one for small talk, decided it was time to discuss the issue at hand. "Very nice, but what the hell is going on?"

Rasta shook his head in acknowledgment of Barnes' anxiety. "We have two very serious issues to discuss and we need resolution on both before we can adjourn."

"Let's get to it!" Barnes gently banged his fist on the table.

"I'm going to discuss the lesser of the two first, mainly because the other issue is so important I believe once we start discussing it, we will have a very difficult time discussing anything else."

"The first issue deals with a member of the committee that both Timmons and I sit on. Her name is Angela Mendoza, who is also a chief advisor to the assistant secretary of health and human services."

"Yes, we are all well aware of Dr. Mendoza's credentials." Wilovsky spoke softly, clearing his throat after a few words.

"Dr. Mendoza is taking a very strong stand, suggesting a major restructuring for the funding of research priorities on a national level. Specifically, she is adamant on recommending a major shift of funding dollars toward primary care and outcome studies and away from basic research. Several of our corporate sponsors from the technological fields and pharmaceutical companies are not happy with Dr. Mendoza's stance on this issue. They're concerned, and justly so I might add, that their efforts in the area of medical research could be irreparably damaged by her efforts. Their concern has made them uncertain as to whether they wish to continue funding our group. As you are aware, their funding is a major source of income for the Gance Foundation."

"Do you think that's true, that the funding will be significantly shifted on a national level?" Timmons asked.

"That's probably irrelevant. If they think it's true and they are paying the bills, then from their perspective it is true." Wilovsky's mind and tongue were still sharp as a razor.

"But is it true?" Timmons insisted.

"Wilovsky's right," Rasta answered. "Your question is impossible to answer at this time."

"So what do we do?" Timmons was rigorously rubbing the back of his neck.

"Can't we try and reason with her?" Barnes said nervously, still gnawing his unlit cigar.

Rasta sighed. "We've tried talking to her, cajoling her, reasoning with her, all for naught. Dr. Mendoza is a very determined and stubborn woman."

"She's a member of the list isn't she?" Barnes scowled.

"Yes, I'm sure we all recall she is a member of the list. As you are all aware, we only use the list as a last resort," Rasta said softly.

"So, aren't we there? At the last resort stage?" Barnes was still scowling.

"Unfortunately, we're beyond that point." Rasta's voice was even softer than before.

"Huh?" Barnes was confused.

"When we realized we had no alternative, we had Gregory's people contact Dr. Mendoza. As with Dr. Cisko, we followed routine procedure and used a former colleague of Dr. Mendoza's to make the initial contact, only using the information from the list if absolutely necessary. In her case, it was deemed necessary and

273

she was presented with the information we had. We emphasized the potential ramifications this sensitive material could have on her career if it got into the wrong hands."

"And?" Barnes interjected.

"And, she laughed in Gregory's face. She challenged him to reveal the information. She said that that was past history and she would gladly stand on her present record."

Wilovsky sat, slowly rubbing his forehead, looking down at the table as if in deep thought. "Victor, if you could review Dr. Mendoza's file for us briefly, it might help matters."

Rasta had the Mendoza file available, but he didn't need it. He had almost the entire file committed to memory. "Angela Mendoza is one of those self-made women, you know, the type that thrives on the challenge of succeeding in a male-oriented world. Anyway, while she was in college she paid someone to write a term paper for her and got caught. The course was a pass–fail course, and she was in jeopardy of failing the course, which would have affected her status relative to her acceptance to medical school. Her advisor threatened to notify the medical schools where she had applied. Angela tried to reason with her advisor, but he was recalcitrant. That's when a friend told her of the Gance organization. With the help of the organization her advisor was convinced not to press the issue and didn't interfere with her acceptance to medical school."

"So she has no concern about any of this information being leaked?" Wilovsky seemed puzzled.

"Not at all. She said she had helped the organization when she was asked and felt it was ethically sound."

"How about when she didn't think it was ethically sound?" Timmons inquired.

"She refused, but we never pressed the issue. It was felt she might be needed for something more significant in the future." Rasta raised his eyebrows as he spoke.

"Like now," Wilovsky said, still rubbing his forehead.

"Exactly, but when we pulled out our ace in the hole, she surprised us by not recanting." Rasta shook his head.

"Isn't she a candidate for the assistant directorship if the position is vacated?" Wilovsky asked.

"Word is she would be the most likely candidate," Rasta said looking at Wilovsky. "That's why I can't believe she would let this information out. It would most assuredly ruin her chance for the position."

"I don't understand what you're talking about," Barnes said. A piece of the cigar broke off in his mouth.

"The assistant secretary of health and human services was recently diagnosed with metastatic lung cancer. The word on the street is he is about to resign for medical reasons. So . . ."

"So, Mendoza is in line to replace him." Barnes nodded.

Wilovsky stood and started to pace, still rubbing his forehead, obviously in deep thought. "She is willing to allow us to reveal the information and isn't concerned about the consequences. Why?"

"Maybe she doesn't want the job," Timmons suggested.

"Unlikely. She's very ambitious and this is the opportunity of a lifetime." Rasta also stood and started to pace.

Wilovsky suddenly stopped and started to smile. "We can use this to our advantage."

"Use what?" Barnes asked.

"Let me explain." Wilovsky had a sly smile on his face. "Instead of threatening Dr. Mendoza, why don't we help her?"

"We need her to cooperate on our committee, and she's resisting. Isn't that right?"

"That's correct," Rasta agreed.

"Then why don't we help promote her off the committee and replace her with someone we know we can control. Once she's promoted, she'll have to resign this committee. Her new job will consume all her time."

Rasta was so excited he was almost jumping for joy. "This is brilliant. We promote her off the committee, and it will be her idea to resign. I'm sure I can talk Jourge into appointing Timmons or myself to head her subcommittee."

"Problem solved." Wilovsky's smile was still evident and some color had returned to his complexion. "We also still haven't used the information we have on her. Once she gets into her new, more prominent position and starts to enjoy the power and prestige of being the assistant secretary, we should have considerably

275

more leverage." Wilovsky confidently folded his arms across his chest.

"I like it, I like it a lot. We can use the organization's resources to virtually assure the position to Mendoza."

"Especially if we leave some subtle signs indirectly connecting Mendoza to the organization. It would then be difficult for her not to cooperate with us, because the evidence would suggest her appointment was aided by the organization. Any denial on her part would only appear as a cover up."

Rasta walked over to Wilovsky to pat him on his shoulder. "Is everyone in agreement with Dr. Wilovsky's recommendation?"

Both Timmons and Barnes nodded.

Rasta started to pace again. "Maybe we can resolve this next issue as well." He hesitated as Wilovsky sat back down. "Remember when we last met and discussed Dr. Steven Callison and Marcus Merker? Well, it seems things have gotten out of hand."

Wilovsky's color again faded. Barnes started to chew harder on his cigar, and Timmons returned to rubbing his neck.

"Let me digress for a moment. Van Gregory had been following Callison after he had met with the detective, Marcus Merker, in Texas. Apparently Callison met Merker again, but this time in Chicago. Gregory was following them in his car. Somehow this turned into a car chase, resulting in an accident. Fortunately, the accident only involved Gregory and another vehicle, and not Merker or Callison."

"Do we know if they knew Gregory was in the car chasing them?" Wilovsky asked shaking his head.

"Yes, we know Merker is aware, and we also assume Callison knows."

"How can you be so sure?" Timmons inquired.

"Gregory wasn't physically injured in the accident, but his ego was bruised and he was extremely upset. After the accident Gregory took it upon himself to pay Merker a visit."

Wilovsky, Timmons and Barnes listened in utter disbelief.

Wilovsky rolled his eyes back and sighed. "What did he do?"

"Gregory actually confronted Merker and Merker got the better of him." Rasta attempted to hold back his smile but he couldn't. He had never been a fan of Gregory's.

"Confronted? I'm not sure what you mean," Wilovsky said hesitantly.

"He tried to assault him physically and lost the fight. This really pissed Gregory off." Rasta looked to Wilovsky for help.

"I knew we should have gotten rid of that macho asshole years ago," Barnes fumed. Wilovsky was speechless.

Rasta continued, "Gregory is so incensed he has sworn revenge against Merker. Smithee intervened at this point and requested I calm Gregory down or else. So I met with Gregory and told him to stay away from Merker. I made this abundantly clear, including the consequences should he decide to ignore our wishes."

"Consequences, what consequences?" Barnes said still feeling the charade about Smithee was unnecessary.

"If he didn't totally back away, we would take him off the case and would call in Valentino."

They all knew of Valentino, who was internationally known as the final solution. They had discussed using Valentino in the past, on one or two other occasions, but had never actually needed to go that far. Valentino was very expensive but was reputably the best.

"Since Gregory has been difficult in the past, I would assume Smithee probably did call in Valentino, but I can't confirm that. Anyway I feel the Gregory–Merker issue is only a subplot of a larger story." Rasta had their undivided attention. "Callison has been inquiring about the Caldo list."

A silence swept over the room—the type of silence which usually portended a storm, and this could be a major storm.

Wilovsky rested his head on his arms as leaned on the table, mumbling, "I'm too old for this; I'm too old for this; I'm too . . ."

"How did he find out about the list?" Timmons stammered, rubbing his neck furiously.

"We're checking that out, but I think it may have been Merker. Anyway, Callison was in my house, looking in my study for the list." Rasta animated his remarks with flailing arms as he talked.

"How do you know this?" Barnes asked.

"I have it on tape. Actually I have a lot on tape." Rasta's mood changed when he thought about the tape. "You see, I was having a party at my home. For security reasons, my home is wired with hidden security cameras. The video camera was on in the study when Callison and a secretary from work, by the name of Maxine Wells, who had been assigned to assist Callison on his subcommittee, sneaked into my study looking for the list. They also did the nasty, and I have it all on tape."

"Are you serious? You caught them in the act?" Barnes was stupefied.

"And some . . . It was really a good show, quite explicit."

Rasta walked over to a table on which a combination TV–VCR was already in place. Rasta turned on the television and inserted the tape. The first part of the tape showed the search for the list, but what followed resembled a poor attempt at pornography.

"Wow, that's disgusting." Barnes, whose sexual mores were a bit to the right of the Puritans, could not even watch the tape.

"More importantly, what are we going to do?" Wilovsky said. He found the search for the list much more distasteful than the sexual exploits.

"Fortunately, they found nothing, but the mere fact they knew to look in my study is very disconcerting."

Wilovsky again stood and started to slowly pace. "So they don't have any hard data."

"As far as I know they're still fishing for the list. I'm not sure they even know if the list is real or just a myth."

Wilovsky stopped pacing and faced the group seated at the table. "From my perspective we have two issues. The first is Gregory and how to control him. The second is Callison and how to control *him*."

Rasta interceded, "The third is what to do with the secretary."

"Then the fourth is what to do with Merker," Timmons added his opinion.

"The fifth is what to do about that disgusting tape." Barnes still could not get the image out of his mind's eye.

"Before we start considering possible solutions, you need to know Smithee's position." Rasta stood.

"Come on, Victor." Barnes said. "We all know there is no Smithee."

"I really don't care whether you believe me or not, but there is a Smithee and it isn't me. The consultant checks that were deposited in the Swiss accounts over the years, well, I think we're finally going to earn some of those dollars." Rasta was referring to an annual deposit placed into an individual Swiss account for each of them. Since they started with the organization, the checks had increased in value, and they had each been collecting one hundred thousand dollars annually for the past several years.

"Smithee does not want any more accidents or deaths," Rasta continued. "He's concerned the deaths of Cisko and Kahn have already brought the organization to a possible point of compromise and feels we cannot afford any more incidents."

"So their deaths were not accidental?" Wilovsky said.

Rasta walked to the opposite end of the table from where the others were seated. "It appears the death of Cisko was of natural causes and truly accidental, but the death of Kahn, well that's another story."

"Was it Gregory?" Wilovsky asked.

Rasta nodded his head. "Smithee is concerned Gregory will do something similar to Merker, even though he has been told to refrain from any contact at all."

"I agree. We need to keep Gregory away from Merker. If he gets careless and gets caught, it's conceivable he can be traced back to us." Wilovsky grimaced as he spoke.

"So where do we go from here?" Rasta asked.

"Why don't we get Smithee here and discuss this with him face to face," Barnes added.

"I agree, I would like to meet with Smithee myself," Wilovsky said.

Timmons nodded.

"I'll be glad to suggest this to Smithee but I doubt he'll agree. I know he feels very strongly about maintaining his anonymity." Rasta had discussed this with Smithee in the past.

"Don't suggest, demand!" Barnes commanded.

"I don't want to get into an argument about this, but Smithee is essentially our boss. He's the one who pays us, has files on each of us, and I am not going to make any demands of him." Rasta's stare matched Barnes' in intensity.

"Let's not argue, gentlemen. I think we've made our point. Now let's come up with some options." Wilovsky spoke more quietly, and this seemed to have a calming effect on both Rasta and Barnes.

"As far as Callison is concerned, has he been approached?" Timmons inquired.

"No he hasn't," Rasta answered.

"We have several options with Callison. First is his grant application. I believe we can help him get over the hump and finally get funded. Only if he is cooperative, of course." Wilovsky resumed rubbing his forehead.

"I believe we can do that," Rasta said.

"If the grant approval strategy isn't effective then we can use the material from the file." Wilovsky continued. "I believe it dealt with some radical movement he was involved with while in college."

"It was something like that and our personality profile on Callison suggests he's very vulnerable to this type of coercion," Rasta added.

"Lastly, if these aren't effective we have the tape." Wilovsky resumed pacing and rubbing his forehead.

"The tape? Why?" Timmons asked.

"He has a wife, doesn't he?" Wilovsky said.

Barnes smiled, "Yeah, he sinned and now he will pay."

Rasta grudgingly agreed. "I think that will work. Now what about the others?"

"The two other people who probably know of the list are Merker and the secretary, what's her name?"

"Maxine, Maxine Wells." Rasta said.

Wilovsky continued. "I think we have little to worry about with Maxine. The tape should invalidate anything she might come up with and it would be the word, the unsubstantiated word, of a secretary against several renowned physicians. I think we're safe with her. Plus, it's possible she was only acting in support of Callison and isn't even aware of what the list is about."

"You really don't believe that, do you?" Rasta asked.

"No, but it is possible. My major concern is with Merker. As a private detective he may have more information and sources than we are currently aware of. We have to find out what he knows." Wilovsky said.

"I agree, but how?" Rasta said.

"What do we know about Merker?" Timmons asked.

Rasta sorted through the various files he had brought. He opened the Merker file and started to read. After reviewing the pertinent background information, Rasta reviewed the information they had gleaned of Merker's connection on this case. "We can't be one hundred percent sure, but we think Merker met with Cisko prior to Cisko's death and that's how he got involved in all this. We think it was Cisko who identified Gregory and Kahn as potential problems and asked for Merker's help."

"What makes you think that?" Wilovsky asked.

"This theory is from Smithee, and after further review I agree with his conclusion." Rasta waited for comments, but there were none.

"Let's agree this is probably true. What else is there?" Timmons asked.

"After the deaths of Cisko and Kahn, Merker started to investigate in earnest. That's why he visited Kahn's lawyer in Los Angeles and that's why he followed Callison to Texas." Rasta was still reading from the file they had compiled on Merker.

"Okay, go on," Timmons implored.

"The next information we have is factual. We know Merker met with Callison in both Texas and Chicago. While in Chicago they also met with Maxine Wells. That meeting in Chicago is where we believe they discussed the Caldo list."

"Is that fact?" Timmons asked.

"No, just an informed guess. I forgot to tell you something important. When we first learned of Merker's inquiries about Harvey Kahn, we asked Gregory to check him out. Much of the information we have is because Gregory is generally very good at his investigative work. Gregory was able to discover several interesting facts about Merker's trip to California. He found out Merker had visited the hospital where Kahn had worked and he asked some questions of the staff implying he thought Kahn's death was no accident. Then one of our people on the coast informed us of a physician who was inquiring about other physicians who were politically active during the Caldo days."

"Why would someone be concerned about that?" Timmons wondered.

"It was the way he was asking which concerned our informant. We thought the timing of this inquiry was more than a coincidence, so we had Gregory investigate. Gregory confirmed that a Dr. Ethan Jasper had been inquiring about another physician named Tyler Trulof, who happened to be one of the proponents of the Caldo theory back in the sixties. Gregory was able to find Dr. Trulof, who had changed his name and was living in Phoenix, Arizona. And take a wild guess at who visited Dr. Trulof in Arizona?"

"Merker?" Timmons said hesitantly.

"Yes, Merker. Merker was meeting with one of the major proponents of the Caldo conspiracy theory."

"So you assume Merker was told of the Caldo list from this doctor in Arizona." Timmons said more deliberately.

"Yes, and then we think he told Callison when they met in Chicago about Caldo. What we still couldn't answer was how they connected me with Caldo." Rasta paused to clear his throat before continuing. "What I surmised was Trulof had a partner when he was in California by the name of Wilcox."

"Our Amos Wilcox?" Barnes remembered Wilcox, as did the others. Wilcox was the first major agenda item when the group was established. His death and the death of Walter Bartolli were the first serious issues they had to deal with. Those names were etched deeply into their memory banks.

"Yes, I'm sure you all remember Dr. Wilcox. I believe he probably mentioned my name to Trulof sometime before he died, and that's how Merker found out about my connection with the organization." Rasta looked depressed.

Wilovsky, who had been silent, stood. He again had gained an infusion of color. "What you have outlined has a certain rhyme and rhythm. If we follow this logic further down this path, it seems to lead us to Gregory and Merker. Since we are already tied to Gregory whether we like it or not, why don't we support him in helping us with Merker? It seems to me Gregory has done most of the work already. If we support him with whatever resources he needs, maybe we can find Merker's Achilles heel." Wilovsky sat as he completed his thought.

Rasta sat up and mulled over what Wilovsky had said. "Aren't you concerned about their previous altercation, and that Gregory's emotional instability could be extremely dangerous?"

"I share your concerns but I really don't see any other option, do you?" Wilovsky again started to rub his forehead.

"Aren't you worried about Gregory implicating us?" Timmons asked.

"Of course I am, but what difference will that really make? Victor has told us tonight Gregory was probably responsible for the death of Kahn, and of course there's Jennifer Chalitz. We are stuck with Mr. Gregory whether we like it or not. Plus, I believe we can convince Mr. Gregory the best way to seek his revenge against Mr. Merker could be with our help and not through physical violence."

"The difference is we haven't been implicated yet but the deeper we get, the more risk we take." Barnes said, clearly concerned about placing too much responsibility on Gregory.

"We need to agree on a plan and then determine our contingencies." Rasta said. "I suggest I contact Smithee and see if he will meet with us. Assuming he won't, I'll discuss with him utilizing Gregory to investigate Merker, using very strict guidelines, so as to not create any further confrontations."

"We also need clarification on this Valentino issue. And are we agreed on the tack to take with Callison and the secretary . . . um." Wilovsky again stumbled over Maxine's name.

"Maxine," Rasta answered.

"Yes Maxine. Plus, if we handle the Gregory issue correctly, we can possibly connect Gregory to Merker on a professional basis, which should free us of being potentially implicated later, if something should happen." Wilovsky sat back down, exhausted.

"I'll find out from Smithee the status of Valentino and will again discuss options utilizing Gregory," Rasta said.

They all agreed on the plan as outlined by Rasta and Wilovsky. They also agreed to meet as often as necessary to resolve this potentially volatile situation.

27

Callison was so preoccupied by the liaison with Maxine, the list took a lesser priority. He had a long conversation with himself on the airplane as to exactly what he would tell Natalie, and decided to tell a half truth. The moment of half truth occurred as soon as he entered the front door of their home.

"What's wrong?" The first words out of Natalie's mouth.

"Nothing's wrong. Why did you say that?" He couldn't believe Natalie could have known about Maxine this soon.

"You know you can't hide anything from me. I could tell immediately from your expression something was wrong. You couldn't find the list, could you?"

Relieved that he didn't have to confess his carnal sin—at least not yet—he sighed a long sigh. "No, we couldn't even find a trace of the damn list, or even any reference to it. It was very frustrating."

"I'm sure it was. But what did you do?" A cold chill ran up Callison's spine. Natalie continued before he could speak. "Was it like the old days, you know, when we infiltrated the registrar's office in college?"

Again a breeze of relief overcame Callison. "Not exactly, this was much more stealthy. We snuck into Rasta's office. As one of us watched for any intruders the other searched the office. Maxine initially checked the computer files and then I checked his paper files; neither of us came up with anything."

"So what are you going to do now?"

"I'm not sure. Part of me wants to drop this whole mess like a bad habit, while another part wants to keep going." Still nervous, Steven sat on the couch.

Natalie sat on his lap. She hadn't done that in years. She slowly stroked his hair as she lay her head on his chest able to hear his heartbeat. They sat silently, gently caressing each other, when the phone broke the silence. Natalie picked it up. The call was from the emergency room.

"Why are they calling me, I'm not even on call this weekend." Steven was aggravated, as if he hadn't enough to deal with.

Steven picked up the receiver and listened carefully. His jaw dropped and the color drained form his face. He hung up the phone and stared at Natalie.

"Steven what's wrong? What's the matter?"

"A patient of mine, I mean the daughter of a patient of mine. Do you remember me talk about a patient named Kodack?"

"Annie Kodack, how could I forget? Has something happened to her daughter?"

"She's been in a car accident and it doesn't look good. She's in surgery now but will need an internist to evaluate her in recovery. Mr. Kodack asked if I could be her doctor."

Natalie put her arms around her husband as tears filled her eyes. She whispered in his ear, "Do you want me to come with you to the hospital, for company?"

He broke from her embrace, looked directly at her and shook his head. "Thanks, but I'll be fine. I'll call you when I know something."

Callison felt as if he was in a fog as he drove to the hospital. When he arrived, Margaret was still in surgery. He met Enos Kodack and his granddaughter Sally in the waiting room. This was the part of his job he hated. Then again, he didn't know a physician anywhere who relished this part of medicine. The light in the waiting room was dim. A bulb had burned out. Sally was sitting on her grandfather's lap resting her head on his chest. Mr. Kodack looked up at Callison, his eyes bloodshot and tearing, his face forlorn, his once formidable body now a shadow of itself.

"I checked with surgery and she's still hanging in there." That was the most positive Callison could be, given the information he had: extensive head and abdominal trauma, with multiple fractures of her right arm and leg, skull, and pelvis. She had needed to be resuscitated twice, once in the ambulance and once in the surgical suite. Her prognosis was grave.

Enos Kodack could not even muster a verbal response. He

just shook his head in acknowledgement of Callison's comment, as he gingerly squeezed his granddaughter, kissing the top of her head.

Callison sat with the Kodacks silently in the waiting room, awaiting any word from the operative suite. His mind wandered back to his excursion in Chicago, the committee, the possibility of a conspiracy, his impending hearing, and the fate of little, silent Sally.

A nurse came in. Dr. Snyder had requested Callison's assistance in the surgical suite. Callison followed the ritual of sterility, scrubbing his hands and robing into the surgical gown, cap, mask and bootees. The surgical suite was crowded, with concurrent surgeries being performed in Margaret's head and abdomen. Snyder noticed Callison's entrance.

"Steven this doesn't look good. She's suffered significant brain damage with bilateral subdural hematomas with an associated intracerebral hematoma on the right. If she survives, I'd anticipate a considerable neurologic deficit."

Callison didn't know what to say. He walked closer to the table to see what was being done in her abdomen. The general surgeon, Paul Lollat, was up to his elbows in Margaret's belly. "Paul, what have you found?"

"Steve, it doesn't look any better here than her head. She ruptured her spleen and lacerated her liver, right kidney and small intestine. I'm now checking for a retroperitoneal hematoma." Paul Lollat pulled a huge blood clot out of her abdomen and showed it to him. "It looks like she has a retroperitoneal bleed too. The only good thing is she somehow spared her chest."

Snyder looked toward Callison over his protective surgical goggles. "She signed a donor card, Steven. Are you aware of that?"

"No, I really wasn't her physician. I took care of her parents."

"Do you think you could verify the donor status, because I think there are several salvageable organs left."

Callison almost shivered at the request, but he also realized the only positive to come of such a disaster was the ability to save others. "I'll check. Do you need me for anything else?" Callison never did like the surgical suite, and this hadn't changed his opinion.

"We'll do everything we can," Snyder said.

"Please, she has a beautiful little daughter and is the only parent." Callison knew little Sally was probably soon to be an orphan.

Callison returned to the waiting room, trying to find a way to ask Mr. Kodack if he knew his daughter had signed a donor card. He had had to do this on occasion and had never found it as difficult as this time. "Mr. Kodack, Margaret is stable but she has sustained significant trauma to her head and abdomen."

"What exactly does that mean in English?" Mr. Kodack said slowly.

"She's damaged her brain and several organs in her belly, such as the spleen, intestine, and liver."

Mr. Kodack looked down at the floor, then to Sally who was asleep on his lap. "Give it to me straight, Doctor, is she going to make it?"

"I really don't know for sure, but it doesn't look good." Callison paused and then asked, "Do you know anything about a donor card?"

The tears were flowing from Kodack's reddened eyes as he spoke. "After the death of my wife, Margaret told me she was going to fill out one of those donor cards. She felt if her death could help others then that's what she'd want to do."

Callison placed his hand on Mr. Kodack's shoulder. He said nothing.

The surgery lasted six hours, and Margaret remained in a coma postoperatively. Callison examined Margaret. Many smaller lacerations had been closed with silk sutures, but her abdominal wound was closed with surgical clips. Her blood pressure had been fluctuating but now appeared to have stabilized, however, her laboratory tests revealed multiple abnormalities consistent with her clinical status. After several hours of manipulating her medications and intravenous fluids, Callison was finally satisfied he had done all he could, at least for now.

Callison escorted Mr. Kodack into the intensive care unit to see his daughter while a nurse stayed with Sally in the waiting area. Mr. Kodack remained controlled while he watched his daughter motionless on the bed, her only movement occurring when the respirator inflated her lungs, a scene too reminiscent of his experience with his wife. Callison suggested Mr. Kodack take Sally home for a while, assuring him they would call if there was any change in her status.

After escorting the Kodacks to their car, Callison returned to the intensive care unit to reevaluate Margaret. Callison noticed Snyder, the midnight club member and head of neurosurgery, examining his patient. Snyder saw Callison as he entered the unit and motioned for him to come over to Margaret's bed.

"Her vital signs are stable but that's it. She's still unresponsive and isn't even triggering the ventilator. If it's all right with you I'd like to order an EEG."

Callison knew the EEG would document whether there was any brain activity. The absence of activity was one of the key components of certifying Margaret as brain dead. "I have no problem with ordering the EEG. If you have a couple minutes, I'd like to talk to you."

Callison and Snyder retreated to the physician dictating room off the intensive care unit. The room was empty, and they took seats at a small round formica conference table. Several half-emptied Styrofoam coffee cups sat on the table.

"This is the part of the job I hate," Snyder said as he collected the used coffee cups and disposed of them in the trash.

"I know what you mean," Callison said, assisting Snyder in his cleanup.

"I was told the accident was caused by a drunk driver who ran a red light and collided head-on with her car. He was killed instantly." Snyder just shook his head.

"What I wanted to talk to you about is the committee I am on." Callison said. "If you recall I discussed some of this with you the other night.

"Yes, I remember. You were asking me about my opinion of our profession." There was no change in Snyder's expression.

"Do you know anything about the merger between the allopaths and us in the 60's?" Callison's question was asked as if

289

he already had the answer.

"Very little, it was before my time. Why do you ask?"

Snyder seemed intrigued.

"At the time of the merger there was a rumor of a list, called the Caldo list. Have you ever heard of the Caldo list?"

"No, should have I heard of it?"

"I guess not. Are you aware that at the time of the California merger many informed physicians, both MD and DO, thought our profession was over?" Callison rubbed his brow.

"No, I wasn't aware of that. Why are you asking me these questions?" Snyder was getting impatient.

"Because I respect your opinion and I need some advice." This calmed Snyder. Callison was concerned about the perception of a certain callousness toward Margaret, but he still continued. "There are some who feel another merger, this time involving our entire profession, is needed. There's also a rumor suggesting the Caldo list still exists."

"What exactly is the Caldo list?" Snyder inquired.

"It's a list of doctors who are susceptible to bribes or blackmail from those who control the list."

"Sounds a bit far-fetched to me."

"I agree. But what would you say if I knew of a letter written in the 60's that talks about this list and a source who says the list is still in existence today?" Callison said in a cold, flat voice.

"So what are you saying?" Snyder leaned forward over the table.

"I'm suggesting there might be a conspiracy of physicians, who for whatever reason, have plotted to use this list to force this merger."

Snyder paused, reflecting before he spoke. "Why? What would be their motive?"

"Power, influence, money, you know, the usual."

"Why are you telling me this?" Snyder said. His face looked uncertain.

"As I said before, I value your opinion, and I'm not sure what to do."

"About what?"

"There are several questions. First, should I pursue the possibility of the list? I've attempted to find the list, but the lead I had wasn't accurate. To be honest, I'm not sure the list truly exists. Plus the person who is theoretically in charge of the list is a very prominent, well-respected physician, and there's the possibility of other prominent physicians also being involved. The second question is really independent of the list. What should I do about the possibility of the merger? My subcommittee has been charged with the task of recommending to merge or not to merge." Callison looked concerned.

Snyder wasn't prepared for a conversation of this magnitude. He was still exhausted from his surgery. "The first question about the list. If it does exist and you can get the list, then I guess you need to do that. If the list contains the names of individuals who are conspiring to amalgamate our profession, then we need to do something about that. On the other hand, if this list doesn't exist, or you can't prove its existence, then you have to be very careful. You said that a prominent physician may be implicated. You better have the proof before you start making any accusations. Remember our credo, *Primum Non Nocere*— 'first do no harm.' This can apply to the medical profession as well as the individual patient. Now what was the other question?"

"The other question was what to do about the merger, independent of the list?"

"To answer this I can only give you my opinion. I'm not speaking for the profession or anyone else." Snyder stood and stared at Callison, squinting his eyes. "Are you sure you want to hear this?"

Callison smiled, a small but sincere smile. "Please."

Snyder sat, then immediately stood again and started to pace. "I feel our profession is on the verge of extinction, and that makes me sad. Over the years many loyal DO's have fought long and hard to maintain a profession they believed in. It was a profession that was based on a different philosophy, a philosophy that espouses the principles needed today and almost exactly what is being asked for by everyone from the government to managed health-care to the population in general. Where my confusion lies is whether the philosophy on which osteopathy

291

was formed still exists. For years our predecessors fought for equal status with our allopathic brothers. Now that battle seems to be all but over, and it may have caused us to lose the war. Do you know why I became a physician?"

Callison looked at Snyder quizzically. "Actually, I have no idea."

"Does the date December 1, 1969 mean anything to you?"

Callison thought about it. "I can't say that date means anything to me. Why?"

"That was the date they instituted the draft lottery. That day changed my life forever. I was in my senior year of college and planning a career as a scientist when the draft changed my career goals. You see, the career I'd chosen was not considered a deferment for the draft and I had a very low draft number, 12. So I quickly applied to medical school, which would qualify as a deferment. From that day on I decided a medical career was my goal. The allopathic schools would have nothing to do with me since my application came in late and they were already swamped with applicants. The DO schools were also swamped, but gave me the opportunity to apply. They were looking for a more rounded applicant than the typical premed student."

Snyder, now feeling more comfortable, took a seat at the table. "Anyway from that day on I felt an allegiance to the osteopathic profession. Initially this stemmed from the profession giving me a chance and a deferment." Snyder paused. "I've reflected on this issue for quite some time, yet I still haven't entirely resolved it in my own mind. In the past it has been said that the osteopathic profession has survived because God loves osteopaths. That hopefully is true, but then he also loves allopaths, nurses, et cetera. I think we survived because we had a mission. For almost a century our mission was equality with the MD's. Now the mission is essentially completed, and our profession's floundering. We have no clear purpose other than to continue to become more like the MD's. This has caused a rift, with one side proclaiming equality is good, while the other side claims we've lost our direction. The result of this is apathy. We're our own worst enemies. Do you know how you form a DO firing squad?"

Callison shrugged his shoulders. "No."

"They form by lining up in a circle." Snyder smiled.

"So what're you saying? The battle's already lost?"

"I told you I still haven't totally resolved this issue, but I do believe our profession is suffering from mural dyslexia."

"Mural dyslexia, what's that?" Callison asked.

"They can't read the writing on the wall. However, there's still hope. More and more, I'm reading varied opinions of options for the profession. They're attempting to redefine our mission away from separate and equal. Other phrases are now bantered about, such as 'parity and plurality,' or 'parallel and distinctive.' I believe they're all struggling with the issue of refocusing the osteopathic profession toward the future health-care needs of our nation. The irony of all of this, is all the redefining and refocusing is returning to the original tenets of A.T. Still, who said 'Seek health, anyone can find disease.' Some mess, huh?"

Callison had heard most of what Snyder had said before, but never presented in such a manner. "So, if you were in my position, what would you recommend?"

"Ours is a profession now over a hundred years old. We take care of millions of people. We've accepted students from all paths of life, many had already succeeded in other careers and brought a broader and more empathetic approach to their medical care. I'd argue that our graduates are equally competent in the care of their patients and have the added knowledge of manual diagnosis and manipulative therapy. We need to emphasize our strengths, and be proud of our heritage and what we've accomplished.

"We as a profession have a track record in providing primary care which is definitely not inferior to anyone's. Our profession forces our students to have early physical contact with patients using manipulative techniques. This hands-on contact allows us to touch our patients and to listen to our patients in a very unique way. In a way our profession has evolved almost as a social movement, and I'd hate to see this end." Snyder furrowed his brow.

"I agree with a lot of what you say, but these qualities aren't unique to our profession. There are many MD's who are as empa-

293

thetic and caring as any DO." Callison needed to clarify in his mind what exactly Snyder was saying.

"I agree that many MD's are osteopathically oriented, just as many DO's are allopathically oriented. Where my concern lies, is with the extinction of our profession, leaving only the allopaths. One can only hope that the osteopathic emphasis, for lack of a better term, will continue to exist."

"So if you were in my position you would not recommend the merger?" Callison asked, but knew the answer.

"I would not recommend the merger." Snyder shook his head vigorously.

There was a break in their conversation, which was interrupted by the nurse. "Mrs. Foster is seizing."

"Who's Mrs. Foster?" Callison asked.

The nurse, confused at his question, responded, "Your patient. In fact, both of you are taking care of her. You know—the lady who just had surgery, you remember her."

"Oh, Margaret. Foster must be her married name. I only knew her as Kodack." Callison and Snyder both left the small dictating room to return to Margaret Foster.

28

Merker again called Callison's office and home; however, he was still unable to contact the doctor. He couldn't help feeling Callison was intentionally avoiding him. Whether or not Callison wanted to talk to him, Merker knew he had to warn Callison about the possibility of his car being tampered with and to remind him to use his security system. Merker had established a fairly good rapport with both Natalie and Helen Hunter, Callison's secretary, both of whom assured him Callison was not avoiding him but was rather inundated with work.

Merker's concern had escalated, and he was convinced he was being followed, although he was unable to identify his stalker. His sixth sense was as strong as ever, and it was indisputable he was being followed by someone much more sophisticated than Van Gregory. Merker reactivated Peter and Paul, asking them to follow him, hoping they would be able to identify his pursuer. Unfortunately, they were unable to identify anyone suspicious. They were convinced Merker's stalker was all in his mind.

Rudolph broke the monotony of Merker's obsession when he told Merker that Truelove was on the line. Merker followed Rudolph back to his apartment. "Hello, Truelove. Merker here."

"I'm glad I caught you. I have someone who would like to say hello."

Merker was in no mood for games and waited impatiently for a response on the other end of the line.

"Hello, Mr. Merker, do you recognize my voice?"

The voice was unmistakable—low pitch initially then ending in a higher pitched squeal. It was Ethan Jasper. "Hello, Dr. Jasper, how are you?"

"Well, very well. Tyler and I have been doing a little investigating, and I think we've found something you might be interested in." The enthusiasm in his voice was contagious.

"The list, you found the list!"

"No, I'm sorry we didn't find the list, but we did find some useful information," Jasper answered.

Merker flopped into the moth ball recliner with a resounding thud and cloud of dust. In a much less enthusiastic tone he asked, "So what did you find?"

Merker could hear Ethan call to Truelove to get on the other line. Ethan then continued. "Tyler and I decided to take a little trip to West Palm Beach, Florida, and the home of Helen Sanford, the former Mrs. Bartolli."

Tyler interrupted, "She's a fine woman, very hospitable and cordial."

Merker, not in the mood for small talk, replied, "So what's this big news?"

Ethan continued. "When we called Helen to confirm the information as you had suggested, she told us she had found something which might be of interest, so we decided to visit her in Florida and see just what she had found. We flew to Florida and met with Helen Bartolli-Sanford. She told us that after we originally contacted her she remembered an old box of papers she had kept from her marriage with Dr. Bartolli. It was mostly nostalgic keepsakes but there was a letter, actually more of a note pad, she had been given from Vigor Truax, the private detective she had hired to investigate the death of her husband."

Merker was intrigued; maybe the detective had found something and it was recorded in his notes. "So do you have this note pad?"

"Yes, in fact I have it in my hand. Some of it is unreadable because the ink has faded. What I can make out often doesn't make a lot of sense. At least to us."

"That's why we decided to call you." Truelove interrupted. "We feel maybe you will be able to decipher this better than we can."

Merker thought for a moment. "Ethan, you say you have the note pad?"

"Yes, I have it in my hands as we speak."

"Read to me what you can." Merker was confident the line

was secure. He doubted any of this would be relevant in the first place.

"Most of this is information detailing the death of Dr. Bartolli, with some references to the widow Tatum, Amos Wilcox, and Van Gregory. Then there seems to be some kind of abbreviations or codes."

"That's okay; read to me whatever you can make out." Merker was hopeful he would be able to explain these codes.

"Here goes; on the second page referring to Bartolli there are several letters, an *O*, a *Y*, an *R*, and the number 22. We're not at all clear to what these letters refer, also whether the number 22 is related to the letters. On the last page of the notebook are the letters *A*, *S* and *E,* then *lwood R Loax*. It's difficult to tell whether this is 'Aselwood R Loax', or 'A Selwood R Loax', or 'A S Elwood R Loax', or possibly 'Asel Wood R Loax.' Does any of this make sense to you?"

Merker concentrated, but none of this made any sense to him either. "Is there anything else?" He hoped another reference or abbreviation might shed some light.

"Yes, there is something else. Another comment written in the margin. The ink had smeared so the words are blurred, but our consensus interpretation is, 'death of a gunfight or sunlight.'"

"What does that mean?" He had no idea what any of this meant. His efforts in deciphering were futile from this distance, and probably futile even in person.

"Yeah, it doesn't make any sense," Ethan said.

"Did you review this notebook with Mrs. Bartolli?" Merker asked.

"No, we felt we wanted to confer with you before we discussed this with anyone else, I hope you don't mind?" Truelove said.

"I think you did the right thing. Don't pursue anything else at this time and wait for me. I'll be there in a day or two, so just enjoy the sun until I get there." Merker wasn't sure this information would amount to anything, but he was sure he didn't want either Truelove or Jasper to investigate this any further.

"Wouldn't it be beneficial if we interviewed Helen Sanford now and got the preliminary information?" Truelove asked confidently.

Merker was resolute in his decision for them to wait for him before they would meet with Helen Sanford. "I'd prefer if you waited for me. Promise me you won't do anything until I get there?"

Truelove and Jasper both agreed to wait.

Merker had one priority before he could meet them in Florida—he had to talk and probably meet with Callison, to warn him. Merker again attempted to contact Callison and was again unsuccessful. His decision was now made. He would first go to Texas to meet with Callison, and then go on to Florida.

Callison was exhausted, not having slept in over a day. Margaret had finally stopped seizing but still had not regained consciousness. The EEG revealed brain activity, and she was breathing spontaneously, triggering the ventilator, so Callison had a small but legitimate sense of hope. Before leaving the hospital he once again stopped into the waiting room to see if Mr. Kodack and Sally were there.

The Kodacks were not in the waiting room and Callison was relieved he didn't have to deal with the emotional turmoil. Realizing he could do no more at the hospital, he went home.

To his surprise, Natalie was talking with a man in their living room. His back was to Callison, but his voice was familiar— it was Marcus Merker. Callison had been intentionally avoiding Merker because he didn't want to deal with him. The words of Sydney Snyder kept replaying in his mind: "first do no harm." Callison still hadn't decided how to apply this principle to his situation. Would he be doing more harm by investigating this further, possibly implicating an innocent renowned physician? Or by forgetting about the whole thing? He still couldn't answer that question. Now, with Merker in his home, there was no avoiding the subject.

As soon as Callison entered the room, Natalie stood and slowly walked toward him with her arms extended. "How are you? You look exhausted. How's your patient doing?" Natalie placed her arms around his neck and gave him a soft kiss on his lips.

"I'm okay." Callison moved his attention from his wife to Merker. "Marcus, I didn't expect to see you here." His eyes deliberately revealed his mixed feelings.

"I was in town and decided to surprise both of you. Surprise." Merker's expression was a mirror image of Callison's, and was likewise intended.

Natalie offered to make them martinis, but they both opted for soft drinks, as did she. Their conversation wandered. Natalie had invited Merker to stay for dinner, which he had accepted, and had offered him their guest bedroom for the evening, which he declined.

The dinner was very good, a new chicken dish. Callison thought they had exhausted every variation, but Natalie kept coming up with new, and in this case, tasty alternatives. Merker offered to help them clear the table, but Natalie insisted on doing it herself.

Callison had an office in the corner of the house. The room had dark walnut paneling, a stark contrast to the modern and airy decor of the rest of the house. The room was compact, housing a desk with a computer and printer. Bookshelves covered the walls, filled on one side with medical textbooks and journals, while on the other wall were novels, various history books, and a smattering of art books. On his desk was a portrait of his wife and next to her was a signed photograph of Babe Ruth. Merker noticed the photo of Ruth and picked it up, reading the inscription.

"Where'd you get this?" Merker asked.

"It was my father's, it's one of the few mementos I have from my parents. The Babe signed the photo for my father when my father was in his early teens. It's hard to read now, but it's very special to me." Callison stared at the photograph while thoughts of his parents flashed through his mind.

"You can say that again. It's wonderful. Never sell this." Merker was as serious about this as anything he had ever discussed with Callison.

"Never entered my mind. This has more sentimental value

for me than money could buy."

Merker smiled approvingly at Callison. "I didn't just appear for no reason."

Callison sat in his oversized lounge chair, the lone remnant of his life before Natalie. Merker sat in the other lounge chair in the room.

"I suspected as much. Why did you come?" Callison already knew at least part of Merker's answer, but he had to ask anyway.

"You haven't been answering my calls and messages." Callison peered down at the floor, cutting off eye contact. "Anyway, we have some important stuff to talk about and I felt it was best to talk about it in person." Merker kept his eyes focused on Callison until Callison looked back at him.

"I apologize for not calling, but my life's been in utter chaos since I returned from Chicago." As Callison finished his remarks he tried to catch himself, but it was too late. He knew he should have called Merker while in Chicago. It would have probably prevented this meeting and saved him the embarrassment.

"Oh, why didn't you call me when you were in the city?" Merker asked.

"I did think about calling you, but to be honest, I really didn't have much to tell you and had very little free time."

"Did I scare you that much with my driving that you wouldn't even call?" Merker gave Callison a wry smile that eased some of the tension.

Callison returned the smile. "No, I really didn't have the time to call."

Merker's smile slowly faded. "I don't mean to pry—" he said slowly, "but were you meeting about the committee?" His eyes held Callison's demanding an answer.

Callison held his gaze, determined not to be intimidated into revealing what he didn't want to. "Yes, we were, as a matter of fact. I had some work to do on the committee."

Merker's face looked expectant. "And . . . ?"

"And what?"

"Did you find anything out that might be of interest to me?"

Callison couldn't remember what he had told Merker. He knew he hadn't talked to Merker in a while, so he decided to start with Maxine and Margo. "Do you recall Margo, the secretary who was going to help us find the list?" He didn't wait for Merker's answer. "She thought she found the list at Rasta's home. Maxine finagled us an invitation to Rasta's house, and we were able to access his computer and his files, all to no avail. I don't think the list exists. If it does, I don't think Rasta's involved."

Merker shook his head, more at his disappointment in Callison's attitude than in his inability to find the list. "So you think this entire conspiracy thing is fiction."

"Yes, I think the so-called conspiracy is a patchwork of isolated facts mixed with some fiction, but with no real substance when you put it all together." Callison was exhausted mentally, physically, emotionally, and he had convinced himself the conspiracy theory was invalid.

"I hear what you're saying, but I have some information that isn't fiction which may change your mind."

Callison was tired, but still was open-minded enough to give Merker his due. "Okay—change my mind."

"My car was messed with in Chicago by someone who was very good. They made it so that it would be very difficult to prove anything if I were to have an accident." Merker waited for a reaction from Callison but got none. "I had a friend, who's an expert, defuse the detonators. They would have wrecked the steering as well as the brakes. Sounds familiar, huh?"

Callison nodded but didn't speak.

Merker continued. "This expert friend of mine told me this was done by professionals, which makes me suspect someone else may be involved besides Van Gregory."

"And what exactly makes you think this?" Callison still wasn't convinced and it showed in his face.

"These detonators were very sophisticated—way beyond Gregory. Plus there's another thing you should know. I think I'm being followed and not by Van Gregory. I haven't been able to figure out who's following me, but my sixth sense tells me there's someone definitely there."

"Your sixth sense! You've got to be kidding me." Callison shook his head in disbelief.

"No, I'm very serious. I feel as strongly about this as any feeling I've ever had with my sixth sense. Even if you don't believe me, I beg you to always use the alarm I put in your car. The alarm works, that's how I figured out my car had been messed with." Merker hesitated a moment. "Please, promise me you'll use the alarm."

"Okay, I'll use the alarm, but I think you're blowing this way out of proportion." Callison rubbed his tired eyes.

Merker was running out of options to convince Callison, he would have to use his ace in the hole, Natalie. Before Callison came home, Merker and Natalie had had a long conversation, in which Merker explained his concerns and how he needed Callison's help. Merker convinced Natalie to allow him to install his alarm system into her car, and while he was doing the installation they talked about Callison. They concluded they both needed him to see this through to its completion for two entirely different reasons. For Merker it was to avenge the death of his friend Jonas Cisko and to rediscover himself. For Natalie it was for Steven to rediscover himself, the man she originally fell in love with.

Natalie entered the room as the conversation had hit a lull. She told Steven he had a call from the hospital and he excused himself.

Natalie appreciated Merker's frustration. "He can be pretty stubborn at times," she said.

"I don't think he believes me about the possible dangers connected to this case. I don't want to frighten either of you, but these people play for keeps. You have to keep your wits about you."

"I believe you. I promise we'll both use our alarm systems in our cars, as you have recommended, as well as keep our wits about us." Natalie said.

Merker had seen this many times before, mostly while still on the force. He called it "television bravery." "TB" as he would refer to it, was a state of artificial confidence that stemmed from television violence. "Please, if either you or Steven find anything unusual, you need to contact the authorities or myself. Don't mess with these people, they're professionals and are very dangerous."

Natalie politely nodded to reassure Merker she wouldn't do anything stupid.

Merker was not convinced he had reached Natalie, but he changed the subject slightly. "How can we now convince your husband this is real?"

"He has been under quite a bit of pressure independent of this conspiracy thing. He has a patient who's quite ill, and has spent several sleepless nights caring for her. Plus he has a hearing tomorrow on a medical problem he had."

Natalie peeked her head out of the study to see if her husband was still on the phone. She listened for several seconds, then heard his voice—it was serious and very solemn.

"So what do you suggest?" Merker followed her into the hallway and was struck by the abstract painting on the wall.

Natalie noticed Merker's interest in the painting and pointed out she was the artist. She had dabbled in both oils and acrylics for several years and was experimenting with the abstract. While discussing the painting and her other works of art, Natalie got an idea how they might convince Steven to take this more seriously. "I have an idea. What we need to do is to get him out of his normal environment and work on him where he's less stressed."

"Okay; I can buy that. You seem to have a plan, where?" Merker asked.

"We have tickets tomorrow evening for the baseball game, why don't you join us and we can work on him there?" Natalie suggested.

Merker thought to himself, *Yes, there is a God.* This had to be a good omen. The only problem, which really wasn't a problem, was he had reservations for a flight to Florida tomorrow. He would just postpone his Florida segment by a day and tell his Florida contingent to soak up the sun for another day.

Steven entered the room, distraught and drained from his telephone conversation. "Margaret has taken a turn for the worse. I doubt I'll be able to do anything." Callison paused, looking deeply concerned, "But I won't be able to sleep anyway, so I'm going in."

"How about if I go with you, to keep you company?" Natalie

placed her arm around her husband's sagging shoulder.

"It's not necessary, but if you want to come I don't care." Steven's tone was depressive.

Merker thought, *this is a guy who needs a vacation.* He was concerned he wouldn't be able to convince him, even at the baseball game. Then he reconsidered. Of course he could convince him at the game—tomorrow would be a great day.

29

The scene in the intensive care unit was chaotic: in bed two, a patient had just self-extubated himself, pulling out his endotracheal tube; in bed four, a man was vomiting blood; and in bed eight, Margaret had started to seize again and was running a fever of 104. A small crowd hovered over Margaret's bed, hastily attempting to stabilize her condition. Callison's presence wasn't noticed until he stood by the bedside. The resident appeared to have control of the situation. The appropriate medications had been administered, the lab tests had been ordered, and the examination had been completed. Callison asked if the family had been notified and was told they were in the waiting room.

The waiting room was overflowing with people. A quiet type of camaraderie can occur among the family members and significant others, who wait together. Although they are complete strangers, brought together by less than optimal circumstances, they all share one thing in common: the concern and love for another individual. When the illness is prolonged, it is not uncommon for the families to interact, forming short-term relationships, and in rare instances long-term relationships are born. This was not so in the case of the Kodacks.

In the corner of the waiting area was seated Mr. Kodack, alone and silent, not altering his stone-like expression save for the occasional shifting of his eyes to notice the movement of a stranger.

Callison had told Natalie to wait for him in the waiting room with the Kodacks, but when he entered neither she nor Sally was visible. Callison approached Mr. Kodack. His darkened eyes, peering out as if from a cave, noticed Callison approach and momentarily exhibited a sign of recognition. The conversation was stifled, but Mr. Kodack told him Natalie had taken Sally to the cafeteria. Callison sat silently with Mr. Kodack, staring into the same oblivion wondering what would happen to this family if Margaret were not to survive. While the seconds passed into minutes, Callison was startled out of his trance by Natalie returning with little Sally.

"Steven, can I have a word with you?" Natalie motioned with her head toward the hall. Natalie placed Sally on her grandfather's lap and met him in the hallway outside the waiting room.

"What? What do you want?" Callison was irritated at her insistence. After all, they were now in his territory, his domain. He was the one who was used to giving the orders here.

"I introduced myself to Mr. Kodack and told him I was your wife." She looked at him with a pitiful, dour expression.

"So?" Steven was still irritated.

"He didn't say a word, he just handed me his granddaughter and motioned for me to leave. I'm concerned for the welfare of this adorable little girl." Natalie looked about to make sure they weren't being overheard.

"So am I. Social services are working with the family; she'll be taken care of. Our social workers are excellent and will find the best solution possible." Callison felt this was the best he could do under these circumstances.

"What does that mean? The best solution possible. Sounds like passing the buck to me." The tone in her voice became perceptively hostile.

"I don't know, they'll do their best. They're professionals and they'll do their job." Callison was still annoyed. He knew it had been a bad idea for her to come with him.

"Don't take that holier-than-thou attitude with me! I know where your warts are, buddy." Natalie's eyes flashed.

"Look, you asked to come. I told you this was a difficult situation. Please don't add to the difficulty." Steven's tone was more conciliatory. He was used to this kind of situation, but Natalie wasn't.

"Would you mind if I keep them company while you do whatever you do?" Natalie's expression now matched his.

Callison realized she was irritated. He also knew the best policy at this point was to not argue and compromise as much as possible. "Sounds like a good idea. I'm going back in the unit.

Hopefully, I won't be too long."

The doors of the intensive unit opened and Callison entered. He felt safe again in his territory, where he was free of his wife's barbs.

In the unit everything was stabilizing. The man who had pulled out his endotracheal tube was now reintubated and sedated. The GI bleed was being stabilized and about to go to surgery. And Margaret had finally stopped seizing.

Callison reviewed the pertinent data with the resident and then performed his own physical examination on Margaret, hoping to find a clue that could lead him to a reversible component of her condition. Callison's exam mirrored the resident's, and the plan of action already formulated seemed reasonable.

It was still too soon to go back to Natalie in the waiting room, so Callison sat and talked hospital politics with the resident for several minutes. This was even more distasteful than the insolence from his wife, so he reluctantly returned to the waiting room.

The hour was now approaching midnight and Callison needed a good night sleep because of his hearing scheduled for the next morning. He suggested Mr. Kodack take Sally home and he would notify them if there was any change in Margaret's condition. The four of them left the hospital together, Natalie with Steven, and Mr. Kodack with Sally draped around his neck, nestled asleep in his arms.

The ring of the telephone awakened Steven. His vision blurred, he could barely read the clock illuminating 5 A.M. It was about Margaret; her blood pressure was dropping, as was her pulse rate. Steven's drive to the hospital was a blur. Natalie wanted to accompany him but he insisted she stay home.

Upon entering the unit he saw the crowd around bed eight. The Kodacks were well known to the staff of each shift in the unit, and the commotion signified things weren't going very well. The code had started thirty minutes ago, and all they had to show for their efforts was the sweat on their foreheads. There was no pulse or blood pressure.

The resident on call, Martin Tupp, was at the bedside and

was well acquainted with the case. Dr. Tupp reviewed what had transpired while Callison was in transit. He told Callison that Dr. Snyder and the family had also been contacted, and both were on their way to the hospital. Callison was determined to save Margaret. Although Dr. Tupp had tried everything he could think of, he had to try again. The second round of resuscitative efforts transiently restored a heart rhythm on the electrocardiogram, although there was no palpable pulse.

Snyder appeared about fifteen minutes after Callison arrived. Assessing the situation, he was confident there was nothing from a neurosurgical point of view that could be of benefit. Callison, still frantically searching for hope when there was none, continued the resuscitation. Snyder stayed by his patient's side, although he knew, as did Callison, that the end result was inevitable. After two hours of intensive, yet futile efforts, and with the insistence of Snyder, Margaret was pronounced dead.

The scene around her body was surrealistic, with all in attendance just silently staring at her lifeless body. The monitor had been straight line for some time when a nurse flicked off the respirator. The new silence added to the solemnity. Tears were in the eyes of most in attendance. This was atypical. Many had died in this unit, even this bed, but this case, this family, continued to tug at the hearts of almost everyone. Sally, the little blonde five-year-old, who had lost her father at the age of three in an auto accident, had now lost her mother at the age of five. Life sometimes wasn't fair.

Callison had to once again tell the Kodacks.

Callison entered the waiting room. It was much less crowded than the previous day, and the Kodacks had their seats tucked away in the corner. Mr. Kodack looked up with his bloodshot eyes and Callison responded with a slow, sorrowful nod. He then asked if they would like some time alone with the body. The slow march through the unit to bed eight was one of the longest walks in Callison's career. Callison led both Mr. Kodack and Sally to the bed where Margaret lay, where Irma Wiggins, the head nurse from the night shift, was tucking the sheets around Margaret, giving the illusion she was just asleep.

Mr. Kodack and Sally silently watched as Wiggins completed

her chores. Wiggins, whose shift had ended hours before, stayed to complete her work. As Wiggins started to pull the curtain to give them the privacy they needed, a small hand grabbed at Callison's pant leg. It was little Sally, her blue eyes tearing and nose running, looking up at the doctor who had attended her mother and grandmother.

Callison was caught in a state of uncertainty, not knowing what she wanted or what he should do. He bent down so he was at Sally's level, looking into her innocent eyes, waiting. "Thank you for taking care of my mommy." The words from Sally's mouth, possibly the first spoken in over two years, were as powerful and moving as any Callison had ever heard.

"Oh, God," Wiggins said as she covered her face with her hands and nearly fell to floor, bracing herself against a counter.

Callison struggled for control, unable to respond as his emotions were lodged in his throat. After swallowing several times and exhaling a giant sigh, he could only mumble, "You're welcome, Sally."

Even her grandfather, Mr. Kodack, was overwhelmed. Mr. Kodack had to sit in the nearest chair to avoid falling. Sally ran over to her grandfather and sat on his lap as they both silently focused their attention on Margaret.

Callison staggered to his feet and assisted Wiggins in closing the curtain to give the mourners their privacy.

The remainder of the morning was lost in a trail of paperwork and counseling of the family. When Callison finally became aware of the time, he realized he had missed his hearing.

Callison called his secretary and asked her if she could find the number to call about postponing his hearing. She said she would try, but he had a message from a Maxine Wells who said it was very important she talk to him.

As if things weren't bad enough, now there was a problem with Maxine!

While dialing Maxine's number a cadre of possible issues swam through his head. Before Callison's vivid imagination could conjure up much, he had Maxine on the line.

"Hello, Dr. Callison, how are you doing?" Her voice was resonant.

"Hello, Maxine, I'm fair. What can I do for you?" As the words left his mouth, he expected the ax to fall.

"I just had a conversation with Margo, and she told me she found the list. She's positive of it, this time."

Callison relieved on the one hand, now had to again deal with the list as an issue. "Why are you telling me this? I thought we had an agreement to drop the list issue until things got sorted out."

Maxine voice became somber and reflective. "I'm sorry, Doctor, but Margo did this on her own and I thought you would want to know."

Callison felt like a heel. "I'm sorry, Maxine, I've just had a pretty traumatic day. I guess I'm taking it out on you."

"There's no reason to apologize, Doctor. I understand, we all have days like that." The resonance was back in her voice.

"How did she find the list?" Callison's curiosity got the better of him.

"She asked me if we found the list. I told her we didn't. That's all I said, I swear. Then she called me today saying she found the list and can get it for us if we still need it." Maxine was calm and collected as she spoke.

"Did we miss it?" Callison could not explain why he was asking but he had to know.

"No, apparently Rasta had brought the disk that contained the list to his other office. He has another office, which he shares with another doctor, where he sees patients twice a week. Rasta asked Margo to help him with some of his insurance forms at his private office and she obliged. While using the computer, she found a disk named Caldo."

"Who has the disk now?" Callison's head was spinning. First, the emotional avalanche from the Kodacks, and now this issue with the list.

"Margo has it. She's still at his private office. That's where she called me from, and I immediately called you. Should I ask her for a copy?"

Callison paused, feeling a moment's respite from his confusion. "Yes, get the copy and let's see what it says."

"I'll call her back. Then I'll get back to you immediately."

"Thank you, Maxine. It seems I'm always saying that to you. By the way, how are you doing?"

"I'm doing well, thank you."

Callison decided not to press the subject. He had enough problems to deal with already.

As soon as he got off the phone, Helen, his secretary, entered his office with a fax from the hearing committee. If Callison would fill out the questionnaire, they would consider rescheduling his hearing on the grounds of extenuating circumstances.

As he sat in his chair, his mind wandered back to little Sally. He thought he was about to cry, but the tears didn't come, they never did. He walked back to the intensive care unit to see if the Kodacks were still there, but they had left. Enervated from the past twenty-four hours, Callison was ready to go home.

Callison was not expecting to see Marcus Merker at his home when he arrived. Natalie and Marcus met him at the door, both grinning.

"What's going on? Why are both of you grinning like you've just won the lottery?" Callison was not in the mood to be jolly, or even to be around people who were jolly.

"Did you forget?" Natalie said. "We're going to the baseball game tonight and I was able to get an extra ticket so Marcus could go with us." The look of excitement would have been contagious on any other evening, but tonight it took all of his strength for Callison to even agree to go to the game.

Steven told them he would only be a couple of minutes as he needed to change his clothes. While he was changing, he reflected on the day and how much he needed to have a relaxing evening. Natalie interrupted his thoughts to tell him he had a long distance call from Maxine Wells.

"Hello, Maxine." He really didn't want to accept the call, but knew he had to hear what she had to say.

"I have some bad news. Margo was unable to copy the disk. Rasta put a lock-out on the disk, making it impossible to copy. She called me and asked if she should just take the original, but I told her no. I hope I did the right thing."

"Absolutely. We aren't criminals, and to our knowledge neither is he. Why don't we sleep on this and I'll call you tomorrow? Again, thanks for all your efforts, and thank Margo for me too." Callison did not want a prolonged discussion and needed to think this list business through.

As soon as he hung the phone up, Callison proceeded to their car where both Natalie and Merker were eagerly waiting. When Callison pulled out of the driveway Merker noticed a tan Acura Integra several homes away also pull away. Merker donned a specially designed pair of sunglasses that contained a miniature pair of reflective side view mirrors. Merker was concentrating on the car following them, and secondarily was listening to Callison's description of his day.

By the time Callison came to the part of the story where Sally spoke, Natalie was beside herself. At about the same time, Merker noticed the tan Acura turn off the street, and a white Buick Skylark took its place. Either they were being followed by a dual surveillance team or this was a simple coincidence. The white Buick stayed three car lengths behind, just as the tan Acura had. It was the way they were following, with the car intermittently peering from the passing lane so not to lose visual contact, which heightened Merker's suspicion.

When Callison completed his story, Natalie was still sobbing. The white Buick turned in another direction with no other car in sight. Merker sat back and relaxed, thinking he was being overly cautious. They were almost at the ballpark when the tan Acura reappeared. This was no longer a coincidence—they were being followed.

Merker could not inform either of the Callisons, who were both distraught. He would have to handle this himself.

The outside of the stadium was adorned with reliefs of longhorn cattle and panels of Texas history. The reddish-brown stone work was highlighted by four green roofed towers, one at each entrance, adding to the park's old-time ambiance.

As the three entered the stadium via the third base entrance, Merker could see out of the corner of his glasses three men in the distance, one of whom was Van Gregory in disguise. Gregory's disguise consisted of normal clothes, nothing black, and no sunglasses. Merker doubted he would have recognized him if he

312

hadn't been looking.

The inside of the stadium was as impressive as the outside. Ample walkways, numerous concession stands, and their seats were perfect behind the first base dugout. The field was green grass. Merker loved grass and despised the artificial turf, which he considered a blight on the sport. Once seated, Merker surveyed the ballpark, first with an eye for escape routes and areas where Gregory and his comrades might be lurking. Merker also surveyed the park as a fan, looking at the asymmetric lines on the field, the white steel latticework of the balconies in center field, the high green wall in left field, and the home run porch in right. Merker approved of this ballpark—it had the ambiance of the older parks with the amenities of the newer parks. But he couldn't waste too much time looking at the park as a fan. He needed to formulate a plan in case he needed a brisk exit.

Once the game started, Merker scanned the stands to see if he could find Gregory and his compatriots. Merker had a small pair of binoculars he frequently used during his work. Merker didn't want to use the binoculars while he was seated; he didn't want Gregory to suspect he was aware they were being watched.

Merker picked a position in a partially hidden alcove, a section away from their seats, which would avail him a panoramic view of the park and hopefully of Van Gregory. Before he could initiate his plan to find Gregory, he needed to work on Callison, and also load his secret weapon. Merker excused himself and returned with several orders of nachos and beer, which would satisfy their appetites and fill Merker with the needed ammunition.

Steven and Natalie were still discussing his day and the fate of poor little Sally and her grandfather. Steven was also concerned about missing his hearing, but was fairly confident it could be rescheduled.

Merker panned the crowd, but with the park filled, it was futile without his binoculars. It was time to work on Callison "So, Dr. Callison."

"Please, call me Steven."

"Steven, I don't want to aggravate you, but I want you to know of the potential danger I feel we're both under."

313

"You told me yesterday. I used the alarm today." Callison wasn't in the mood for this.

"That's good, but you need to keep your wits about you until this case is settled." Merker was looking past him at Natalie as he spoke.

"As far as I'm concerned the case is closed, so I guess I have nothing to be concerned about." Callison's tone was noticeably agitated.

"Steven, stop being difficult. Marcus is just trying to be helpful," Natalie said.

"Okay, I'll listen without being difficult." His acerbic tone was unmistakable.

"Listen, I'm not trying to be difficult either," Merker said. His tone was businesslike. "All I want is for you to know how serious this may be. After all, this is your profession on the line, not mine. I'm doing this for a friend. I know why I'm doing this, do you?"

Callison thought for a several seconds. "At first, I was helping you because it seemed the right thing to do. Now honestly I'm not so sure. The matter regarding my profession isn't the issue. I'll have to deal with that regardless of the situation with the list or Rasta."

Natalie couldn't believe what she was hearing. "Steven, are you telling me this hasn't infuriated you?"

"What are you talking about?" Callison said, perplexed.

"What am I talking about? Didn't this group or whatever it is plan to extinguish your profession in the past, and now there's every reason to believe they're trying to do it again. They might have killed or at least contributed to the deaths of several people, many of whom were your colleagues. And now Marcus is telling us his car has been tampered with, and maybe ours is next. And you're still not sure?"

Merker couldn't have said it better.

Callison was about to reply when they were interrupted by a roar from the fans in the stadium, which was followed by music and fireworks. A Texas Ranger had just homered and they had missed it. Fortunately the replay captured the moment so they could share in the excitement.

314

Once the roar had dissipated, Callison returned to the previous conversation. "Natalie, everything you've said, I've said to myself a hundred times, but I can't get away from the fact that none of this can be proven. The California merger didn't ruin the profession and ironically may have given the profession the status it needed to survive and flourish. The fact that a list may exist is still speculative. I thought it was worth the risk to find it, but I now think I was wrong. I literally committed a crime and found nothing. I broke into the study of a respected physician, for God sakes!"

Callison paused for a moment reflecting on his recent conversation with Maxine. He decided against complicating matters further by introducing new information about the list.

Merker had finished his large order of nachos and started on the Callisons'. Callison, nervous, also started to munch on the chips, cheese, and jalapenos. The latter were too spicy for his taste, causing him to gulp down the beer Merker had bought.

Once the burning in his mouth subsided Steven continued. "The information we have about the deaths of Dr. Cisko and the others is totally theoretical, and before I go way out on a limb I'd need some real confirmation, and not speculation. Lastly, I have no doubts your car was tampered with, but you have no evidence that someone involved with this case did it. Isn't it possible someone else did this? Someone involved in another case? Someone from your past, who's holding a grudge? Isn't that possible?"

"Pretty unlikely," Merker answered.

"But possible. Could you tell me, without any doubt, the car was altered by someone involved in this case? Didn't you say earlier you didn't think Van Gregory was capable of this type of sophistication?" Merker nodded. "Then, by your own reasoning you're implicating another party. Who is this mysterious party? What's their motive? I'm sorry, there are too many holes in your theory."

Merker understood Callison's reasoning and couldn't answer, but he was positive there was a relationship between his car, Van Gregory, and this case. His sixth sense told him so. He also hadn't had a case in months, and the likelihood of anyone else having the least interest in him was remote at best. Merker decided his best option was to prove to him Gregory was following them tonight, or better yet, have Gregory tell him why he was following them. Then he was fairly confident Callison would be convinced. It was time for Merker to set his trap for Gregory. The nachos were eaten, the beer was gone, the secret weapon was loaded, and it was time to deploy.

Merker's plan was simple, he would perch himself several sections away to afford him the best view of the park. He would scan the sections in search of Gregory who would be watching Callison, while he was waving. Merker would then approach Gregory and force him to reveal himself to Callison. Merker was sure once Callison realized Gregory was still following him, it would turn the tide and Callison would be glad to help.

Merker asked Callison to wave his hands above his head for about ten seconds at a time. He asked him to start waving about ten minutes after Merker left and to repeat the sequence every minute for five additional minutes. Merker told Callison he was testing his new binoculars and wanted to see how effective they were from a distance. He also asked Callison to mouth the following sentence, "I know where you are," with each sequence, to see if he could read his lips from the outfield. Callison initially refused but Natalie convinced him to be a good sport, although he felt like a fool.

Merker slowly scanned the stadium from his vantage point, looking for the person or persons whose attention were aimed at the stands and not the field. To his surprise, there were many people looking into the stands, at the sky, at each other, anywhere but the field. This was so inconceivable to Merker, he interrupted his surveillance to make sure the game was still in progress. Merker noticed the score was tied in the fifth inning. He couldn't believe the crowd was not fixated on the field, as he wished he could be. He returned to scanning, only after watching Callison to see if he would do his wave.

To Merker's surprise both Callison and Natalie started waving. They looked foolish. Merker wasn't in position to read their lips, since he was to their side but he assumed if they were doing the wave they would likewise mouth the sentence. There was no sign of Van Gregory or anyone else looking in their direction.

Two waves down, Merker noticed him. Van Gregory also had binoculars, but he wasn't watching Callison, he was watching Merker. They were eye to eye, binocular to binocular. Merker realized they were probably following him and not Callison.

Merker saw a smile appear on Gregory's face, who then motioned with his free hand. Merker looked behind him and noticed two men dressed in slacks and Hawaiian shirts approaching. Merker was strategically situated on the aisle where he could exit by either of two routes. Both his pursuers were approaching in the same direction. Merker exited in the opposite direction, which emptied into a large walkway. Hastening his pace, Merker accidentally bumped into a man standing in the corridor between the inner and outer portions of the stadium. Merker excused himself for the accidental bump, when he felt something hard prodding his side. It was a gun. The man told Merker to hold his position. Within seconds his two accomplices were at his side. Without saying a word they escorted Merker to Van Gregory.

Merker realized why Van Gregory wore the glasses and black clothing—he was a very unattractive man. His face was pockmarked, he had an unappealing bulbous nose, multi-tiered bags under his eyes, and yellow-stained teeth. Gregory smiled when Merker sat next to him. The gap between his two front teeth was more noticeable when he was smiling.

"So nice of you to drop by, Mr. Merker."

Merker thought about using his secret weapon. He was in a crowd and the commotion would certainly create the diversion he would need to escape, but he first needed to know what Gregory wanted. "Listen, Gregory, what's all this about? I'm here with company."

"We know you're here with the Callisons, but it's you we need to talk to. You've been a hard man to pin down recently." Merker noted a fine mist which sprayed intermittently through the gap between Gregory's teeth.

"What's so important you had to track me down here?" Merker needed to find out if it was Gregory who had activated his alarm system.

"I needed to find a place to talk to you, where I knew I'd have your attention. This place seemed as good as any." The spray increased every time Gregory emphasized a word with an *S* sound.

"Okay, you have my attention." The crowd erupted as a Ranger doubled in two runs, giving the Rangers the lead.

"You need to drop the Cisko case." The look on Gregory's face was much more serious.

"Why would I do that?" Merker returned the serious expression.

"Because I have a signed statement from Gus Amacorde, that says you received a bribe from Simon Escobart while you were on the force. And I don't think you'd like your old department to reopen the investigation, would you? And I doubt Dr. Callison would want to be associated with a pimp either, do you?"

The words struck a sensitive chord in Merker. The Gus Amacorde case was the reason Merker left the force and had almost put him behind bars. Gus Amacorde was an acquaintance of Merker's from the old neighborhood. Amacorde was running a small brothel on the south side of Chicago, which was fairly well known and frequented by several local politicians. It was one of these politicians, a local councilman by the name of Simon Escobart, who was caught in a raid on the brothel, which started a chain of events eventually causing Merker to resign from the force.

The night Escobart was caught, Merker had been assigned to escort him to the police station. Escobart pleaded and begged Merker, promising him a substantial sum of money if he would let him go home first, before taking him in. Merker was in debt, up to his ears, from the doctor bills, hospital bills, and private nursing bills he accrued during his wife's protracted illness. She was still very ill and needed around-the-clock care. Merker was out of cash. He thought a little diversion en route to the station, was innocent enough and would provide him the cash necessary to pay his bills. Merker insisted on accompanying Escobart to his home, which was filled with illicit drugs. Merker had no warrant and had no reason to be there, so he was caught in a very tenuous situation.

Amacorde was in Escobart's home when they arrived. He had

been sent there by Escobart to retrieve additional drugs for their party. Amacorde hid in the closet, and watched and listened as Escobart scurried about collecting all the drugs scattered throughout the premises. Merker demanded they leave, but Escobart continued his task, just in case the police decided to search his home.

Merker eventually escorted Escobart to the police station, never mentioning the side trip to Escobart's home. When Escobart was released on bail, he sent an envelope containing thirty one-hundred dollar bills to Merker's home. Merker kept the money.

Escobart was eventually caught for trafficking in drugs, but committed suicide before he was convicted. During the trial, Merker was approached by Amacorde, who told him he had been hiding in the closet that night and he would reveal that fact if he were implicated in the Escobart trial. Escobart died before the trial ended, so Amacorde was never implicated and neither was Merker.

Somehow Gregory had gotten to Amacorde and now he would reopen this wound which had festered for many years. Gregory was right, he didn't want Callison to know about this. Merker's secret weapon was of no use, Gregory had the upper hand and now Merker had to regroup.

Merker had been quiet for some time, thinking of his options before he answered Gregory. "I'll drop out of the case but I need to know something."

"What?"

"Did you do something to my car?" Merker was studying Gregory's body and facial language closely as he answered.

"No, I didn't touch your car." There was no hesitation in his answer and no evidence he was lying.

Merker's sixth sense also told him Gregory was not responsible for the car. But—*if not him, then who?* "Can I return to the Callisons now?"

"Sure. Not that I don't trust you, but I don't. I don't trust any cops . . . not even the crooked ones." Gregory's words hurt Merker as only the truth could. A fact that didn't escape Gregory, who took great pleasure in Merker's uneasiness. "We'll be keeping an eye on you just to make sure you keep up your end of the agreement."

Gregory winked at Merker before placing his sunglasses on.

Indignant, yet under control, Merker slowly walked away.

The game had temporarily taken Callison's mind off his problems. But as for Merker, he needed a new plan.

30

Merker had formulated another plan, realizing Van Gregory, et al, would be watching him. If anything, Merker was more determined to find the list and avenge the death of his friend, Dr. Cisko. He would deal with Mr. Gregory in due time, and this time he would not underestimate his abilities. The information Gregory had collected on Merker's past rekindled memories he had tried to forget, but realistically never could.

Merker contacted the boys of Florida, Drs. Jasper and Truelove, and told them to meet him at the marina next to the Marriott, at pier 61, in Fort Lauderdale. Merker changed his flight reservations from West Palm Beach to Miami. He assumed he would be followed, and in Merker's estimation, Miami Beach would be a more logical destination for relaxation than West Palm Beach.

Boarding the airplane, Merker noticed one of the goons still wearing the same shirt he wore when he accompanied Gregory to the ball game. Merker went out of his way to let him know he was aware of his presence and told him he should enjoy watching Merker fish and lie on the beach. He wondered if the man ever changed his clothes.

Upon arrival, Merker rented a Camaro. He would need a car with good acceleration later. Merker drove down Miami Beach past the massive complexes, looking for the right hotel. He was in the art deco hotel area when he pulled into the Algiers Hotel. The man in the Hawaiian shirt pulled in behind Merker.

After checking into his room, Merker changed to his bathing suit and tank top. His body had changed over the years—hair was growing in places he had previously thought it impossible for hair to grow. Merker was sure the hair on his back and in his ears was being seeded from the hair falling from his head, but he was long past caring. He tried to stay in shape, but his outfit couldn't hide the ample love handles he had acquired.

At the pool Merker relaxed with a Polynesian concoction topped with a little umbrella: it was cool, tasty and refreshing. Merker remained poolside until the sun set and then mentioned to the man in the Hawaiian shirt that he was going to shower and then have dinner, again eliciting no comment or reaction.

The next day, Merker went to the restaurant in the hotel for their continental breakfast. He was followed by the same man, now in a different colored Hawaiian shirt. If someone else was following him, Merker hadn't noticed. It would be a clever ruse to use the man in the Hawaiian shirt as a distraction, while another was really doing the surveillance. Merker couldn't detect an accomplice, but was highly suspicious. Once breakfast was over, Merker retrieved his car from the attendant and returned it to the rental agency. He complained there was something wrong with the steering mechanism, which there wasn't. He just wanted another car. He was positive the Camaro was armed with a tracking device and he had places to go and didn't want any company.

Pulling out of the rental agency with his Buick LeSabre, Merker saluted the man in the Hawaiian shirt, who was waiting. Merker could see he was irritated, and he assumed it was because his homing device was now useless.

On the highway, Merker tested his pursuer's driving skills in a cat-and-mouse mini-chase. He was better than average, but definitely not in Merker's class. Merker had to meet the doctors in Fort Lauderdale in two hours, so it was time to lose his tail. He exited off the highway, the Thunderbird in pursuit. He reentered the highway immediately and repeated this sequence with the next two exits. With the third exit, Merker signaled to exit but at the last second swerved back onto the highway, the Thunderbird still hot on his trail. The man in the Hawaiian shirt actually smiled. It was the first sign of emotion Merker had seen from him.

Now Merker was ready to have some fun. A group of teenagers in a reconditioned Mustang convertible were speeding down the highway. Merker accelerated past them, cutting off the Mustang. The teenagers were in close pursuit, with the Thunderbird a distant third, but closing the gap quickly. Merker changed lanes repeatedly; the Mustang followed each move, with the Thunderbird in close pursuit. Merker started to change lanes once again, signaling to the left, and then he started to veer left. Suddenly he switched and crossed to the far right lane, slamming his brakes.

The Mustang had also started left and as it cut to the right there was no room, since Merker had hit his brakes. The Mustang turned into the oncoming Thunderbird, whose tires were screeching as the cars skidded into each other. Merker exited from the highway and doubled back to the intersection of U.S. 1, which would take him to his rendezvous in Fort Lauderdale.

Pier 61 had an impressive array of expensive yachts and sailboats docked along its intricate maze of wooden platforms. The sun was bright and hot, and there were many people about. Some were there because of the sea and their interest in sailing, but most seemed to be just hanging out. Merker surveyed the area, keeping a watchful eye for anyone questionable. He was sure he lost the man in the Hawaiian shirt, but his sixth sense told him somebody else was following, someone much more cunning and deceptive. Merker considered stopping somewhere else first to see if he could flush someone out, but he decided against complicating his day any more than was necessary.

Merker stationed himself on the roof of the Marriott. If the good doctors were being followed, it would be very easy to spot from his vantage point. Merker was a half hour early, so he made himself comfortable and watched the crowds mill around the dock, using his binoculars.

Time passed quickly. Merker noticed two men walk tentatively onto the pier, Truelove and Jasper. Merker watched them aimlessly wander for several minutes until they landed on a bench overlooking the marina. Perusing the crowds, Merker could not find anything out of the ordinary. If someone was following Truelove and Jasper, he couldn't find them, so he implemented the second phase of his plan.

Merker requisitioned a bellboy to ask the elderly gentlemen to meet him in the lobby of the hotel. Again, Merker was able to observe the bellboy talking to the doctors on the pier. As before everything appeared to be safe. The bellboy escorted Truelove and Jasper to the lounge as Merker had instructed and told them their party would meet them there momentarily. Merker observed the lobby from his vantage point before he approached, feeling confident they were alone.

Neither Truelove nor Jasper noticed Merker before he called their names. Both jumped slightly, as the secretive maneuvering had unnerved them.

"Gentlemen, it's nice to see the both of you." Merker smiled, as the two attempted to settle in their seats.

"Why all this moving around and secret rendezvous?" Jasper asked.

"Can't be too careful. Anyway, I was watching you pretty closely for the last ten minutes or so. I'm sure we're safe here." Merker wasn't as sure as he would like to have been, but had no real reason to be concerned. Just his intuition.

"I guess we should review the notebook before we do anything else." Truelove wanted to get down to the business at hand. He handed Merker the small notebook, which hopefully contained the clues that could help them find the list.

Merker studied the notebook, which was aged and tattered but still intact. The pages were held together by multiple small spiral rings. Merker turned to the first page.

As he opened the first page, Jasper started to talk. "As you can see, much of this is self-explanatory but there are segments that are either uninterpretable or unreadable."

When Merker turned to the second page, which explained some of the details relative to Bartolli's death, Jasper pointed a to a specific notation. "See this reference here—it doesn't make any sense." Merker read the notation, which was an obvious abbreviation "O. Y. R.," just as they had described over the phone.

Each page had at least one reference, which was either blurred, faded, or confusing. However, they were able to understand the gist of each page by piecing it together. The exception was the last page, which made no sense at all. On this page was a name or reference, which might have been written at a different time, and regarding a different case. Merker thought this was possibly a red herring and had nothing to do with this case. The rationale for this was that there were several blank pages between the last notation regarding Van Gregory and this notation. It read: "A S E lwood R Loax," and underneath was scribbled "death to the gunfighter." Merker studied this for several minutes. He wanted to believe this was gibberish, but his sixth sense told him otherwise.

Truelove suggested the possibility of the letters being an anagram. Truelove said he was an avid anagram solver, but neither he nor Jasper could make any sense out of these letters.

Both Jasper and Truelove had pondered the last page of the notebook for days and had come to the same conclusion—they had no idea what it meant. They decided it was time to revisit Helen Bartolli and see if she could help shed any further light on this dilemma. Merker insisted he drive just in case they were being followed.

The drive to West Palm Beach from Fort Lauderdale passed quickly as they all discussed the last page of the notebook, trying to decipher the riddle. Who was a gunfighter and who was Aselwood or was it Selwood or Elwood or Loax? It made no sense. If there was someone named any of these names, how would they ever find this person over thirty years later? Maybe Mrs. Bartolli had the answer.

The Palm Meadows Estates was one of those expensive, all-inclusive communities for the elderly. To enter the development you passed through a security gate which was manned twenty-four hours a day, and entrance was allowed only after confirmation by one of the tenants. The entrance to the complex was adorned with a wide array of beautiful flowers: roses, tulips, hibiscus and numerous other colorful flora surrounding a fountain separating the entrance from the exit lanes.

Jasper had called ahead, and Mrs. Bartolli had already informed the front gate she was expecting company. When they entered the lush grounds of the estates, Merker noticed in his rearview mirror a minivan slow slightly before it regained its speed and passed the entrance. Merker wondered for a moment why a car would slow down, but dismissed the notion and decided he was being overly cautious.

Beyond the entrance, it was as if they entered a city unto itself. They initially passed a section of individual homes, all magnificently maintained and landscaped. The streets were wide and immaculate. They passed a small medical clinic, which posted a sign signifying 24-hour coverage.

Helen Bartolli-Sanford and her husband lived in one of the large duplexes in the development. It was tastefully decorated with a glass-enclosed atrium housing a large palm and numerous colorful plants. The atrium was the central focus of the home, and it availed a view from four different rooms, giving the entire indoor living area an open, airy effect.

They were greeted by Helen Bartolli Sanford, who was dressed in white shorts and an emerald green tank top. Although she was in her sixties, she still had a firm, trim figure and walked with a pert bounce. Helen introduced her husband, Jack, to the group. The reference to Jack Sanford immediately reminded Merker of the old baseball pitcher who had the same name.

Off the entrance was a sitting area where Helen had a pitcher of fresh lemonade and a vegetable platter placed on a glass table surrounded by four wicker chairs.

Jack quickly excused himself and returned to his garden work. The four remaining, Helen, Merker, Truelove and Jasper, sat in the four chairs around the glass table. Helen offered lemonade and they all accepted. As she poured the lemonade, she inquired why they returned.

Merker answered. "I'm sorry if we're disturbing you but I wonder if you could help us understand some of the notes written in this book?" Merker placed the notebook on the glass table.

"I hope you don't mind?" Jasper added.

"No bother at all, but I have to tell you, I don't know if I'll be able to remember." Helen smiled. Her white hair was shaped to outline her long face, and her green eyes sparkled, nicely contrasting with her green tank top. Merker thought she was still an attractive woman, and years ago she must have been a knockout.

They sat around the table drinking the lemonade, reviewing each page of the notebook, but focusing on the uncertain passages. Helen was able to explain what the initials, O, Y, R, and number 22 meant. The initials stood for Old York Road and the 22 referred to the date, March 22, the day Bartolli died. The road was the street where the fatal accident occurred.

One question was answered but the last page was still the real mystery. Helen had no more idea than they did what "A S E lwood R Loax" meant.

But when she saw the reference, "death to the gunfighter," her body stiffened and shuddered.

"Back when I hired Truax, he visited Mrs. Tatum the wife of Dr. Tatum." Helen was excited. "Anyway, Truax said he had a hunch that Rasta was working with somebody and he called him the gunfighter. Truax felt this gunfighter was the person behind everything."

"Behind everything. What do you mean by that? Merker looked at both Truelove and Jasper and shrugged his shoulders.

"I mean he was the one who had my husband killed, not Rasta. He also somehow got to Truax, who backed off the investigation abruptly after he told me about the gunfighter. I pressed him at the time, but he told me he had to resign from the case for personal reasons. That's when he gave me the notebook, and he returned the retainer check I'd given him."

"So he never took any money for his work?" Merker asked.

"Exactly. After that I personally visited Mrs. Tatum and we had a very long, cordial talk. We discussed our husbands, their careers, and the sacrifices we'd made to support those careers. If Mrs. Tatum is still alive, she might be able help you answer the remaining questions."

Merker had already planned a visit to Clearwater to visit the widow Tatum, this only further strengthened his previous decision. They said their good-byes to Helen and Jack and started to back out of the driveway when Merker noticed in his rearview mirror a van parked in the shadows of a large palm. This was the same minivan he had noticed when they were entering the complex. What bothered Merker was the lack of an escape route. There was only one way to exit the development. They were trapped.

Before Merker could formulate a plan, Jasper, who was

seated in the front passenger seat, tapped Merker on the shoulder. As Merker turned in his direction, he first noticed Jasper's face, it was pale and drained of all color with large beads of sweat emanating from his forehead. His eyes suggested sheer terror. Before he spoke, Jasper leaned forward and Merker could see the gun pointed at his head by a man with a shaved head and sunglasses. "We have company," was all Jasper could muster.

31

There were only about twenty people at Margaret's funeral. Mr. Kodack and Sally sat alone in the front row with no one else sitting closer than row three. Natalie was visibly upset, not only by the pathetic sight of little Sally sitting quietly, but for Mr. Kodack, who was torn by the paradox of not wanting to live for himself yet now having to survive for Sally.

The funeral was sad, the only redeeming factor being it was short. Following the funeral, Steven and Natalie had an argument. She was saddened by the funeral and used her sadness as an entree to discuss Steven's state. What Natalie could not understand was how Steven had become so dispassionate about not only matters of the heart but also matters of political concern.

The events of the past several weeks had caused Steven to reconsider his goals and priorities. Was this mid-life crisis or just some bad luck? He had hit a new level of low and needed some time to sort things out.

On their way home Callison noticed a white car following them. He had noticed the car at the funeral. What made the car somewhat unique was the sticker identifying the car as a rental. Callison wondered *why would someone rent a car to go to a funeral? An out-of-town relative, perhaps?* But why would this car be following him? The white car continued on the highway after Callison exited—so much for Merker and his concerns.

A message from Jourge was waiting for Callison when he returned home. The message had a sense of urgency, so Callison decided to immediately return the call.

The phone conversation with Jourge was relatively short but to the point. The White House was receiving increased pressure from the Senate Finance Committee to submit their plan for health-care reform. The White House had remained steadfast in their commitment to guarantee universal health care. What they had to show was how the medical profession could ensure adequate primary-care access to the over thirty million Americans who were now uninsured, while simultaneously maintaining adequate coverage for those currently on government-sponsored programs. Jourge had been told a group of lobbyists representing the nursing profession were challenging the premise that the medical profession could effectively render the primary-care needs for the nation.

The effect of this pressure had now filtered down to their committee, whose report had to be finalized in a week. The subcommittees had been working on a schedule to finalize their presentations in three weeks, thus the shortened timeline created a critical situation. Callison asked if they could ask for a delay, but the answer was an unqualified no.

When Jourge asked Callison if his committee was close to completion with their charge, he lied and told him they were. Callison was embarrassed to admit he had let the committee work slip because of the other issues he had been dealing with. His mind flashed images of Margaret and Sally, Rasta and Merker, Maxine and Natalie. Where had the time gone and to what end? Then other images entered his thoughts; the delayed hearing with the Texas Medical Foundation was still pending and carried with it a fair amount of anxiety, and then there was the issue of the profession, and the committee. He needed some space to clear his mind so he could focus.

Callison told Jourge he would have the committee report for the pre-committee meeting next week. Jourge said the formal meeting would follow the next day, when a panel representing the White House, the Department of Health, the surgeon general's office, and the Senate finance committee would all be in attendance.

When he got off the phone with Jourge, Callison could feel the rage building inside his body. Like a volcano about to erupt, he felt as if he could explode. He knew he had no choice but to call Maxine to help organize the meeting of his subcommittee.

Maxine was not home, so Callison left a message on her answering machine. As he finished the call the doorbell rang.

330

Opening the door, Callison noted the same white car parked in his driveway, while three men stood on his doorstep. The men were all dressed in suits and ties. They ranged in age from approximately thirty to sixty and were neatly groomed.

Before Callison could close the door, the oldest of the three spoke. "Dr. Callison, Dr. Steven Callison?" The man had gray hair and a small, closely trimmed gray beard. His skin was tanned and his blue eyes were riveting. It was still very warm outside in the Texas summer and beads of perspiration were apparent on his temples.

Before Callison could respond, the man continued.

"We apologize for disturbing you at home, but we were afraid to approach you at your office." His voice was gentle and soft, but Callison wasn't about to be lulled into a possible trap. He was about to slam the door in his face, when he was distracted by a man in the shadows to his left, who was smiling.

"Hello, Steven."

"John, is that you?" John McQueen was Steven's roommate his first year in medical school. John was several years older than Steven, but he still looked the same, except without hair.

So what is John McQueen doing on my doorstep? And who are these other men?

Callison opened the door so the three could enter, warmly greeting John with a handshake and embrace. It had been several years since they last saw each other, and seeing John reminded Callison how much he had missed him.

John made the introductions. The older gentleman was Foster Ehrlich, one of the past presidents of the AOA, and the younger man was James Williams, who was hired by the AOA to help them with difficult political situations.

Natalie joined her husband in welcoming their visitors and especially in greeting John. Natalie had always liked John—everybody did—and was thrilled to see him again. The five sat in the living room and talked for several minutes, small talk primarily, catching up on family and mutual friends. But both Foster and James were growing impatient as they had a different agenda to discuss.

All three removed their jackets and ties, exposing their

331

undergarments, which were soaked with perspiration. Natalie offered them towels and T-shirts. They accepted the towels but declined the shirts. When Natalie left the room for the towels Foster suggested they change the conversation to a subject they needed Callison's input on: the Hargrove Bill.

"What's the Hargrove Bill? I don't think I ever heard of it," Callison asked.

Foster was about to answer when Natalie returned with the towels. The three men dabbed their faces and their shirts. Foster looked at Callison and then at Natalie. John noticed this and intervened. "Foster, I don't think we have anything to say that Natalie can't hear."

Natalie immediately blushed, feeling out of place, and she excused herself.

When Natalie left the room, Foster said. "I hope we didn't run your wife out of here." Callison winced and shook his head as Foster continued. "The Hargrove Bill was a piece of legislation which died with its author, Senator Douglas Hargrove of Michigan. Senator Hargrove was a tremendous advocate for the osteopathic profession, and when he died, so did the bill."

Callison had never heard of Hargrove. "What was the bill about?"

"There was a rumor emanating from the AMA suggesting all physicians not trained with at least three post-graduate years would be used to meet the inner city and rural needs stemming from the new health-care initiatives."

Callison looked at John. Now he realized why they all were here. "So, what you're saying is, someone like John would have to sacrifice his practice, which he has spent his entire career creating, and he would be forced to practice in an area of need." The anger in Steven's voice was noticeable.

"Not exactly." John gave a half smile before he continued. "They're far too clever to force anyone to do this. They would have this as an option for any doctor who would like to pursue this career choice, realizing that if you had less than three years of post-graduate training and you declined the offer, you couldn't participate in any government-sponsored programs. The Hargrove Bill would have allowed those who are either board eligible or certified without three post-graduate years to maintain and preserve their practices and not be displaced to an area of need. In addition, the bill provided for an alternative incentive program to fill the void in areas where health-care was most needed."

Foster stood and walked over to John and placed his hand on John's shoulder. John looked up toward Foster. Foster then looked at Callison and resumed the conversation. "What had happened after the death of Hargrove was a total reversal of the select steering committee on health-care reform regarding the status of physicians who only had one or two years of postgraduate education."

"What changed?" Callison asked.

"They first sent up a test balloon. They included language in the Omnibus Budget Reconciliation Act which mandated that physicians who treat Medicaid beneficiaries under the age of twenty-one must meet certain requirements."

Callison interrupted Foster. "I'm aware of this act." He pondered whether he should tell them about what Timmons had said.

"So you're aware this act was passed by Congress without any resistance." Foster leaned on the table looking into Callison's eyes.

"Yes, but I was told this entire act was a mistake. Someone inadvertently overlooked the issue of DO training and certification." Callison decided not to discuss Timmons' proposal with them—at least not at this time.

"You don't really believe that, do you? That would be some mistake, don't you think? I contend it was their test case. If the passage of the Omnibus Act went without a hitch, it led the way for the Hayes Bill to be introduced and passed."

"The Hayes Bill?" Callison asked.

"When the committee changed their tune, they instead considered recommending the Hayes Bill. This bill was primarily authored by Senator Hayes of Georgia, who just happens to be in the pocket of the AMA lobbyists. His version of the bill recommends that the universal health-care initiative and all government-sponsored programs, such as Medicare, Medicaid,

Champus, et cetera, all follow the same managed care, capitation format which limits its providers . . ."

"To only those with a minimum of three years post graduate training," Callison interrupted.

"Exactly." Foster was still standing next to John. Natalie entered the room with a pitcher of iced tea and a bowl of pretzels.

"So where is this Hayes Bill now?" As Callison asked the question he could see Foster was uncomfortable with Natalie in the room.

Once Natalie left, Foster continued. "The Hayes Bill is being reviewed by the AMA, and also by one of the subcommittees of your group, the one headed by Victor Rasta."

Here we go again, thought Callison.

"What we're concerned about is this bill will not get the attention it deserves at the committee level and will get thrown in with everything else. The way this is written it will essentially single-handedly wipe out the practices of many of the family practitioners in our profession. As a friend I ask you to help us make sure this doesn't happen." Callison had never seen John as distraught as this evening.

"What exactly would you like me to do?" Callison said uncertainly.

"First, when Rasta gives his report, ask him specifically to discuss the Hayes Bill." Foster drank another glass of iced tea and grabbed a handful of pretzels.

"Also try to see if you could muster some support from the other DO's on the committee. We suspect some are already on the payroll of the AMA, but we're not sure who. Do you have any idea?" John peered into Steven's eyes.

"I really don't know, but I have my suspicions. If you don't mind, I'd rather not voice them without evidence." Callison was honest but calculating, not allowing his concerns to backfire on him.

"I mind." The silent man in the corner, James Williams, dark-haired, military cut, mid-thirties, athletic build, very intense, and no longer silent. "You asked if we minded—well, I do mind. You see, my job is to find the traitors in the ranks and expose them, so if you have suspicions let me know and I'll investigate. If they're on the AMA payroll I'll find out and you'll be doing the profession a service." His words were harsh and ardent.

Callison was taken aback by the man's tone. He was about to reply when John interrupted. "Listen James, if Steven has something to tell us, he will, when he's ready."

"I don't buy that for second." James' voice was still harsh. "If one of your own is selling out the rest of you, why would you protect him? Why would someone be unwilling to share the truth when the truth makes such a difference? It makes no sense to me, none at all."

"I don't think Steven's protecting anyone." John was about to continue when he noticed Callison raise his hand.

"John, please let me speak. I'm not sure who can or can't be trusted. When I am sure, I'll let you know. But I'll tell you I don't appreciate your threats." Callison looked hard at James.

"Fine, I'll be eagerly waiting to hear from you." James' tone was still caustic.

The hour was getting late. Natalie invited John to stay for the evening but he declined. After assuring they would be in touch, they all left.

Natalie mentioned Maxine had called and requested he call her back.

Before he could dial Maxine's number, the doorbell rang. It was James Williams.

"Did you forget something?" Callison said.

Looking into Williams' face, Callison could see he was fuming. "Listen, you little shit. I don't know if you're on the take, but if you are I'll nail your ass and all your friends too. My threats are not idle and you'd be wise to heed them. I want the names and I want them soon. I wrote my number on this piece of paper. I expect to hear from you within two days." Williams held out a piece of paper which Steven refused to take. Williams then shoved the paper into his shirt pocket and left.

"I'll contact you when and if I feel like it." Callison angrily shouted as James faded into the darkness. He removed the piece of paper from his pocket. He was unable to read because he was so furious.

Callison, still unnerved, decided not to call Maxine until the morning. Natalie asked what had upset him so, but he denied being upset. Natalie asked again, only this time she insisted.

Before he could answer, Natalie informed him Maxine was on the line.

Callison had to talk to Maxine, even though he was still distraught. "Hello, Maxine."

"What's wrong?" Maxine asked.

"Wrong, why do you think something is wrong?"

"Because you left a message for me saying something has come up that we need to address immediately. In my book, that suggests something's wrong."

Callison felt foolish. He was so upset from Williams' onslaught, he had forgotten why he called Maxine originally. "I'm sorry to upset you, but something has come up. Jourge has moved up the group meeting to next Thursday, and we have to have a subcommittee meeting before the big meeting. Do you think you can arrange that?"

"I can try but this is very short notice," she said slowly. "When would you like to meet?"

"Since the group is meeting Thursday and Friday, I guess we should meet on Tuesday, in case we need Wednesday to finish."

"Tuesday? I've got some work to do. I assume you want the entire subcommittee and their respective reports for review prior to the meeting." Her voice was less than enthusiastic.

"Yes, I'm sorry for the short notice but Jourge only informed me tonight." Callison's tone was apologetic.

"Is there anything else, Doctor?" Maxine said sarcastically.

"No. And again I'm sorry."

"I know it's not your fault, we'll get it all done. By the way, Margo said she was going back to Rasta's office and asked if we still wanted her to get the disk. Do we?"

Callison thought for a minute. If he had the disk and the names, then he might have something to tell Williams and John.

"If she thinks she can get the disk without being caught, ask her to take it." Callison couldn't believe his own words.

"Are you sure?" Maxine sounded surprised by Callison's answer.

"Yes, I'm sure." Callison said, tentatively.

"Okay, then." Maxine paused. "Are you sure you're all right?"

"I'm fine." His tone was upbeat. "I'll call you tomorrow." Callison hung up the phone.

Natalie walked into the room, her arms crossed in front of her chest, a worried look on her face. "What's going on?"

"How much of the conversation with John did you hear?" He asked but he already knew the answer.

"I heard most of it, but in bits and pieces. What are you going to do?"

"Well, it was a brilliant maneuver to recruit John, whom I trust implicitly. But this other guy, Williams, threatened me." Callison sneered as he said Williams' name.

Natalie's arms fell to her side. "He what?"

"He threatened me. He said if I didn't cooperate with him, he would . . ."

"He would, what? What would he do?"

Callison thought for second. What could he do? Nothing. "I don't know what he would or could do, but I definitely didn't like his manner."

"So are you going to help John or not?" Natalie's tone made it clear she needed him to commit to this.

"How could I not at least try to find out if this is true? And if this Hayes Bill is for real, I'll do what I can to find out what this is all about."

Natalie walked and hugged him tightly.

While she was hugging him, thoughts of the DO committee members raced through his mind. Who could he trust and who might know about the Hayes Bill? He decided he knew Harold Teitelman the best and never knew him to be anything but honest and forthright. He would start there.

32

Callison's conversation with Harold Teitelman was short and to the point. Harold had not heard of either the Hayes or the Hargrove Bill, which seemed strange to Callison, since Teitelman was the other member on the subcommittee Rasta chaired. According to Foster, this bill was to be reviewed by that subcommittee and then presented to the committee of the whole. Both Callison and Teitelman were perplexed. Harold said he would personally discuss this matter with Rasta. During the conversation Callison could detect a sense of uneasiness with Harold, but he decided not make any judgments until he heard back from him.

Since the other DO members of the committee were essentially strangers to Callison, he deferred contacting them until he talked again to Teitelman.

While at work, Callison's attention was shifted toward the problems of the day. The resident clinic had been overbooked and one of the residents called in sick with a stomach virus. The attending assigned to the clinic, Malcolm Petrie, had jury duty. The clinic was utter chaos with patients waiting and complaining. The three doctors in attendance, Callison and two first-year medical residents, did the best they could under the circumstances, but it left everybody on edge. Fortunately for Callison, none of the patients that morning were unstable.

During all this commotion, Helen Hunter interrupted Callison to tell him he had an urgent call from Maxine Wells.

Callison was midway through an evaluation of a patient who was having a proctoscopic examination when he was interrupted by Helen. There could hardly be a more inopportune time to interrupt. Callison was not pleased. After he completed the exam, he returned Maxine's call.

"Maxine, what's so important that you insist I call you back immediately?" Callison wanted to be angered by her interruption, but in actuality it was a welcome break to a hectic morning.

"I don't know how to say this, so I'll just tell you." Her voice quivered.

"Maxine, try to calm down and just tell me what's the matter." Callison spoke calmly and tranquilly.

"Margo took the disk." Maxine hesitated, and Callison knew she had been caught, implicating him. His career was about to explode in his face. Callison could feel his heart start to flutter.

Maxine continued, her voice unchanged. "We were able to pull up the main menu and access the file using the password Caldo." Maxine continued, her voice barely audible. "There's a list of 112 DO's, including almost everyone on your committee."

"My committee? You mean our committee?" Callison voice was no longer self-confident and serene.

"Yes, our committee. On the list are the names Susanna Michelson, Jacob Danzinger, Harold Teitelman, Chester Timmons, and you."

The word "you" reverberated in Callison's head as if a firecracker had gone off in his ear. His heart was pounding. He needed to brace himself with his hand supporting his head while he rested his head on the desk.

"Are you still there, Dr. Callison?" Maxine's voice had a staccato quality.

"Yeah, I'm still here." Callison was able to vocalize the words, but his head was still spinning. "Maxine, check the list for Jonas Cisko; see if his name is on the list?"

With no hesitation she answered, "Yes, he's there also."

Callison was now over the initial shock. His heart was still beating fast, but not pounding, and his head was clearing. "Are there any MD's on the list?"

"I don't know for sure. The list is just a list of names with no initials after them. However, every name I've pulled up was a DO, and none of the MD's on our committee are named." Maxine's voice was also more stable.

"What do you mean pull up?"

"We can access each name on the list. It gives some background historical information, telephone numbers, addresses, and other pertinent data."

"What pertinent data?" Callison said, feeling his privacy had been invaded.

"The reason why the name's on the list."

"What did my pertinent data say?"

Maxine read Callison a detailed summary of his collegiate activities involving the SDS and the sit-in, with the resultant assault of a professor. The information was accurate but incomplete. However, it did make a compelling argument.

Callison needed to review this list before he could make any rational decision about what he should or could do. He could not risk using FedEx or faxing or even e-mail because a security breach could be devastating. "Listen, Maxine, is there any way you could bring the disk down here?" Callison had no time to travel to Chicago. He was already behind schedule with patient care responsibilities, administrative responsibilities, the subcommittee work, his hearing being rescheduled for Monday, and the meeting scheduled in Chicago on Tuesday.

"You want me to come to Texas?" Maxine was taken off guard by Callison's request.

"I know it's a lot to ask, but I'd really appreciate it if you could bring the disk down here." Callison knew he was asking more than he should but he had to ask.

"Well, I have the meeting scheduled for Tuesday as you asked. Both Doctors Michelson and Percy will be there with their reports, so I guess I can come to Texas tomorrow and get back in time to finish things up here."

"Maxine, you're an angel. I don't know how to thank you for this."

"I'll see you tomorrow."

Callison sat silently in his chair, staring at the ceiling, wondering how things had gotten so out of control and what he could do about it.

Truelove and Jasper were pondering what had happened. After they were separated from Merker by their captors, they were released with the admonition to return to their respective homes and forget about Florida, Merker, and anything else related to the case. Prior to their release they were taken separately for interrogation where they were both told not to reveal anything to anyone, especially not to each other. When they were released, they were placed on a plane back to Phoenix. Neither had told the other what had transpired. Jasper had not flown coach in years, but didn't have the nerve to ask for an upgrade. The Boeing 727 was half full when they left Miami International, however they noticed they were being followed by two men in dark sunglasses.

The conversation on the plane was stilted because of their concern over the men in the sunglasses. Finally Truelove couldn't take it anymore and asked Jasper what he thought was going on. Jasper, unnerved by the question, cautiously looked at the two men in sunglasses. They appeared to be asleep, so he answered Truelove in a whisper. "I don't know what's going on but whatever it is has gotten a lot of people very excited."

Truelove's response was in his normal voice. "I've run and hid my entire life, but I'm not hiding any more. I don't know what they said to you, but they threatened me and my family, and I'm not going to take it."

Jasper's eyes dilated. "Shhhh." Jasper placed his index finger to his mouth. Then he peeked another look at the men in the sunglasses: they still appeared to be asleep.

Jasper whispered, "Listen, I'm upset too, but there's a time and place, this is neither. Let's wait until we get back to your place to discuss this, please."

Truelove knew Jasper was right, but he was infuriated. "Okay, I'll wait, but we will discuss this." His voice was softened, but was definitely not a whisper. They didn't speak the remainder of the flight.

Earl, Truelove's roommate, met them at the airport and drove them both back to the their Scottsdale home, followed by the men in the sunglasses. Once secure in his own home Truelove turned to Jasper.

"Ethan, can we talk now?" Truelove enunciated each word to emphasize their importance.

"Of course, but can I get something to drink first?"

341

"Earl!" Truelove's command needed no further explanation. Earl immediately went to the kitchen to prepare something for them to drink.

"So what did they tell you?" Truelove said.

"They took me to this room. No windows, only an iridescent light." Truelove nodded. He also had been taken to the same room. The room had a square wooden table, and four wooden chairs. Nothing on the walls except an obvious two-way mirror on the far wall.

"Don't you think that room was too perfect?" Truelove said. "I mean it looked like a interrogation room right out of a movie."

"Yeah, it did." Jasper was not as concerned with the room as Truelove. "Anyway, they asked me a lot of questions about Merker and you. Then they started in on why we were in Florida and what we were doing at the home of Helen Bartolli."

"What did you tell them?" As Truelove finished his question, Earl returned with a large pitcher of lemonade. They all took a break to drink a glass.

"Earl, this is excellent lemonade," Jasper said.

"Freshly squeezed with my own secret ingredient." Earl said proudly.

"Can we please continue?" Truelove intervened. "What did you tell them when they asked what we were doing?"

"I said we needed to ask Mrs. Bartolli some questions about her former husband." When Jasper finished his sentence he reached for the pitcher to pour himself another glass of lemonade.

"Did you elaborate much?" Truelove was curious. They asked him almost the identical questions.

"Some. I elaborated a bit, but they seemed to have most of the answers already." Jasper gulped down the remaining lemonade in his glass.

"They asked me the same questions and I feel as do you they already knew the answers. So what was this all about?" Truelove's anger had subsided. He was now more confused than angry.

"I think they want us out of the way. There's something bigger here than we're aware of."

"Let's assume you're right. What's the bigger picture?" Truelove poured himself another glass of lemonade, emptying the pitcher.

Earl, who was quietly listening to their conversation, retrieved the empty pitcher and returned to the kitchen to prepare another batch.

"I'm not sure, but they did say something that I thought to be quite peculiar." Jasper paused. "First, they warned me about Merker. They said he was way out of his league on this one and we should keep our distance from him. Then they threatened me with auditing my income taxes. I think they assumed I did something illegal with my taxes."

"You know, they said the same thing to me. They must think everybody cheats on their taxes."

"Or just doctors." They both chuckled.

Earl reappeared with another pitcher of the lemonade. They both immediately refilled their glasses.

Jasper set down his lemonade and asked, "Do you think they were really FBI?"

"I suppose. They acted like they were."

"Why would an FBI agent pull his gun? All he had to do is show his badge." Jasper inquired.

"You know there was something bothering me about this and I couldn't put my finger on it. But you're right. Then who are those guys?"

"These people seem to be very serious about all this, I'm not sure we should get involved any further." Jasper was concerned not only for his welfare, but for that of his family.

"I completely understand, but what I said on the plane still goes for me. I'm not going to hide any more, and I'm going to do whatever I can to help Merker solve this case."

"Well, I'm not as sure as you." Jasper said, his hands trembling. "Jonas Cisko was a good friend and a good person, and Merker believes his death may be tied up in this whole mess. But I don't know." Small beads of sweat appeared on his upper lip and forehead.

"Listen, Ethan. You don't have to do anything else. You've already done more than your share. Let me follow this through and if I need your help I'll call you." Truelove didn't want to force Jasper into anything he really didn't want to do.

It had been two days since they had last seen Merker in Florida. Truelove decided to start by calling the special number Merker had given him, to see if he could reach him and find out what he should do next. Truelove dialed Rudolph's number.

"Hello?"

"Rudolph, this is Dr. Truelove. Do you know if Mr. Merker is home?"

There was silence on the line. Truelove waited for about a minute before he broke the silence. "Rudolph, are you still there?"

Silence again, this time for fifteen to twenty seconds before Rudolph responded, "Dr. Truelove, Merker is dead."

Truelove's expressionless stare was a haunting sight for Jasper. He had seen this type of response in the past, usually associated with the news of a major trauma.

Truelove never noticed Jasper. He was so overwhelmed by Rudolph's statement. "What did you say?" Truelove hoped he had not heard Rudolph correctly.

Rudolph was also upset and needed a few seconds to control his emotions. "I said, . . . " Rudolph again faltered, sighing and then coughing. "Merker died in a car accident two days ago; that's all I know."

"Do you know where he was when he died?" Truelove composed himself to ask the question slowly and clearly.

Jasper, hearing Truelove's question, shook his head.

Rudolph answered the question as best he could. "He died somewhere in Florida, that's all I know. I got a phone call from a friend of Merker's, a Chicago policeman, who asked me if I had a key to his apartment."

"Do you remember this policeman's name?" Truelove was still upset, but now his mind began to clear.

"Let me think." Rudolph thought for a few seconds. "Oh yeah, Barnes. His name was Sergeant Barnes."

"Can you think of anything else?" Truelove asked.

"No, nothing, but if I do, can you leave me your number and I'll call?"

Truelove gave Rudolph the number and then hung up.

Jasper walked over to Truelove as he hung up the phone and patted him on his shoulder. "What are you going to do?"

Truelove thought for a moment, biting his lower lip. "I don't know. But I do know I'm going to do something."

"Before you get too carried away, let's go over some facts. First, we were accompanied here by some men in sunglasses who say they're with the FBI. We had our doubts, but now I'm sure they're associated with the people responsible for Merker's death."

"You think Merker was killed?" Jasper looked at Truelove with a wide eyes.

"Don't you?" Truelove was irritated at Jasper's question.

"It could've been an accident." Jasper didn't even believe his statement, but he couldn't deny the possibility.

"Yeah, right; you know as well as I do that Merker was an excellent driver and the possibility that he died in an accident is as remote as a snowball in hell."

Truelove started to pace.

"Okay, let's assume Merker was killed and the men outside and those who interrogated us are responsible. Do you think they'll leave us alone now?" Truelove was still determined to find out who was behind all this.

"Yes, I believe they'll leave us alone if we leave them alone. If we're killed, then the authorities will surely investigate and whoever's behind this would be in jeopardy of being caught. I think we're pretty safe if we do nothing from this point on." Jasper wanted to believe what he just said.

"I wouldn't be so sure, and I'm not going to sit around and wait to find out you're wrong." Truelove said. He stopped pacing and focused on Jasper. "I understand if you don't want to pursue this, but I feel I have to."

Jasper could feel the acid building in his stomach. His mind told him to stay out of this, but his heart knew he had to see this through with Tyler Truelove. "Okay—so what's your idea?"

They had to devise a plan. They reviewed the letter from Amos Wilcox, and Truelove explained to Jasper who Callison was. They decided he might be someone they would need to meet with later. They then took out their notes from their Florida trip and the notebook of Vigor Truax, which they both thought contained the secret to the Caldo list. They needed to decipher the meaning of who or what was Aselwood R Loax.

Their plan would start with a trip to Clearwater and a visit to Mrs. Tatum, who might be able to shed some light on the their dilemma. Then a side to trip to Texas might be in order depending on how things went in Florida. They now had a plan—granted it was a fairly weak plan—but nonetheless it was a plan. The question was, how were they going to get there without being followed? Earl had the answer: A *Phantom* party.

Ever since Earl and Tyler had seen the play *Phantom of the Opera* they would hold a masquerade party every month or so. Their friends would dress to the hilt, exhibiting a cavalcade of glorious costumes, adorned with exotic makeup, and a multitude of masks.

The men in sunglasses who had been monitoring the house were aghast when the partygoers started to arrive by the carloads. Men dressed in drag by the dozen (they stopped counting the Mae West impersonators at five), and there were similar numbers representing Marilyn Monroe or Madonna, they couldn't distinguish. A smattering of other high-profile women were also in attendance, such as Diana Ross, Bette Midler and Barbra Streisand, but the majority of the partygoers were dressed in elaborate costumes commemorating the masquerade scene from *Phantom of the Opera*. Everybody was in mask and costume. During the party Truelove and Jasper exchanged costumes with two of Earl's friends who were dressed as Beauty and the Beast. Earl had taken out three thousand dollars from the bank, so Truelove and Jasper wouldn't need to use their credit cards for their airline tickets, thus limiting the ability of their pursuers to locate them.

Truelove and Jasper left in a large crowd, about twenty revelers, and drove directly to Tucson International, just in case the pursuers were watching the Phoenix airport. Earl had his friends pack a suitcase of their clothes and deposit them in the trunk of their Lexus. Once they were out of the city they changed

346

into regular clothes, leaving Beauty and the Beast in the trunk, and continued their drive to Tucson where they left the car in a remote airport parking lot. There was no indication they were being followed. The parking lot where they left the car was practically abandoned, with no one in sight; it appeared their plan had worked.

While the men in the sunglasses were monitoring the gates in Phoenix, Truelove and Jasper were boarding a plane in Tucson destined for Tampa.

33

Maxine was looking forward to dinner with her current male companion, Spencer Dalrymple, a CPA, with whom she enjoyed an occasional evening.

Spencer was in his late fifties but had not one gray hair. He wore bifocals, otherwise there was nothing to suggest he was as old as he was. Maxine enjoyed his company and his sense of humor, but wasn't attracted to him physically. She did, however, think they looked good together. He was tall, about six foot three, so she could wear any type of heels she wanted, and he was trim and fit as was she. They had met at a party of a mutual friend and had been dating for the last month.

The small bistro, featuring a global, eclectic menu, was crowded and, although they had reservations, there would be a small delay. "I hate that! We have reservations and we still have to wait," Maxine complained.

"Maxine, what's wrong?" Spencer knew her well enough to know the delay was not the reason for her distress.

Maxine didn't feel comfortable confiding in Spencer, but knew she had to say something. "It's work. I have to go to Texas tomorrow and I don't want to go."

"Then don't go. You work too hard as it is. You don't have to do this if you don't want to." Spencer placed his arm around her shoulder.

"I know, but I feel I have to. I'll get over it." Maxine smiled at Spencer and rested her head on his chest.

The hostess indicated their table was ready. They made their way through the crowd, winding over to the table.

After they ordered, Maxine excused herself to go to the ladies room. Two men at the bar followed Maxine's every move, as she walked to and from the ladies lounge.

"Do you see those men at the bar?" Maxine queried. Spencer

didn't have to look. He already knew who she meant.

"You mean the two guys ogling you?" Spencer smiled.

"Are they still looking this way?"

Spencer had a more direct eyeline, but he had to shift slightly in his seat to see over Maxine's right shoulder. "No, they're talking to each other."

"Do they look familiar to you?" Maxine asked.

"No, never saw either of them before."

Maxine was sure they were following her, but had no explanation why. "I don't feel well, do you think we could leave now?"

The disappointment was evident on Spencer's face. "Sure. Let me get the check."

Spencer paid the bill and they left the restaurant. Maxine noticed the two men from the restaurant getting into a black sedan. Who were they and what did they want?

The morning was warm, warmer than usual, already mid-eighties and it was only nine o'clock. Callison had just returned from his morning jog and was seated outside cooling down, drinking a large glass of water, when Natalie told him he had a phone call. She handed him the portable phone.

"Hello, Steven, this is Harold Teitelman."

"Hi, Harold did you find anything out?"

"Before I tell you what I found out, could you tell me why were you were inquiring about the Hayes Bill in the first place?"

Callison was quiet for a minute, then said, "A friend of mine, who knows I'm on the committee, told me about the bill and asked me if I knew anything about it. Since I had never heard of either the Hayes or the Hargrove Bill, I thought I would check them out."

"Can you tell me who your friend was?" Harold's tone was friendly enough. If Callison hadn't known about the Caldo list and Harold's presence on that list, he would have thought nothing about telling him, but he did know Harold's name was on the list and therefore questioned whether he could be trusted.

"Before I tell you who told me about the bill, why don't you tell me what Rasta said." Callison said.

"Okay, but promise me you'll tell me later."

349

Callison promised.

Harold continued, "The official line from Rasta is, the bill's not an issue at this point. The unofficial word is, there is a Hayes Bill which is still in committee and deals with the medical services for areas of the country in which there are physician shortages."

"Is that it? I know there's more than that." Callison was agitated at the overt simplification.

"That's all you need to know. Believe me, the more you know, the more you don't want to know."

Callison was furious. "Don't patronize me, tell me the truth, damn it! I'm a big boy, I can handle it."

"Listen, control yourself." Harold's tone remained calm. "All I'm trying to do is to keep you out of something that could only cause you grief. Believe me."

Callison thought of dropping the Caldo information on him but decided against that. "I appreciate your concern for me, but if I'm to do my job on this committee, the information contained in the Hayes Bill could have a significant impact on my final decision." Callison regained his composure and talked in a slow, monotone voice.

"Believe me, what this bill's about will have no bearing on your subcommittee nor mine."

"Then why don't you tell me what you know?" Callison was not going to let this go.

Harold's tone increased several octaves. "What I know is you're dealing with powerful people who could destroy you with a single phone call and think nothing of it." As the words left his mouth, Harold realized he had said too much, but there was no turning back now. "What I'm about to tell you is in the strictest confidence. Do you understand?" His voice lowered with the last three words.

"Yes, I understand." Callison said, somewhat ponderously. "Please go on."

As Harold collected his thoughts, there was a moment of silence. "There's a group of men, some physicians, some not, who are shaping health-care reform independent of what we do or say. I don't know who they are, or for that matter I don't even want to know. But I can tell you, if you get in their way or cause a problem, they'll squash you."

"How do you know this?" Nothing Harold had said was surprising, but he now indicated he was afraid for his life.

"I won't tell you who threatened me; that isn't important. What is important is the fact that I was threatened. It happened shortly after the death of Jonas Cisko. I started to ask some questions and was told to stop. I thought they were kidding, so I continued. I received a letter, outlining a plan to systematically wipe out my professional career using information that I thought was long ago buried."

The information from the Caldo list, thought Callison.

"Anyway, I backed off. It was shortly after that I was asked to become dean. I think I mentioned this to you." Harold didn't wait for a response from Callison, but proceeded on. "I then received another letter, detailing an organized plan for my career to reach levels I never imagined. The second letter had a message attached: 'the choice is yours.' So I chose." Harold's voice tailed off.

"So you won't tell me about the Hayes Bill?" Callison knew this would get a reaction from Harold.

Callison was right, Harold was furious. "Haven't you heard a word I said?" He was screaming. "If you fuck with them, they'll ruin your life, and if you don't concede they'll kill you, like they did . . ."

"Cisko?" Callison answered for Harold. There was a prolonged pause. "Do you know for a fact Cisko was murdered?"

"I told you earlier, I don't know and I don't want to know. But I can tell you, Cisko was causing trouble on the committee and wound up dead. It was all the wake-up call I needed. It isn't worth it."

"What isn't worth it?"

"The profession. If they want to speed up a process that's inevitable, then so be it. You know as well as I do that we're just marking time. We already have more DO's in MD residencies than in DO residencies. Once they start asking for dual degrees, the game's over. The way I look at it, if we can help our own careers, then at least something positive can come out of all this."

351

Callison couldn't believe his ears. "What about the careers of the thousands of DO's who will have their practices destroyed. Doesn't that bother you?"

"So you do know about the Hayes Bill. Who told you?"

Callison knew he was going to lie, but he had to pick a person who Harold would believe and more importantly, who would convince the person or persons whom Harold would call after their discussion. "His name is Marcus Merker, he's a private detective, investigating the death of Jonas Cisko."

"How did he find out about the bill?"

"You know, I really don't know. I guess you'll have to ask him yourself."

"Steven, as a friend and colleague—"

Callison was about to vomit when he heard those words out of Harold. "Don't be stupid, this is so big nothing can stop it, just go along for the ride and end up on top."

"I'll do that." Callison hung up the phone.

Callison remembered he had to pick Maxine up at the airport and he was already late. After assuring Natalie he was fine, he convinced her he didn't need her company for the drive. Callison needed some time alone to sort his thoughts and decide what he should do.

While driving to the airport, Callison's mind was abuzz with issues and images. The issues meshed one into another: the committee, the Caldo list, the Hayes Bill, the medical profession, health-care reform. And then there were the images, Harold Teitelman, Victor Rasta, Marcus Merker, Natalie, and of course Maxine. What was he going to say to Maxine? Should he kiss her hello, or shake her hand? By the time he reached the airport and parked at the gate, Callison had little time to think about anything. He was late.

After first missing Maxine at the gate, Callison finally caught up with her at the baggage claim area. Maxine offered her hand, which was a great relief to Callison. Since she only had a carry-on, they went directly to Callison's car, where he had activated the Merker alarm. The little light on his key ring indicated the car was safe, so they started their drive to Fort Worth.

352

Maxine had never visited Texas before and like many, had preconceived notions about the state and its residents. The DFW airport appeared as most of the other modern airports she had visited—the only indication she was in Texas, were the local Texas retail stores scattered throughout the airport. The roads looked much like Chicago, except they were in better condition and less crowded. The first difference that distinguished Texas from Chicago was the heat. The sky was a vivid blue, sans clouds and it was hot, but the humidity was perceptively less than Chicago.

Callison functioned as a tour guide for most of their ride into Fort Worth. He turned into the downtown area. Maxine's preconceived notions were not even close. There were no horses or cactus or cowboys or dirt roads. Instead, there were modern office buildings and banks. The area her hotel was situated in was called Sundance Square. The red bricked streets accented the restored buildings, new restaurants, a state-of-the-art movie complex, a world class jazz club and symphony hall all within walking distance of her hotel.

Once Maxine checked into her room and freshened up, they were off to Callison's office to review the disk. The ride to the office again didn't fulfill Maxine's expectations of Fort Worth, Texas. "I thought this city was nicknamed Cowtown. I don't see any cows or cowboys."

Callison laughed. "There's a section of the city that has retained the western flavor, it's called the Stockyard area. They have a rodeo there and down the street is a place called Billy Bob's Texas, the world's largest honkytonk. Maybe if we have some time later I'll show you."

"I think I'd like that." Maxine smiled back. This trip might work out better than she had expected. When Callison pointed to the large white buildings of the medical center, her mind shifted to other issues—why she was there and who those men were who followed her yesterday.

The clinical office building of the medical school was essentially empty on Saturdays, and this Saturday was no exception. Aside from the usual security personnel, there were only a few people on the floor of Callison's academic office. They noticed

Mitchell Abbott, who was hurriedly working on a research grant which had to be submitted on Monday. Another colleague was meeting with a resident in his office. Otherwise, the floor was empty. Callison's office was situated at the end of a long corridor and could only be entered through an ante office, which was Helen's domain.

Callison nervously fumbled with the switch to turn on his computer. He knew the information on the disk could probably ruin his professional career. He placed the disk in his PC.

The names on the list were not in alphabetical order, but appeared to be listed in a random fashion. Callison found his name about a third down the list. He reviewed the information pertaining to his past and found it was just as Maxine had indicated. There was enough information in his file to make it extremely difficult, if not impossible, to maintain his current academic status, let alone have any chance for career advancement.

While Callison reviewed his file, Maxine wandered around his office. She studied his diplomas and awards displayed on the wall. The office, for the most part, was neat, with most things in their place, save a couple of medical journals and papers stacked on his desk.

Callison grunted as he reread his file. Maxine leaned over his shoulder to see what he was grunting about. Callison could feel her gently pressing against his left shoulder; the smell of her perfume titillated his senses. Her touch and smell reminded Callison of their night at Rasta's party, a night he would never forget. It took all of Callison's concentration to stay focused on the computer screen.

"Pretty interesting stuff," Maxine said, still leaning over his shoulder.

Callison, never taking his eyes off the screen, commented, "I guess you could say that." He studied the file of Harold Teitelman. Just as in his case, there was enough in Harold's file to alter his career permanently, and not in a positive way.

After reviewing the files of all the committee members, Callison scanned the list for other people he knew or heard of, there were several. All the list could do was to place Callison in an untenable position. If he exposed the list, he was only compromising his osteopathic colleagues, placing them as well as himself in jeopardy. Callison asked Maxine, "Do you know of any files or original documents that could verify the data on this disk?"

"No, I have no idea if Rasta has any other files."

"Without some hard data, the information on this disk is useless. Anyone could say anything. What we need is the original information on which the data on the disk was based."

Callison realized the only way he could use this information was if he had some additional information to substantiate the validity of what was on the disk, because from his review of his own file, he presumed the data on the disk was probably accurate.

Callison compiled a list, noting pertinent facts about members on the committee, as well as other colleagues. After an hour, Maxine was growing impatient. "So what do we do now?"

Callison looked up from the screen and could see in Maxine's face how bored she was. "I'm sorry, Maxine, I just got caught up in all this."

"I understand." Maxine was polite as usual.

While driving to the airport to pick Maxine up, Callison had thought of a question. "Do you know how the committee was put together?"

Maxine was a step ahead of him. "You know, I thought about that myself. It seemed too great a coincidence that most of your committee was also on this list. So I asked around. You know, very casual-like. The original group was picked from a larger list of names submitted from both the AMA and the AOA."

"Who did the picking?" Callison asked.

"From what I can surmise, the names were picked by Nathan Slinger."

"*The* Nathan Slinger?" Callison was impressed.

"Yes, the head man for the Health Care Reform Initiative straight from the White House."

"Shit, you know what this means?" Callison furrowed his brow.

"You mean he might be in on this?" Maxine realized the mag-

355

nitude of such a statement. It had the potential to undermine the entire Health Care Initiative.

"How can we prove this?" Callison's mind was racing. If this went this deep, he really needed to be one hundred percent sure.

"I have a copy of a letter to Dr. Jourge asking him to chair the committee. The letter's signed by Nathan Slinger," Maxine proudly stated.

"But does the letter say he selected the committee members himself? I doubt that."

"Here's the letter, read it yourself." Maxine handed Callison her copy of the letter.

"How did you get this?"

"I have my ways." She coyly smiled back.

Callison began to carefully read the letter. It appeared to be on the White House stationery and was dated November 10.

Dear Dr. Jourge,

You have been nominated by your colleagues to sit on a committee that will be instrumental in deciding official policy relative to the President's Health Care Reform Initiative. I have recommended your name to the President to head this critical committee. I am fully aware of your very busy schedule, but I would appreciate if you could consider this most important task. I will be contacting you in several days with the details. Please keep this letter confidential until all the committee appointments are finalized.

Sincerely,
Nathan Slinger
Head, the Presidential
Task Force on
Health Care Reform

Callison looked up at Maxine, who had been intently watching him read the letter. "This doesn't definitively implicate Slinger but I have to admit it doesn't look good."

"Told you so." Maxine shrugged her shoulders.

"So, if we assume Slinger formed the committee, he must know about the list. How can we prove any of this?"

Maxine again shrugged her shoulders.

"Maxine, do you know how I was chosen?"

"Yes, and I'm certain of this. When Dr. Cisko died, Dr. Jourge was told to find a replacement out of the remaining names from the original list. I know this because I had to make the packets for the meeting. Jourge met with Rasta and Timmons and they decided on you. Do you know who pushed your selection?"

"Don't tell me Rasta?" Callison winced.

"Bingo!"

Callison thought every time something suspicious occurred in this mess, Rasta's name was involved. He also thought of Harold Teitelman's comments, "Don't ask, because you really don't want to know." Harold was right.

"So—anything else in your little black bag, Ms. Wells?" Callison flippantly asked.

"That's all I have. I hope it was sufficient." Maxine gave Callison a smile.

Callison thought for a second. He hated to ask more from Maxine, but she was his best inside source. "Maxine, do think there might be *another* disk? A disk that would list the MD's involved in all this. It could be named Gance or Tatum. Maybe Rasta has access to that disk also."

"Margo didn't say she saw another disk, but she really was just looking for Caldo. If he has it, we can find it. Assuming he hasn't discovered the other disk is gone."

Callison noticed the time. It was already late in the afternoon and he was hungry. "Listen, I have an idea. Why don't I call Natalie and the three of us go out for dinner?"

"Great idea."

"Before we leave, were you able to copy the disk?"

Maxine shook her head. "The disk is protected and I haven't figured out a way to copy it."

Callison anticipated her response. He was already dialing the number of Herman Wingfield, the best computer hacker in the institution. Herman loved a challenge, and Callison had hinted to Herman he had a disk he knew Herman wouldn't be able to copy. Herman's response to Callison's challenge was, "Any time, any place."

Callison reached Herman at his home and told him, "The time is now, and the place is my office." Herman was on his way.

Callison then called Natalie and told her to meet them at his office.

While they waited for Herman to show, Callison inquired how Maxine was doing. Maxine told him about the two men who followed her. Callison tried to reassure her she had nothing to be overly concerned about, but he was less than convincing. Before they could discuss this any further, Herman had arrived.

Maxine had envisioned Herman to look like a typical nerd, but to her surprise Herman was just the opposite. He was about six-three, two hundred pounds of well-sculpted muscle, blond hair, blue eyes, bronze tan, and tank top.

"So what's the deal, Doc?" Herman asked as he sat at Callison's desk, not even acknowledging either Callison or Maxine.

Maxine answered, "The disk is protected."

"Piece of cake. Time me," Herman said with such self-assured arrogance he was almost charming.

Maxine watched Herman's fingers masterfully play the computer keyboard. He looked so young and athletic, like a California surfer from the sixties, not a computer hacker from the nineties.

"Time," Herman said.

"Excuse me." Callison wasn't sure what he had said.

"Time, time," Herman shouted.

Callison looked at his watch. "Twenty after five."

"No, no. The time it took me to break the write protect," Herman said with even more arrogance than before.

"Three-and-a-half minutes," Callison answered, while he looked at Maxine in utter disbelief.

"Damn." Herman's response was no longer as arrogant.

"What's the matter?"

"Got a disk?" Herman looked up from the screen for the first time since he sat down.

Callison handed him a blank disk. Herman inserted it and within minutes Callison had several copies of the disk.

"Why did you act so discouraged when I told you the time?" Callison asked.

"Because my record was two minutes forty. I thought I might have broken my record. Oh well. Got anything else, Doc?" A large smile appeared on Herman's face.

Callison looked at Maxine. "No, Herman, I think that's adequate. Very impressive, I must say."

"I know. You owe me a dinner." Herman winked at Maxine, who smiled. "Got to go. Got a hot date tonight. Catch you later." On his way out the door, Herman popped his head back through the doorway. "Nice to meet you." Then he was gone.

Maxine looked at Callison and they both broke into laughter. "Interesting guy," was all Maxine could muster. Callison could only nod in concurrence.

Minutes later Natalie arrived, both Callison and Maxine were giggling.

"Did I miss something?" Natalie said, as if she was on the wrong side of a private joke.

When Natalie asked Maxine what type of food she was in the mood for, Maxine indicated she wanted something unique to the area. Natalie suggested Mexican, and Maxine thought that was a great suggestion.

Callison recommended they kill two birds with one stone. Maxine wanted to see the Stockyard area of the city, they could go to Joe T Garcia's Restaurant and then tour the more rustic section of the city. The dinner was just what Maxine wanted, Mexican food with an authentic flair. She particularly enjoyed the refried beans and guacamole, and was grateful the Stockyard area was close so she had an opportunity to walk off part of her meal. Since Maxine had an early flight back in the morning they decided to call it an evening by nine o'clock. Callison drove them back to his office, where Natalie picked up her car, while Callison drove Maxine back to the hotel.

Maxine told Callison how nice his wife was and never mentioned anything of their brief encounter in Chicago. Callison reviewed Maxine's assignments as they were driving back to the hotel. Maxine would contact Margo to see if she could find another disk. Also Maxine and Margo would both explore the possibility of another set of files, the original documents from which the computer files were based. Lastly she would see if she could find some further documentation implicating Nathan Slinger.

Callison let Maxine off in front of the hotel his mind still abuzz with issues and images.

Natalie was waiting for Steven at the door, a look of concern on her face.

"What's the matter?" Callison had only left her minutes ago. What could have gone wrong in such a short period of time?

"You've had three calls from the same man left on the answering machine," Natalie said.

Natalie's words so surprised Steven he was dumbfounded.

"Steven, did you hear me? A man, a Sergeant Marvin Powell of the Chicago Police Department, called three times. He said it was important and left his home number."

"What? Who? Who is this person?" He was still in a fog.

"I don't know. Why don't you listen to the message yourself?" Natalie wanted to be annoyed, but was actually more concerned.

Callison took her advice and listened to all three messages. He had no idea who this person was, but it was unmistakable he wanted to speak with Callison that evening.

Callison called the number Sergeant Powell had left.

"Hello, the Powell residence." A deep masculine voice answered the phone.

"Sergeant Powell, please." Callison asked.

"May I ask who's calling?"

"Dr. Steven Callison, I'm returning the sergeant's call."

"Dr. Callison, thank you for returning my call, I'm Marvin Powell."

"So, Sergeant, why did you call?"

"I'm sorry. I have some bad news to tell you. You see, I'm a friend of Marcus Merker and he gave me your name and number to call if anything should happen to him." Powell paused. "Merker's dead. He died in a car accident a couple of days ago."

Callison was standing when Powell told him about Merker and with the news his knees weakened and he fell to the floor. "He died in a car accident?" Callison's words were barely audible.

"Yeah, his car ran out of control and hit a bridge. It happened

360

somewhere in Florida." Callison could feel the emotion in Powell's voice.

"But he was such a good driver," Callison mumbled.

"Yeah, right."

"Do you know why he asked you to call me?"

"No, he just gave me instructions about what to do if anything happened to him. Calling you was one of his instructions. But I have to say this. I don't know what you and Marcus were up to, but I can tell you, be careful. Marcus was a good cop and good man, but whatever he was into was major. My advice to you is, if you can, get out now while you can. If you can't, then I guess I can help you. I owe that much to Marcus." Powell gave Callison his phone number and address. Callison already had Powell's phone number on his answering machine, but he wrote it down anyway.

Natalie found her husband seated on the floor, a blank look on his face, staring at the wall. He told her about Merker's death. Although neither knew Merker well, somehow he had made an impact that far exceeded the scope of their relationship.

Natalie joined Steven on the floor and they hugged together, silently sitting, remembering Marcus Merker. A thought struck Callison as powerful as a lightning bolt. If Merker was killed, then it was possible he, Steven was in danger. That was okay, but what if Natalie was also in danger? That was *not* okay. Callison decided not to say anything at this time, but he seriously considered sending Natalie to her sister's home while he traveled to Chicago.

34

Truelove and Jasper felt fairly secure they weren't followed to Tampa. Since they both were novices in the surveillance game, they decided to not attempt any deceptive moves, because they had no way of measuring their effectiveness.

The drive to Clearwater from Tampa was picturesque: sailboats in the bay, the blue of the ocean sparkling under the bright sunlight, and the palms gently bending in the summer breeze. They had called ahead and Mrs. Tatum had given them directions to her home. Shorewood Estates was a moderate community by Clearwater standards for the well-to-do. As with Palm Meadow Estates where Helen Bartolli-Sanford resided, there was a security gate but it differed because here there were two gates, one at each end of the complex. The flora was even more lavish than the Palm Meadows, and the entry drive was lined by large palms forming an arch over the entrance. Inside the complex all the residences had an impressive water view, and most had their own private docks. Mrs. Tatum's home was a pale yellow, single dwelling with a terra-cotta roof.

As they pulled into the driveway, Jasper noticed a woman peeking through the drapes in the house. An elderly woman shuffled out of the door supported by a walking stick. She exhibited a marked gait disturbance, as she dragged her left leg.

"Hello! My name's Ethel Tatum; you must be Ethan Jasper and Tyler Truelove." Mrs. Tatum met them halfway down the walkway as her Siamese cat darted into the bushes.

Both Truelove and Jasper looked at each other. Neither understood what she had said.

Mrs. Tatum, noticing their confused expressions, repeated her remarks very slowly. She had been left with a severe speech impediment, a dysarthria and a weakened left side as a result of a stroke four years ago.

After a few minutes her speech, although still distorted, was understandable. Both Doctors Truelove and Jasper had patients with similar difficulties in articulation and they were accustomed to a slow, garbled speech pattern.

They introduced themselves to Mrs. Tatum and then accompanied her into her home. There was a lavender fragrance that emanated throughout the home. As opposed to Helen Bartolli-Sanford's home, Ethel Tatum's decor was not modern, it was antique. The antiques included four bergeres, which Ethel explained differed from the usual French armchair in that the area between the armrest and the lower seat rail was closed with upholstery. They all sat in bergeres which surrounded a small Chippendale table, forming a cozy sitting area.

Ethel Tatum looked the way a grandmother was supposed to look: kind, gentle, and caring. "So why have you gentlemen come all this way?" Her voice was high pitched and cracked at the end of each sentence, but was understandable.

"We've come to see if you could help us solve a puzzle." Truelove looked at Jasper as he answered.

"I love puzzles." Ethel said as she positioned herself on the edge of her bergere, precariously close to falling off.

"The first part has to do with your husband." Truelove moved to the edge of his seat, just in case Ethel fell from her chair.

"Wayne? What do you want to know about Wayne?" A somber, reflective aura came over Ethel as she slipped back in her bergere.

"What do you remember of the Gance list, which your husband created many years ago?" Truelove could see Ethel still missed her late husband very much, even after all these years.

"The list was started for a man, Miles Gance, who saved my husband's life during the war. The list and the organization from which the list came, meant a great deal to the both of us. When my husband became ill, he still wanted to maintain the list and its purpose as a testament to Miles Gance. After his death I wanted to maintain the list and its purpose, as a testament to my husband." A tear welled in Ethel's right eye, which she brushed away with her hand.

"And what purpose was that?" Jasper asked.

"Actually I felt there were several. The main purpose was to help those who really wanted a career in medicine to achieve that dream. Of course, the people who we helped were somewhat unconventional, but very special." Ethel gave them both a half smile. "I believe another purpose was one of continued hope and perseverance. Many of our alumni had tried to pursue their dreams but were thwarted by circumstances, some by their own doing, while with others it was out of their control. But the purpose I feel the most deeply about is, the list of our alumni is a living testament to the memory of my husband, manifested by the lives saved by the hundreds of doctors who were given their opportunity because of this organization." Ethel sat upright, her head regally poised, as she completed her statement.

"Do you know what became of the list after your husband's death?" Truelove asked Ethel, who still beamed with pride.

"When my husband became ill, it became impossible for him to administrate the Gance Society, as he called it. Wayne had entrusted a physician named George Alexander who was a young, very bright, energetic type. In many ways, George actually became the son Wayne never had, *we* never had." Ethel looked away for moment.

Jasper noticed a frown on Ethel's face as she turned. "Mrs. Tatum, how did you feel about George?"

Ethel's expression changed. She closed her eyes and began to speak. "After Wayne's death, George was given the responsibility of carrying on Wayne's legacy." She stopped and started to look for something, a tissue, a towel, anything she could use to blow her nose, which had become congested. Ethel had a mild tremor, which caused her hands to shake slightly. This shaking increased when she was under stress, and she was shaking noticeably now, and her words were becoming progressively more difficult to understand. Her nose started to freely run as her eyes started to tear.

Jasper handed her a handkerchief, so she could blow her nose and dab her eyes. Ethel thanked Jasper and then excused herself and shuffled off to the bathroom.

"What do you think?" Truelove asked Jasper.

"I don't know. She seems as if she's with it, but I'm not sure.

What upset her so much, anyway?"

"I don't know. Do you think we should leave?" Truelove was starting to feel guilty that they had traumatized this little old lady.

"No way, we literally snuck out of your house to come here. We have to follow this through, if at all possible."

Ethel returned to her bergere. "If you would like, I could continue now." They both nodded. "This is painful for me, but you both have been so nice and patient, I hope you'll understand. This list, as you refer to it, was truly my husband's pride and joy. So when I saw what George was doing with the list, well I had to confront him."

"What was he doing?" Jasper asked as he moved to the edge of his seat.

"At first it appeared it was business as usual. Then I was told by a friend that George was using members of the group for political purposes. I confronted George with this accusation but he denied everything and I believed him. I lost touch with George after that. He moved to New York and I lost touch with the organization. I was always invited to the board of directors' annual retreat, but I even stopped attending those after a while." Ethel had to stop as she was again becoming congested with emotions, her words once again garbled. After clearing her nasal passages, she was able to continue. "I had no idea what George had done to my husband's dream. It was only when a doctor contacted me about the organization, his name was . . . "

"Dr. Bartolli?" Truelove said.

"Yes, how did you know?" Ethel stopped and studied the faces of both Truelove and Jasper. "Please tell me how you knew about Dr. Bartolli?"

Truelove decided to give the abridged version. "We met with Dr. Bartolli's widow several days ago and she referred us to you."

"Why were you visiting with Mrs. Bartolli?"

Truelove looked at Jasper, who looked back and said, "You or me?"

Truelove decided he would continue and tell Ethel the whole story. The story about Caldo and Amos Wilcox, the story about Jonas Cisko and Marcus Merker, the story about Dr. Bartolli and

Helen Bartolli-Sanford. He stopped before he reached the note-book of Truax, the detective.

Ethel sat for moment as if she was compiling the data in her head. Without saying a word she got up and walked over to a restored ice chest, the kind of ice box that had used large ice blocks at their base to keep the food cold. Ethel opened the brass latch to the cabinet that housed the ice a century before and pulled out a bottle of apricot brandy. "Would you boys like a drink?" Ethel smiled and they responded in kind.

As they sipped the brandy, Ethel again took her seat. "I have suspected such a story for years. I believe you're telling me the truth, at least as you know it. Now I'm going to tell you some truths, as I know them." Ethel finished her glass and poured another. Her speech impediment seemed to improve after she completed her drink.

Truelove smiled at Jasper, who returned the smile.

Ethel took another sip of brandy and continued. "Years after I lost contact with the organization, a man visited me, Dr. Bar-tolli. Dr. Bartolli told me a story about how George Alexander, the same George who said his role model was my husband, used the organization for monetary profit and political power. He asked me if I still had any of Wayne's files on the organization. The two of us spent hours rummaging through file cabinets and boxes from Wayne's practice. Although we never found the exact information he needed, we did find some information about the early days of the Gance society. These files were apparently destroyed with Dr. Bartolli when he died in the car accident."

"Did you have any copies?" Truelove inquired.

"No, no copies. I never thought Dr. Bartolli's death was any-thing but an accident, until I was visited by a private detective."

"Truax," Jasper said.

"You boys have done your homework. I would have never remembered that name on my own, but now that you mention it, I do recall his name was Truax." Ethel hadn't thought about Truax, or about much of what she was discussing, for over twenty-five years. "Anyway, Truax asked many questions, simi-lar to yours. He also mentioned he was hired by the widow of Dr. Bartolli who was convinced her husband was killed."

"Do the names Smithee and Rasta mean anything to you?" Jasper asked.

"Victor Rasta was a member of the Gance society, I remember him well. He was always polite and respectful, two qualities I admire. The other name I do not recall."

"Was Dr. Rasta involved in the administration of the Gance society?"

"Not that I recall, but remember I was only peripherally involved. My husband was the one who did the administration." Ethel finished her second glass of brandy and poured a third, only halfway filling the glass.

"You mentioned you were going to tell us some truths." Truelove said, not sure if these were the truths or there was more.

Ethel smiled a knowing smile at Truelove. "Several days ago I had a visit from the FBI." Truelove and Jasper looked at each other. "You know, sometime people can be very stupid." Ethel paused.

Truelove looked down at the floor, he thought she was talking about him. "I'm sorry if I offended you."

Ethel laughed, "No, I wasn't referring to you. I was talking about the FBI agents. They think that because you are old, you are senile and feeble-minded. A lot of people treat age as a disease, but I can assure you my mind is as sharp as ever." Mrs. Tatum sipped her brandy, the spark of youthful exuberance was still illuminated in her eyes.

"I never doubted that for a minute." Truelove smiled back at Ethel.

"Me neither," Jasper added.

"So when these FBI agents asked for information, I played the part they wanted. I played dumb. But for some reason I like you, both of you, so I'll tell you what I didn't tell them." Ethel grinned and sipped her brandy.

Truelove and Jasper clicked their glasses together. They had no idea what they were about to hear, but whatever it was, they knew the FBI didn't know it.

"After Mrs. Bartolli visited me those many years ago, I decided to do a little investigating on my own. I knew why my husband started the Gance society and I wanted to make sure its

367

essence still existed. After the death of Dr. Bartolli, I asked several close friends of Wayne's to help me investigate the organization. What we were able to piece together greatly disturbed me. Dr. George Alexander had ruined the organization. It had no resemblance to the society my husband had worked so hard to create. I wanted to lash out at someone, but George was gone and it was now being run by Victor Rasta. He had been recruited by George to take over the organization. I had known Victor in the old days, and he assured me he would attempt to bring the organization back to its previous status. Victor organized a steering committee of qualified, dedicated physicians and reestablished the mission of the organization, recreating the Gance society."

Truelove and Jasper were surprised at her commendation for Rasta. "So you were pleased with what Victor Rasta did."

"Very much so. Some people told me he was only telling me what I wanted to hear, but he opened up the books to my accountant and everything seemed in order. Young students who were unable to get into school were again recruited and assisted by the society. I was satisfied the organization was once again headed in the right direction."

"You said you never heard the name Smithee before, but we were told it was Smithee, along with Rasta, who took over the organization." Truelove then handed the Amos Wilcox letter to Ethel. "Maybe you need to read this first."

Ethel asked Jasper to get her reading glasses, which were on the bed stand, adjacent to her bed. Her bedroom had a large antique brass bed flanked on either side by an English side table. On both tables were pairs of glasses and a book. The glasses looked the same, but the books were different, one fiction, the other nonfiction. Jasper grabbed the nearest pair and returned to the sitting area. Ethel explained she was an avid reader, and always read two books simultaneously, one usually fiction, the other non-fiction. Her mood would dictate which book she would read at any given time.

Ethel put on her glasses. She bit her lip in an attempt to refrain from crying when she read the part pertaining to Douglas Kern. Ethel looked up her eyes reddened and watery. "Douglas Kern was a good and gentle man, I had no idea." Ethel returned to the letter. Ethel's mood changed as she finished the letter. She was angry, the spunk in her body was awakened.

"People told me Rasta was fronting for another organization with a totally different agenda, which used the good name of Gance for their cover. I never believed that, probably because I never wanted to believe it. So I take it you think this Caldo list is a spinoff of the Gance Society?" Ethel was hurt as much as she was angered.

"Yes, that's exactly what we think." Truelove stood as he answered.

"If this is true, then I was very wrong about Victor Rasta—and I feel very stupid and used." There was a fire in Ethel's eyes. Her body might have been old, but her spirit was still young.

"We're fairly confident Rasta has something to do with this and we need your help." Jasper stood next to Truelove as he spoke.

Ethel remained seated in her chair while the two men stood, all three energized by the heat of the moment.

"What type of help can I be?" Ethel said deliberately.

"We have a riddle for you. It's from Truax's notebook, the private detective hired by Mrs. Bartolli."

Truelove showed Ethel the copy of the last page of the notebook. "Does any of this make any sense to you?"

Ethel concentrated intently. After several minutes of studying the sheet of paper she just shook her head. "I'm sorry, I have no idea what this might mean."

Both Truelove and Jasper sat back, as they could not hide their disappointment.

Ethel seemed to sense their frustration. "Remember, I was talking about my visit with the FBI." They both nodded. "Well, there is something I do have; it's my files of the early members of the society."

Truelove pushed himself forward, knocking over his glass in the process. A small amount of brandy fell onto her oriental rug, staining the carpet. Embarrassed, Truelove used the tail of his shirt to attempt to mop up the brandy.

Ethel laughed and assured him she had to deal with worse stains almost on a daily basis, a result of her pets: her Bichon

Frise, Pebbles, and two Siamese cats, Hank and Norm. Truelove felt better, and Jasper went to the kitchen to get a wet towel to clean the stain.

Jasper returned with a damp towel and rubbed the carpet in an attempt to remove the brandy. Truelove offered to pay for her carpet to be cleaned. Ethel slowly pulled herself out of her chair and without saying a word, shuffled into her bedroom.

Truelove, distraught over his faux pas, asked Jasper if they should leave. Before Jasper could answer Ethel emerged from her bedroom.

"Please don't worry about the carpet. I have it cleaned regularly. Believe me, this stain is nothing compared to the stains Pebbles has made." She held up a manila folder and waved it like a banner. "This is the file I have on Rasta. I also have about fifteen others, including George Alexander and Douglas Kern. I decided against telling the FBI I had these because they were being so evasive and secretive in their questioning."

"Why didn't you give these files to Dr. Bartolli when you went through your husband's files?" Jasper was perplexed.

"I forgot I had them. These files were actually mine, not Wayne's. I had a separate set of files I kept in the early days of the society, so I could plan social events for the group. Wayne had his own set. Since I only used a portion of the file for my needs, I placed the remainder of the files in a storage container. I remembered I had the files after I had met with Mrs. Bartolli years ago. I remember calling her and telling her I had some information which might be of some use to her, but she told me she was no longer interested and had dropped her investigation."

"Do you know why she did that?" Jasper asked.

"No, she wouldn't elaborate, and I didn't feel it appropriate for me to ask. It really wasn't any of my business. I assumed she felt her theory was invalid, so I also lost my interest. At that time in my life, I had just met someone and had other interests. Unfortunately, I later learned the man I was interested in wasn't interested in me, he was interested in my money." A half smile, half frown, appeared on Ethel's face. "Anyway I kept the files safely hidden waiting for a rainy day. Today I think I hear the rain drops starting to fall." The smile was now full and a sparkle appeared in her eyes.

"Let me see if I understand you." Jasper said slowly. "These files have the original documents of the first people in the society and these are the only copies?"

"Yes, that's correct. I thought about copying the files but never got around to it." Ethel shrugged her shoulders. By this point in the conversation neither Truelove or Jasper had to strain to understand Mrs. Tatum. Her broken speech pattern was as clear and lucid to them as their own.

"Can I see the file on Rasta?" Truelove asked, and Ethel handed him the file. Jasper positioned himself behind Truelove so he could also read the file. The file had several black and white photographs in it and the information documenting Rasta's indiscretions in college. They reviewed the information in a haphazard manner, partially because they were excited and partially because they knew they would have time later to go over the file piece by piece.

"Are all the files similar to this?" Jasper asked.

"I'm not sure what you mean," Ethel countered.

"Do they all have photographs along with the documents?"

"Oh yes, I was very big on pictures in those days. At one time I thought about writing a book on the society, in which the pictures would be included." Ethel finished the brandy remaining in her glass.

"How large is the container where the files are kept?" Truelove asked hoping the container was in her home.

"It's not that large, but it's too heavy for me to lift by myself. Let me show you." Ethel led them into a small room off her bedroom, many antique knickknacks were lying about. This was her storage room. In the corner was a large secretary from the Louis XV period, which was rather elaborate with a chiseled leaf and shell motif and a fall-front. Ethel opened it, revealing a large metal case. "These are the files."

"Not very secure," Jasper said.

"Nobody even knew they existed until now."

"Good point," Jasper conceded.

"Do you mind if we copied the files and returned the originals to you?" Truelove asked.

"No, but why don't you keep the originals and leave the copies with me?" Ethel wanted to be as cooperative as she could. These files had lain dormant for almost forty years, if someone could use them, that was fine with her.

"At this time, I feel the original files are safer with you, but there might be a time we may ask for them." Truelove appreciated her support, but he knew that where they were going could place the files in jeopardy.

Truelove and Jasper left with the metal cabinet containing the files. It took them about an hour to copy all the files and return the originals to Ethel.

Truelove and Jasper thanked Ethel for all her help and assured her they would be in touch. They now had a new destination: Texas.

"What do you mean you lost them?" J.T.'s voice had escalated to a scream.

"I'm sorry, sir. They must have left in a crowd." William Katte, assigned to J.T. for surveillance purposes, was nervous for a good reason. This case had been ongoing for over six months. They were finally closing in on one of the top assassins in the world, the infamous Valentino, and now two key leads had slipped through their fingers. Katte was in charge and thus shouldered the responsibility.

Katte's two partners were equally concerned, because all their careers were precariously dangling by a very fine thread. They had to produce Truelove and Jasper before they inadvertently tipped off Valentino. If Valentino had any inkling the FBI was this close, Valentino would disappear and all their effort would have been for naught.

Katte knew it was wrong to apologize, but he was so upset he couldn't think of another response.

"Sorry? Sorry your ass! Listen, you're not a rookie, a novice maybe, but not a rookie." J.T. was still screaming. "And what do you mean a crowd?"

Katte explained about the costume party and how everyone was dressed up and wearing masks. When they left in large groups it was impossible to identify them. After checking Truelove's home, Katte and one of the agents went to the airport but could not locate the missing doctors. The other agent remained at Truelove's home just in case they returned.

"So they're gone." J.T. said, mixing frustration with his anger.

"We have one possible lead." Katte said. "Truelove's room-mate, Earl, said they took off for Sedona."

"Listen, you go to Sedona, in the remote possibility this guy Earl's telling the truth. Call me when you find something out." J.T. wasn't screaming but he was still at moderate roar.

"I'm on my way. I'm going to keep agent Johnston here, in case they return." Katte said, heedfully.

"Fine. By the way, this goes without saying. If I go down on this, I'm taking you with me. So you better hope we find these guys before Valentino does." J.T. slammed the phone down.

35

The Algonquin Hotel had become a second home to the group and now they had yet another priority meeting. None of the them were in a good mood, especially Marvin Barnes. Dr. Barnes had been outspoken before, but he was livid this evening. "I'm getting sick and tired of this bullshit. We need to make some decisions tonight so we can go on with our lives and practices."

Timmons nodded. He couldn't understand the need for another meeting, especially this close to the last. Wilovsky wasn't holding up well and it showed.

Rasta, who had again called the meeting and arranged the agenda, needed to gain control of the group. Rasta walked over to Barnes. "The reason we have to meet here is to provide us the utmost security and secrecy, while bringing us all up to speed on matters critical to all of us."

Barnes never moved or blinked as he stared intently at Rasta. "Where's our friend Smithee?"

"I contacted Smithee about our suggestion or was it a demand, that we all meet. He declined and advised me again, it was better for all of us if we remained ignorant of his identity."

"Why is it better for all of us?" Wilovsky softly asked.

"Smithee feels that if something should happen, then we can't implicate him, nor he us." Rasta was tired of his role as messenger, but he could not find a way out.

"How can you say that?" Wilovsky asked.

"Because we've never had any contact, therefore it is impossible for us to say who Smithee is."

It was apparent this conversation was going nowhere. Barnes only mentioned Smithee to agitate Rasta. "Can we start to discuss the emergency that brought us here?" Barnes grumbled as he took a seat around a conference table.

The others joined Barnes around the mahogany table. A

pitcher of water was set in the middle of the table surrounded by glasses. Rasta decided to start with a safe subject.

"I'm sure you're all aware Dr. Mendoza resigned her position on the committee after she was promoted to assistant secretary of health and human services. Dr. Timmons was appointed her replacement heading the subcommittee." Wilovsky and Barnes softly clapped, as Timmons bobbed his head.

"I know we're here for something other than that." Barnes pulled out one of his cigars, which he placed in his mouth unlit.

"There were several issues left unresolved from when we last met. To review, there were concerns with several people. First, there was Van Gregory, who has kept a low profile. However, he did meet with Merker and convinced him to drop the case. Which brings me to Merker. I don't have the full story, but Merker was killed in an automobile accident in Florida."

"Was this a set-up?" Wilovsky asked, realizing this was the way Harvey Kahn had died.

"No, we had nothing to do with this and that is confirmed. However, the death of Merker has created a bit of a problem." Rasta picked up the pitcher and poured himself a glass of water.

"What kind of problem?" Timmons started to rub the back of his neck.

"We're concerned his death might bring some inquiries about our organization. It seems Mr. Merker had been talking to a Mrs. Bartolli prior to his death. I don't know if you remember her husband, Walter Bartolli—he used to be an associate of mine. He died in the sixties and his wife blamed me for his death. She even hired a private detective to investigate his death, but he found nothing."

"How did her husband die?" Wilovsky questioned.

"A car accident, I believe," Rasta answered. Automobile accidents appeared to be a constant theme.

"Interesting. Please go on."

"Anyway, we're attempting to find out why Merker was meeting with Bartolli's wife. Van Gregory had made it very clear to him, he had to cease all inquiries about the committee."

"Guess what, he didn't comply, and I'll bet our friend Van Gregory killed him and that's why you're so concerned." Barnes was chewing off the end of his cigar.

"No, I believe Gregory, and he said he had nothing to do with Merker's death. Nevertheless, we need to keep our wits about us. I'm fairly confident there's nothing significant Merker could have learned from Mrs. Bartolli, but I need to remind you, Dr. Bartolli was inquiring about the Gance list at the time of his death." Rasta was deadly serious.

"What do we know about Dr. Bartolli?" Wilovsky was also serious.

"After his death, his wife hired a private detective by the name of Vigor Truax. Truax had found some information about the committee, and we were able to buy him off. He dropped the case and Mrs. Bartolli lost interest, so I doubt if all these years later something new would arise. But we're not taking any chances. Van Gregory's checking this out."

"Do you think having Gregory investigate is a wise move?" Barnes was still chewing his cigar.

"I have no concern in that regard. I'm positive Gregory had nothing to do with the death of Merker, and he's very good at investigation." Rasta leaned back in his chair, folding his hands behind his head.

"How can you be so sure?" Timmons said.

Rasta hesitated and swallowed hard. "I know because Van Gregory was with me at the time of Merker's death."

"Why couldn't he have arranged Merker's death or used someone else to do it and used you as his alibi?" It was clear Rasta was concealing something and Wilovsky was going to find out what it was.

"I know because Mr. Gregory and his team were all in Chicago at the time of Merker's death." Rasta never wanted to broach this subject and now that he had, he regretted it.

"I'm sorry, this still doesn't explain why he couldn't have arranged his death." Timmons was now as curious as Wilovsky.

"Because Gregory was with me when we found out about Merker's death. He was as surprised as I was." Rasta was becoming defensive.

"I'm sorry I have to agree. He could have arranged this and acted surprised," Barnes added.

"Okay, Gregory was told by Smithee if he harmed Merker in any way, he would have to deal with Valentino." Now Rasta had said what he wanted to avoid saying.

"How do you know this?" Wilovsky said.

"Because both Gregory and Smithee told me, independent of each other. I could tell this upset and actually frightened Gregory, who said if I ever told anyone of his reaction, he would make me pay." Rasta was unnerved even saying the words. He never liked Gregory and his tactics, but now he was genuinely afraid.

"Gregory threatened you?" Wilovsky was stunned and angered.

"It appears that way." Rasta again swallowed hard.

"This is unacceptable! We must do something." Wilovsky was becoming more upset.

"Believe me, I've thought about this a lot and haven't been able to come up with any logical solution. The problem is Gregory isn't logical in his reaction, so I have no idea if he's serious or not."

"He's just trying to scare you. Anyway, you haven't done anything." Timmons tried to reassure Rasta.

"Gregory's concerned if word gets out he's afraid of Valentino, his effectiveness would be severely compromised."

"Hogwash, he's not serious. And if he does try something I'll hire this Valentino myself to kick his butt," Wilovsky said. "Should we arrange to check out the circumstances of Merker's death?"

"This has already been done," Rasta said.

"By whose authority?" Wilovsky asked.

"Smithee's, of course." Barnes answered for Rasta, who nodded in agreement.

"Some day we really do need to meet this mystery man." Wilovsky said realizing it was futile to discuss this issue further. "What else is on the agenda? We've reviewed the status of Gregory and Merker, but we haven't discussed Callison or the secretary, Maxine Wells. That's her name isn't it?"

"Yes. She was approached by Gregory—and she unraveled. She fell apart and said she needed her job and would do what-

377

ever she could to help us, if we would assure her job security."
Rasta was less tense talking about Maxine Wells than when he
addressed his own problems with Gregory.

"So how comfortable are we? Can we be sure she can be
trusted?" Barnes asked as he began chewing on a new cigar.

"I think she's so frightened of the consequences of her prior
activities she can be trusted. We told her to maintain her current
position and relationship with Callison so we can use her for
inside information if he becomes a problem. We have already
reaped some benefit from this agreement." Rasta had a brash
look about him.

"What happened?" Timmons seemed distraught at the mention of Callison, another of his colleagues.

"Ms. Wells reported to Gregory, that Callison was inquiring
about the Hayes Bill." Rasta poured another glass of water.

"Isn't the Hayes Bill about redistribution of the physician
pool to supply physicians to the rural and inner city areas of
need?" Wilovsky asked.

"That's the essence of the bill, but we cannot have this bill
brought up in discussion at our committee," Rasta answered.

"Why not?" Timmons couldn't see any harm in discussing the
bill as a committee.

"Because this could polarize our group and reverse much of
the work we've done toward the merger."

"How? I don't understand." Timmons was still confused.

"We have all the members on the committee in agreement
with the concept of a merger. This bill can only work if the
merger is completed and the DO's are merged into the AMA. The
bill can be implemented once both sides are under one organization."

"I'm sorry for being so dense, but why can't we talk about this
as a group?" Timmons still couldn't understand why Rasta was
so adamant about this.

"You haven't read the bill, have you?" Rasta eyes pierced
Timmons.

"No, I haven't seen the bill." Timmons shrugged his shoulders.

"The major point of contention is a requirement that all practitioners have three years of an approved allopathic residency training program to provide care to any government-sponsored program. If this bill is approved before the merger, then we were told the osteopathic community would be exempt. However, if a merger precedes the bill, then we can grandfather all the prior training in osteopathic programs as approved allopathic programs, since there no longer would be any osteopathic programs or osteopathic physicians for that matter."

"So what happens to those physicians who don't have three years of post-graduate training?" Timmons was realizing the reason Rasta was adamant about keeping this topic off their agenda.

"There are choices. They can maintain their current practices, they can go back for further training to complete the three-year requirement, or if they wish they can be assigned to a need area and have the three-year requirement waived."

Timmons shook his head. Rasta didn't have to say another word. A significant number of Timmons' colleagues had only one or two years of post-graduate training. Their practices would be ruined by such a bill. If Timmons went along with this, he would be an accomplice in the destruction of the practices of many of his friends and colleagues.

"Do you have any further questions about the bill?" Rasta knew Timmons was too involved in the group to voice an objection. He had already been bought out and they all knew it.

Timmons said nothing and shook his head looking down at the table. His fate had already been determined.

"There's another issue we have to discuss. Sort of a good news, bad news story." Rasta wanted to move the agenda forward to avoid further embarrassing Timmons.

"Give me the good news, I could use some good news." Barnes grinned, but he was serious. Anything positive would be a welcome relief.

"Okay, the good news is there is a large bonus for all of us if the merger takes place." Rasta managed a half-hearted smile.

"What do you mean by large?" Barnes asked.

"Two hundred thousand apiece will be deposited in our foreign account."

Barnes' lower lip protruded and he bobbed his head in approval. Timmons lifted his head from the table.

"So what's the bad news?" Wilovsky brought them all down to reality.

"The merger and then the Hayes Bill are now non-negotiable. Plans have been implemented and large sums of money have exchanged hands. We have to deliver. Also, Timmons..."

Chester Timmons' mind had gone off in another direction. He momentarily returned to reality with the news of the bonus, but again wandered off. When Rasta mentioned his name, Timmons was again forced to deal with the reality of the situation.

Rasta repeated Timmons' name and waited until he was sure he had the doctor's attention. "You have to deliver the research recommendation. I've prepared a copy for your review, which you will report to the committee when we meet on Thursday." Rasta handed Timmons a file of papers.

Rasta then looked at Barnes. "Timmons and I will do our part to force the recommendation for the merger from our committee. What you need to do is to contact a Senate aide by the name of Lance Darby. He'll instruct you on what you need to do to help push the Hayes Bill through committee."

"Who's this Lance Darby?" Barnes asked.

"He works for Nathan Slinger, and it's integral that Slinger be supportive of this bill."

They all recognized the name Nathan Slinger, senator from Oregon and the hand-picked golden boy in charge of the health-care reform initiative.

"Lazlo, your task..." Before Rasta could complete his sentence, Wilovsky raised his hand.

"Before you go any further, I have a question which needs a direct answer." Wilovsky paused to gather his thoughts. "Who is directing you with these assignments and why is there no discussion?" Wilovsky's eyes were cold and penetrating.

"The question is a reasonable one and I'll answer it to the best of my ability." Rasta could feel Wilovsky driving his point. "The people who are paying us for these bonuses are setting the agenda. I got my information from Smithee, whom I know some of you don't believe even exists. As you all know, these people

380

have been paying our expenses for decades and have asked for relatively little in return. It has been through their generosity, for lack of a better term, that we have been able to use the resources of this organization to advance our careers and those of the others whom we have chosen. They never second-guessed our decisions, and we were able to form a powerful and formidable infrastructure. Over the years, we all have been asked to support certain legislative actions, endorse certain political candidates, assist members of the organization with our collective influence. I'm sure you get the picture. Now it's time for us to pay the piper, so to speak. Health care reform will be devastating to many medical-related industries, while on the other hand, many companies will flourish like never before. Our supporters need to be in the latter group. Their success will be ours. Their fortunes will be shared by those who assist them. It has been suggested the little bonus they have recommended is just a starting place. There's the potential for much more."

Wilovsky couldn't remain silent any longer. "Look, I'm old and sickly. I don't want to do this. What if I refuse?" The look on Wilovsky's face indicated he was worn out and ready to give up.

"Smithee made this very clear to me. If any of us refuse to do what they ask, they'll ruin us. They will use all the resources at their disposal and they are monumental. They will destroy our lives, reputations, families and anything else they can think of. They have access to the files on all of us. I don't see we have much choice."

Wilovsky despondently shook his head. "Maybe. I need to think about this."

"Lazlo, we need your vast connections to help this legislation pass." Rasta pleaded. "Specifically, we need you to use your skills to convince Congressman Wilder and Senator Paxton to support the Hayes Bill. They're both assigned to a bipartisan review committee dealing with rural health-care needs. We're aware they are both close personal friends of yours and we need their support."

Wilovsky could feel the tremor start in his legs and slowly ascend up his thighs to his torso and then consume his entire body. He was so outraged, he was shaking uncontrollably. "How dare you ask that of me? I will not do this and I don't care what you do to me." Saliva was spewing as he screamed, and his face turned crimson with anger. "I won't do this."

"Calm down, Lazlo, this was just a suggestion and I'm sure they will understand." Rasta was calm and collected. The stress Wilovsky was under could precipitate a cardiac event, and he needed to calm down.

"But you just said how they will ruin us if we don't cooperate. How can you talk out of both sides of your mouth?" Timmons asked.

"You're right, I did contradict myself, but maybe I overstated their requests. I'm only the messenger here and therefore can only convey what I feel is their intent. If they have a problem with Dr. Wilovsky, or for that matter any of us, they'll let us know in no uncertain terms. But Lazlo has the right, as do all of us, to decline, and wait and see what happens, if anything."

Wilovsky had calmed down considerably. "If I were to approach Congressman James Paxton and Senator Philip Wilder, what would I be expected to say?"

"What they want is for you convince both the congressman and the senator of the necessity to support the Hayes Bill. They both are key figures, each representing a constituency critical to the eventual passage of this bill. And you're in the unique position to influence both of their decisions."

Wilovsky surmised that passage of the Hayes Bill must be worth hundreds of millions of dollars, maybe billions, to various pharmaceutical and technology firms, not to mention the insurance companies. He also realized there were issues in his past he would not want to be made public. Wilovsky knew he was on the tail end of the curve of life, a life he had dedicated to medicine, sacrificing so much. Now it all could be undone by not cooperating with this invisible force.

"In all my years I have never used my friendships to better my career, and I have a great deal of difficulty considering this now, as my career is ending." Wilovsky appeared defeated, his head bowed, his arms hung limp at his side and his eyes closed.

"I understand, we all understand. We must do what we must

do." Rasta's voice lowered, as he also felt Wilovsky's despair.

The room was silent. Wilovsky's surrender was a powerful message. They really had no choice.

"If you want to reach our foreign division, please press 3." This was the message on the voice mail menu for Hitherto Industries. Pressing the key for 3, the recorded message now said, "We are not in at the moment, if you will please leave your name, the time and phone number we will return your call at our earliest convenience."

Smithee picked up the code book that Valentino had given him, so he could properly code in the message for Valentino to return his call. Smithee had a secured telephone line, on which he encoded a message for Valentino to return his call at 10 P.M.

At 10 P.M. sharp the secured line rang. The interference on the line was no different than in the past, distorting the voices to mask the tone and pitch, yet allowing the words to be understood. "Valentino here." The muffled voice sounded distant but understandable.

"We need to go to phase two. Do you understand?" Smithee was concerned and needed to insure there would be no problems with him fulfilling his contract with the "Overlords." Smithee knew by moving to phase two it would cost him an additional million dollars, but he needed the insurance. His profit would still be substantial. He had already spent their good faith money as a down payment on his own debt. Smithee knew if he didn't meet all their demands, there was no place safe for him to hide. If he wasn't successful, he was a dead man. Smithee had everything in place to pay off all his debts, fulfill all the expectations, and maintain his current status. The additional million for Valentino was a small price to pay for such piece of mind.

"I understand. I'll initiate phase two when the foundation is completed."

The line disconnected. Smithee had already initiated the transfer of funds to the account number given to him by Valentino into the Royal Bank of Montreal located on Grand Cayman Island. The million would complement the 3 million dollars already transferred to the account. Valentino had used banks all over the world, but had become recently enamored with the banks in the Caymans because these banks were very discreet and safe, even when compared to the Swiss.

36

The hearing was scheduled in downtown Fort Worth in the Summit Avenue building of the Texas Medical Foundation. It was a four-story edifice constructed in the 1950's, white-bricked, inconspicuous, and well maintained.

The hearing was scheduled for 9 A.M., and Callison arrived twenty minutes early. He wasn't taking any chances this time. Even though Callison had been assured he had nothing to worry about, he was worried. The Level III medical mismanagement implied Callison's treatment could have caused a significant adverse event, possibly leading to unconsciousness or death. Maybe some of his colleagues would have taken this lightly but to Callison this was very serious. Callison had reviewed the medical record of Valerie Williams a hundred times, he also had a number of his partners review the chart and critique the care which had been provided. Callison did an exhaustive literature search on the medication, which apparently caused the adverse event to occur. He was prepared with a concise explanation for the care rendered and a logical explanation for the adverse event.

At nine o'clock sharp, Callison was summoned into a conference room on the second floor. Seated at a head table were three men all wearing white shirts, with extra starch, and all had their suit jackets off. It was already ninety degrees outside, but the temperature in the room was cool, although Callison could feel his body start to perspire as soon as he entered. The man seated in the middle was busily reading the file when Callison entered. His glasses precariously clung to the tip of his nose while he read. He was flanked by two other men also wearing glasses. The man on the left was talking to the secretary, who was seated at the end of the table and the man on the right was resting his chin in his hand, while motioning with his free hand for Callison to sit in the chair situated in the middle of the room

After Callison took his seat the man on the left nudged the middle man, who hadn't noticed Callison until that moment.

"Dr. Callison, so nice to see you." The man in the middle then introduced himself and other gentleman, as well as the secretary. Although Callison heard the words he immediately forgot all their names. He was concentrating on his presentation.

Once the introductions were completed, the man in the middle then described the quality issue and the reason for the possible Level III sanction. The case was identified by a beneficiary number, and the secretary began recording all the information. Once the charge had been stated for the record and the reason why Callison's original written appeal had been turned down, it was time for Callison to state his case.

Callison was nervous, more nervous than he could ever remember being while doing a presentation. Because his job required him to lecture frequently, he was and always had been comfortable in front of an audience. But he was nervous today, in front of three men in white shirts and no jackets.

Callison defended the reasons for his management. His statements had been rehearsed and memorized, using current medical references for emphasis. The questions they asked he answered with ease. After thirty minutes, the man in the middle asked Callison if he would wait in the hall. The process was painless to this point, and Callison knew the rigorous interrogation was about to start. After a few minutes the secretary asked Callison to return to the meeting room. Callison again sat in the chair facing the table, trying to read their faces. Their expressions had not changed since the start of the hearing, so Callison prepared for the worst.

The man in the middle peered at Callison over the rim of his glasses, which remained carefully balanced on the tip of his nose. "The decision of this Reconsideration Hearing is to reverse the decision of the original denial." There was a small smile on his face as Callison sat motionless, still contemplating what he had said.

"You will be receiving a letter detailing this decision in several weeks. Thank you for your time."

Callison remained motionless in his chair. He thought to himself, *Is it over? Where were the hard questions, the grilling over the care he delivered? It couldn't be this easy, could it?'* The three men slowly stood, and each had a smile on his face. Callison's adrenaline was still pumping and he was still waiting for the *but* . . . but there was no *but.*

"Excuse me, are we done?" Callison still couldn't believe the hearing was over.

"Yes, Dr. Callison. We were impressed with your presentation and the explanation justifying your care. We're not here to judge you, only to ensure that the quality of care rendered to our patients was up to the standards of the community. It was obvious you gave your patient excellent care and at no time placed the patient in danger."

Callison couldn't believe it was over; it was as if a giant cloud had been lifted. He felt great. He thanked each of the three men individually, shaking each of their hands.

Leaving the building, the sun seemed to shine a little brighter and the air was a little cleaner. Callison had a little more bounce to his step. He noticed it was only slightly after ten. This would allow him time to complete his paperwork before his afternoon patient rounds and to prepare for his meeting in Chicago. Maybe things were finally turning his way.

Truelove and Jasper deplaned at DFW. It was midafternoon and they needed to meet with Callison. The stalkers who trailed them from Florida to Phoenix had not been seen since the party, and the men were cautiously optimistic they were still disengaged from their pursuers.

They rented a car at the airport, paying cash as they had during their entire adventure. Their plan was to contact Callison at work and set up a meeting at a safe place, to be determined by Callison, just in case Callison was being followed.

The drive to the medical school took longer than anticipated. They hit rush hour traffic and an accident had occurred in the mixmaster, a complex web of highways intersecting in downtown Fort Worth. By the time they arrived at the school, the clinics were closed and Callison's business number was relegated to the answering service. Before they would call Callison, they decided to eat dinner and plan their strategy.

There were several restaurants in the area, and they were referred to a quaint Italian restaurant that specialized in Northern Italian cuisine.

Steven and Natalie had just sat down to dinner when the phone rang.

"Hello, Dr. Callison?"

"Yes."

"I don't know if Marcus Merker mentioned me, my name is Tyler Truelove, I'm a friend of Marcus."

Callison's day had gone so well. He had had time to finish his work, return home at a reasonable hour, spend a leisurely evening with his wife, and now this call was about to ruin it all. "What can I do for you?"

"Is it possible we can meet tonight? My friend Ethan Jasper and I have some important information to tell you." Truelove was being as direct as he could over the phone. It was a calculated risk but one they felt necessary to lure Callison away from his home. They were more concerned about Callison's home being watched than they were about his phone being tapped.

"Why tonight?" Callison had no idea who these men were and he wanted to spend the evening with his wife.

"Please don't hang up. We're both physicians who helped Merker on the Caldo case. We need to talk to you confidentially tonight. We're concerned that Merker's death may not have been an accident."

Natalie could see Steven was upset and mouthed to him the words, "What's the matter?"

Steven mouthed back to Natalie. "Merker." Then he answered, "I really don't think I can meet with you tonight. Can you tell me what this is about over the phone?"

"It concerns the Caldo list."

Callison had the list, but he wondered if they did. "What about the list? I doubt it even exists."

"What if we could prove to you the list does exist."

Callison thought, *they must also have a copy, but how?* He

was intrigued. *What if the lists were different?* "How can you prove the list exists?"

"If you meet us we'll show you."

"But I can't tonight, and tomorrow..." Callison stopped before he revealed that he was about to go out of town. He had no idea who these men really were, and his business was none of their concern.

"Tomorrow? I think we need to meet tonight. Do you know somewhere we could meet you? Somewhere private?" Truelove was reeling him in, slowly.

Callison had no intention of meeting anyone—Merker had made him paranoid enough to not even consider a private meeting. "No, I know of no place I could privately meet with you."

"We'll be happy to meet you at your home if you like."

"No, that's not an option." The last person he met with at his home about this case was Merker—and now Merker was dead.

"Then please tell us a place where you would feel comfortable meeting."

Callison thought for several seconds: first, he was intrigued by their comments; second, maybe they had some information about Merker, whose death still haunted him; third, he would need a place to meet where he would feel safe and in charge. There was only one place he could think of: the hospital. "Okay, I'll meet you at the hospital in thirty minutes, the sixth floor conference room off the main elevator."

"We'll be there." Truelove had him, and hung up before Callison could change his mind.

Callison hung up the phone as Natalie hovered over him. "What was that about?" Natalie asked.

"It was a phone call from a man named Truelove who said he worked with Merker on the Caldo case and has some information for me." He didn't know what to think. Maybe he shouldn't meet with them after all.

"What information do they have?" Natalie had also been affected by the death of Merker and was curious about his death.

"They wouldn't say. What they did say was, they would show me evidence that the Caldo list existed. I assume they have the same information I have. They also said they were with Merker before he died, so they might have the details about his death." Callison did not want to mention their concern that Merker's death might not have been accidental, since this would probably unsettle Natalie.

"So what are you going to do?" Natalie curled her hair in her fingers nervously.

"I'm going to meet with them tonight if that's okay with you." He planned to meet with them even if Natalie disagreed, but he thought he owed her the courtesy of asking.

"Do you think that's a good idea?" She continued to play with her hair.

"I'm not sure. That's why I arranged to meet them at the hospital. I'll make sure there's someone around just in case. Plus, I know the nooks and crannies of the hospital and they don't." He could see Natalie was still worried. "I promise I'll be careful. Anyway, doesn't this remind you of the old college days?" There was no way she would argue against that.

"Please be careful."

"Let me eat something before I go." Callison followed Natalie to the kitchen where he hurriedly ate the meal he thought he would be able to leisurely enjoy.

Truelove had Jasper wait for Callison outside in the doctors' parking lot. They figured that if Callison was being followed, Jasper would be able to spot the pursuer. Jasper stationed himself in a corner of the lot, hidden in the shadows. He had never met Callison, but knew what time he was expected. If someone was following him, he would know.

Callison pulled into the doctors' parking lot on time, activated the Merker alarm system, and proceeded to the hospital, never noticing Jasper stalking in the shadows. Jasper waited for several minutes to see if another car would appear. He didn't have to wait very long. In the darkness a man got out of his car and walked into the parking lot. The car he vacated was double-parked on the street opposite the lot.

The man studied the parking lot for a second, scanning the lot with a powerful flashlight. Jasper was crouched behind a cement post, totally hidden. The man then focused the light on

Callison's car and attached something to the rear of the car under the bumper. He then moved to the driver's door, but a voice called to him from the darkness and he left the lot.

Jasper remained in the shadows for several minutes, waiting to see if they would return, but all was quiet in the lot. He noticed that the pursuers had left in a dark sedan, but he couldn't determine the make of the car. Jasper gingerly walked out of the darkened lot, searching for the sedan. As Jasper made his way to the hospital's back entrance, he noticed the sedan hidden in a driveway at the end of the street. A streetlight silhouetted the car, which appeared to be empty.

Truelove waited for Callison on the sixth floor. He had stationed himself opposite the conference room off the main elevators. Callison entered the floor via the back staircase, so he could approach the conference room from the opposite direction. Callison immediately noticed Truelove. Callison knew there should be at least one other person, but he could see only the lone figure. The hall was empty except for a nurse on her rounds.

Before Callison would approach Truelove and his partner, he needed to assure himself there would be help if he needed it. Callison backtracked to the nursing station on the sixth floor, where the ward clerk was reading the newspaper. Callison greeted her and asked her to check who was the medical resident on call. The ward clerk told Callison that Dr. Warren was on call. Callison didn't know Warren very well, but he would have to do.

Callison called Warren, who was busy in the Intensive Care Unit, and told him he might need his assistance later. Warren grunted a response.

Returning to the conference area, Callison still saw only the lone figure of Truelove. He was able to sneak behind Truelove, whose eyes were fixed on the elevators. "Dr. Truelove, I presume."

Truelove jumped and nearly screamed, but was able to control himself. "You startled me. I take it you're Callison?"

"Yes, and I thought you had a partner." Callison looked around curiously.

"He'll be joining us in a couple of minutes. Is there some place we can talk?" Truelove's voice was softer as he relaxed.

"Sure; let's go into the conference room." Callison led Truelove into a large conference room. Callison choose this room because of the hidden exit, which provided him an escape route if he needed it. The escape door was masked by a wall to wall mural. The door was almost impossible to discern unless you already knew it was there.

"I want to thank you for meeting with us, and I'm sure you'll find this meeting of interest to you."

Callison wasn't as sure as Truelove. He already had the list, and he was fairly sure this was Truelove's big surprise. "Okay, what's so interesting?"

"Before I show you, I wonder if you could answer a question for me? You said something during our phone conversation which troubled me." Truelove looked to the doorway expecting to see Jasper, but it was a maintenance man walking by.

"What troubled you?" Callison had purposely said little during their conversation, so he was puzzled by Truelove's concern.

"You said you doubted the list existed. Didn't Merker show you the letter?"

"What letter?" Callison thought he knew what letter he was referring to, but wanted to be sure.

"It was a letter written many years ago by a friend of mine, Amos Wilcox."

"Yes, I recall reading that letter."

"Well, the letter discussed the Caldo list over thirty years ago. Why do you doubt its existence today?"

"For just that reason. If the letter is accurate, which is debatable, then why would a list compiled thirty years ago be relevant today?"

"Are you serious? You don't think this list could be relevant today? Isn't it possible the list is ongoing? If it was used years ago during the California merger, it could be used again."

Callison knew Truelove was correct. "I can see your point, but I still don't see the definitive evidence that the list exists."

As Callison completed his remarks, Jasper rushed into the room, sweating and short of breath.

"Did you see anyone else?" Jasper had to take a breath between words.

"What are you talking about? Where were you?" Truelove was troubled by Jasper's state.

Jasper was bent over with his hands leaning on his knees, catching his breath. He looked up at Truelove. "He was followed." Jasper pointed at Callison.

"What?" Callison was dumbfounded. "By whom?"

"I don't know, but they did something to your car. And I'm pretty sure they're in the hospital now looking for you."

"Did you get a good look at them?" Truelove asked.

"No, I only saw the one who came into the parking garage. It was dark so I couldn't see his face but he was six foot or so and stocky. There was at least one other, who parked a dark sedan at the end of the street." Jasper had caught his breath.

"Did you see what type of car it was?" Truelove asked.

"No, I'm not very good at that anyway and it was too far away for me to see. I wasn't about to go up to the car and inspect it."

"Do you have any idea who might have been following you?" Truelove asked Callison.

"I have no idea. Are you sure about this?" Callison looked at Jasper nervously.

"Yeah, I'm positive. I think we'd better get out of here."

Jasper peeked through the doorway of the conference room into the hall. At the end of the hall walking in their direction was the maintenance man, leading two other men toward them. One of the men was a stocky man about six feet tall. Jasper was certain he was the man from the parking garage.

"I don't know who these guys are, but I'm not in favor of sticking around to find out. I think if we go now we can beat them to the stairway and get out of here." Jasper's voice had a tinge of panic.

"I have a better idea. Follow me." Callison led them to the mural on the wall and pushed the center panel, revealing a stairwell concealed by the mural. Callison recalled how he had criticized the prior administrator for the hidden doors. He was told they would be useful in escorting grieving families out of the facility, so as not to upset the already nervous patients and families who were waiting. For once, Callison was pleased his objections were discounted.

As they left through the hidden door, Jasper twisted his neck and craned his head to see if they were followed.

Moments after they exited through the concealed door the maintenance man led the stocky man and his companion into the conference room. "I know they were here. I saw them right before I saw you. There's no way they could've left without being seen."

The stocky man growled and his partner went back into the hallway to see if they were there.

The maintenance man was scratching his head. *How could they disappear?* Then it occurred to him. "I know where they are." The maintenance man ambled over to the mural and revealed the hidden panel and the back stairwell. "I bet you they went here." With a large smile he held out his palm. The stocky man placed a twenty-dollar bill in the maintenance man's palm, then charged into the stairwell followed by his partner.

The stairwell emptied into the main hospital corridor. Callison peeked his head through the door: the hallway was empty. "Follow me." Callison led them down another corridor past the CT scanner and the MRI to the back entrance of the hospital. Callison headed toward the back stairs, Jasper and Truelove close behind.

When Callison opened the door to the back stairs he was greeted by a blond man talking into a walkie-talkie. The man shouted into the walkie-talkie and grabbed for something inside his jacket. Callison and his two visitors didn't wait to see what he wanted, as they frantically reversed directions heading back to the other stairs.

Callison yelled to Truelove to turn left instead of returning to the first staircase. Truelove turned left, followed by Jasper, who was huffing and puffing. Callison was in the rear, but he rushed past the two older men and turned the corner, entering yet another stairway. Callison scampered up one of the stairs to the third floor, where he exited the stairwell past the sign, 3 WEST-ONCOLOGY.

Callison entered a room marked Chemotherapy. The room was dark, but the shadows revealed eight lounge chairs, four each on opposite sides of the room. In the back of the room was another door which led to the bathroom. Callison told Jasper and

Truelove to go into the bathroom and lock the door, and he would check the hallway to see if they were still being followed.

Standing next to the door, Callison could hear the faint static of the walkie-talkie. Straining to hear, he could tell the static was getting closer.

A voice from the walkie-talkie broke the low-pitched static, "Where are you?"

Another voice whispered, "I followed them to the third floor. They must have gone into a room. I had to leave my position at the exit, but if you station someone to block the stairs exiting 3 West we'll have them trapped."

"Good, I'm on my way."

Callison was frozen against the doorway to the chemotherapy room, not breathing for fear of attracting attention. He closed his eyes so he could concentrate harder on the sound in the hall. From the bathroom, Callison could still hear Jasper's labored breathing. Again concentrating on the sounds in the hall, he could hear only the faint static. Callison's eyes were adjusting to the darkness, and he surveyed the room trying to form a plan. He knew there was only one entrance, and it was too high to jump.

Callison wondered why he had directed them to this room. Subconsciously he had been drawn there from the stairway. He remembered earlier that day, he was visiting one of his patients receiving chemotherapy—but there was something else. Callison thought hard, and then it came to him. His patient had asked him to remove a wart from his arm. Callison had frozen the wart with liquid nitrogen and had left the container next to the chair.

Callison moved as quietly as he could. Next to the chair was the metal container holding the liquid nitrogen. Callison bent over to pick up the container. A loud cough resonated from the bathroom. It was Ethan Jasper.

The door to the chemotherapy unit opened and the beam of light was directed toward Callison, who had just bent over to pick up the liquid nitrogen canister, and was fortuitously hidden from the view of the blond man with the walkie-talkie. Callison remained hidden behind the recliner where his patient had received his chemotherapy earlier that day. The coughing from the bathroom continued, and Callison could hear Truelove whispering for Jasper to be quiet. The man with walkie-talkie slowly walked toward the bathroom at the other end of the room. He walked past Callison, focused on the men in the closet.

The man with the walkie-talkie attempted to turn the handle of the bathroom door but to no avail. The door was locked. "I know you're in there, I can hear you coughing. Open up the door and nobody will get hurt." The man's voice was soft and calm, as he reached inside his jacket and removed a revolver. Callison saw this and involuntarily reacted.

The man was pointing his gun at the lock, when Callison lunged, spraying the liquid nitrogen in his direction. The spray from the container struck the man in the face, some hitting his eyes. The man dropped both the gun and the walkie-talkie as he screamed. Callison yelled for Truelove and Jasper to open the door. They needed to get out of there. The door to the bathroom opened, hitting the man who was still writhing on the floor. Truelove and Jasper hopped over the man, who was now reaching for his gun, squinting through the pain. Callison instinctively reacted, hitting the man on the head with the metal canister holding the liquid nitrogen. He fell to the floor unconscious, a small amount of blood staining his blond hair.

Always physicians, all three stopped in their tracks and looked at the man lying unconscious on the floor. They all bent down to examine him, to make sure he was not dead. A large bruise was forming on his head where Callison had struck him, but the bleeding was minimal, and he was breathing and appeared to be close to regaining consciousness. They looked at each other and decided it was time to leave.

In the hallway they heard sounds coming from the opposite end of the hall. They were on the run again, turning the corner and entering the stairwell. Callison was in the lead and headed up the stairs, followed closely by a gasping Jasper and Truelove. They exited on the fourth floor. Callison knew he couldn't push Jasper to climb more than one floor, so they ran down the hall looking for an empty patient room. When Callison noticed an empty room, he motioned for them to enter. He pointed at Jasper as he whispered, "Why don't you get into the bed. You definitely look bad enough to be a patient."

Jasper panting, responded, "Thanks a lot," but followed Callison's suggestion and got under the covers. He did look like a patient. Callison suggested Truelove lie down next to the bed, between the bed and the wall, so he would be hidden from view.

Callison was surprised at how clearly he was thinking. The incident with the liquid nitrogen had emptied his mind and he was in a definite survival mode. He thought the pursuers would expect them to go down the stairs, looking to leave the building rather than go up. The latter seemed the better choice, since Callison was fairly sure they had all the exits blocked. Callison also hoped this would give them a little extra time to implement his plan.

Jasper was once again breathing normally and Truelove was totally concealed on the floor next to Jasper's bed. Room 445 appeared to be no different than any of the other patient rooms on the floor. Even though there was considerably less staffing at night, there were still enough employees around to discourage a room-to-room search. If worst came to worst, they could stay there all night.

Callison's plan apparently was working, since there was no evidence of any of the men for over ten minutes. Callison, who was hiding in the bathroom, decided to check the hall to see if it truly was clear. To his dismay, he noticed a security guard accompanying a man in a navy sports jacket coming out of a room down the hall. They were doing a room-to-room search. He needed a new plan immediately.

Callison waited until the security guard and the man in the sport coat went into the next room before they dashed for the nearest stairwell. Callison knew these stairs would empty into the back of the cafeteria. As the door opened to the cafeteria everything was quiet. The cafeteria was empty.

Callison had an idea. Maybe the midnight club was in session, they could meet with them and all leave together. Callison led Jasper and Truelove to the physicians' dining room where the midnight club convened. A light was on in the room. Maybe they were in luck? He glanced in the room but it was empty. So much for the midnight club.

"Who are these guys?" Jasper asked.

"I don't know. But now they have security helping them." Callison said, rubbing his forehead.

"What do we do now?" Jasper said. His tone was more frantic.

"How the hell do I know? But contacting security is now out." Callison said, frustrated.

The three sat in the doctors' dining room discussing their options. If they remained there, it was likely they would be discovered. They could backtrack to a room already searched, remain there for the night, and then go out an emergency exit, but that would initiate an alarm. Then Callison thought of another option. They could leave via the emergency room. Tiny would be on duty. If Callison could talk to Tiny, he would be able to escort them out safely.

The emergency room was relatively slow that evening. One woman was in labor, screaming something uninterpretable each time a contraction occurred. Another patient had been transferred from a nursing home with a high fever and an altered state of consciousness. Another was being evaluated for chest pain. Tiny was quietly reading the paper when Callison crept beside him and tapped him on the shoulder.

"Can I have a word with you."

Over the years Tiny and Callison had become friendly, if not friends. Callison had been Tiny's physician for several years, and recently also Tiny's parents'. Callison asked Tiny to check the lobby of the emergency room and the area around the exit for anyone looking like they didn't belong.

Tiny returned to Callison in less than a minute. There were two men in the lobby who fit his description. The plan was simple: Tiny would detain the two men, and Callison, Truelove, and Jasper would slip out the entrance rather than the exit door to the emergency room.

Tiny agreed to help, but Callison had to promise to buy him dinner. They both smiled and Tiny strolled down the hall of the emergency room to greet the two men. Tiny's size, six feet-six-inches, three hundred pounds, blocked their view of the hallway as Callison, Jasper, and Truelove tried to sneak out without creating any attention.

Jasper was the first to hear the shouts coming from the other end of the emergency room, it was the stocky man from the garage and his companion. They were yelling into their walkie-talkies and started to run down the corridor of the emergency room.

The plan changed. They had to run for the car and hope they could get away before getting caught. Jasper was a weak link, and he knew it. He told them to leave him, but neither Callison nor Truelove could do that.

The noise and clamor caused by the men running down the emergency room corridor, triggered Tiny into action. Tiny was able to push both the men into their seats with his powerful arms, and then pivoted, stepping into the oncoming traffic. He hit the stocky man with such force, he knocked him into his partner, sending both their bodies sprawling to the floor. By the time Tiny returned, the first two men were already heading for the exit. There was no way Tiny could stop them. He could only hope he had given Callison and his friends enough time to get away.

The driveway in front of the emergency room was clear of traffic, and Callison ran up the small hill to the side of the building toward the doctors' parking garage. Both Jasper and Truelove were able to keep pace to this point, but Callison noticed the two men from the lobby in pursuit. Callison thought if he could get to his car and get the car started he could pick both Truelove and Jasper on the run and they might make it. When he got to the garage, he pressed the Merker alarm. It was flashing. Callison remembered Jasper had said somebody had messed with his car. They were screwed.

By the time Truelove and Jasper caught up to Callison they were rapidly running out of options. Truelove said their car was parked in a direction opposite of the men pursuing them, so they still had a slim chance of outrunning them. Those odds diminished quickly when they noticed another group, including the blond man from the chemotherapy room, approaching from the other direction. They had nowhere left to run. All their options were cut off. When the men in pursuit saw they had stopped running, they also stopped running, but continued to walk briskly in their direction. Callison still wasn't sure who these men were.

The street was dark and empty, and the three of them waited as the two groups slowly converged on them. Out of the darkness a car started up the street, almost knocking over the blond man and his friends. The groups were less than fifty feet away from the threesome when this same car sped up and stopped next to them. A door flung open and from within the car a voice yelled, "Get in!" Without thinking, the three jumped into the car. The men on foot looked at each other, then hopelessly sprinted after the car as it sped away into the night.

37

Callison did not recognize the two men who had rescued them, but assumed they were with Truelove and Jasper. They were on the highway before anyone spoke. Callison asked Truelove to introduce him to his friends.

Truelove gave Callison a quizzical look. "By the way you jumped into the back seat, I thought they were *your* friends. I don't know who these men are."

Callison didn't know what to think. He didn't know who had been chasing him before, and he didn't know who was driving him now.

The men in the front seat had smiles on their faces. The man driving was wearing glasses, and his companion had his hair tied in a ponytail. The man with the ponytail turned toward the three men crammed in the back seat. "Let me introduce us. My name is Paul, and his is Peter, we're friends of Marcus Merker's."

The three in the back seat were stunned. Paul then explained. "We were working with Marcus on this case. Marcus had told us he was concerned for his own safety and when Marcus says something like that, we take it very seriously. When we heard of Marcus' death, we came down here to follow you around." Paul pointed to Callison.

"Why me?" Callison asked

"Marcus told us to watch you if anything happened to him. He was worried you could also be in danger. I guess he was right." Paul shrugged his shoulders.

"How long have you been following me?" Callison had never seen either of these men before and had no idea he was being followed. This was somewhat disconcerting, because Callison had believed he was being very cautious and observant.

"Just the last two days. You know we weren't the only one following you," Paul said, matter-of-factly.

"This is great. Here I am thinking I'm being cautious, watching for people following me, and now you tell me not one but *two* people were following me?"

"Well that isn't exactly correct, it's more like two *groups* have been following you."

Callison placed his face in his hands. Truelove asked, "Do you know who the other group is?"

"We're not sure. Could be the police, but I don't think so. They acted more like the FBI or CIA. I doubt it was the mob or anything like that."

"Why do you doubt that?" Truelove said.

"Their actions were too regimented, but I guess it could have been. We're going to check it out." Paul paused for a second and changed the subject. "By the way, who are you?" Paul directed his question at Truelove.

"My name is Tyler Truelove and his is Ethan Jasper. We were also working with Marcus on this case." Truelove smiled at Paul.

"Really, how were you helping?" Paul asked skeptically.

Paul repeated his question, but Truelove was still preoccupied. Jasper answered. "We were with Merker when he—actually, we—were picked up. They said they were the FBI, but we had some doubts about that. Anyway, they put us on a plane back to Phoenix, that's where Tyler lives, and told us to stay out of this." Jasper stopped to clear his throat. "For some strange reason we didn't listen." Jasper looked at Truelove, who still had a distant look about him. "Actually, the reason wasn't that strange. When we found out Merker had died we had to do something. As far as we know, we were the last people to see Marcus alive, other than the people who kidnapped us."

"This is all really interesting, but does anyone know where we're going?" Peter asked as he crossed the county line. They were now in Dallas county.

"Listen, we have to go back to my house," Callison said forcefully.

"I don't think that's a very good idea," Paul said. "Remember I told you, you were being watched. Well I can guarantee you, they are watching your house."

"My wife's home alone. I have to get her and ensure her safety." Callison was adamant.

"They won't hurt your wife," Paul said in an attempt to reassure Callison.

"Can you guarantee him they won't hurt his wife?" Truelove glared at Paul.

"No, I can't guarantee it, but it doesn't make any sense. Why would they bother her?"

"Does any of this make any sense? We don't even know who *they* are." Truelove didn't want anything else to worry about. "I agree. I think we need to get her."

"Okay, but we need a plan," Paul said.

"I have a plan. First, stop the car," Jasper said.

Peter turned off at the next exit and pulled into a parking lot. Jasper then detailed his plan to the group.

"Hello, Sylvia. This is Steven, I have a favor to ask of you. It's a little bizarre but bear with me."

"Okay, Steven." Sylvia, the Callisons' next-door neighbor, was a close friend of Natalie's.

"I'd like you to get Natalie at our house and bring her to your phone."

"You want me to go over to your house and tell Natalie to come over here to talk to you? I know there must be a logical explanation for this, but I'm not going to ask. I'll go get her. Hang on."

"Thanks a lot, Sylvia. Someday I'll explain."

Callison looked over to the group and gave a thumbs up. Truelove slapped Jasper on the back.

Several minutes passed, finally Natalie was on the line.

"Steven, what's going on?" Her voice was a mixture of worry and anger.

"I can't go into it now. Let me just say, you need to get out of town. I know this is going to upset you, but please don't let Sylvia notice."

"I understand." Her voice was softened, but he could tell she was upset.

"This is what you need to do. Do you have your purse with you?"

"No, it's at home."

"No problem, what I want you to do is change clothes with Sylvia. I want you to wear her clothes and she yours. Are you with me so far?"

"Yes."

Callison continued. "Okay, after you change clothes, ask Sylvia if she will lend you her car. I assume she will."

"I'm sure she will, go on."

"I want you to drive to the Texaco station off Cooper and 820. I'll be watching for you there. If we're sure you're not followed we'll pick you up."

"Who's we? Who are you with?"

"I'll explain all that later. Now before you leave, Sylvia must go back to our house dressed as you. Do you understand?"

"Of course, I understand, Steven, I'm not stupid. This isn't that complicated."

"I'm sorry, I know. I'm concerned we're being watched. It's possible someone is watching our house as we speak."

"Really, where?"

"This is real important. Neither you nor Sylvia can act like anything is out of the ordinary, it's critical everything appears totally normal."

"I think we can manage that." Natalie paused. "Steven, can I at least go home to get my purse and change my clothes?"

"No, it's too risky. You'll have to buy some new clothes. Sylvia can watch your purse if you like."

"No, I don't like. I don't like this at all. How long are we going to be on the run or whatever this is?"

"I'm not sure, hopefully not too long. I'll stay on the line while you speak to Sylvia." He could hear her talking in the background.

"Steven?" Natalie had picked up the phone again.

"Yes, I'm here."

"Sylvia agreed. Her only question is when she'll get her car back."

"Tell her we'll call her in about an hour. Ask her to stay at our house until she hears from us. When we call, we'll tell her where she can pick up her car." Callison gave another thumbs up to the group.

"Okay, I'll see you at the gas station in a couple of minutes."

"See you soon, hon. Be careful."

Natalie and Sylvia exchanged clothes. Natalie was a little taller than Sylvia and her hair was darker and longer but they had a similar physique. Ordinarily no one would ever mistake one for the other, but it was night and if she moved quickly it might work. Sylvia left wearing Natalie's blue jeans, T-shirt and sandals. Natalie waited several minutes before leaving in Sylvia's van wearing Sylvia's tank top and shorts.

The gas station at Cooper street was well lit and could be seen from the highway. The group had stopped the car, feigning a flat tire. Truelove and Jasper were pretending to change a tire while the others were studying the roads for anyone following them. The van pulled into the station. There were no cars following. The plan appeared to have worked, but they waited several minutes to make sure.

Natalie was seated in the driver's seat of Sylvia's van, nervously waiting. She had parked the car in the corner of the lot so she wouldn't obstruct the traffic flow to the filling pumps. Her husband's manuevers had frightened her, but she kept telling herself to be calm, he will be here any second.

The knock on the glass startled her—she had locked the doors as a precaution, and Callison couldn't open the door. Natalie was relieved to see her husband, so she quickly opened her door.

Callison introduced Natalie to the group. After the introductions, Jasper explained his plan. He surmised that the Callison house was being watched and there was a good chance the telephone line was tapped. They would drive to the airport, where Natalie would call Sylvia and tell her where she left her car. If the line was tapped and they traced the call, then they would assume they were at the airport. Jasper grinned as he explained the next part. "After we complete the call, we're going to drive to San Antonio and leave from there. Whoever's following us will be looking all over DFW for a group that doesn't exist."

On the way to the airport, Steven had them exit so he could access an ATM machine. He needed cash for the plane ticket, but to his dismay, he was only able to take out $400.

At the terminal, Natalie used a pay phone to call Sylvia and thank her for her help. Natalie instructed Sylvia where she could find her car and told her she would be in touch in a day or so. The final part of Jasper's plan was set, now they had the long drive to San Antonio.

The back seat was overcrowded, and Natalie would have to sit on her husband's lap for the duration.

The discussion of the group turned to cash. They all emptied their wallets. Their combined largess would be enough for everybody.

On the highway to San Antonio, Truelove remembered he had left the files back at the hospital.

"Turn around," Truelove shouted. "We have to go back to the hospital."

"Are you crazy?" Callison said. He couldn't believe his ears.

"No, I left a very important file at the hospital. If they get their hands on it, well, it could be big trouble." Truelove really didn't know what trouble the files could cause, he just knew it was important.

"What file? What are you talking about?" Callison asked. His voice squeaked as he talked.

"Remember before all hell broke loose, I told you I had something that would definitely interest you. It was the files." Truelove had a look of panic on his face.

"You don't mean these files, do you?" Jasper smiled as he pulled out a manila envelope he had tucked into his shirt. "I picked these up from the table when we went out the back way."

Truelove showed Callison the files, which included the records on Rasta. "These files can substantiate the fact that Rasta's involved. They're complete with records, pictures, everything."

Callison was excited. Merker had been right. Callison was holding up each page trying to read what was written from the headlights from the oncoming traffic and the intermittent lighting on the highway. Callison looked at another page, but it was a

406

duplicate. "Do you have more than one copy?"

"Yes, we made two copies. We were considering giving you a copy, just in case something happened to us." Truelove watched Callison squint attempting to read what was written on the paper.

"I have an idea. Why don't we give a copy to my wife? Since we'll be traveling together, her copy can be our insurance policy." Callison squeezed Natalie's thigh as he completed his thought.

Natalie leaned back against her husband and kissed him softly on his cheek. She was pleased he included her in this.

"I think that's a good idea." Peter said.

"I agree," echoed Jasper.

Callison, still straining to read the files, noticed some additional papers had fallen to the bottom of the envelope. "What's this?" Callison inquired.

Truelove held the paper up. "These are notes. Do you recall a Walter Bartolli from the Wilcox letter?"

Callison vaguely remembered. "Sort of, why don't you refresh my memory?"

"Dr. Bartolli was a former partner of Rasta's."

Callison interrupted, "Oh yeah, he was the guy Rasta screwed."

"Correct. Anyway, he died in a car accident. Sound familiar? His wife thought his death wasn't accidental and actually hired a private detective to investigate. For some reason the detective dropped the case but gave Mrs. Bartolli his note pad. Most of the pad was information we already knew, but there was a cryptic message on the last page we can't figure out. It mentions an Elwood or Selwood or Aselwood R. Loax. Do any of those names mean anything to you?"

"No, never heard of any of those names."

Truelove and Jasper simultaneously sighed with disappointment.

"How about the phrase 'death to the gunfighter'? Does that ring any bells?" Jasper added.

"No, I don't know what that means either," Callison answered.

"We feel the same way. It makes no sense. Anyway we're not

407

even sure these notes have anything to do with this." The disappointment in Truelove's voice was clear.

"How did you get these files?" Callison was so overcome by the data on Rasta, he had neglected to ask for their source.

"I'll tell you if you really want to know, but before I say anything consider this: if you should get caught or if someone tries to force the information from you, it might be to your benefit to be unaware of the source."

"Let me think about it. We can discuss this point further on the plane to Chicago." Callison wasn't sure about Truelove's suggestion, but they had the luxury of not having to make that decision now.

J.T. was so infuriated he couldn't talk. He was screaming into the phone, but there was just a high-pitched squeal, which probably traumatized the dogs in the neighborhood. Using every ounce of self control in his body, J.T. again attempted to talk. "Let me see if I understand you correctly. You had found Truelove and Jasper. They met with Callison. But now they're all gone and you don't know where any of them are?"

As he continued to talk his voice started to crescendo into a scream. "How can you keep losing these people? You're supposed to be professionals, aren't you?"

William Katte was watching his career disintegrate before his eyes. "Somebody picked them up right in front of our eyes. We're running the plates now; it was a rental car. So we're assuming they used a false name, but we'll check it out anyway."

"Do you have any idea who it was?" The fury in J.T.'s voice was still there.

"No, but I think it was someone they knew. They got in the car too fast for it to have been a stranger."

"You were chasing them and they were trapped. They would have jumped into a garbage truck, you idiot." J.T. was usually very tolerant of his coworkers, even when they screwed up, but this was different. This was the biggest case he had ever been assigned and his ass was on the line. The CIA wanted total control, but the FBI had jurisdiction, so they compromised. J.T. was to cooperate with the CIA, but the FBI would have primary responsibility. J.T. had twenty years in the Bureau and a meritorious record. Now it was falling apart. He was concerned Valentino had them and they would never be seen or heard from again.

Katte decided now was as good a time as any to drive the final nail in his coffin. "That's not all." Katte hesitated but there was no response, although he could feel the steam oozing out of the line. "We also lost his wife."

"Whose wife?" J.T. was shaking his head.

"Callison's. She gave us the slip. She worked out some kind of scam with her neighbor and we fell for it. They must have picked her up because she abandoned her neighbor's car at a local gas station. We're interrogating the neighbor now, but she doesn't know anything. We also monitored a call from Mrs. Callison to their home. This occurred a little more than two hours ago. We traced the call to the airport and have been combing the airport for the last two hours, but there's no sign of the car or of them."

J.T. was silent on the other end. He was the one who suggested the false FBI scenario, which worked a little too well. He now had innocent people, who were potentially on a hit list from one of the most notorious assassins in the world, running away from the FBI.

"J.T., are you still there?"

"Yes." J.T. could feel his ulcer starting to flare. He grabbed for a bottle of antacid and took a large gulp.

"We have an all-out on them. We have agents at both DFW and Love Field in Dallas. We're distributing Callison's, Truelove's and Jasper's IDs to all local officials and the airlines. We have instructed the airlines to notify us of any group purchasing airline tickets with cash. We believe that was how Truelove and Jasper got out of Phoenix. And we have an all-out on their car as well."

"What about other airports. Do we have people there?" J.T. was concerned they were missing something.

"No, I haven't dispatched any agents to any other airport out of this locale."

"How much time has elapsed?"

"Almost four hours since we lost them. I guess it's possible they could have driven to another city."

J.T. thought to himself, four hours at sixty miles, two hundred and forty miles. "Put agents in all airports within five hundred miles of Dallas, maybe we'll get lucky."

One of the other agents handed Katte a fax. "J.T., we have something on the rental car. It was rented by a man named Paul Abnus under the name of Sixth Sense Inc. This was Merker's firm. We think this guy worked for Merker, so it looks like Valentino doesn't have them."

"We'll check this Abnus out on our end. Meanwhile you try to find them." J.T. breathed a sigh of relief. If Merker's men had them, then he still had a chance to find them before Valentino.

The remainder of the ride to San Antonio, the group exchanged information and tried to put the various pieces of the puzzle together. They discussed the people involved, including Marcus Merker. Then they discussed the men who chased them earlier that evening. Callison was the only one who actually saw a gun, and Peter and Paul questioned Callison repeatedly to assure them that the gun was real and not a fabrication of his imagination. When Callison became irritated by their persistent questions, they dropped the subject, but continued discussing the identity of the men at the hospital.

They reached San Antonio at three in the morning. The earliest flight out to Chicago was 7 A.M. and to Denver at 8 A.M. They were all exhausted and decided to see if they could get a couple hours of sleep before their flights. A hotel by the airport had vacancies and they checked in, agreeing to regroup at 6 A.M.

They purchased their airline tickets with cash, now a common policy for Truelove and Jasper. The ticketing agent at the terminal had just arrived and hadn't yet been briefed on the memo from the FBI, so she had no reason to question Callison, when he purchased five seats to Chicago and one to Denver, paying cash for all the tickets.

The group, still weary after only a couple hours of sleep, would all be flying to Chicago for the big meeting, except for Natalie, who would fly to Denver to visit her best friend from college. Natalie's flight was scheduled to leave an hour later, so she accompanied them to their gate.

Steven and Natalie spent time discussing everything and nothing. Natalie also remembered to tell him Maxine had called while he was at the hospital, and had left a message for him to contact her. Maxine had said she had found some valuable information, which he would be very interested in. Callison decided to contact Maxine when he reached Chicago. For now he had enough on his mind. He kissed Natalie good-bye, telling her he would call her tomorrow with an update.

The flight to Chicago was on time. Peter and Paul entered the plane first and scanned the passengers for anyone who looked suspicious. It appeared they were still free and clear.

38

"We found the car. It came up on the computer at the airport in San Antonio." Katte was excited this possibly was the break they needed, he needed.

"Do we have men there?" J.T. couldn't allow himself to get too optimistic. They had been down this path before and to date had come up empty.

"Yes, Jackson and Wilbinder are at the airport. They're checking the outgoing flights. If that doesn't pan out, they'll check the rental cars."

J.T. thought that would be just like them, to turn in one rental and then rent another. "I thought we left their photos with all the airlines?"

"We did, maybe someone screwed up. The airline computers don't show any of their names, but we're checking for groups of tickets recently purchased with cash."

"When did they arrive at the airport?" J.T. knew that all the airports kept a record of every car entering the airport grounds.

"They arrived . . ." Katte looked at his watch and calculated the time differential in his head. " . . . around three hours ago."

"Call me back, when you find something out." J.T. hoped they had taken a flight and were currently in the air. Then he could arrange to meet them when they landed and take them into custody. It was possible his career might be salvaged.

It wasn't even fifteen minutes later when Katte called back. "J.T., we found them. They left on an American flight, and get this, it's going to Chicago."

"What's the number of the flight?" J.T. couldn't believe his luck.

"It's flight number 1118 and it arrives at nine thirty."

"Shit, that's less than ten minutes from now. Thanks, Katte, good work." J.T. slammed the phone down. "Do we have anybody at O'Hare?" The two agents in his office shrugged their shoulders. "Don't just sit there, get going. I need agents to meet flight 1118 American, now! Move it! Also, check out any cars registered to Marcus Merker and Paul Abnus, maybe they left a car at the airport." J.T. hastily grabbed his coat and headed out his office, grabbing agent Simmons on the way.

"Simmons, come with me. We're going to the airport."

The flight arrived on time, and the group had deplaned by the time the local authorities arrived at the gate. Checking the baggage area the local authorities were met by two agents. Agent Johnson called J.T. with the news. Simmons was making record time getting to the airport, but it appeared they had just missed them.

"Have all the cars and cabs checked. We'll be there in five minutes. Simmons, step on it!" J.T. realized there was no way to go faster; Simmons was maneuvering within the midmorning traffic flawlessly, and J.T. would have to accept that.

Agent Johnson contacted the toll booths of the airport and instructed them to hold all outgoing traffic until they arrived. The message was received and the people in the toll booths initially complied. However, after about one minute the first horns started to sound their displeasure. By the end of two minutes it was a symphony of horns. Shortly after the noise reached a fever pitch, the first toll booth person sent a motorist through his gate. Within seconds the booths were operational as usual. The cab with the group was through their toll booth and on their way downtown just as J.T. and Simmons reached the airport.

Agent Johnson and his partner were waiting for J.T. when he arrived at the outbound booths.

"Johnson, I thought I told you to hold the traffic until I arrived." J.T. was livid as he watched the traffic flow out of the airport.

"From what I can tell, there was nearly a riot, so they took it upon themselves to start letting the traffic through," Johnson said, shaking his head as he joined J.T., watching the traffic leave the confines of the airport.

Frustrated, J.T. blurted out, "Doesn't anyone follow orders

anymore?" He saw one of the agents about to speak. "You don't have to answer."

J.T. wanted to yell but he couldn't figure out where to place the blame. "Okay, we know they're here. Let's check all the downtown hotels. They'll have to have some identification, maybe we'll luck out. Also check out the address of this Paul Abnus, they might be going to his house. I want it monitored around the clock, and get a tap on the line. We have to get to these guys before Valentino does."

J.T. knew Valentino had been given a contract, but his sources couldn't identify the victim or victims. They also knew money had been transferred, which meant a hit was imminent. It could be any or all of the group. J.T. had to find them before Valentino, because once Valentino completed the job, he would be gone and with him, J.T.'s career.

The cab dropped Callison, Truelove, and Jasper off at the downtown Marriott, which was reasonably close to the AMA building on LaSalle Street, where Callison's meeting was scheduled for later that day. Maxine had told Callison she had made reservations for him at the Marriott, so that seemed a logical place to go.

Peter and Paul would meet them later at Jerry's on Lincoln, a neighborhood bar where they could assemble and have a private conversation.

As they were about to enter the Marriott, Jasper grabbed Truelove's arm and pulled him back. "Look in the lobby over there." Jasper pointed at a figure through the glass window in the lobby of the hotel. Jasper squinted. "Isn't that one of the men who followed us to Phoenix?"

Both Truelove and Callison stopped and looked in the direction Jasper was pointing. "I can't tell for sure, but I think you're right. That does look like one of the men."

The traffic on the sidewalk was minimal, as the morning rush hour had subsided and the early lunch crowd had not yet started. They all looked toward the street, keeping their back to the lobby, and started to walk down the street away from the hotel.

"Maybe we should check into a different hotel, at least until

414

we can decide on our plan," Truelove suggested.

"Do either of you have any other fake identification?" Jasper asked.

"Why?" Truelove asked back.

"Because any hotel we register in will ask for identification and if they already followed us here . . . "

"Then they would probably find us easily, no matter what hotel we registered at." Callison finished Jasper's line of reasoning. "I have an idea." Callison removed his wallet from his back pocket and pulled out a card with a phone number scribbled on it. "This is the card of a policeman friend of Merker's. Maybe he can help us."

Callison called the home of Marvin Powell. Marvin's wife told them he was working at the police station at Foster and Damen.

"Before we visit Sergeant Powell, we have to do one more thing." Callison smiled. They walked up the block to the Chicago Hilton and Callison entered the lobby, followed by Truelove and Jasper. "I'm going to register here with my credit card. Maybe they'll spend their time staking out this hotel and we'll be elsewhere."

Jasper and Truelove both agreed with this tactic. The hotel was not filled, so they had no trouble getting a room with two double beds. After registering, the three of them got into a cab headed for the police station at Foster and Damen.

By the time they arrived at the police station it was late morning, and the station was bustling with business. Callison inquired at the front desk for Sergeant Powell and was instructed to follow the main hallway. His office was second door on the left. The sergeant was seated at his desk engrossed in his paperwork when they knocked on his door and entered. Powell looked over his reading glasses at the three men standing in front of him.

"Can I help you gentlemen?"

"We're looking for Sergeant Marvin Powell," Callison said.

"You found him. What can I do for you?"

"My name is Callison, we talked the other day."

"Callison? Oh yeah, Callison. Marcus' friend. Sit down." Powell smiled as they sat. There were two chairs situated in front of his desk. Truelove pulled over a third chair.

Callison started, "The other night you said you would help if you could. Well, we need help."

Powell stared at Callison, a penetrating stare. Then he got up from his seat. "Follow me, the walls have ears around here."

Powell led them down the hall to an empty interrogation room. They all entered and Powell placed an IN USE sign on the door before he closed it. "We can talk in here. Now what do you mean, you need my help?"

Callison started, but both Truelove and Jasper added their input as they told the story of the last twenty-four hours, including their latest concern about being followed all the way to Chicago.

"So how can I help?" Powell wasn't convinced, but he owed it to Marcus to hear them out.

"We have a plan, but we need to be safe and secure, at least until Thursday," Callison said. "We're concerned if we stay at a hotel we'll be found. Can you help us find a safe place to stay?".

Powell thought for a minute, then decided he would help. "Go to this address, it's my home. I'll call my wife so she'll be expecting you. You can be my guests for the next two nights."

Callison called Maxine before they went to Sergeant Powell's home. He wanted to call from a public phone, just in case her phone was tapped. Maxine asked if they could rendezvous before the meeting that afternoon with his subcommittee. She had some important information to tell him.

Callison left Truelove and Jasper with Marvin Powell's wife, Janet, while he went to meet Maxine. Maxine had left instructions for Callison to meet her at a small coffee shop a block away from the AMA office building. The lunch hour crowds had started to arrive by the time Callison got there.

The patrons were primarily from the downtown blue-collar work force: policemen, construction workers, cab drivers, and the like. Maxine was already seated in the back of the coffee shop and she stood and waved as Callison entered, to grab his attention. The grease spurting on the grill caught Callison's attention. It had been quite a while since he last frequented such a place.

Although the shop was air conditioned, the heat from the street mixed with the grill and the crowds made the temperature of the coffee shop uncomfortably warm. Callison sat at the table with Maxine who already had completed her glass of water.

"Why all the secrecy?" Callison asked.

"Margo's been busy, and I think you'll be shocked at what she's found." Maxine's face was somber and serious, not her usual chipper self.

Maxine handed Callison an envelope which he opened. It contained several copies of cashier's checks and a letter. Callison looked at the checks, which were all made out to Citizens for a Better Oregon. Each check was for a sum of $25,000 except for one check of $50,000. "What does this mean?" Callison was bewildered. He had no idea what this had to do with him or the committee.

"The Citizens for a Better Oregon is the group primarily responsible for funding the campaign of Nathan Slinger. Also see if you can read the name of the signature of the person who signed the check."

Callison hadn't looked at the signature until she mentioned it, but the name was one he was familiar with: Alan Smithee. "Where did you get this from?"

"You won't believe it." Maxine's eyes dilated as she spoke. "You remember the night at Dr. Rasta's house?" Callison didn't need to respond to that question, as Maxine continued. "Do you remember the rug in the study?"

Did he ever—the Oriental carpet they had made love on and had stained. "Yes, I recall an Oriental carpet." Callison fought to maintain a straight face.

"Under that rug was a floor safe. That's where Rasta kept this disk." Maxine lifted a disk from her lap. "Over a thousand names, many of whom you will recognize; it's called Gance."

"Are you telling me you got these from Rasta's house?"

"Exactly."

"How did you get this?"

"Margo. She said not to ask how, but we owe her." Maxine raised her eyebrow.

"I'll say." Callison's mind was swimming with possibilities.

417

With the information he had from Truelove and Jasper added to this, their case was getting some powerful teeth.

"Read the letter," Maxine suggested.

Callison pulled out the letter from the envelope and began to read.

Dear Dr. Smithee,

Thank you very much for your most generous contribution. The committee and I are both very fortunate to have such loyal supporters as yourself. I have received your list of prospects and believe we are in agreement. I am sure we can accommodate your needs and ours in ensuring a better tomorrow. Much work still needs to be done, but I believe we are well on the way.

Sincerely,
Nathan Slinger

Callison read the letter twice before he looked up at Maxine.

"The letter is dated the day after the fifty-thousand-dollar check was deposited. Two days after that the committee assignments were sent out of Slinger's office." Maxine peered at Callison, who was definitely jolted.

"I can see why you felt the urgency to talk to me." Callison's mind was racing.

The waitress came by, but left since they were still conversing.

"Could this mean Rasta is Smithee?" Callison's mind was only partially functioning, but the inference seemed to be there.

"I'm not sure; but if he isn't, it sure looks like he knows who Smithee is." Maxine answered. The waitress returned only to again be rebuffed.

"Also the disk is the original with the same protection as before. We can probably make a copy before our meeting if we leave now," Maxine suggested.

During the walk to her office on LaSalle Street, Callison was in a fog. He couldn't help but be distracted by the avalanche of information. When they reached the building, Maxine escorted Callison to the second floor where she knew they would have privacy and access to a computer. "You do have Herman's number, don't you?" Maxine asked.

"What? Who?" Callison tried to listen.

"Herman, your computer wizard. We need to call him." Maxine held Callison by the shoulders and looked him in the eyes as she spoke.

"Yes, I'll get Herman. You start up the computer." Callison took Herman's work number from his wallet and called.

Herman was at his desk when Callison called. Callison gave Maxine the phone and within five minutes they had a copy of the disk. They both thanked Herman and hung up.

Callison's curiosity was now raging. Who was on this disk? As with the Caldo list, the names were randomly listed, and there were a lot of names. Steven leaned over the back of Maxine's chair so he could read the list. He could feel her breath on his face and the smell of her perfume further distracted him. Scanning the list he noticed Rasta's name, and Robert Thornhill, but had difficulty concentrating.

Maxine twisted her neck to see if he was all right. He had been studying the list for several minutes without saying anything.

Callison finished studying the list. "It seems everybody's listed except McMillan and Jourge."

Maxine nodded.

Callison was relieved he didn't have to read the list any further, which allowed him to stand upright and keep his distance from Maxine's intoxicating scent.

Maxine told Callison, if she left now she could return the original disk to Margo, who could replace the disk before Rasta was aware it was ever gone. Callison thought this was a great idea. It would allow him time to clear his senses, plus this plan had previously worked with the Caldo list, which Margo had been able to replace without any difficulty.

The meeting with the subcommittee was scheduled to begin in a half hour on the fifth floor. Maxine had told Callison she would meet him there.

Both Susanna Michelson and Andrew Percy were in the room when Callison arrived. They were quietly talking while looking out at the street traffic.

Callison's mind was still reeling from his meeting with Maxine. The issue he needed to resolve was whether he could separate the Gance-Caldo list from the merger. Since almost the entire committee was on a list, it had to be more than a coincidence, but was it part of a larger plan? For Callison's part, he hadn't been aware of the list when he accepted the assignment. For all he knew neither were the others. So maybe the list wasn't a reason to sway his opinion on the merger. Maybe these were separate issues, only related by circumstances. But what about these circumstances: the deaths of Cisko and Merker; the lists; the tie with Rasta and Slinger; the men who chased him and Truelove and Jasper less than twenty four hours ago. Callison was very confused.

When Maxine entered the room, Callison suggested they get started. Jourge had asked Callison to discuss briefly the schedule of events for later that week. Callison used Jourge's instructions as an introduction. He explained that the reason for their meeting today was to formulate a consensus statement relative to the merger. If they were unsuccessful today they would reconvene tomorrow, because they needed a written statement for the meeting on Thursday. The Friday meeting was going to be a media circus, with representatives from every advocacy group dealing with health-care reform. The work would be done on Thursday, the show on Friday.

The meeting started with Percy rehashing his report from the last meeting. He again reviewed the statistics and trends, which all suggested the merger was, in his opinion, inevitable. He concluded the major reasons to push the merger at this point were twofold. First, there should be considerable cost savings by going to a single system for everyone. Second, it was a way to maintain the viability of the osteopathic schools as a training site for primary-care physicians.

Michelson's stance was much softer than the previous meeting. She again talked of a different philosophy that osteopathic medicine espoused, but was dismayed at the overall apathy she encountered when she approached the rank and file of the profession. In the end she agreed with Percy. If the merger could be shown to be cost effective, maybe it was time to recommend it.

420

Callison could see in her face that Michelson didn't totally believe the words she was saying, yet they were her words. When Andrew Taylor Still introduced the philosophy over a hundred years ago, it was in response to his disenchantment with how the public was being cared for by traditional medicine. He was sure Dr. Michelson could see some strong parallels between Still's time and today, and how the profession could flourish rather than perish with the right leadership.

Callison couldn't tell for sure, but he had his suspicions that both Percy and Michelson were not exactly speaking for themselves. What Callison still couldn't piece together was for who and why. Both Percy and Michelson had extremely successful careers; neither needed the power of another group. Why were they compromising? Could the list be that powerful a tool, to make these highly skilled professionals jeopardize a hundred-year-old profession so they could maintain their own status while sacrificing thousands of others? Or did they truly believe the inevitability of all this?

The "who" part really bothered Callison. Who was really behind all this? Rasta? Unlikely. What would he gain out of all this and why would he be willing to sacrifice the lives of others for the sake of a merger? No, there had to be someone else or another group that had another motive, a powerful motive to go to such lengths to structure this committee to their liking.

Callison decided to make the recommendation a consensus, with the stipulation that they could change their opinion pending the receipt of new information. He knew this decision would buy him some time, so he could try to make some sense out of this. By ending the meeting early, he still had ample time to meet with Truelove and Jasper to reevaluate their plan and make changes, if necessary.

Maxine asked if she could accompany Callison, but he thought it would be best if she kept her distance from him.

Callison hadn't noticed anyone following him, but he had a strong feeling he was not alone. He now had to think of a way to return to Sergeant Powell's home without including his pursuers in the process.

39

Smithee hung up the phone, irritated and annoyed. How dare they call him to remind him of the importance of the recommendations coming forth from Friday's committee meeting! Smithee had worked for months setting the entire scenario and had as much to lose as anyone if it didn't go as planned.

It was just a little more than ten years since Smithee had been approached by L. Gorman Tuttle, king of the Overlords, with an offer he couldn't refuse. Tuttle had put together a business proposition with which they could become rich beyond their dreams. Tuttle had the knowledge of how the governmental bureaucracy functioned, and how to survive and even thrive within the mazes of red tape. Smithee had the knowledge of how the medical community functioned and through the Gance organization had insight and influence over many of the top physicians in the country. By combining their resources, they created a new order in the business of medicine. Both Tuttle and Smithee invested most of their own resources into the business. All was going well—extremely well, and then came health-care reform.

Tuttle would frequently quote Thomas Starzl, "All triumphs in medicine are the forgotten sorrows of past days." Then he would talk of the progress medical science has made in the treatment of heart disease, kidney failure, organ transplants, and various infectious diseases. Tuttle would then paraphrase the Starzl quote, "All triumphs in medicine are the financial sorrows of those who never tried." Tuttle would then discuss in great length the struggles of the individuals whose research and vision created the monumental breakthroughs, usually rewarding those individuals with fame and fortune. It was the fortune part of the equation Tuttle was most interested in, and it was the new health-care reform that would either make or break his chance at the golden ring.

As a result of decreasing governmental dollars and increasing governmental restrictions, Tuttle discovered there was a void in the research community. Tuttle was able to marry private industry with bureaucracy and, for a piece of the action, he was in business. What Tuttle needed to expand his business was a large referral base to bring together the medical community and the public. Smithee had the resources to accomplish that. Everything was going well, until some of the new powers in health-care reform decided to attack businesses such as Tuttle's, stating conflict of interest among other reasons, while simultaneously forcing legislation to disband them. One such power was a Senator Hargrove from Michigan, whose untimely death almost canceled the efforts dealing with conflict of interest issues. But others had taken the torch, and one in particular was in a position to force the legislation and thus destroy Tuttle and Smithee.

Smithee did not need Tuttle's reminder as to the importance of the recommendation of the committee. He was well aware Tuttle had invested millions in the Gance organization, for which he expected the organization to use its vast resources in both the medical and legal communities. Smithee had his contingency plan in place, and assured Tuttle he had nothing to be concerned about.

Callison took the long way to the Powell residence. He was concerned about the possibility of being followed, so he changed cabs, interspersed with a stop at a hotel.

While at the hotel, Callison decided to call Natalie, who should be safe at her friend's home in Denver.

"Hello, Linda, this is Steven. Is Natalie there?" It had been hectic and Callison felt guilty he hadn't called earlier.

"She's right here, let me get her."

"Thanks, Linda." The relief was noticeable in his voice.

"Hi, hon."

"I take it you had no problems with your flight?"

"Everything was fine, no problems at all. How was yours?"

Callison decided not to tell her about the people waiting for them at the hotel. There was no reason to concern her any more than she already was. "Our flight was okay. You didn't notice anyone following you?"

"No, Steven, no one followed me. But I do have some news for you." Natalie's voice sounded cheery. "I think Linda and I have figured out part of your puzzle."

"What are you talking about?"

"I'd rather not tell you until tomorrow, but we have an idea what the riddle means and who Aselwood R Loax is. I hope you don't mind that I showed Linda the riddle. You know she was always so good at those type of things."

Callison couldn't decide whether he should be angry or grateful, but he doubted they could possibly figure out what the riddle meant. "Fine, when you figure it out call me. Wait a minute, that's not such a good idea. I'il call you back tomorrow."

"Okay. We should have the answer to the riddle by then." Natalie said confidently.

"I'll call you tomorrow. Good night." Callison was agitated, probably because his wife was having fun without him and he was having no fun at all.

The remainder of the trek to Powell's house took an additional forty minutes as Callison made one more stop, just as a precautionary measure. The added time and expense was worth the effort in the event he was being followed. Since he noticed no one, he felt safe when the cab pulled up to Powell's home on Mozart Street.

As Callison entered the home of Marvin Powell, he didn't notice the car slowly pull around the corner. The infrared binoculars allowed them to follow Callison's every move from a safe distance, without being noticed. The agents in the car were given specific instructions not to intervene unless they thought someone was endangered. Otherwise, they needed to be invisible. J.T.'s plan was once again in motion, his career once again given a breath of life. If Valentino was to make a move against Callison or Truelove or Jasper, they would be there, and J.T. would be the one responsible for his capture. They knew from their source within Valentino's organization that a hit had been ordered and was imminent, but they didn't know the mark. J.T. had to cover all the potential victims he could think of. Callison, Truelove, and Jasper were just three of many J.T. was watching.

It was a little after nine when Callison, Truelove, and Jasper entered Jerry's watering hole on Lincoln. The bar was crowded and there was a large group of rowdies huddled around the pool table where a hotly contested match was ongoing. In the corner beyond the smoke, Truelove noticed Peter and Paul sitting and sipping their beer, quietly talking.

The table was only large enough to accommodate four comfortably, but they squeezed all five around the table. The smoke was annoying, and Truelove asked if there was a no-smoking area. Peter and Paul escorted them to another room where the smoke was tolerable and the noise level was markedly diminished. Paul returned with their pitcher of beer, and the waitress said she would bring clean glasses to their new table. Peter also asked for a new bowl of peanuts.

The conversation lasted only a few minutes before Callison asked Peter and Paul what they had found out. They couldn't prove it conclusively, but they surmised that the men who had followed them were either FBI or CIA. They also found out that there was a rumor on the street that the mob was somehow involved. Callison asked them to explain what they meant by all this. Peter tried to explain that if the list was revealed it could ruin the careers of many prominent people and therefore the powers behind the list would do whatever was necessary to make sure that didn't happen. So they concluded there were at least two groups who wanted their files; the Feds and the other guys.

Truelove and Jasper, meanwhile, had met with Foster Ehrlich, the past president of the AOA, who had visited with Callison in Texas. Jasper knew Ehrlich from the old days and they hoped he might be able to help shed some light on who was behind this and what was their motive. Instead, they were given a totally new perspective on their friend, Steven Callison. Ehrlich told them about his meeting with Callison and his plea for support. He explained about the Hayes Bill and its possible

425

ramifications on the profession. Ehrlich then told them of Callison's reticence to cooperate, in spite of his own personal plea, as well as that of his old roommate. Finally, Ehrlich told them of the ongoing investigations involving not only Callison, but the other osteopathic members on his committee.

Ehrlich's research had found that almost every member on the committee had a reason to be in the pocket of the AMA. Specifically, Callison's reason was a Primary Care Preventative Medicine Grant for which he had applied but hadn't been funded. The grant was currently under reconsideration, with the funding possibly dependent on the outcome of the committee.

In parting, Ehrlich warned them to be wary of Callison.

Neither Jasper or Truelove mentioned the details of their conversation with Ehrlich. They only stated he was of little help. Before they could confide anything to Callison, they needed some assurances, and even then they would be skeptical.

As Truelove completed his short report on his meeting with Ehrlich, he asked a question. "Why are you doing this?"

Jasper was the first to answer. "I do care about the osteopathic profession, since it gave me the opportunity to become a physician, but the reason I'm pursuing this to the end is out of respect for Jonas Cisko. He was a great man, and if his death was because of some conspiracy, then I'll do what I can to expose his killers."

Peter followed Jasper. "I think I can talk for Paul also. Whoever killed Marcus Merker will pay, and we'll do whatever we have to find and avenge his death."

Paul finished his glass of beer and simply said. "Ditto."

Truelove was the next to speak. "As strongly as you feel about Dr. Cisko and Merker, that's how I feel about Amos Wilcox. Amos was my partner. Over twenty-five years ago he died, and I believe he was murdered, possibly by the same people who did Cisko and Merker, and I did nothing. I hid. But I'm not hiding anymore, I'm with the rest of you. I'm in it until it's over."

All eyes then fixed on Callison. Truelove and Jasper had planned this and were anxious to hear his answer. Callison on the other hand, had heard all their explanations, while he wondered what he was doing there. He didn't have a mentor or partner to avenge. His reason was just as personal but not as well defined.

Callison poured himself a glass of beer and took a swig before he started. "My reason is not as clear-cut as yours. All my life I wanted to be a doctor, and the osteopathic profession gave me that opportunity, for which I'll always be grateful. Like any organization it isn't perfect, not by a long shot, but it's a survivor. I promised myself when I graduated I would try to give back to the profession. And I think I did. I've been active in teaching medical students and residents, active on committees when asked, and always tried to do the best job I could.

"Then came this opportunity, which came at a period in my professional career when I needed to be rejuvenated. The more I learned of the committee and its potential impact on medicine in general and osteopathic medicine specifically, the more nervous I became. The responsibility of this committee could quite literally change the face of osteopathic medicine forever."

The group stared at Callison, who had stopped to scan the room. "Today my subcommittee voted to recommend merging the two professions."

"As usual, conventional wisdom has it wrong," Truelove said as he looked at Jasper.

"I've debated with myself," Callison said. "Confided in a few others whom I truly respect, but still couldn't come to a concrete decision. The words of a friend of mine continue to haunt me, and I really don't know what to do. His words were simply, 'first do no harm.' But I'm still not sure—which way does the least harm? I've been told that if a merger doesn't take place, a number of our physicians taking care of Medicaid patients will be denied access to their patients."

"You're talking about the Omnibus Reconciliation Act. That will never go," Truelove said with staunch conviction.

"I hope you're right, but as of now I believe it's still on the books. If the merger were to take place, the act would be voided because we would all be grandfathered in."

"Good point! Never thought of it that way." Truelove nodded.

"Anyway, there's another issue called the Hayes Bill. This one is more secretive, but I believe it states that all physicians with less than three years post-graduate training would not be able to take care of government-sponsored patients, which as we all know may be virtually everybody in the near future, unless they practiced in an area of need. Thus many of our family practitioners would lose their practices and would either have to get additional training or be relocated to an area of need."

Truelove and Jasper looked at each other, bewildered. If Callison couldn't be trusted, why was he saying all this? Truelove still wanted Callison to answer his original question. "So why are you doing this?"

"I told you my answer was not as straightforward as yours, I'm getting to it." Callison's thoughts were crystallizing and he hoped he would be able to clearly express them. "The reason I agreed to vote for the merger today was to buy time until I could reach my final decision. I knew if I went the other way, I would be barraged by members of the committee trying to convince me to reverse my decision. This seemed the best approach for the time being."

"So by agreeing to support the merger, you thought it would be easier to change your mind than if you opposed it?" Jasper said. He still had his doubts.

"Correct. Not necessarily easier but less controversial, at least for now."

"If you say so." Jasper still wasn't convinced. "But I'd imagine you'd cause a significant amount of controversy if you changed your mind and came out against the merger at the last second."

"No doubt about it. But if I do that, I'll have more ammunition than I currently have and hopefully will be able to convince others to agree with me." Callison picked up a peanut, shelled it and swallowed.

"I'm sorry, I don't get it. What ammunition?" Truelove still felt he hadn't the answer he wanted from Callison.

"Okay, I'll explain. The reason I'm here tonight is for my own self-esteem and pride. I might have kidded myself all these years, but I think I'm honestly looking at myself now. Back in college I made a huge mistake, one that I have never really come to grips with. I've often, hell, *always* taken the path of least resistance, and for the most part have done fairly well with that approach. When I critically analyzed why I was chosen for this committee, I realized it wasn't for my knowledge or insight into the area. Others have more experience, are brighter, and have more insight, but I have one thing they don't have. I have a strong track record for taking the path of least resistance, and in this case that is to acquiesce in favor of the merger. They knew I would, and that's why I was chosen."

"So are you saying you're not in favor of the merger?" Truelove asked, still confused.

"No, what I said earlier is the truth. I'm still not sure. To disagree for the wrong reason could possibly be worse than acquiescing. What I decided, was to try to build a case which will allow me to change my mind using facts not fiction. This is where I need all your help."

"I'm not sure I follow, but continue," Truelove said.

"I have a plan which might get all of us what we want out of this mess. It might implicate the people responsible for the deaths of Jonas Cisko and Marcus Merker, while justifying the cause that Amos Wilcox might have died for."

"So let's hear this plan," Paul said as he grabbed a handful of peanuts.

Callison scanned the crowd around the pool table. They were even more raucous than before. Their table was isolated enough to insure a modicum of privacy, which seemed sufficient since no one had paid any attention to them at all. "My plan is based on the assumption that Victor Rasta is the key player in this whole deal. My reason for saying this is based on some fairly substantial documentation." Callison then reviewed the details from the Wilcox letter, the files from Mrs. Tatum, and the new information about his ties with Nathan Slinger, which put Rasta in the middle of this. Callison withheld his information about the Caldo list, since he was attempting to do this without decimating his own career.

"Okay, let's say we agree Rasta's a critical part of all of this. What's the plan?" Jasper was starting to believe Callison was forthright and wanted to hear his strategy.

Callison continued with his plan. The premise was to pit Van Gregory against Rasta, hoping Rasta would crack and be willing to turn on Gregory to save himself. Callison reasoned, if Rasta feared Gregory would turn on him, then Rasta would probably give up Gregory to save himself. The key was the ability to offer Rasta a deal that would offer him some protection, but only if he disclosed the details of the conspiracy.

The group asked how they could offer any deal to Rasta.

Callison expected the question. "The men who have been chasing us are either CIA or FBI. Right?" They all nodded. "I'll let them catch me at the Marriott. Whoever they are, hopefully they will have the authority to offer Rasta a deal." Callison realized this wasn't the only solution but it was the best he could think of.

They discussed the other options at their disposal, but agreed to try Callison's plan. This plan did not put either Callison or his career on the line and thus if it didn't succeed, he would not be any worse off than he was now. In this plan, Callison didn't have to force the merger situation, and if it made sense to support the merger he still had the option to do that. If, on the other hand, Rasta revealed that the conspiracy existed, that would most likely result in having to curtail any further discussion about the merger until everything could be sorted out.

They agreed to try Callison's plan and reconvene the next night to see where they were. Truelove and Jasper were to return to Florida to see if they missed anything that could help make their case.

Peter and Paul had an idea of how to get to Gregory, as well as send a message to Rasta. If their plan worked both Rasta and Gregory would be pitted against one another.

Callison, on the other hand, had to find out who these other people were. He knew this was risky, but felt it was a risk he needed to take. Once Callison found them, assuming they were from some type of government agency, he then had to convince them that Rasta was responsible for the conspiracy, in order for his plan to work. Callison hoped he had enough information to convince them, but if he didn't, maybe Truelove and Jasper could find another piece of the puzzle in Florida.

Before they left, they agreed to meet at Peter Moiner's home at nine on Wednesday, at which time Truelove and Jasper would call from Florida so they could formulate their new plan.

40

Wednesday, the day before the group meeting. Callison had a full agenda. First he would accompany Truelove and Jasper to the airport. Meanwhile, Peter and Paul were working on their plan to undermine Van Gregory.

Peter and Paul offered to take Truelove and Jasper to the airport, but Callison persuaded them to initiate their plan, since time was at a premium. The taxi let Truelove and Jasper off at O'Hare with plenty of time to spare for their flight to Fort Lauderdale.

On the return ride downtown, Callison thought he noticed a blue sedan following him, but he couldn't tell for sure, and at this point he really didn't care. The taxi let him off at the Marriott. The lobby was virtually empty when Callison approached the reception desk.

The reservation was initially made for Tuesday through Friday, and Callison had to explain to the front desk clerk why he hadn't canceled the previous night. From the corner of his eye, Callison noticed a man watching the interchange. The person watching them was wearing khaki pants and a navy blue, short sleeve shirt. Callison thought he must be with some governmental service.

As Callison walked across the lobby toward the elevator bank, he felt the man's eyes following him. Callison pressed the up button on the elevator panel. While waiting for the elevator he turned and stared directly at the man. Callison thought it comical that he caused this professional to become uncomfortable. The man first looked away, in a natural manner, but Callison continued to stare. When the man again looked in his direction, Callison smiled at him. The man again looked away, this time for a more protracted period, and when he again looked in the direction of the elevators Callison was gone.

The man in the navy shirt approached the elevator bank studying the elevator he believed Callison had taken. He talked into a walkie-talkie to his partner on the fourteenth floor who was awaiting Callison's arrival. He never noticed Callison sneak behind him from the opposite direction. Callison had walked around the elevator shaft and was able to position himself directly behind the man while he was speaking on his walkie-talkie. If Callison startled him, he didn't show it, he just glared coldly.

"We have to talk," Callison said to the man in the navy shirt.

"We do, do we? And who are you? Do I know you?" The glare was still there.

An awkward pause was interrupted by a static voice transmitting on the walkie-talkie. The glare faded and a half smile took its place. The man mumbled something into the walkie-talkie and then turned it off. "Come with me," he said as he led Callison to a lounge off the lobby.

They sat at a table. Since the lounge was officially closed this early in the morning, it would afford them the privacy they needed.

"Who are you?" Callison asked.

"My name is Roberts." The intensity with which he carried himself made Callison uncomfortable.

"I mean, who do you work for?"

Roberts hesitated, squinting his left eye. "I'm not sure what you mean."

"I think you do. What organization do you work for?" Callison asked.

They were joined by another man. This man was dressed in a plaid sports coat and plain white shirt. He approached the table where they were seated. "Hello, Dr. Callison, my name is Clark Grimes."

Callison shook his hand as Grimes took a seat at their table.

"Can you tell me who you work for?" Callison was not going to say anything of any significance until he saw some identification.

"We're FBI," Grimes stated, matter-of-factly.

"Got any ID?" Callison believed him, but also wanted to see his identification.

Both Roberts and Grimes showed Callison their ID's. The badges looked official but Callison knew he wouldn't be able to distinguish between a real ID and a fake.

"I wonder if you'd mind coming with us. We have someone who would like to speak to you," Grimes said as he stood and backed away from the table.

Callison had committed to see this to the end. "Okay, let's go," Callison said and they left. His plan was now in motion.

They drove to a three-story walk up off Clark Street. The neighborhood was primarily residential, and the morning traffic was now merging with the early lunch-hour crowd. Roberts told Callison to stand away from the door of the building as Grimes placed a plastic card into a slot by the door and then punched in a code into the panel adjacent to the slot. The door automatically opened. It was apparent this was not an ordinary door: it was at least six inches thick and opened slowly as if it were on a hydraulic system.

They entered a foyer and were greeted by another man, who frisked Callison. After he declared Callison safe, he opened the far door, using a remote control unit. This door led to a stairway that they climbed to the third floor and entered the first door on the left.

The room contained a wooden table and six chairs, and a mirror on the east wall. Seated at the head of the table was a man who stood as they entered the room. He was wearing a plain gray suit and an extra-wide tie that appeared to be a leftover from the sixties.

"Hello, I'm Agent Tartorino—but everybody calls me J.T. Please have a seat, Dr. Callison."

Callison sat at the table, as did Grimes and Roberts. Before he sat, J.T. asked if anyone would like something to drink. They all declined and J.T. then took his seat.

"You've been quite a busy man lately, Doctor. Would you mind if I called you Steven?" J.T. smiled at Callison as he asked the question.

Callison was not a formal type of person. "No, not at all."

434

"Steven, we have a good idea what you're up to and we need your help." J.T. leaned his forearms on the table with his hands clasped.

"If you know what I'm up to, why would you need my help?"

J.T. pressed a button on a recorder he had in front of him. Callison heard his voice as well as the voices of Truelove, Jasper, Peter, and Paul. Somehow J.T. had obtained a complete tape of their conversation at Jerry's on Lincoln. Callison reflected on what was actually said and just as important, what he didn't say, specifically his involvement with the Caldo list.

Callison was impressed with the clarity of the recording. J.T. asked Callison about the Wilcox letter, the files from Mrs. Tatum, and the information he had on Nathan Slinger. The information on Slinger intrigued J.T. the most. Callison felt if they could tape a conversation in a loud, crowded bar then they could easily obtain the information he had on these topics, so he cooperated.

"Will you be able to get us a copy of the files and the letters?" J.T. asked. He told Callison they would be taping their conversation. Since he had nothing to hide, Callison agreed.

"I think I can manage a copy of the letter and the files." Callison hoped if he cooperated now, they would cooperate when he suggested his plan.

"Your plan to confront Rasta. Exactly how were you planning to do this?" J.T. asked.

"I'll tell him I have proof Van Gregory was involved in the deaths of Jonas Cisko and Marcus Merker. Then I'll tell him, Gregory has implicated him in these deaths. Hopefully that will get Rasta's attention, then I'll say I've been approached by men who had worked with Merker and warned that both Rasta and myself were targeted by Van Gregory.

"What proof do you have to say that?" J.T. knew Gregory by reputation only, but he had trouble believing this tactic would work.

"None really, but if he's guilty, he won't know that. If he's innocent, he won't know what I'm talking about."

"He won't buy that, it's way too thin." J.T. shook his head and looked at Roberts, who was likewise shaking his head.

"What I'm hoping for, is that because I know about their deaths and also his involvement, which will so upset him, he'll believe whatever else I say implicitly. Plus, we have another source who'll get a message to Rasta that Gregory's after him."

"Too risky." J.T. was concerned Rasta and/or Gregory could interfere with his apprehension of Valentino.

"Well, do you have a better idea?"

"Yes, I do. Remember I said we needed your help? Well, what I am about to tell you is highly classified. Do you understand?" J.T. spoke slowly and waited for Callison to acknowledge before he would continue.

J.T. stopped and looked at Roberts. "Will you please tell Martinez to bring them in."

Agent Roberts left the room and returned in a few minutes followed by two men.

The first man was dressed impeccably wearing a three-piece suit, the other man wore a simple sport coat. J.T. introduced them: the one in the three-piece suit was named Garrison Hammer, an attorney, and the man in the sport coat was named Harris Terbanion, who was a physician. Both men appeared in their forties, maybe early fifties, both were neatly groomed, but Hammer carried himself more stately, like a dignitary or celebrity.

"By the way, Dr. Terbanion is also a DO," J.T. mentioned. A brief conversation ensued between Callison and Terbanion.

Once they agreed on several DO's they both knew, J.T. intervened. "The reason I wanted you to meet these gentlemen is to show you the depth and seriousness of this situation."

J.T. motioned with his hand, as if he were introducing Hammer to center stage. Hammer followed his lead and stood at the head of the table, leaning on his hands while watching Callison.

"J.T. allowed us to hear the tape and we need to fill you in on some details, to avoid you or anyone else possibly getting hurt." Hammer stood upright and slowly walked around the table as he continued to talk. His posture was perfect. "I worked for Senator Douglas Hargrove of Michigan, do you know of him?"

Callison knew he heard that name, but his mind had blanked it out. "The name sounds familiar."

"Senator Hargrove was a good man, maybe a great one," Hammer said.

"And a good friend of our profession," Terbanion added.

"Anyway he died several months ago," Hammer said. "The cause of his death was officially noted as due to a pulmonary embolism, but we think differently. The autopsy was inconclusive, and the possibility of foul play was considered. I personally took the responsibility for the subsequent investigation, because I not only worked for the senator but was a very close friend, as was Harris." Hammer nodded in the direction of Terbanion.

Harris nodded his head in agreement.

"To make a very long story short, after the senator's death I hired a private detective to investigate the circumstances surrounding his death. This detective unfortunately had a fatal boating accident. This so-called accident just increased my suspicions. I hired another detective to investigate further. His investigation resulted in a wild goose chase, involving a very prominent family in the state of Michigan. I realized at that time, this was way above my head. So, I contacted a friend in the Justice Department, who introduced me to Agent Tartorino. Combining our information led us to a former aide of the senator's. His name is Lance Darby. After the senator's death, Mr. Darby was hired by another senator, Nathan Slinger."

Callison looked toward the ceiling and bit his lower lip.

"I know you have information about Senator Slinger and Rasta; hopefully this will help you make up your mind. Anyway, we have reason to believe Mr. Darby had been working for Slinger long before Senator Hargrove's death." Hammer stopped and looked at J.T. "Can I show him the pictures?"

J.T. nodded and handed a packet of photographs to Callison. The photos were pictures of two men talking at various places, a park, a McDonald's, a lobby of a hotel, etc.

"I take it these men are Darby and Slinger," Callison asked.

"Correct. Anyway, from the dates on some of the photos, it can be appreciated they were taken long before the death of Senator Hargrove."

"So?" Callison was growing impatient.

"So, this documents the connection between Darby and

437

Slinger occurred before the death of Senator Hargrove."

Even if he wasn't told, Callison would have guessed Hammer's profession, by his repetitive, seemingly inane statements. "So they knew each other," Callison said sarcastically.

Hammer then slid another packet of pictures across the table, Callison stopping them before they hit the floor.

"Look at them," Hammer barked.

Callison opened this packet. They were pictures of men meeting, only this time he recognized the men. There were pictures of Darby, but this time he was meeting with Victor Rasta, while the last few pictures featured a Rasta and Slinger meeting.

"A *ménage à trois*." Suddenly Callison wasn't as impatient. He looked up at Hammer, who was standing at the far end of the table.

"Look at the dates on the photos in which Rasta and Slinger are meeting. Then compare those dates with the canceled checks you have signed by Alan Smithee. Each check is dated within one to three days from the time Rasta met with Slinger."

"Slow down. You're losing me. What's the significance of that?" Callison could sense this was important, but couldn't tie it together.

"In our investigation we were able to trace some of these checks to a Swiss account, while others went to Slinger's reelection fund. What we can't prove is who issued the checks. But it seems more than a coincidence that a check was deposited after each meeting between Rasta and Slinger, with the largest amount being deposited before the committee was selected."

"Okay, I'm with you so far," Callison said.

"What we have is Darby working for Hargrove and possibly for Rasta and/or Slinger. Then we have large sums of money deposited into an account that supports Slinger's campaign or his secret Swiss account, and then we have your committee being formed with most, if not all, its members being on a special list. Yes, we know about the list."

Callison could feel much of his confidence fade.

"So now comes the good part. J.T., do you want to do the honors?" Hammer grinned at J.T.

J.T. cleared his throat before he started. "Ever since the

death of Senator Hargrove, we have been investigating the possibility of the senator having been assassinated. We have been able to trace a check originating from the same account, which had previously sent money to Slinger. But this new check had transferred funds to an account in the Caymans. This account, we believe, is the one used by Valentino." J.T. waited for a reaction, but there was none.

Callison threw his hands in the air. "I take it I'm supposed to know who Valentino is?"

"Valentino is only the preeminent assassin in the world," J.T. said.

"Oh," Callison said, mildly embarrassed.

"A week before the death of Senator Hargrove we traced a sizable deposit into Valentino's Cayman account. At the time we didn't put the death of the senator together with Valentino, but now we are very suspicious. We have been a step behind Valentino for over a decade and we think Valentino is about to strike again."

"Really?" Callison asked.

"Several days ago another million was deposited, and our sources indicate something is about to go down. Our problem is we don't know who, when, or where. Only it's soon, real soon."

"So you think Valentino is going to kill someone associated with the committee?" Callison finally put the pieces together.

"We're almost positive. That's why we have been monitoring all the key players on the committee. If Valentino strikes, we want to be there to get Valentino before the hit is history." J.T. leaned back in his chair, confident he had Callison convinced.

"So where do I fit into this?" Callison was interested, but wasn't about to volunteer for anything.

"We know Rasta is part of all this, but we don't know who Smithee is. We have followed Rasta closely and still can't locate Smithee. If Smithee is calling the shots, Rasta has to be in close contact and we need someone on the inside."

"So you think Rasta is the front man for Smithee?"

"Yes, we believe that, but we can't prove it. That's where you come in."

439

"How exactly do you want me to help?" Callison said reluctantly.

"First, can you fill us in on your plan and what exactly Truelove and Jasper are doing in Florida and what Peter and Paul are going to do with Van Gregory?"

Callison could see no harm in explaining their plan, as J.T. knew most of it anyway. He filled them in on the details. J.T. told Callison that Truelove and Jasper were wasting their time in Florida. They had already found all there was to be found, and the FBI already had Gregory in custody for questioning. They were planning to keep him there until they either had something to charge him with or the meeting was over.

"What we'd like you to do, is to confront Rasta with the pictures, the files, and the list," J.T. said.

This was exactly what Callison wanted to avoid doing. Once he did this, there was no retreat. His career would be on the line, and that was not an option he desired. If he pressed the issue, Rasta would most likely threaten to take Callison and many other innocent physicians with him. "What if I refuse?"

"We would prefer you didn't. You see this a federal investigation involving the possible assassination of a senator of the United States. You don't want to obstruct justice, do you?" J.T. was serious in his manner, but kept his voice controlled.

Callison knew the path of least resistance was to submit to J.T.'s request, but he decided to question their logic. "If I do as you ask and if Rasta is as involved, I've effectively ruined my career and for what?"

"Why do you think your career would be ruined?" Terbanion said.

"Once I accuse Rasta as a possible conspirator, he will probably react by at least exposing the Caldo list, which will place many DO careers in jeopardy, including myself. The information on Senator Slinger is all circumstantial, although suggestive, and to be accusing one of the most powerful senators in the country of manipulating the health-care reform initiative, we better have a good reason why."

"Did you ever hear of the Hargrove Bill?" Hammer asked.

"Yes. I've heard of it." Callison recalled his conversation with

Foster Ehrlich and the discussion about both the Hargrove and Hayes Bills.

"Then you're aware the bill died the day Senator Hargrove died." Callison nodded. "There were several others who supported the concept of the bill, but none with enough clout or grit to carry on the fight." Hammer repositioned himself in his chair. "Enter center stage Senator Hayes, whose bill will have the opposite effect. We know several powerful lobbies have contributed heavily to Hayes' campaign. His bill will change the flow of dollars from one self-interest group to another, without regard to what might be best for the country."

Terbanion interjected. "There's a point that needs to be emphasized. What they're doing is wrong. You know it and so do they. You're a professional, which means you can do your best work, even when you don't feel like it. Are you going to let them get away with this?"

Callison couldn't help but fixate on Hammer. "I'm not as convinced as you. I can still see both points of view, and yet emotionally I want to support our profession."

"Then do it!" Terbanion said.

While Callison, Terbanion, and Hammer continued their debate, J.T. was quietly having a conversation with agent Roberts. After several minutes of whispered dialogue, Roberts left the room, only to return several minutes later.

Roberts whispered something into J.T.'s ear while the debate continued between Callison and Terbanion.

"Excuse me, gentlemen, may I interrupt?" J.T. stood at the end of the table and slowly walked toward the door, where he stood holding the knob. "I find the conversation interesting but not very productive. If I might suggest an alternative: Dr. Callison, I have one other person I would like to introduce you to."

J.T. deliberately opened the door. Standing in the doorway was an image Callison thought he would never see again, Marcus Merker. Merker smiled as he entered the room. Callison rose from his chair to greet him. They shook hands and then hugged.

"What's going on?" Callison couldn't believe his eyes. Merker's death had upset him to a far greater extent than he had imagined. Now that Merker was alive Callison didn't know if he should be overjoyed or indignant, because he had been duped.

Merker explained the reason for his sham death. J.T. had been working with Merker indirectly on the case when J.T. learned Merker was being followed. They discussed their options and decided on faking Merker's death, which would have several benefits. First, he would no longer be followed but would be able to help in the investigation. Second, his death should be a stimulus for Callison to remain involved. Third, the FBI wanted Merker under their control and used the obstruction of justice scheme with him just as they did with Callison.

"So you planned your death to keep me interested in this." Callison didn't take Merker's remarks as a compliment.

J.T. needed to redirect the conversation back to the original topic. "Dr. Callison, Mr. Merker has been watching our discussion through that two-way mirror over there." J.T. pointed to the mirror. "I think it might be beneficial for all of us to hear his point of view."

Merker smiled: it was a smile but wasn't a smile, all at the same time. "My point of view, huh?"

"We need to hear your opinion, please." J.T. couldn't afford to alienate Merker.

"All right, what I see is the FBI needing to find this guy Smithee, which will allow them to get to Valentino." J.T. protruded his lower lip and nodded. "And I think what the doc needs is a way to protect himself, yet help you, and possibly help his profession."

"Is that pretty accurate?" Terbanion asked of both J.T. and Callison.

Neither Callison nor J.T. said anything.

"Since nobody's saying anything, I must be in the ballpark. If Dr. Callison agrees to what you asked, he needs some kind of assurance that he'll be protected," Merker said while looking at Callison.

"What kind of assurance?" J.T. asked, turning his attention toward Callison.

"If I approach Rasta with the files and the pictures, what do I say when he comes back with the Caldo list?" Callison was still concerned about the list becoming public.

"We'll do what we can to prevent the list from hurting you or your profession," J.T. said.

"I'll also do what I can to help you," Hammer said.

"Can I have a moment alone with Mr. Merker?" Callison asked.

They left the room leaving only Merker and Callison.

"Okay, what is it?" Merker appeared a little agitated.

"They're probably watching us right now, aren't they?" Callison asked.

Merker nodded.

"What do you really think I should do?"

"You're the only one who can answer that. Without you they'll have to come up with a different plan. They've removed me from most of what's going on, but I can tell you Truelove and Jasper really had them going. Whatever you did caused them to pucker their behinds." Merker grinned.

"I really don't see a way out other than to cooperate," Callison said, waiting for Merker to contradict him.

"Like I said before, this is your call. You have to follow what's best for you. Once this is over, they'll all be gone and there will only be you. When you look in the mirror, you have to feel you did what was best for you. Once you decided that, it really doesn't matter what they say or think."

"I guess you're right," Callison said despondently, looking down at the floor.

"Don't let them force you into something you really don't believe in or want to do."

"I won't." Callison looked up from the floor toward Merker.

"My father told me this story of a cat he had when he was a kid. One day the cat jumped on a hot oven burner, the cat learned from that experience and never jumped on a hot burner again— but that cat never jumped on a cold burner either." Merker winked at Callison.

Callison knew Merker was probably aware of his past and how he was burned by his college misadventure. Since then he hadn't returned to a burner, either hot or cold. Maybe it was time to try again.

"One last question" Callison said. "Do you think I'll be in any danger?"

"I'm not sure but I'd say you'll be in some danger. Possibly a lot. People have died, maybe even murdered, and millions of dollars are at stake. You're definitely taking a risk."

Callison thought to himself, *why should I take this kind of risk? What is in it for me?* The only answer he could come up with was, he had to look at himself in the mirror.

"By the way, that cat story, isn't that a Mark Twain story?" Callison asked of Merker.

"Could be, but I heard it from my old man. Anyway who cares?"

Callison approached the mirror and said it was all right for them to enter. After no response, he opened the door. To his surprise they were all congregated in the hall. He knew that his discussion with Merker was probably taped, but it was a nice gesture to give the appearance that they had been allowed some privacy.

Callison told them he would do what they asked. They also asked him to wear a wire so they could tape his conversation with Rasta. Roberts fitted Callison with the wire and J.T. gave him his instructions. It was time to go to work.

41

The drive to Victor Rasta's home was entirely different in the daylight. Maybe it was because Callison was now driving, or he was without the distraction of Maxine, but the trip seemed much longer. During the drive he kept thinking about what he was going to say, how he would broach the subject and how he would handle Rasta's retaliation.

Rasta was waiting as Callison pulled up in his rental car. Rasta's greeting was cordial, which was not unexpected since all he had been told was that they had to meet before the group meeting scheduled for the morning.

Rasta offered Callison some refreshment. He declined, and they retreated to his study, the scene of Callison's liaison with Maxine Wells. Callison couldn't help but look at the Oriental rug in front of Rasta's desk to see if the small stain was still apparent. He also walked over the middle of the rug to see if he could determine the location of Rasta's floor safe but he felt nothing.

They both were seated in the large leather armchairs which were arranged to form an intimate conversation corner. Rasta sat and crossed his legs. He was holding a large brandy snifter. "So, Steven, why the honor of your visit?"

Callison could feel the sweat trickle down the side of his face, his armpits were already moist, and his mouth was dry. "I've been given some information which I feel needs to be addressed before our meeting tomorrow."

Rasta took another sip from the snifter. "Please continue." Rasta exuded confidence, while Callison was the opposite.

"Are you aware of a list called the Caldo list?" The words seemed to stick in Callison's throat before coming out.

"Yes, I know of the list and I know you happen to be named on the list." Rasta knew Callison had been inquiring about the list. "I just want to assure you that the list is kept in the strictest confidence and would never be used in any manner that would be detrimental to you or anyone else on our committee." Rasta was so self-assured in his delivery.

Callison could feel his body regaining control. Maybe it was Rasta's arrogance or Callison's knowledge of the bomb he was about to deliver, but his sweating stopped and his mouth regained its moisture. "Then you must also be aware of another list. I believe this list is sometimes referred to as the Gance or Tatum list. And I assume you're aware your name is included on this list." Callison sat back in the leather chair. The coolness of the leather felt good against his back. He now wished he had a brandy so he could slowly sip, as Rasta had done moments before.

Rasta's complexion turned green as his self-confidence waned. "Where did you get that?" His voice had a guttural quality.

"I'm sorry, I'm not at liberty to say. So I take it you are aware of this list?" Callison glared at Rasta.

"I don't believe you have the list, and even if you did, the list itself is meaningless." Rasta sat upright and leaned on the edge of his seat.

"Why do you say that?" Callison remained calm, sitting back in his seat, enjoying seeing Rasta squirm.

"First, because I'm not even aware the list you are referring to exists, and second, a list is just that, a bunch of names with no real meaning." Rasta glared back at Callison.

"Well let me assure you the list does exist, and there are many prominent physicians and lawyers on it." Callison said, savoring the moment. "Plus there's also historical data, which if revealed could be very embarrassing. In some cases, perhaps career ending."

"Let me see it. Let me see the list." Rasta demanded.

Callison handed him a paper copy of the list. Surprised, Rasta turned page after page of names. "I can't believe this. How did you get this information? Who are you working for and what do you want from me?" Rasta was rambling.

"I really can't tell you where I got this information but if I can get it, so can others. And I'm not working for anybody. I'm just trying to do my job on the committee, just as you are." Callison smiled, the same self-assured, arrogant smile that Rasta had had at the beginning of their conversation.

"You realize this list is all but useless unless you have the documentation to corroborate it." Rasta was calming down, but his voice still was less secure than before.

"You mean a file like this?" Callison delivered his first knock-out punch. He gave Rasta a copy of his file that Truelove and Jasper had gotten from Mrs. Tatum.

Rasta opened the file and scanned the information. The data was accurate, with copies of information he believed had been destroyed years ago. Rasta had a lump in his throat which made it difficult for him to speak, but he forced the words out. "Okay, what do you want?"

Callison now had the edge and needed to optimize his opportunity. "First, I need to know who has access to the Gance account. Second, I need to know how to find Alan Smithee."

"Over my dead body. You asshole, who the hell do you think you are?" Rasta's ire was raised. Callison had miscalculated his opportunity. "Listen, before we go any further with this conversation, why don't you take a look at the videotape in the VCR over there." Rasta pointed to a VCR and monitor he had set up on his desk. "Go on, take a look, and then we'll talk some more."

Callison walked over to Rasta's desk and turned on the tape. At first he couldn't tell what was going on, then it hit him like a two-by-four across the forehead. He was watching his foray with Maxine in living color. Callison was at once amazed and humiliated. Rasta had definitely done him one better.

"I don't have to say what type of impact this tape could have on your wife. So, now let's start over, shall we?" The confidence was back in Rasta's voice as he swaggered over to the desk where Callison was still watching the tape. "Not bad quality, huh? Old Maxine looks like she's still in pretty good shape." Rasta chuckled.

Think, think, Callison said to himself. He was losing it and had to regain his composure. "Yeah, she does have a great body, doesn't she? So what's the big deal? My wife knows all about this. Let's get back to the issue at hand." Callison kept his voice and demeanor under control hoping Rasta would be convinced.

He wasn't. "Yeah sure, your wife knows you were with Maxine but I doubt she realizes you were with her this way. I can't wait to see her reaction when I personally deliver this tape to her. And you'd better believe I'll do that. You won't be only ruining your career but your marriage as well. I think you need to consider that." Rasta's bitterness increased with each word as he pounded his hand on his desk.

Callison needed to change the subject quickly, so he pulled out his ace card. "Take a look at these pictures."

Callison slid the envelope of pictures of Rasta's meeting with Slinger across the desk. The tape had run its course, and Callison wanted to destroy it before it destroyed him. He knew Rasta probably had copies, so he restrained himself.

Rasta briefly studied the pictures and then looked up at Callison with a bewildered expression. "I don't get it. These are pictures of me meeting with Nathan Slinger, so what?"

"I'll show you so what." Callison unveiled the canceled checks from the Gance society made to Slinger's organization and signed by Alan Smithee. "See these canceled checks. Each one was cashed within days of your meeting with Slinger."

"So?" Rasta still looked confused.

"We know that you and Smithee bribed Slinger to form the committee, made almost exclusively of members from the list."

"You got to be kidding. You have no proof of that. These photos could have been taken any time, and our discussions had nothing to do with this committee."

"Look at this letter and tell me we have no proof." Callison handed Rasta the letter written to Smithee from Slinger.

"First, this is addressed to Smithee not me. Second, it's so vague that you can't prove anything." Rasta scratched his eyebrow as he reread the letter.

"I'm not sure the authorities will look at it that way." Callison was surprised by Rasta's reaction. He had reacted so vehemently to Gance list and so differently to this.

"Go to your authorities and make your case, you have nothing. You're grasping at straws and you know it." Rasta chuckled cynically.

This wasn't going as planned. Callison could see Rasta was correct, although the circumstantial evidence was compelling, it proved nothing. The only way they had a case was if somebody cracked, and it appeared it wasn't going to be Rasta.

"What about the Hayes Bill?" Callison was now grasping at straws.

"What about it?" Rasta was becoming arrogant again.

"I think you're using this committee to get the merger so the Hayes Bill can pass."

"Don't be ridiculous. Why do we need the merger for the Hayes Bill to pass?"

"Because you need the DO's to make the proper impact with the bill. Without a merger, it could be argued the DO's are exempt."

"Why would they be exempt?" Rasta looked perplexed.

"Because the vast majority had their training in osteopathic institutions and were not in approved allopathic programs. Once the merger takes place, all the osteopathic programs would be grandfathered into the allopathic family and the bill could then apply."

"I don't see how the two issues overlap. The merger has nothing to do with the bill."

"Now who's grasping at straws?" Callison said.

"Fine, what's your bottom line? What do you want?" Rasta was becoming progressively more irritated.

"I want you to help me find Smithee." Callison leaned forward resting his elbows on his knees.

"I told you I won't do that, I've never tried to contact Smithee and I'm not about to start." Rasta shook his head.

"Then would you help me defeat the motion to proceed with the merger?" Callison's body language still revealed how serious he was.

"Why would I do that? I agree with your subcommittee, the merger's the best option." Rasta again started to sip his brandy.

"Why do you say that?" Callison sensed he was losing the argument.

"Because it's a cost effective way of increasing our primary-care pool, while at the same time preserving the practices of many of your physicians." Rasta sat back in his chair, again in control.

Callison could tell this was a rehearsed performance and it would be of no benefit to belabor the issue. "I can see no sense in arguing with you about this. Let's agree to disagree."

"What are you going to do?" Rasta was still concerned about the Gance list and his file and his reputation.

"I guess you'll have to wait and see. I can tell you this, I'd be less likely to create a scene if I knew I could have your cooperation on the merger issue."

"Listen, I don't do well with threats. If you pursue this course I promise you, your career and life will be ruined, and if I go down, you'll go down farther." Rasta glared at Callison and slammed his brandy snifter onto the table.

"I also don't do well with threats, so I guess we'll leave it at that." Callison walked out without saying another word.

Callison stopped at the first gas station on his way back to the city. J.T. had given him a telephone number to call to confirm they had the conversation on tape. He was rattled by Rasta, and the tape.

J.T. was not happy. He thought Rasta would break and lead them to Smithee and Valentino The tape, definitely, was unexpected.

Sensing Callison's anxiety, J.T. assured him he would do everything in his power to make sure Callison's career was not ruined. However, J.T. carefully avoided the home life topic. J.T. told Callison he could drop off the monitoring device at the office either later that evening or the next day.

After he completed his abbreviated conversation with J.T., Callison decided it was time to call his wife.

"Hello, Linda—this is Steven. Is Natalie there?"

"Sure, I'll get her, and does she have something to tell you." Linda's voice seemed more vibrant and excited than he had ever heard.

"Steven, is that you?" Natalie also sounded exhilarated.

Callison wondered what could make them both this excited. "Hi, hon. What's going on?"

"Linda and I have been doing a little homework on your case, and I think we're close to finding Smithee for you." Natalie's voice reverberated out of the receiver into Callison's head.

"What do you mean you found Smithee? How?"

"Remember I told you I asked Linda to help me with the puzzle or riddle or whatever you want to call it." The enthusiasm was still in Natalie's voice.

"Yes, I remember."

"Well, Linda figured out part of the riddle. The gunfighter part, and we're close to deciphering the Aselwood R Loax part also."

"Okay, tell me what you found." Callison's tone was less than enthusiastic.

"Remember how you used to give Linda grief because of her minor in communication? You used to call it movie credits. Remember?"

"Yes, I remember. Are you going somewhere with this?"

"Well, Linda remembered from one of her classes a reference to an Allen Smithee. Here, let her explain."

Callison waited for Linda to pick up the line. "Steven, how are you?" Linda said, still enthused.

"Yes, Linda. I'm fine. Tell me about Smithee."

"He's the worst director in Hollywood." She giggled.

"I don't get it. Is that supposed to be funny?"

"No, really he's the worst director in Hollywood. But he doesn't exist." Linda chuckled as she spoke.

"What are you talking about?" Callison was getting perturbed.

"Let me explain. Smithee was invented in the sixties. You see, the name Allen Smithee was substituted for the real director's name when the director didn't want to use his name on the credits for whatever reason. Usually it was because the director of the film felt he had lost creative control or some garbage like that. Even today, if a director feels he wants no part of the credit for a film, he can petition the Director's Guild to have Smithee's name replace his in the credits."

"So Smithee really doesn't exist?" Callison said. He was now very interested in what Linda was saying.

"Guess what Smithee's debut film was called?" Linda asked.

"I haven't a clue."

"Try *Death of a Gunfighter,* made in 1967, starring Richard Widmark."

"You're kidding?" Callison said cautiously.

"Nope, this is no joke."

"Then you feel our Alan Smithee doesn't exist either."

"Bingo!" Linda's voice exploded out of the receiver.

"Then if he doesn't exist, who's signing the checks with his signature? Who's behind all this?"

"That's the million dollar question. But from just the little information Natalie has told me, whoever's responsible for compiling this list of yours has some very powerful people on it. It's conceivable they could have created this Smithee person to shield their own identity."

What Linda said made perfect sense. Why hadn't he or the FBI thought of this? Maybe the FBI knew this already, but if they did, why all the charade with Rasta?

"Do you think the other part of the riddle, the Aselwood R Loax has anything to do with this?"

"Yes, I think it's also a clue. I have a strong suspicion Aselwood R Loax is the real Smithee." Linda's voice was still confident.

"Well, then who is this Loax guy?"

"I don't think that's his name. It's some sort of code. I have an idea how to break the code but I'm waiting for a call from a friend of mine whose help I need."

"Listen, I can contact the FBI and they can assist you if you need help.

"I may do that later, but at this point I think it's probably premature."

Callison thought maybe she was right but for the wrong reason. He didn't trust J.T., and this information could backfire. J.T. had placed him in a terrible position. He already had accused one of the most powerful and prestigious physicians in the country of participating in a conspiracy. Linda was right, they all would be better off if they could solve this on their own.

"I don't know how to thank you, but I'm sure you'll think of

452

something." Linda laughed on the other end of the line. Callison continued. "When do you think you'll have the answer?"

"Hopefully first thing tomorrow, if we're lucky."

"Okay, I'll call you some time around our first break in the morning. It should be between nine and ten your time."

"We'll be here. Let me put Natalie back on."

"Linda," Callison said before Linda could hand Natalie the phone.

"Yes," Linda answered.

"Before you go, thanks again and I take everything back about those communication courses."

Linda laughed and handed the phone to Natalie. "Pretty neat stuff, huh?"

"This is great. It may be a lifesaver for me. Literally." Callison said.

"So how is everything going up there?" Natalie's voice changed to that of a concerned wife.

"It's been interesting. When we have the time I'll tell you all about it. But for now I have to go. Got another meeting. Miss you." Callison felt guilty about avoiding the details, but an extended conversation would be more than he could handle at this point. Linda's comments gave Callison an idea and maybe, he could get out of all of this without losing his career, his wife, and his self-esteem.

42

Peter Moiner's home was in a two-story walk-up on the near north side of the city, not far from Jerry's on Lincoln, where they had met the evening before. Peter's home was furnished in hand-me-downs and wicker, yet the place had a cozy feeling. By the time Callison arrived, Paul and Peter had finished a six pack between them and a large bag of Bavarian pretzels, the ones with extra salt. Callison knew they would be frustrated and depressed because of their inability to find Van Gregory, who was in the custody of the FBI.

Peter and Paul had spent the day following every lead they had accumulated during the weeks in which they were tailing Gregory and his men. They were able to find Larry the Weasel and Tommy the Toad, as they had affectionately called them, but neither knew of Gregory's whereabouts. They did accomplish one thing—they spread the word implying that Rasta had given Van Gregory's name to the authorities to save his own skin. If Gregory was in town they were fairly confident the message would get to him. They ended their day at Gregory's home, where the mail had not been picked up for several days.

When Callison apprised them of Gregory's status, they were upset. They had wanted the pleasure of being responsible for his incarceration.

As they awaited the call from Truelove and Jasper, Callison updated Peter and Paul on some of the details of his day. Callison told them that the FBI were watching all of them and probably had someone watching them that evening. He also discussed his meeting with Rasta and explained how Rasta lost his composure when told about the list, yet remained calm when confronted with the conspiracy theory involving Nathan Slinger. Peter and Paul were confused, as was Callison.

At precisely nine the phone rang; it was Tyler Truelove.

Callison recapped the day's activities for Truelove. Once Callison finished, he asked Truelove about his day.

"While at the airport, Ethan and I decided to split up. I would visit Mrs. Bartolli and he would visit Mrs. Tatum. We thought this would maximize our productivity."

While Callison listened, J.T.'s comments on their trip being futile passed through his mind. Callison was just glad they were out of town and out of harm's way. They were one less headache he had to worry about.

Truelove's conversation was essentially a rehashing of the material they already knew. Mrs. Bartolli was still unable to solve the riddle, as was everyone else. Callison had kept that part of his day his secret, at least until he could talk with Linda again.

Truelove told Callison he thought the plan would work as they had decided, but he hadn't heard from Jasper.

Callison was still talking with Truelove when Peter responded to a knock on the door. It was J.T. While attempting to listen to Truelove, Callison was also straining to hear what J.T. was saying at the front door. The few words Callison could put together suggested something had gone wrong. Callison excused himself from his conversation with Truelove and told him to follow the plan as before and call Peter if there were any problems.

J.T. had bags under his bloodshot eyes, he looked exhausted. His clothes were disheveled, a portion of his shirt was sticking out of his pants, and his tie was loosely tied about four inches below his neck. "What a day. What a week. What the hell," J.T. whined.

"What's the problem?" Callison asked.

"This case is the problem." J.T. was definitely feeling sorry for himself.

Callison then introduced Peter and Paul to J.T. Following the introductions, J.T. removed his coat and tie and untucked his shirt completely. "I have some good news and some bad news. What do you want to hear first?"

"Good news. I always ask for the good news first," Callison said.

Peter asked J.T. if he would like something to drink. J.T.

asked for a large, cold glass of water.

"So, first with the good news," J.T. said.

Peter handed J.T. the glass of water, which he gulped down without taking a breath.

"So, where was I? Yes, the good news. Your little talk with Rasta has already provided some dividends. After he finished talking to you, he made some calls. He used his secured line to make the calls. Guess what? The line wasn't secure."

J.T. laughed a deep belly laugh, and soon they were all laughing. Joking about how no one's privacy is safe anymore. One bad joke led to another, and soon they were hysterically laughing at how the FBI could secure a phone tap on anyone, even if the line was supposed to be immune to taps.

"Anyway." J.T.'s chest was still heaving slightly. "Rasta called some people. First he called Lazlo Wilovsky, a semi-retired doctor from Cleveland, then Marvin Barnes, who's some big shot doctor in New Orleans, and Chester Timmons, a doc in Detroit. They're all on the board of directors of the Gance Foundation. We've known about them for a while, but never thought they were involved in this. We're going to bring them all in for questioning. Maybe if we're lucky, one will crack.

"The last call he made was possibly the most interesting. It was to a phantom corporation, which forwarded his call to another number. Until recently it would have been impossible to trace. But due to modern technology and a genius called Milo Aspermonti we were able to track and tape the conversation.

J.T. paused for effect. "The call went to Nathan Slinger's office. But even stranger was the conversation. Rasta hung up immediately, without saying a word. Now granted, Slinger himself didn't answer the phone, but why wouldn't he at least ask to talk with him?"

"Maybe he could tell the line was bugged," Peter answered.

"Highly unlikely. It didn't stop him from talking to the other three. Anyway, it looks mighty suspicious. He called Slinger immediately after your conversation." J.T. finished his second glass of water and refilled his glass. "Because of his high profile, we're just going to keep watching Mr. Slinger and see what he does."

"Is that the good news?" asked Peter. If implicating one of the most powerful senators in the country was good news, then what was the bad news?

"Yes, I consider that good news. We now have something to go on. Maybe we'll get lucky. I can sure use the luck, which brings me to the bad news." J.T. walked over to Callison and put his hand on his shoulder. "Remember earlier today you asked me how we could keep Van Gregory, and I told you we had our ways. Well, Gregory's lawyers found out he was in our custody. They were able to spring him."

"So Gregory's out?" Callison asked.

"Yes, and the worst part is, I don't know where he is. When his lawyers arrived I was out of the office, and he left before we could put a tail on him. What I'm concerned about is Gregory has a tendency to be a loose cannon. I don't need him screwing things up. We have several agents out in the streets looking for him, but I wanted to warn you to be on the lookout. He could be dangerous."

Peter gave Paul a smile.

"We'll find him," Paul said confidently. "We know his habits, his friends, his associates, we'll find him for you."

"I hope you do. If you do happen to find him, please don't approach him. We can't afford an incident at this point. If you could call this number and tell whoever's there where Gregory is, we'll do the rest." J.T. handed Paul his card.

Paul showed the card to Peter and they started to discuss their strategy.

Meanwhile J.T. took the opportunity to pull Callison aside. Whispering, J.T. asked Callison, "Do they know Merker's alive?"

"I don't think so. At least I never mentioned it to them."

"Well, Merker's gone." J.T. frowned as he spoke.

"Do you know where he is?" Callison asked, sensing J.T.'s concern.

"No, maybe he and Gregory are partying somewhere." J.T. laughed, as did Callison. Their laugh, however, was half-hearted. "If Merker contacts you, could you give him a message for me, to stay away from Gregory."

"I'll tell him. Why do you think he left?"

"Primarily because he heard about Gregory. You know he has a thing for him. Anyway, we're close, and you deserve some of the credit for getting us there. I know you didn't want to do what you did today. I just want to say, thanks."

"You're welcome." Callison knew J.T. didn't have to say that, and it meant a lot to him, to know what he did today was appreciated. Especially since it could be the beginning of the end of his career.

Peter and Paul were still discussing their plans to find Gregory. J.T. had to leave and asked Callison if he needed a ride. Callison told him he had a car but would leave with him.

As J.T. and Callison left Peter's apartment, they agreed to meet same time, same place, tomorrow.

Callison decided to stay at the Marriott where he had registered earlier that day. J.T. told him they would keep an agent on him, twenty-four hours a day, just as a precaution. His talk with Rasta might have placed him in some danger, and J.T. wasn't about to take any chances.

The lobby of the Marriott was packed with people dressed in formal attire. Callison was maneuvering through the crowds when he walked into a barricade of tuxedoed bodyguards. He was told he would have to wait until the secretary of health and his party cleared the area before he could access the elevators. Callison then inquired why they were there. The bodyguards ignored his request, but a woman standing in the crowd wearing enough gold and diamonds to feed a small nation told him they were sponsoring a fund-raiser that evening and were in town for a meeting on health-care reform. Callison realized the meeting they were in town for was his meeting.

Once the secretary's party cleared the lobby, Callison was permitted to go to his room. Upon entering, he noticed the red light flashing on the phone next to his king size bed. The message was from Maxine, who said it was urgent she talk to him.

Callison called Maxine. She said she would be right over, she had something she needed to give him. Callison thought of meeting her in the lobby, but determined it might be better to meet in his room if the material she had to give him was confidential.

458

Maxine was at Callison's room in less than a half hour. It was difficult for Callison to read the expression on her face. She seemed preoccupied.

"Thank you for seeing me this evening; I have something you might want to see before your meeting tomorrow." Maxine handed Callison a letter to read. "This letter was sent to Rasta yesterday, it's from Nathan Slinger."

Dear Victor,

If all goes well over the next few weeks, I would like you to consider a position on my staff. The position would be chief of operations for coordinating the merger of the allopathic and osteopathic professions. It would also include lobbying support for the Hayes Bill, which should solidify our image in the Health Care Reform Initiative. As you are aware, the polls are starting to sway to the opposition and the timeliness of the merger should buy us the time to shift the political climate back to our side.

None of this could have been accomplished without the stalwart efforts of many loyal supporters, such as yourself. Your efforts have been noticed, and I know your contribution will reap many rewards in the future.

I hope you seriously consider this offer. I know you have many options in your career, but I believe this option has unlimited possibilities. Please join me in reshaping the health-care of our country for the new millennium.

Fondly,
Nathan Slinger

Callison thought about the letter, especially in light of the phone call Rasta had made to Slinger's office.

Maxine was seated on the edge of the bed intently watching Callison read the letter. "What do you think this all means?"

"It appears Slinger will offer Rasta the position if Rasta can deliver the merger. And from my discussion with Rasta today, he can make my life unbearable if I don't cooperate."

"What are you going to do?" Maxine asked, sucking her fingertip.

"I don't know." Callison looked at Maxine. Should he tell her

459

about the tape? What possible benefit could she derive from knowing about the tape? Callison had to control his need to tell someone about the tape, at least for now.

"I can't believe Rasta can get away with this. This is really unbelievable," Maxine said shaking her head.

"Believe it. I think he had the committee set up to recommend the merger, and the man in charge of the reform movement is behind it all. I don't know if there's anything I can do to stop it, even if I wanted to."

"You mean you're in favor of this merger?"

"I can see both sides of the issue. Right now I could go either way."

"Are you serious? You could actually support the dissolution of your profession? Especially knowing Rasta probably set the whole thing up?"

"I know what you're saying is probably right, but I feel like I'm between a rock and a hard place." Callison wanted to agree with Maxine, but knew if he did, he would be committing personal career suicide.

"Is there anything I can do?" Maxine said sympathetically.

"No, what I need is another ally on the committee. Some one else who could support my position so I wouldn't feel so alone." Callison rambled, not really thinking what he was saying.

"Are you saying there's no one on the committee you can trust?"

"Yeah, I guess I am saying that." Callison thought about that for a moment. Who could he trust on the committee? Since he didn't know any of the committee members well, he didn't feel comfortable confiding in any of them, especially since most of them were on one list or the other.

"Not even if they were aware of the facts you now have?" Maxine was astounded.

Again Callison reviewed the committee members in his mind. He imagined how they would respond to the information he had. "Maybe I could convince one of them."

Of the members on the committee, Probst seemed the logical choice since he wasn't on the Caldo list. But he was a virtual stranger, which left Callison feeling extremely uncomfortable discussing this issue with him. Callison knew Danzinger no better than Probst and he was on the list, so he was excluded. Timmons had already indicated he was in favor of the merger, as did Michelson, which left only Teitelman. Although Teitelman had previously tried to sway Callison not to cause any trouble, he wasn't convincing. Callison had a feeling Teitelman would support him if he were given the information. Like Callison, Teitelman was younger than the others, and had other career options in the event everything fell apart.

"Who would you ask?" Maxine anxiously said.

"Possibly Harold Teitelman. I've known him the longest and I think he could be persuaded if he knew the facts."

"He's staying at this hotel. We could call him right now to discuss this," Maxine said as she slid across the bed to the phone on the night stand. "Do you want me to ring his room?"

Without thinking of the consequences, Callison agreed. Maxine assured him he had done the right thing.

When Teitelman entered the room, Maxine asked if she should leave. There was nothing Callison would say to Teitelman that she didn't already know, so he gave her the choice of staying or leaving. She decided to stay.

Teitelman was wearing a T-shirt and blue jeans with loafers and no socks.

"You look nice and relaxed considering the meeting is tomorrow." Callison said.

"I'd like to say the same about you, but you really look ragged." Teitelman could see the stress all over Callison's face.

"Well, I've had a bad couple of days." Callison could feel his stomach churning. If he couldn't confront Teitelman with this information there would be no way he could confront the committee tomorrow. "I'd like to tell you something, and I'd appreciate it if you would hear me out before you respond. But I do need to hear your honest response once I've finished."

"Sure, I can listen," Teitelman replied.

"The last time we talked you gave me some advice. You said to go with the flow, that there were powerful people who could ruin my career or worse. Do you remember that conversation?"

Teitelman didn't look quite as relaxed as he did when he first

461

sat down. "Yes, I remember the conversation."

"Since our talk I've done a lot of thinking, and I'm not sure either of us grasped the total scope of this committee. Do you know who I ran into in the lobby?"

"I have no idea who you ran into." Teitelman was growing agitated.

"The secretary of health, he's in town to attend our meeting Friday."

"So?"

"It made me rethink the importance of what we're about to recommend and its potential impact on possibly thousands and maybe millions of people."

"I think you're getting a little carried away with the importance of our little committee," Teitelman snickered.

"Maybe you're right and the committee is just one of many insignificant committees. But maybe I'm right and this committee will play a critical role in the final health-care proposal which may literally impact millions. If, for the sake of argument, I am right, how can any of us sit idly by and let some of these self-interest groups determine the fate of our profession? Do you know about the Caldo list?"

"How do you know about the list?" Teitelman gasped.

"I not only know about the list, I've got a copy of it. Do you want to see? Your name's on it and so's mine. And for that matter so is most everyone else on the committee, including the MD's."

"I don't believe you." Teitelman said, woefully furrowing his brow.

Callison handed Teitelman both the Caldo and Gance lists. He had highlighted the members of the committee in yellow. Teitelman couldn't believe the number of people involved.

"Don't you think it an odd coincidence that our committee is predominantly made up of people on that list? I did, and I investigated a little. Guess what I found?" Callison had gone too far to turn back now. He would either have an advocate or an enemy.

"I'm not sure I want to hear what you found. In fact, I'm positive I don't want to hear what you found." Teitelman already knew more than he wanted. It could only mean trouble.

"Oh yes, you do," Maxine said from the corner of the room

where she had situated herself.

"Who are you to say that to me?" Teitelman growled.

"I'm just a secretary, but even I can see what's happening here isn't right. And I know that you know I'm right." Maxine's voice was firm but conciliatory.

Callison interjected, explaining the Rasta-Slinger connection and how it appeared they were manipulating the health-care system for their own personal and political gain, while possibly ruining the practices of thousands of doctors, destroying the osteopathic profession, and compromising the medical care of millions of patients. When he had finished, Teitelman sat staring at the letter Maxine had brought, which promised Rasta a position if he delivered on the merger.

"Tomorrow I plan to bring up the Hayes Bill and see if we can table our decision about the merger until we have discussed the Hayes Bill and how it would be impacted by the merger. Can I count on your support on this?" Callison solemnly looked at Teitelman, begging him with his eyes.

"You know if we take on Rasta, we have a good chance of getting annihilated." Teitelman slapped Callison's thigh.

"Then you'll do it," Callison said enthusiastically.

"Hell, I never really wanted to be a dean anyway," Teitelman chuckled.

"Do you think we need to contact anyone else before the meeting for support?

Teitelman reviewed the other members of the committee one at a time and explained why it would be dangerous to reveal this information to them at this time. Teitelman thought their best tactic was surprise. Since Teitelman knew the committee members much better than he, Callison deferred to Teitelman's recommendation.

With Maxine's assistance, they sketched out their game plan of how they were going to address the committee and confront Rasta using the Hayes Bill as the pivotal issue. It was after one in the morning when they completed their plan. They all needed some rest, because tomorrow would be a stressful day.

43

The room was arranged to accommodate a large audience. Microphones and video cameras were in place and there was even a special section dedicated for the press. Callison had no idea this was to be a media event. He started to have second thoughts about voicing his concerns in front of the cameras and the press. Today was the day Callison needed to state his case. If he waited for tomorrow it might be too late.

However, today there were no crowds, no media, no press, no political dignitaries, but there was something in the air that Callison could feel would still make this day special.

Callison arrived twenty minutes before the meeting was scheduled to start. Most of the committee members were already there, including Harold Teitelman, who avoided eye contact with him. The head table was designed in a semicircle, with placards placed in front of each chair. Callison was positioned on the left hand side of the dais, between Robert Thornhill and Jacob Danzinger. However, for their meeting today, a separate room off the main conference area was to be used, to ensure the privacy they needed.

The meeting room was much smaller and much less formal. There were no microphones or cameras, and the atmosphere was less conspicuous and more comfortable. Callison conversed with Susanna Michelson, craftily asking if she still held any reservations about the merger. He felt better when Susanna said she also had reservations, giving him some hope of gathering her support later in the day.

The meeting started on time, with Jourge reviewing the agenda. The first item was an update from Jourge, which would be followed by the subcommittee reports. Finally they would produce a consensus report, which would be presented the next day to the select panel and then sent onto the White House. An evening meeting was tentatively scheduled if they needed additional time to finalize the consensus report.

Jourge initiated the discussion with the news from the health-care reform front. The White House was under siege from the Senate Finance Committee and several other powerful groups pressuring them to present their proposal. Time was running out. The president had many unexpected issues which had taken priority, thus delaying his health-care agenda. It was now becoming a political time bomb. Advisors close to the president counseled him to present his plan expeditiously or he could suffer irreparable damage in the polls. Several components had been made crystal clear and were non-negotiable, such as a universal health-care policy which would initially reduce the uninsured population to less than 10 million and eventually to zero, while simultaneously decreasing the cost for administering health-care. The second caveat from the White House was to increase the proportion of primary-care physicians. These were the two major issues the committee was to address in their consensus report. There were other issues related to research, preventative care, and the like, but these were intertwined and could be discussed in conjunction with the two major issue.

Before the subcommittee reports were reviewed, Jourge highlighted some of the recent opinion polls, which again suggested that doctors were still perceived by the public as the primary cause of the spiraling health-care costs—more than managed care, the insurance companies, or the government. Jourge further detailed a recent survey conducted by a bipartisan research team that concluded that the greatest concern about health-care coverage was the cost. However, when the public was asked what would they would be willing to sacrifice, almost no one was willing to sacrifice security or quality in their health-care. Thus creating what Jourge termed "the health-care paradox."

A heated debate followed Jourge's report. Almost every member of the committee resented the fact that the president was attempting to manipulate them.

When Rasta said he couldn't be bought, Callison, who was drinking a glass of water at the time, choked on the water, spraying the table. Several other members laughed, probably at Callison's spray rather than Rasta's remarks, but not Teitelman. He was somber as ever.

Callison watched Rasta pontificate and knew he would have to wait for the appropriate time to make his move. The committee was to proceed with the subcommittee reports and then reevaluate the president's requests to see how they might coincide.

Jourge suggested they would review one subcommittee report before they would break. Prior to the meeting they had all received a packet with a synopsis of all the reports. The purpose of the meeting today was to review the reports and vote on each of them. Then they would combine the subcommittee reports to formulate their consensus report.

Jourge asked Dr. Thornhill to present first. Thornhill's voice filled the room as he began to speak. As always he was understated and controlled in his presentation, with each word and phrase carefully thought out. Thornhill talked of the system working cohesively to produce the best health-care system in the world. The system was far from perfect and too expensive, but it was difficult to ignore the quality of care and dedication of its practitioners. The medical schools, many functioning as health science centers, also train other health-care professionals such as nurses, physician's assistants, pharmacists, technologists, et cetera. All contributing to the quality, as well as the cost, of medical care.

As Thornhill continued, Callison found his mind starting to wander. He was watching the clock, waiting for a break so he could call Natalie and Linda.

Thornhill's deep raspy voice deliberately followed a logical path to his recommendations. He concluded by referring to the public survey Jourge had presented. It was obvious a new emphasis in all undergraduate medical curriculum was needed and to make this happen funding would have to be reallocated. Since much of the funding for medical schools was tied into their post-graduate programs his subcommittee would have to work in concert with the post-graduate subcommittee. He said the two committees had met and a combined recommendation would be forthcoming at the conclusion of Danzinger's report.

Jourge thanked Thornhill for his thorough and informative presentation and then recommended they take a break before hearing Danzinger's report.

As Callison began to get up from his chair, Rasta sat next to him. "Can we talk privately for a minute?" Rasta said politely.

"What do you want?" Callison asked, not pleased.

"Please, can we go somewhere more private to talk?"

Callison followed Rasta down a hall to an empty office. Rasta opened the door and let Callison enter first.

"Listen, I did a lot of thinking after our talk yesterday and I just want to tell you I appreciate your concerns." Rasta appeared genuine. "I made a couple of calls, and I can assure you a favorable response if you resubmit your grant for next year."

"You mean if I don't make any waves, you'll assure me?" Callison knew Rasta probably had the power to assure him the funding, but he didn't want to get funded that way.

"All you have to do is nothing. Let the committee do its work and give your report as it's written. That's it." Rasta smiled, the same self-assured, arrogant smile that Callison had seen before. "And as an added benefit I'll give you the original tape. Nobody will know."

Callison closed his eyes, trying to control himself. As much as he wanted the tape and the grant, he wanted to nail Rasta more. "I appreciate your interest in my career, but I'd rather have my grant approved on its own merits. Please don't take any offense, but that's how I feel."

"I understand. Actually, I feel the same way, but if you wouldn't mind I'd like to write a letter of support for your application." Rasta's smile persisted.

"I'll tell you what—if I decide to reapply I'll send you a copy of the grant. If you still feel the same way, I'd be honored by a letter of support from you."

Callison excused himself, stating he needed to make a phone call. As he left the room he knew Rasta was anxious, and that pleased him. It was time to call Natalie and Linda. Although he told himself to expect little, his inner voice couldn't wait to hear what they had found.

467

Callison found an alcove of phones, but he needed more privacy. Fortunately there was a private booth.

Natalie was expecting his call. "Steven, it's about time you called." Her voice teemed with expectation and excitement.

"The meeting went a little longer than I expected. So what did you find out?" Natalie's excitement was contagious.

"We found Smithee. His real name is George Alexander." Natalie's voice was still resonant with enthusiasm.

George Alexander, the name reverberated in Callison's head. Where did he know that name? "Do you have any idea who this person is?"

"That's the interesting part; he's dead. In fact he died in 1968 according to the file you left with me."

"What file?" Callison had no idea what file Natalie meant.

"The files you left with me for safekeeping. One of the files was on a George Alexander, who had taken over control of the Gance organization after the death of Dr. Tatum. According to the files, he was Tatum's hand-picked successor and was a brilliant physician to boot."

Callison's insurance policy was now paying an unexpected dividend. "So what else does the file say?"

"There's a large gap of time missing from the file. I guess Mrs. Tatum lost contact with Alexander for about six or seven years. The last entry is a clipping from a medical bulletin. It's an obituary, and scribbled on the margin is the word 'suicide.'"

"So he committed suicide in 1968. I don't get it." Callison rubbed his forehead, trying to understand what Natalie was saying.

"That was our dilemma and was the reason I didn't tell you all this yesterday. Aren't you curious how we found out about all this?" Natalie eagerly said.

"Yes, very."

"The secret is in Aselwood R Loax."

"Okay, I give. Tell me what it means."

"Actually it was Linda who figured this out. Aselwood is a strange name." Natalie almost laughed when she said the name again.

"Granted."

468

"But we knew the name Allen Smithee, and the initials A.S. And if you look at the sheet of paper from the notebook, it doesn't say Aselwood, it says A S Elwood. Such as Allen Smithee Elwood."

"So who's Elwood?" Callison was still perplexed.

"Who or what's Elwood? This is where the R Loax comes into play." Natalie stopped momentarily. "Linda had a thought the letters represented something other than a name. She recalled that in the sixties telephone numbers all began with a name, such as Elwood or Elmwood and the R Loax represented the rest of the number. People used to use names instead of numbers so they could more easily recall the number from memory. So Elwood R Loax actually represented the telephone number of Allen Smithee, EL-7–5629. Since the detective who discovered this was investigating the death of Dr. Bartolli at that time, we assumed the number was referable to that locale. Linda knew someone who was able to check out who was listed in the phone book with the number EL-7–5629 at the time of the detective's inquiry."

"So they found the name Allen Smithee," Callison said confidently.

"Yes, but they changed the spelling to A-L-A-N."

"Why did they change the spelling of his first name?"

"We don't know. Maybe it was their attempt at originality." Natalie mused. "But now the strange part. At the time of the detective's investigation, the telephone listing was under the name of Alan Smithee but we already knew the name of Smithee was fictitious. We asked Linda's friend to see if she could find out who actually paid the phone bill. This morning she called us with the name George Alexander. But the strange part is the bill was paid in October, and Alexander had died in March. How could a dead man pay the bill?"

"Good question?" Callison began rubbing his forehead again.

"Well, that's about it," Natalie said proudly.

Callison was still waiting for the punch line. "Well, how did Alexander pay the bill when he was dead?"

"I don't know. I thought we did a great job hunting down Alexander to begin with."

469

"You did." Callison felt as if all this were foreplay and he was ready for the big send-off, only to find out he was being teased. He tried to sound grateful. "You both did a brilliant job at figuring this all out. I can tell you the FBI couldn't do it. But you really don't know how Alexander paid the bill after his death?"

Natalie could sense his disappointment which also disappointed her. "No, Steven, that's still a mystery."

"To review for my sake." Callison wanted to verbalize what he was thinking. He grabbed a piece of paper to write down his thoughts. "Aselwood R Loax stands for Alan Smithee's telephone number, which was actually George Alexander's number, correct?"

"Correct," Natalie said emphatically.

"But Alexander was dead and still paying the bills, which suggests either he wasn't dead or someone else was paying the bills. Does that make any sense?"

"I guess. But that's where we are."

"Is there anything else?" Callison asked. He was already late for the meeting.

"I don't think so, but if so I'll call you. Give me your number."

Callison was afraid if she called they would trace the number and find her. "No, I'll call you later. For now I'd rather not have you call me, let me call you. Love you. Got to go."

Walking back to the meeting the name of George Alexander kept recurring in his mind. Suddenly it came to him, Dr. Alexander, the mystery name from the Amos Wilcox letter. Just knowing where he had heard the name was a great relief.

44

Jourge was not pleased at Callison's tardiness and had directed Jacob Danzinger to start his report. Callison could feel Jourge's penetrating gaze admonishing him as he took his seat. Danzinger had just started and was still discussing Thornhill's presentation, which eased Callison's guilt.

Once settled, Callison poured himself a drink of water as he surveyed the participants seated around the table. Most were intently listening to Danzinger. The exception was Teitelman, who seemed preoccupied and would frequently look in Callison's direction only to rapidly turn away if he sensed Callison acknowledging his stare. And then there was Rasta, pompous as always, giving the appearance he was listening to Danzinger... but Callison knew he already had orchestrated Danzinger's presentation along with the others. Rasta was reveling in his creation of the perfect committee, all committed to his agenda. This sickened Callison, but he was about to do something about it.

Danzinger reiterated much of what Thornhill had said about the need to support the primary-care effort without destroying the present system. Danzinger expressed a rationale for why more primary-care providers are needed—highlighting them as gatekeepers and cost savers. With managed health-care becoming the dominant force in the market, it will naturally adjust, and primary care will become an even greater focus of need. Danzinger and Thornhill outlined twelve steps that would increase the emphasis of primary care over the entire spectrum of medical education, from undergraduate to postgraduate, while still allowing the teaching hospitals to function effectively.

Following the report there was a great deal of back slapping and congratulatory adulation for both Thornhill and Danzinger. Callison was half expecting a standing ovation. The programs they presented appeared to the naked eye as revolutionary and innovative, but in fact were a drop in the bucket. Increasing the budget from one hundred million to two or even three hundred million, wouldn't be functionally significant, but it would be politically significant. With regard to the six billion dollar budget for specialty care, the subtraction of a couple hundred million could easily be absorbed without causing any harm. Thus everyone was pleased. The primary care people doubled or even tripled their funding, the lobbyists were able to keep their programs functioning as usual, the president would appear to be taking a hard stand, and Rasta would have his new position on Nathan Slinger's staff.

Jourge finally had to intervene to keep the group on schedule. The next to present was Chester Timmons.

Timmons' report was more of the same. He presented the need to increase the research efforts in the field of primary care, but noted the research funding averaged almost 20 percent of the average medical school budget and in many accounted for a third of the budget. Timmons' recommendations were in concert with those earlier recommendations, suggesting funds would be shifted to stimulate and support research in primary care, where applicable. Timmons proposed ratios similar to those proposed by Thornhill and Danzinger. The response was also similar.

Callison knew this was the same scenario as before. The research dollars would essentially remain unscathed, while a nominal amount of funds would be redirected to primary care, so the politicians could claim the victory in the war against the health-care crisis.

Callison still remained silent, as did Teitelman, but the discussions in the afternoon session would be entirely different. Jourge seemed pleased at the rapidity of the meeting and was hopeful the evening session could be canceled. Before breaking for lunch, Jourge directed the group to be on time for the afternoon session, keeping his eyes on Callison.

Upon exiting the meeting, Callison was greeted by Maxine, who escorted him out of the building. Once out of the building, she told Callison where they were to meet Truelove and Jasper, along with their guests, Mrs. Bartolli and Mrs. Tatum.

The streets were packed with the lunchtime crowds. Callison didn't notice the man following them until he bumped into him from behind. "Keep walking and turn into the next building on your right." Callison could feel something hard and cold poking him in the back. He assumed it was a gun.

Maxine immediately noticed what was happening, but didn't recognize the man who grabbed her by the arm and guided her into the building following Callison. The lobby of the large office building was virtually empty as the men led Maxine and Callison to an alcove where they were greeted by a dark haired man with a military hairstyle. Callison recognized him as James Williams. The man shoved them toward Williams, causing Maxine to lose her balance and fall to the floor.

"I'm sorry for the disturbance." Williams bent over to help Maxine.

Maxine pushed away from him and uprighted herself. "What the hell is going on here?"

Callison had never seen Maxine like this and was surprised at her aggressiveness.

"I needed to talk to both of you privately and I was afraid you wouldn't cooperate if I asked nicely." Williams attempted a smile, which quickly vanished when he looked at Maxine's scowl.

"Listen, Williams, isn't it? I'm on a very tight schedule so let's skip the formalities." Callison didn't feel threatened by Williams and noticed that the men who accosted them were not carrying weapons. They had used hairbrush handles to make their point.

"I told you I would follow you if you didn't contact me." Williams said. "Actually I think we're on the same side. I have found something that might help you on the committee."

"Listen, I don't want to be rude but can I leave?" Maxine said.

"No, what I have to say is for both of you."

Callison started to panic. Did he have a copy of the tape that Rasta had shown him? What would Maxine say once she saw it?

To Callison's relief, Williams handed them a photograph envelope. Inside were pictures of most of the members of the group, congregating in front of a building.

"We took these photos last evening. As you can see, most of the members of the committee were present, and we were able to monitor much of their discussion. They discussed their strategy for the meeting today and had some concern about you." Williams pointed to Callison. "But Rasta assured them you were under control. Then they theoretically adjourned; however, a smaller group remained behind to discuss other details." Williams raised one eyebrow as he spoke.

"And what other details are you referring to?" Callison asked.

"The members who remained were Rasta, Danzinger, and Percy, and their topic was the merger. The bug we planted wasn't the best but we've reviewed the tapes and I believe we have enough to nail them. Basically they talked about the need for the merger, so they can accomplish the goals of the committee without negatively affecting their ongoing programs or those initiatives of their supporters. Plus they refer to osteopaths as pond scum, and would use this merger to eliminate them once and for all."

"Can I hear the tape?" Callison wasn't convinced Williams was telling the truth, but his ire awakened.

"I don't have it here, but I'll let you hear it later. I just wanted to let you know it existed, just in case you were planning to do something stupid, like supporting their cause for your own benefit." Williams gave Callison a smirk and then winked at Maxine.

"I still don't know why I have to be involved in all this."

"Without going into details, you were also discussed, and Rasta also assured the other committee members you would be no problem."

The absence of the tape made Callison even less convinced of Williams' sincerity. However, he thought he knew to what Williams was indirectly referring and immediately changed the subject. "Can we go? I can't be late for this meeting."

"Sure, I'll contact you later. Sorry for the dramatics, but I needed to get your attention. I apologize if we scared you." Williams seemed sincere in his apology.

Callison and Maxine exited the building. "Listen, Maxine, I don't have time to meet with Truelove and Jasper now, but if you could have them available this afternoon, I might need them then. I'm not sure what's going to happen."

"No problem. What was that all about, anyway?"

"Williams is working for the AOA and has an inflated sense of self-worth. He's an asshole."

"You can say that again."

"He's just an asshole. See you later." Callison walked back to the meeting, while Maxine went in the opposite direction to retrieve Truelove and company.

Callison rushed back in time for the afternoon session and even had time to devour a piece of pizza before the meeting started. Teitelman appeared restless and still wouldn't even look at Callison. Callison had asked Jourge if he could present last, thus he knew Rasta was next to present. He wanted to be there for every minute of Rasta's presentation.

Rasta was in his glory, all eyes aimed at him. He stood to present his report rather than remain seated as the others had, presumably to distinguish himself from the rest. Rasta presented data on the health-care needs of the medically underserved and those with inadequate or no insurance coverage.

Rasta paused for effect before he changed topics. Scanning the room to ensure he had the full attention of those present, he lectured on the need to critically evaluate the registered nurse baccalaureate programs and physician assistant accredited programs in this country, to see how they might be integrated into a multidisciplinary approach to the problem. Rasta suggested that if they implemented the changes made earlier, along with his recommendations, they would be able to significantly impact the health-care needs of the medically underserved and uninsured.

Jourge asked Teitelman if he had anything to add to Rasta's presentation. Teitelman was noticeably nervous and declined. Callison was worried that Teitelman would reject their plan if the pressure became too intense, but he decided to pursue Rasta with or without Teitelman's assistance.

"Can I ask a question?" Callison asked.

Rasta's smile changed to a look of scorn and contempt. "Yes, what is your question?"

"Can you explain how the Hayes Bill will impact the rural

health-care needs of the underserved?" Callison glared back at Rasta.

"I don't think that's relevant to this discussion," Rasta replied nastily.

"But isn't this bill directed toward providing health care to those underserved areas you previously mentioned?" Callison asked.

"I'm not sure of the details of the bill, so for me to reply to your request wouldn't be appropriate."

"I happen to have a copy of the entire bill, which I will pass out. Also, a summary sheet is attached to acquaint any of us who aren't familiar with the bill." Callison sneered back at Rasta and then smiled.

Callison stood and personally handed each member of the committee a copy of the bill, stopping at Rasta first. "Now we can discuss this bill?"

Rasta looked toward Jourge for support. "Dr. Jourge, this is highly irregular. First, I have no idea if this bill is fact or fiction, and second, I still don't see its relevance to our discussion."

Before Jourge could respond, Callison intervened. "Maybe we should all take some time to review the bill to see if it has any merit to our discussion."

Jourge readily agreed to Callison's recommendation, against Rasta's protestations. After ten minutes, Jourge asked for any comments.

"I have to agree with Dr. Rasta, I don't see the relevance of this bill pertaining to this issue." Percy commented.

"Have you heard of this bill prior to today?" Callison inquired.

"No." Percy answered as he cleared his throat.

Callison was impressed by the cool way Percy had lied. He expected him to support Rasta, but he was astonished at how effortlessly he lied.

"Maybe Dr. Callison can enlighten us on how he perceives this bill to impact our committee," Jourge asked, not wanting to discourage open dialogue, but also not wanting to spend time discussing irrelevant topics either.

"This bill recommends a quick fix for some of the underserved areas. It suggests physicians who are in active practice but without three years post-graduate training be reassigned to these areas of need. Since the majority of physicians in this particular situation are family practitioners, who also happen to be DO's, this bill will unfairly affect their practices and careers." Callison centered himself in his seat.

"This bill says nothing about DO's, it just states that for reimbursement from government-sponsored programs you need to have three post-graduate years of training or practice in an underserved area," Rasta snarled.

"Yes, but the majority of physicians in this predicament are DO's." Teitelman came to Callison's defense. He weakly smiled at Callison, but avoided any eye contact with Rasta.

"Correct me if I'm wrong, but aren't the majority of DO's graduating from three-year residency programs?" Percy asked.

"Yes, they are now," Callison said. "But this bill will apply to all physicians, and many who have trained even several years ago wouldn't meet the three-year requirement, yet have been successful practitioners."

"I still don't see how this affects our committee," Percy said.

"By using the DO general and family doctors, their MD counterparts will be spared of meeting the demands of the health-care needs in the underserved areas."

"So?"

"So, this will unfairly affect one group of physicians," Callison said defensively.

"I have to agree with Dr. Percy," McMillan said. "The bill doesn't stipulate any type of physician and doesn't mandate anything. It just seems to give a choice to those who wish to take that option."

"Plus, the bill isn't even official yet; it's still in committee," Percy said.

"I thought you had never heard of this bill before. If that's true, how do you know it's still in committee?" Callison got the break he was hoping for. Maybe now he could muster some support from the other DO's on the committee.

"I guess I didn't explain myself clearly. I had heard of the bill, just not of the details." Percy looked away, embarrassed and aggravated.

"Dr. Jourge, I appeal to you to have this bill reviewed before we can finalize our recommendations," Callison said.

"Do you wish to propose a motion?" Jourge suggested.

Callison moved and Teitelman seconded the motion. It was defeated six to one, with Teitelman and Susanna Michelson abstaining. Callison had lost the first round, but he still had his report to come.

Rasta then presented his recommendations, which were approved with one abstention.

The merger committee headed by Callison was the last committee report of the day. Callison reviewed the rationale for the decision of the committee and their recommendation to support a merger between the osteopathic and allopathic professions. There was little discussion and no argument from either side of the issue.

Callison took a deep breath, fully aware that his next step could result in professional suicide. It was the seminal moment of his medical career, an instant in time that belonged to him. "I would like to suggest that there is a conspiracy which has orchestrated this merger to benefit a select group of individuals who have a financial and political investment in the merger taking place."

"What are you saying?" Jourge's jaw dropped.

Rasta gasped as the words left Callison's mouth. He was so stunned he couldn't talk, but could only listen to what Callison would say next.

"I said there is a group which has set this whole thing up. Specifically, they have organized the merger by influencing various committee members." Callison couldn't believe he was saying this.

"Do you have proof of this?" Jourge asked incredulously.

"I myself have been approached," Callison said with conviction.

Jourge cleared the room of all personnel other than the committee members before he would allow any more dialogue on the subject. Once the room was cleared of everyone except the committee members, Jourge again addressed Callison.

"Dr. Callison, you have just proposed the most outrageous, contentious accusation I believe I have ever heard. I hope you have documentation to substantiate your allegation."

Callison then discussed the Caldo and Gance lists in general terms, suggesting that several members of the committee were probably unaware of their names being on the list, while others were probably well aware. Callison inferred that the list might also implicate himself, thus he had as much to lose as anyone. Before he could recommend any kind of merger, he needed to be sure it was the right thing to do and not make the recommendation due to coercion. Callison was careful not to name names. There was still the remote possibility he could achieve his goal without having to expose those on the list.

"You mentioned that there are members of this group who are part of some type of conspiracy. Do you mind if I ask who?" Jourge asked in total disbelief.

"Before I answer that question, I would like to give the members of the committee who are involved the opportunity to comment." Callison slowly surveyed the group awaiting a response.

Silence filled the room. The committee members were stunned and no one appeared to be willing to admit to anything.

"Dr. Callison, you have made some outlandish statements. It is up to you to provide substantive proof." Jourge was miffed at Callison's disruption of his meeting.

Callison looked at Rasta. This was the moment of truth. He was putting his career and reputation on the line. "I think Dr. Rasta can answer your concerns."

Rasta sprang to his feet, his head spinning. He started to scream, "It's a lie! A damned lie! He's setting me up. He has no proof of any of this."

Jourge was shocked by Rasta's outburst, as were the other members of the committee. "Calm down, Victor. I didn't hear anyone accuse you of anything," Jourge said in an attempt to regain control.

Callison smiled. "I apologize to Dr. Rasta for upsetting him so. If I may, I would like to answer your concerns." Callison focused on Jourge as he talked, but kept Rasta in view.

"Please do," Jourge said.

"May I get something?"

"Fine, but be prompt."

As Callison left, the room was abuzz. They were still in shock when Callison returned followed by Truelove, Jasper, Mrs. Bartolli, Mrs. Tatum, and Maxine.

"Who are these people?" Jourge asked.

"These people will corroborate what I have said and will provide the added proof you wanted," Callison answered.

Rasta stood at his seat, pounding the table with his fist. "I can't believe this. This is outrageous! First these accusations, and now a group of strange people who are going to further confuse this whole issue."

"Dr. Rasta has a point. Exactly who are these people?" Jourge was curious about Callison's allegations, but needed to restore order to the meeting.

Callison then introduced his party. Truelove and Jasper reviewed their credentials before the committee. Since they were both physicians, it gave them a modicum of credibility. The other committee members were not overly upset at their presence, but were rather perplexed at what they could add to the discussion.

Then Callison introduced the two ladies, first Mrs. Helen Bartolli-Sanford. When Callison mentioned her name, Rasta fell in his seat.

When Callison introduced Mrs. Ethel Tatum, Thornhill stood to greet her.

"Ethel is that you? It's Robert, Robert Thornhill!" Thornhill approached the elderly woman, who shuffled over in his direction, stabilized by a walking cane.

"Robert Thornhill, I haven't seen you in what, forty years." Ethel smiled as he approached her. Her speech pattern was dysarthric and difficult to understand.

"Yes, something like that. How are you involved in all of this?" Thornhill caught himself before he said anything else. "Well, I guess I'll find out soon." Thornhill assisted Mrs. Tatum to her seat.

Callison's introduction of Maxine was not necessary, since the committee were all acquainted with her.

"I'd like to move that these witnesses or whatever they are

supposed to be, be escorted to another room so we may privately discuss this." Rasta was watching Helen Bartolli as he made his request. It had been many decades since they last met and she was still a striking woman, but she was now striking him with fear and anxiety.

Percy seconded the motion, and Callison's party was escorted out of the room. Thornhill personally assisted Mrs. Tatum and returned once she was situated.

Before Callison could speak, Rasta stood. "This is a disgrace, bringing in senile old ladies and washed-up physicians—what kind of sham is this? Please, can we get on with the agenda?" Rasta looked around the room, rallying support with his glaring eyes.

"I agree with Victor. This is really quite a show, but we do have work to do." Percy as usual came to Rasta's defense.

"May I say something?" Callison asked.

"Please do," Jourge responded.

"Each of these individuals has something pertinent to say. Both Doctors Truelove and Jasper were involved with the California merger between the osteopathic and allopathic professions in the sixties, and they had some concerns about a conspiracy then. It may have spanned the decades to today! Mrs. Bartolli's husband was a partner of Dr. Rasta's many years ago and has some information which could enlighten us all. Finally, Mrs. Tatum is the source of the files we have obtained and her husband founded the Gance organization, which I believe is behind the entire conspiracy. Plus both Mrs. Bartolli and Mrs. Tatum have come from Florida because they feel this is important. I think we owe them the courtesy of hearing what they say."

"The older one is senile and the other has hated me ever since I fired her husband. I don't think this is fair at all." Rasta scanned the room for support.

Percy was about to speak when Thornhill stood. "I knew the Tatums very well many years ago. Finer people I have never met in my life. You have no cause to call this woman senile—old, yes; but I would bet you her mind is sharper than any in this room. I want to hear what she has to say." Thornhill spoke with authority.

Jourge agreed with Thornhill, and Rasta didn't argue. Jourge then asked, "Other than Dr. Thornhill's prior acquaintance with Mrs. Tatum and Dr. Rasta's with Mrs. Bartolli, are there any other relationships or possible conflicts of interests I should know about relevant to any of these individuals?"

There was no response. Jourge then set the parameter for the meeting: he alone would ask the questions. If another member of the committee wanted to ask a question they could write it down and Maxine would bring the question to Jourge for review. He would then determine whether the question should be asked. Jourge made one last condition: once everybody had their say, they would convene and come to a group recommendation, with the majority opinion as the final solution. Both Callison and Rasta agreed.

Maxine was sent to retrieve the party.

Jourge started the questioning with Truelove and Jasper who confirmed that the Caldo list not only existed but possibly had had a role in the previous merger. Part of the plan they had agreed upon at Peter Moiner's apartment was to avoid discussing issues that pertained to the FBI investigation. So Truelove and Jasper, as well as Callison, would avoid any discussion of the deaths of Jonas Cisko, Marcus Merker, Amos Wilcox, or anything else not dealing with merger. No such agreement had been made with either Mrs. Bartolli or Mrs. Tatum.

Jourge reminded them all of the sensitivity of this issue and how this could compromise not only the work of the committee but all their careers.

The session with Truelove and Jasper lasted the entire afternoon, exhausting the group and their guests. Details of the merger in California were discussed, and the Caldo list was mentioned, but only in vague terms. Nobody specifically was named. Jourge needed resolution that evening because they had to present their final report in the morning. He asked if Truelove, Jasper, Bartolli-Sanford, and Tatum could stay the night at the committee's expense so they might continue their dialogue after dinner. They all agreed.

Before breaking for dinner, Rasta suggested that maybe he

and Callison could discuss some of the issues to facilitate the process.

Jourge championed Rasta's suggestion. "The issue of the merger is at the heart of this controversy and I am still not sure how I stand. Since Doctors Rasta and Callison seem to be the major antagonists in this debate, I would like to ask a favor. Could you two meet before we reconvene at 8 P.M. and hopefully reach a solution? I am confident you will be able to put aside any personal differences, for the good of the committee and the medical profession. I know I would greatly appreciate it, and I think I speak for the rest of the committee as well. I know I do not have to say this, but nothing that has been said can be repeated outside this room. We will resolve this issue tonight." Jourge's request was more like an order—one which Callison and Rasta were obligated to at least attempt to work out.

45

During the meeting Callison had a thought cross his mind which quickly became an obsession. He needed to review the Gance list again.

Rasta suggested a restaurant nearby where they could meet to discuss their differences. Callison agreed to meet him in forty minutes, because he had several things to do beforehand.

Before leaving he asked Maxine about the guests. Maxine assured him they all had rooms at the Marriott, and she had made dinner reservations for them at the hotel. Callison also needed to call Peter and Paul, to inform them he might not attend their meeting because of the conflicting evening session. Instead of calling, he asked Maxine to inform Truelove and ask him if he would be able to update Peter and Paul.

Callison had a copy of the Gance list in his room. He had less than two hours to meet with Rasta and review the list before the meeting was to reconvene. Maxine asked if she could accompany him, so they could coordinate their plans for the remainder of the evening. In his room he immediately pulled out the hard copy of the list and slowly read each name listed. Once he was finished, Callison looked up at Maxine, who had been unsuccessful in attempting to contact Peter and Paul.

"He's not there. I knew it," Callison repeated to himself.

"Who's not there? What are you talking about?" Maxine asked.

"George Alexander isn't on the master list of the Gance organization but we know he's part of the original list. He must have taken himself off." This meant something, but Callison couldn't decide what. He would think about this later. For now he was relieved that his instincts were correct.

"Where are you meeting Rasta for dinner?" Maxine wanted to make sure Callison had his arrangements taken care of.

"I'm not sure. I'm meeting him in the lobby in a couple of minutes."

"I'm going to check on our reservations, and I'll see you back at the meeting after dinner. Good luck with Rasta." Maxine gave Callison a peck on the cheek. She still smelled good, and her fragrance lingered after she had left the room.

Several seconds after Maxine left there was a knock at the door. Callison assumed Maxine had left something, but when he opened the door, to his surprise it was J.T.

"We have to talk." J.T. barged into the room and sat on the edge of the bed. "First, how did the meeting go?"

"Not real well," Callison moaned.

"Don't worry about the list. I told you we'll take care of you."

"How did you know about the list?"

J.T. gave Callison a knowing look. "We have the room bugged. We have all of it on tape."

"I should have known. So you know it all. Why don't you tell me how it went?" Callison began to pace. He didn't have much time and he still wanted to call Natalie.

"Not bad. I think you got to him, but it's all academic now." J.T. grinned ear to ear.

"What are you talking about?" Callison stopped pacing.

"We got him." A glint of victory emanated from J.T.'s eyes.

"Got who?" Callison didn't like this guessing game.

"Rasta, he's our man. He hired Valentino."

"What are you talking about? Rasta hired an assassin? Why?"

"Probably for the usual reasons, money and power. Rasta fits the pattern of a certain type of sociopath, very intelligent, successful, but still not satisfied, at least in the regular world. They have huge egos and lust for power and dominance. They will go to whatever lengths necessary to feed their overblown egos."

"Sounds like I know a lot of sociopaths," Callison joked.

"No shit." J.T. chuckled. "Anyway, after Rasta made those calls we picked up some of his friends for questioning and struck it rich. Marvin Barnes, a member of his group, sang like a bird. When we suggested he was involved in a possible conspiracy with Rasta, Barnes started to talk. He said he always suspected

485

Rasta was Smithee and he was sure he was behind it all. He promised to testify in court if he's granted immunity from prosecution, and he'll tell us all about Rasta and Valentino." J.T. fell back on the bed.

"You're kidding me?" Callison suspected all along that Rasta was behind this, but had never felt right about it, not even now.

"The bad news is, I think we lost Valentino. I think Rasta called him off the case yesterday because today Valentino transferred $300,000 back into the original account." J.T. sounded disappointed.

"Why would he do that?" Callison asked.

"Valentino returned the $300,000 probably because the hit was canceled. The remainder of the money covered incidentals and his expenses. So I think we're temporarily out of the picture with Valentino, but I'm still hopeful we'll be able to use Rasta to close in on him. That's where we still can use your help. Neither Rasta or Timmons know about Barnes' confession, and we need you to see if you can find out about the Slinger connection before we confront Rasta." J.T. pulled out the wire he had used before. "I also want you to wear the wire again. This is partly for your protection." J.T. tried to be reassuring, but Callison knew the wire was for them, not him.

"So, can I use any of this in my conversation with Rasta?" Callison unbuttoned his shirt. He had already done the routine before.

"This is very important." J.T. stopped Callison from undressing momentarily to ensure his attention. "Because this information may be used in a federal offense, you cannot use this information at all. Anywhere."

"Not even at the meeting?" Callison knew if he could use this at the meeting, they would have to agree to defeat the merger. Without any of this information, it would be unlikely he could garner enough support.

"Especially not at the meeting. You could screw up our whole case and also be convicted of a felony yourself. It could be construed legally that you were obstructing a federal investigation involving the assassination of an elected official." J.T. could not have been more serious.

"You would do that to me?" Callison was angered by the threat.

"Not me, the lawyers. What more can I say?" J.T. lifted his brows and shook his head. "Just don't bring any of this stuff up and we'll all be okay." J.T. finished attaching the wire to Callison's chest.

Callison buttoned his shirt, still angered by J.T.'s threats. He wasn't sure whether J.T. was deceiving him, but he wasn't going to take the chance to find out.

"Don't you have to meet with Rasta now?" J.T. asked.

"Yes." He looked at his watch. It was time to go. He wanted to call Natalie, but not from the phone in his room and not when he was wired. He would call her after the meeting.

Rasta had been waiting for Callison in the lobby, but didn't seem upset that Callison was late.

"Let's get a cab. I have a reservation at O'Brien's Restaurant in Old Town."

Callison got in the cab with Rasta, as Rasta instructed the driver on their destination. Callison had resolved to remain steadfast in his stand on reversing the decision regarding the merger. He now was positive the merger was wrong, and he would do what he could to convince Rasta and the others of that fact.

Once at the restaurant they were immediately seated, and Rasta instructed the waiter to bring them the usual. "I come here frequently. Because of the time constraints I thought I would order for both of us. I hope you don't mind?"

Callison couldn't believe Rasta's audacity, but would hold his comments for the real discussion.

"What do you want?" Rasta asked Callison.

Callison didn't particularly like Rasta's brazen style, but he knew Rasta was in big trouble, so he would humor him. "I want you to help me vote down the merger, I want all copies of the tape, and I want to know how Slinger fits into all of this." Callison handed Rasta the latest Slinger letter which Rasta hastily read.

Rasta shook his head and looked down at the table. "Where

did you get this stuff on Slinger? I never saw any of this."

Callison knew he had enough information to connect Rasta to Slinger, but he couldn't understand the charade. "Look, I have the letters, photographs, and canceled checks. What I don't have is the reason. Why?"

Rasta looked at the ceiling for several seconds before replying. "Somebody is setting me up and I don't know why. I've met with Slinger a couple of times, but always with other people and never about anything specific. As far as these letters are concerned, I have no idea where you got them I never saw that letter, ever."

"Whatever you say." Callison wasn't about to play Rasta's game.

Rasta reclined in his seat, seeming to drift away for a moment. Then suddenly and triumphantly, he smiled. "It must be Smithee."

"What?" Callison couldn't believe Rasta was using Smithee as his excuse.

"Alan Smithee must be setting me up, but why?" Rasta appeared to be verbalizing his thoughts.

Callison knew J.T. was listening, but he couldn't resist taunting the arrogant Rasta. "Stop the pretense, I know you're Smithee."

"Why do you say that?" Rasta appeared surprised by Callison's comment.

"Let's say I have it from a very good source." Callison looked at his watch. Time was running out and they were going nowhere.

"Your source is wrong. I don't know Smithee, but I can say he's probably the one setting me up." Rasta paused and reflected on what he was about to say. "I recently attempted to contact Smithee and his number was forwarded to Slinger's office. At first I didn't understand why, but if he's setting me up, then my phone records would indicate I contacted Slinger."

"Did you speak to Slinger?" Callison asked. Callison knew the call Rasta was referring to.

"No, I immediately hung up. I talked to no one," Rasta said emphatically.

488

Maybe Rasta was telling the truth?

The waiter served the salad, and Callison thought this would be an opportune time to change the subject. "What's your favorite movie?"

"What?" Rasta blurted out as he gave Callison a double-take.

"I know we're on a limited time schedule, but humor me. What's your favorite movie?" Callison asked again.

"I don't know. Can we get back to Smithee, please?"

"You must have a favorite movie, everybody does."

"I don't know, I've never been much of a moviegoer. I like opera, myself. Now can we go back to Smithee, please?" Rasta was becoming annoyed.

"Okay, then can you remember the last movie you saw?"

Rasta thought for several seconds and then answered. "I remember, *Schindler's List*. Maybe that's also my favorite movie."

"Can you remember the last movie you saw before that?"

That was the last straw. "Why are you asking me these inane questions? No . . . I can't. It's been years and I just can't remember, okay?" Rasta was fuming.

Callison had gotten his answer. Maybe Rasta was telling the truth and really wasn't Smithee. Whoever Smithee was had to be some type of movie enthusiast, and it was apparent Rasta wasn't. One last question might give Callison the insight he needed. In his most apologetic tone he asked Rasta. "The last movie question, I promise." Callison crossed his heart as he said the words and gave Rasta a pathetic smile. "Did you ever see a movie called *Death of a Gunfighter*?"

There was no change in Rasta's expression. "No, now can we talk about Smithee?" Rasta was not amused.

Callison had a feeling Rasta was telling the truth about Smithee. "Okay, if I help you find out who Smithee is and why he's setting you up, will you help me with the merger?"

Rasta bit his lower lip and extended his hand across the table. "It's a deal. But with the condition that I don't want either Mrs. Bartolli or Mrs. Tatum to testify. Plus I don't want you to expose the list. I appreciate you keeping my name out of the discussion when you mentioned the list. I realize you intentionally kept the discussion fairly vague, probably hoping we could come to some compromise. Well, I guess this is it. Maybe you're willing to have your career go up in smoke, but I'm not."

Callison didn't need either Mrs. Bartolli or Mrs. Tatum to talk if Rasta agreed to support him, and the issue of not revealing the list appealed to Callison almost as much as it did to Rasta. "I think I can live with those conditions."

"By the way, why did you bring in those two women, anyway?"

"Mrs. Bartolli had information about the death of her husband which tied in nicely with the conspiracy theory, and Mrs. Tatum could confirm the origins of the list. None of which needs to be brought up if I have your support. I guess we can now recommend that the list is not pertinent to our discussion and go on from there." Callison intentionally told Rasta enough to ensure that he was serious about this, but still withheld some information as insurance.

"Well, I think it would be best for all involved to keep these ladies out of all of this. If we can agree on that, I think we have a deal." Rasta forced a smile.

Callison thought he would jump out of his skin. He had the support of the leader of the pack! He had done what he had thought was impossible. He would be able to stop the merger and preserve the osteopathic profession without exposing the list. Callison hadn't felt this elated since the day of his marriage, and maybe not even then.

Callison struggled not to reveal his almost uncontrollable excitement. "So, before I can help you with this Smithee thing, I need to know why he would set you up?" As Callison completed his question the waiter served their main course.

"I can only speculate, but I think Smithee has made some promises to some very powerful people and needs a scapegoat if he can't deliver. I'm his scapegoat. You see, for many years I've acted as Smithee's liaison with the group, never knowing who he is or what he looks like. I've never told anyone this before but when I was recruited into the group, Smithee was the one who contacted me. Even then it was always by phone and never personal contact. Smithee made it clear to me back then, he was in charge and had enough material to ruin my career, but if I played ball, he also had enough influence to make my career. I was young and ambitious so I went along. For the most part it has worked out fine. Along with Smithee and the group we have helped many physicians and supported many in their research and administrative efforts. Why I'm being set up now is a mystery to me."

Callison reflected on this, trying to collate Rasta's information with that which J.T. had given him. If Rasta wasn't Smithee, then J.T. was wrong, but more importantly, *who was Smithee?* Natalie and Linda had proved Smithee was fictitious, and the evidence pointed strongly in the direction of Rasta, but his total lack of knowledge about the movies suggested he knew nothing about Smithee. Callison had to ask, "Do you know where the name Smithee comes from?"

"What do you mean? I guess from his family. Why?" Rasta again seemed sincere in his answer. Either he was accomplished at lying or he was telling the truth.

"No reason, I just thought the name was made up."

"Me too. I tried several years ago to find Smithee, but was never successful. I always thought Smithee was a false identity but I don't know for whom."

"So if I help you, you'll support me in deferring the merger."

"I'll say we discussed some of your concerns and before we can make any final decisions about the merger we need to look into the Hayes Bill in more detail. Would that suffice?" Rasta smiled at Callison, who couldn't believe his ears.

"Why are you agreeing to do this?" Callison said.

"Several reasons. First, I never imagined in my wildest dreams you would have had the courage to jeopardize your career and home life for this. Once you did that, I knew I either had to compromise or have my career likewise ruined." Rasta paused for a second, "In addition, many other innocent hard-working physicians would also have their careers placed in some sort of compromised position. I don't think either you or I really wanted to do that." Callison nodded in agreement.

"Also, the committee's work is important. I don't want all that effort ruined. Don't get me wrong, the merger's an important issue, but the larger issue needs to be discussed without this added controversy. Finally, bringing in Helen Bartolli reminded me of memories I'd rather not resurrect. They need to remain in the past, and bringing them up now would open wounds that needn't be opened."

"What about Smithee?" Callison asked.

"Oh yes, Smithee. The documents you showed me suggest this was thought out very carefully. I have my faults, but whoever Smithee is, he has set me up beautifully. I've worked long and hard on my career, and I'll be damned if I'm going to take this sitting down. I won't be the fall guy for Smithee. I can promise you that."

"We better get back for the meeting," Callison said. They paid the check and hailed a cab back to the meeting.

Callison had about fifteen minutes until the meeting was to reconvene and would use this time to call Natalie. He removed the wire before he called. Callison was still exuberant from his triumph with Rasta and had to tell his wife.

"Natalie, guess what?" Callison's voice was animated.

"What, what's the matter?" Natalie wasn't sure whether the news would be good or bad.

"You won't believe it." Callison then described his stand on the merger and how he used his trump cards, Helen Bartolli and Ethel Tatum.

Natalie was thrilled. "Steven, I'm so proud of you! I know your parents would also be proud of you."

"Anyway, Rasta agreed to support me at the meeting, and I can't believe it." His enthusiasm was still evident. "Before I go to my meeting, I have a question to ask Linda."

Natalie called for Linda to pick the other line. "Hello, Steven. How are you?"

"Fine, Linda, and thank you again for everything." Callison paused and then said, "I still have one question for you."

"Shoot."

"Do you feel George Alexander would have to be a movie buff? In other words, how else could someone know about Alan Smithee?"

"I can't answer how anyone would find out about Smithee. It would make sense that someone who knew the business would be more likely to know about Smithee, but I guess it's possible someone could pick up this information from other sources."

"Other sources? What other sources are you referring to?"

"I have no idea. Just idle speculation," Linda answered.

"So you would assume the person would be well versed in movie trivia?"

"Yes, I guess I would assume that." Linda answered.

"Thanks, Linda."

"You're welcome."

Callison looked at his watch. He was late again, but this time he didn't fear the wrath of Jourge He was about to deliver a compromise that should expedite the meeting and maintain Callison's integrity.

The mood was subdued when Callison entered the room. Jourge had already started questioning Mrs. Bartolli, who was reviewing the circumstances which surrounded the death of her husband. Jourge again glanced in Callison's direction, giving him the evil eye, but this time Callison didn't care.

Callison wanted to interrupt, but didn't want to be rude. Plus, Rasta hadn't returned to the meeting, and he would need Rasta to present his new recommendation; to reverse the decision on the merger. He could then recommend dismissing both Mrs. Bartolli and Tatum, to fulfill his agreement.

Several minutes into Mrs. Bartolli's discussion a security guard entered the room and approached Dr. Jourge. The expression on Jourge's face was of shock and horror, causing Mrs. Bartolli to stop in mid-sentence.

The room remained eerily silent, waiting for Jourge to reveal whatever he had just been told. Jourge's eyes welled with tears and his voice rattled, as all he could muster were the words, "Victor Rasta is dead."

46

A pall overcame the room. Several members of the group started to cry, while others sat paralyzed by the news. Mrs. Bartolli couldn't speak.

Callison was ashamed, as his first thought after hearing the news was how Rasta's death would undermine his proposal. Rasta was the key ingredient in Callison's plan. Now he was gone, leaving a gaping hole Callison could not fill. If he said that Rasta and he had agreed to stop the merger, he would have to give the reasons, which would implicate them both. If he said they agreed on reviewing the Hayes Bill before they would suggest anything definitively, then it would appear he was using Rasta's death as an excuse for obfuscating the merger issue. Callison then realized Rasta was dead. He felt ashamed he had put his own concerns over Rasta's death.

Jourge asked the security guard if he had any details. The guard told them he was found dead, the victim of an apparent suicide. He had shot himself once in the head. The somber mood of the room became even more melancholy.

Callison realized he might have been the last person to have seen Victor Rasta alive. On reviewing Rasta's demeanor when they parted, Callison couldn't recall any indication that Rasta was this desperate. It made no sense.

Percy asked if Rasta left a note. The security guard didn't have any knowledge of a note, but added that the police had isolated the area, so he didn't really have that type of information.

Several others asked the security guard questions, but he was also visibly shaken from the experience. Jourge thanked him for his time and then asked for a moment of silence in the memory of Victor Rasta.

Callison could feel Percy's stare during the moment of silence and so was not surprised when Percy asked, "What did you and

494

Victor talk about that would have made him kill himself?"

Callison expected the question but still didn't have an answer. "I don't know." Callison shrugged his shoulders. "Really, I'm not trying to be flippant or anything. But when we left for our respective rooms, he gave no indication he was depressed or anything remotely suggesting he was about to kill himself."

"What exactly did you talk about?" Percy persisted.

"We talked about the merger and its implications. Also, how the Hayes Bill might be related to the merger." Several of the issues they discussed Callison thought should remain confidential. Did Rasta's suicide indicate he really was Smithee and now that he had been caught he couldn't live with his identity being revealed? Callison could only speculate, but didn't think it appropriate to smear Rasta's name and reputation now that he was dead.

"You didn't talk about anything else?" Percy pressed. He and Rasta had been close friends and he had no idea Rasta was suicidal.

"Nothing of consequence. We barely had enough time to discuss the merger in any detail. Oh yes, there was one thing." Callison decided to go for it. "We both concluded to hold off any final decision on the merger until we could study the Hayes Bill in more depth."

"Yeah, sure," Percy said sarcastically. "I know for a fact, Victor was in favor of the merger, as were you at our last meeting. Remember?" Percy scowled.

"Yes, I remember, but I wasn't aware of the Hayes Bill and all its implications at that time," Callison sternly replied.

"Okay, gentlemen—enough," Jourge interrupted.

Callison thought to himself, *I could taste it—and now it's all gone* . . . There was no way he would be able to convince any of them that the merger decision should be reversed. Less than an hour before, Callison had felt elated and exhilarated. Now he was depressed and dejected. Rasta's death had also killed Callison's hope for reversing the merger decision.

Jourge asked the group if they wanted to take a fifteen-minute break before deciding what to do. They all agreed.

Several members of the group remained in their chairs, still stunned by the news of Rasta's death. Jourge left the room to find a quiet area where he could think without any interruptions. Percy followed Jourge out of the room, only to be dismissed. Callison had watched Percy chase Jourge and was pleased when he saw Percy rejected. As Percy returned, he was followed by J.T., who motioned for Callison to meet him in the hallway.

J.T. looked stressed. His hair was disheveled with strands going in all different directions. A large coffee stain covered his shirt and his eyes conveyed concern. J.T. grabbed Callison by the jacket and pulled him into an empty room at the far end of the hall, closing the door behind them.

J.T.'s nervousness rattled Callison. "What's the matter?" Callison didn't think this was all due to Rasta's death.

"We got trouble. Big trouble." J.T. shook his head and looked down at the floor, purposely avoiding eye contact with Callison.

"What trouble?"

"I had almost all my case based on Rasta and I thought we had him, but now . . ." J.T. stopped. Callison thought he was about to cry. "Anyway, I don't know what you know about his death."

"Only what was said in the meeting. You were listening, weren't you?"

"Yeah, but there's more. The only reason I'm telling you this is for your own safety, but you can't tell a soul. I need your word on this."

"You have it."

"We have reason to believe Rasta didn't commit suicide." Callison raised an eyebrow and J.T. continued, "I had one of my men at the scene. He says it looks like someone set Rasta up. He can't be positive because we have to wait for forensics, but he's reasonably sure Rasta never fired the gun. The residue left after a close range shot should have left some splatter on Rasta's shooting hand and there was none. This leads us to suspect he was killed and then the scene was made to look like a suicide."

"So who do you think killed him?" Callison asked.

"This is where you have to maintain total secrecy."

"Agreed."

"When Van Gregory was released, we put the word on the streets that Rasta had given him up."

"Given him up?"

"We put the word out that when we pulled in Rasta, he gave up Gregory to save his own ass."

"How did you put out the word?"

"That's very easy. We have a saying around the bureau, 'A lie will be halfway around the world before the truth can get its shoes tied.' We've never had trouble getting bad news on the streets."

"So you think Gregory killed Rasta?"

"It's a definite possibility. Plus we already have someone fitting Gregory's description in the building around the time of Rasta's death." J.T. shook his head.

"Sounds suspicious." Callison shook his head too.

J.T. crinkled his nose. "There's another suspect."

"Who?"

"You."

Callison couldn't believe his ears. "Me, you have to be kidding!" Suddenly the air in the room became hot and stuffy causing Callison to breathe deeper.

"No, you have a motive and you were the last person known to have been with Rasta." J.T.'s tone was deadly serious.

"How could I have killed him? I wasn't even with him." Callison could feel his heart pounding, his hands shaking. He was having difficulty catching his breath.

"Can you prove that? We know you had taken off the wire. Why? Were you trying to hide something?"

"Yes, I removed the wire because I wanted to have a conversation with my wife without having you listen in. Check the telephone records, it will show I called my wife." Callison could feel his body calm down as the telephone record should verify his alibi.

"Your wife in Denver. Yes, we already know about the call." J.T. smiled an obnoxious smile.

"If you already knew, why did you say all those things?" Callison was irritated and didn't appreciate the game J.T. was playing.

"I just want to remind you not to cross us because we'll find out. We always do."

"Fine. I get the point." Callison was not amused at J.T.'s glib manner. "Listen, I have to get back."

"Just be careful. And remember we'll be listening."

"See you later." Callison started to leave when J.T. pulled him back into the room.

"One last thing. When the meeting's over, we're going to bring in Timmons for questioning."

"Why are you telling me this?"

"It could get embarrassing, especially if he overreacts. I just thought I'd extend the courtesy of letting you know, in case you wanted to avoid any potential scene."

Callison thanked J.T. and returned to the meeting.

Jourge had not started the meeting. Callison was late again. Jourge stared, but Callison had too many other things on his mind to care.

Callison took the same seat between Thornhill and Danzinger, who were in the midst of a conversation. As he sat, both of them gave him an unseemly look.

Callison viewed the group to get a sense of the mood of the room, when he felt a hand tap him on the shoulder. Jourge wanted to talk with him, and asked Callison to step into the hall for a moment.

"I looked for you at the break but I couldn't find you." Jourge said.

Callison didn't bother to respond.

"Anyway, I am concerned over the issues you mentioned. If these were cogent concerns, why hadn't you advised me earlier?" Jourge adjusted his collar and coughed after he asked the question.

"I wasn't sure what to do. I've been under a lot of pressure, as I'm sure we all have, and I just did what I thought was the right thing to do." Callison didn't need a lecture now, and wasn't in the mood to justify his actions.

"Well, hopefully we can resolve this. I've taken the liberty of dismissing Mrs. Bartolli and Mrs. Tatum. I hope you don't mind but I think the news of Victor's death really unsettled the both of them."

Callison thought for a second before he replied. "I agree. There's no reason to traumatize them further. I assume they'll still be available if a question occurs which they would be able to clarify?"

"Of course. They are staying at our expense until the meeting tomorrow is concluded. I wanted you to know just in case you had another reason for their presence."

"No, they were here primarily to substantiate Dr. Rasta's complicity with the Gance organization. Now that he's gone, well, most of my case is gone too."

"Shall we return and wrap this meeting up?" Jourge placed his arm around Callison and gave him a pat on the back.

Everyone was still seated and quietly conversing when Jourge and Callison returned.

"I know today has been a long and emotionally devastating day, but unfortunately, we still have some more work to do." Jourge almost groaned as he completed his statement. Jourge once again started to slowly move his head in a circular manner, coughing at the completion of the circle. "The issue of the merger remains a topic for discussion. I would like to ask Dr. Callison to review his concerns and the dialogue he and Dr. Rasta shared tonight relative to this issue."

Callison was nervous. He knew what he wanted to say, but with the death of Rasta, he wasn't sure how this would be received. "I have concerns over the merger. I know our subcommittee voted unanimously for a merger, but that was before we had information on the Hayes Bill. I know some of you believe there's no connection between the Hayes Bill and the merger, but I repeat, I have concerns. Tonight after our conversation, Dr. Rasta also shared my concerns and was going to support my motion to table the decision on the merger until these concerns could be addressed."

"I thought we already discussed this," Percy stated, prepared to confront Callison on this issue all night if necessary.

Jourge's mission was to facilitate a decision as quickly as possible. "We do not have the luxury of a prolonged debate on this issue. I would agree to a limited discussion period and then a vote, majority decides." This was really not a question but a statement, and Callison had no choice but to agree.

Callison again gave his reasons for concern, but they were getting old.

His opposition consisted of speeches by Percy and Thornhill, which were to be expected, but when both Timmons and Probst added their support, Callison knew it made no sense to press the issue.

The remainder of the meeting was a blur for Callison, and he didn't even bother to abstain when the final vote was tallied. Jourge thanked the group for their perseverance under extremely difficult circumstances.

The room where they met seemed different as they left. Rasta's papers, still scattered around where he had been seated, remained. Tears were still visible on the faces of several of the committee members. The day had drawn the marrow out of their bones leaving them all exhausted, depressed, and dejected. Jourge left with his consensus document, but without his friend and colleague.

As Callison left the room he was once again confronted by J.T. waiting for him in the hallway.

"Can I have a moment of your time?" J.T. politely asked.

"I'm really tired and would like to just get some rest." Callison was more mentally than physically exhausted. The meeting and the death of Rasta had taken their toll.

"This shouldn't take very long."

"Okay," Callison reluctantly agreed.

As J.T. led him away from the room, Callison noticed out of the corner of his eye two men in navy suits approach Chester Timmons. "Are those guys with you?"

J.T. nodded as they left the building. J.T. walked Callison back to the hotel. They retired to a quiet booth off the lobby next to the bar. J.T. then produced some papers and handed them to Callison. "I feel I owe you this much. If you tell anyone you saw this I could get in a lot of trouble, as could you. This is Rasta's suicide note."

Callison began to read.

Dear Friends and Family,

I know this has come as quite a shock to most of you and for that I apologize. I hope you will be able to forgive me and understand why I had to do this.

First let me explain some things. I know I have not been perfect, but I want you all to know my intentions were always honorable. Many years ago, I was approached by a physician named George Alexander, who presented me with a proposition to manage the Gance organization. He explained the need to keep the organization strictly confidential and under the control of a single individual. I agreed to be that person with the condition that I could appoint a committee to assist me with the oversight of the organization.

I realized to be most effective I would need to create another fictional person who would function as the leader of the organization. This would allow me to continue my career, yet still allow me the ability to fully participate in the Gance organization. Thus, I created the name Alan Smithee. Through Smithee I was able to run the Gance organization and still maintain my own career.

Over the years the organization did many things, most positive, and all were based on enhancing and supporting the medical profession, which I truly love. Retrospectively, some of the decisions were bad, and for those I take total responsibility. I, and I alone, was the responsible party, not the others on the executive committee. They did not know I was Smithee, and they were not privy to the negotiations which have brought me to this place.

Over the years, I thought I was doing what was right for medicine. Recently, I think my judgment was wanting. In the past few years I felt compelled to negotiate for political power in the ever-changing climate of health-care reform. Because of this, some of the groups with special interests, specifically those who were interested in maintaining the status quo, donated significant funds to our organization, and I felt an obligation to support their interests with our group. Maybe I was wrong.

In supporting the interests of some, I may have neglected what was best for the whole and now I must pay the price. The decisions I made, I thought were correct, but I was misguided.

To say I'm sorry is not enough. I have inadvertently implicated many of my colleagues in some practices which could be construed as illegal. I want to reiterate they had no knowledge of any illegal actions. I do not want their careers tarnished by my stupidity. That is why I chose this option. If I had to testify, many people would get hurt and for no good reason other than they were innocently involved. I hope my death will clear the air and let the process continue without any recrimination against those who are innocent. I've dedicated my life to my family and my profession, but if I am to be judged by my recent mistakes then so be it.

Please do not feel sorry for me, as I have had a good life, full of joy and satisfaction. I could not tolerate watching my career dragged through the mud because of my recent mistakes. It is better this way, for me, and for medicine.

Please do the right thing and do not punish the innocent, so I might rest in peace.

Good-bye,
Victor Rasta, M.D.

Callison sighed as he finished the letter, looking up at J.T., who had been studying him as he read.

"We're sure he committed suicide. His were the only prints on the gun, which was registered to him, and his were the only prints on the disk on which the note was written." J.T. took the papers from Callison and placed them in an attaché case, then looked around the room and grunted, taking the papers out again.

"Then your suspicions about Gregory are unfounded?"

"To put it in a word, yes," J.T. answered. The note plus the evidence was convincing.

"What about your concerns with the blood. You know the splatter pattern?" Callison was intrigued by J.T.'s prior theory, plus he didn't want to believe Rasta had actually killed himself.

"Actually our expert did say it was possible because of the angle of the entry wound, for the blood not to splatter on his shooting hand. The forensics will give us that answer. But for now, we are reasonably confident he did commit suicide." J.T. looked away for a moment, contemplating what he would say next. "There is one more thing I have to say."

"I guess I'm ready." Callison was drained and didn't want to hear any more bad news, but he really didn't have any choice.

"We deleted some of the text because it implicated some very respectable people and we need to check it out first. See here . . ."

502

J.T. pointed to a section on the page. "Right after this 'misguided' line, he talked about some specific areas in which he made mistakes. What I can tell you is, one of the mistakes deals with the merger decision. He says he thinks a merger is inevitable, but not now and not for these reasons. I wanted you to know that, because if this becomes public record, people might point in your direction. I want you to know this was not about tonight. Whatever Rasta had planned was done well in advance of your meeting tonight. He had already typed this message and had brought his gun to the hotel room. His suicide was premeditated. I wanted you to know that. I'm sure someone will try to blame you for driving him over the edge. I just want you to know he was already there." J.T. put his powerful hand on Callison's right shoulder and squeezed.

Callison placed his left hand on J.T.'s hand and squeezed back. "Thanks for telling me this. It really means a lot to me." Callison thought for a second before asking, "Now that Rasta's dead, can I use some of this to delay or table the merger issue?"

J.T. frowned. "Sorry, you can't use any of this. We're still in the process of investigating, and there's a strong possibility there may be some indictments coming out of this mess."

"So I can't use any of this?" Callison frowned.

"Nothing from this. In fact, you don't know this note exists. Correct?" J.T.'s voice was once again serious.

"Correct," Callison said reluctantly. Every time he was close, the door would slam in his face.

"You look tired. Get some sleep. You still have a big day ahead of you tomorrow." J.T. shook Callison's hand and left, as Callison veered for the elevators so he could go to bed.

Upon entering his room, Callison noticed the flashing light indicating he had a message. He called the operator for his messages and there were three. The first was from Truelove, the second was from Peter Moiner, and the third was from Mrs. Tatum. Callison looked at his watch. It was too late to meet with the group at Peter Moiner's home, but maybe they were still there. That would be his first call.

"Hello, Peter, Callison here." The exhaustion carried in Callison's voice.

"Where are you?" Peter asked, as if he were surprised by Callison's absence.

"Didn't Truelove tell you I probably wouldn't be able to make the meeting?" Callison inquired. Maxine had been so efficient in the past, he naturally thought she would have followed through.

"No, but he's here. Let me ask him." Callison could overhear Peter yelling at Truelove and Truelove denying he was aware of Callison's prior commitments.

"That's strange. Didn't Maxine tell Truelove about the other meeting?" Callison said.

Peter again yelled in the direction of Truelove, who again had no idea what Callison was referring to. He hadn't seen Maxine all day.

Peter continued, "Anyway, we were unable to find Gregory. The word on the street is he left town. But there's another rumor out there, that he's after this guy Rasta."

"Rasta's dead," Callison said.

"We know. The other rumor is, Gregory did him," Peter said with half-hearted confidence.

"I have it from a reliable source Rasta's death was self-induced. He committed suicide." Callison said.

"Maybe. Homicides can be made to look like suicides."

Callison considered telling Peter about the suicide note, but restrained himself after he considered the consequences. "I agree there's some doubt, but like I said, I have very reliable sources who are convinced he committed suicide."

"Do you want to talk to Truelove?"

"Sure, but before you go, what did you decide tonight?" Callison's inside information from J.T. should allow him to protect them from any actions that could interfere with the ongoing FBI investigation.

"Basically, we're waiting for you. Paul and I will try again tomorrow to find Gregory, but we doubt we'll be successful. I'll let Truelove tell you what he found out." Peter handed the phone to Truelove.

"Hello, Steven. Quite a day."

"Yeah, quite a day. You and Ethan did a great job." Callison was serious.

"They didn't buy our story, did they?"

"The story was fine, what was lacking was the corroborating evidence. That was to be Rasta. When he died, so did our case." Callison wanted to tell Truelove how he had convinced Rasta to cooperate, but decided against it. It was time to let Rasta be. Enough was enough.

"So where do we go from here?" Truelove asked, his voice carrying the disappointment they were all feeling.

"I don't know. The merger will be recommended tomorrow. Although we can oppose it, we really don't have a strong case."

"Have you talked to Mrs. Tatum? I know she wanted to tell you something."

"No, I got a message to call her but I called you instead," Callison said. "Anyway it's probably too late to call her now. I bet all she wanted was to tell me she was sorry she didn't get a chance to testify today." Callison felt sorry that both Mrs. Tatum and Mrs. Bartolli had to experience the trauma of the day.

"I'm not sure. I only know she really wanted to speak to you and only you. She wouldn't tell me why, but she did say she was waiting for your call. Although she didn't specify, I believe she wanted to talk to you tonight."

"I got the message. Before I go, how do you think we did?" Callison was concerned he had let them down.

"I think we did fine. Rasta and his group have been exposed and are probably out of commission. Gregory's on the run and with the help of the FBI, I'm sure he'll get what's coming to him. Hopefully when this is investigated further the deaths of Amos Wilcox, Jonas Cisko, and Marcus Merker will be avenged, and those responsible will be held accountable. The merger probably will happen sooner or later. I don't know what else could be done to prevent it. On the whole, I think we all did a great job."

"I'll see you tomorrow. You'll be at the conference?" Callison said dejectedly.

"We'll be there." Truelove hung up.

Callison looked at the time, it was getting late but he had two more calls to make. First, he had to talk to Natalie.

Callison told Natalie of Rasta's death and how his case had

fallen totally apart, apparently irreparable. He told her how he wanted to leave and not even participate in the conference tomorrow. He told her about his conversation with J.T. and how he was forbidden to reveal any of the information he was privy to. And he told her how he couldn't muster any support to preserve his profession.

Natalie's response surprised him. Instead of her usual support, she lambasted him. She told him to stop whining and feeling sorry for himself and use his ingenuity and come up with a solution. He had the data, and he needed to take a stand. If he really believed the profession needed to be saved, then he had to do whatever he could to save it. If his career needed to be sacrificed, then so be it. He needed his integrity more.

By the time Natalie had finished, Callison was rejuvenated and had decided to try one more time to reverse the merger decision. He didn't know how he would do it, but he knew he would try.

Before he could concentrate on a new strategy, he had to call Mrs. Tatum. He knew the hour was late, but she had requested he call. He would honor that request.

47

Callison had spent most of the night reviewing notes and files while developing a plan. Tormented by J.T.'s implied threats, he designed several variations of a scheme in which he might be able to halt the merger proposal without destroying himself in the process.

The room where the conference was to be held looked different from when he first saw it. The television cameras were situated in the far corners of the room, with a section roped off to prevent any curious participants from manhandling the equipment. A section of chairs were centralized in the room, which would accommodate about seventy people. Several large flood lights were strategically located to illuminate the room for television. The committee table was arranged in a horseshoe configuration to allow each member access to the audience, with each chair having its own individual microphone to ensure that each and every word would be clearly heard and recorded. The names of the members of the committee were placed on placards. Callison noted he was seated between Robert Thornhill and Susanna Michelson, thus keeping his subcommittee together for their presentation.

Another area separated from the flow of the room housed several large conference chairs. Callison concluded this was the dignitary section. However, just who those dignitaries were was still unknown.

A security guard approached Callison and told him the room was closed to the public. Callison explained who he was and asked if he could examine the room before he presented. The security guard understood Callison's concerns, but explained to him they also had a protocol to follow. He escorted Callison to another man, who identified himself as Secret Service. Callison was frisked and his identification was inspected before he was allowed to explore the room. Callison meandered around while several technicians were completing their work and a security team was inspecting the room one last time.

Callison likewise surveyed the room one last time. In less than two hours the conference would start and it would be show time. He returned to the hotel to get dressed for the event. He would wear his most conservative suit—navy blue, pin-striped, the one Natalie said made him look like a banker, or worse, a lawyer. For some reason he couldn't make the knot in his tie look right. Where was Natalie when he really needed her?

By the time Callison returned to the conference room the television crews were in place, the security system was in effect, and several members of the press were in attendance. A small room on a separate corridor was reserved for the committee members before the meeting. Jourge had mentioned he wanted to meet with the group an hour before the conference was to start, ostensibly to review any last minute details. It was imperative the meeting went off without a hitch.

Most of the committee were already seated in the small meeting room, with the exception of Teitelman and Percy. The atmosphere was somber. The death of Rasta had deeply affected every member of the committee, leaving them all in a reflective state. Michelson looked as if she hadn't slept at all, and the others didn't look much better. Callison had noted the deep, darkened circles under his own eyes and realized he probably looked as bad as the others. Jourge was the only member who looked refreshed, even though he probably slept less than most. He was ready to go and mark his place in history.

"How are you doing?" The voice startled Callison, who was looking out the window.

"I'm okay, I guess," Callison said as he turned around to face Jourge.

"Yesterday was very traumatic. Victor Rasta was a close friend, and his death was excruciatingly painful for me. I know yesterday wasn't easy for you either. There's a line from the movie *I Never Sang for My Father,* where Gene Hackman is eulogizing his father, Melvyn Douglas, which epitomizes my feelings: 'Death ends a life, but it does not end the relationship, which struggles on in the survivor's mind toward some resolution it may never find.'" Jourge squeezed his eyes, nose, and mouth tightly. It wasn't a pretty sight. "I just wanted you to know you're not alone."

"Thanks." Callison didn't know what else to say. Fortunately, before he had to say anything else both Teitelman and Percy arrived.

Jourge reviewed the agenda for the conference: first, the secretary of health would make some introductory remarks. Jourge would then introduce the committee members. Next, Jourge would present the executive summary statement, which be followed by a question and answer period. Afterward they were all asked to remain for a media briefing and press conference.

"Before we formally convene for the meeting, I would like to personally thank each and every one of you. The mandate to expedite this report has created quite a strain on each of us and even under these most trying of circumstances we prevailed. For that you have my utmost gratitude and respect. I know Victor would have wanted us to proceed, and proceed we will. What we are about to accomplish is nothing less than actuating an epiphany out of entropy. I am confident that our efforts will herald the president's health-care reform initiative." As he completed his remarks Jourge motioned for the committee to follow him to the conference room.

The room looked much smaller, with all the seats filled. A group of what appeared to be Secret Service men were stationed against the far back wall.

Scanning the crowd Callison recognized the faces of his group: they were all there with the exception of Ethan Jasper, waiting for the opportunity to actualize their plan. Also in the crowd was J.T.

Callison took his place on the raised platform, which afforded him an excellent view of the audience. Everything was set. Callison knew his plan was risky, but with a little luck it would work.

Moments after Callison was seated he was blinded by the flood lights for the television cameras, a circumstance he hadn't accounted for. Callison could not see past the first row of the audience. This could be a factor in his ability to implement the plan, because he needed to maintain eye contact with his group. Out of the corner of his eye he noticed the secretary of health enter with his entourage and security escort, accompanied by a murmur of whispers acknowledging his presence.

Jourge stood at the podium which was positioned on the left side of the platform stage and waited for the noise to dissipate. Several members of the media continued their private conversations, but finally succumbed to Jourge's cold, silent stare. Once the room was silent, Jourge introduced Horace Jamison, the Secretary of Health.

Horace Jamison walked with confidence. Some would call it a swagger, but it fit his deportment. A handsome man, graying at the temples, slim and riveting blue eyes. "It is truly an honor to address such a prestigious group on this memorable day. The journey which we started many months ago to reform the health-care of this great nation will take a quantum leap forward today. The tireless efforts of these men and women before you cannot be praised enough, for no reform can be achieved without the physicians trained in the art of primary care to fulfill the medical needs for the millions now without access to health care. The recommendations today will be an integral component of the health-care reform package the president will present to Congress later this month. Without further ado, I would like to present the chairman of the committee, Dr. Alexander Jourge."

Jamison initiated the applause, and the audience followed politely.

Jourge stood at the podium exuding confidence and poise. He had a written text from which he would read his summary statement. The cameras were rolling, the chatter subsided, and Jourge stood alone in the spotlight, reading the consensus statement. It took Jourge seventeen minutes to conclude his address. Callison was impressed at the elegance and clarity of Jourge's statements. Although he knew the holes and warts in Jourge's logic, it was still an impressive presentation. Callison expected applause at the conclusion of Jourge's presentation, but there was none. Instead there was the press, ready with their questions.

Callison had his troops positioned for their assault on the merger issue. According to their plan, the first wave was to come from an unlikely source, James Williams, the man who had once threatened Callison but would now initiate the dialogue. Truelove was to follow Williams, and then either Jasper or Mrs. Bartolli would add their contribution. Lastly, Mrs. Tatum as the coup de grace.

Callison had orchestrated the production and would signal Williams at the appropriate time. Callison wanted to have Jasper in attendance before Williams started, just in case he needed him.

The initial questions from the media were general and non-controversial, with Jourge needing very little support from the other committee members to answer. A man in a gray suit approached the microphone and announced he was from the Associated Press. Callison did not catch his name but the question caught his attention.

"Dr. Jourge, can you confirm or deny the allegation that a member of your committee was involved with a noted senator and the result of this involvement preferentially influenced your committee's recommendations?" As he spoke a flurry of side comments were made throughout the press corps. The man raised his voice over the noise and continued his questioning. "And furthermore, when this issue was brought to the attention of said committee member, he committed suicide?"

The mild din was now a resounding uproar, forcing Jourge to bang his gavel and demand quiet.

"Mr.?" Jourge had also forgotten the man's name.

"Wentzel, Arthur Wentzel," the man in the gray suit obliged.

"Mr. Wentzel, I have no idea to what you are referring, and I find it offensive that you have denigrated a highly respected colleague of mine with your innuendo. I hope you have a *procès-verbae*."

"I have a what?"

"A *procès-verbae*, an official written record to substantiate your remarks." Jourge sneered at Wentzel.

"I beg your pardon, sir." Wentzel was not about to back down from his issue. "I have, from reliable sources, information confirming these allegations and also of your knowledge of these issues."

Jourge was infuriated, but needed to stay in control. He closed his eyes and slowly counted to ten. He started to turn his head in a circular motion and cough after each turn while he straightened out his collar. Once he finished counting, Jourge felt he could continue without shouting. His voice took on a disagreeable, strident quality, which was extremely intimidating. "These sources you claim to have—they had better be as reliable as you allege, because I have no idea to what you are referring."

"I can assure you they are." Wentzel smirked.

Several reporters darted out of the room to call their respective bosses. The cameramen were honing in on Jourge as he commented, hoping for some type of histrionics. Unfortunately, Jourge was disappointing to them. The members of the committee were all stunned by the question, by Jourge's response, and the implications this entailed.

Callison focused onto Williams, who shrugged his shoulders as if to say, "I had nothing to do with this." Callison's attention then moved to J.T., who had summoned one of his men and was in the midst of a heated discussion. J.T. was animated in his discourse, and it was evident he wasn't pleased. J.T. paused momentarily to look toward Callison, who averted his accusatory glance.

Before Jourge could respond further, Horace Jamison bolted to the platform and gently but firmly pushed Jourge aside, taking control of the conference. "Before we go any further, I want this room cleared. Only the committee members and Mr. Wentzel can remain. I promise we will have this matter sorted out momentarily, and I will personally conduct a press conference at the conclusion of this closed meeting to update everyone on this issue." Jamison waved his hands, instructing the security guards and the Secret Service to clear the room.

J.T. showed his identification and was allowed to stay. Several members of the press protested their forced exit from the meeting, claiming their rights had been violated. Jamison had little sympathy for their claim. He had a much larger problem to grapple with and didn't need the press to complicate matters any further. The group Callison had arranged to effectuate his plan were also all removed.

As the room was being cleared and Callison watched his group leave, he thought, *This is a disaster; what else could possibly go wrong?* Then J.T. approached Callison and whispered in his ear. "I'll get you for this."

Callison could feel the warmth of J.T.'s breath and his saliva spray his ears. Callison wanted to tell J.T. he was innocent, but he couldn't speak. He realized he shouldn't speak.

Callison had visions of prison race through his mind. How could he prove he had nothing to do with this? Since no names had been mentioned, maybe the reference was to another senator and not Slinger. Callison had to wait and see.

The room was finally cleared. All the cameras remained in their places, and security guards were placed at all the exits. Jamison had resolved to get to the bottom of this. His career, and possibly the career of the president of the United States, depended on it.

"Okay, Mr. Wentzel. I'm shocked at your audacity by making these accusations at this meeting." Jamison never had a fondness for the press and this didn't help his impression. Jamison continued, "But we need to get to the bottom of this mess, so can you please continue."

"I have information from two sources that a senator intimately related to the health-care reform initiative was given substantial campaign contributions in exchange for certain favors which were to be forthcoming from this committee."

"May I ask your sources?" Jamison inquired.

"That information is privileged," Wentzel replied.

"May I add something here?" J.T. interrupted.

"And who are you?" Jamison asked.

"I'm with the FBI, sir. And we have an ongoing investigation regarding some of these allegations," J.T. answered.

"So this is real?" Jamison couldn't believe what he was hearing. If this became public, it had the potential to be a political nightmare.

"We're not sure what's real at this point. But one thing is real, and that is the fact Mr. Wentzel here could be looking at some serious jail time if he doesn't cooperate." J.T. turned from Jamison and coldly stared at Wentzel.

Wentzel knew this was possibly the story that would make his career. Was it worth going to jail for? "If I reveal my sources, will that information remain in this room?"

"I can't guarantee that." J.T. said matter-of-factly. "But I have someone, as we speak, obtaining a warrant for your arrest for obstructing justice in a federal investigation. I promise you, it's not worth it."

"My sources are from an aide in the office of Nathan Slinger, a man named Lance Darby, and from a secretary who has worked closely with Dr. Rasta, Dr. Jourge, and the committee as a whole, by the name of Maxine Wells."

Callison would have fallen if he hadn't already been seated. What did Maxine have to do with this? He also realized he hadn't seen Maxine since the previous evening in his hotel room. Where was she?

"What exactly did you find out?" Jamison was heartsick. Nathan Slinger had been handpicked by the president himself.

"Darby told me that after the committee was disbanded, Dr. Rasta would conditionally be promised a position by Senator Slinger, only if his committee delivered on specific issues which would support Slinger's needs. I don't have all the details with me, but I have some notes which include policies on the care of the indigent and rural areas, as one of the major issues which Slinger has as part of his personal agenda. My sources also suggest special interest groups contributed heavily to Senator Slinger's campaign, and these same groups might benefit greatly from these reforms. This was confirmed by Ms. Wells, who said she had information that a conspiracy was in place and Dr. Rasta was heading the conspiracy."

"So let me restate this so I am totally clear. You're saying you have proof that Dr. Victor Rasta had worked with Senator Slinger in some sort of conspiracy which involves this committee?" Jamison squinted his left eye as if he was in pain.

"That's a fair statement," Wentzel answered.

"What else can you tell us about either Mr. Darby or Ms. Wells?" Jamison asked.

"Darby appears to be one of those spit-and-polish politician types. A real go-getter, but to be honest I'm still somewhat lacking on my research into his background. And for Ms. Wells . . ."

Before Wentzel could reply, Jourge answered, "I personally brought in Ms. Wells and it is evident I miscalculated. I offer no whiny attempts to justify her malignity. The grace that might have redeemed her seemed to be her breathtaking lack of hypocrisy. But that was misconstrued by myself and I contend she's an economic woman on an intricate and divinely sociopathic rampage."

"Why do you say that?" Jamison was struck at Jourge's vindictiveness.

"Because both Dr. Rasta and myself encouraged and supported Ms. Wells. Her treachery can only be construed as pathologic. She's a doctor hater," Jourge said plainly without emotion.

"Do you agree?" Jamison asked Wentzel.

"I really don't feel comfortable commenting." Wentzel replied.

Callison sat frozen to his seat. His worst fears were realized. Both Rasta and Slinger were named, his plan was rendered useless, and Maxine was crucified by Jourge. Should he defend Maxine? He really didn't know her. If she was involved with Wentzel, maybe Jourge was right. Plus there was always the tape. Callison couldn't afford to blow his credibility defending Maxine, at least not at this time.

The committee sat silent, while Jamison changed the subject. "So for this conspiracy to work, Rasta must have had some help on this committee?" Jamison's response was as much a statement as a question. He scanned the group seated around the table hoping for a response.

"I agree with your logic but I don't know for sure," Wentzel said.

Jamison looked toward Jourge with his brow furrowed. "Dr. Jourge, are you telling me you know nothing about any of this?"

Jourge answered without hesitating. "That is correct."

Jamison then turned toward Wentzel. "Can you get your sources here so we can get to the bottom of this?"

"I have no idea where either of them are. I haven't seen

either of them today. Other than trying to contact them at work or home I would have no idea how to reach them."

Darby had approached Wentzel, and it was Darby who recommended he investigate Rasta. It was during Wentzel's investigation of Rasta that he stumbled across Maxine Wells.

"Sir, I'm sending some agents out immediately. We'll find them," J.T. said confidently.

Jamison stood in the middle of the half-circle, rubbing his chin in deep thought. He slowly looked at each person sitting around the table before he spoke. "Let me ask the same question of you. Do any of you have any insight into any of this?"

The moment of truth had arrived for Callison. This was not at all as he planned, but the cards were on the table and he would have to play the hand he had been dealt.

Callison summoned up all his strength before responding. "I have some knowledge that may shed some light on this."

The group looked as stunned as when Wentzel initially brought up the subject. Teitelman shook his head while looking at Callison, silently pleading with him to not continue. Callison returned Teitelman's silent plea with one of his own.

"I have been privy to some of the data that Mr. Wentzel has presented, but I differ with him over several points. I met with Victor Rasta last evening before his untimely death, and I'm convinced he was not in charge of any conspiracy. I would agree he was part of the group which led the conspiracy, but I have a strong feeling he was set up." Callison waited for any type of response from the group. There was none.

"So are you confirming a conspiracy exists? Do you have any proof of this?" Jamison asked, dejectedly shaking his head.

"Yes. The leader of this conspiracy goes by the name of Alan Smithee. There is some evidence that suggests Alan Smithee was actually Victor Rasta, but I don't think that's true. Rasta told me he was set up, and I believe he was telling the truth." Callison had started and now he had to see this through to the end.

"Why do you say that?" J.T. said.

"Because he had no reason to lie to me. Last evening we talked about all of this and Dr. Rasta was not talking like a man

516

who was about to kill himself. We agreed to help each other. I would help him find out who Smithee was, and he would help me defeat the merger proposal."

"That's a lie! Rasta would have never agreed to that." Percy stood and shouted instinctively, then became self-conscious when he realized he was standing and everyone was staring at him.

"How do you know, were you there?" Callison responded, knowing Percy was wrong.

"Because Victor and I had discussed this in the past, and he was adamant about the merger. I know he wouldn't change his mind." Percy was still standing at his seat.

"But he did change his mind. I was there," Callison answered confidently.

"I doubt that." Percy said.

Callison looked toward J.T., asking with his eyes whether he could reveal the tape recording of their conversation which would confirm his statement. J.T. was still angry over Callison's apparent breach of confidence, shook his head.

"The merger was a negotiable issue with Rasta. After our discussion he agreed we needed more information before finalizing our recommendation." Callison knew he had no way to prove this without the tape.

"I know this was a non-negotiable issue with Rasta, but I don't know why you're changing your decision." Percy said.

Before Callison could reply Jourge interrupted. "Look—this isn't going anywhere, let's drop this." It was not a question but a command.

"Dr. Callison, do you have anything else to say?" Jamison asked.

"Yes. I have proof that Alan Smithee is actually a person named George Alexander and that person is present here today under another name," Callison said. "Also, I have proof that George Alexander is the leader of the conspiracy and had Victor Rasta set up, in an effort to protect himself."

"And what is that proof?" Jamison asked.

J.T.'s jaw dropped at Callison's statement.

"First I would like to ask a question of the committee." He

517

paused. "Can you tell me your favorite movie?" Callison smiled as he asked the question.

"I don't see the relevance here," Jourge protested.

"Please humor me on this," Callison pleaded.

"Mr. Jamison haven't we heard enough of this banal dribble? I implore you to move the agenda." Jourge said in frustration.

Callison looked at Jourge and recalled his earlier reference to the movie *I Never Sang For My Father*. He knew he had to continue with this topic. "I know this seems a bit far-fetched, but if you could indulge me for just a few minutes, I assure you this will be pertinent to our discussion." Callison knew this would further aggravate Dr. Jourge, but he was willing to take that chance.

Jamison agreed and everyone then spoke about their favorite movie.

"Can you explain why we just did that?" Jourge was irritated at the apparent frivolity.

"It will become clear in several minutes, if you allow me to bring in someone who can verify my statement, help explain the details of the conspiracy, as well as clarify the logic behind the movie question." Callison crossed his fingers, hoping he would be allowed to bring his group into their meeting.

Jamison thought for several seconds before responding. "I'd very much like to get to the bottom of this, so if I don't hear an objection, I would like to comply with the request."

Jourge started to protest, but waited to see who Callison would bring in before he would make his decision. The others were too overwhelmed by the entire scenario to dissent.

The security guard opened the back door of the conference room and led Callison to the room where the participants of the session had been sequestered. When Callison entered he was immediately mobbed by reporters. Ignoring the press, Callison located his group which was minus Ethan Jasper, who still was absent, and James Williams, who had left. Callison escorted the remaining members of his group back to the meeting.

48

The group followed Callison to the first row where they took their seats. Percy protested, saying he was under the impression Callison was bringing in one person, not an army. Jamison ignored his remarks, and none of the other committee members joined in Percy's protest.

The committee recognized the group from the meeting the previous day: Truelove, Mrs. Tatum, and Mrs. Bartolli. Jamison asked for Callison to introduce each member of the group, which Callison did. Callison then informed Jamison of both Dr. Thornhill's previous contact with Mrs. Tatum and the late Dr. Rasta's relationship with Mrs. Bartolli. Finally Callison again asked if there were any other prior relationships which might cause a conflict of interests. The remainder of the committee denied any prior contact with any of Callison's witnesses.

Callison then called for his first witness, Dr. Tyler Truelove.

"Before we proceed any further I want to caution all of you that everything said in this room is classified," Jamison said. "Although we are not in court, you are under oath to tell nothing but the truth."

Callison asked Truelove to testify first. Truelove reviewed an abbreviated version of the history of the prior merger in California. He then showed the committee Amos Wilcox's letter which mentioned both Rasta and Smithee by name, as well as a Dr. Alexander. The letter mentioned the list, and Truelove explained about their investigation of the list.

Teitelman could sense what was about to happen next and excused himself as Truelove showed them a copy of both the Tatum–Gance list and the Caldo list. Between the two, they named them all, save McMillan, Probst, and Jourge. Truelove ended with the files from the original list which were provided by Mrs. Tatum, containing the unseemly details on Rasta and

George Alexander, who had died in 1968 of an apparent suicide. He also mentioned there was no record at all of an Alan Smithee.

By the time Teitelman returned from the restroom, Mrs. Bartolli had started to describe her husband's stormy relationship with Rasta. She also told them of the private detective she hired after her husband's death and of his mysterious notebook. She described how they had deciphered the code in the notebook and how the cryptic AS Elwood R Loax actually translated to Alan Smithee's phone number. She then explained how that number had been billed to George Alexander and not Alan Smithee.

Jamison was becoming annoyed. "Dr. Callison, I appreciate the amount of effort that has gone into your presentation, but you must be aware the press corps is waiting for an answer. Can we move this along?"

Callison motioned for Mrs. Bartolli to continue. Helen Bartolli smiled at the group. She then proceeded to hold them spellbound as she unraveled the web of Alan Smithee.

Mrs. Bartolli continued, "The next part of this puzzle had us baffled for a while. It seems Dr. Alexander was paying the bills for Alan Smithee after he had committed suicide."

"Who, Smithee or Alexander?" Jamison asked.

"Alexander was the one who supposedly committed suicide. This led us to two conclusions: Alexander wasn't dead and Smithee wasn't real. Which led us to the third conclusion, that Smithee and Alexander were probably one and the same. This opinion was confirmed when we discovered the origin of Alan Smithee. Alan Smithee is a fictitious name used by motion picture directors who refuse to have their identity associated with their films. In other words, Smithee doesn't exist. His name is used only when the true director wants to remain anonymous. What's also of interest is the omission of Alexander's name from the Gance list. We know he had to be on it, because Mrs. Tatum had the original files in which he was included. We believe the real Smithee had no knowledge of Mrs. Tatum's files, so we can only surmise that the name was intentionally deleted by Smithee–Alexander. Without any records, Alexander would have never existed. Thus, we concluded if we find Alexander, we'll find Smithee and therefore the leader of the conspiracy."

Callison then entered the conversation. "Now hopefully you can appreciate the question I asked you about your favorite movie. All of us could readily recite our favorite movie without any hesitation. However, Victor Rasta couldn't. He literally had to strain to think of any movie. As he stated, he wasn't a fan, he preferred the opera. I doubt he would have used Alan Smithee for his code name." Callison grinned triumphantly.

"Are you suggesting Dr. Rasta wasn't involved in spite of the evidence presented, the evidence you presented, just because he wasn't a movie buff?" Jamison was confused.

"No, I'm not saying he wasn't involved. I'm just saying he wasn't in charge. He wasn't Smithee." Callison's grin faded.

"But Rasta was listed along with Smithee and Alexander in the letter you presented. Plus, he appears to be the common denominator connecting the stories of Dr. Truelove and Mrs. Bartolli. Rasta is also the person implicated in Mr. Wentzel's investigation, tying him with Senator Slinger. Not to mention he killed himself. How can you be so sure there's someone else?" Jamison asked.

Callison could see in the eyes of the others seated around the table, including J.T. The evidence pointed to only one person, Victor Rasta.

Before Callison could answer, Jourge sneezed. Then he stood as he started to talk. "Dr. Callison, I appreciate your concern, but as the newest representative on the committee I feel compelled to remind you of the numerous sacrifices both personal and professional we have all made. I was as close to Victor Rasta as anyone in this room and I mourn his passing. But the evidence appears overwhelming. Victor was unfortunately associated with this list and for whatever misguided reason shared this information with Senator Slinger as evidenced by the letter Mr. Wentzel presented. Can we please let him rest in peace?" Jourge bowed his head, as his words faded.

Jamison lowered his head and without looking up asked Callison if he was through.

"I appreciate Dr. Jourge's sentiments, but I have a question to ask Dr. Jourge." Callison had a gleam in his eye.

"Of course." Jourge responded.

"What letter are you referring to? I don't recall Mr. Wentzel discussing any letter." Callison turned from Jourge toward Wentzel.

"Mr. Wentzel, did you mention a letter?" Jamison asked.

Wentzel looked first at Jourge, then at Callison, then again at Jourge. "I don't know of any letter. My information was from a verbal statement from Lance Darby, which I have on tape."

A hush fell over the room. Callison sat back in his chair.

Jourge blushed, while he moved his head in a circular motion and coughed. "Victor had told me of a letter he had received from Slinger, offering him a position in the administration if he finessed our committee into satisfying Slinger's agenda."

"Why didn't you mention this before?" Jamison asked, his tone harsh.

"Victor was a dear friend of mine and I couldn't further denigrate his memory. I now realize I was wrong in withholding this information. I apologize." Jourge's usual strong voice trailed off as he completed his apology.

"What else do you know about this conspiracy that you have not told us?" Jamison was growing angry.

"Honestly, that's all I know. When Victor—I mean Dr. Rasta—told me of this letter, he assured me he would have nothing to do with the senator. Because of the tremendous time constraints we both agreed to not pursue this until the committee work was completed. I guess Dr. Rasta succumbed."

"Then you know nothing else of the conspiracy?" Jamison asked.

"Nothing," Jourge said.

"Dr. Callison, do you have anything else?" Jamison inquired.

"Before I conclude my report, I would like Mrs. Tatum to speak. She has come all the way from Florida and I believe her presentation should clarify most if not all of your questions." Callison looked at the frail elderly woman and then at the committee members. No one appeared to disagree.

Mrs. Tatum looked old; she had a kyphotic hump of her back due to osteoporosis and had a mild resting tremor.

Her voice started to crack as she spoke and was barely audible and totally unintelligible. Jamison strained to hear what she was saying, when he politely interrupted her. "Excuse me, Mrs. Tatum, could you please speak louder?"

Jourge then spoke. "Please do not take this in any manner as an insult, but is there anyone here who can vouch for her mental competence? I know I am not alone in my consternation about the accuracy of Mrs. Tatum's pending testimony. We need to be absolutely confident of Mrs. Tatum's faculties, since there is so much contingent on her presentation. Before we proceed, I implore you to accede her competence."

Percy added, "I must agree with Dr. Jourge. I couldn't understand a word she just said and I feel very uncomfortable hearing her testimony without some assurance that she does have all her faculties."

Jamison thought for a second before agreeing. "I apologize to Mrs. Tatum, but because of the importance of her statements, we need some assurance that she is competent."

"You have to be kidding! This is preposterous," Callison exclaimed, flinging his hands in the air.

"Dr. Callison, please calm down. I could barely hear, let alone understand Mrs. Tatum when she first addressed us and if she has some, some . . . " Jamison struggled for a word. " . . . impairment, then we should hold off on hearing her testimony."

All eyes focused on Thornhill, who had defended her honor the previous day. Thornhill felt compelled to say something in her defense. "I have known the Tatums for many, many years. In her youth Mrs. Tatum had a mind that was razor sharp, but I haven't had any contact with her in nearly forty years. In all good conscience, I cannot honestly vouch for her competence. I'm sorry, Ethel."

The others in the room began mumbling.

"I'm sorry, Mrs. Tatum, but without someone to support your mental competency, it would be improper to hear your testimony at this point," Jamison said apologetically.

"I can't believe this," Callison said. "Ask her a question. Ask her a hundred questions. Give her a mental status exam, but don't dismiss her. Mrs. Tatum had a stroke, but her mind is totally intact and she has extremely critical information to present." Callison was beside himself. His key witness was being discarded because she was *old*.

"I would question whether a mental status exam would even suffice," Percy said.

"I'm sorry, Dr. Callison, we don't have the time to conduct a full mental competency exam now. Without some proof I cannot, in all fairness, allow her to testify." Jamison was not going to change his mind.

"Would you have this concern if Mrs. Tatum was younger?" Callison asked.

"It's not only her age but her status, post-stroke, which has me concerned. She probably has multi-infarct dementia," Percy said emphatically.

"I assure you she has neither dementia or senility, she just has a post stroke dysarthria," Callison countered.

"Can we please move the agenda? No one can vouch that Mrs. Tatum has a dysarthria rather than a dementia and we can argue this forever." Jourge could see the pain in Mrs. Tatum's eyes, but it didn't alter the facts.

"Dr. Callison, are there any other people you would like to have testify?" Jamison asked, tapping his finger impatiently on the desk.

Callison frowned. "I know this is a bit out of the ordinary, but I would appreciate if we could revote the merger issue." Callison was desperate.

Jamison looked at Jourge, since this fell under his jurisdiction.

Jourge addressed Callison. "The information presented has not dissuaded my opinion on this matter. The list, however, is another matter and should be reviewed at a different venue."

Before Jourge completed his remarks, a security guard entered the room and whispered to Callison that the rest of his group had arrived.

Callison's expression changed from dejection to relief. "The guard informed me my last witness just arrived. I'll go out and get him." Callison looked at Jourge and winked as he left the room.

Seconds later Callison reentered, followed by Ethan Jasper and another man. The other man was bald and wore wire-rimmed glasses. Dressed in a finely tailored suit, he strolled into the meeting as if he were in charge. Several of the committee members recognized him immediately, as did Jamison.

"Dr. Prentiss, how nice of you to honor us with your presence."

C. Arnold Prentiss was the most renowned physician in the country, a Noble Laureate, and beyond reproach. His reputation superseded everyone's in the room. "My friend and colleague, Ethan Jasper, has explained to me some of the issues, significant issues that you are deciding today. I was also told that an old friend of mine, Ethel Tatum, was not permitted to address this group because she had no one to vouch for her mental alertness. I would be honored to vouch for this wonderful woman and would very much like to hear what she has to say."

Dr. Prentiss sat in the first row, crossed his legs and arms, awaiting to hear what Mrs. Ethel Tatum had to say.

"By all means let us proceed with Mrs. Tatum's statement," Jamison said.

Dr. Prentiss smiled and said, "Please, Ethel, enlighten us."

Callison sat back in his chair awaiting her presentation, smiling at Percy, who slowly sank in his seat. Several of the other members of the committee started to squirm in their seats, having no idea what she might say, but fearful that anything in their past was now fair game.

Mrs. Tatum slowly maneuvered herself into a comfortable position before she started to speak. Because she was aware of her speech impediment, Mrs. Tatum attempted to clearly articulate each word. Her words were garbled but understandable as she started her testimony.

"I have heard what has been said and I must say I am glad for one thing, that my husband, who so loved this profession of yours, is not alive to see what you have done. I know you all must have started with honorable intentions of helping mankind and practicing the art of healing. I remember my husband's face the time he came home and told me he had delivered his first baby. He maintained that type of enthusiasm his entire life, always proud and honored to be a physician, a healer. He frequently said there was no greater responsibility on earth than that of a physician, a job where people would literally place their lives or the lives of their loved ones in your hands for safekeeping. It was the ultimate responsibility and compliment. Wayne felt so strongly about medicine that he created an organization and named it after a man who was as dedicated as he, Miles Gance. The organization was dedicated to help those whose lifelong ambition was to become a physician and to serve mankind. You have distorted that mission and have thus impugned my husband and his name. And for that you must be held accountable. I know which one of you is the real George Alexander, a man whom my husband and I trusted and loved. Under ordinary circumstances I probably would have never known, since you have all changed so much over the years and so many of you have obviously had cosmetic surgery to further alter your appearance. But you still have that nervous habit you had forty years ago. That's what gave you away Alexander, or is it George, Dr. Jourge?"

A hush fell over the room, an eerie silence as all eyes moved toward Dr. Jourge. Jourge peered at the old lady.

"I'm sorry, Mrs. Tatum. I must have not heard you correctly. I thought you said I was someone else. I find that to be a ludicrous statement." His voice controlled, not a shred of evidence that he was unnerved or provoked. Then he started to slowly move his head in a circular manner coughing at the completion of the rotation, followed by the readjustment of his collar.

"I see you still haven't been able to rid yourself of that annoying habit, George." Mrs. Tatum gave a knowing glance in his direction.

"Dr. Prentiss, I know you are a reasonable man. I hope you can see the folly in all this. Yes, I have a nervous reflex, but everyone in this room has seen me do this these last few days. To take a nervous tic and from that make these outrageous accusations is an egregious miscarriage of justice."

"Mrs. Tatum, what have you to say to Dr. Jourge's reply?" Prentiss calmly asked.

"Now, Doctor, do you think I would make such an outlandish statement without more proof than a nervous twitch?" Mrs. Tatum smiled at Prentiss and then turned to Jourge. "The trust we had given you, the friendship and love, you betrayed us all.

Why? Maybe even you don't know, but I have been waiting many years to right this wrong. If it wasn't for the twitch I would have never suspected, and thus never have thought to check my files again. I doubt you remember, but the first members of the Gance organization were all fingerprinted, including yourself. I still have the copy of your fingerprints from all those many years ago. You may have been able to alter your face, but I believe your fingers are still the same. If they are then you must be the late George Alexander resurrected from the grave. Shall we compare?"

Jourge's eyes flittered from one side to the other. "I can't believe the audacity of all this! This is so outlandish, it is beyond reason."

"How so?" Callison asked.

"She could have gotten my fingerprints any number of times in the past." Jourge's voice was raised as he spoke.

"How so?"

Jourge responded, "Assuming the prints are mine, how can you verify this particular set of fingerprints were ascertained at the time you have claimed?" Jourge's voice was once again calm and collected.

"What do you mean?" Callison asked.

"I think it is obvious these prints could have been extracted on any number of occasions, there is no way you can corroborate your assertion," Jourge said smugly.

"But, Dr. Jourge, how could Mrs. Tatum have ever gotten your fingerprints if you have never met? By your own admission you had never met before, yet now you are saying Mrs. Tatum could have gotten your prints any number of times in the past. Which statement is true, or are you still trying to protect the reputation of Dr. Rasta?" Callison leaned both arms on the table and coldly stared into Jourge's panic-stricken eyes.

The color drained from Jourge's face as he stared at the old woman, then at Dr. Prentiss, not saying a word. If he accused Mrs. Tatum of lying, it was tantamount to challenging Dr. Prentiss' integrity. Jourge swallowed hard and then mumbled, "I need to call my lawyer."

J.T. approached Jourge and read him his rights. Jourge sat

in his seat in a state of shock.

Callison thanked the group for all their efforts and especially thanked Dr. Prentiss for his help.

"I actually owe you." Prentiss said. "Dr. Jasper's medical acumen saved my sister's life; this is the least I could do. If any of you well-intentioned colleagues ever need my assistance, please do not hesitate to ask. Now, if you no longer require my assistance, I must be off. It was a pleasure to make all your acquaintances." Prentiss shook each of their hands and exited out the back door.

Jamison, stunned by the events of the day, sat on the podium trying to envision what he would say at the press conference. "Listen, gentlemen and ladies. I believe we still have some unresolved questions to answer before our press conference. Can we all take our seats and return to the business at hand? Please?"

The committee returned to their seats as Jourge was being escorted by J.T. out the back door.

49

Jamison didn't know which way to turn. With Jourge gone he knew he had to assume the leadership role and organize a strategy to appease the media. Arthur Wentzel had been privy to the entire fiasco. If he reported all he knew, Jamison's career would be history.

Callison's group remained. They couldn't believe the plan had actually succeeded. They sat muted in disbelief.

Jamison offered a supportive smile and motioned for Callison to follow him. Callison followed Jamison to the corner of the room. Jamison placed his arm on Callison's shoulder as he whispered in his ear, "Dr. Callison, would you mind excusing your friends? I want to express my gratitude to all of you for your laudable efforts in uncovering the conspiracy, but we have some policy decisions to make."

Callison understood, and explained to Truelove and Jasper why they were required to leave. They also understood. Before the group left, Jamison personally thanked each one for their part in the meeting. Callison thought the gesture was thoughtful, appropriate, and politically savvy. Truelove suggested they all meet later for a congratulatory drink. Callison said he would call them when he was finished and accompanied them out the same door from which Jourge had been escorted just moments earlier.

The committee, meanwhile, was numbed by the events of the past two days. Victor Rasta's death and Alexander Jourge's indiscretions were more than most could stand. Fortunately, cooler heads prevailed. Now they had the task of controlling the damage and picking up the pieces.

"Gentlemen and ladies, can we please take our seats?" Jamison said. "We are all in this together whether we like it or not, and if we can't agree on a solution to this mess, there's a good chance all our careers will be over."

Jamison's last statement penetrated the fog. "What are you going to do?" Percy asked.

Jamison had removed his coat, there were perspiration stains around his armpits and on his back. "I think this needs to be decided as a group. But if I may, let me summarize where I think we are." Jamison wiped the sweat off his brow and poured a glass of water before he began. "From my perspective, I need to present something of substance to the media, and I will need Mr. Wentzel's cooperation to accomplish this."

Wentzel smiled, quite aware he was sitting on the story of his life. He acknowledged Jamison's remark with a nod and a grunt.

Jamison continued. "I'm prepared to give Mr. Wentzel exclusive rights to this story, but first we have to agree what information needs to remain confidential."

"I don't think so," Wentzel said.

"Mr. Wentzel, we need to be absolutely positive of the facts before we report any of this, otherwise this can get totally blown out of proportion." Jamison was defensive and for a good reason. He was one of the major proponents who had endorsed Nathan Slinger's appointment to lead the president's health-care reform team. If Slinger was acting autonomously or illegally, Jamison could be out of a job.

Wentzel started to laugh. "Blown out of proportion. Are you kidding? This mess is so out of proportion already, there's no way I can make it any bigger. As far as I can see, we have the key advisor to the president as part of a conspiracy, linking him to the chairman of one of his major committees on health-care reform. To boot, one of the other key members of this committee had committed suicide probably because of his involvement in this mess. I don't need to blow anything out of proportion. Believe me, this story will sell itself."

"But you don't even know if what you said is true! Most, if not all of this, is secondhand information or worse. Nobody here will go on record to support your claims." Jamison looked around the room, shaking his head. "If this information is released before it can be confirmed, it could ruin the careers of everyone in this room, and if you were wrong, you could be held liable."

"No way, I'm absent of malice. I'm just reporting the facts," Wentzel said.

"Really? What facts are they? All the media heard to this point was your ranting allegations, that's all. No proof, no documentation, and no support. You don't have your story yet." Jamison trusted he made his point.

"Okay, for argument's sake, let's say I agree. What's in it for me?"

"First, like I said, I'll give you the story 24 hours before I release it to the press. What I need from you is your word not to write anything until we can confirm or deny the allegations that have been made. Second, you have to write a story about our meeting today, but the committee has to approve the text."

"Absolutely not. Freedom of the press, you've heard of that, haven't you?" Wentzel sneered at Jamison.

"Freedom does not give you the right to print every rumor you hear and ruin the lives of these people. If you print what was said here today without confirming your data, I promise you I will use every means at my disposal to make sure that is the last story you ever write." Jamison considered his deal more than fair.

Wentzel reconsidered his position. He could see in Jamison's eyes he was not bluffing. "I'll work with you, if you promise me exclusive rights to this story and you will allow me to quote you in my article."

"Deal," Jamison said.

The committee members said nothing but they traded stares with each other. "What about us?" Percy finally said.

"I was about to get to you." Jamison appeared more relaxed knowing he had the press under semi-control. "This list that has all your names on it. Where did it come from?"

Callison realized he was the only one who could answer that question. "I got it."

"Yes, and where did you get it?" Jamison was in no mood for a guessing game.

"From Victor Rasta," Callison said, choking on Rasta's name. He felt guilty using Rasta even though it was the truth.

"He gave you the list?" Jamison asked.

"Actually, it's two lists, and he didn't actually give them to me." Callison knew where this was going, and he didn't want to go there.

"Then how did you get the list?" Jamison's voice was more determined.

"Rasta's secretary got the list and gave it to me," Callison admitted.

"His secretary? Do you know how we might find this secretary? So we may confirm your story?"

"No, I actually used Maxine Wells as my intermediary. I haven't spoken to her since last evening. I honestly don't know where she is." Callison hadn't thought of Maxine for some time because of all the commotion. Realizing how atypical her absence was, he was worried something might have happened to her. "But I believe the FBI is tracking her as we speak."

"Is this the same person Mr. Wentzel referred to earlier?" Jamison seemed confused as he glanced in the direction of Wentzel.

"One and the same," Callison replied.

Jamison thought for a second before asking, "I believe you mentioned another secretary?"

Callison then explained to Jamison and the committee about Margo and her scorn for Rasta.

At the completion of Callison's story, Jamison asked, "How did she get the list?"

"She took it, at my suggestion," Callison said.

"So you believe the list is genuine?" Jamison asked.

"No doubt about it, and there are people in the room who could also confirm its validity." Callison intentionally avoided eye contact with Teitelman. He didn't want to embarrass him into testifying.

Callison didn't have to; Teitelman spoke up immediately. "The list is real. I know because it was used against me." Teitelman's voice grew louder with each word.

"Me too," said Thornhill.

"Same here," echoed Danzinger.

One by one they all admitted to knowing about the list and that their names were on it. Even McMillan and Probst claimed

532

to have knowledge of the list. Everyone but Percy, who froze in his seat unable to talk.

Jamison finally addressed Percy. "Dr. Percy, are you aware of this list and of your connection with it?"

Percy looked up at Jamison with tears in his eyes. He was a very proud and stubborn man. Jamison could see the pain and anguish in Percy's face. "Dr. Percy?"

Percy broke down and started to weep, mumbling in between his sighs, "This can't be happening."

Susanna Michelson placed her arm around his shaking body and comforted him as a mother would comfort her child. After several minutes, Percy controlled his sobbing and admitted that he too was aware of the list. He was mortified he hadn't the courage to do anything about it.

"So where do we go from here?" Jamison lamented. "I have to meet with the press and tell them something. Since Dr. Jourge is no longer with us, I think it would be best if I meet with the press alone. I will tell them we are investigating the allegations suggested by Mr. Wentzel, but at this time we cannot confirm or deny anything. I will also say that the consensus report from this committee will be postponed until this matter is completely investigated, at which time we will reconvene the committee and reveal all the information to the press involving the events of today."

Jamison approached Wentzel. "I will promise to give you the press statement and all the background information I'm allowed to reveal prior to any formal meeting with the press, and with enough lead time to break the story. In addition, I'll give you, and only you, an exclusive interview after the press conference." Jamison extended his hand and Wentzel reciprocated.

"What I ask of you now is just to report what I say at the press conference. The FBI and the Secret Service are probably meeting with Senator Slinger as we speak. If he's charged, you'll have the story first, but if he's innocent I don't want to start spreading malicious rumors, and I know you don't either."

Wentzel reluctantly agreed.

"The press is waiting. Why don't you all exit out the rear door. When you're gone, I'll conduct the conference."

They all started to rise, all except Percy. Still devastated, Percy had to be helped to his feet. McMillan and Danzinger supported Percy, one on each arm as they made their way to the exit.

"I'll try to keep this list out of the press, but I can't promise I'll succeed," Jamison hollered as they were leaving.

Thornhill turned around. " You know, it's a relief having this out in the open. If the list is revealed, we'll all survive. You do what you have to. We'll all understand."

They were gone and Jamison fell into his seat exhausted. He sat silently for ten minutes with his eyes closed thinking about what he was going to say. Once he was told they were all safely out of the building, Jamison opened his eyes, fixed his tie, put on his jacket and his politician smile, and said, "Let's get the show on the road. Bring them in, boys."

The security guards went to retrieve the press while Jamison took the podium.

Callison thought about the meeting with Truelove and the others, but first he needed some time alone. The committee splintered in all directions as they left the building. It appeared they all required some time to reflect on everything that had happened and the possible consequences.

Callison had a message waiting for him when he returned to his room. The message was from Maxine, asking him to call her as soon as possible. Hearing the message and knowing Maxine was all right immediately made Callison feel better. He had envisioned many unpleasant things.

"Hello, Maxine, this is Steven."

The voice on the other line seemed tentative, "Steven, I need to talk to you tonight. Can you come over?"

"Why? What's the matter?" Callison could sense her consternation.

"We have to talk. I have a videotape you need to see." Her voice faded at the word "videotape."

Callison couldn't believe how naive he was, thinking she had no knowledge of the tape. "Okay, where should I meet you?"

Maxine gave him her home address. It appeared he wouldn't get the rest he wanted, at least not yet.

The cab took twenty minutes to reach Maxine's house. The street was dark and quiet. When he paid the driver, Callison instinctively looked down the street to see if he had been followed. There was no activity at all on the small one-way street of two-story apartment buildings, lined by large maple trees. Maxine had said he should go to the second floor of the building and knock three times.

The front door was ajar, leading to a central stairway that led to the second floor. The stairway had a turn at the halfway point. The upper half was unlit due to a burned-out bulb. The streetlight and the pale silver moonlight silhouetted the trees against the far wall where the long purple shadows gave off an image resembling emaciated hands reaching into the sky. At the top of the stairs was a door marked 2A, and Callison knocked three times as instructed.

The door opened and a man, probably in his fifties, answered. The man held a photo of Callison, which he studied before he spoke, "Steven?"

"Yes, I'm Steven."

"I have a message for you from Maxine. She said for you to take the cellar exit into the alley, turn right on Clifton, and go to the third house, 902 Clifton. She'll be waiting for you there. She said you would understand why she was taking these precautions."

Callison did understand, but was surprised Maxine was going to this extent. "How do I get to the cellar exit?"

The man showed him the door to the cellar and instructed him to follow the light which would lead him to the adjacent building. Callison thanked the man and proceeded to the cellar.

The back stairway to the cellar was through a large metal door. Callison strained to move the door, but it was stuck. Holding the door knob with both hands, he pulled with all his strength. Over his grunts and straining muscles, Callison could sense the door move. The door opened slightly and again became stuck, as if it had been glued into position. Callison was able to slide through the narrow doorway sideways and followed the dark stairway down three flights to the cellar.

This stairway had no light from the outside and was old and

rickety. The air in the stairwell was scant and felt hot and steamy, smelling of mildew. As he approached the bottom of the stairwell he had a startling thought. *What if he had been set up?* There was no escape. Considering he really had no other option, he decided to follow the instructions.

There was limited light emanating from a single bulb hanging precariously from a wire in the middle of the room. The light created bizarre shadows throughout the cellar, which was strewn with boxes and other discarded relics of the past. Large pipes traversed the ceiling, which intermittently transmitted a high pitched squeal. The air was musty and dank reminding Callison of a root cellar in his grandparents old house.

Callison thought he heard a sound from the room he was about to enter, a sound distinctively different from the squealing of the pipes. His heartbeat quickened and his mouth became dry as he attempted to make his way through the maze of boxes. Peeking into the adjoining room, Callison could barely see the far wall. The room appeared similar to the first, except darker, and the shadows were even more ominous. As he slowly entered, he reached down and picked up a metal leg that had been broken off a chair. Having something in his hand gave him some comfort.

At the far end of room, Callison could see a stairway going up, just as the man had described. Another fifteen feet or so and his journey through the cellar would be over, and not a minute too soon. Then he heard the noise again; this time it was unmistakable. He was not alone in the cellar.

The noise came from behind him. His eyes were fully dilated, his mouth dry as the desert, his palms sweaty. He tightened his grip on the metal leg. He was still too far to run to the stairs since the path before him was dark and full of obstacles. Callison planted his right foot, pivoting quickly to his left, arm raised. A high pitched screech startled him as he saw two eyes vanish into the darkness of the other room. It was either a cat or a monster rat. Either way, he was out of there.

Callison dashed up the stairs, which emptied out onto the alley. He discarded his weapon and reminded himself he needed to thank Maxine for this little adventure.

902 Clifton was exactly where it was supposed to be. Callison knocked on the door and Maxine greeted him, a look of concern on her face. Callison was so relieved to be safely in a house, he didn't notice the man standing next to the door. The cold steel of the barrel of the revolver pressing against his neck caught Callison's attention immediately.

"How nice of you to join us, Doctor." The voice was familiar but Callison couldn't place it. As he felt the gun lower from his neck, Callison saw the image. It was the man in black, Van Gregory.

"Is the gun necessary?" Callison said calmly.

"I'm sorry, Doctor, I'm afraid it fucking is." Gregory lowered the gun to his side and smiled. "Let's go to the living room."

Callison followed Maxine to the living room with Gregory in the rear. The room was simply decorated; a small couch with a coffee table, two easy chairs, a console TV, and a cheap reproduction of Picasso's *Guernica* adorned the wall.

Callison stopped in the doorway to the living room, only to be forcibly pushed into the room by Gregory. He stumbled into the room, nearly tripping over the coffee table.

"Watch it!" Callison shouted.

"Sit down," Gregory commanded.

Callison sat on the couch next to Maxine. He was confused. What was going on? Callison turned to Maxine with a quizzical look, but she simply shrugged. Callison changed his attention to Gregory, who had his gun raised and pointed at Maxine.

"I want some answers now," Gregory barked, his face distorted with anger. "Why'd you set me up?"

Callison didn't know whether he was addressing him or Maxine, so he didn't answer.

"I said, why'd you fucking set me up?" Gregory's finger slowly tightened the trigger.

"I don't know what you are talking about. I didn't know before and I don't know now," Maxine cried. Tears ran down her cheeks, tears of fear.

"Why'd you call me to meet with Rasta yesterday? Why?" Gregory was furious. "I thought we had a deal?"

Callison's eyes lit up. A deal? What kind of deal did they have?

"I didn't call you, I swear." Maxine was shaking, her entire body convulsed in a shudder of fear.

"Don't play dumb. You told me Rasta was about to crack and I had to meet with him. You fucking set me up, you bitch." Gregory pulled his hand back.

Maxine, anticipating the blow, contorted her body to avoid Gregory's swing. "It wasn't me, I swear, it wasn't." Maxine looked up at Gregory, begging him with her eyes to believe her.

"If it wasn't you then who was it that called me?" He dropped his hand. "Who else even knew how to contact me? We had a deal, remember? And you fucking betrayed me." Gregory placed the barrel between Maxine's eyes.

"I swear I didn't," she said as she watched the barrel of the gun press against her forehead.

"Oh what the hell." Gregory removed the gun. Maxine sighed in relief and readjusted herself onto the couch. Gregory winked at Callison while keeping the gun pointed in the direction of Maxine. "Let me tell you a little story about your friend here."

Callison wanted to rush Gregory and be the hero, but common sense prevailed. Gregory was a professional and Callison was a doctor. Unless they choose dueling stethoscopes, he was out of luck. "Really, Mr. Gregory, what's all this about?"

"It's about betrayal and deception. First, let me explain how you were used and betrayed. Did you know Ms. Wells here was really hired by Jourge to make sure you didn't get out of line?" Gregory maintained his distance from the couch, but kept his gun aimed in their direction.

Maxine didn't say a word, but her face indicated Gregory was telling the truth.

Gregory continued, "The little episode you and Maxine had at Rasta's home was planned by her to be used against you." Gregory chuckled as he explained Maxine's betrayal.

Callison was aghast. He looked at Maxine not wanting to believe any of this. "Is this true?"

"Of course not. It's a total fabrication," Maxine said . . . but her face said otherwise.

"How would I know about this if I were making it up?" Gregory asked. "Let me continue and you'll see I'm telling you the truth."

Callison needed to hear Gregory out before he could make any decisions. Since Gregory had the gun, he really had no choice.

"I was asked by Jourge to watch Rasta's group because he needed to know the group was functioning as ordered. I learned that Jourge had contracted an insurance policy, who I later found out was none other than Maxine Wells."

"That's a lie," Maxine shouted defiantly.

"Really? I had my men follow you and I have proof you secretly met with Jourge. Besides, when I confronted Maxine with the tape, she countered by offering to help me with Merker. She knew I was having trouble with Merker and said she could help me with Merker by using you." Gregory pointed at Callison. "Then she said, if I helped her get the list, we could both use the information later to bribe Rasta and the others. I thought we had an agreement. But then things started to get complicated. So yesterday I get a call from her telling me to meet with Rasta at his hotel room. I show up and there's no Rasta, so I leave."

"Don't listen to any of this, it's all a great big lie!" Maxine jumped from the couch toward Gregory, who struck her with the butt of his gun, knocking her to the floor, lacerating her forehead which was now bleeding.

Callison moved to assist Maxine, a look of vengeance in his eyes, as he lifted her back to the couch, dabbing her forehead with his shirt tail.

"Now, Doc, let's not be the dead hero!" Gregory handed Callison a clean towel to place on Maxine's wound. "Now I hear the Feds are investigating Rasta's death and they found my prints in the room, and the word on the street was I was looking for him. And the only person who fucking knew I was going to meet with Rasta was Maxine. She set me up, just like she set you up, Doc."

Callison looked down at Maxine who was lying on his lap as he wiped the remaining spots of blood off her skin.

Gregory shook his head and continued, "I've even heard through my sources that I was seen leaving the hotel around the time of Rasta's death. Now if that isn't a set-up, what the fuck is?" Gregory pointed the gun in Callison's direction. "Doc, I need your help. I need you to help clear me. I'm not taking the rap for Rasta's death. The phone call you made to Ms. Wells here will give both of you a motive to kill Rasta. I'm sure the Feds had the conversation taped and it will be an open and shut case of blackmail. I got a copy of the tape starring the both of you. I'll leave this tape in a place they're sure to find, along with a little note from Rasta." Gregory's eyes were crazed. "Now you have a choice. Either you both cooperate and help me, which might save your lives. Or you don't and I kill you both. Either way, I don't care."

Callison could see that Gregory was probably telling the truth.

"Now for the last time, why did you set me up?" His rage was escalating.

Callison looked at Maxine, pleading with his eyes for her to answer the question.

Maxine's bleeding was under control and she was fighting the pain. "I don't know what else to say, it wasn't me. Why would I set you up?"

"You're really pissing me off. I don't know how much you're getting paid, but I think you under-fucking-estimated me. I'm not that dumb."

Callison started to get up, but again Gregory pointed the gun in his direction. Behind Gregory, Callison could make out the outline of a person appearing out of the darkened hallway. A muffled sound was immediately followed by Gregory's head exploding, his blood jettisoning out of the hole in his forehead. A look of astonishment filled Gregory's eyes as life left his body and he collapsed to the floor.

The person was now recognizable, a dark-skinned woman wearing a wrap-around head-piece. It was Margo.

"Here, hon." Margo emptied the chamber and tossed the gun to Callison as she bent over to examine Gregory's corpse. "Never did like him. He didn't even know how to curse. He always put his vulgarity in the wrong place. Fuck him."

Callison carefully caught the gun, looking at the silencer. He had never seen a silencer before.

Margo looked up from Gregory's body. "Hon, I'm not sure, but he might have friends around. We have to be careful."

Maxine was seated upright and spirited. "I thought you'd never get here."

"I wanted to hear what he had first." Margo smiled at Maxine.

"He would have killed us. I could see it in his eyes." It was Callison's way of thanking Margo for doing something he considered reprehensible.

"I'm sure he would have but . . . " Margo held Gregory's dead hand in her gloved hand, and pointed his revolver at Maxine, and fired.

Maxine's face was similar to Gregory's, a combination of shock and death. Maxine slumped over onto Callison's lap as life drained from her body.

All this happened so fast Callison had no time to think. He just reacted, squeezing the trigger of the gun in his hand toward Margo. There was nothing but the sound of the click. The chamber was empty.

"Here, I forgot to give you these." Margo tossed three bullets to Callison, which he caught.

Callison's hands were shaking; he was unable to load the bullets into the chamber of the revolver. He gazed at Margo, still not comprehending what was happening. "Why?" was all he could mutter.

"Don't take it personally; it's just my job." Margo shifted Gregory's dead hand so she could aim his gun at Callison.

Callison closed his eyes, seeing his life flash before him. An image of Natalie appeared and froze as his last conscious thought. He heard the shot fired. Then he heard a voice. He wasn't dead. The voice said, "Muck it." It was Merker.

Callison opened his eyes and saw Margo's body lying on top of Gregory's corpse, a truly gruesome sight. The bullet had gone through Margo's right shoulder which was actively spewing blood.

Callison couldn't believe the sight before his eyes: Marcus Merker triumphantly standing over the bodies of Margo and Gregory. Merker pulled out a set of handcuffs, grabbing Margo's uninjured left arm, forcing it behind her back. As he grabbed for her right arm, Margo activated the stiletto hidden in the bracelet on her right wrist. Concealing the razor sharp dagger in her palm, she suddenly extended her wrist exposing the lethal blade. When Merker reached for her right hand, Margo slashed out at Merker, slicing his forearm. Blood spurted everywhere as Merker dropped his gun and instinctively grabbed his lacerated arm. Margo swiftly and adroitly rolled away from Merker, who was momentarily distracted. Margo reached for Merker's gun, but he was able to kick it away, out of Margo's reach.

Callison sat frozen, watching the events unfold in front of him, mesmerized yet unable to move.

Both Margo and Merker struggled to their feet. Their bodies entangled in a bloody mess, a dance of death. Margo was able to free her leg and powerfully kick Merker in the knee, forcing him to the ground. Merker's fall was partially broken by a chair which he grabbed on his way down. The chair shattered as he awkwardly grabbed for support.

Margo moved swiftly and fluidly toward Merker. Using her left hand to help guide her now limp right arm, she aimed her stiletto at Merker's carotid artery. Merker groped for a piece of the broken chair, but to no avail. The point of the stiletto was on track, when Merker summoned every ounce of concentration in his body, sending a spew of vomit into Margo's face and eyes.

Margo's stiletto missed its primary mark but still cut flesh, opening a large gash in Merker's upper chest, leaving a gaping hole as it penetrated his lung. Merker was able to roll out of the way with his last seconds of consciousness, while she cleared the vomit from her eyes.

Margo crawled over to Merker's unconscious body. She stopped as she heard Callison's voice. "Stop, or I'll shoot."

Margo slowly turned toward Callison, blood smeared over her face, washing off some of her dark makeup. She looked like the monster she was. Margo noticed Merker's gun several feet away and reached for it.

Callison warned her. "Stop, or I'll have to shoot!"

Margo glared at Callison studying his frightened eyes. "No, you won't." She lunged, grabbing the gun with her left hand and in one motion pivoted and fired.

Callison standing, his hand shaking while he pointed the gun at Margo. "No bullets, you have the wrong gun. *I switched the guns.*" Callison's pseudo-smile turned into a scowl.

Margo, enraged, sprung to her feet and charged Callison with her stiletto blade. Callison squeezed the trigger and the gun reverberated in his hand. Margo slumped to the floor at Callison's feet, clutching her chest.

50

The intensive care unit staff had to place Merker in an isolation room, not because he was contagious but because of the commotion he created. The stab wound had punctured his lung, which had required emergency surgery. However, Merker was now off the critical list and was in stable condition. Although he was appreciative, Merker nevertheless resented having to be in the hospital. He hated hospitals.

Callison had discussed Merker's condition with the unit resident. He had a perforated lung, hemopneumothorax, and they were monitoring him for post-shock syndrome, because he had presented in shock to the emergency room. Merker said he survived because of his crusty personality, but nonetheless he responded to the fluids and transfusions. His post-operative course was one of continued improvement.

When Callison entered the unit, he could see the back of J.T., who was at Merker's bedside. J.T.'s shoulders were bobbing up and down, as if he were crying uncontrollably. Callison rushed over to Merker's bedside. Had something happened?

Callison never envisioned J.T.'s body bobbing because of laughter, but that was the case. Merker was explaining to J.T. his heroics and described how his secret weapon saved his life. Callison couldn't laugh because the memory of that evening was still frighteningly fresh in his mind. The best he could do was muster a smile.

J.T. wiped away his tears, his body still bent at the waist and aching in the midsection, when he noticed Callison standing next to him. Suppressing his laugh, J.T. straightened himself to address Callison. "Yesterday, I wanted to kill you and today I'd marry you."

Callison backed away from J.T. "Is that supposed to be a compliment or a threat? I can't tell."

J.T. chuckled. "What you did last night showed a lot of guts, real balls." Callison stood tall and pushed his chest out. "I don't know if you're even aware of what you did." J.T. became more earnest in his remarks.

Callison shrugged his shoulders.

"Margo, the woman you shot," J.T. said seriously.

"Yes, I shot her." Callison's response was reserved as he looked at the ground, still distraught over the shooting.

"Margo's not her real name. Actually, I don't know what her real name was, but we knew her as Valentino. The primo assassin of the past decade, and you stopped her."

Callison was stunned by J.T.'s announcement. "You're kidding?"

"No, it's true. Valentino was the one I was after all along. She managed to give us the slip, but you, you son of a bitch, you got her. Way to go!" J.T. slapped Callison on the back.

Merker repositioned himself in his bed. "You know she was there to kill you?"

"Kill *me*? Why?" Callison asked, surprised at Merker's comment.

"Because you saw her. She'd kill anyone who could identify her. She planned to kill all three of you last night, which would've left no one to identify her." Merker coughed. The pain was evident on his face.

J.T. walked to his side, and placed his hand on Merker's shoulder. "Marcus is right, you would've been a dead man. It was all a set-up."

Merker continued, "Margo planned this real well. She convinced Gregory to meet with Maxine. What's funny is, that Margo had never even met Gregory, but she'd spoken to him over the phone several times. She used some type of voice adapter to change her voice to sound like Maxine's, then over time she left these clues for Gregory to piece together. Gregory figured from Margo's clues that *Maxine* was actually Valentino. Meanwhile, it was actually Margo who had hired Maxine to spy on you and Rasta. Maxine was probably told the reason she was hired was to make sure the merger would take place, when in fact, she was there to take the fall for Margo, if the need arose. It's not clear whether Maxine actually knew Margo was Valentino, but I believe she probably did. I'll bet she just never suspected Margo was using her in that way."

"She knew." J.T. said. "We traced her background, she'd been an operative for Valentino in the past but always as a messenger. As far as we can tell, this was the first time she actually had contact with Valentino, thus making her expendable." J.T. looked around the intensive care unit to make sure they weren't overheard. The nurses in the unit were busy doing their chores and everyone else seemed oblivious to them.

"Really, I didn't know you guys were on to Maxine." Merker thought he was the only one who had the inside information on Maxine.

"Give us a little credit, will you," J.T. feigned insult.

"Sorry," Merker said.

"How did you know about Maxine?" Callison had trusted Maxine and was confounded by her duplicity and how they both knew she was a traitor.

"Remember when we first met her, I told you she wasn't to be trusted?" Merker proudly barked.

"Your sixth sense." Callison reluctantly nodded.

"Yeah. From the beginning I kept tabs on her. I knew she was up to no good, but I didn't want you to know. I had a feeling she'd lead me to whoever was behind this, and she did. At least she helped." Merker managed a half smile through the pain.

"So Margo was planning to kill us all. How was she going to get away with all this?" Callison still had some major pieces missing from his puzzle.

"That would've been simple. The scene when the police arrived would look something like this." Merker coughed again. "You and Maxine would have been shot dead by Gregory, and Gregory would be shot by your hand."

Callison thought about the melee of the previous evening. Margo had used Gregory's gun to kill Maxine and then used her gun to shoot Gregory, which she also tossed to him. Callison realized his fingerprints were not only on the gun, but also the bullets, which she had also tossed to him. No doubt about it, Margo had the circumstantial evidence down to the bullets. Under those circumstances it would have made a very convincing case. What Merker said made sense.

Callison started to think out loud. "So, Margo would have made it look like a gunfight, but why would I be involved?"

"Because of the tape. She had it set up as if Gregory was blackmailing the both of you," Merker said.

Callison thought to himself, *Does everyone know about this tape, or what?* "So I kill him over the tape?" He said aloud.

"Basically, yes. It would appear there was a struggle and then things got out of hand. Before you know it, there are three dead bodies. We have the murder weapons, the motive, a cut-and-dried case. This type of case isn't that uncommon and wouldn't be hard to sell."

"It probably would have worked, and I'm sure Margo or Valentino, whatever, would have been out of the country before morning, leaving not a shred of evidence to connect her to any of this," J.T. agreed.

Callison looked troubled. "How could Margo be this assassin Valentino while she held a full-time job working for Jourge?"

J.T. shook his head. "She never worked for Jourge. She just took the name of his secretary who was out on medical leave and used Maxine to cover her in case you asked."

"So there is a real Margo?" Callison asked.

"Sure, but not the one you met. Maxine was there to help protect our Margo's real identity."

"Let's assume we agree on your theory—how does Rasta tie into this?" Callison had questioned Rasta's death ever since J.T. suggested it might not have been a suicide.

"This is where it gets a little more complicated," Merker smugly said. "Rasta never knew for sure that Jourge was Smithee, but I believe he had a strong suspicion. Jourge had Rasta set up and I believe murdered to look like a suicide."

"Why do you say that?" J.T. was curious.

"Because my sixth sense tells me so. So does common sense." Merker knew J.T. well enough not to reveal all he knew at this time. "I think Jourge was afraid he was about to be exposed and had Rasta set up as the fall guy. Once he had Rasta set up as Smithee, all he had to do was to get rid of him and he was in the clear. That's why I think Rasta's suicide was staged. It makes sense, and from what I can tell of Rasta, he wasn't the suicide type. Too arrogant." Merker pressed the buzzer for the nurse. His pain had increased.

"So let me see if I understand this. Jourge used Margo and Maxine to set up Rasta and then he had Rasta killed." Callison scratched his head.

"Sure, Margo was given the information Jourge wanted leaked and Maxine would then forward that information to you and others." Merker attempted to smile through his pain. "It was beautiful. Rasta couldn't even deny it, because he didn't even know about it. Yet, it was all set up so that he was the *man*, and Jourge was free and clear."

"I'm impressed." J.T. said. He had been working on this case for months, with the resources of the FBI supporting him—and here Marcus Merker had been able to ascertain all this in a few weeks with virtually no help. It was impressive.

"Don't be so impressed, there's still one part of this that doesn't make any sense." Merker winced as he spoke.

"What's that?" J.T. inquired.

"There's a piece missing." Merker grabbed Callison's arm, his grasp still strong despite his weakened state. "Steven, do you remember the meeting in the FBI office?"

Callison nodded.

Merker continued as the nurse entered the room. "Nurse Thomas, would you mind excusing us for just a few minutes, please."

Nurse Thomas muttered something to herself and said she would return in five minutes.

Merker winked at Callison. "I didn't want her to hear this." Merker hesitated as another wave of intense pain passed through his chest. "I've been bothered by that meeting with the FBI. There were two men who had worked with Senator Hargrove . . ."

J.T. interrupted. "Garrison Hammer and Harris Terbanion."

"Yeah. Well, anyway they were concerned that Rasta had been involved in some larger plot involving Senator Hargrove and Senator Slinger to name a few. What's that all about? And

how do Rasta and Jourge fit into this? This is what I've been trying to figure out."

"Your questions are very perceptive and I can tell you we had
the same questions . . . "

The nurse reentered the isolation room while J.T. was in
mid-sentence. She asked both Callison and J.T. to leave, so she
could attend her patient.

"I'll come back later and we can finish this discussion," J.T.
said as nurse Thomas was pushing them out of the room.

"I've learned over the years when a nurse gets that crazed
look, it's best not to argue," Callison whispered to J.T. as they left
the unit.

"Can I ask you something?" J.T. asked.

"Sure," Callison replied.

Callison followed J.T. out of the unit and down the hall,
where J.T. found a vacated patient room. J.T. closed the door
behind Callison after he entered. "There's something I have to
ask you."

Callison was tired of all the secretive meetings behind closed
doors. "What's the matter now?" Frustration and exhaustion
were noticeable in Callison's voice and mannerism.

"Did you put the word on the street about Slinger?"

"No, it wasn't me. I told you I wouldn't and I didn't say a word
about Senator Slinger to anyone. I don't know how that reporter
got his information, but it wasn't from me." Callison was as
earnest as he could be.

"If you would have told me this yesterday, I wouldn't have
believed you, but today's a different story." J.T. didn't want to
believe Callison had deliberately disregarded his request.

"I could tell you thought I had given that reporter the information on Slinger and that bothered me. That you had so little
trust," Callison said, but his attempt for sympathy fell on deaf
ears.

"It's my job not to trust anyone, and at the time you were the
most likely candidate," J.T. answered frankly. "Because you did
prove to be trustworthy, I'm going to tell you something, but you
have to promise to keep this quiet."

"No problem," Callison answered.

"We have evidence Rasta was probably killed and didn't commit suicide. The gun wound was from close range and there was no evidence of a struggle, so the person who killed Rasta was probably someone he knew and felt comfortable around. Forensics also said the angle of the shot suggested the gun was aimed from someone about five foot five or six."

"How tall was Margo?" Callison asked.

"Five six, very good." J.T. smiled at Callison's perceptiveness. "As you have already guessed, we feel Margo or as we prefer, Valentino, killed Rasta. But the question is why?"

J.T. hesitated as a doctor peeked his head into the room asking if they were part of the Thurmond family. They said no and the doctor left.

"It was like Merker said. If Jourge had set Rasta up, then by killing him there would be no way Rasta could deny he was Smithee, and Jourge would be free and clear. But it isn't that simple."

Callison had bought that line of reasoning, but was somewhat surprised J.T. had a problem with it. "It isn't? It makes sense to me."

"That's what we initially thought as well. But there were several other factors that also needed to be explained. First and foremost, why would Jourge go to all this trouble? What was in it for him?" J.T. asked, but he already knew the answer.

"The power?" Callison answered.

"He already had that."

"The prestige?" Callison countered.

"No, he didn't need that either."

"Well, what else could he get from this? Was he promised some position, like Rasta?" Callison could see J.T.'s dilemma.

"No, it wasn't for a position either. What we found was that the good doctor was living beyond his means. Way beyond his means. It appears he has this gambling problem and he has lost a veritable fortune. Jourge had his problem under control until his recent marriage several years ago. It seems his new, young wife likes the finer things in life and is quite high maintenance. If you get my drift?" Callison nodded and J.T. continued. "She wiped out Jourge's savings, so he decided to return to gambling for additional funds. At first he did okay, but then he ran into a streak of bad luck. Real bad luck. This wasn't the first time Jourge had gotten in over his head because of gambling."

"That's interesting," Callison said.

"Do you remember Mrs. Tatum suggested Jourge had some type of, um, cosmetic makeover? We asked him about that, and he admitted to changing his name, face, and identity to hide from a gambling debt many years ago."

"Is that when he changed his name from George Alexander to Alexander Jourge?" Callison smiled.

"Yes, he changed his name then because of his gambling and some other issues dealing with the Gance organization. Anyway, his latest gambling escapades left Jourge down over three hundred grand. That's when he first met L. Gorman Tuttle. It was because of Tuttle, Jourge developed his little scheme to set up Rasta."

"How so?" Callison's curiosity was now piqued.

"When Jourge became involved with Tuttle, he decided to use the Gance organization to further both their interests. We had known about Tuttle and his concerns, but weren't able to make the connection to Rasta, and we didn't know who Smithee was. That was where you came in. Gorman Tuttle refers to himself as King of the Overlords. The Overlords are a group of financiers, venture capitalists, opportunists who capitalize on the misfortunes of others. Of course, they see themselves as helping those down on their luck, but in reality they're parasites who live off the hard work of others. The Overlords' most recent dealings were with the pharmaceutical and biotech industries, specifically with their research and development."

"So you're saying Tuttle is influencing the research and development of new drugs and technologies?" Callison understood how this could be lucrative but couldn't determine what this had to do with his committee or the merger.

"Not exactly, but close. Tuttle, with the help of Jourge and others, found a loophole in the law that allowed them to connect the pharmaceutical industry with biotech and academics, giving them the inside track on everything from dot.coms to gene therapy to new medicines. Obviously this type of information can be very profitable. The Overlords have virtually locked this thing up, especially since the government has cut back on their funding of research." J.T. stopped to check the hallway. He wanted to ensure they were alone.

"You mean they can speculate on the stock market with the knowledge that a specific drug or techno-stock is going to be released." Callison excitedly continued. "Or a certain experimental trial will be reported to have some significant benefit, and they already know about it." Callison smugly nodded.

"It's much larger than that. We know they have inside information on products, trials, technologies, the Internet—but they also have their network involved in the banking industry and Wall Street. This partnership between medicine, high tech and big business has the capacity to manipulate the market and create unbelievable opportunities for those on the inside. You realize that between the pharmaceuticals, the dot.coms and the biotechs, we're talking in the hundreds of billions of dollars. We're not talking spare change here."

"Interesting, but I still don't see the connection." Callison wondered how this scenario involved the committee. He knew one thing for sure, he wasn't profiting from any of this.

"I was about to get to that," J.T. said. "The Overlords weren't satisfied with the tens of millions they were making with their inside information. They extended their area of interest and greed to the selling of their information to interested parties who had the financial resources to pay the fees the Overlords charged. For example, Ronald Sutherland, the Wall Street whiz kid, was one of their first clients. His investments brought huge profits to his investors and gave Mr. Sutherland the reputation as the *king* of the money market managers, along with a hundred million dollars or so.

"But wasn't he convicted for that?" Callison inquired.

"Yeah, he was prosecuted and then a congressional committee was assigned to investigate. Guess who chaired the committee?" J.T. asked.

"I don't know. Slinger?" Callison answered.

"Close, he was a member of the committee. The chairman was Senator Douglas Hargrove. Hargrove used the information he learned from the committee to form the Hargrove Bill, which involved issues not only relative to the merger, but also to this conflict of interests with the pharmaceutical and biotech industries."

"So the Hargrove Bill also dealt with this Overlord issue?" Callison protruded his lower lip and nodded.

"Yep, I believe he was killed for that reason, and Jourge was able to set up Rasta to redirect attention away from industry and toward the merger."

"So the merger issue was really a front for this Overlord thing?"

"It was a brilliant ploy. You see, if no one ever suspected Hargrove was killed, that was fine with Jourge and Tuttle. When Garrison Hammer hired a private detective to investigate the death of Hargrove, the Overlords led him to a dead-end investigation of a wealthy Michigan family. Hammer, though, still had his suspicions, but couldn't prove anything. They had it set up, that if there was any further investigation, it would direct attention to Hargrove's osteopathic connections and the merger issue. It was a beautifully conceived deception where the real issue would never be suspected."

"So you're saying Hargrove was killed?" Callison wanted to be certain.

"Yes, we have evidence he was probably killed by Valentino, who masqueraded as a nurse and injected air into the senator's intravenous line."

"An air embolus," Callison interjected.

"Yeah, right. Whatever you say. Anyway it appears Senator Slinger took up Hargrove's cause, but Tuttle and his friends decided it was too dangerous to kill off another senator . . . so they set out to ruin his reputation." J.T. frowned.

"So Slinger was also set up?" Callison was surprised and possibly even disappointed that Slinger wasn't a central character in this conspiracy. Callison didn't know much about Slinger, but assumed he must be guilty. After all, he was a politician . . .

"As far as we can tell, Slinger has no knowledge of any of this." J.T. had investigated Slinger, only to surmise he was an innocent victim, set up by Jourge and Tuttle.

"Then where did the memos and the photographs come from?" Callison was finding this hard to believe.

"It appears the memos were either regarding other issues which were taken out of context, or were totally falsified on Slinger's stationery by Lance Darby, who was on Tuttle's payroll. While on the other end, either Maxine or Margo took care of Rasta's correspondence. They were able to set them both up without either of them suspecting a thing." J.T. raised his brow. "By the way, Mr. Darby has disappeared, and I'd be very surprised if he was ever found."

"What about the photos then?"

"They're legitimate, but as far as we can tell they were discussing other issues and the checks were deposited without Slinger's knowledge."

"You mean the checks to support Slinger's campaign funds?"

"Among others. We also found other checks that tied Rasta to Slinger, and we're sure neither had any knowledge of them. Many were cashed by Darby, who forged Slinger's signature and deposited them in an account only Darby could access. He did quite well by this scam."

"So Darby was freelancing?" Callison inquired.

"Something like that. Anyway, Jourge probably told Margo to leak the list to you. My guess is Rasta never actually had the list, but Jourge wanted you to believe he was the source behind the list. Thus implicating Rasta with the merger conspiracy and deflecting any attention away from himself and Tuttle."

"Let me review what I think you just said." Callison said. "It seems Tuttle had to get rid of Hargrove first and then Slinger. He used Valentino to kill Hargrove and then with the help of Jourge set an elaborate trap for Slinger. A trap so devious that by the time Slinger's name was cleared, even if he was successful at clearing his name, his reputation would be so compromised that he would have lost his political clout."

"Go on."

"With both Hargrove and Slinger out of the way, I assume Tuttle had his own political horses to run his agenda." Callison smiled, waiting to see J.T.'s response.

"Very good." J.T. shook his head. "We know of several politicians who are tied to either Tuttle or one of the other Overlords."

"Jourge was brought into this primarily because of his gambling debt?" This was the only confusing issue for Callison. How could a man of Jourge's reputation allow himself to come to this?

"Yeah, he was an asshole. It was the gambling debt that led Jourge to Tuttle, but once Tuttle had his claws into Jourge, Jourge had no choice. Since we've had Jourge in our custody, he's been singing like a bird. He's scared to death about going to prison and will do anything to prevent that. Jourge said Tuttle had promised to leave him alone after all this was over. Jourge's share of the profits would've easily paid off his debtors and would have left him with a very tidy sum. I guess he felt he could walk away."

"Is that realistic?" Callison couldn't believe Jourge would be naive enough to think he could just walk away from all of this.

"Probably not, but possibly he could have pulled it off. Once Slinger was out of the way and the Overlords had control, they really didn't need Jourge any more. What they needed was the list, and they could have easily put in another person to control the Gance organization. It was the power of the list, which when married to their industry connections allowed them to manipulate the system. Jourge was expendable. I think they might have let him be, but more likely he would have been killed."

"So what's going to happen to Jourge?" Callison had liked Alexander Jourge prior to the revelation of his involvement with the conspiracy. Even though Jourge was at least partially, if not totally responsible for Callison's death warrant via Valentino, he still felt sorry for him.

"I don't know," J.T. said.

What J.T. wouldn't tell Callison was the information they had learned about the death of Walter Ambercrombie, a chief advisor to the president of the United States. J.T. had pieced together enough information to implicate the Overlords in the murder of Walter Ambercrombie. Apparently the Overlords had invested so much into the health-care initiative, they couldn't take the chance that the president would not emphasize this issue in his campaign. By killing Ambercrombie, they were able to refocus the president onto their health-care agen-

555

da while misdirecting the investigation of Ambercrombie's murder to the Colombian drug cartel.

"You don't know, or you won't say?" Callison countered.

J.T. shrugged his shoulders. "Anyway, I want to personally thank you. If you hadn't discovered that Jourge was Smithee, it's very likely none of this would have happened."

"You're welcome." Callison was more perplexed than embarrassed by J.T.'s remarks, but he was glad to hear that J.T. appreciated his efforts. Callison thought for a few second. "How much of this is going to be in the media?"

"I can't say for sure, but they're all over this," J.T. said shaking his head.

"I could only imagine, this must be a media orgy." Callison smirked.

"You got it." J.T.'s face turned serious. "I hope you realize it's going to be difficult, if not impossible, to keep the list out of the papers. This reporter, Arthur Wentzel, really had the inside track on all of this. I have to give him some, if not most of what we have discussed. What burns me is this story will probably make his career and could destroy yours, as well as many others. You know they're going to need scapegoats?"

"You have to do what you have to do. I realized that when I committed myself to following this to the end. Whatever happens, happens." Callison wrinkled his forehead and looked away. He could envision his academic career evaporating under the media's scrutiny.

"I admire you for your commitment."

"Thanks." Callison had a moment of clarity in the haze. "Was this whole thing just about money?"

J.T. laughed. "Isn't everything? Yeah, I guess that about sums it up."

"What about the merger?" Callison had thought long and hard about the merger. For him, this was still a major issue.

"As I said, the merger was used as a decoy by Jourge to discredit Slinger, while not revealing his ulterior motives. I believe Tuttle and Jourge saw an opportunity to use the merger issue to allow them to set up both Rasta and Slinger, after they had disposed of Hargrove. This was the perfect way to misdirect any investigation away from their real agenda. Otherwise, I don't think they really cared one way or the other."

"Okay, they used the merger as a decoy. Was Rasta part of this?" Callison knew what Rasta had told him and realized he was probably right. He was being set up.

"I think Rasta knew of the list. On the other hand, I think Rasta had seriously considered the merger as a way of salvaging his and many of his friends' careers. Your insight in the Hayes Bill is probably fairly accurate. I believe they were more than willing to sacrifice your profession to maintain their piece of the academic and health-care pie."

J.T. stopped and extended his hand, which Callison shook firmly. "You know, I believe you have effectively killed the merger, at least for now—as well as the Hayes Bill. We both know you'll never be acknowledged for what you've done, but I want to again say thanks."

Callison, humbled by J.T.'s praise, said. "You're welcome."

J.T. expression again changed, a pensive, troubled look appeared on his face. "There is one other item. I think you should know."

"What?"

"Do you remember James Williams?"

Callison thought of his last encounter with James Williams and Maxine. The thought of Maxine and her death made Callison even more despondent. "Yes, I recall James Williams. Why?"

"It appears Mr. Williams was following you last evening when you went to visit Maxine Wells."

Callison had a surprised look on his face. "Oh?"

"We found his body this morning in a cellar about a half a block away from Maxine's apartment."

Callison thought to himself about the sounds he had heard in the cellar. "I was in that cellar," Callison said in a reflective tone.

"We know. Valentino had that all arranged. She wanted to make sure you were alone, so she had you traipse through the cellar, knowing if you were followed she'd be able to intervene and eliminate any surprise visitors. Unfortunately, Mr. Williams was caught in her trap."

Callison looked away—another dead body. A thought crossed

his mind. "How did Merker get through then?"

"Ah, yes . . . Merker." A wry smile appeared on J.T.'s face. "He was following Maxine all along, and avoided the cellar trap all together."

"I see." Callison studied his watch. He was late. "I really do have to go." He started to leave but paused for a second. "I feel like I have to thank you, but I'm not sure for what."

"You know I feel the same way." J.T. smiled and shrugged his shoulders.

Laughing, Callison and J.T. embraced in mutual respect.

"I'll keep you informed, if you like," J.T. yelled as Callison started to exit the room.

"Yeah, I'd appreciate that." Callison was pleased with J.T.'s offer.

"I think I'll see if Merker wants any company. I still have a lot to discuss with him." J.T. headed back to the ICU, while Callison left for the airport.

Natalie's flight from Denver was delayed, so Callison's tardiness was not noted. Natalie looked distraught as she exited the plane and rushed into his arms. They embraced in a grip so strong neither was able to take a deep breath. "I'm so glad to see you," Natalie said as she loosened her grip.

"Likewise, I never realized how much danger I was in." Callison had only explained part of what he had known to Natalie the previous night when he called her. He realized there was no benefit in upsetting his wife, especially after the fact. It was Natalie who insisted on meeting him in Chicago.

During the cab ride to the hotel, Callison explained events as he now knew them. Natalie was mesmerized. He even had difficulty believing all that had occurred.

While Callison checked out of the hotel, Natalie went to the newsstand to buy the local papers, to see if there was any information on the events of the previous day. A small article noted the meeting on health-care reform was delayed because of rumors involving possible interference from the Senate. In a long line of potential scandals, it didn't even warrant front page coverage. When Natalie showed him the articles, Callison just smiled. No Pulitzer for Wentzel yet, but J.T. was about to give him the story of his life.

Natalie held his hand tightly as they left the lobby and hailed a cab. "Can we go home now?" Natalie said to her husband. He kissed her on her forehead and instructed the cabbie to drive to O'Hare. It was time to leave Chicago.

Epilogue—One Year Later

Callison sat in his chair looking out the window into space. His thoughts drifted back to one year ago, a day that had changed his life forever. He was now in a different city, with a different job, and a new family. It was definitely different. Callison had intentionally kept his morning patient load light so he could have some time to reflect. Over the past year Callison had done quite a bit of soul searching and reflecting, and felt he was a better person, a better husband, a better doctor because of it. Faces from the past flashed across his mind, highlighting various incidents and memories that together formed his recollection of the those fateful days.

Callison slowly moved his feet from his desk top where they had been propped, to the floor. As he stood, he caught a reflection of himself in the mirror. The lines on his face were looking back, and the gray in his hair seemed to increase daily. This was all fine with him; he was content, possibly for the first time in his life. The events of the past year had transformed him into the man he had hoped he would become, and for that he was grateful.

The scandal that peaked in the cold winds of winter was later imbued with a warmth of forgiveness and righteous spirit of the spring. In its wake many physicians were subsumed, along with more than a smattering of lawyers and politicians. By the summer the medical profession, both allopathic and osteopathic, had rallied behind their leaders, putting the scandal behind them. The medical profession decided to take control of its own destiny and reestablished itself as the preeminent profession in the country, prepared to meet the challenge of health-care reform, while maintaining the ideals which would allow the citizens of the United States access to the best medical care anywhere in the world. Callison was once again proud to be a doctor, proud to be a DO.

A knock at the door startled him from his daydream. His receptionist reminded him of his patient waiting in the exam room. Callison was irritated. He had planned on this time to be quiet and thoughtful. Now he had to examine a new patient who had inadvertently been scheduled for this morning, even though his entire office staff insisted the morning had been blocked. Not one to turn down new business, Callison donned his white coat and marched off to the exam room.

Callison almost gasped as he entered the exam room. There sitting on the exam table was an enormous man, incredibly obese, with day old stubble and a shiny bald head. He looked like a medical catastrophe waiting to happen. Callison had taken care of many patients such as this, but today was supposed to be different. Today he wanted to let his mind drift aimlessly, but this man would change all that. He would have a myriad of complaints, and Callison would be forced to think, *medicine.*

"Hello, my name is Dr. Callison." Callison extended his hand to greet his new patient while reading the chart his nurse had prepared. "Mr. Minton is it?"

"Yes, it's nice to meet you, Doctor. I've been told you were a very good diagnostician and I have a major diagnostic problem."

Mr. Minton was so obese the zipper of his pants was bursting forcing the zipper to be partially undone. However, almost the entire zipper was hidden by his pendulous abdominal fat pad, which flopped over his waist onto his lap as he sat. Callison was prepared for an extensive evaluation.

"I have this bump, Doctor, and I hope you can tell me what it is." Minton lifted his shirt and revealed a very large mass on his abdomen which was obviously not normal.

Callison thought the mass would be soft and fluctuant but on palpation it was rock hard. The skin overlying the mass also felt strange, it was coarse and didn't feel real. The mass was somewhat movable and not totally fixated to the abdominal wall. "How long have you had this?" Callison asked.

"I don't know, but it's been there for some time."

Callison knew a mass this large and this hard had to have been present for many months, and possibly even years. He was concerned the mass was associated with a malignancy but would need to be biopsied to make a definitive diagnosis. Whatever this was, it was the first one Callison had ever seen or felt. "I think, it would be wise for me to perform a complete exam before we discuss this mass," Callison said, being a firm believer in obtaining a complete patient history and perform a complete physical examination before rendering any conclusions.

"How long is this going to take, Doc? I got things to do," Mr. Minton said as he nervously sat on the edge of the exam table.

Callison thought to himself. He also had other plans and had to alter those plans to accommodate this overweight, unappreciative slob of a man. "Listen, Mr. Minton, if you have to leave that's your choice, but for me to do the best job I can, I'll need to fully examine you." Callison's words were direct and without emotion.

Minton, still with his shirt off, looked at the mass protruding from his abdomen. He gently caressed the mass in his large palm. "Really, I don't mean to be disrespectful or anything but isn't there a way to remove this thing now?" His hand squeezed down on the mass.

Callison cringed as Minton squeezed the mass, half expecting the thing to pop. "Mr. Minton, I really would suggest not squeezing that, it could make it worse." Callison winced as he noticed Minton's grip tighten.

"What if I just pulled the thing off?" Minton's face flushed as he was now grasping the mass in a death grip.

Callison's was astonished at this barbaric approach and jumped toward him in an attempt to dislodge Minton's hand. Screaming, "Don't do that!"

Callison was too late. It one violent motion Minton yanked at the mass, pulling it out of his body. The suction-like sound was almost as gross as the visual image. Callison had seen many grotesque behaviors in his career but this had taken the cake. A wave of nausea overtook him when Minton tossed the mass in his direction.

Callison instinctively caught the whitish mass in his right hand. It was still firm and round. Callison looked down into his hand and could see the stitching on the ball. Minton was now audibly laughing, and his laughter was accompanied by laughter coming from the hallway.

Callison, still aghast from this macabre scene was thoroughly confused. "What the hell?" Callison mumbled to himself, as he repeatedly looked down at the ball and then up at Minton laughing.

A figure entered the room. He was partially bent at the waist from laughter but there was no mistaking the profile. It was Marcus Merker. Unable to talk because he was laughing so hard, Merker was able to eventually force the words, "Say hello to my partner, Barney Minton."

Callison was still too grossed out to laugh, as he cleaned the pasty substance off the ball to read the inscription. The ball was autographed by Hack Wilson, Merker's hero.

"The ball's a gift from me to you," Merker said as he squeezed Callison's shoulder in an expression of friendship and appreciation.

"This ball is signed by Hack Wilson," Callison said.

"Yeah, it's my pride and joy," Merker said proudly.

"I can't take this."

"Please, Doc, I want you to have it. If it wasn't for you I would have never solved the death of Dr. Cisko, nor would I have teamed up with my new partner here." Merker slapped Minton on the back. "Our business is doing real well, and this is a way for me to say thanks. Besides, every time you look at the ball you'll think of me."

Callison didn't know what to say. He always had problems accepting gifts graciously, but as with many of his old habits, he was trying to change his reactions. "Thank you, I'm honored. By the way, what new business?"

"We're in the security alarm business," Minton said.

"Yeah, we started with the Merker car alarm and have now expanded to home and business security. We also have a deal pending with the police department. Ironic isn't it, since we were both, ah, encouraged to leave the force," Merker added.

"Well I'm happy for the both of you." Callison was genuinely pleased that Merker was doing well.

"Thanks, the business is making more money than I could have ever imagined. But enough about me. How are you doing?"

Merker asked in a concerned voice. He had kept minimal contact with Callison over the year. Merker was aware Callison had left his academic position at the medical school but not much after that.

"I'm doing just fine. Thanks." Callison returned a contented smile back to Merker.

"So fill me in. What happened? How'd you wind up here?" Merker leaned on the counter propping his head in his hand.

"After the news broke about the conspiracy and the list was revealed to media, my life became unbearable. The dean at the medical school was supportive, but was getting tremendous pressure from all sides to act on those faculty on the list."

"So you get the ax. Like my father used to say, no good deed goes unpunished." Merker's cynicism was still intact.

"Well maybe. Anyway, this wasn't unique to our institution. There were similar pressures at almost every medical school in the country, both DO and MD. Most of those on the list were either terminated or resigned. Several presidents and deans were on the list, as well as many noted and highly regarded physicians. I'm sure you read that Senator Hayes along with a dozen or so other senators and congressman were also removed from office, along with several lobbyists."

Merker was aware of the impact this scandal had on the committee members, as well as the resultant fallout, culminating with the conviction of L. Gorman Tuttle for his part in the murder of Senator Douglas Hargrove among others. J.T. received a promotion and Arthur Wentzel received his Pulitzer for the Tuttle-gate story. Although Callison was among those who were negatively affected, he was not alone. Even though Senator Slinger was exonerated of any wrongdoing, his name had frequently been associated with Tuttle, Jourge, Valentino, etc. in the media, and the president had been forced to remove him from his position in the health-care reform movement.

The president was also harmed by the investigation. Although there was never a direct link, much was made of his relationships with Doctor Jourge and Senator Slinger. Additionally, the Health Insurance Association of America spearheaded an aggressive campaign that showed how the changes in the organization and financing of health-care would negatively affect a large segment of the voting population. When this issue was combined with the potential of higher taxes, it created enough concern and more than enough ammunition for the opposition in the Congress to defeat the president's proposal.

"So what happened to you? After you resigned from the school, you disappeared." Merker asked.

"Natalie and I needed some time to think. I had always followed the path of least resistance. You know, I went to medical school because it was an automatic deferment from the draft. Back then I felt I had no choice—it was either medical school or Viet Nam, so the choice was easy. I never really thought much about what I wanted to do, it was more like what I *needed* to do. If that makes any sense?" Merker nodded. "Then I did the medicine residency because it seemed the right thing to do, and I took the job at the medical school because it had the least risk of all the job offers I had."

"What do you mean, the least risk?"

"When I interviewed for jobs as I was completing my residency, I chose the school because it was the easiest one to leave. What I mean is, all the other offers needed a more substantial commitment of either time or money . . . but the school job was a one-year commitment. It was easy to accept because I always had an out."

"I see."

"But last year forced me to reevaluate it all. I even took the easy route with Natalie. It was easier for me to charge ahead with my career while avoiding the commitment of parenthood. Natalie had also taken a similar stance, and we never really took the time to discuss it honestly. When I had to seriously evaluate my job, I decided to extend my self-analysis to my marriage, my life, everything."

"So are you sorry with your choices?" Merker was confused.

"No, don't get me wrong. The decisions I made were mine and I don't regret any of them. I've had a really good life and I don't know if I would change any of it. But this gave me cause to think whether the direction I was heading was where I wanted to go. Natalie and I both needed time to decide on where we wanted to go. So we spent the time and made some hard choices."

"What choices are you talking about?" Merker inquired.

"Some of the choices were personal between Natalie and myself, but others were career choices." Callison stopped and momentarily looked out the window. He then refocused on Merker. "I had gradually, almost imperceptibly, distanced myself from patient care. With all the meetings and academic responsibilities, I had effectively shunted my efforts and energy into areas that didn't give me the same satisfaction that the practice of medicine did. I decided, with the total support of my wife, to do something different and not take the easy way out. I had never had a private practice and everything I read told me that this went completely against the grain of medicine, but it was what I wanted to do. After I quit my academic job, I was contacted by Foster Ehrlich with a proposition to take over the practice of Jonas Cisko. I found the symmetry of this very intriguing, and with Natalie's counsel, I took the plunge." Callison stopped when he heard a noise.

There was commotion in the lobby of his office. Several voices could be heard and the patter of feet running up the hall was evident. A little girl jumped into Callison's waiting arms and hugged him tightly around his neck.

"Hello, Daddy," she said.

"Sally, I'd like to introduce you to Mr. Merker and Mr. Minton," Callison said as he kissed Sally on her forehead.

"Hello, nice to meet you," Sally said coyly as she nestled in her father's arms.

Natalie stood at the door and looked at her family. Her expression was one of contentment and love. "Marcus, how nice to see you again."

"Look at you. Don't you look the picture of health," Merker said examining Natalie's profile.

Natalie looked much different from the last time Merker had seen her. She had gained weight, predominantly in the middle; she was obviously in the late stages of pregnancy.

Merker smiled at Callison, a knowing smile. Callison had found himself, it was evident. Merker didn't even need his sixth sense to see it.

Callison sat with Sally on his lap as he turned up the volume on the radio, a song was on that he wanted to hear.

The music filled the room. *"These are the good old days."* Callison looked at his pregnant wife and his adopted daughter. He thought of his new life and smiled. As a tear ran down his cheek, he realized, these are the good old days.